THE JULIANTHES

(The Weathered Isles)

Pireth
Vanguard

of
Corona

Pireth
Dancard

MIRIANIC

OCEAN

Pireth
Tulme
Tinson

Macomber

The Broken Coast

N

THE DEMON SPIRIT

THE
DEMON
SPIRIT

THE BALLANTINE PUBLISHING GROUP • NEW YORK

This one's for Scott Siegel and Jim Cegeilski, two guys who have made this business such a pleasure for me.

CONTENTS

PART III
THE DEMON WITHIN

PART IV
DOWN THE ROAD OF SHADOWS

THE DEMON SPIRIT

PART ONE

▼

WILDERLANDS

I am afraid, Uncle Mather, not for myself, but for all the goodly people of all the world. Pony and I rode south from the Barbacan with our hearts heavy in grief, but with hope. Avelyn, Tuntun, and Bradwarden gave their lives, but in destroying the dactyl, we had, I believed, taken the darkness from the world.

I was wrong.

Every running stride Symphony carried us south would bring us to more hospitable lands, so I thought, and so I told Pony, whose doubts were ever greater than mine. I cannot count the numbers of goblins we have seen! Thousands, Uncle Mather, tens of thousands, and with scores of fomorian giants and hundreds of cruel powries as well. It took Pony and me two weeks and a dozen fights to reach the area near Dundalis, and there we found only more enemies, firmly entrenched and using the remnants of the three towns as base camps for furthering their mischief. Belster O'Comely and the raiding band we set up before we went to the Barbacan are gone—to the south as we discussed, I pray. But so vast is the darkness encompassing the land that I fear nowhere will be safe.

I am afraid, Uncle Mather, but I vow to you now that no matter how bleak the situation becomes, I will not surrender my hope. That is something not the demon dactyl, not the goblins, not all the evil in all the world, can take from me. Hope brings strength to my sword arm, that Tempest may cut true. Hope allows me to keep fashioning arrows as score after score are lost to goblin hearts—a line of monsters that seems not at all diminished by my efforts.

Hope, Uncle Mather, that is the secret. I think that my enemies are not possessed of it. They are too selfish to understand sacrifice in the hope that it will bring better things for those who come after them. And without such foresight and optimism, they are often easily disheartened and chased from battle.

Hope, I have learned, is prerequisite for altruism.

I will hope and I will fight on, and with every battle I am reminded that my attitude is not folly. Pony grows strong with the stones, and the magical forces she conjures are indeed incredible. Also, our enemies, for all their numbers, no longer fight in any coordinated fashion. Their binding force, the demon dactyl, is gone, and I have seen signs that goblin battles goblin.

The day is dark, Uncle Mather, but there may yet be a break in the clouds.

—ELBRYAN WYNDON

❖ I ❖

Another Day

Elbryan Wyndon collected his wooden chair and his precious mirror and moved to the mouth of the small cave. He blinked as he pulled the blanket aside, surprised to see that the dawn was long past. Climbing out of the hole seemed no easy task for a man of Elbryan's size, with his six-foot-three-inch muscular frame, but with the agility given him in years of training with the lithe elves of Caer'alfar, he had little trouble navigating the course.

He found his companion Jilseponie, Pony, awake and about, gathering up their bedrolls and utensils. Not so far away, the great horse Symphony nickered and stomped at sight of Elbryan, and that image of the stallion would have given most men pause. Symphony was tall, but not the least bit lanky, with a powerful, muscled chest, a coat so black and smooth over those rippling muscles that it glistened in the slightest light, and eyes that projected profound intelligence. A white diamond-shaped patch showed on the horse's head, above the intelligent eyes, but other than that and a bit of white on the forelegs, the only thing that marred the perfect black coat was a turquoise gemstone, the link between Symphony and Elbryan, magically set in the middle of the horse's chest.

For all the splendor, though, the ranger hardly paid Symphony any heed, for, as was so often the case, his gaze was locked on Pony. She was a few months younger than Elbryan, his childhood friend, his adult wife. Her hair, thick and golden, was just below her shoulders now, longer than Elbryan's own light brown mop for the first time in years. The day was lightly overcast, the sky gray, but that did little to dim the shine of Pony's huge blue eyes. She was his strength, the ranger knew, the bright spot in a dark world. Her energy seemed limitless, as did her ability to smile. No odds frightened her, no sight daunted her; she pressed on methodically, determinedly.

"Do we look for the camp north of End-o'-the-World?" she asked, the question shattering Elbryan's contemplation.

He considered the thought. They had discerned that there were satellite camps in the region, clusters of goblins, mostly, supplied by the larger encampments set up in what used to be the three towns of Dundalis, Weedy Meadow, and End-o'-the-World. Because the towns were each separated by a day's walk, Dundalis west to Weedy Meadow, and Weedy Meadow west to End-o'-the-World, these smaller outposts would be key to regaining the region—if ever an army from Honce-the-Bear made its way to the borders of the Wilderlands. If Elbryan and Pony could clear the monsters from the dense woods, there would remain little contact between the three towns.

"It seems as good a place as any to start," the ranger replied.

"Start?" Pony asked incredulously, to which Elbryan could only shrug. Indeed, both were weary of battle now, though both knew that many, many more fights lay before them.

"Did you speak with Uncle Mather?" Pony asked, nodding toward the mirror. Elbryan had explained Oracle to her, that mysterious elven ceremony in which someone might converse with the dead.

"I spoke at him," the ranger replied, his olive-green eyes flashing as a shiver coursed his spine—as always happened when he considered the ghost of the great man who had gone before him.

"Does he ever answer?"

Elbryan snorted, trying to figure out how he might better explain Oracle. "I answer myself," he started. "Uncle Mather guides my thoughts, I believe, but in truth, he does not give me the answers."

Pony's nod showed that she understood perfectly what the young man was trying to say to her. Elbryan had not known his uncle Mather in life; the man had been lost to the family at a young age, before Olwan Wyndon— Mather's brother, Elbryan's father—had taken his wife and children to the wild Timberlands. But Mather, like Elbryan, had been taken in and trained by the Touel'alfar, the elves, to be a ranger. Now, in Oracle, Elbryan conjured his image of the man, an image of a perfect ranger, and when speaking to that image, Elbryan was forcing himself to uphold his own highest ideals.

"If I taught you Oracle, perhaps you could speak with Avelyn," the ranger said, and it wasn't the first time he had suggested as much. He had been hinting that Pony might try to contact their lost friend for several days now, ever since he himself tried, and failed, to reach Avelyn's spirit at Oracle two days after they had started south from the blasted Barbacan.

"I do not need it," Pony said softly, turning away, and for the first time Elbryan realized how disheveled she appeared.

"You do not believe in the ceremony," he started to say, more to prompt than to accuse.

"Oh, but I do," was her quick and sharp retort, but she lost momentum just as abruptly, as if fearing the turn in the conversation. "I . . . I might be experiencing much the same thing."

Elbryan stared at her calmly, giving her the time to sort out her response.

As the seconds passed into minutes, he prompted, "You have learned Oracle?"

"No," she answered, turning to look at the man. "Not quite the same as your own. I do not seek it. Rather, it seeks me."

"It?"

"It is Avelyn," Pony said with conviction. "He is with me, I feel, somehow a part of me, guiding me and strengthening me."

"As I feel about my father," Elbryan reasoned. "And you about yours. I do not doubt that Olwan is watching over . . ." His voice trailed away as he looked at her, for Pony was shaking her head before he finished.

"Stronger than that," she explained. "When Avelyn first taught me to use the stones, he was badly injured. We joined, spirit to spirit, through use of the hematite, the soul stone. The result was so enlightening, for both of us, that Avelyn continued that joining over the weeks, as he showed me the secrets of the gemstones. In a mere month my understanding and capabilities with the stones progressed far beyond what a monk at St.-Mere-Abelle might learn in five years of training."

"And you believe that he is still connecting with you in that spiritual manner?" Elbryan asked, and there was no skepticism in the question. The young ranger had seen too much, both enchanting and diabolical, to doubt such a possibility—or any possibility.

"He is," Pony replied. "And every morning, I wake up to find that I know a bit more about the stones. Perhaps I dream about them, and in those dreams see new uses for any given stone, or new combinations between them."

"Then it is not Avelyn, but Pony," the ranger reasoned.

"It is Avelyn," she said firmly. "He is with me, in me, a part of who I have become."

She went quiet, and Elbryan did not respond, the two of them standing in silence, digesting the revelation—one that Pony had not made even to herself until this very moment. Then a smile spread across Elbryan's face, and Pony gradually joined him, both taking comfort that their friend, the Mad Friar, the runaway monk from St.-Mere-Abelle, might still be with them.

"If your insight is true, then our business becomes easier," Elbryan reasoned. He held his smile and offered a wink, then turned, moving to pack Symphony's saddlebags.

Pony didn't reply, just methodically went about closing down the camp-site. They never stayed in a place more than a single night—often not more than half the night if Elbryan determined there were goblin patrols in the area. The ranger finished his task first, and with a look to the woman, to which she responded with an assenting nod, he took his sword belt and wandered away.

Pony hurriedly finished her task, then silently stalked after him. She knew his destination to be a clearing they had passed right before they set camp, and knew, too, that she would find ample cover in the thick blueberry bushes on its northeastern end. Stalking quietly, as Elbryan had taught her, she finally settled into place.

The ranger was well into the dance by then. He was naked, except for a green armband set about his left biceps, and was holding his great sword Tempest, which had been given by the Touel'alfar to his uncle, Mather Wyndon. Gracefully, Elbryan went through the precise movements, muscles flowing in perfect harmony, legs turning, body shifting, keeping him always in balance.

Pony watched, mesmerized by the sheer beauty of the dance, which the elves called *bi'nelle dasada*, and her love's perfection of form. As always when she spied on Elbryan's dance—no, not Elbryan, for in this fighting form he was the one the elves had named Nightbird, and not Elbryan Wyndon—Pony had pangs of guilt, feeling quite the voyeur. But there was nothing sexual or prurient here, just appreciation of the art and beauty of the interplay between her love's powerful muscles. More than anything, she wanted to learn that dance, to weave her own sword in graceful circles, to feel her bare feet become so attuned to the moist grass below them that they could feel every blade and every contour in the ground.

Pony was no minor warrior herself, having served with distinction in the Coastpoint Guards. She had battled many goblins and powries, even giants, and few could outfight her. But in looking at Elbryan, the Nightbird, she felt herself to be a mere amateur.

That dance, *bi'nelle dasada*, was perfection of the art form, and her lover was perfection of *bi'nelle dasada*. The ranger continued his slashing, weaving maneuvers, feet turning, stepping to the side, front, back, body going down low and then rising in graceful sequences. This was the traditional fighting style of the day, the slashing routines of the heavy, edged swords.

But then, abruptly, the ranger shifted his stance, heels together, feet perpendicular to each other. He stepped ahead, toe-heel, and went into a balanced crouch, his knees bending out over his toes, front arm cocked, elbow down, and rear arm similarly bent except that his upper arm was level with his shoulder, his hand up high and hanging loose. He went forward then retreated in short, measured, but impossibly quick and balanced steps, and then suddenly, right from one such retreat, his front arm extended and seemed to pull him. It happened in the blink of Pony's eye, and this morning, as with every such strike, it stunned her. So suddenly, Nightbird had come forward, the tip of Tempest covering at least two feet of ground, his back arm turning down so he made one long and balanced line.

A shudder coursed down Pony's spine as she pictured an enemy impaled on that deadly blade, staring wide-eyed in disbelief at the suddenness of the attack.

And then the ranger retracted, again quickly and in balance—no opening in his defenses throughout the move—and went back to his weaving dance.

With a sigh of both appreciation and frustration, Pony snuck away, back to finish closing down the camp. Elbryan returned to her soon after, showing sweat on his exposed arms but looking revitalized and ready for the trials of another day on the road.

They set out soon after, both astride the great stallion, with Symphony easily carrying them along. Elbryan guided them north, away from the line of the three towns, and then west, toward End-o'-the-World, and before midday they had found the smaller goblin encampment. A quick survey of the area provided the information they needed, and they retreated to the deeper woods to unladen Symphony and prepare their assault.

By early afternoon the ranger was creeping through the woods with Hawkwing, his elven-crafted bow, in hand. He came upon a group of three goblin perimeter guards soon enough, and, as was usually the case, the slovenly creatures were not on their best guarding posture. They were clustered about a wide elm, one leaning on the tree, one pacing before it and grumbling about something, and the third sitting at the base, back against the trunk, apparently asleep. The ranger was somewhat surprised to see that one of these guards carried a bow. Goblins usually fought with club, sword, or spear, and the sight of the bow tipped him off that there might well be powries in the vicinity.

The ranger did a silent circuit of the area, ensuring that no others were about, then found his best angle of attack. Up came Hawkwing, so named for the three feathers set on its top end, which separated like the feathered "fingers" on the end of a hawk's extended wing when he drew back the bowstring. Those feathers went widely apart now as Elbryan lined up his shot.

Hawkwing hummed; the ranger had a second arrow up and away almost immediately. He was the Nightbird now, the elven-trained warrior, and the mere mention of his name sent trembles through the hearts of even the sturdiest powries.

The first arrow nailed the leaning goblin to the tree. The second took out its pacing companion before the creature had time to cry out its surprise.

"Duh?" the third asked, coming from its slumber when Nightbird prodded it. The goblin looked up just in time to see Tempest's descent, the mighty sword cleaving its head in half.

The ranger retrieved his arrows, then took a couple from the goblin's quiver. They weren't well-crafted, hardly straight, but would suit his purposes well enough.

On he went, drawing a complete perimeter of the encampment. He encountered two more guard positions, and dispatched them with equal efficiency. Then he went back to Pony and Symphony, better detailing the layout, his attack plans already formulated. The goblin camp itself was well-placed on a low bluff amidst a tumble of boulders. There were only two apparent approaches: one on the southeast up a trail between shoulder-high walls of stone, a path that turned in from a thirty-foot sheer drop; the second up the gentler-sloping western side of the hillock, a wide track of empty grass.

Nightbird positioned himself in a copse of trees on the western side, where he could find clearer shooting, while Pony made her tentative way along the top of the cliff face.

The ranger moved to a higher position, climbing from Symphony's back to one of the lower branches of an oak. That still left him below the level of the goblin camp, but with more than half of it exposed. Pony would wait for him, he trusted, and so he took his time in selecting his first target, trying to get a feel for the hierarchy of this patrol. No two groups of goblins were alike, the ranger had learned, for the smallish, yellow-green creatures were purely selfish and not devoted to any greater cause than fulfillment of their present desires. The demon dactyl had changed that—that sudden coordination of the monsters was the element that had made the darkness so complete—but now the dactyl was gone and the wretched creatures were fast reverting to their previous, chaotic nature.

This encampment reflected that clearly. All the place was a tumult, pushing and shoving, shouting and grumbling.

"We goes south for killing!" Nightbird heard one creature shout.

"We goes the way I says we goes!" replied one especially weasely little runt, a spindly-armed and bow-legged wretch, short even by goblin standards—which meant that it barely topped four feet—and with a nose and chin so narrow that they appeared to be arrow shafts protruding from its ugly face.

The ranger saw the larger goblin standing before the runt clench its hands in rage, saw the group of three goblins closest him—all carrying bows, he noted with disdain—put hands near their quivers. The tension held, silent for many seconds, just below an explosive level, and then another form rose up, a giant form, fifteen feet tall and more, two thousand pounds of muscle and bone.

The fomorian stretched away its sleepiness and ambled over to join the conversation. The giant beast said not a word, but stood right behind the weasely goblin—and how that creature puffed its skinny chest with its bodyguard so near!

"South," the other said again, but in a calm and unthreatening manner. "Peoples to kill to the south."

"We was told to stay here and guard," the weasely goblin insisted.

"Guard from what?" the other whined. "From bears or boars?"

"Me bored," offered another, from the side, drawing a few halfhearted snickers—laughter that died away quickly when the weasely goblin put an unrelenting stare on the jokester.

It was all taking shape perfectly from Nightbird's perspective, except of course for the appearance of a fomorian giant. His first instinct told him to put an arrow into that behemoth's face, but as he considered the general dynamics of the group, another, more insightful plan began to unfold.

The arguing continued, followed by more than a few loud threats by the weasely goblin, the creature gaining in confidence with the giant standing right behind it. The goblin ended by promising a cruel death to any that defied its commands, and then it turned about, walking away.

Nightbird, using one of the arrows he had taken from the goblins, nailed it in the back, at an angle that sent the missile right between two of the archers at the camp's edge. The goblin went down hard, squirming and screaming, trying to reach about to grab the painful bolt, and all the gathering erupted in pushing and shoving, in accusations and cries of murder.

The three archers were the most confused, each yelling at the other two, each counting the arrows in their counterparts' quivers. One cried for a check of the shaft of the arrow in their leader's back, claiming that its own arrows had specific markings.

The enraged fomorian had no such patience for any investigation, though. The giant stalked over and slugged the protesting archer in the face, launching it head over heels down the grassy slope. The giant grabbed a second archer as the third scrambled away, lifting the unfortunate creature and squeezing the life out of it. All the rest of the camp fell upon the third, taking its flight as an admission of guilt. Their blood lust in full, they pounded and stomped long after the poor creature had stopped squirming.

For the ranger, watching the brutal spectacle was a confirmation of his belief in the absolutely irredeemable nature of the wretched beasts. The killing was over quickly, but the pushing and shoving and accusations did not relent. He had seen enough, though. There were perhaps a dozen goblins left in the camp, not counting the leader, who wouldn't be up for any fighting anytime soon, and, of course, the one fomorian. Thirteen against three, counting Symphony.

The ranger liked the odds.

He hopped down from the tree, onto the back of waiting Symphony. The great stallion gave a snort and rushed away, out the back side of the copse. The last thing Nightbird wanted was bring the goblins charging down the slope, where they could scatter. He went west, and then south, and then turned back to the east, coming in sight of Pony, who was in position at the end of the long and narrow trail. They shared a wave, and the ranger searched out a new vantage point. Now came his turn to wait.

The goblin camp remained astir, with accusations flying. The creatures seemed perfectly oblivious to the notion that an outsider might have shot down their leader, until Pony struck hard.

A goblin appeared at the end of the trail, leaning on one wall of stone. It removed its metal helmet—another oddity for the crude creatures—and scratched at its hair, then replaced the cap, talking all the while with another who remained out of Pony's line of sight. She focused on the one goblin, on its helmet, as she held before her a black, rough-edged stone, magnetite, or lodestone, by name. Pony fell into the stone, saw through it, down the trail. Everything blurred and fogged over—everything except for that one helmet, the image of it sharpening to crystal clarity. Pony felt the energy building within the stone, energy she lent to it, combined with its own magical properties. She felt the attraction to that helmet growing, growing, the stone beginning to pull against her grasp.

As she reached the pinnacle, as it seemed the stone would verily explode with tingling magic, she let it go. In the blink of an eye it covered the distance and smashed against then through the helmet, and the goblin flipped over once and lay dead.

How its companion shrieked!

Pony was not surprised when the fomorian giant turned down the narrow trail, running full out and bellowing with rage. She held forth another stone, malachite, the stone of levitation, and before the behemoth had gone three strides, it found that its feet were no longer touching the ground. It was moving, though, its momentum propelling its suddenly weightless form in a straight line.

The trail curved slightly and the giant brushed the wall. It tried to reach down and find a hold, but the movement came too late and only sent the creature tumbling head over heels, twisting and turning, reaching desperately for any potential handhold.

Pony could hardly believe the effort needed to keep the behemoth aloft, and knew she would not be able to hold it there for long. She didn't have to, though. She ducked very low—the giant spinning over more quickly as it grabbed for her—and let the creature soar past her. Then, as soon as the giant moved out over the cliff, she dropped her concentration, releasing the stone's magical energy, and let the brute drop.

Looking back the other way, she saw a handful of goblins at the far end of the trail, gaping at her but not yet daring to approach. Quickly she went for her third stone, the graphite, and reached deep inside herself to find some more magical energy. Already she had done more magic in rapid succession than ever before, and she had little faith that her next casting, a bolt of lightning, would have much power behind it.

She took hope, then, in the commotion that sprang up on the hillock behind the goblins, at the screams and cries of agony, at the sound of charging Symphony off to the side and the thrum of the ranger's deadly bow.

But her love could not get there in time to help her, she knew. A line of five goblins came on, rushing down the narrow trail, howling. One let fly an arrow that barely missed the young woman.

Pony stood resolute. She dismissed her fears and focused on the graphite, only the graphite. The bolt came forth more quickly than she had intended, wrung from her by sheer urgency as the nearest goblin closed to within three running strides.

Pony staggered as if hit; the expenditure of energy was more than she could tolerate. Her knees wobbled and she instinctively ambled away, her eyes hardly open as she glanced back, with some relief, to see that the lightning had pushed the goblins back. Three of the five were down, jerking spasmodically, while the other two fought hard to hold their balance, their muscles trembling violently.

Up on the hillock, Nightbird shot one last arrow, catching a nearby goblin right through its skinny nose, then turned the bow over in one hand, whipping it like a club as Symphony pounded past another creature. That creature dispatched, he dropped the bow altogether, drawing out Tempest, the elven blade, light and strong, forged of precious silverel and crackling with energy, from both elven magic and the gemstone set in the sword's pommel. The ranger turned Symphony in line and let the great stallion run down the next goblin, and as Symphony passed, hardly stumbling, Nightbird swung out with his sword at the next. This goblin held a metal shield and had it up to block, but the gemstone in Tempest's ball hilt, a blue stone clouded with white and gray, flared with power and the fine blade smashed right through the shield, snapping the straps that fastened it to the goblin's arm, then charged on past the turning metal to crease the creature's face.

The hillock was clear, the only goblin in sight in fast flight down the grassy slope. The ranger, his blood lust high, thought to pursue, but changed his mind when he heard Pony's lightning bolt behind him, a sparking crackle and not a thunderous blast, and then heard the groans of goblins still very much alive.

He rolled backward off the saddle, landing lightly on his feet. Symphony skidded to a stop and turned about to regard him, and Nightbird couldn't help but pause and do likewise. The horse's black coat glistened with sweat, accentuating the powerful muscles. Symphony looked hard at his companion and stamped the ground, ready, eager for more battle.

The ranger looked from the horse's intelligent eyes to the turquoise set in his breast, the gift of Avelyn, the telepathic bond between Nightbird and Symphony. Elbryan used that bond now to instruct the horse.

With an agreeing snort, Symphony wheeled and charged away, and the ranger went fast for his bow, in full run on his way to the narrow trail.

He came to its lip, sliding to one knee, Hawkwing up and drawn. Only one goblin remained down now, with two starting off after Pony and two others still struggling to secure their balance. Off went the arrow, zipping between the two standing nearby and over the head of the third, to strike the lead goblin in the back. The creature went into a weird hop then, seeming to fly for several feet before falling facedown. Its running companion, fearing a similar fate, howled and dove to the ground.

Elbryan's second shot got the closest goblin in the chest, and then he was up, Tempest in hand. He came in hard, sword flashing back and forth, maneuvers designed more to put the goblin off-balance than to score a hit. The creature struggled to keep up with the flashing blade, its own crude sword ringing against Tempest only a couple of times in the ten-stroke routine. In short order the goblin was staggering again, nearly tripping on its own feet as it tried to twist and turn in tune with the darting blade. Tempest went left, then right, then right again, then Nightbird started back for the left but cut short the swing, and then came that signature lunge. Suddenly, immediately, he was simply there, fully extended, his sword tip two feet farther ahead than it had been, stabbing the goblin hard through the shoulder.

Down went the goblin's arm, its sword falling uselessly to the ground. One step brought the ranger to the side, where he chopped down hard on the head of the remaining goblin even as it struggled to stand. Then he came back in, ignoring the last goblin's cry for mercy, driving his blade through the creature's ribs and into its lungs.

The ranger glanced down the trail, to see that Pony, no unskilled fighter in her own right, had come back in, with sword this time and not gems, to finish off the goblin who had dived for cover. The woman looked up at Nightbird and nodded, then opened wide her eyes as the ranger let out a startled shout and launched himself toward her.

He went right by Pony as she turned, throwing her sword up defensively in fear that something had come in at her back. Indeed, the giant had returned, stubbornly climbing the cliff face. It had both hands and one shoulder over the lip when Nightbird met it, Tempest flashing. The ranger slashed one arm, then the other, then again and again, all the while dodging the behemoth's futile attempts to grab at him. Finally the beating opened wide the giant's defenses and its grasp on the ledge weakened, and Nightbird calmly strode ahead and kicked the creature in the face.

Down it went again, bouncing along the thirty foot descent. Stubbornly, it shook its head and rolled to its knees, intent on climbing once again.

Pony was beside Elbryan in a moment. "You might be needing this," she remarked, handing Hawkwing over.

His fourth arrow slew the giant, while Pony walked back along the trail and encampment, finishing the wounded goblins. Symphony returned during that time, the horse's rear hooves splattered with fresh goblin blood.

The three friends regrouped shortly after.

"Just another day," Pony said dryly, to which the ranger only nodded.

He noted that there was an almost dispirited edge to her tone, as though the battle, as smoothly as it had gone, had been somehow unsatisfying.

2

St.-Mere-Abelle

His wrinkles seemed even deeper now, shadowed by the torchlight. Deep grooves in that old and weathered face, the visage of a man who had seen too much. By Master Jojonah's estimation, Dalebert Markwart, the Father Abbot of St.-Mere-Abelle, the highest ranking person in the Abellican Order, had aged tremendously over the last couple of years. The portly Jojonah, no young man himself, studied Markwart carefully as the pair stood atop the seaward wall of the great abbey, staring out into All Saints Bay. He tried to compare this image of the Father Abbot, unshaven, with eyes sunken deep into sockets, against the memory of the man just a few years previous, in God's Year 821 when they had all waited eagerly for the return of the *Windrunner*, the ship that had delivered four of St.-Mere-Abelle's brothers to the equatorial island of Pimaninicuit, that they might collect the sacred stones.

Things had changed much since those days of hope and wonderment.

The mission had been successful, with a tremendous haul of gemstones taken and properly prepared. And three of the brothers, with the exception of poor Thagraine who was stricken in the meteor shower, had returned alive, though Brother Pellimar had died a short time later.

"A pity that it had not been Avelyn who was hit in the head by a falling stone," Father Abbot Markwart had often said in the years hence, for Avelyn, after achieving the greatest success in the history of the Church as a Preparer of the sacred gems, had returned a changed man, and in Markwart's eyes had committed the highest heresy possible in the Order. Avelyn had taken some of the gemstones and run off, and in that flight, Master Siherton, a peer of Jojonah's and a friend of Markwart's, had been killed.

The Father Abbot had not let the theft pass. Indeed, he had guided the training of the remaining brother from the party of four, a stocky and brutish man named Quintall. Under Markwart's strictest orders, Quintall had become Brother Justice and gone after Avelyn, with orders to bring back the man or his broken body.

Word had come back to the library only the month before that Quintall had failed and was dead.

Still, Markwart had no intention of letting Avelyn run free. He had set De'Unnero, the finest fighter at the abbey—and, by Jojonah's estimation, the most vicious human being alive—to training not one, but two Brothers Justice as replacement for Quintall. Jojonah didn't like De'Unnero at all, considered the man's temperament unbefitting a brother of the Abellican Church, and so he had not been pleased when the still-young man had been named to the rank of master as a replacement for Master Siherton. And the choice of hunters, too, had bothered Jojonah, for he suspected that the two young monks, Brothers Youseff and Dandelion, had only been admitted to St.-Mere-Abelle for this purpose. Surely neither of them qualified above others who had been refused their appointment.

But both could fight.

So even that choice of admission to the Order, the greatest responsibility of abbots and masters, had fallen victim to Markwart's desire to clear his own reputation. The Father Abbot wanted those stones back.

Desperately, Master Jojonah thought as he looked upon the old Father Abbot's haggard visage. Dalebert Markwart was a man possessed now, a snarling, vicious thing. If at first Markwart had wanted Avelyn captured and tried, he merely wanted the man dead now—and painfully killed, tortured, rended, his heart torn out and put on a stake before the front gate of St.-Mere-Abelle. Markwart hardly talked of dead Siherton these days; his focus was purely the stones, the precious stones, and he meant to get them back.

All of that had been put aside for the moment, though, out of necessity even greater than Markwart's obsession, for the war had at last come to St.-Mere-Abelle.

"There they are," Father Abbot Markwart remarked, pointing out across the bay.

Jojonah leaned on the low wall, squinting into the darkness, and there, rounding a bend along the northern spur of the rocky seacoast, came the lights of a vessel, obviously sitting very low in the water.

"Powrie barrelboat," Markwart said distastefully as more and more lights came into view. "A thousand of them out there!"

And so confident that they approach in full view with lights burning, Jojonah silently added. And that wasn't even the extent of their problems, though the master saw no need to remark on the potentially greater troubles facing the abbey.

"And how many by land?" the Father Abbot demanded, as though he had read Jojonah's mind. "Twenty thousand? Fifty? The whole powrie nation is upon us, as if all the Weathered Isles had been dumped at our gate!"

Again the portly Jojonah had no practical response. According to the reports of trusted sources, a vast army of the four-foot-tall dwarves, the cruel powries, had landed less than ten miles down the coast from St.-Mere-Abelle. The brutal creatures had wasted no time in laying waste to the nearby villages, slaughtering any humans who could not escape. The image of that brought a shiver along Jojonah's spine. Powries were also called "bloody caps" for their practice of dipping their specially treated berets—caps made of human skin—into the blood of their slain enemies. The more blood one of those berets soaked, the brighter its crimson stain, a sign of rank among the barrel-bodied, spindly limbed dwarves.

"We have the stones," Jojonah offered.

Markwart snorted derisively. "And we'll tire our magics long before we diminish the ranks of the wretched powries—and of the goblin army that's said to be moving south of here."

"There is the report of the explosion far to the north," Jojonah offered hopefully, trying in any way possible to improve Markwart's surly mood.

The Father Abbot didn't disagree; whispers from reliable sources spoke of a tremendous eruption in the northern land known as the Barbacan, reputedly the land of the demon dactyl who had gathered this invading army. But while those rumors offered some distant hope that war had been brought to the dactyl's doorstep, they offered little in the face of the force now moving against St.-Mere-Abelle, something Markwart emphasized with his next derisive snort.

"Our walls are thick, our brothers well-trained in the fighting arts, and our catapult crews second to none in all Corona," Jojonah went on, gaining momentum with every word. "And St.-Mere-Abelle is better suited to withstand a siege than any structure in Honce-the-Bear," he added, preempting Markwart's next glum statement.

"Better suited with not so many mouths to feed," Markwart snapped at him, and Jojonah winced as if slapped. "I wish that the powries had been quicker!"

Master Jojonah sighed and moved a few steps to the side then, unable to tolerate his superior's grating pessimism and that last remark; obviously aimed at the multitude of pitiful refugees who had recently come swarming into St.-Mere-Abelle, it had, in Jojonah's estimation, been on the very edge of blasphemy. They were the Church, after all, supposedly the salvation of the common man, and yet here was their Father Abbot, their spiritual leader, complaining about giving shelter to people who had lost almost everything. The Father Abbot's first response to the influx of refugees had been to order everything valuable, books, gold leaf, even inkwells, locked away.

"Avelyn started all of this," Markwart rambled. "The thief weakened us, in heart and soul, and gave hope to our enemies!"

Jojonah tuned out the Father Abbot's ranting. He had heard it all before—indeed, it had by now been disseminated to all the abbeys of Corona that Avelyn Desbris was responsible for awakening the demon dactyl, and thus setting into motion all the subsequent tragedies that had befallen the land.

Master Jojonah, who had been Avelyn's mentor and chief supporter through the man's years at St.-Mere-Abelle, couldn't, in his heart, believe a word of it. Jojonah had studied at the abbey for four decades, and had never in all that time met a man as singularly holy as Avelyn Desbris. While he had not yet come to terms with Avelyn's last actions at the abbey—the theft of the stones and the murder, if it was a murder, of Master Siherton—Jojonah suspected there was more to the story than the Father Abbot's version would indicate. More than anything, Master Jojonah wanted to speak at length with his former student, to discover the man's motivations, to find out why he had run and why he had taken the gemstones.

More lights appeared in the dark harbor, a reminder to Jojonah to stay focused on the grim situation at hand. Avelyn was an issue for another day; the morning light would bring the full fury of war to St.-Mere-Abelle.

The two monks retired then, seeking to gather all of their strength.

"Sleep well in God's bosom," Master Jojonah said to Markwart, the proper and traditional nighttime parting.

Markwart waved a hand absently over his shoulder and walked away, grumbling something about the wretch Avelyn under his breath.

Master Jojonah recognized a growing problem here, an obsession that could only bring ill to St.-Mere-Abelle and all the Order. But there was little he could do about it, he reminded himself, and he went to his private room. He added many lines about Avelyn Desbris, words of hope for the man's soul, and of forgiveness, to his evening prayers, then rolled onto his bed, knowing he would not sleep well.

Father Abbot Markwart, too, was speaking words about Avelyn when he entered his lavish quarters, four rooms sectioned off near the middle of the massive abbey's ground-level floor. The old man, consumed with anger, muttered curse after curse, spat Avelyn's name in succession with the names of the greatest traitors and heretics in the history of the Church, and vowed again to see the man tortured to death before he, himself, went to view the face of God.

His reign at St.-Mere-Abelle had been unblemished, and having been fortunate enough to preside over the Order in the generation of the stone showers, the tremendous haul of stones—the greatest ever taken from Pimaninicuit—seemed to solidify his place among the most revered Father Abbots of history. But then the wretch Avelyn changed that, brought a black mark to his reputation: as the first father abbot to ever suffer the absolute indignity of losing some of the sacred stones.

It was with these dark thoughts, and none for the invasion fleet that had entered All Saints Bay, that Father Abbot Markwart at last drifted off to sleep.

His dreams were as razor-edged as his anger, showing stark, clear images of a faraway land that he did not know. He saw Avelyn, thick and fat and haggard, snarling orders to goblins and powries. He saw the man fell a giant with a streak of searing lightning, not out of any hatred for the evil race, but because this one had not obeyed him without question.

In the background an angelic figure appeared, a winged man, large and terrible. The personification of the wrath of God.

Then Markwart understood.

A demon dactyl had been the source of the war? No, this disaster had been caused by something greater even than that dark power. The true guiding force of evil was Avelyn, the heretic!

The Father Abbot sat bolt upright in bed, sweating and trembling. It was only a dream, he reminded himself.

But had there not been some shred of truth buried within those visions? It came as a great epiphany to the tired old man, an awakening call as clear as the loudest bell ever chimed. For years he had been proclaiming Avelyn as the root source of all the problems, but much of that had been merely a self-defense technique aimed at deflecting his own errors. He had always known that hidden truth . . . until now.

Now Markwart realized that it had indeed been Avelyn, beyond any doubt. He knew that the man had unraveled all that was holy, perverted the stones to his own wicked use, worked against the Church and all of Mankind.

Markwart knew, without doubt, and in that profound knowledge he was at last able to dismiss all of his own guilt.

The old man pulled himself from his bed and ambled over to his desk, lighting a lamp. He fell into his chair, exhausted, overcome, and absently took a key from a secret compartment in one drawer and used it to open the lock on a secret compartment in yet another, revealing his private cache of stones: ruby, graphite, malachite, serpentine, a tiger's paw, a lodestone, and his most precious of all, the strongest hematite, the soul stone, at St.-Mere-Abelle. With this heavy gray stone Markwart could send his spirit across the miles, could even contact associates though they were separated by half a continent. He had used this stone to make contact with Brother Justice—no easy task since Quintall was not proficient in use of the stones, and since his single-minded training had given him a level of mental discipline that was hard to penetrate.

Markwart had used this stone to contact a friend in Amvoy, across the Masur Delaval from Palmaris, and that friend had discovered the truth of Brother Justice's failed quest.

How precious these sacred stones were—to the monks of St.-Mere-Abelle, there was no greater treasure—and it was more than Markwart could stand to know that he had let some get away.

He looked at the handful of stones now as if they were his children, then sat up straighter, blinking quizzically. For he saw them now more clearly than ever before, as if a great truth had been revealed to him. He saw the powers buried within each stone, and knew he could reach them with a mere thought, hardly an effort at all. And some of them seemed almost to blend together, as the old man recognized new and more powerful combinations for various stones.

The Father Abbot fell back and even cried out, tears of joy dripping from his eyes. He was free of Avelyn's dark grip, he suddenly believed, for now he understood, beyond doubt. And with his revelations had come a greater knowledge, a deeper understanding. It was always a sharp thorn in Markwart's side that Avelyn, this supposed heretic, had been the most powerful stone user in the history of the Church. If the stones came from God, it followed that their power was a blessing, yet how could that be so if Avelyn Desbris, the thief, was so proficient with them?

The demon dactyl had given Avelyn the power! The demon dactyl had perverted the stones in Avelyn's hands, allowing him the insight to use them.

Markwart clutched his stones tightly and moved back to his bed, thinking that God had answered the dactyl by showing him equal—no, greater— insights. This time he would find no sleep, too consumed with anticipation for the morning's fight.

Dalebert Markwart, the Father Abbot, the highest-ranking member of the Abellican Church, had it all exactly backward, a thought that pleased the spirit of the demon dactyl immensely. How easily Bestesbulzibar had linked with this craven old man, how easily it had perverted Markwart's assumed truths!

Nearly all of St.-Mere-Abelle's more than seven hundred monks turned out on the seawall before the dawn, preparing for the approach of the powrie fleet. With two notable exceptions, Master Jojonah realized, for Brothers Youseff and Dandelion were nowhere to be found. Markwart had put them safely away for what he considered their more important task.

Most of the monks manned the abbey's long parapets, but others moved to their strategic positions in rooms below the level of the wall top. Two dozen catapults were readied as the vast powrie fleet made its way in toward the rocky cliff. Even more deadly, the older and more powerful monks, the masters and immaculates, monks who had studied for ten years and more, prepared their respective stones, and among them was the Father Abbot, with his new insights and heightened power.

Markwart kept most of the monks in position on the seaward side of the structure, though he had to place more than a score of brothers on the opposite wall, watching the many approaches for the expected land attack. Then all of St.-Mere-Abelle hushed and waited as score after score of powrie vessels rounded the rocky spur and moved in line with the great abbey, most resembling a nearly submerged barrel, but others with flat, open decks set with catapults.

A catapult let fly from one of the rooms just below the Father Abbot's position, its pitch ball sailing high and far, but well short of the nearest vessel.

"Hold!" Markwart yelled down angrily. "Would you show them our range, then?"

Master Jojonah put a hand on the Father Abbot's shoulder. "They are nervous," he offered as an excuse for the premature firing.

"They are foolish!" the Father Abbot snapped back at him, pulling from his gentle grasp. "Find the one who fired that catapult and replace him on the line—and bring him up to me."

Jojonah started to protest, but quickly realized that to be a fool's course. If he angered the Father Abbot any more—and he saw no way he could even speak with the man without doing that—then Markwart's punishment of the young monk would only be more severe. With one of his customary sighs, a helpless expression that he thought he seemed to be making far too often these days, the portly master moved off to find the errant artillerist, taking with him a second-year student to replace the man.

More and more powrie ships came into view, but those closest did not move into catapult range, or stone magic range.

"They await the ground assault," remarked Brother Francis Dellacourt, a ninth-year monk known for his sharp tongue and severe discipline of the younger students, attributes that had made him a favorite with Markwart.

"What news from the western walls?" Markwart asked.

Francis immediately motioned for two younger monks to run off for information. "They will hit us harder from the ground at first," Francis then offered to Markwart.

"The reasoning that led you to such a conclusion?"

"The sea cliff is a hundred feet, at least, and that at its shortest juncture," Francis reasoned. "Those powries in the boats will have little chance of gaining our walls unless we are sorely taxed in the west. They will hit us hard by ground, and then, with our numbers thinned on this wall, their fleet will strike."

"What do you know of powrie tactics?" Markwart said loudly, drawing all of those nearby, including the returning Master Jojonah and the errant artillerist, into the conversation. Markwart knew what Francis would say, for he, like all of the older monks, had studied the records of previous powrie assaults, but he thought that a dissertation by the efficient Francis would be a prudent reminder.

"We have few examples of a powrie dual strike," Francis admitted. "They usually attack primarily from the sea, with incredible speed and ferocity. But I suspect that St.-Mere-Abelle is too formidable for that, and they know it. They will thin our line by attacking from the west, by ground, and then their catapults will put their strong lines up over our wall."

"How high will any climb with us standing defense at the top of those ropes?" one monk asked impertinently. "We'll cut them down, or shoot arrows or magics at the climbing powries."

Master Jojonah started to respond, but Markwart, preferring to hear from Francis on this matter, stopped him with an upraised hand, then motioned for the ninth-year monk to proceed.

"Do not underestimate them!" Francis fumed, and Jojonah noted that Markwart cracked his first smile in many weeks. "Only months ago the powries struck at Pireth Tulme, a fortress on a cliff no less high than our own. In this manner they gained the courtyard before the majority of the garrison had even arrived at the walls to offer defense. And as for those who were in place along Pireth Tulme's seemingly defensible walls . . ."

Francis let the thought hang. It was common knowledge that no survivors had been found among Pireth Tulme's elite Coastpoint Guards, and also that those remains found had been horribly mutilated.

"Do not underestimate them!" Francis yelled again, turning as he spoke to ensure that every monk in the area was paying attention.

Master Jojonah watched Francis closely. He didn't like the man, not at all. Brother Francis' ambition was obviously large, as was his ability to take every word muttered by Father Abbot Markwart as though it had come straight from God. Jojonah did not believe that piety was the guiding force behind Brother Francis' devotion to Markwart, though, but rather, pragmatic ambition. Watching the man reveling in the attention now only reinforced that belief.

The two monks returned from the western wall, trotting, but with no apparent sense of urgency. "Nothing," each reported. "No signs of any gathering army."

"Several villagers came in just minutes ago," one of them added, "reporting that a large force of powries was spotted moving west of St.-Mere-Abelle village, heading west."

Jojonah and Markwart exchanged curious looks.

"A ruse," Brother Francis warned. "Moving west, away from us, that we might not be prepared for the sudden assault over land."

"Your reasoning is sound," Master Jojonah offered. "But I wonder if we might not turn their ruse, if that is what it is, back against them."

"Explain," said an intrigued Markwart.

"The fleet might indeed be waiting for the ground assault," Jojonah said. "And that assault might indeed be delayed so that we might lower our guard. But our powrie friends in the harbor cannot see St.-Mere-Abelle's western walls, nor the grounds beyond them."

"They will hear the sounds of battle," another monk reasoned.

"Or they will hear what they believe to be the sounds of battle," Master Jojonah replied slyly.

"I will see to it!" cried Brother Francis, running off even before the Father Abbot gave his consent.

Markwart ordered every second man off the wall and out of sight.

Moments later the commotion began, with cries of "Attack! Attack!" and the swooshing sound of ballistae firing. Then a tremendous explosion shook the ground and a fireball rose into the air, the magical blast of a ruby.

"Authentic," Master Jojonah said dryly. "But our exuberant Francis should conserve his magical energy."

"He has powries to convince," Markwart retorted sharply.

"Here they come," came a call before Jojonah could reply, and sure enough the powrie craft began gliding across the bay, right on schedule. The tumult continued in the west, the cries, the ballistae firing, even another fireball from excited Francis. The powries, spurred on by the sight and sound, came in hard, their barrelboats bobbing.

Markwart passed the word to let them in close, though more than one catapult let fly its payload prematurely. But the ships came on fast and were soon in range, and with the Father Abbot's eager blessing, the monastery's two dozen seaward catapults began their barrage, throwing stones and pitch. One powrie catapult barge went up in flames; a barrelboat got hit on its rounded side, the force of the boulder rolling the craft right over in the water. Another barrelboat took a hit squarely on its prow, the heavy stone driving the front of the craft under the water, its stern reaching skyward, its pedal-driven propeller spinning uselessly in the empty air. Soon many of the evil dwarves were in the water, screaming, thrashing.

But the cheering on the abbey's wall did not hold, for soon enough the lead powrie ships were right below the Father Abbot's position, right at the base of the seawall, and now their catapults went into action, launching dozens of weighted, knotted ropes tipped with cunning, many-pronged grapnels. The hooked instruments came down on targeted areas as thick as hail, sending the monks scrambling. Several monks were caught by a hooked tip, then pulled in screaming to the wall, the grapnel digging right through an arm or shoulder.

A group of seven immaculates stood in a circle to Jojonah's right, chanting in unison, joining their power, six with their hands locked, the seventh in their center, holding forth a piece of graphite. A sheet of blue electricity crackled over the bay, sparking off the metallic cranks of powrie catapults, laying low the dozens of exposed powries on the barge decks.

But the burst lasted only a split second, and dozens more powries rushed to take the places of the fallen. Up the ropes they came, hanging under, climbing hand over hand with tremendous speed.

Monks attacked with conventional bows and with gemstones, loosing lightning bolts, springing fire from their fingertips to burn the ropes, while others went at the grapnels with heavy hammers or at the ropes with swords. Dozens of ropes went down, sending powries diving into the bay, but scores more came flying up as more craft crowded into the base of the cliff.

With still no sign of any approaching ground force, all of the monks came to the seawall, all of St.-Mere-Abelle's power focused on the thousand powrie vessels that had swarmed into All Saints Bay. The air came alive with the tingling of magical energy, with the stench of burning pitch, with the screams of freezing, drowning powries. And with the screams of dying monks, for as soon as all the ropes were up, the powrie catapult barges began hurling huge baskets of pinballs, wooden balls an inch in diameter set with a multitude of metal, often poison-tipped needles.

Despite all the talk of Pireth Tulme, all the warnings of the older, more studied monks, the defenders of St.-Mere-Abelle were indeed taken aback at the sheer ferocity and boldness of the assault. And of the skill, for the powries were as efficient and disciplined a fighting army as any in all the world. Not a monk, not even stubborn Brother Francis, doubted for a moment that if the enemy ground force had made its appearance then, St.-Mere-Abelle, the most ancient and defensible bastion in all of Honce-the-Bear, would have fallen.

Even without that ground force, Father Abbot Markwart appreciated the danger of the situation.

"You!" he called to the monk who had fired the first catapult shot. "Now is the chance to redeem yourself!"

The young brother, eager to regain the Father Abbot's favor, rushed to Markwart's side and was presented with three stones: a malachite, a ruby, and a serpentine.

"Do not use the malachite until you descend near to the ship," the Father Abbot explained hastily.

The young monk's eyes went wide as he discerned the intent. The Father Abbot wanted him to leap from the cliff, plummet to one particularly large tangle of powrie ships, enact the levitational malachite and the fire-shield serpentine, and then loose a fireball across the vessels.

"He'll not get close," Jojonah started to protest, but Markwart turned on him with such ferocity that the portly master abruptly backed away. Markwart was wrong in sending this young monk, Jojonah maintained privately, for the three-stone usage was more suited to an older and more experienced monk, an immaculate at least, or even a master. Even if the young man managed the difficult feat, the explosion would not be extreme, a puff of flame, perhaps, and nothing to deter the powries.

"We have no options," Markwart said to the young monk. "That group of ships must be dealt with, and immediately, or our walls will be lost!"

Even as he spoke, a pair of powries came over the wall to the side. The immaculates fell over them at once, beating them down before they could get in defensive posture and then cutting free the ropes in the area. But still, Markwart's point had been clearly reinforced.

"They'll not notice you coming, except to think you were thrown over by one of their own," he explained. "By the time they realize the truth, they will be burning and you will be ascending."

The monk nodded, clutched the stones tightly and leaped up to the top of the wall. With a look back, he jumped far and high, plummeting down the cliff face. Markwart, Jojonah, and several others rushed to the wall to watch his descent, and the Father Abbot cursed loudly when the malachite turned that plummet into the gentle fall of a feather in a stiff breeze—with the monk still many yards above the deck level.

"Fool!" Markwart roared as the powries focused on the man, throwing spears and hammers, raising their small crossbows. To the young monk's credit—or perhaps because of his sudden terror, or perhaps because he simply did not possess the magical knowledge and strength—he did not reverse direction and begin floating back up the cliff, but continued down, down.

A crossbow bolt dove into his arm; a stone tumbled from his hand.

"The serpentine!" Jojonah cried.

The young monk, clutching his arm, twitching and turning in a futile effort to dodge the growing barrage, was obviously trying to float back up.

"No!" Markwart yelled at him.

"He has no shield against the fireball!" Jojonah yelled at the Father Abbot.

The young monk jerked spasmodically, hit by a crossbow bolt, then another, then a third, in rapid succession. His magical energy left him along with his life force, and his limp body dropped the rest of the way, bouncing off a powrie barge and into the dark waters of All Saints Bay.

"Fetch me one of our peasant guests!" Markwart yelled at Brother Francis.

"He was not strong enough," Jojonah said to the Father Abbot. "That was no task for a mere novice. An immaculate might not complete such a feat!"

"I would send you, and be glad to be rid of you," Markwart screamed in his face, stunning him into silence. "But you are needed."

Brother Francis returned with a young villager, a man of about twenty, looking sheepish. "I can use a bow," the man said, trying to appear brave. "I have hunted deer—"

"Take this instead," Father Abbot Markwart instructed, handing him a ruby.

The man's eyes widened at the sight and smooth feel of the sacred stone. "I cannot . . ." he stammered, not understanding.

"But I can," snarled Markwart, and he held forth another stone, his mighty hematite, the soul stone.

The man looked at him blankly; Brother Francis, understanding enough to know that he should distract the peasant, smacked him hard across the face, knocking him to the ground.

Master Jojonah looked away.

Francis closed on the man, meaning to strike him again.

"It is done," the man announced, and Francis held back the blow and reverently helped him to his feet.

"Possession," Jojonah spat distastefully. He could hardly believe that Markwart had done this wicked thing, which was normally considered the absolute darkest side of the hematite. By all edicts, possessing another's body was an act to be avoided—indeed, an act that monks spirit-walking with hematite often guarded against by preparing other protective stones. And when he thought about what he had just seen, Jojonah could hardly believe that the possession, perhaps the most difficult of any known task for the gemstones, had been completed so easily!

The Father Abbot in the peasant's body walked calmly to the wall, glanced out over the edge to locate the greatest tangle of powrie vessels, then, without a moment's hesitation, calmly leaped over the side. No malachite this time, no screaming, no fear. The Father Abbot focused on the ruby as he plunged the hundred feet, bringing the stone's energy to a peak and loosing a tremendous, concussive fireball just before he slammed the deck. His spirit deserted the peasant body immediately, flying through the flames, away from the agony and back to his own waiting form atop the seawall.

He blinked his tired old eyes open, acclimating to his own body and fighting past that instant of sheer terror when he had neared the powrie decks, when he consumed his own borrowed form in magical fires. All the monks around him, with the notable exception of Master Jojonah, were cheering wildly, many looking over the wall at the burning mass of powrie vessels, uttering praises of disbelief that anyone could ignite so tremendous a fireball.

"It had to be done," Markwart said curtly to Jojonah.

The master didn't blink.

"To sacrifice one for the sake of others is the highest precept of our Order," Markwart reminded.

"To sacrifice oneself," Master Jojonah corrected.

"Go from this place, to the catapult crews," a disgusted Markwart ordered dismissively.

Though Jojonah realized that his stone skills were still needed up on the roof, he was glad to comply. He glanced back at Markwart many times as he departed, for while others were purely awestruck by the magical display, Jojonah, who had known Markwart for more than forty years, was simply confused, and more than a little suspicious.

*   *   *

There was one entrance to St.-Mere-Abelle from the wharf area at the level of All Saints Bay, but so great were the doors down there—oak wood, two feet thick and reinforced with metal banding, backed by a portcullis with pegs as thick as a man's thigh, and that backed by another falling wall, as thick and strong as the outer doors—that no powries, not even the huge fomorian giants, could have broken through them if they had spent a week at it.

That was assuming, however, that the doors were closed.

If they could have seen over the cliff well enough to spot the doors, neither Father Abbot Markwart nor Master Jojonah would have been surprised to see those great portals swing open in invitation to the groups of powries that had managed to escape the blast and drag themselves onto the rocky shore. In fact, both men had expected this very thing when Master De'Unnero had volunteered, indeed insisted, that he be the one heading the contingent of twelve at the low station guard post. That group had two ballistae, one on either side of the great doors, but their firing range was severely limited by the narrow scope of their shooting slits, and Markwart had known full well that De'Unnero would never be satisfied with launching a few, usually ineffective bolts.

So the young and fiery master had opened the doors, and now he stood exposed in the corridor just inside, laughing hysterically, daring the powries to enter.

A group of nearly a score of the bloody caps, battered already but never afraid, did come roaring in, brandishing hammers and axes and cruel short swords.

As the last of them passed under the portcullis, it fell with a resounding crash, its vibrations reaching all through the abbey, all the way up to the seawall.

Startled but not stopped, the bloody caps yelled all the louder and charged on. A dozen crossbow bolts whipped out into their ranks, taking down a few but hardly slowing the charge.

There stood De'Unnero, alone, laughing, his honed muscles straining so tightly against his skin that it seemed they might tear right through. Other monks, principally Master Jojonah, had often voiced their belief that De'Unnero's heart would simply explode, for the young master was too intense for the wrappings of any human coil. He seemed to fit that image now, verily trembling with inner energy. He held no weapon that the powries could see, only a single stone, a tiger's paw, smooth brown and with black streaks.

Now he brought forth the magic of that stone, and as the first powrie neared, De'Unnero's arms were transformed, taking the shape of the mighty forelegs of a tiger.

"*Yach!*" the lead powrie cried, lifting its weapon defensively.

De'Unnero was too quick for that, springing ahead like a hunting cat, slashing his right arm down across the powrie's face, tearing away its features.

The master seemed to go into a frenzy then, but in truth, he was in perfect control, springing from side to side to prevent any powries from getting past him, though a dozen other monks stood in the corridor to meet their charge. The stone had stayed with his transformed paw, melding to the skin, and De'Unnero fell deeper into its grasp now, and though his outward appearance changed no more, his inner muscles became those of the cat.

A swipe of his tiger arm sent one of the powries flying; with a flick of his legs muscles, he darted to the side, avoiding a smash from a hammer. Then a second muscular twitch brought him back in front of the attacking powrie before the startled dwarf had even lifted its hammer.

The claws raked viciously, and that powrie's face disappeared, too.

Those powries behind were giving ground now, but De'Unnero's battle lust was far from sated. His legs twitched, launching him fully twenty-five feet ahead, landing in the midst of the dwarves. He became a whirlwind of flailing claws and kicking feet. Powries were no minor enemy, but though they outnumbered this creature nine to one, they wanted nothing to do with him. They scrambled and rushed. Two went back for the portcullis, crying to their comrades who were still outside, while several others staggered past the fighting De'Unnero, stumbling down the corridor, where they were met by a second volley of crossbow quarrels.

All but one of the monks dropped their crossbows and drew weapons for close melee, though a handful rushed forward to finish the dwarves with only their bare hands.

Farther down the corridor, De'Unnero held the last powrie standing before him by the head, between his great paws. His claws had dug right through the powrie's skull, and he whipped the creature back and forth now as easily as if it was a down-filled child's doll. Then he threw it aside and started an advance on the two at the portcullis.

Beyond them, a powrie leveled a blowgun and let fly, scoring a hit on De'Unnero's belly, just below his rib cage.

The monk roared, a tiger's roar, and tore the dart free, along with a considerable amount of flesh, continuing his determined advance. The powrie gunner popped another dart into place; the two dwarves at the portcullis screamed and tried to squeeze through.

Then the inner sliding door fell, snapping the blowgun and squashing the two powries flat.

De'Unnero skidded to a stop as a spray of blood washed over him. He turned about and roared again, a battle cry that became a call of frustration as he realized that his soldiers had efficiently dealt with the remaining dwarves. The fight was over.

The fierce master came back fully to his human form, exhausted by the effort both physical and magical. He felt the profound sting in his belly then, a burning, washing sensation, and realized he had been poisoned. Most of that poison, a paralyzing and painful concoction, had been defeated by the sheer energy of the magical transformations, but enough remained to bring such a fit of trembling to the monk that he was soon down on one knee.

His soldiers crowded around him, concerned.

"Man the ballistae!" he growled at them, and though De'Unnero was fully human once more, his voice was as ferocious as the roar of the hunting tiger. The younger monks obeyed, and by sheer determination Master De'Unnero soon joined them, directing their shots.

With the main tangle of powrie vessels burning and out of the fight, the watching monks dispersed from that area, running to bolster the wall defenses wherever necessary. Many powries gained the wall through that long and vicious morning, but none found a lasting hold, and by midday, with still no sign of any approaching ground force, the outcome was no longer in doubt. The powries fought on, as powries always will, and more than fifty monks were slain, and several times that number injured, but the powrie losses were staggering, with more than half the thousand vessel fleet going to the bottom of All Saints Bay, and the hundreds that escaped slipping out into deeper waters, manned by only skeleton crews.

By mid-afternoon Master Jojonah had joined with the other older monks proficient in stone use in tending the many wounded, while younger brothers had already organized burial detail for those beyond the help of the soul stones. The battle had slipped into its last stage, the cleanup, as the chaos of fighting died away. Soon the discipline of the brothers put the duties into order, pragmatic and efficient. One thing did strike Master Jojonah as curious, though. The Father Abbot, who had in his possession, Jojonah knew, the most powerful soul stone in all St.-Mere-Abelle, walked among the wounded and offered hopeful words, but seemed to be tending none. The concussive fireball, and a couple of other lightning blasts that Markwart had screeched along the wall top, were hours old now, and so Markwart's remarks that he had no magical energy left made little sense.

The portly master could only shrug helplessly and shake his head, then, when Master De'Unnero arrived at the wall, his side torn open wide, though the fierce man was hardly limping or showing any sign that he felt any pain at all. Still, Markwart moved near and promptly sealed the wound with the soul stone. Jojonah had known that the bond between these two was tight, as tight as the one between the Father Abbot and Brother Francis.

He went about his work quietly, digesting it all, filing it away until he could find enough private time to properly reason it through.

*   *   *

"You insist upon thrusting yourself in danger's way," Markwart scolded De'Unnero as the gaping wound sealed under the influence of the hematite.

"A man must find his enjoyment," the master replied with a mischievous grin. "Enjoyment you continue to deny me."

Markwart stepped back and looked harshly at him, understanding the complaint all too well. "How goes the training?" he asked sharply.

"Youseff shows promise," De'Unnero admitted. "He is cunning and will use any weapon and any tactic to find victory."

"And Brother Dandelion?"

"A mighty bear, strong of arm but weak of mind," said De'Unnero. "He will serve our purposes well, as long as Youseff guides his actions."

The Father Abbot nodded, seeming pleased.

"I could defeat them both together," De'Unnero asserted, stealing his superior's smug look. "They will hold the title of Brothers Justice, yet I could crush them both, and easily. And I could go and retrieve Avelyn and the gemstones."

Markwart had no practical argument against the claim. "You are a master, and have other duties," he said.

"More important than the hunt for Avelyn?"

"Equally important," Markwart said with a tone of finality. "Youseff and Dandelion will serve this purpose, if Master Marcalo De'Unnero properly trains them."

De'Unnero's face crinkled severely, his eyes narrowing, throwing imaginary daggers at the Father Abbot. He did not like to be questioned, not at all.

Markwart recognized the look, for he had seen it often. He knew, though, that De'Unnero would not cross him, and given that, such intensity could be put to good use.

"Let me go hunting," De'Unnero said plainly.

"You train the hunters," Markwart shot back. "Trust me, you will find rewards for your efforts." With that, the Father Abbot walked away.

"We were valiant this day," Master De'Unnero proudly offered to Markwart and the other masters at their summary meeting after vespers.

"But also fortunate," Master Jojonah reminded them all. "For neither the powrie ground force nor the goblin army that has been oft sighted in the region made its appearance."

"More than luck, I would reason," Francis piped in, though it was not the man's place to speak at such a meeting. Francis wasn't even an immaculate yet, after all, and was only at the meeting as an attendant of the Father Abbot. Still, Markwart made no move to silence him, and the other masters afforded him the floor. "This is uncharacteristic of our enemy," Francis went on. "Every tale from the battle lines north of Palmaris indicate that our monstrous foes fight with cohesion and guidance, and it is obvious from the success of our ruse that those powrie ships were indeed waiting for the ground army to engage."

"Where, then, were—are—the enemy ground armies?" Markwart asked impatiently. "Will we awake on the morrow to find that we are besieged once again?"

"The fleet will not return," another master responded immediately. "And if the monsters come at us from the ground, they will find our fortifications even more formidable than those that protected us by sea."

Master Jojonah happened to be looking at De'Unnero when these words were spoken, and was disgusted to see the man's almost feral smile, a grin truly unbefitting a master of the Abellican Order.

"Triple the guard along the walls this night, land and sea," the Father Abbot decided.

"Many are weary from the fighting," said Master Engress, a gentle man and a friend of Jojonah's.

"Then use the peasants," Markwart snapped at him abruptly. "They have come in to eat our food and hide behind the shelter of abbey walls and brother flesh. Let them earn their keep at watch, this night and every night."

Engress looked at Jojonah and at several other masters, but none dared question Markwart's tone. "It will be done, Father Abbot," Master Engress said humbly.

The Father Abbot pushed his chair back forcefully, the legs screeching on the wooden floor. He rose and waved his hand dismissively, then walked out of the room, the meeting at its end.

By Markwart's reasoning, all important business had been concluded. The man wanted to be alone with his thoughts, and with his emotions, some of which were troubling indeed. He had sent a man flying to his death this day, an act that still required a bit of rationalization, and he was also conscious of the fact that he had not been greatly involved in the healing process after the fight. There had remained magical energy within him—he had known that even as he spoke falsely to excuse himself—but he simply hadn't *felt* like helping out. He had gone to one injured monk, a man sitting against the seawall, his arm badly torn from a sliding powrie grapnel, but when he moved to heal the man with the hematite, an action that required an intimate connection, he recoiled, feeling . . . what?

Loathing? Repulsion?

Markwart had no practical answers, but he trusted in his instincts completely. There was a perversion, a weakness, growing within the Order, he realized. Avelyn—always it was that foul Avelyn!—had begun the rot, and now, it seemed, it was a more general thing than even he had believed.

Yes, that was it, the Father Abbot understood. They were growing weak and so full of compassion that they could no longer recognize and properly deal with true evil. Like Jojonah and his foolish sympathy for the peasant whose sacrifice had saved so many lives.

But not De'Unnero, Markwart thought, and he managed a smile. The man was strong, and brilliant. Perhaps he should concede to the man's wishes and let him be the one to hunt down Avelyn and the gemstones; with Marcalo De'Unnero set to the task, success would almost be assured.

The Father Abbot shook his head, reminding himself that he had other plans for the master. De'Unnero would be moved high in line as his successor, the Father Abbot silently vowed. As soon as he had seen De'Unnero's wounds, Markwart had desired to heal them, as though the sacred soul stone had called to him to act, had shown him the truth.

It was all sorting out neatly for Father Abbot Markwart. He made a mental note to properly eulogize the fireballing peasant, perhaps even to erect a statue in the man's honor, and then he went to bed.

He slept soundly.

Scouts went out from St.-Mere-Abelle the next day, scouring the countryside and then returning to report that no sign of monsters was to be found anywhere near the abbey. Within a week the situation was made clear: the powrie invasion force had gone back to their ships and departed—for where, no one knew. The goblin army, and indeed there was a huge force in the region, had fractured, with rogue bands running haphazard, sacking towns.

The Kingsmen, Honce-the-Bear's army, were tracking down the rogue bands one at a time and destroying them.

At St.-Mere-Abelle, the implications of this seemingly good news went far deeper.

"We must look to the source of our enemy's disarray," Father Abbot Markwart told his senior monks. "To the Barbacan and this rumored explosion."

"You believe that the demon dactyl has been destroyed," Master Jojonah reasoned.

"I believe that our enemy has been decapitated," Markwart replied. "But we must know the truth of it."

"An expedition," Master Engress stated plainly.

Brother Francis was the first out of the room, eager to put together the plans for a trip to the Barbacan, eager, as always, to please the Father Abbot.

❖ 3 ❖

Roger Lockless

"He's in there," the old woman groaned. "I know he be! Oh, the poor child."

"Might be that he's dead already," said another, a man of about thirty winters. "That would be the most merciful. Poor child."

A group of a dozen villagers crouched on a bluff a quarter mile north of their old home, Caer Tinella, watching the powries and the goblins. A pair of fomorian giants had also been in the town earlier that day, but were out now, probably hunting refugees.

"He should not have gone down there, and I told him so," the old woman asserted. "Too many, too many."

Off to the side, Tomas Gingerwart gave a knowing smile. These people didn't understand the lad named Roger. To them he was Roger Billingsbury, an orphan boy who had been taken in by the town. When Roger's parents had both died, the common thinking was to send him south to Palmaris, perhaps to the monks of St. Precious. But the folk of Caer Tinella, truly a bonded community, decided to keep Roger with them, with all of them helping him get through the trials of grief and sickness.

For Roger was a poor, skinny waif, so obviously frail. His physical development had been stunted at the age of eleven, stolen by the same fever that killed his parents, and his two sisters, as well.

That was several years ago, but to these worried townsfolk, Roger, who looked much the same, was still that little lost boy.

Tomas knew better. The lad's name was no longer Billingsbury, but Lockless, Roger Lockless, a tag given him for good reason indeed. There was nothing Roger couldn't open, or slip through, or sneak around. Tomas reminded himself of that often as he looked to Caer Tinella, for in truth, he was also a bit worried. But only a bit.

"A line o' them," the old woman cackled, pointing emphatically toward the town. Her eyes were sharp, for indeed a group of goblins moved across the town square, escorting a line of ragged-looking human prisoners—those people of Caer Tinella and the neighboring community of Landsdown who had not been quick enough or hidden deep enough in the woods. Now the monsters were using the towns as encampments, and the captured humans as slaves.

All of the refugees understood what grim fate would befall those captives when they were no longer useful to the powries and goblins.

"You should not be looking upon them," came a voice, and the group turned as one to see the approach of a portly man, Belster O'Comely. "And we are all too close to the towns, I fear. Would you have us all captured?" Despite his best efforts, Belster, the jovial innkeeper who used to run the very respectable Howling Sheila in Dundalis, could not manage too sharp an edge to his voice. He had come south with the refugees from the three towns of the Timberlands: Dundalis, Weedy Meadow, and End-o'-the-World. Belster's companions from the northland were a far different group, though, quite unlike the more recently displaced people of Caer Tinella and Landsdown, and those of the handful of other smaller communities along the road south to the great port city of Palmaris. Belster's group, trained by the mysterious ranger known as Nightbird, were far from pitiful and far from afraid. They hid from the goblins, to be sure, but when they found the terms favorable, they became the hunters, with goblins, powries, even giants, their prey.

"We will make a try for them, as I promised," Belster continued. "But not so soon. Oh no. We'll be no good to our fellows dead! Now come along."

"Is there nothing to be done?" the old woman said angrily.

"Pray, dear lady," Belster replied in all sincerity. "Pray for them all."

Tomas Gingerwart nodded his agreement. And pray for the goblins, he silently added, thinking that Roger must be having a grand time of it by now.

Belster didn't miss the smirk, and moved to speak with Tomas alone.

"You wish that I would do more," the portly innkeeper said quietly, misinterpreting Tomas' look. "And so do I, my friend. But I have a hundred and fifty under my care."

"Closer to a hundred and eighty, counting those from Caer Tinella and about," Tomas corrected.

"And only two score and ten fit for fighting, to guard them all with," Belster remarked. "How might I risk my warriors on a raid against the town with so many lives at stake?"

"I do not doubt your wisdom, Master O'Comely," Tomas said sincerely. "You vow to raid the town when the time is right, but I fear that you will find no such time. The goblins are lax, but the powries not so. A cunning lot, well trained for war. Their guard will not drop."

"Then what am I to do?" asked a distressed Belster.

"Keep to your duty," Tomas replied. "And that duty is to the hundred and eighty, not to those already in powrie clutches."

Belster eyed the man unblinkingly for a long while, and Tomas could see the pain in the gentle man's eyes. The innkeeper did not want to let a single human slip through his protective web.

"You cannot save them all," Tomas said simply.

"But I must try."

Tomas was shaking his head before Belster finished. "Do not play the fool's game," he scolded, and Belster realized for the first time that Tomas' earlier smirk was not derisive, was not in response to his hesitance in going into Caer Tinella. "If you attack openly," Tomas continued, "then expect to be routed. And I fear that our powrie and goblin friends would not be satisfied with that, but would expand their search of the forest until all of us were hunted down and taken prisoner—or slain, in the case of many, the older folk and children too young to be of any use."

"So you agree with my decision to hold? Even to retreat our line?"

"Reluctantly," Tomas replied. "As reluctantly as do you. You are a man of conscience, Belster O'Comely, and fortunate are we of Caer Tinella that you and yours have come south."

Belster took the compliment in stride, needing the support. He couldn't help another glance in the direction of the occupied town, though, his heart breaking at the thought of the torment those poor prisoners must now be experiencing.

Another curious onlooker was watching the procession of slaves as the goblins led them to the dark forest on the edge of Caer Tinella. Roger Lockless knew the workings of the town better than any other. Ever since the invasion, he had been in Caer Tinella nearly every night, moving from shadow to shadow, listening to the goblins and powries lay their plans for the area, or overhearing talk of the greater war being waged not so far to the south. More than anything else, the crafty Roger Lockless knew his enemy, and knew where they were vulnerable. When he left the town before dawn each day, his slight frame was usually laden with goods for the refugees in the nearby woods. And so careful was he in his stealing that the monsters rarely realized they were being robbed.

His work three nights previous remained his shining achievement to date. He had stolen a pony, the boss powrie's favorite mount, and taken it in such a way as to implicate a pair of goblin sentries, who, as Roger had previously discovered through some fine spying, happened by coincidence to be feasting that very night on a horse.

Both were hanged in the town square the next morning—Roger watched that, too.

The young man, barely more than a boy, knew that today was different. Today the goblins meant to kill one of their prisoners; he had heard them talking about it before dawn, which prompted him to stay around as the day brightened. The goblins had caught Mrs. Kelso stuffing her mouth with an extra biscuit, and the powrie boss, a thoroughly disagreeable fellow named Kos-kosio Begulne, ordered her slain in the morning as an example to the others.

She was out there, chopping at the trees with the rest of the poor prisoners, oblivious to the fact that she had only hours left to live.

Roger had witnessed much cruelty in the last few weeks, had seen several people butchered for no better reason than the fact that a goblin or powrie didn't like the way they looked. Always, the pragmatic young thief would shake his head and look the other way. "Not my business," he often reminded himself.

This was different. Mrs. Kelso was a friend, a dear friend who had often fed him when he was younger, an orphaned waif running the streets of Caer Tinella. He had spent years sleeping in her barn, for though her husband had little use for him and kept telling him to get away, gentle Mrs. Kelso usually ushered the man aside, glancing back and winking at Roger, then nodding toward the barn.

She was a good lady, and Roger found it hard this day to shake his head and say, "Not my business."

But what could he do? He was no fighter, and even if he were, there were a pair of huge fomorians in or about Caer Tinella, more than a hundred goblins, half that number of powries, and probably ten times that number of monsters running around in the forest and the neighboring villages. He had hoped to get Mrs. Kelso out of town before the dawn, but by the time he heard the grim plans for her, the prisoners had already been roused, lined up, and placed under heavy guard.

One problem at a time, Roger repeatedly told himself. The prisoners were chained to each other ankle-to-ankle, separated by five-foot lengths of chain, each person chained to two others. For added security, the shackles on each prisoner were not a matching pair and were finely made, with one chained to the shackle on the leg of a slave to the right, the other chained to a slave on the left. Roger estimated he would need nearly a full minute to get through both locks, and that only if Mrs. Kelso and the two prisoners chained to her kept still and cooperated.

A minute was a long time with powrie crossbowmen nearby.

"Diversion, diversion, diversion," the young thief muttered repeatedly, slipping from shadow to shadow about the occupied town. "A call to arms? No no no. A fire?"

Roger paused, focusing his thoughts on a pair of goblins taking some rest on the piles of last season's hay just inside Yosi Hoosier's barn. One of them had a pipe stuck in its mouth and was blowing gigantic rings of noxious smoke.

"Oh, but I love fire," Roger whispered. Off he went, silent and quick as a hunting cat, taking a wide circuit of the barn, slipping into the structure— as he had so often in the last few years—through a broken board far in the back. Soon he was crouched behind the hay within a few feet of the oblivious goblins. He waited patiently for nearly ten minutes, until the smoker tapped out his pipe and began loading fresh weed.

Roger was good at making fires—another of his many talents. He moved back so he wouldn't be heard, then struck flint to steel over a few pieces of straw.

Then he crept back and pushed the straw in carefully, in the general area where the smoker had tapped out his pipe.

Then he was gone, back out of the barn before the first wisps of smoke tickled the noses of the goblin pair.

The hay went up like a giant candle, and how the goblins howled!

"Attack!" some yelled. "Enemies! Enemies!" cried others. But when they went to investigate and saw their comrades batting wildly at the flames, including one goblin with a lit pipe still stuck in its mouth, they changed their song.

Those goblins out with the woodcutting prisoners did not go in to fight fire, but their attention was diverted enough for Roger to easily scamper around the back of the group, coming to a stop behind the large oak that Mrs. Kelso was halfheartedly chopping. She let out a chirp when he peeked around, but he quickly hushed her and those nearby.

"Hear me quick," he whispered, crawling halfway around, his hands immediately going to work on her shackles while he locked Mrs. Kelso's gaze with his own. "Now stand still! They mean to kill you. I heard them."

"You cannot take her out or they'll kill us all!" one man complained, his voice loud enough to draw a growl and an order to "Work!" from the goblin guards.

"You must take us all, then," demanded another.

"That I cannot do," Roger replied. "But they won't kill you, they won't even blame you."

"But—" the first man started, before Roger hushed him with a look.

"When I get her free, I will put her shackles about that sapling," he explained. "Give us a five-count to get away, then here is what you do . . ."

"Stupid Grimy Snorts and that smelly pipe o' his," one of the goblin guards remarked, sorting out the mess in the town proper. "Ugly Kos-kosio ain't to be giving us extra food tonight."

The other laughed. "Might that we'll be eating Grimy Snorts!"

"Demon!" came a cry that sent the goblins spinning. They saw the prisoner line, tools thrown down, the people struggling mightily, trying to run away.

" 'Ere now!" one of the goblins yelled, charging up to the nearest human and laying her low with a shield rush. " 'Ere now!"

"Demon!" yelled the other humans, precisely as Roger had instructed them. "Demon dactyl!"

"He turned her into a tree!" one woman shrieked. The goblins guards looked on curiously, even scratched their heads, dumbstruck, for the two lines of prisoners—and there did seem to be two lines now—were stretched out to the length of the chains, and were both anchored by a small but sturdy sapling.

"A tree?" one goblin croaked.

"Blimey," said another.

All the attention of the encampment shifted from the now dying fire in the barn to the bustle at the forest's edge. Many goblins ran over, along with the powrie host, led by their merciless leader, Kos-kosio Begulne.

"What'd ye see?" the powrie demanded of the man who had been chained to Mrs. Kelso's right and was now closest to the sapling.

"Demon," the man sputtered.

"Demon?" Kos-kosio echoed skeptically. "And what'd the demon look like?"

"Big and black," the man stammered. "Big winged shadow. I . . . I didn't stay nearby to watch. He . . . it turned poor Mrs. Kelso into a tree!"

"Mrs. Kelso?" Kos-kosio Begulne repeated a couple of times, until he remembered the woman and the fate he had planned for her. Had Bestes-bulzibar, the demon dactyl, the lord of the dark army, returned? Was this a signal from the dactyl that it was again with him, Kos-kosio, watching over his operation?

A shudder coursed the powrie's spine as he remembered the fate of a former leader of this band, a goblin named Gothra. In a fit of its all-too-typical rage, Bestesbulzibar had ripped the skin from the goblin while it remained alive to watch and to feel. That was when Kos-kosio had been put in charge, and the powrie had known from the beginning that this was a tentative command.

The powrie studied the tree closely, trying to remember, without success, if the sapling had been there all along. Had Bestesbulzibar really returned, or was it a trick? the ever-suspicious powrie wondered.

"Search all the area!" Kos-kosio ordered his minions, and when they started out cautiously, eyes darting about, the powrie roared even louder, promising death to any who did not hustle.

"And yerself, human dog," Kos-kosio said to the man nearest the tree. "Pick up yer stinking axe and cut Mrs. Kelso down!"

The man's horrified expression was convincing enough to bring a smile to the ugly powrie's square-chinned face.

Roger realized he was taking a chance in coming back near the town, but with Mrs. Kelso safely on her way to Tomas and the others, he simply couldn't resist the sport of it all. He relaxed comfortably, his back against a tree, as two stupid goblins wandered right below him. When that patrol had moved farther along and no others were in the immediate area, he moved in even closer, climbing into the same oak he had slithered around to get to Mrs. Kelso in the first place.

Then he watched contentedly. The humans were back to work—the two men who had been flanking Mrs. Kelso now shackled together—and the powries had returned to the town, leaving a handful of goblins to guard the humans, and another dozen or so of the nervous wretches searching the woods.

Yes, it was a perfectly wonderful situation, Roger mused, for never in his young life had he found so much fun.

❖ *4* ❖

At the Gates of Paradise

Graceful and strong, Nightbird slipped down from Symphony's side while the horse was in mid-gallop. The ranger hit the ground running, stringing Hawkwing as he went, while Pony, who had been sitting behind him on the horse, hopped forward, took up the reins and kept Symphony's run true and in control, for the muddy ground was treacherous. She expertly veered the horse to the left, around the base of a wide mound, while Elbryan went right.

Before Pony and Symphony were halfway around, they spotted the trio of goblins they had been chasing. Two were far ahead, running wildly for the cover of a copse of trees, but the third had doubled back and was going around the mound the other way. "Coming fast!" Pony yelled and bent low on Symphony, angling the horse more sharply about the hillock.

Symphony broke stride as the goblin came staggering back out from behind the mound, clutching at the arrow lodged in its throat. A second arrow hit it in the chest, dropping it to the mud.

"They made for the trees," Pony said to the ranger as he came running into sight. "They will lay up in there," she reasoned.

The ranger slowed and glanced at the copse, then, apparently agreeing, he went to the dead goblin and began extracting his arrows. That done, he stood again and scanned the landscape, a curious expression crossing his handsome face.

"We can do a circuit of the copse," Pony reasoned. "Find the best way to get in and strike at them."

Nightbird seemed not to be listening.

"Elbryan?"

Still the ranger kept looking around, his mouth open now, his face full of wonderment.

"Elbryan?" the woman said again, more insistent.

"I know this place," he replied absently, his gaze darting from spot to spot.

"The Moorlands?" Pony asked incredulously, her face scrunching with disgust as she looked around at the desolate region. "How could you?"

"I passed this very way on my road back to Dundalis," he explained. "When I left the elves." He ran to a nearby birch tangle, bending low as if he expected his long-ago campsite to still be under there. "Yes," he said excitedly. "I slept here in this very place one quiet night. The gnats were horrific," he added with a chuckle.

"The goblins?" Pony asked, nodding in the direction of the distant copse.

"I did find some goblins in here, but farther to the east, on the edges of the Moorlands," Elbryan replied.

"I mean *those* goblins," Pony said firmly, pointing ahead.

Elbryan waved his hand dismissively. The goblins were not important to him at the moment, not with that long-ago traveled road coming clearer and clearer in his mind. He scrambled to the side, past Pony and Symphony, and looked over the splotchy brush and the rolling clay to the black silhouette of mountaintops just visible far in the west, their outlines silver under the light of the descending sun.

"Forget the goblins," Elbryan said suddenly, grabbing Symphony's bridle and leading horse and rider away, on a course that would bring them well to the side of the copse of trees and more directly in line with the distant mountains.

"Forget them?" Pony echoed. "We chased that tribe twenty miles, into the Moorlands and more than halfway through. I've got a thousand gnat bites swelling on every part of my body, and the smell of this place will follow us for a year to come! And you want me to just forget them?"

"They are unimportant," Elbryan said without looking at her. "The last two out of thirty. With their score-and-eight companions slain, I doubt they'll head back toward End-o'-the-World for some time to come."

"Do not underestimate goblin mischief," Pony replied.

"Forget them," Elbryan said again.

Pony lowered her head and growled softly. She could hardly believe that Elbryan was leading her farther west, away from the Timberlands, even if he meant to dismiss the goblin pair. But she trusted him, and if her guess was right, they were closer to the western edge of the Moorlands than the eastern. The sooner they got out of this wretched, bug-ridden place, the better she would like it.

They went on for a short while, until the sun began to set over the distant mountains, then Elbryan went about the task of setting up camp. They were still in the Moorlands, still haunted by the buzzing insects, and, even more to Pony's dislike, they were still too close to the copse of trees wherein the goblins had disappeared. She repeatedly tried to point this out to her companion, but he would hear none of it. "I must go to Oracle," he announced.

Pony followed his gaze to the base of a large tree, one root pulled up out of the soft ground to create a small hollow underneath. "A fine place to be sitting when the goblins come charging in," the woman replied sourly.

"There were only two."

"You doubt that they'll find friends in this wretched place?" Pony asked. "We could set our camp with thoughts of a quiet night, only to find that we are fighting half the entire goblin army before the dawn."

Elbryan seemed to have run out of answers. He chewed his bottom lip for a bit, looking to the nearby tree, its hollowed base inviting him to Oracle. He had to go to Uncle Mather, he felt, and soon, before the images of that long-lost trail faded from his thoughts.

"Go and do what you must," Pony said to him, recognizing the true dilemma etched on his face. "But give me the cat's-eye. Symphony and I will scout about for any signs of enemies."

Elbryan was genuinely relieved as he took the circlet from his head and handed it to the woman. It was a gift from Avelyn Desbris that he and Pony had been passing back and forth as needed. He couldn't use it in Oracle anyway; it would defeat the whole mood of the meditation, for the gemstone set in the front of the circlet, a chrysoberyl, more commonly known as cat's-eye, would allow the wearer of the circlet to see clearly in the darkest of nights, even in the darkest of caves.

"You owe me for my indulgence," Pony informed him as she placed the circlet about her thick mop of blond hair. Her tone, and the sudden grin that lifted the edges of her mouth, told the ranger what she might have in mind, a notion reinforced when she hopped over to him a moment later and kissed him passionately.

"Later," she said.

"When we are not surrounded by goblins and insects," Elbryan agreed.

Pony swung up onto Symphony's saddle. With a wink at Elbryan, she turned the horse about and trotted away into the growing gloom—but with the cat's-eye securely in place, the images before her remained distinct.

Elbryan watched her go with the deepest affection and respect. This was a trying time for the young ranger, a time when all his skills, physical and mental, were being put to the absolute test every day. Every decision could prove tragic; every move he made could give his enemies the advantage. How glad he was to have Pony, so thoughtful, so skilled, so beautiful, at his side.

He sighed when she passed out of sight, then turned to the business at hand: the construction of a proper sight for Oracle and a meeting with Uncle Mather.

It didn't take Pony long to discern that the goblins had not given up the chase, and had in fact begun trailing her and Elbryan. And the tracks she found when she circled back indicated that the goblin pair had indeed found some friends, more goblins, perhaps as many as a dozen. Pony looked ahead, back toward her camp, which was now no more than a mile away. She would be hard-pressed to ride by the goblins and get to Elbryan in time, she realized.

"Oracle," she said, shaking her head and giving a great sigh. She bade Symphony to stay put, then reached into her pouch for her malachite. She slipped her feet out of the stirrups as she put her thoughts into the gem, summoning its power. Then she began to rise, slowly, into the nighttime sky, hoping the darkness was complete enough to keep her hidden from sharp goblins eyes.

She had only gone up about twenty feet when she spotted the creatures, gathered about a small, well-concealed fire in another copse of trees, barely a couple hundred yards from her position. They hadn't settled for the night, she knew, but were up and agitated, sketching in the dirt—probably approach routes or searching routes—pushing each other and arguing.

Pony didn't want to expend too much of her magical energy, so she gradually released the malachite's levitational powers, drifting back down to land atop Symphony. "Are you ready to have some fun?" she asked the horse, replacing the malachite in her pouch and taking out two different stones.

Symphony nickered softly and Pony patted his neck. She had never tried this particular trick before, and especially not while taking a horse in with her, but she was brimming with confidence. Avelyn had taught her well, and, given her newfound insights into the gemstones—an understanding that went beyond anything she had ever known—she believed with all her heart that she was ready.

She started Symphony walking in the direction of the goblin camp, then took up a serpentine and began gathering its magic. In her other hand she held both bridle and a ruby, perhaps the most powerful stone in her possession.

With the cat's-eye, Pony picked her path carefully, a trail that would take her and Symphony in fast and hard. Barely twenty yards away, Symphony's hoofbeats covered by the sounds of arguing goblins, the woman communicated her intentions to the horse via the turquoise, then kicked the powerful stallion into a dead gallop and let her own thoughts fall into the serpentine, bringing up a glowing white shield about her and the horse, making it look as though she and Symphony had fallen into a vat of a sticky, milky substance.

Pony only had seconds to secure the shield about them both, to switch hands on the bridle and bring the ruby up high, dropping the serpentine shield about the ruby, then completing the protective bubble about her hand under the gemstone.

Goblins howled and reached for their weapons, diving and rolling as horse and rider thundered into their midst. One ugly brute had a spear up and ready to throw.

Pony paid it no heed, could see nothing but the red swirls within the ruby, could hear nothing but the wind in her ears and the simmering, mounting power of the gemstone.

Symphony ran straight and true, right to the goblins' fire, then skidded to an abrupt halt and reared.

Goblins shouted; some charged, some continued to scramble away.

Not far enough away.

Pony loosed the destructive power of the ruby, a tremendous, concussive fireball that exploded out from her hand, engulfing goblin and tree alike in a sudden blazing inferno.

Symphony reared again and whinnied, pulling wildly. Pony held on and called comforting words to the horse, though she doubted that Symphony could even hear her through the tremendous roar of the blaze, or even sense her calming thoughts with the sheer commotion of the conflagration. Pony could hardly see, smoke rolling all about, but she urged Symphony forward, and so solid was her serpentine shield that neither she nor the great horse felt any heat whatsoever. They passed by one fallen goblin, the one who had raised its spear to throw, and Pony looked on in disgust as the blackened creature, still holding fast the charring spear, settled, its super-heated chest collapsing with a crackle.

Soon after, horse and rider came out of the copse, into the cooler night, and moved away, an exhausted and coughing Pony dropping the protective shield. "Oracle," she said again and sighed again, glancing back at the blaze.

No goblins would emerge from that catastrophe, she knew.

When she got back to her camp, she found Elbryan standing on the edge, staring at the continuing fire nearly a mile away.

"Your doing," he stated more than asked.

"Somebody had to see to the goblins," Pony replied, slipping down from the still-agitated black horse. "And it should interest you to know that their numbers had swelled."

Elbryan gave her a disarming grin. "I had confidence that you could handle whatever situation arose," he said.

"While you played at Oracle?"

The smile left the ranger's face and he shook his head slowly. "No play," he said gravely. "A search that might save all the world."

"You are being very mysterious this night," Pony remarked.

"If you took a moment from your insults and considered the tales I told you about my time away from Dundalis, you would begin to understand."

Pony cocked her head and regarded the man, the ranger, the elven-trained ranger.

"Juraviel?" she asked suddenly, breathlessly, referring to an elf she had once known, friend and mentor to Elbryan.

"And his kin," Elbryan said, nodding his chin toward the west. "I believe that I have remembered the road back to Andur'Blough Inninness."

Andur'Blough Inninness, Pony echoed in her mind. The "Forest of Cloud" wherein lay Caer'alfar, home to the Touel'alfar, the slight, winged elves of Corona. Elbryan had told her many tales of the enchanted place, but always answered her pleas to go there with a frustrated reply that he could not recall the trail, that the elves desired their privacy even from him, the one they named Nightbird, a ranger trained in their home. If he was right now, if he could indeed find the trail back to the elven home, then his words about the unimportance of a couple of goblins suddenly rang with more conviction.

"We shall set off in the morning," Elbryan promised into her eager expression. "Before the dawn."

"Symphony will be packed and waiting," Pony replied, her blue eyes twinkling with excitement.

Elbryan took her hand and led her to the small tent they shared. "Have you any enchantments which will repel insects?" he asked on a whim.

Pony considered the thought for a moment. "A fireball would give us a short reprieve," she replied.

Elbryan glanced back to the east, to the still-burning, thoroughly decimated copse, then scrunched up his face and shook his head. He'd suffer the inconvenience of a few thousand gnats.

No goblins bothered them the rest of that night, nor the next day as they exited the Moorlands through the western border. Both rode atop Symphony as soon as the ground became more firm, and Elbryan pushed the horse at a swift pace. Joined telepathically through the turquoise, the ranger understood that Symphony wanted to run hard, had been born to run hard. And so they made their swift way, setting camps for only short hours in the darkest part of the night, and, on Elbryan's insistence, avoiding any goblins or giants or powries, or any other distraction. His purpose was singular now, while the ever-elusive trail to Andur'Blough Inninness remained clear in his thoughts, and Pony didn't argue with the wisdom of trying to enlist the elves in their continuing struggle.

And there was an added benefit for the woman. With all the enchanting tales Elbryan had told of his days training as a ranger, she dearly wanted to see the elven forest.

She used the reprieve from battle for another purpose, as well. "Are you ready to begin your new career?" she asked one bright morning, Elbryan breaking down the camp and grumbling that they had overslept and should have been on the trail before the dawn.

The ranger cocked his head curiously.

Pony held aloft the pouch of gemstones, and gave them a definitive shake when Elbryan's expression soured. "You have seen their power," she protested.

"I am a warrior, and no wizard," Elbryan replied. "And certainly no monk!"

"And I am not a warrior?" Pony asked slyly. "How many times have I put you down to the ground?"

Elbryan couldn't suppress a chuckle at that. When they were younger, children in Dundalis before the goblins came, he and Pony had wrestled several times, with Pony always emerging the victor. And once, after being caught by the hair by Elbryan, the girl had even laid the boy out cold with a punch to the face. The memories, even of the knockout, were the brightest of all for Elbryan, for then had come the dark time, the first goblin invasion, and he and Pony had been separated for so many years, each thinking the other dead.

Now he was Nightbird, among the finest warriors in all the world, and she was a wielder of magic, a wizard trained in the use of the sacred gemstones by Avelyn Desbris, who had been perhaps the most powerful magic-wielder in all the world.

"You must learn them," Pony insisted. "At least a bit."

"You seem to do well with them on your own," Elbryan replied defiantly, though he was privately a bit intrigued by the prospects of using the powerful gemstones. "Would we not be weakened as a fighting team if some of the stones were in my possession?"

"That would depend on the situation," Pony answered. "If you get wounded, I can use the soul stone to mend your injuries, but what if I get wounded? Who will heal me? Or would you just leave me sitting against a tree to die?"

The image conjured by that thought nearly buckled Elbryan's knees. He couldn't believe that neither he nor Pony had thought of that possibility before—at least not enough to do anything about it. All objections gone, he said, "We must be on the trail." He held his hand up as Pony began her expected protest. "But with every meal and every break, I will be tutored, particularly with the soul stone," he explained. "All our waking hours will be filled, then, with traveling and learning."

Pony considered that for just a moment, and nodded her agreement with the concession. Then, with a sudden wistful smile, she took a step closer to Elbryan, hooked her finger in the top of his tunic and pursed her sensual lips. "Every waking moment?" she asked coyly.

Elbryan couldn't find the breath to reply. That was what he most loved about this woman: her ability to keep him always off-balance, to surprise him and entice him with the simplest statements, with movements subtly suggestive. Every time he thought he was planted firmly in the ground, Pony found a way to make him realize that the ground was as tentative as the shifting silt of the Moorlands.

They were late for the trail, the ranger knew, and he knew, too, that they wouldn't be going anywhere for a little while.

* * *

What struck them most was the pure majesty of the mountains—there was simply no other word for it. They walked along rocky trails, with Elbryan in the lead, checking the trail and watching for tracks. Pony, walking behind, held Symphony by the bridle, though with its telepathic connection to both these humans, the horse would have followed anyway. Neither Elbryan nor Pony spoke, for the sound of voices seemed out of place here, unless those voices were raised in glorious song.

All about them great mountains reached up their white caps of snow to touch the sky. Clouds drifted by, sometimes above them, sometimes below them, and often they walked right through the gray air. The wind blew constantly, but it only dulled the sound even more, making this majestic place utterly silent, utterly serene. So they walked and they looked, and were humbled by the sheer power and glory of nature.

Elbryan knew he was on the right trail, knew he was closing in on his intended destination. This place, so powerful, so overwhelming, *felt* like Andur'Blough Inninness.

The trail forked, going up and to the left, down and to the right, around an outcropping of stone. Elbryan started left and motioned for Pony to move on to the right, figuring the paths would cross again soon enough. He was still climbing, and still veering left, when he heard Pony cry out. Down he sprinted, cutting over the rough ground between the paths, leaping atop any boulders in his path and springing away, as sure-footed as any mountain cat. How often Nightbird had run along such terrain during his years of training with the Touel'alfar!

He slowed his pace when he spotted Pony standing calmly with Symphony by her side. When he got up beside her and followed her gaze over the lip of a steep descent, he understood.

There was a valley below them, obviously, but it was hidden from view by a wall of thick fog, an unbroken blanket of gray.

"It cannot be natural," Pony reasoned. "No cloud as I have ever seen."

"Andur'Blough Inninness," Elbryan replied breathlessly, and when he finished his statement, the corners of his mouth rose in a wide smile.

"The Forest of Cloud," Pony added, the common translation of the elven words.

"There is a cloud above it all the day, every day—" Elbryan started to explain.

"Not a cheery place," the woman interrupted.

Elbryan gave her a sidelong glance. "But it is," he replied. "When you want it to be."

Now it was Pony's turn to regard her companion curiously.

"I cannot even begin to explain it," Elbryan stammered. "It seems so gray from up here, but it's not like that underneath, not at all. The blanket is illusionary, and yet it is not."

"What is that supposed to mean?"

Elbryan gave a great sigh and searched for a different approach. "It is gray down there, and melancholy, beautifully so," he said. "But only if you want it to be. For those who prefer a day in the sun, there is plenty to be found."

"The gray blanket looks solid," Pony remarked doubtfully.

"Appearances are often far from the truth where the Touel'alfar are concerned."

Pony couldn't miss the reverence with which Elbryan spoke of the elves, and having met a couple of them, she could understand his respect—though she wasn't so enamored of them, and in truth found them to be a bit arrogant and callous. Still, looking at Elbryan now, she noticed that he was beaming, as obviously delighted and charmed as she had ever seen him.

And the source of that charm, she knew, was right below them. She stopped her arguing then, taking the ranger at his word.

"It was not until this very moment that I realized how much I miss my days in Caer'alfar," Elbryan said quietly. "Or how much I miss Belli'mar Juraviel, and even Tuntun, who made my life quite difficult in those years."

Pony nodded grimly at the mention of Tuntun, the gallant elf maiden who had given her life in Aida saving Elbryan and her from one of the demon dactyl's monstrous creations, the spirit of a man encased in magma.

Elbryan chuckled, stealing the somber mood.

"What is it?" Pony prompted.

"The milk stones," the ranger replied.

Pony looked at him curiously; he had told her quite a bit about his days with the elves, but had only mentioned the milk stones in passing. Day after day, week after week, month after month, young Elbryan had spent his mornings with the stones. They were spongelike, though harder and more solid. Each day they would be placed in a bog, where they would soak up the liquid. It was Elbryan's job to fish them out and carry them to a trough, where he would squeeze the now-flavored water out of them, a concoction that the elves used to create a sweet and potent wine.

"The warmth of my meal would depend on how fast I could get those stones milked," Elbryan went on. "I would gather a basket and run to the trough, then return again and again until I had collected my quota. Meanwhile, the elves would set out my meal, piping hot."

"But you were not fast enough and had to eat it cold," Pony teased.

"At first," Elbryan admitted in all seriousness. "But soon enough I could complete my task fast enough to burn my tongue."

"And so you ate many a hot meal."

Elbryan shook his head and smiled wistfully. "No," he replied. "For Tuntun was always there, setting traps, slowing me down. Sometimes I was the trickier, and got the meal hot. Many times I wound up sitting in the brush, my feet entangled by invisible elven cords, and often right in view of

the meal, watching the steam go off the soup." Elbryan could talk about it
wistfully now, could remember with the wisdom of hindsight, with the
knowledge of the great value of the often brutal lessons that the Touel'alfar
had taught him. How strong his arms had become from squeezing those
stones! And how resilient his spirit had become from dealing with Tuntun.
He could laugh about it now, but the treatment had brought him near to
blows with the elf many times, and had actually put him in a very real fight
with her once—a fight that he lost badly. Despite the rough treatment, the
humiliation and the pain, Elbryan had come to realize that Tuntun, in her
heart, had only his best interests in mind. She was not his mother, not his
sibling, and, at that time, not even his friend. She was his instructor, and
her methods, however punishing, had been undeniably effective. Elbryan
had come to love the elf maiden.

And now all that he had of Tuntun were his memories.

"Blood of Mather," he said with a sneer.

"What?"

"That's what she always used to call me," Elbryan explained. "And, at
first, she always edged it with heavy sarcasm. Blood of Mather."

"But you soon proved to her that it was a true enough title," came
a melodious voice from within the shroud of fog, and not so far below
the pair.

Elbryan knew that voice; so did Pony. "Belli'mar!" they called together.

Belli'mar Juraviel answered that call, emerging from the fog blanket, his
gossamer wings beating to help him navigate the steep angle of the mountainous slope. The sheer beauty of the elf, his golden hair, his golden eyes,
his angular features and lithe form, gave both humans pause and added to
the already majestic aura of this place. Elbryan and Pony could almost hear
music with every one of Juraviel's short, hopping steps, with every beat of
his nearly translucent wings. His movements were a dance of harmony, of
perfect balance, a compliment to Nature itself.

"My friends," the elf greeted them warmly, though there was also an
edge to his voice that rang unfamiliar to Elbryan. Juraviel had started with
them on the quest to Aida, as the sole representative of the elven race, but
sacrificed his place in the journey to serve as a guide for a band of haggard
refugees.

Elbryan walked over and clasped hands with the elf, but the ranger's
smile did not hold. He would have to tell Juraviel of the fate of his friend,
for the elves had not known that Tuntun was following the band. The
ranger glanced back to his companion, his expression revealing his distress
to Pony.

"You know that the demon dactyl has been defeated?" Pony asked, to
get things moving.

Juraviel nodded. "Though the world remains a dangerous place," he
answered. "The dactyl has been thrown down, but the fiend's legacy lives

on, in the form of a monstrous army rampaging through the civilized lands of your human kin."

"Perhaps we should talk about these dark matters down in the valley," Elbryan put in. "Hope is ever-present under the fair boughs of Caer'alfar." He started moving down the slope, but Juraviel put out a hand to stop him, and the elf's suddenly grim expression showed that there was no possibility of debate on this subject.

"We will speak here," the elf said quietly.

Elbryan stood straight and studied his friend for a long moment, trying to decipher the emotions behind the unexpected declaration. He saw pain there, and a bit of anger, but not much else. Like all the elves, Juraviel's eyes possessed that strange and paradoxical combination of innocence and wisdom, of youth and great age. Elbryan would learn nothing more until Juraviel offered it openly.

"We have killed many goblins and powries, even giants, on our passage back to the south," the ranger remarked. "Yet it seems as if we have made little progress against the hordes."

"The defeat of the dactyl was no small thing," Juraviel offered, a hint of his smile returning. " 'Twas Bestesbulzibar who bound the three races together. Our . . . your enemies are not so well organized now, and fight with each other as much as they battle the humans."

Elbryan hardly heard the rest of the sentence after the elf had shifted possession of the enemies solely to Elbryan's people. The Touel'alfar had stepped out of the fight, he realized then, and that was something the world could ill-afford.

"What of the refugees you escorted?" Pony asked.

"I delivered them to Andur'Blough Inninness safely," Juraviel replied. "Though we were accosted by the demon dactyl itself—a meeting in which I never would have survived had not Lady Dasslerond personally come forward from the elven home to stand beside me. We did get through to safety, and those beleaguered people have been delivered back to the southland with their kin, safe." Juraviel managed a chuckle as he finished the thought. "Though they returned south lacking quite a few of their more recent memories."

Elbryan nodded, understanding that the elves could work a bit of their own magic, including some to erase directions, as they had enacted that magic on him. Lady Dasslerond meant to keep the location of her valley secret at any costs. Perhaps that was why Juraviel was upset at his appearance here; perhaps, by returning, he had violated some elven code.

"As safe as any can be in these times," Pony remarked.

"Indeed," said the elf. "But safer now than before, due to the efforts of Elbryan and Jilseponie, and to the sacrifices of Bradwarden the centaur and Avelyn Desbris." He paused and took a deep breath, then looked Elbryan squarely in the eye. "And of Tuntun of Caer'alfar," he finished.

"You know?" the ranger asked.

Juraviel nodded, his expression grave. "We are not numerous. My people and our community are joined in many ways which humans cannot begin to understand. We learned of Tuntun's death as Tuntun realized it. I trust that she died valiantly."

"Saving us both," Elbryan was quick to say. "And saving the quest. Were it not for Tuntun, Pony and I would have perished before we ever reached the lair of the dactyl."

Juraviel nodded and seemed satisfied with that answer, a great peace washing over his fair features. "Then Tuntun will live on in song forever," he said.

Elbryan nodded his agreement with the sentiment, then closed his eyes and imagined the elves, gathered in a field in the valley, under a starry sky, singing of Tuntun.

"You should tell me the details of her death," Juraviel said. "But later," he added quickly, holding up his hand before Elbryan could begin. "For now, I fear, the business is more pressing. Why have you come here?"

The bluntness of his question, the almost accusing tone, set Elbryan back on his heels. Why had he come? Why wouldn't he, once he had remembered the way? It had never occurred to Elbryan that he might not be welcomed in Andur'Blough Inninness, a place he considered as much his home as any he had ever known.

"This is not your place, Nightbird," Juraviel explained, trying to sound friendly, sympathetic even, though the mere words he spoke could not help but wound Elbryan. "And to bring her here without the permission of Lady Dasslerond—"

"Permission?" the ranger balked. "After all that we have shared? After all that I have given to your people?"

"It was we who gave to you," Juraviel promptly corrected.

Elbryan paused and thought it over. Indeed, the Touel'alfar had given him much, had raised him from a boy, had trained him as a ranger. But the generosity had been reciprocal, the young ranger now realized, as he considered the relationship in the sober tones of Juraviel's attitude. The elves had given him much, that was true, but in return he had given to them the very course of his life. "Why do you treat me so?" he asked bluntly. "I had thought we were friends. Tuntun gave her life for me, for my quest, and did not the success of that quest benefit the Touel'alfar as well as the humans?"

Juraviel's stern expression, exaggerated by his angular features, softened somewhat.

"I wield Tempest," Elbryan went on, drawing forth the shining blade, a weapon forged of the secret silverel by the elves. "And Hawkwing," he added, pulling the bow from his shoulder. Hawkwing was fashioned from the darkfern, a plant the elves cultivated and which leached the silverel from the ground. "Weapons of the Touel'alfar both," the ranger went on.

"Your own father crafted this bow for me, for the human friend and student of his son. And Tempest I rightfully carry, having passed the challenge of my uncle Mather's ghost—"

Juraviel held up his hand to stop the speech. "Enough," he begged. "Your words are true to me. All of them. But that does not change the details of this moment. Why have you come, my friend, unbidden, to this place which must remain secret?"

"I came to find out if your people will lend aid to mine in this time of great darkness," Elbryan replied.

A great sadness washed over the face of Belli'mar Juraviel. "We have suffered," he explained.

"As have the humans," Elbryan replied. "Many more humans have died than Touel'alfar, if all the elves of Andur'Blough Inninness had perished!"

"Not many of my people have perished," Juraviel admitted. "But death is only one measure of suffering. The demon dactyl came to our valley. Indeed, Lady Dasslerond had to take the foul fiend there to defeat it when it came upon me in my quest to rescue the refugees. The demon was sent away, but Bestesbulzibar, curse his name, left a scar upon our land, a wound in the earth itself that will never heal and that continues to expand despite all our efforts."

Elbryan looked to Pony, and her expression was grave. He did not need to explain the implications.

"There is no place in all the world for us save Andur'Blough Inninness," Juraviel went on somberly. "And the rot has begun. Our time will pass, my friend, and the Touel'alfar will be gone from this world, a children's fireside tale to most, a memory for those descendants of the few, like Nightbird, who knew us well."

"There is always hope," Elbryan replied past the lump in his throat. "There is always a way."

"And so we shall seek one," Juraviel agreed. "But for now, our borders are closed to any who is n'Touel'alfar. If I had not come out to you, if you had descended into the mist that veils our home, it would have choked you and left you dead on the mountainside."

Pony gave a surprised gasp. "That cannot be," she said. "You would not kill Nightbird."

Elbryan knew better. The Touel'alfar lived by a different code than did humans, one that few people could understand. To them, any who was not of their race, even those few selected to be trained as rangers, was considered inferior. The Touel'alfar could be among the greatest allies in all the world, would fight to the death to save a friend, would risk everything, as Juraviel had done with the refugees, out of compassion. But when threatened, the elves were unbending, and it didn't surprise Elbryan in the least to learn that such a deadly trap had been set up to keep strangers from their land in this time of peril.

"Am I *n'Touel'alfar?*" the ranger asked boldly, looking Juraviel right in the eye. He saw the pain there, a profound disappointment within his elven friend.

"It does not matter," Juraviel offered halfheartedly. "The mist distinguishes only physical form. To it, you are human, and nothing more. To it, you are indeed *n'Touel'alfar.*"

Elbryan wanted to press that point, wanted to hear how his friend felt about the situation. This was not the time, he decided. "If there was any way in which I might have asked permission to come, and to bring Pony, I would have," he said sincerely. "I remembered the path, and so I came, that is all."

Juraviel nodded, satisfied, then managed a sudden and warm smile. "And I am glad that you have," he said cheerily. "It is good to see you again, good to know that you—and you," he added, looking to Pony, "survived the ordeal at Aida."

"You know of Avelyn and Bradwarden?"

Juraviel nodded. "We have ways of gathering information," he said. "That is how I knew that two too-curious humans were approaching the warded borders of Andur'Blough Inninness. By all reports, only two forms, Nightbird and Pony, left the blasted Barbacan."

"Alas for Avelyn," Elbryan said somberly. "Alas for Bradwarden."

"A good man was Avelyn Desbris," Juraviel agreed. "And all the forest will mourn the passing of Bradwarden. Gentle was his song, and fierce his spirit. Often I would sit and listen to his piping, a melody so fitting to the forest."

Both Elbryan and Pony nodded at that notion. When they were children in Dundalis, in better, more innocent times, they had sometimes heard the melodious drift of Bradwarden's piping, though at that time they had no idea who the piper might be. The people of the two Timberland towns, Dundalis and Weedy Meadow—for End-o'-the-world was not in existence then—called the unknown piper the Forest Ghost and did not fear him, for they understood that no creature capable of making such hauntingly beautiful music would pose any threat to them.

"But enough of this," Juraviel said suddenly, pulling the small pack from his back. "I have brought food—good food!—and *Questel ni'Touel.*"

"Boggle," Elbryan translated, for *Questel ni'Touel* was the elvish wine made from the water filtered through the milk stones. It was sometimes traded through secret channels to humans under the name of boggle, an elvish joke signifying both the bog from which the liquid originally came, and from the state of mind it readily produced in the humans.

"Let us go and set a camp," Juraviel offered. "Out of this wind and sheltered from the chill of the approaching night. Then we might eat and talk in a more comfortable manner."

The two friends readily agreed, and both realized then that their previous agitation had only been due to the search for the magical valley. Now that the issue of Andur'Blough Inninness was decided, they could both relax, for neither feared any goblin or powrie, or even giant-inspired trouble, this close to the borders of the elven home.

When they sat down to eat, Elbryan and Pony found that Juraviel wasn't exaggerating in the least concerning the quality of the food he had brought: berries, plump and sweet, fruit fattened under the gentle boughs of Caer'alfar, and bread flavored with just a touch of *Questel ni'Touel*. Juraviel hadn't brought much with him, but it was immensely satisfying, and truly this was the finest meal that either of the weary travelers had enjoyed for many, many months.

The wine helped, too, taking the edge off the uncomfortable nature of their meeting, allowing Elbryan and Pony, and the elf, as well, to put aside the dangers of the continuing battle for just a while, to sit and relax and forget that their world was full of goblins and powries and giants. They spoke of times long past, of Elbryan's training in the elvish valley, of Pony's life in Palmaris and her time serving in the army of Honce-the-Bear's King. They kept their chatter lighthearted, mostly relating amusing anecdotes, and many of Juraviel's tales concerned Tuntun.

"Yes, I will find quite a bit of material for the song I plan for her," the elf said quietly.

"A rousing war song?" Elbryan asked. "Or a song for a gentle soul?"

The notion of Tuntun being described as a gentle soul brought laughter bubbling to Juraviel's lips. "Oh, Tuntun!" he cried dramatically, leaping to his feet, throwing his arms heavenward and taking up an impromptu song:

Oh gentle elf, what poems hast thee written
To best describe thyself?
What lyrics spring from thy lips to Nightbird's waiting ears?
But since you hold his head in the trough, 'tis doubtful he can hear!

Pony howled with laughter over that one, but Elbryan fixed a nasty stare over his friend.

"What troubles you, my friend?" Juraviel prompted.

"If I remember correctly, it was not Tuntun, but Belli'mar Juraviel, who put my head in the trough," the ranger replied grimly.

The elf shrugged and smiled. "I will have to write another song, I fear," he said calmly.

Elbryan couldn't maintain the facade, and he, too, erupted in laughter.

Their boggle-enhanced mirth rolled on for several minutes, finally dying away to quiet titters, the occasional chuckle. That was followed by simple, reflective silence, all three sitting, none moving to be the first to speak.

Finally Juraviel walked back over and plopped down across the small fire from Elbryan. "You should go to the south and east," he explained. "To the towns halfway between Dundalis and Palmaris. There you are most needed, and there you will do the most good."

"That is the battle line?" Pony asked.

"One of the battle lines," Juraviel replied. "There is greater fighting raging in the far east, along the coast, and up north, in the cold land of Alpinador, where mighty Andacanavar holds the elven-bestowed banner as ranger. But I fear that Elbryan and Pony would be only minor players in those greater battles, whereas you two might turn the tide in the more immediate area."

"The area closer to the borders of Andur'Blough Inninness," Elbryan said slyly, suspicious of the elf's motives.

"We do not fear any attacks from goblins or powries," Juraviel was quick to reply. "Our borders are safe from that enemy. It is the deeper evil, the stain of the demon dactyl . . ." He paused, his voice trailing away, letting the dark thought hang in the air.

"But you two should go to those towns," he said at length. "Do for those folk what you did for the people of Dundalis, Weedy Meadow, and End-o'-the-World, and all the region might soon be freed of the legacy of the demon dactyl."

Elbryan looked to Pony, and both gave a nod to the elf. Elbryan studied his diminutive friend closely then, seeking unspoken signals that would clue him in to the importance of it all. He knew Juraviel well, and had a feeling that many things were not as set in stone as the elf had indicated.

"You two are formally betrothed?" Juraviel asked suddenly, catching Elbryan off his guard.

Pony and Elbryan looked to each other. "In our hearts," the ranger explained.

"There has not been time nor opportunity," Pony said, and then with a great sigh she added, "We should have asked Avelyn to perform the ceremony. Could any have been more fitting to such a task than he?"

"If you are married in your hearts, then married you are," Juraviel decided. "But there should be a ceremony, a formal declaration made openly, to friend and to kin. It is more than a legality, and more than a celebration. It is a declaration, openly made, of fidelity and undying love, a proclamation to all the world that there is something higher than this corporeal form, and a love deeper than simple lust."

"Someday," Elbryan promised, staring at Pony, the only woman he believed he could ever love, and understanding every word Juraviel had just said.

"Two ceremonies!" Juraviel decided. "One for your human companions, one for the Touel'alfar."

"Why would the Touel'alfar care?" Elbryan said, a hint of anger in his tone, which surprised both his companions.

"Why would we not?" Juraviel replied.

"Because the Touel'alfar care only for the affairs of the Touel'alfar," Elbryan reasoned.

Juraviel started to protest, but saw where the trap was leading and only laughed instead.

"You do care," Elbryan said.

"Of course," Juraviel admitted. "And glad I am, and glad are all the elven folk of Caer'alfar, that Elbryan and Jilseponie survived the quest to Aida and have found each other. To us, your love is a shining light in a dark world."

"That is how I knew," Elbryan said.

"Knew what?" Juraviel and Pony asked together.

"That I . . . we," he corrected, indicating Pony, "are not *n'Touel'alfar*. Not in the eyes of Belli'mar Juraviel."

The elf gave a great, exaggerated sigh. "I admit it," he said. "I surrender."

"And that is how I know the other thing, as well," Elbryan said, grinning from ear to ear.

"And what is that?" Juraviel asked, his tone one of feigned disinterest. "What else does the wise Nightbird know?"

"That Belli'mar Juraviel intends to accompany us to the south and east," Elbryan replied.

That widened Juraviel's eyes. "I had not considered that!"

"Then do," Elbryan instructed, "because we, all three, leave at first light." He rolled back from the fire then, nestling into his bedroll. "Time for us to sleep," he said to Pony. "And time for our friend to go back to his valley, that he might tell his Lady Dasslerond that he will be away for a while."

Pony, weary from the road and the wine, and content with the meal, was more than happy to fall back into her blankets.

Juraviel said not a word and did not move for some time. Before him, both Elbryan and Pony were soon breathing in the rhythms of a deep and contented sleep, and behind him, Symphony nickered softly in the quiet night. Then the elf was gone, slipping away silently into the darkness, running with his thoughts and running to his lady.

Quiet though he was, his departure woke Pony, whose sleep had become filled with troubling dreams. She felt the weight of Elbryan's strong arm about her, felt the warmth of his body curled against her. All the world should have been warm and happy for her in that embrace.

But it was not.

She lay awake for a long while, and then Elbryan, too, as if sensing her anxiety, awoke.

"What troubles you?" he asked softly, nuzzling closer and kissing the nape of her neck.

Pony stiffened, and the ranger felt it. He pulled away and sat up, and she could see his dark silhouette against the starry sky. "I was only trying to be comforting," he apologized.

"I know," she replied.

"Then why are you angry?" he asked.

Pony considered that for a long while. "I am not angry," she decided. "I am only frightened."

Now it was the ranger's turn to pause and reflect. He lay back down beside Pony, shifting to his back and looking up at the stars. He had never known Pony to be frightened—not since the day their homes were sacked, at least—and he was certain now that her fears were not based on any powries or giants, or even the demon dactyl. He considered her tenseness when he had touched her. She was not angry with him, he knew, but . . .

"You were quiet when Juraviel spoke of marriage," he said.

"There was little you had not already said," Pony replied, rolling over to face Elbryan. "We share hearts, and are of like mind."

"But?"

Her face clouded over.

"You are afraid of becoming with child," Elbryan reasoned, and Pony's expression shifted to one of wonderment.

"How did you know?"

"You just said that we were of like hearts," the ranger replied with a slight chuckle.

Pony sighed and draped her arm across Elbryan's chest, kissing him softly on the cheek. "When we are together, I feel like all the world is wonderful," she said. "I forget the loss at Dundalis, the loss of Avelyn and Bradwarden, of Tuntun. The world does not seem so terrible and dark, and all the monsters run away."

"But if you were to become with child now, out here," Elbryan said, "then those monsters would become all too real again."

"We have a duty," Pony explained. "With the gift the Touel'alfar gave to you, and the one Avelyn gave to me, we must be more to the folk than observers. How could I fight on if I become pregnant? And what life would our child know in these times?"

"How could I fight on if you could not remain beside me?" Elbryan asked, running his fingertips across her face.

"I do not wish to refuse you," Pony said. "Ever."

"Then I shan't ask," Elbryan replied sincerely. "But you told me that there were times each month when it was not likely that we would conceive a child."

"Not likely?" Pony echoed skeptically. "What chance is acceptable?

Elbryan thought on that for just a moment. "None," he decided. "The stakes are too high, the cost too great. We will make a pact, here and now. Let us finish this business at hand, and when the world is put aright, we will turn our attention to our own needs and our own family."

He said it with such simplicity, and such optimism that this pact would be a temporary thing, that the world would indeed be put aright, that a smile found its way across Pony's troubled face. She snuggled closer then, wrapping herself around Elbryan, knowing in her heart that he would be true to his pact and that their lovemaking would wait until the time was right.

Both of them slept soundly the rest of the night.

Juraviel was back at the small camp when Pony awoke, to find their belongings already packed and in place atop Symphony. The sun was up, though still low in the eastern sky.

"We should already be on the road," a sleepy-eyed Pony said through a yawn and a stretch.

"I gave you this one night of sleep," Juraviel replied, "for I doubt you'll find another anytime soon."

Pony looked to Elbryan, still sleeping contentedly. Long and restful sleep, like other pleasures, would be a rarity now.

But only for a short while, she reminded herself determinedly.

❖ 5 ❖

To Seek the Truth

The mountainous ring surrounding the Barbacan was fully twelve hundred miles from the stone walls of St.-Mere-Abelle, and that as a bird might fly. By road, in those places where a traveler would be fortunate enough to even find a road, the distance was much closer to two thousand miles, a trek that would have taken a conventional caravan twelve weeks to traverse—and that, only if the caravan ran into no unforeseen problems and did not stop a single day for any respite. In truth, any merchant planning such a journey would allow for three months of travel, and would have carried enough gold to replace his horse team several times. And in truth, in these dangerous times, with goblin and powrie forces running wild even along the normally tame areas of Honce-the-Bear, no merchant, not even the soldiers of the famous elite Allheart Brigade, would have made the attempt.

But the monks of St.-Mere-Abelle were not merchants or soldiers, and were possessed of magics that could cut tremendous amounts of time from their journey and keep them well-hidden from the eyes of potential enemies. And if it so happened they were discovered by goblins or other monsters, those magics would make them a formidable force indeed. The planning for such a journey from the abbey had already been done, centuries before. The monks of St.-Mere-Abelle were the original cartographers of Honce-the-Bear, and even of the Timberlands, northern Behren, southern Alpinador, and a good deal of the western reaches of the Wilderlands, as well. In those long past times, journey logs had been turned into travel guides, detailing supplies needed, magic stones recommended, and fastest routes. Those guides, in turn, were updated on a regular basis, and so Brother Francis' biggest task that day after the repulsion of the powrie attack was to find the proper guide tomes, and convert the recommended supply figures to accommodate a party of twenty-five, the number of brothers that Father Abbot Markwart had determined would make the journey.

After vespers on only the second day, Brother Francis reported to the Father Abbot and the masters that the lists were complete and the route confirmed. All that needed to be done was rounding up the supplies—a task that Francis assured the Father Abbot could be done in a matter of two hours—and the naming of the journeying monks.

"I will lead the team personally," the Father Abbot informed them, drawing gasps from Francis and all the masters, except for Master Jojonah, who had suspected that all along. Markwart was obsessed, Jojonah understood, and in such a state, his decision-making was greatly flawed.

"But Father Abbot," one of the other masters argued, "this is unprecedented. You are the leader of St.-Mere-Abelle and all of the Abellican Church. To risk your safety on such a perilous trek—"

"We would risk less by sending the King himself!" another master protested.

Father Abbot Markwart held up his hand, silencing the men. "I have thought this through," he replied. "It is fitting that I go—the greatest power of good sent to do battle with the greatest power of evil."

"But surely not in your own body," offered Master Jojonah, who had also done quite a bit of thinking on this very subject. "Might I suggest Brother Francis as a suitable vessel for your inquiries as to the progress of the troupe?"

Markwart looked long and hard at Jojonah, the Father Abbot obviously caught off his guard by the perfectly reasonable suggestion. With a telepathic connection between the two bodies, facilitated by a soul stone, physical distance would mean little. Father Abbot Markwart could make the trip, or could check in on its progress personally—in spirit—without ever leaving the comfort of the abbey.

"You would be honored at such a position, would you not, Brother Francis?" Master Jojonah went on.

Brother Francis' eyes shot daggers at the sly master. Of course he would not be "honored" by such a position, something that he, and Jojonah, understood well. Possession was a horrible thing indeed, and nothing to ever be desired. Even worse, Francis knew that serving as a mere vessel for Markwart would reduce his role significantly, should he be chosen to go along on the journey. How could he be placed in any position of leadership, after all, if there was the possibility that he would not even be there, if his spirit and will were thrown out into empty limbo while Markwart used his body?

Brother Francis looked from Master Jojonah to the Father Abbot, to the other seven masters in attendance, all of them eyeing him expectantly. How could he refuse such a proposal? His angry gaze fell back over Jojonah, the younger monk staring unblinkingly at the master even as he mouthed, through gritted teeth, "Of course it would be the highest honor that any brother could expect or desire."

"Well done, then," the victorious Jojonah said, clapping in his hands. In one fell swoop he had prevented Markwart from leading the caravan and had put the too-ambitious Brother Francis in his place. It wasn't that Jojonah wanted to protect Markwart from any perils; far from that. It was simply that he feared the mischief Markwart might cause if the journey proved successful. More than a few speculations placed Avelyn Desbris at the scene of devastation in the north, and Jojonah feared that Markwart might cover whatever truth was to be found there with calculated tales that fell more in line with his hatred of Avelyn. If Markwart was in control of the caravan that reached the Barbacan, then Markwart would determine what had happened there.

"I do fear, though, that my work will have then been wasted," Brother Francis added suddenly, even as Father Abbot Markwart started to speak.

All eyes turned to the young brother.

"I have planned the trip," Francis explained—improvising, Jojonah and several others realized. "I am familiar with the course we must take and the amounts of supplies that should be remaining at each stop. Also, I am well-versed and, by all accounts, proficient with the stones, a necessary ingredient if we are to meet the timetable of three weeks offered in the guide tomes."

"Twelve days," Father Abbot Markwart said, drawing looks from all, and a gasp of disbelief from Brother Francis. "Our timetable will be twelve days," the Father Abbot clarified.

"But . . ." Brother Francis started to respond, but if the old man's tone left little room for debate, his glare left none, and the young monk wisely fell silent.

"And Master Jojonah is correct, and his suggestion is accepted as the wiser course," Markwart went on. "Thus I will not go, but will look in on the expedition on a regular basis, through the willing eyes of Brother Francis."

Jojonah was pleased by that announcement; he had feared that stubborn Markwart would hold out longer. He wasn't surprised that his recommendation of Francis as the vessel had been accepted, though. The ambitious brother was one of the few in St.-Mere-Abelle trusted by the old Father Abbot, who had grown increasingly paranoid ever since Avelyn Desbris absconded with the gemstones.

"Since I will not personally, or at least not physically, lead the quest," Markwart went on, "one of you masters must go." His gaze drifted about the room, settling for a moment on eager De'Unnero before falling fully over Jojonah.

The portly old master returned that look with an incredulous expression. Surely Markwart would not choose him, he prayed. He was among the oldest of the masters of St.-Mere-Abelle, and was easily the least physically prepared for any long and hard road.

But Markwart did not back down from that gaze. "Master Jojonah, the senior master of St.-Mere-Abelle, is the logical choice," he said aloud. "With an immaculate to serve as his second, Brother Francis to serve as his third, and twenty-two others working the wagons and the horse teams."

Jojonah stared long and hard at the Father Abbot as Markwart and the other masters began discussing which of the younger and stronger brothers would be best suited for the road. Jojonah offered no input into the selection process, just sat staring and thinking, and hating the man. Markwart had chosen him for no practical reason, he knew. He was being punished by the old man for his friendship and mentoring of Avelyn and for his continued arguments against so many of Markwart's decisions on every issue, from the abbey's role in the larger community to philosophical discussions about the true value of the gemstones and the true meaning of their faith. Markwart had voiced his displeasure with Jojonah on more than one occasion, had even once threatened a College of Abbots gathering to discuss, as he had put it, "Jojonah's increasingly heretical way of thinking."

Jojonah had almost hoped for that meeting, for he was convinced that many of the other abbots of the Abellican Church would see things his way. He saw the bluff for what it was, for he knew that Markwart probably feared the same judgments. Over the last few years, Markwart had purposefully lessened St.-Mere-Abelle's contact with the other abbeys, and the last thing the old Father Abbot wanted was a showdown with the rest of the Church over philosophical matters.

Despite that, Master Jojonah had feared that Markwart would find a way to get back at him, and so, it seemed, it had come to pass. Twelve hundred miles in twelve days, with much of that time, no doubt, spent dodging disaster in the form of powries, goblins, and giants. And then the troupe would spend weeks, perhaps months, trying to decipher the riddles left behind in the inhospitable wasteland of the Barbacan, tormented by a climate, according to the tomes, where water might freeze even on a summer night, and surrounded by vast hosts of their enemies, perhaps even including the demon dactyl itself. They did not know, after all, whether the fiend had really been destroyed. It was all speculation.

Ambitious Brother Francis desperately wanted to make this journey—though with his own spirit inhabiting his own body—but for Master Jojonah, having passed the mark of his sixth decade and with no further aspirations for power or for glory, and certainly not for adventure, this was indeed a punishment, and quite possibly a death sentence.

There would be no debate, however. The twenty-two were selected quickly, based on their strengths both magical and physical. Most were fifth- or sixth-year students, men in the prime of their physical life, though a pair of immaculates, a tenth-year and a twelfth-year student, had been included.

"And your selection for your second?" the Father Abbot asked Jojonah.

The master took his time considering his options. The obvious choice, from a purely selfish point of view, would have been Brother Braumin Herde, a close friend and often a confidant. But Jojonah had to consider the wider picture. If this caravan met with disaster, a very real possibility, and both he and Braumin Herde were killed, that would leave Markwart virtually unopposed. The other masters, with the possible exception of Master Engress, were too entrenched in their trappings of power and wealth to even argue with the Father Abbot, and the other immaculates and even ninth-year students were too ambitious, too much like Brother Francis.

Except for one, Jojonah mused.

"Must it be an immaculate?" he asked.

"I'll not spare another master," Father Abbot Markwart was quick to reply. His tone, full of surprise and with an edge of anger, revealed to Jojonah that he had expected and hoped that Jojonah would select Braumin Herde.

"I was thinking of one of Brother Francis' peers," Master Jojonah explained.

"Another ninth-year student?" Markwart asked skeptically.

"But we have selected two immaculates among the twenty-two," Master Engress pointed out. "They may not take kindly to the fact that a ninth-year student has already been appointed as the third in rank."

"Though they will accept it, since said ninth-year student is serving as the vessel for the Father Abbot," another of the masters quickly and reverently put in, bowing his head in deference to Markwart.

Master Jojonah resisted the urge to run over and punch the man.

"But to give them a ninth-year student as a second, as well," Master Engress continued, not to be argumentative, for that was not his nature, but only to play a necessary dissenting voice here.

Markwart looked at the master, who had stood up for the decision to name Francis as third, and gave a slight nod, one that Jojonah was sure the old man wasn't even aware of doing, which tipped Jojonah off to the coming decision.

"Who did you plan to name?" Father Abbot Markwart asked.

Master Jojonah shrugged noncommittally. It was a moot point, as far as his journey was concerned, he realized, for Markwart had already made up his mind that no ninth-year student would serve as second. The Father Abbot was merely fishing now, he realized, trying to find out if there were any other potential troublemakers among the underlings at St.-Mere-Abelle, any other conspirators in Master Jojonah's little gang.

"I only hoped that Brother Braumin Herde might accompany me," Jojonah remarked offhandedly. "He is a friend, and one I consider a bit of a protégé."

The Father Abbot's face screwed up with confusion, his smug expression disappearing.

"Then what—" one of the masters started to ask.

"Brother Herde is no peer of mine," Brother Francis interrupted. "He is an immaculate."

Jojonah put on his best confused look. "Is he?"

Several masters began speaking all at once, most voicing their fears that their portly fellow might be going soft in more than the belly.

"You wanted Herde?" Father Abbot Markwart said loudly, calming the din.

Jojonah grinned and nodded sheepishly. "So he is a tenth-year student," the master answered, feigning embarrassment. "The years do pass so quickly, and they all seem to blend together."

The nods and chuckles about the table told Jojonah that he had managed to wriggle out of that tight spot. Still, he wasn't thrilled about the fact that both he and Braumin Herde were going off together so far from St.-Mere-Abelle and so near to mortal danger.

Brother Braumin Herde was a handsome man with short black, curly hair and strong features, including dark, penetrating eyes and a face that was always shadowed by hair, no matter how often the man shaved it clean. He was not tall, but his shoulders were broad and his posture straight, giving him a solid appearance. He was into his early thirties, having spent more than a third of his life at St.-Mere-Abelle, and since his first love was for his God, many of the women in the area surely lamented that decision and devotion.

He glanced both ways along the corridor in the upper level of the abbey, then backed into the room, softly closing the door behind him. "I should be going on this journey," he said in his rich and resonating voice, turning to face Master Jojonah. "Through my years of work, I have earned a place on the caravan to the Barbacan."

"A place with me, or with Markwart?" Master Jojonah replied.

"You were given the pick of a second, and that after the others, not including me, had been selected," Braumin Herde was quick to reply. "And you chose me, though I know that you meant to choose otherwise."

Jojonah looked at him quizzically.

"I heard the story. You could not have forgotten that I was an immaculate, since you yourself presented me the scroll of honor," Braumin reasoned. "You meant to choose Brother Viscenti."

Jojonah rocked back on his heels, surprised that such detailed information concerning the meeting had already spread. He studied Brother Braumin carefully, and had never seen such pain and anger on the man's face. Braumin Herde was a forceful and physically imposing man, all hair and muscle, and with a huge square jaw. His broad chest angled down in a V to a narrow waist, for there was nothing soft about him; it seemed as if he had been cut from stone, and there were few in all of St.-Mere-Abelle who could match him in feats of sheer strength. Master Jojonah knew him well, though, his inner being, his compassionate heart, and understood that the man was not a fighter. For all his great strength, Brother Braumin had never been anything exceptional in the martial training, a fact that had so often frustrated Master De'Unnero, who saw such potential in the man. To De'Unnero's dismay, Brother Braumin was a gentle soul, and Jojonah was not worried that he might act out his anger now.

"You would have been my first choice," the master answered honestly. "But I had to consider the implications of naming you. The road to the Barbacan is fraught with peril, and we have no idea what we might find when—if—we do get there."

Braumin gave a deep sigh and his shoulders slumped a bit. "I am not afraid," he replied.

"But I am," said Jojonah. "What we two have come to believe must not die with us on a road to the Wilderlands."

Braumin Herde's disappointment could not hold against the logical reasoning and Jojonah's clear concern. "We have to make certain that Brother Viscenti and the others understand," he agreed.

Jojonah nodded, and the two stood silent for a long while, each considering the dangerous course they had taken. If Father Abbot Markwart came to know the level of what was in their hearts, if he came to realize that these two above all others in St.-Mere-Abelle saw his leadership as errant, and had even begun to question the entire direction of the Abellican Church, then he would likely, without hesitation, brand them as heretics and have them publicly tortured to death—an act not without precedent in the often brutal history of the Abellican Church.

"What if it is Brother Avelyn?" Braumin Herde asked at length. "What if we find him there alive?"

Master Jojonah gave a helpless chuckle. "No doubt, our orders will be to bring him back in chains," he replied. "The Father Abbot will not suffer Avelyn to live, I fear, and will not rest easy until the gemstones Avelyn took are returned to St.-Mere-Abelle."

"And will we bring him back?"

Again the helpless chuckle. "I do not know if we could restrain Brother Avelyn if we wanted to," Jojonah replied. "You never had the pleasure of seeing Brother Avelyn at work with the magic stones. If we find that it was indeed he who caused the explosion in the north, if Avelyn destroyed the dactyl and is still alive, then pity us if we try to wage battle against him."

"Twenty-five monks?" Braumin Herde asked skeptically.

"Never underestimate Brother Avelyn," came the curt reply. "But it would not come to that, in any case," Jojonah was quick to add. "I pray that we do find Brother Avelyn; oh, how I would love to see him again!"

"It would force conflict," Braumin Herde reasoned. "If Brother Avelyn is alive, then we must take a side, either with him or with the Father Abbot."

Master Jojonah closed his eyes, recognizing the truth of his young friend's words. Jojonah and Herde, and, to a lesser extent, several others at St.-Mere-Abelle, were not pleased by Markwart's leadership, but if they were to side with Avelyn, who had been called a heretic openly by the Father Abbot, and who would likely be formally branded as one in the College of Abbots that was to convene later that year, they would find themselves against the whole of the Church. Jojonah, believing in the righteousness of his position, didn't doubt that many other monks—in St.-Mere-Abelle, in St. Precious of Palmaris, and in all the other abbeys— might join in his cause, but did he really want to split the Church? Did he want to begin a war?

And yet, if they did indeed find Brother Avelyn alive, how could Jojonah in good conscience go against him, or even turn away from any others' actions against him? Brother Avelyn was no heretic, Jojonah knew—in fact, was quite the opposite. Avelyn's crime against the Father Abbot and against all the Church was that he had held a mirror up to them, showing them the truth of their actions when measured against the honest precepts of their faith. And the brothers, Markwart most of all, had not liked the image in that mirror. Not at all.

"I believe that it was Brother Avelyn in the Barbacan," Jojonah said with confidence. "Only he could have gone against the demon dactyl. But which survived, if either, remains to be determined."

"We have evidence that the dactyl is no more," Braumin Herde replied. "The monster army has lost its direction and its cohesiveness. Powries and goblins no longer closely ally, by all reports, and we have personally seen their disarray in their attack on our walls."

"Then perhaps the dactyl has been badly wounded, and we will go and finish the task," Jojonah said.

"Or perhaps the demon is destroyed, and we will find Brother Avelyn," Braumin Herde said grimly.

"If the dactyl is dead, and thus the business at the Barbacan finished, it is likely that Brother Avelyn will be far gone from that cursed place."

"Let us hope," said Braumin Herde. "We are not ready to go against the Father Abbot yet."

That last statement caught Jojonah off guard and gave him pause. He and Herde had never discussed going against the Father Abbot at all. By the implications of all their conversations, they would hold fast to their beliefs about the way the Church should behave, and would funnel those beliefs to others through example and voice in council. But never once had they discussed, or even intimated, any formal plans to "go against" Markwart or the Church.

Braumin Herde caught the nonverbal cues and sank back a bit, embarrassed by his forward stance.

Jojonah let the slip pass with yet another chuckle. He remembered when he was younger, much younger, a firebrand like Herde, who thought he could change the world. The wisdom, or perhaps just the weariness, of age had taught him better, though. It was not the world Master Jojonah meant to change, not even the Church, but only his own little corner of both places. He would let Markwart have his direction, would let the Church follow the course that others decided. But he would remain true to his own heart, and would follow a course of piety, dignity, and poverty, as he pledged those decades ago when he had taken his vows at St.-Mere-Abelle. He would spread the word of truth to those younger monks, like Braumin Herde and Viscenti Marlboro, who wished to listen, but it was neither his intent nor his desire to see the Abellican Church split apart.

That was his fear.

And so Master Jojonah, the gentle man, the true friend of Avelyn Desbris, hoped that Avelyn was dead.

"We will be leaving in the morning," Jojonah said. "Go to Brother Viscenti and reinforce all that we three have discussed. Bid him to study well and hard and hold fast to the truth. Bid him to always offer charity, to believers and unbelievers alike, to tend the wounds of the body and the soul for friend and for enemy. Bid him to speak out against injustice and excess, but to temper his voice with compassion. The good will win out in the end, by the truth of their words and not the swing of their sword, though that victory may be centuries in the making."

Braumin Herde considered the wisdom of those words for a time, then gave a respectful bow and turned for the corridor.

"And prepare yourself well for the road," Master Jojonah added before he opened the door. "Brother Francis speaks for the Father Abbot, and do not doubt the loyalty of the other twenty-two in our party. Rein in your temper, brother, or we will find trouble before we ever leave the civilized lands."

Again Braumin Herde bowed respectfully, and he nodded as he came up straight, assuring his mentor that he would indeed heed the words.

Master Jojonah didn't doubt that for a moment, for Herde, both firebrand and gentle soul, was a disciplined man. He knew Brother Braumin would do the right thing, and so would he, though Jojonah feared what the right thing might become should they find Brother Avelyn Desbris alive and well on the road.

"You know what I suspect, and what I expect," Father Abbot Markwart said sharply.

"I am a willing vessel, Father Abbot," Brother Francis said, lowering his eyes. "You will find entrance to my body whenever you so desire."

"As if you could stop me," the old abbot boasted. The words were hollow, Markwart knew, for possession, even with his new understanding of the stones, was a difficult thing, and even more so when the vessel was a man trained in the magics. "But this is about more than that," he continued. "Do you understand the true purpose of this journey?"

"To discover if the dactyl was destroyed," the younger monk replied without hesitation. "Or to see if ever there was a demon dactyl."

"Of course there was," snapped an impatient Markwart. "But that is not the issue. You are going to the Barbacan to determine the fate of the demon, that is true, but you are going, more importantly, to determine the whereabouts of Avelyn Desbris."

Brother Francis' face screwed up with confusion. He knew the Church sought Avelyn, knew it was suspected that Avelyn had been involved in the reputed explosion far to the north, but he never imagined that the Father Abbot would place Avelyn's whereabouts as more important than the fate of the demon dactyl.

"The demon dactyl threatens the lives of thousands," the Father Abbot conceded. "The suffering caused by the emergence of the beast is truly horrifying and regrettable. But the demon dactyl has appeared before and will appear again; the cycle of suffering is the fate of Man. Brother Avelyn's threat, however, is more insidious, and potentially more long-lasting and more devastating. His actions and his tempting heretical viewpoints threaten the very foundations of our beloved Abellican Order."

Still Francis appeared doubtful.

"From those few reports of his actions on the run, it seems that Avelyn masks his heresy with pretty words and seemingly charitable actions," Markwart went on, raising his voice in frustration. "He disavows the importance of ancient traditions without understanding the value of such traditions and, indeed, the utter necessity of them if the Church is to survive."

"My pardon, Father Abbot," Brother Francis said quietly, "but I had thought that Avelyn was long on tradition—too long, some would say. I had thought that his errors went the other way, that he was so devoted to outdated rituals, he could not see the truth and the realities of the modern-day Church."

Markwart waved his bony hand and turned away, chewing his lip, trying to find some way out of the logic trap. "True enough," he agreed, then turned back fiercely, forcing Francis to back away a step. "In some matters, Avelyn was so seemingly devoted as to appear inhuman. Do you know that he did not even care, did not shed a single tear, when his own mother died?"

Francis' eyes went wide.

"It is true," Markwart went on. "He was so obsessed with his vows that the passing of his own mother was to him an unimportant matter. But do not be fooled into thinking that his actions were wrought of true spirituality. No, no, they were the product of ambition, as he proved when he murdered Master Siherton and absconded with the gemstones. Avelyn is dangerous to all the Order, and he, not the dactyl, remains the first order of business."

Brother Francis thought it over for a few moments, then nodded. "I understand, Father Abbot."

"Do you?" Markwart replied, in such a tone that Francis doubted himself. "Do you understand what you are to do if you encounter Avelyn Desbris?"

"We are twenty-five strong—" Francis began.

"Do not count on the support of twenty-five," Markwart warned.

That, too, gave Brother Francis pause. "Still," he said hesitantly and at length, "there are enough of us to take Avelyn and return him and the gemstones to St.-Mere-Abelle."

"No." The simple manner in which Markwart replied put Francis on his heels yet again.

"But—"

"If you encounter Avelyn Desbris," Markwart explained grimly, "if you even catch the slightest hint of his scent, you will return to me that which was stolen, along with the news of wandering Avelyn's demise. You may bring me back his head, if possible."

Brother Francis squared his shoulders. He was not a gentle man, and probably would have been ranked higher in his class except for several brawls he had been all too willingly involved in. Still, he never expected such a command from the Father Abbot of St.-Mere-Abelle. Francis was an ambitious and blindly loyal monk, though, and never one to let conscience get in the way of following orders. "I will not fail in this," he said. "Master Jojonah and I—"

"Beware Jojonah," Markwart interrupted. "And Brother Braumin Herde, as well. They serve as first and second for the journey to the Barbacan and in any matter concerning the disposition of the demon dactyl. Where Avelyn Desbris is concerned, if Avelyn Desbris is concerned, Brother Francis speaks for Father Abbot, and the Father Abbot's word is unquestionable law."

Brother Francis bowed deeply, and seeing the dismissive wave of Father Abbot's hand, turned about and left the room, full of anticipation, full of possibilities.

The night was deep about St.-Mere-Abelle as Brother Braumin made his way across the upper levels of the ancient structure. Though his mission was vital—he had already passed word to Brother Viscenti to await his arrival in his private chambers—he took a circuitous route, moving through the long, long corridor that ran along the abbey's seawall, overlooking All Saints Bay. With no torches burning along the structure's outer walls, and none on the few docks far below, Braumin was afforded the most spectacular view of the evening canopy, a million million stars twinkling above the dark waters of the great Mirianic. He had been born too late, he mused as he stared out one of the tall and narrow windows, for he had missed the journey to Pimaninicuit, the equatorial island upon whose shores the monks of St.-Mere-Abelle collected the sacred stones. Such journeys only occurred every six generations, every 173 years.

Braumin Herde wasn't even supposed to know the details of such things, for he was not yet a master, but Jojonah had told him the story of the most recent journey, of how Brothers Avelyn, Thagraine, Pellimar, and Quintall had traveled to the island aboard a chartered ship, the *Windrunner*. It was the subsequent destruction of the *Windrunner* by the monks as it sailed away from St.-Mere-Abelle, its mission complete, that had set Brother Avelyn fully at odds with the Abellican Church, Master Jojonah had told Braumin. Looking out now, the young monk tried to imagine that scene, all the power, the ballistae and catapults, the tremendous energies of the ring stones, loosed upon a single sailing vessel. Braumin had witnessed St.-Mere-Abelle's fury against the powrie invasion; he shuddered when he thought of that power brought to bear against a single ship and her unsuspecting crew.

What a fateful night that had been, the man mused. If Avelyn had not learned of the destruction, might he have remained a loyal and dedicated servant of Father Abbot Markwart? And if, as they suspected, Brother Avelyn had played no minor role in the possibly momentous events in the northland, in the Timberlands and all the way to the Barbacan, then what darkness would still hold the world fast in its grip if Avelyn had indeed remained at the abbey?

Braumin Herde sent his fingers through his tight-curled black hair. Everything had a purpose, his mother had so often told him. Everything happened for a reason. In the case of Brother Avelyn Desbris, those words rang true indeed.

He pushed away from the window and went on his way, moving quietly but swiftly along the corridor. Most of the monks were asleep now—it was required of the younger monks, and recommended for the older, though ninth- and tenth-year students could make their own curfew if they had important matters to tend to, such as penning passages from ancient texts, or, Braumin thought with a snicker, conspiring against the Father Abbot. Braumin, too, wanted to get to his bed as quickly as possible; he would be up before the dawn, and soon after that out on the road, a long and dangerous road.

He nodded when he saw a line of dim light underneath the door of Viscenti Marlboro's room. His knock was gentle; he didn't want to wake any in the nearby rooms, nor did he want to draw any attention to his presence at this man's door.

The door opened; Braumin slipped inside.

Brother Viscenti Marlboro, a skinny and short man with darting dark eyes and perpetual stubble on his weathered face, was quick to close the door behind his friend.

Already rubbing his hands together, Braumin noted. Brother Viscenti was perhaps the most nervous person he had ever met. He was always rubbing his hands together, and always ducking his head as if he expected someone to slap him.

"You will both be gone, and both be dead," Viscenti said suddenly, sharply, his squeaky voice seeming more fitting for a weasel or a squirrel than a man.

"Gone, yes," Braumin conceded. "But for a month, two at the most."

"If the Father Abbot has his way, you'll not return," Viscenti remarked, and he ducked low and spun about, and put a finger to his own pursed lips, as if speaking openly about Father Abbot Markwart would bring a host of guards bursting through his door.

Braumin Herde didn't even try to hide his amusement. "If the Father Abbot wanted to move against us openly, he would have done so long before now," he reasoned. "The hierarchy does not fear us."

"They feared Avelyn," Viscenti pointed out.

"They hated Avelyn because he stole the stones," Braumin corrected. "To say nothing of his killing of Master Siherton. The Father Abbot despised Avelyn because in taking the stones, Avelyn took Markwart's reputation, as well. If Father Abbot Markwart passes from this world with those stones unrecovered, then his time of leadership will be viewed by future Abellican monks as a failure. That is what the man fears, and no revolution because of Brother Avelyn."

Brother Viscenti had heard it all before, of course, and he threw up his hands in surrender and shuffled across the floor, taking a seat at his desk.

"But I'll not diminish the danger to myself and to Master Jojonah," Braumin Herde said to him, taking a seat on the edge of Viscenti's bed, a small and unremarkable cot. "Nor, in that event, should we diminish the responsibility that will fall upon your shoulders, my friend."

Viscenti's look was one of sheer terror.

"You have allies," Braumin Herde reminded him.

Viscenti snorted. "A handful of first- and second-year novitiates?"

"Who will grow to ninth- and tenth-year students," Braumin replied sternly. "Who will achieve their status as immaculates even as you, if you are wise enough, attain the rank of master."

"Under the auspices of Father Abbot Markwart," Brother Viscenti came back sarcastically, "who knows that I have befriended you and Master Jojonah."

"The Father Abbot does not determine rank," Brother Braumin replied. "Not alone. Your ascension, at least to master, is a foregone conclusion as long as you remain steadfast in your studies. If the Father Abbot went against that, he would be inviting whispers from every abbey, and from many of the masters of St.-Mere-Abelle. No, he cannot deny you a position."

"But he decides upon assignment," Brother Viscenti argued. "He could send me to St. Rontelmore in the hot sands of Entel, or even worse, he might assign me as a chaplain to the Coastpoint Guards in lonely Pireth Dancard, in the middle of the Gulf!"

Braumin Herde did not blink, only shrugged as if such possibilities did not matter. "And there you will hold fast to your beliefs," he explained quietly. "There, you will keep our hopes for the Abellican Order alive in your heart."

Brother Viscenti wrung his hands again, got up and began pacing about the room. He had to be satisfied with his friend's answer, he knew, for their fates were not their own to decide. Not now. But still, it seemed to Viscenti as if the whole world was suddenly moving too fast for him, as if events were sweeping him along without a moment to consider his next move.

"What do I do if you do not return?" he asked in all seriousness.

"You keep the truth in your heart," Brother Braumin replied without hesitation. "You continue to speak with those younger monks who share our tenets, fight back in their minds against the pressures to conform that they will know as they move higher in the Order. That is all that Master Jojonah has ever asked of us; that is all that Brother Avelyn would ever ask of us."

Brother Viscenti stopped his pacing and stared long and hard at Braumin Herde. The man was right, he believed with all confidence, for he, like Brother Braumin Herde, like Master Jojonah, and like several other younger monks, had Avelyn's spirit within him.

"Piety, dignity, poverty," Braumin Herde recited, his Abellican vows. When Brother Viscenti looked at him and nodded, he added the one word that Master Jojonah, in light of Avelyn's work, had secretly tagged on: "Charity."

There was no fanfare, no general announcement, as the caravan of six wagons rolled through the gates of St.-Mere-Abelle. Four of those wagons carried five monks each, while another, full of supplies, held only the two drivers. The second in line was also manned by two monks, and held Master Jojonah, the maps and the logs.

The three monks in the back of the fourth wagon, including Brother Braumin and another immaculate, worked continually with gemstones, quartz mostly, though the other immaculate also held a hematite. They used the quartz, a stone for distance sight, to scout out all the area around the caravan, and if anything looked the slightest bit suspicious, the immaculate would then use the hematite to project his spirit into the area to better discern the situation. These three were the eyes and ears of the caravan, the guides to keep the wagons away from trouble, and if they failed, the monks would surely see battle, perhaps long before they had even left the so-called civilized lands of Honce-the-Bear.

They rode throughout the morning, traveling the northwestern road toward Amvoy, the small port across the great Masur Delaval from Palmaris. Normally such a large caravan would travel southwest, to Ursal and the bridges over the great river, for there were no ferries large enough to get them across to Palmaris in one trip. But the monks had their own methods; their line to the Barbacan would be as near to straight as possible, and with the magic stones, quite a bit was possible.

The horses, two for each wagon, were soon exhausted, some drawing breath so forcefully that they seemed near to death, for each wore a bridle set with magical turquoise that allowed the drivers to communicate with the animal, to push the beast beyond its limits with mental intrusions. They took their first break at noon, in a field off to the side of the road, an appointed rendezvous. Half the monks went to work on wheels and under-carriages immediately, tightening, straightening, while others prepared a quick meal, and the three with the scouting stones sent their eyes out wide to make contact. The Church was well-prepared for such undertakings as this journey, for all along the roads of Honce-the-Bear were allies, pastors of small congregations, missionaries, and the like. The previous day, several of St.-Mere-Abelle's masters, using the maps and logs provided by Brother Francis, had used hematite to make contact with these strategically placed allies, informing them of their duties.

Within an hour of their noontime break a dozen fresh horses were brought to the field. Master Jojonah recognized the friar leading the procession, a man who had gone out into the world after a dozen years at St.-Mere-Abelle. Jojonah watched him from the flaps of his wagon cover and did not go out to greet the man, for familiarity would breed questions, he knew, questions it was neither this friar's place to ask nor Jojonah's to answer.

To the friar's credit, he stayed no longer than the couple of minutes it took him and his five helpers to make the exchange.

Soon the teams were yoked, the supplies repacked, and the caravan on its way, running hard across the miles. In mid-afternoon they veered from the road, turning more to the north, and soon thereafter, amazingly, the great Masur Delaval was in sight, with more than seventy miles already behind them. To the south lay Amvoy, and across the twenty miles of watery expanse, beyond their sight, was the city of Palmaris, the second largest city in all of Honce-the-Bear.

"Take good meals and gather your strength," Master Jojonah instructed them all. The monks understood; this would likely be the most difficult and taxing part of their journey, at least until the Timberlands had been left behind.

An hour passed, and though Brother Francis' detailed itinerary had only allowed for that much of a respite, Master Jojonah made no indication that he meant to get them going.

Brother Francis came to him in his wagon. "It is time," the younger monk said quietly, though firmly.

"Another hour," Master Jojonah replied.

Brother Francis shook his head and began to unroll a parchment. Jojonah stopped him.

"I know what it says," the master assured.

"Then you know—"

"I know that if we get halfway across that water and any of us weaken, we will lose a wagon, or all the wagons," Jojonah interrupted.

"The amber is not so taxing," Brother Francis argued.

"Not for one to walk across the water," Jojonah agreed. "But to carry such a load?"

"There are twenty-five of us."

"And there will remain twenty-five of us when we exit onto the river's western bank," Jojonah said sternly.

Brother Francis gave a slight growl and spun on his heel, starting away.

"We will travel long into the night," Jojonah said to him, "using diamonds to light the way, and thus make up the time lost resting here."

"And drawing attention to us with our beacons?" Francis asked sourly.

"Perhaps," Jojonah replied. "But that is less a risk, by my estimation, than is crossing the Masur Delaval with weary brothers."

Brother Francis narrowed his eyes and set his jaw, then turned about and left in a huff, nearly running over Brother Braumin Herde, who was on his way up the few stairs at the back of the wagon.

"We are not on his schedule," Jojonah explained dryly as his friend entered.

"He will report this to the Father Abbot, of course," Brother Braumin reasoned.

"It is as if Father Abbot Markwart were right here beside us," said Jojonah with a great sigh. "The joy of it all."

His frown melted into a smile, though, and then that turned into a laugh when Braumin Herde gave a chuckle.

Outside the wagon, Brother Francis heard it all.

An hour later, with a proper landing found along the banks of the river, and the sun riding low in the western sky, they were on the move again. Now Master Jojonah, the most seasoned and most powerful with the magical stones, led the way, with two first-year novitiates beside him and only a single driver up front. Eighteen of the twenty-five monks, all except for the actual drivers and one whose duties remained scouting with the quartz, were divided equally among the six wagons, the three in each joining hands in a ring about a piece of enchanted amber. They pooled their powers, sent their energy into the stone, calling forth its magical properties. Amber was the stone used for walking on water, and as each wagon rolled off the landing and onto the river, it did not sink, horses' hooves and the bottom of the wheels making only slight depressions on the liquid surface.

The eighteen monks fell deep into their meditative trance; the drivers worked hard, constantly angling their teams to compensate for the current. But this part of the journey proved easy going. The ride was so very smooth, a gentle reprieve on the wagons, on the horses, and on the monks.

Less than two hours later Jojonah's driver, using diamonds to light the course ahead, found a smooth and easy slope along the western bank and put his wagon back on dry ground. He went back then to inform the master, and Jojonah came out of his trance and moved outside for a good stretch and to watch the other five wagons come ashore, one by one. To the south, a handful of miles in the distance, the lights of Palmaris could be seen; to the north and west was only the darkness of night.

"The line will be tightened for our evening drive," Master Jojonah informed them, "with no more than a single horse's length between the back of one wagon and the noses of the team of the next. Go easy on the turquoise intrusions and take your rest and your last meal in the seat. We will ride long into the night, as long as the horses can take it, but at a comfortable pace. I wish to put twenty more miles behind us before we set a proper camp."

He dismissed the group then, except for Brother Francis. "When do we next exchange horses?" he asked the young monk.

"Not until late afternoon," Francis replied. "We may be taking a dozen fresh ones in exchange for only six who will ever be able to pull a cart again."

"As it must be, so it shall be," Master Jojonah said, and headed back for his wagon, truly regretting having to work the poor animals so hard.

❖ 6 ❖

Underestimated

H e thought it curious to find powrie sentries on the outskirts of
Caer Tinella this late at night. Usually the dwarves and goblins
moved back into the town proper soon after sunset. While the
goblins, in particular, did favor the cover of night for their misdeeds, with
the town secured, they normally used this active period to play their gambling games, drinking and shoving each other until fights inevitably broke
out among them.

That was before Mrs. Kelso had supposedly been turned into a tree,
though, an action the monsters attributed to their god figure, the demon
dactyl. So now they apparently meant to be more vigilant, just in case the
dactyl showed up to personally scrutinize their work.

Roger smiled; he was glad his little ruse had caused so much trouble for
the wretches. As for the guards, he wasn't overly concerned. He had come
this way to go into Caer Tinella, and so into Caer Tinella he would go,
whatever the powries might try to do to stop him. Oh yes, the guards would
slow him down, he realized, but not in any manner they had foreseen.

The two powries stood calmly, one with its hands in its pockets, the other
drawing deeply on a long-stemmed pipe. Roger noted that their caps shone
a crimson hue, even in the dim light. These were seasoned veterans, he
understood. Powries were called "bloody caps" for their practice of dipping their berets, hats fashioned of skin, often human, in the blood of their
enemies. The berets were treated with special oils that would allow them to
retain the color of the blood, with each new victim's essence brightening
the hue. Thus, a powrie's standing could often be determined by the color
of its cap.

Roger was repulsed by the sight and the implications of those shining
berets, but he was not deterred. If anything, the realization that this pair
had dipped their caps often only made him more determined. To his
thinking, this little action would avenge those killed, at least a little bit. A
low fire burned between the powries, and they had set three torches out a

dozen feet in a semicircular pattern, leaving open only the short path back to the nearby town. Roger slipped beyond that semicircle, moving as silently as a cloud drifting across the path of the moon. As he passed by the circle, the town was open to him, but he turned about, moving in behind the dwarven pair, sliding down behind a hedgerow a few feet away. He waited there a few moments, making sure the powries were off their guard and that no others were in the immediate area. Then he slithered around the edge of the bushes, belly-crawling for his prey.

"Could use a draw myself," one of the dwarves remarked, and it pulled one hand from its pocket, holding a pipe of its own.

Even as the dwarf's hand came out, Roger's fingers slipped in.

"Weed me up," the dwarf said, handing the pipe to its companion. The other powrie took it and lifted a packet of pipe weed, while the first moved its hand back to its pocket—even as Roger's hand came sliding out with a pair of gold pieces, the strange, eight-sided coinage of the Weathered Isles.

Roger smiled widely as the dwarf retrieved its pipe—with its other hand, thus opening the second pocket.

"You are sure?" Belster O'Comely asked for the tenth time.

"Saw them myself," the man, Jansen Bridges, answered. "No more than an hour ago."

"Big?"

"Could eat a man with room left in their bellies for his wife," Jansen replied.

Belster stood up from his tree-trunk seat and walked to the southern edge of the small clearing that was serving as a base camp for the refugee band.

"How many went to town?" Jansen asked.

"Just Roger Lockless," Belster replied.

"He goes in every night," Jansen said in a somewhat derisive tone. Jansen had come from the north, with Belster's group, and had never been enamored of Roger Lockless.

"Yeah, and we all eat the better for it!" Belster retorted, turning about to regard the man.

He saw then that Jansen's tone was more wrought of frustration than of any anger aimed at Roger, and so the gentle Belster let it pass.

"If any can get by them, it's Roger Lockless," Belster continued, talking as much to himself as to Jansen.

"So we all hope," said Jansen. "But we cannot wait to find out. I say we put another five miles between us and the dwarves, at least until we see how dangerous these new additions might be."

Belster considered the notion for a short while, then nodded his assent. "Go and tell Tomas Gingerwart," he instructed. "If he agrees that it is better we are on the road this very night, our group will be ready to march."

Jansen Bridges nodded and moved off across the clearing, leaving Belster to his thoughts.

He was growing tired of it all, Belster realized. Tired of hiding in the woods and tired of powries. He had been a successful tavernkeeper in Palmaris, a town he had called home since the tender age of five, relocating with his parents from the southland near Ursal. For more than thirty years he had lived in that prosperous city on the Masur Delaval, working first with his father, a builder, and then on his own in a tavern business of his own making. Then his mother had died, peacefully, and less than a year later, his father, and only then had Belster learned of the debt his father left behind, a legacy that fell squarely on the large shoulders of the man's only son.

Belster had lost the tavern, and was still in debt to the point where he would either have had to accept a decade of indenture to the creditors or go and rot for a like period in a Palmaris jail.

He had created his own third option instead, packing his few remaining belongings and fleeing for the wild north, to the Timberlands and a place called Dundalis, a new town being raised from the ruins of one destroyed by a goblin raid several years earlier.

In Dundalis, Belster O'Comely had found his home and his niche, opening a new tavern, the Howling Sheila. There weren't many patrons—the Timberlands were not heavily populated, and the only visitors who passed through were the seasonal merchant caravans—but in the self-supporting lifestyle of the wilderness town, the man didn't need much money.

But then the goblins had come back, this time with hosts of powries and giants. And so Belster became a fugitive again, and this time the stakes were much higher.

He looked back to the dark forest, in the direction of Caer Tinella, though the town was too far away, and beyond too many hills and trees, to be seen. The outlaw band could not afford to lose Roger Lockless, Belster knew. The young man had become a legend to the beleaguered refugees, their leader of sorts, though he was rarely among them, and even more rarely ever spoke to any of them. Since Roger's daring rescue of poor Mrs. Kelso, that status had even increased, if possible. If Roger was caught and killed now, the blow to morale would be heavy indeed.

"What do you know?" came a question. Belster turned about to see Reston Meadows, another of his fellow Dundalis refugees, standing behind him.

"Roger is in town," Belster replied.

"So Jansen told us," Reston replied grimly. "And he told us of the new additions, too. Roger will have to live up to his reputation and more, I fear."

"Has Tomas spoken on the matter?"

Reston nodded. "We will be on the move within the hour."

Belster rubbed his thick jowls. "Take a pair of your best scouts and make for Caer Tinella," he said. "Try to determine the fate of Roger Lockless."

"You think that three of us might get in to save him?" Reston asked incredulously.

Belster understood the sentiment; few in the camp wanted any encounters with Kos-kosio Begulne and his tough powries. "I only asked you to learn of his fate, not to determine it," the portly man explained. "If Roger was taken and killed, we will have to concoct a more fitting tale of his absence."

Reston cocked his head curiously.

"For them," Belster finished, motioning his chin in the direction of the encampment. "It did not break us when the Nightbird, Pony, and Avelyn went off for the Barbacan, but how heavy might our hearts have been if they were slain?"

Reston understood. "They need Roger," he reasoned.

"They need to believe that Roger is working for their freedom," Belster replied.

The man nodded again and scampered off to find two appropriate scouting companions, leaving Belster alone again, staring into the forest. Yes, Belster O' Comely was tired of it all, particularly of the responsibility. He felt like the father of a hundred and eighty children, and there was one risk-taker in particular who kept his nerves tingling.

Belster dearly hoped that one troublemaker would return safely.

His booty secured, Roger began to slither away. As he crossed back into the brush, though, he noticed a length of coiled rope, one used by the slaves to haul logs. Roger couldn't resist. He looped the middle of the rope around a sturdy tree trunk, then took both ends with him as he returned to the oblivious pipe-smoking powries.

He was back in the woods soon after. He decided that he would come back this way on his departure and startle the pair. If, as was usually the case with powries, they had not moved much in the meanwhile, they would find a bit of trouble, and Roger would find a bit of fun, when they took up the howling chase and the loops he had put about their feet tightened and they fell flat to the ground.

He might even be able to get back to them and snatch one of their precious caps before they managed to extricate themselves.

Roger filed the thoughts away for a later time; the town was in clear sight now, quiet and dark. A couple of goblins milled about, but even the central building, usually used for gambling, was quiet this night. Again Roger considered his ruse about the dactyl and Mrs. Kelso. The monsters were on their best behavior, fearing that their unforgiving master was about.

Given that on-guard stance, Roger almost wished he had used a different explanation concerning Mrs. Kelso's disappearance.

Too late to worry about that now, the young man told himself, and into the town he went. He would be careful this night; instead of his normal rounds, moving from building to building, picking pockets—and often placing not-so-valuables in the possession of other monsters, just to see if he might start a fight—he went straight for the larders, thinking to get a good meal and to bring some food back out to the folk hiding in the forest.

The larder door was locked, its hoop handles wrapped in heavy chains and secured by a heavy padlock.

Where did they get that? Roger wondered, rubbing his chin and cheeks and glancing all around. And why did they bother?

With a bored sigh, Roger pulled a small pick out from behind his ear and slipped it into the padlock's opening, bending low that he might better hear his work. A couple of twists, a couple of clicks, later, and the lock popped open. Roger lifted it free and started to unwrap the chains, but paused and considered his actions. He wasn't really hungry, now that he thought about it.

He glanced all about, taking in the silence, trying to measure the level of wariness in the town. Perhaps he could find a bit of sport this night. Then he could return and gather some food for his friends.

He took the lock and the chain, and left the door unopened.

Good fortune was with him, he realized before he had gone two steps, when he heard the low rumbling behind him. He skittered back to the door, bent low and put his ear to the wood.

Growling and snarling came from behind the door, and then, with sudden ferocity that stood Roger up straight in the blink of an eye, a loud and angry bark.

The young man sped away, slipping behind another building. He stashed the chains and lock—they were too noisy for flight—under a loose board along the alley, then went up to the roof, climbing easily and silently.

A powrie crossed the open ground to the larder door, cursing every step. "Bah, what're ye howling about?" the dwarf grumbled in its stone-against-stone voice. The powrie reached for the door, but stopped and scratched its head, recognizing that something was missing.

"Drat," Roger muttered when he saw the powrie run off, back the way it had come. Roger's normal tactics would have called for him to sit tight, but the hairs on the back of his neck were prickling, his instincts telling him to get away, and quickly. He went down the far side of the building, then sprinted away into the darkness. Behind him, all through the town, torches went up, one after another, the commotion mounting, cries of "Thief!" echoing through the night.

Roger went from rooftop to rooftop, scrambled down one wall and up another, then over a split-rail fence into a corral on the northwestern edge of town. Down low, the young man picked his way among the cows, trying not to disturb them, touching them only gently and whispering softly, urging them to keep quiet.

He would have gotten through without incident; the resting cows weren't overly concerned with him.

Except that not all of them were cows.

If Roger hadn't been so concerned with waking powries and goblins, he would have realized that this was Rosin Delaval's farm, and that Rosin had a bull, the most mean-tempered animal in all of Caer Tinella. Rosin usually kept the bull separate from the cows, for the bullying beast often hurt them and didn't make it easy for him to go in and get any milk. But the powries did not separate the animals, taking sport in the wounded cattle, and in the antics of their goblin lessers whenever they sent the goblins in to get milk, or a cow for slaughter.

Roger, looking over his shoulder more than ahead, and walking through a veritable maze of cow bodies, gently nudged one beast aside, then pushed softly on another. He noticed immediately that this animal seemed sturdier than the others, and less willing to give ground.

Roger started to push again, but froze in place, slowly turning his head around to regard the animal.

The bull, all two thousand pounds of it, was half asleep, and Roger, thinking that to be a half too little, backed away slowly and quietly. He bumped into a cow, and the animal moaned its complaint.

The bull snorted, its huge, horned head swinging about.

Roger darted away, cutting a path right behind the spinning bull, then turning back, right behind it again. He entertained some brief fantasy about getting the thing so dizzy that it would just fall down. Brief indeed, for despite his darting movements and strong foot speed, the bull was turning inside him, those deadly horns gaining ground.

Roger took the only course that seemed open: he leaped on the bull's back.

Rationally, he knew he shouldn't be screaming, but he was anyway. The bull bucked and snorted, hooves slamming the ground in absolute rage. It twisted and leaped, ducked its head and cut a tight turn, nearly pitching Roger over its shoulder.

Somehow he held on as the bull worked its way to the far end of the corral, with only the dark forest beyond the fence. It was a good thing, too, Roger realized, for back the other way, goblins and powries were all about, most yelling and pointing toward the corral.

The bull ran flat out for a short burst, then skidded to an abrupt stop, cutting hard to the right, then back to the left. Again Roger held on for all his life, even grabbing one of the bull's horns. On the second cut the bull overbalanced, and quick-thinking Roger saw his chance. He pulled one leg up under him and tugged with all his might on the horn, turning the bull's head even farther.

The bull pitched over and Roger leaped away, hitting the ground in a stumble that quickly turned into a dead run. He made the rail fence before the squirming bull even managed to regain its footing, and was over in the blink of an eye.

The bull trotted up to the fence; Roger, though he saw goblins running both ways along the rail back by the town, paused long enough to boast, "I could have broken your fat neck." He ended by snapping his fingers in the air just in front of the bull's nose.

The bull snorted and pawed the ground, then ducked its head.

Roger's mouth fell open. "You cannot understand me," he protested.

The point was moot; the bull charged the fence.

Roger bolted for the woods. The bull thrashed and kicked, taking out rails, knocking logs high into the air.

Then it was free, bursting onto the small clearing just beyond the corral. Goblins were closing in both directions by then, and suddenly the bull was on Roger's side.

"*Aiyeeee!*" one of the goblins squealed. Considered a quick-thinker among its dim-witted friends, the goblin grabbed its nearest companion and threw the poor fool right in the bull's path.

That goblin was soon airborne, spinning two complete somersaults before landing hard on the ground. It crawled away, trying not to groan, trying not to do anything that would get the bull's attention, for the enraged beast was giving chase to the rest of the fleeing goblins.

From a tree not so far away, Roger watched with sincere amusement. His chuckles turned into a sympathetic groan, though, when the bull gored one scrambling goblin, the sharp horn stabbing into the back of the goblin's leg, then coming right out through its kneecap. The bull snapped its head back, and over the goblin went, screaming, falling flat out across the bull's huge neck. The bull ran on, bucking wildly, the goblin flopping all about, until finally the horn tore free of the knee and the goblin pitched away. The bull wasn't done with it, though, and turned about, throwing sod, running down the goblin before it could begin to crawl away.

Up in the tree, Roger moved along the limb, out from the trunk, and leaped out to the branch of another tree, making his way to the north, back toward the encampment.

"Another night," he promised himself, remembering the chain and padlock. He could create more than a little mischief for the powries with those items, he mused. So even though he hadn't gotten into the larders, and in spite of the encounter with the bull, the ever-optimistic Roger considered the night a success, and it was with a light heart and dancing feet that he came down from the trees and began picking his trails back to the first two powries. He spotted them from a distance, both sitting on the ground, trying to pull their ankles out of the rope. The commotion in town had stirred them, and the rope had tripped them, it seemed.

Roger was sorry he had missed it. He took some satisfaction in the two pipes lying in the dirt, and in the muttered curses of his victims. That only made his heart skip lighter, a mischievous grin widening across his face as he made his way into the deep forest.

But then he heard the baying.

"What?" the young man asked, pausing, studying the strange sound. He had no experience with hunting dogs and didn't understand that they were calling out a trail, his trail. He knew from the continuing sound, though, that they were getting closer, and so he scrambled up a tall and wide oak set apart from any other trees and peered back into the darkness.

Far to the south he saw the glow of torches. "Stubborn," he muttered, shaking his head, confident that the monsters would never find him in the dark woods.

He started back down the tree, but reversed his course almost immediately as snarling sounds came up at him. From a low branch he could make out the four forms. Roger had seen dogs before—Rosin Delaval kept a pair for working his herd. But those dogs were small and friendly, always wagging their tails, always happy to play with him, or anyone else, for that matter. These dogs seemed to Roger to be a different species altogether. The tone of their barking was not friendly, but threatening, and deep and resonating, the stuff of nightmares. He couldn't make out much detail in the darkness, but realized from the sound of the barking and the black silhouettes that these dogs were much larger than Rosin's.

"Where did they get those?" the young thief muttered, for indeed the dogs were a new addition to Caer Tinella. He glanced around, looking for a way down the tree, far enough to the side to get him away from the animals.

It struck him almost immediately that to come down from that tree was to be eaten. He had to trust his luck, and up he went to the highest branches of the oak, hoping the dogs would lose sight of him, and lose interest in him.

He didn't understand the training of these animals. The hounds stayed right at the base of the tree, snuffling and scratching, and then baying. One kept jumping high, scratching at the bark.

Roger glanced anxiously to the south, to see the torches moving closer, closer, following the commotion. He had to shut the dogs up, or find some way to get away from this area.

He didn't know where to begin. He carried only one weapon, a small knife, better suited to picking locks than fighting, and even if he had a great sword with him, the thought of facing those dogs appalled him. He scratched his head, glancing all around. Why had he gone up this particular tree, so far from any others?

Because he hadn't understood his enemies.

"I underestimated them," Roger scolded himself as powries entered the clearing beneath the oak. In moments his tree was encircled by the dwarven brutes, a smiling Kos-kosio Begulne among them. Roger heard the powrie leader's fellows congratulating him on acquiring the dogs—Craggoth hounds, they called them.

Roger understood then that he had been outsmarted.

"Come on down, then," Kos-kosio Begulne bellowed up the tree. "Yeah, we see ye, so come on down, or blimey, I'll burn the damned tree out from under ye! And then I'll let me dogs eat up what's left of ye," he added slyly.

Roger knew that the fierce Kos-kosio wasn't kidding, not at all. With a resigned shrug, he slipped down to the lowest branches of the tree, in clear sight of the powrie leader.

"Down!" Kos-kosio Begulne demanded, the dwarf's voice suddenly stern and terrifying.

Roger looked doubtfully at the frenzied dogs.

"Ye like me Craggoth hounds?" the powrie asked. "We breed 'em on the Julianthes just to catch rats like yerself." Kos-kosio Begulne motioned to several others, and they quickly went to the dogs, looping choke chains and hauling the animals aside—no small feat, given the dogs' level of excitement. Roger got a good look at them then, in the torchlight, and saw, as he had suspected, that these beasts hardly resembled Rosin's dogs. Their heads and chests were huge, great muscled torsos, tall on thin legs, with coats of short brown and black hair and eyes that blazed red in the forest night, as if with the flames of hell. They seemed to be fully restrained by that point, but still, Roger could hardly bring himself to move.

"Down!" Kos-kosio Begulne said again. "Last time I'm asking."

Roger dropped lightly to the ground right in front of the powrie leader. "Roger Billingsbury at your service, good dwarf," he said with a bow.

"Roger Lockless, they call 'im," another powrie piped in.

Roger nodded and smiled, taking it as a compliment.

Kos-kosio Begulne laid him low with a heavy punch.

7

The Long Night of Fighting

Their journey on the road had thus far been surprisingly uneventful. They had encountered a band of goblins on the southern edge of the Moorlands, but dispatched that group with typical efficiency—three shots from Juraviel's bow, a lightning bolt from Pony, and Elbryan and Symphony running down those couple that managed to scamper away from the main, doomed group. Searching the area afterward, the ranger and the elf, both expert trackers, had found no signs to indicate that any greater number of the monsters might be in the immediate area, and so the fighting, for the present, was at its end.

Things got even quieter when they left the always wild Moorlands far behind, crossing into the kingdom of Honce-the-Bear, just south of the Timberlands. The northwestern corner of Honce-the-Bear was not heavily populated, and there was really only one path that could be considered a road, that covered the ground between the Wilderlands and the main road connecting Palmaris and Weedy Meadow. Apparently the goblins and powries hadn't found enough sport in the immediate region, for there was no sign at all that any were about.

Soon, though, the trio was farther south, in more populated regions, crossing fields lined by planted hedgerows and stone walls, and with many roads to choose from. And all of those roads showed many sets of tracks, powrie, goblin, and giant, and the deep grooves of the wheels of laden carts and powrie war engines.

"Landsdown," explained Pony, pointing to a plume of smoke rising in the distance, just over a short hill. She had been through this area only a couple of times, but from even those short passages, knew it far better than either of her companions. When the invading monstrous army had first come to the three towns of the Timberlands, it was Pony who traveled south to warn the folk of Landsdown and the neighboring community of impending danger.

"Occupied by monsters," the ranger reasoned, for it seemed unlikely to him that humans could still be in the towns, given the sheer number of enemy tracks along the roads. And the smoke was not that of a sacked village, not the angry, billowing blackness of buildings burning, but rather the simple gray plumes of a hearth.

"And likely we'll find the neighboring town in a similar position," Belli'mar Juraviel reasoned. "It seems as if our enemies are well-entrenched and mean to stay."

"Caer Tinella," Pony remarked after some thought. "The next town in line is Caer Tinella." She looked back to the north as she spoke, for the group had veered from the one main road, the one between Palmaris and Weedy Meadow. They were moving through the forest, and had come in from the west, below the level of Caer Tinella, the northernmost organized township in Honce-the-Bear, and thus the closest to the three towns of the Timberlands.

"And beyond Caer Tinella?" Elbryan asked.

"The road back home," Pony answered.

"We should start in the north, then," the ranger reasoned. "We will swing back around Caer Tinella and see what we might find, then come back to Landsdown to take up the fight."

"You will probably find a fight waiting for you right over that hill," Juraviel remarked.

"Our first order of business is to locate the refugees, if there are any in the area," Elbryan replied, and it was not the first time he had expressed those sentiments. He didn't say it aloud, but hoped he might find Belster O'Comely and the other folk of Dundalis among any resistance bands operating in this area.

The ranger looked to Pony, saw a smile on her fair face, and knew that she understood the reasoning behind the urgency in his voice, and knew, too, that she was of like heart. It would be good to be among trusted allies again. At Elbryan's bidding, Pony climbed up behind him on Symphony's broad back.

"The town is right on the road?" Belli'mar Juraviel asked.

"Both of them are," Pony replied. "Landsdown to the south and Caer Tinella just a few miles to the north."

"But we'll give Caer Tinella a wide berth to the west, going right around the town," Elbryan explained. "It is possible that any resistance bands would be encamped farther in the north, where the fields and roads are less, and the forest is thicker."

"You go west," Juraviel agreed, eyeing the north road. "I will go closer to Caer Tinella to see if I can get a good measure of our enemy's strength."

Elbryan, fearing for his diminutive friend, started to protest, but bit the words back, considering the stealthiness of the Touel'alfar. Belli'mar Juraviel could walk right up behind the most alert deer and pat it twice on the rump before it ever knew he was there.

Juraviel wouldn't have listened to any arguments anyway, Elbryan knew from the sly expression on his angular face, an observation confirmed when Juraviel shot Elbryan and Pony a wink of a golden eye and added, "And our enemy's weaknesses."

Then the elf was gone, slipping away, a shadow among shadows.

"Ye will tell me what I wants to know," Kos-kosio Begulne promised.

Roger sat as straight as his tight bindings would allow and painted a disarming smile on his face.

Kos-kosio Begulne's head snapped forward, the powrie's bony forehead crushing Roger's nose and knocking the man over backward.

Roger sputtered and tried to roll away, but the cords held his arms fast behind the chair back and he could get no leverage. A pair of powries were beside him suddenly, roughly pulling him back up.

"Oh, ye'll tell me," Kos-kosio Begulne declared. The powrie smiled evilly and raised one gnarly hand, snapping its fingers.

The sound jolted poor Roger's sensibilities; he could only groan as the door to the small room opened and another powrie entered, leading on a short leash the biggest, meanest dog Roger had ever seen. The dog strained in his direction against the powrie's strong pull, baring its formidable teeth, growling and snarling and snapping its powerful jaws.

"Craggoth hounds eat lots," the grinning Kos-kosio Begulne said. "Now, boy, ye got something to tell me?"

Roger took several deep breaths, trying to steady himself, trying hard not to panic. The powries wanted to know the location of the refugee encampment, something Roger was determined he would not divulge, no matter what torture they exacted.

"Too long," said Kos-kosio Begulne, snapping his fingers again. The powrie dropped the leash and the Craggoth hound came on, leaping for Roger's throat.

Roger threw himself over backward, but the dog only followed, its fangs scoring the man's cheek, cracking at his jawline.

"Don't ye let the beast kill him," Kos-kosio Begulne instructed the others. "Just make him hurt real bad. He'll talk to us, don't ye doubt." With other matters to attend to, the powrie leader left the room then, though he was surely enjoying the spectacle.

For poor Roger, all the world was blood and snapping jaws.

Belster O'Comely eyed the approaching torches with the greatest fear he had known since leaving Dundalis. According to the returned scouts, the powries had Roger, and now the appearance of so large a monstrous force in the forest, moving unerringly to the north, led the portly man to believe that Roger had been forced to give them up. Maybe Jansen Bridges had been right in his disdain for Roger's nightly antics.

There was no way that nearly two hundred refugees, many very old and many very young, would get away from such a force, Belster realized, and so he and his fellows had only one apparent option: the able-bodied would go out and fight the powries in the woods, occupy them with hit-and-run tactics until those who could not fight could get far, far away.

Belster wasn't thrilled with the prospects, and neither was Tomas or the other leaders of the refugee band. Hitting at an organized and prepared group of monsters would cost them greatly and probably spell the end of any real resistance in the region. Belster suspected that any humans surviving this night would have to move farther south and try the dangerous maneuver of slipping around the monster lines to get into Palmaris. Many times over the last couple of weeks, Belster and Tomas had considered just such an option, and each time had dismissed it as too perilous. There simply wasn't yet enough pressure being exerted on the monsters from the forces of Palmaris; the monster lines were too thick and too well-entrenched.

Still, the innkeeper had suspected all along that it would come to this, and in fact had known that the primary mission for him and his fellow warriors was to get the noncombatants far from the field of battle. The run to Palmaris would be fraught with danger, but the summer wouldn't last forever, and many of the old and young would not likely survive the cold nights of winter in the forest.

Belster blew all those thoughts away with a profound and helpless sigh. He had to concentrate on the business at hand, on directing the coming battle. His archers had already gone out to both the east and west of the advancing monstrous horde.

"The eastern flank is ready to strike," Tomas Gingerwart said, moving near the innkeeper.

"They hit hard, and retreat fast," Belster explained.

"And those in the west have to come in hard and fast as soon as the monsters make their turn to the east," Tomas replied appropriately.

Belster nodded. "And then comes our job, Tomas, the most critical of all. We must assess the strength of our enemy at once, and determine if they are weak enough, and disorganized enough, for a full assault. If so, then we send our fighters straight in, and signal for east and west to close like the jaws of a wolf."

"And if not," Tomas interrupted, for he had heard all of this before, "those in the west flee into the forest and those in the east come back in hard at the rear of Kos-kosio Begulne's turning line."

"While you and I and our fellows go to the others and begin the long circuit to the south," Belster finished, his deflated tone showing he did not like that prospect.

"You would begin that at once?" Tomas asked, somewhat surprised. He had thought that they would finish the night, however it was to be decided, in the forest, and wait for the revealing daylight to lay their plans.

"If we mean to go south—and if this force is on to us, then we have few options—it would be better that we go while the monsters are preoccupied with our archers," Belster decided.

"We have to get word to them, then," Tomas replied. "When they finally break ranks, they must know where to find us."

Belster considered that for a moment, then shook his head, his expression grave. "If in their fear they turn directly to the south, they will be chased, and thus we will be chased," he reasoned. "They have already been instructed to flee into the forest if the attack is routed. They will find their way from there, wherever they choose to go." Those were indeed the most difficult words Belster O'Comely had ever spoken. He knew the reasoning to be correct, but still felt as if he was abandoning his comrades.

Tomas' first reaction called for an immediate protest, but he sublimated it quickly, seeing Belster's pained expression, and, because of that, taking the moment to consider the wider situation. He found he had to agree with the decision, and understood that no matter how difficult the situation might become for the archers, it would be no less so for Belster's retreating group, for by all reports they would have to cross miles and miles of land even thicker with monsters.

Another man came running toward them then, from the south. "The powries and goblins have four giant allies," he reported. "They've just crossed Arnesun's Creek."

Belster closed his eyes and felt weary indeed. Four giants, any one of which could probably wipe out half of his warriors. Even worse, giants could return the arrow volleys by hurling huge stones or spears the size of tree trunks.

"Should we change the plan?" Tomas asked.

Belster knew it was too late. "No," he said gravely. "Send the eastern flank into action. And may God be with them."

Tomas nodded to the scout and the man ran off, passing the word. Barely ten minutes later the forest to the south erupted with screams and roars, with the sound of zipping arrows and the thunder of giant-hurled boulders.

"Powries, goblins, and giants," Juraviel explained to Elbryan and Pony when he caught up to them northwest of Caer Tinella. "A strong force, heading north, with purpose, it would seem."

Elbryan and Pony exchanged concerned looks; they could guess easily enough what that purpose might be.

"Up with us," Elbryan bade, lowering his hand to the elf.

"Three on Symphony?" Juraviel asked doubtfully. "He is as fine a horse as ever there was, I do not question, but three is too many."

"Then run, my friend," Elbryan bade the elf. "Find where you might best fit into the battle."

Juraviel was gone in the blink of an eye, scampering through the forest.

"And keep your head low!" Elbryan called after him.

"And you, Nightbird!" came the already distant reply.

The ranger turned to Pony, giving her that prebattle expression, a look of sheer determination she had come to know so well. "Are you ready with the stones?"

"Always," Pony answered grimly, marveling at the change in the man. In the span of a few seconds he had gone from Elbryan to Nightbird. "You just remember all that I taught you with the hematite."

The ranger chuckled as he turned back and kicked his great stallion into a run. Pony had a diamond out, calling forth its magics to light the way, and as they rode she removed the cat's-eye circlet from around her head and set it on her companion's. Then she let the diamond light die away. Nightbird would guide Symphony, for with his telepathic connection to the horse through the magical turquoise, it was almost as if the horse could see through his eyes. Even with that guidance, though, the ranger found the trail difficult, with thick brush and tightly packed trees, and paths that seemed to always lead him farther to the west instead of directly north, and so it was Juraviel, cutting a straighter course than the riders, for trees were hardly an obstacle to the nimble elf, who actually got within hearing distance of the battle first. He saw the monsters soon after, running hard left to right, to the east, apparently in pursuit.

"Giants," the elf said grimly, spotting the huge forms. Even as he watched, one of the behemoths launched a heavy stone through the tangle of trees, smashing branches.

A man came tumbling down hard from that tree. A host of goblins and the stone-throwing giant made for him, while the other monsters continued their chase.

Juraviel glanced all around, hoping that Nightbird and Pony would come onto the scene. Alone, what might he do against so powerful a force?

The noble elf shook those thoughts away. Whatever he might do, he had to try; he could not stand idly by and watch a man be murdered. Up a tree he went, running along a solid branch.

The fallen man was still alive, his head lolling, groans escaping his lips. On came a goblin, spiked club in hand.

Juraviel's first bowshot took the creature in the kidney.

"Blimey!" the goblin howled. "I been stuck!"

Juraviel's second arrow took it in the throat, and it fell over, gurgling, clasping futilely at the mortal wound.

The elf wasn't watching, though, after having seen the giant's tactics. Sure enough, a heavy stone came slamming into the tree, where Juraviel had just been standing.

The elf, far to the side in another tree, giggled loudly—giants hated that. "Oh, big and stupid is not the way!" Juraviel sang out, emphasizing his point by shooting an arrow right into the giant's face.

Even so perfect a shot had little physical effect, though, the behemoth waving the tiny arrow away as if it was no more than a stinging insect. The emotional toll, however, was more to Juraviel's liking. The giant roared and charged blindly, smashing through trees, ordering the goblins to follow.

Soon the elf was running, skipping lightly along high branches and stopping every so often to hurl a taunt, or, when the opportunity presented itself, to shoot an arrow, just to keep his pursuers on course. He doubted he would kill the giant, or would even get enough of a clear shot to bring down a goblin, but he figured that having the behemoth and half a dozen goblins chasing him far from the field of battle was a solid contribution.

The elf's keen ears picked up the sound of battle again soon after, but it was far to the north now, or at least he and the pursuers were far to the south, closer to Caer Tinella than the spot where the man had fallen.

Juraviel meant to keep them running all night if need be, past Caer Tinella and all the way to the south of Landsdown.

"Oh, well done," Elbryan congratulated when he saw the second band of human archers moving east, behind the monstrous force.

Pony looked at him curiously.

"I know this tactic," the ranger explained. "They hit side to side, trying to confuse their enemies." A smile widened on the ranger's face.

"I know it, too," Pony agreed, catching on. "And so does—"

"Belster O'Comely," the ranger reasoned. "Let us hope."

"And let us see where we might fit in," Pony added, kicking Symphony's flanks. Off the great stallion surged, thundering along the path, closing ground to the second wave of Belster's army. Elbryan took care to guide Symphony to the south of the opposing forces—except for one monstrous group that, for some reason Elbryan and Pony could only guess at, had gone charging off far to the south. Pulling up behind the cover of a line of thick pines, the ranger slid down from the horse and handed Pony the reins.

"Stay safe," he whispered, reaching up to touch the woman's hand. To his surprise, Pony handed the small diamond over to him.

"I cannot use it without drawing too much attention," she explained.

"But if they get close—" Elbryan started to protest.

"Do you remember the copse in the Moorlands?" Pony replied evenly. "They were close then."

That image of carnage quieted the ranger's concerns. If the monsters did get close to Pony, pity them, not her.

"You take the diamond and mark out targets for me," the woman explained. "If you can use the hematite, you can also use the diamond.

Seeking out the magic of each stone is much the same process. Put a glow on a band of powries, and then run clear."

Elbryan grabbed her hand more tightly and pulled her down to the side, going up on tiptoes that he could give her a kiss. "For luck," he said, and started away.

"For later," Pony replied slyly just as Elbryan moved out of sight. She remembered their pact as soon as she had spoken the words, though, and gave a frustrated sigh. This war was getting too long for her liking.

For Elbryan's liking as well. With the cat's-eye, the ranger could see well in the night. Still, when Pony's teasing reply drifted to his ears, he almost fell over a log.

He took a deep breath and put aside any images her comment had inspired, bringing himself fully into the present, to the situation at hand. Then he was off and running, using the sounds of fighting to guide his movements, to bring him closer to the action. Adrenaline coursed through his veins; he fell into that almost trancelike state, the warrior incarnate, the same perfect balance and honed senses that he found in *bi'nelle dasada*, his morning sword-dance.

He was Nightbird now, the elven-trained warrior. Even his step seemed to change, to grow lighter, more agile.

Soon he was close enough to view the movements of the combatants, both human and monster. He had to keep reminding himself that they, unlike he with his gemstone, could not see very far ahead, that the powries and goblins were perfectly blind outside the tiny perimeter of their torch-light. And for those not carrying torches, this night fighting in the dark forest was as much a matter of feeling their way along as of seeing their enemies. The ranger watched, measuring the situation, trying hard not to chuckle at the utter ridiculousness of it all, as humans and powries often passed right by each other, barely ten feet apart, without ever noticing.

The ranger knew that it was time to find his place. He spotted a pair of goblins huddled low at the base of a tree, peering to the west, the direction from which the most recent assault had been launched. He saw the pair clearly, but without any source of light, they did not see him. Silent and swift, Nightbird put himself along a clear run to them, then inched closer, closer, and leaped into their midst. Mighty Tempest flashed left, then right, then Nightbird turned back to the left, driving his sword out straight with all his weight and strength behind it, a sudden, explosive thrust that skewered the first.

He tore the blade free and pivoted back the other way, to find the other goblin down on its knees, clutching its belly, staggered from the first strike. Tempest slashed across, powerful and sure, lopping off the creature's ugly head.

Nightbird ran on, cutting swiftly across open patches of grass, climbing into trees at times to gain a better vantage of the unfolding scene around him. Always he tried to remain cognizant of where Pony might be waiting and of what help the woman might offer.

Seconds seemed like long minutes to anxious Pony, sitting quiet on Symphony within the sheltering boughs of the pine grove. Every so often she spotted or heard some movement not so far away, but could not tell if it was human or powrie, or perhaps even a deer frightened by the tumult of the battle.

All the while, Pony rubbed her fingers about several chosen stones: graphite and magnetite, the powerful ruby and protective serpentine and malachite.

"Hurry along, Elbryan," she whispered, anxious to get into the fray, to launch the first blows that she might be rid of this typical nervousness. That was how battles—except, of course, for unexpected fights—always started for her, with the churning stomach and the beads of sweat, the tingling anticipation. One strike would rid her of that edginess, she knew, when purpose and adrenaline would surge through her body.

She heard a commotion not far ahead and spotted a form, a huge silhouette. Pony needed no diamond light to discern the identity of that massive creature. Up came the graphite, the lightning stone, Pony holding it up at arm's length, gathering its energies. She hesitated a bit longer, letting the power mount, letting the giant and its handful of allies settle into position on a ridge across a short depression of thin trees.

Still she waited—she doubted that her lightning stroke would kill many of the creatures, and certainly it would not destroy the giant. If she loosed the magic, her position would be given away and she would indeed be in the thick of the fight. Perhaps a better opportunity would be presented to her.

But then the giant roared and hurled a huge stone to the west, where a group of humans was fast approaching, and the issue was settled. Goblins and powries howled in glee, thinking they had ambushed and would quickly overrun this one small band.

Then came the stroke, a sudden, jarring, blinding burst of searing white energy. Several goblins and a pair of powries went flying to the ground; the giant was thrown back so forcefully that it uprooted a small tree as it stumbled.

And most important of all, from Pony's perspective, the human band had been warned, had seen the full extent of the enemies crouched in this area in one sudden, brightening instant.

But so, too, was Pony's position surrendered. Fires flickered to life in the small vale between her and the monsters, lightning-clipped trees going up like candles. The giant, more angry than hurt, came right back her way, reaching into a huge sack to produce another boulder.

Pony thought to loose another lightning blast, but graphite was a particularly draining stone, and she knew that she would have to be more focused this time. She fumbled with the stones; she saw the giant's arms go up high, and could only pray that his throw would be off the mark.

Another light appeared, bright and white, the glow of a diamond, backlighting the giant and its allies. It lasted only a second or two, giving Pony a clearer picture of the enemy and distracting the giant for just an instant.

All the time Pony needed. Out came the magnetite, the lodestone. The woman focused on the stone's magics, saw through its magnetic energy, seeking an attraction, any attraction. She "saw" the powrie swords, the belt buckle of one dwarf. The image of the giant in the diamond backlight came clear in her mind, particularly its upraised arms, the great hands that held the boulder.

The giant was wearing metal-banded gauntlets.

Pony quickly focused the magnetite energy, blocked out all other metallic influences except one giant gauntlet. She brought the power of the stone to an explosive release and let it fly, many times the speed and power of one of Elbryan's deadly bowshots.

The giant dismissed the flash of light behind it and brought the boulder over its head again, thinking to throw it in the direction of the unseen lightning caster. But suddenly its right wrist exploded in searing pain and lost all strength, and the boulder fell from its grasp, bouncing off one square shoulder before tumbling harmlessly to the ground.

The giant hardly felt the bruise on the shoulder, for its wrist and hand were thoroughly shattered, what little remained of the metal gauntlet crushed in against the behemoth's hand. Two fingers hung loose on flaps of skin; another finger was altogether gone, just gone.

The giant staggered back a couple of long strides, blinded by surprise and agony.

Another lightning bolt slammed in then, driving the monster right over backward, dropping it, groaning, to the ground. Hardly conscious, the behemoth did hear the sounds of its few remaining comrades, all of them running away into the dark night.

Pony eased Symphony out of the pines and into the valley, picking her way through the tangle. She drew out her sword as she rode, and found no opposition when she came upon the squirming giant.

She killed it quickly.

Confident in Pony's abilities and judgment, Nightbird didn't stay around after he had marked out the target with the diamond light. Back in the darkness again, the ranger made his way farther north, cutting right across the monster and human lines.

He saw a group of men crawling through some ferns, and, on a low branch above them, a pair of goblins holding cruel spears, both peering down at the fern bed, trying to find an open shot.

Up came Hawkwing, and a split second later one of the goblins dropped heavily from the branch.

"Huh?" its companion said, turning to where the other had been standing, trying to figure out why it had jumped away.

The ranger's second shot took it through the temple, and it, too, fell away, dead before it hit the ground.

The men in the ferns scrambled, not knowing what had dropped about them.

Nightbird moved ahead quickly, closing the distance. One man came up, hearing his approach, bow drawn and ready. "What?" he asked incredulously, and then added in a whisper as the ranger rushed by him, "Nightbird."

"Follow me," the ranger instructed. "The dark is no obstacle; I will guide you."

"It is Nightbird," another man insisted.

"Who?" asked another.

"A friend," the first explained quickly, and the small group, five men and three women, set off after the ranger.

Soon enough the ranger spotted yet another band of allies crouching in the dark, and led his group that way. Suddenly his force was twenty strong, and he led them out to find enemies. He understood the realities of night-fighting in the dark forest, and the huge advantage the cat's-eye afforded him and his band. All around the group the larger battle quickly deteriorated into pockets of screaming and cursing frustration, with arrows launched blindly into the darkness, or opponents inadvertently stumbling into each other, or even comrades stumbling into one another, often lashing out before they paused long enough to identify their allies. Somewhere far back in the distance there came a cry, the grating voice of a powrie, followed by a tremendous explosion, and Nightbird knew that another unfortunate enemy had stumbled upon Pony.

He bit his lip and resisted the urge to rush back and check on his love. He had to trust in her, had to remind himself repeatedly that she knew how to fight, day or night, and that, in addition to her expertise with a sword, she carried enough magical power to carry her through.

Another battle erupted far in the opposite direction, a group of goblins stumbling across the northern end of what remained of the human line. This time the results were less clear-cut, with screams of outrage and agony, both human and goblin, splitting the air. The fighting drew more combatants, spreading until all the forest seemed thick with tumult, monsters and humans rushing this way and that. The ranger set his band in a purely defensive posture, then moved out to walk a perimeter. Any humans who ventured near were ushered in, the numbers of the group soon rising to more than thirty. Whenever any enemies ventured near, Nightbird circled about them, bringing up the diamond light so his archers could take their sudden and deadly toll.

When the immediate area finally appeared clear of monsters, Nightbird got his group moving again, putting the men in a tight formation, that they could guide each other by touch.

Torches flared to life in several places deeper in the forest, screams issued from the darkness in many others, and there were no clear lines of combat for the group to engage. But those with the ranger held their calm, methodical way, moving along in their tight and organized formation, the tireless Nightbird continually circling about them, guiding them. More than once the ranger spotted enemies moving in the brush, but he held his forces in quiet check, not willing to reveal them. Not yet.

Soon the sounds of fighting withered away, leaving the forest night as quiet as it was dark. A torch flared to life in the distance; Nightbird understood it to be powries, the cocky dwarves likely confident now that the battle had ended. He moved to the nearest of his soldiers and bade the man to pass the word that the time to strike was near.

Then the ranger settled the group once more into a defensive posture and moved out alone. No stranger to powrie tactics, he figured that those with the torch would form the hub of their formation, with their forces encircling them like the spokes of a wheel. The torchlight was still more than two hundred feet away when the ranger encountered the tip of one of those spokes, a pair of goblins crouched beside a tight grouping of small birch trees.

With all his great skill, Nightbird slipped around and moved in behind the oblivious pair. He thought to flash his diamond light, that his archers could mow the goblins down, but decided against that tactic, preferring to make this one strike decisive. He went in alone, inch by inch.

His hand clamped over the mouth of the goblin to his left; his sword drove through the lungs of the goblin to the right. He let Tempest fall free with the dead goblin, and grabbed the remaining creature's hair with his now free right hand, sliding his left down enough to cup the monster's chin. Before the goblin could begin to cry out, the ranger drove both arms across his body, right to left, left to right, then violently yanked them back the other way.

The goblin hardly found the chance to squeal, and the only sound was the snapping of its neck bone—it might have been a footstep on a dry twig.

The ranger retrieved Tempest and moved in deeper, nearer the hub, surveying the enemy formation, which was exactly as he had suspected. Taking as accurate a count as possible, he silently went back to his waiting force.

"There are monsters about," he explained. "A trio of powries within that torchlight."

"Then show them to us and let us be done with this night," one eager warrior piped in, and his words were echoed many times over.

"It is a trap," the ranger explained, "with more powries and goblins waiting in the darkness and a pair of giants lurking behind the trees."

"What do we do?" one man asked, his tone very different now, more subdued.

The ranger looked around at all his men, a wry smile widening on his face. They thought they were outmatched—that much was obvious from their expressions. But Nightbird, who had been fighting bands of monsters all the way from the Barbacan, knew better. "We kill the giants first," he coolly explained.

Belster and Tomas watched and listened from a distant hilltop. The innkeeper rubbed his hands repeatedly, nervously, trying to guess at what might be happening down there. Should he retract his forces? Should he press the fight?

Could he? The plans seemed so logical when they were made, so easily executed and, if need be, retracted. But the truth of battle never worked out that way, particularly in the dark and confusing night.

Beside him, Tomas Gingerwart was fighting an equally difficult dilemma. He was a tough man, battle hardened, but for all his hatred of the monsters, Tomas understood that to engage them in drawn-out conflict was a fool's game.

But he, too, could not get a clear picture of what might be happening. He heard the occasional screams—more often a monster's voice than a man's—and saw the flares of light. A couple of surprising flashes, brilliant and sudden, caught his and Belster's attention more keenly, though, for they were not the fires of torches. Belster recognized them well enough as an obvious stroke of lightning magic.

The problem was, neither Belster nor Tomas had any idea which side was tossing the magic about. Their little band possessed no gemstones, and wouldn't have known how to use them if they did, but likewise, powries, goblins, and giants had never been known to wield such magic.

"We must decide, and quickly," Tomas remarked, his voice edged with frustration.

"Jansen Bridges should return soon," Belster replied. "We must find out who loosed that magic."

"We haven't seen it in a long while," Tomas went on. "The point may be moot, with the magic expended or the wielder dead."

"But who?"

"Roger Lockless, likely," Tomas replied. "Ever has he a trick to play."

Belster wasn't so sure of that, though the notion that Roger had a bit of magic about him was nothing new to the innkeeper. The legends of Roger might be exaggerated, but his exploits were indeed amazing.

"Call them back," Tomas decided then. "Light the signals and send runners with the word. The battle is ended."

"But Jansen—"

"We haven't time to wait," Tomas interrupted firmly. "Call them back."

Belster shrugged, and couldn't rightly disagree, but before either he or Tomas could give the retreat signal, a man came loping up the side of the hillock.

"Nightbird!" he cried to the two. "Nightbird, and Avelyn Desbris!"

Belster ran down to meet him. "Are you sure?"

"I saw Nightbird myself," Jansen replied, huffing and puffing as he tried to catch his breath. "It had to be him, for no other could move with such grace. I saw him kill a goblin, oh, and beautifully, too. Sword left and right." He waved his arm about, imitating the move as he spoke.

"Who does he speak of?" Tomas asked, coming down to join them.

"The ranger," Belster replied. "And Avelyn?" he asked of Jansen. "Did you speak with Avelyn?"

"It had to be him," Jansen replied. "The flash of lightning, scattering powries, felling giants. They have returned to us!"

"You assume much," pragmatic Tomas put in, then to Belster he added, "Are we to hope that this man's observations ring true? If he is wrong—"

"Then still it would seem as if we have found some allies, powerful allies," Belster replied. "But let us indeed light the torches. Let us regroup and see how strong we have become." Belster eagerly led the way from the hillock, silently hoping that his old comrades from Dundalis had indeed returned to help in the cause.

Their expressions were mixed, some nodding eagerly, others hesitantly, and still others glancing doubtfully to their fellows.

"The torchlight marks the hub of the powrie defensive position," Nightbird quickly explained. "The way is open to it if we are quiet enough and clever enough. We must strike hard and sure, and be prepared for any attacks that come in about us."

"The hub?" one man echoed doubtfully.

"The center of the powrie defensive ring," the ranger clarified. "A small grouping in the middle of a wide perimeter."

"If we attack there, right in the middle, then we will be surrounded," the man replied, and several incredulous grunts of accord sprang up about him.

"If we hit them strong enough at the center and kill the giants, the others, particularly the goblins, will not dare to come in against us," the ranger countered with confidence.

"The torches are naught but bait," the man argued, raising his voice so that the ranger and several others had to motion for him to be quiet.

"The torches are indeed meant to bring in enemies," Nightbird conceded. "But those enemies are supposed to be identified and engaged on the edge of the ring. If we move without further delay, the path is open all the way to the hub; our enemies will not expect so strong an attack."

The man started to argue again, but those near him, their trust in the ranger growing, hushed him before he could begin.

"Go in quiet and in a line three abreast," Nightbird explained. "Then we shall form a tight circle about the hub, and kill it before any reinforcements can arrive."

Still, many of the others exchanged doubtful glances.

"I have been fighting powries for many months, and these are powrie tactics, to be sure," Nightbird explained.

His tone, full of absolute confidence, bolstered those nearest him, and they in turn turned back to nod to the men behind.

The group set off immediately, with Nightbird far in the lead. He went back to the spot where he had slain the two goblins, and was relieved to find their bodies as he had left them, and that no new tracks were about the area. The enemy force was not numerous and the spokes of this defensive wheel were few, he reasoned, for when he searched both left and right, using the light of the powries' own torches as his guiding beacon, he saw no other monsters.

Nightbird led his force straight in, then fanned them out, barely thirty feet from the powries—and the giants, he realized, for the behemoth pair was still in place, their lanky forms pressed up tight against the back side of the oak tree, using its girth to shadow them from the revealing light.

The ranger picked his course quietly. He moved along his line, signaling for all to be ready, and clutched the diamond tight in his fist. Far out to the left of the powrie trio, he found a low, thick limb. He went onto it slowly, easing his weight up so it would not rustle, then picked his careful path along the solid wood, moving nearer, nearer, to the trunk.

Nearer to the giants.

Nightbird concentrated on the stone, building its energy, but not yet releasing it.

Building, building—all his hand was tingling from the stone's magic, begging release.

Nightbird ran along the branch; the powries looked up at the sound.

And then they, and the giants, looked away, blinded by the sudden burst of radiance, a brilliant white light, brighter than the day itself.

Nightbird rushed above the stunned powries and bore down on the nearest giant, its head even with his own. He knew he wouldn't get many swings; he grabbed up Tempest in both hands and came in running, jerking to a stop and transferring every ounce of his momentum and strength into that one downward chop.

The blade, trailing a line of white light hardly discernable in the brilliant diamond glare, smashed down through the giant's forehead, cleaving bone and tearing brains, and the behemoth, howling, grasped at its head and tumbled backward.

The other giant rushed in, only to be met by a hail of stinging arrows.

Nightbird changed direction, scampering straight up the tree.

Powries and goblins cried out and scrambled all about the area; the archers had to shift their rain to nearer, closing targets.

The remaining behemoth shrugged away the initial volley and grabbed hard on the tree, thinking to tear it right from the ground, thinking to smash the ranger, the miserable rat who had just inflicted a mortal wound on its brother. It looked up, roaring in pain and outrage, and then went quiet, seeing the ranger looking back at it, down the arrow set on his strange-looking bow.

Nightbird had Hawkwing drawn all the way back. With corded muscles perfectly taut, arms locked with the bow, legs locked about the branch and trunk, he had held the pose until the giant was in position, directly below him, and the behemoth glanced up at him.

Then he released, the arrow burrowing into the monster's face, driving deep, deep, disappearing.

The giant's outstretched arms flailed wildly, helplessly, and then it slumped to its knees, crumbling right beside its brother, dying even as its brother continued to squirm in the dirt.

Nightbird wasn't watching, was too busy climbing, realizing he was vulnerable at this low position. Then, from a branch higher up he watched the fight and carefully picked his shots, taking out those couple of monsters too well hidden, from ground level, for his companions to spot them.

"To hiding!" the ranger called, and a moment later he dropped the diamond light, leaving the area black, save one fallen torch flickering in its death throes on the ground.

Nightbird closed his eyes, then opened them slowly, letting them adjust to the new lighting, letting the cat's-eye take control once more. The monsters were far from defeated, he realized immediately, for several groups had banded together and were stubbornly coming in, mostly from the south. He had to make a decision, and quickly. The element of surprise was gone, and the enemy still badly outnumbered his meager force of thirty.

"Take to the north," he called down, keeping his voice as low as possible. "Stay together at all costs. I will rejoin you as soon as I can."

As his soldiers slipped away through the brush, the ranger turned his attention back to the south, to the many monstrous groups, thinking he would find some way to deter them, perhaps to lead them on a long and roundabout chase back to the south.

But then he looked behind the monstrous lines, saw the blue-glowing form of a woman on a horse.

"Run on!" the ranger cried to the humans. "Run for all your life!" And Nightbird began to climb, scampering wildly up the tree, and not in fear of any powrie crossbow.

Trusting in Symphony's superior senses to get her through the tangle,

Pony urged the horse ahead. She crossed by a pair of startled powries—who hooted and gave chase—and strengthened her serpentine shield.

They were all about her, rushing in, crying in savage glee.

And then, in the blink of a powrie eye, they were all burning, and so were the trees.

Using the light to guide her way, Pony moved through the conflagration, straining to keep the protective fire shield in place. She blinked in disbelief as she neared a huge oak on the very edge of the fires, for coming down the far side, dropping frantically from branch to branch, came Nightbird.

Pony guided Symphony under the lowest branch, and the ranger dropped to the ground right before her, immediately diving into a roll to smother a few errant flames. He rolled to his feet and scrambled away. "You might have warned me!" he scolded, wisps of smoke trailing from his leather tunic.

"The night is warm," Pony remarked with a snicker. She took Symphony right by him then, leaning to the side and offering him her hand. He grabbed on—falling into the protective shield as soon as their fingers touched—scrambled up behind her, and away they trotted, confident that no monsters were anywhere near in pursuit.

"You should be more careful about where you blow up," the ranger scolded.

"You should be wiser about where you hide," Pony countered.

"There are options other than the gemstones," the ranger argued.

"Then teach me *bi'nelle dasada*," the woman said without hesitation.

The ranger let it go at that, knowing all too well that with Pony, he would never get the last word.

❖ 8 ❖

Intervention of Conscience

In a meadow a score of miles east of the town of Landsdown, the caravan from St.-Mere-Abelle made its last exchange of horses. Friar Pembleton, who brought the fresh animals, also brought news that was not welcomed by the leaders of the caravan.

"We must go farther to the east, then," Brother Braumin Herde reasoned, looking to the northwest, their intended course, as if he expected a host of monsters to rush down upon them.

Brother Francis eyed Braumin dangerously, the young and ambitious monk taking every little change to his itinerary personally.

"Be at ease, Brother Francis," Master Jojonah remarked, seeing the anxious man chewing hard on his lip. "You have heard good Friar Pembleton. All the lands between Landsdown and the Wilderlands are thick with our enemies."

"We can hide from them," Brother Francis argued.

"At what magical cost?" Master Jojonah asked. "And at what delay?" Jojonah gave a sigh, and Francis growled and spun away. That settled, for the moment at least, Jojonah turned back to Friar Pembleton, a large and round man with a thick black beard and bushy eyebrows. "Pray tell us, good Pembleton," he bade the man. "You know the region far better than we."

"Where are you going?" the friar asked.

"That I cannot say," Master Jojonah replied. "You need know only that we must get through the Timberlands, to the north."

The friar rubbed a hand over his bushy chin. "There is a road that will lead you to the north, though into and through the eastern sections of the Timberlands, not the western reaches, as you had originally planned. It is a good road, though little used."

"And what word of powries and goblins up there?" Brother Braumin asked.

The friar shrugged. "No word," he admitted. "It appears as though the monsters came from the northwest, sweeping through the Timberlands past the three towns of Dundalis, Weedy Meadow, and End-o'-the-World. From there they have extended south, but, as far as I have heard, not to the east.

"It seems a reasonable detour," the friar added hopefully, "for there is little in the east that would give the monsters sport. No towns, and very few, if any, homesteads."

A younger monk joined the group then, bearing a satchel full of rolled parchments, their ends sticking from the leather bag. Brother Francis moved immediately to intercept, and yanked the satchel away.

"Thank you, Brother Dellman," Master Jojonah said calmly to the young monk, and he made a gentle motion for the startled young man to go back to the others.

Brother Francis flipped through the various rolls, finally settling on one and pulling it forth. He unrolled it gingerly, spreading it on a tree stump as Master Jojonah, Brother Braumin, and Friar Pembleton huddled around him.

"Our path was right through Weedy Meadow," Brother Francis remarked, tracing the line on the map with his finger.

"Then expect to be fighting every step of the way," Friar Pembleton answered sincerely. "And Weedy Meadow, by all accounts, is now a powrie outpost. Lots of giants up there, too."

"Where is this more eastern road?" Master Jojonah asked.

The friar moved in close to the map, studied it for just a moment, then ran his finger to the east of their present position, and then north, cutting through the narrower region of the eastern Timberlands and right into southern Alpinador. "Of course, you can turn back to the west before you get through the Timberlands, circling north of the three Timberland towns."

"What terrain might we find?" Master Jojonah asked. "Have you ever been up there?"

"Once," the friar replied. "When they first rebuilt Dundalis after the goblin raid—that was several years ago, of course. It's all forest, settled on the hillsides, hence the name of the region."

"All forest, and thus not well-suited for wagon travel," Brother Braumin put in.

"Not so bad," the friar replied. "It's old forest, with great and dark trees, but not much undergrowth. Except of course for the caribou moss; you will encounter more than a bit of that."

"Caribou moss?" All eyes turned to the questioner, Brother Francis, his fellow monks surprised indeed that he did not recognize the name. Francis met Jojonah's curious gaze head-on, the younger man again narrowing his eyes threateningly. "No tomes told of it," he answered the master's unspoken question.

"A shrub, white and low to the ground," Friar Pembleton explained. "Your horses should have no trouble pushing through, though it will grab at your wheels. Other than that, the canopy is too dark for much under-growth. You will get through, no matter where you turn to the west."

"We will get through along the original course," Brother Francis replied sternly.

"I beg your pardon, good brother," Friar Pembleton said with a gracious bow. "I never said that you would not. I only warned you—"

"And for that, we are truly grateful," Master Jojonah said to the man, though he was looking directly at Francis as he spoke. "I ask you now, in good faith, which road would you, who are more familiar with this terrain, select?"

Pembleton scratched his thick beard, mulling over the options. "I would go east," he said. "And then north, right up into Alpinador. The land is sparsely populated, but you'll find the barbarians living along the route to be cordial enough, though probably of not much assistance."

Master Jojonah nodded; Brother Francis started to protest.

"Will you go and speak with the drivers now, that you might guide them to the entrance of this eastern road?" Jojonah bade the friar. "We must be back on the trail at once."

The friar bowed again and walked away, glancing back several times.

"Father Abbot—" Brother Francis began.

"Is not here," Master Jojonah promptly interrupted. "And if he were here, he would agree with this new course. Sublimate your pride, brother. It is unfitting to one of your training and station."

Brother Francis started to argue, but the words were lost in a swirl of absolute rage before they ever got out of his mouth. He quickly gathered up the parchment, creasing it in many places with his rough handling—the first time the others had seen him treat one of the maps in that manner—and stormed away.

"He goes to contact Father Abbot," Brother Braumin reasoned.

Master Jojonah chuckled at the thought, confident that his choice was the correct one and that Francis was simply too blinded by his anger and wounded pride to see past the inconvenience.

The caravan was on its way soon after, moving onto the eastern road without incident. Brother Francis did not emerge from the back of his wagon all that day, though the monks riding with him were quick to get out and away from him. He was pouting, by their accounts.

"In some situations, Father Abbot Markwart can be counted on," Master Jojonah whispered to Brother Braumin, offering a sly wink.

The younger monk smiled widely, always thrilled to see the ambitious Francis put in his proper place.

As Friar Pembleton had told them, the road was easy and clear. Those monks searching the area with the quartz reported no monstrous activity at all, just the wild forest. Master Jojonah set the pace at steady and smooth. They couldn't afford to drive these horses beyond their limits, for they expected no replacements the rest of the way to the Barbacan and all the way back again, until they met with Friar Pembleton in the very same field they had just left behind, swapping these horses for the ones they had given into the man's care.

Of course, that was assuming that Pembleton's little hamlet would survive over the next few weeks, and given the reports of monsters just a score of miles away, the monks could only pray that would be the case.

They traveled late into the night, with Master Jojonah even daring to put up substantial diamond light to guide their way. They camped right on the road, circling the wagons for protection. Great care was given to the precious horses, with hooves cleaned and shoes carefully inspected. The animals were toweled down and brought to graze in a nearby meadow, and more guards were posted about them than about the wagon ring.

The going was easy again the next day, but their new track would be much longer, and there was no way they could meet the timetable without pushing the horses. Brother Francis ran up behind Master Jojonah's wagon and climbed in precisely to make that point.

"And if we drive them so hard that they cannot continue?" the master argued.

"There is a way," Brother Francis said evenly.

Master Jojonah knew what he was talking about: in the old tomes, Francis had stumbled upon a formula, a combination of magic stones, that could steal the life force from one animal and give it to another. Master Jojonah thought the process truly barbaric, and had hoped they would find no cause to even discuss the matter. Or at least, he had hoped he could keep the caravan on schedule, thus giving him the ability to deny Francis, for he knew that the eager and ambitious brother would surely want to try this new combination of magics, if only to add a major footnote to his account of the journey. Now, facing the reality of a longer road, the master glanced to Brother Braumin, who could only shrug, for he, too, had no practical answers. Finally, Jojonah threw up his hands in defeat. "See to it," he instructed Brother Francis.

The monk nodded, couldn't hide his smile, and was gone.

Using turquoise and hematite, the monks under Brother Francis' charge brought the first few deer to the wagons within the hour. The unfortunate wild animals were lashed beside the horses, and again the hematite and turquoise combination was used upon them, this time to draw their very life force from them, transferring their strength and energy to the horse teams.

The deer were soon left behind in the road, two of them dead, the other three too exhausted to even stand. Master Jojonah looked back at them with sincere sympathy. He had to keep reminding himself of the urgency of the mission, of the fact that many, many more animals and people would suffer greatly if the answers were not found and the monsters not turned back.

Still, the sight of the drained animals on the road saddened him greatly.

The Abellican Order should not be about such dark things as this, he thought.

More deer were brought in, and even, at one point, a large bear, the creature posing no threat, for it was overwhelmed by telepathic intrusions. Continually refreshed by the stolen energy, the horses crossed more than sixty miles before the sun was down, and again the caravan rolled on long into the night.

With the abundance of wildlife and absence of monsters, neither Jojonah nor Francis doubted they would be back on schedule within a couple of days, despite the roundabout detour.

"Just goblins!" one man declared, slamming his mug of ale down on the oaken table so forcefully that the metal handle broke apart at its top brace, sending the golden liquid flying about. The man was huge and powerful, with bulging arms and chest, thick hair and beard. He hardly stood out in this gathering of thirty adult men of Tol Hengor, hardy folk all, tall and strong from a life in the harsh climate of southern Alpinador.

"A hundred goblins, at the least," another man put in. "And with a giant or two, do not doubt."

"And them stupid little dwarf things," added another. "Ugly as an old dog's arse, but tougher than stewed boot!"

"Bah! But we'll smash them down, every one!" the first man promised, growling with every word.

The door to the town's mead hall opened then, and all eyes turned to see a man, tall even by Alpinadoran standards, enter. He had seen more than sixty winters, but stood as straight as any twenty-year-old, and there was nothing slack about his muscles or his posture. About the town, about all of Alpinador, it was often whispered that this one had been touched by "faerie magic," and in a sense, that was true enough. His hair was flaxen and long, well below his shoulders, and his face adorned with a well-trimmed golden beard, accentuating his eyes, which remained as sparkling and blue as a clear northern sky. All boasts ended at that moment, in deference to the great man.

"You have seen them?" one man asked, a perfectly silly question in the minds of all who knew this man, the ranger Andacanavar.

He walked up to the long table and nodded, then pulled his tremendous claymore over his shoulder and laid its bloodstained blade across the table.

"But is there any sport remaining for us?" a man said with a burst of laughter, which was joined by all in attendance.

All except for one.

"Too much sport," Andacanavar said grimly, and the room went silent.

"Just goblins!" the man who had spilled his mead repeated determinedly.

"Goblins and giants and powries," the ranger corrected.

"How many giants?" came a call from the far end of the great table.

"There were seven," the ranger replied, lifting his gleaming blade up before their eyes. "Now there are five."

"Bah, not so many," two men said in unison.

"Too many," Andacanavar said again, more forcefully. "With their smaller allies holding our warriors at bay, the five giants will destroy Tol Hengor."

Nervous glances met angry glares, the proud northlanders not knowing how to respond. They held Andacanavar in the greatest respect—never before had he led them astray. Over the last few months, with the invasion by sea and by land, all the towns of Alpinador had been sorely pressed, and many overrun. Whenever tireless Andacanavar was about, though, the odds were more even, and the Alpinadorans had fared well.

"What are we to do, then?" a bear of a man named Bruinhelde, the chieftain of Tol Hengor, asked, leaning forward over the table to stare the ranger in the eye. He motioned to a woman standing in waiting at the side of the tent, and she took up a cloth and approached the great ranger.

"You will take your people out to the west," Andacanavar explained, handing his claymore to the woman, who reverently began to clean it.

"And hide in the woods like women and children?" the ale-spiller roared, leaping up from his seat. Having had too many drinks, he wobbled on unsteady feet, and the man next to him promptly shoved him back down.

"I will try to keep striking at the giants," the ranger explained. "If I can defeat them, or lead them away, you and your warriors can strike back at the rest and reclaim Tol Hengor."

"I do not wish to leave my home," Bruinhelde replied, and then paused, and all the room hushed. Bruinhelde was the leader, a title won in battle, and the tribe would follow his words, whatever Andacanavar might suggest. "But I trust in you, my friend." he added, and reached out and dropped his hand on the ranger's shoulder. "Strike fast and strike hard. It would be better if these filthy creatures did not set foot in Tol Hengor. And if they do, I wish to have them out quickly. I do not enjoy weathering the open forest at my age." He said the last with a wink, for he was more than fifteen years Andacanavar's junior, and it was well-known that the nomadic ranger lived almost exclusively in the deep forest.

The ranger nodded to the chieftain, then to all gathered. He took the cloth from the woman and finished wiping the giant blood from his blade, then lifted it up, gleaming for all to see. It was an elvish blade, Icebreaker by name, the largest item ever constructed of silverel. Icebreaker did not nick and did not dull, and in Andacanavar's strong arms, it could cleave down small trees in a single swipe. The ranger slid the blade back into its sheath over his shoulder, nodded to Bruinhelde, and was gone.

* * *

Master Jojonah and Braumin Herde stood on the edge of a high ridge, looking down upon a small village of stone houses set in a wide and shallow vale. The sun was low in the west, sending long shadows along the valley.

"We have come farther than we believed," the brother reasoned.

"Alpinadoran," Master Jojonah agreed. "Either we have crossed through the Timberlands or these barbarians have settled beyond their accepted southern border."

"The former, I would guess," Brother Braumin replied. "Brother Baijuis, skilled in use of the sextant, agrees."

"The magic used on the wild animals is effective, however immoral," the master said dryly.

Brother Braumin glanced sidelong, studying his companion. He, too, had not been thrilled by the life-draining of innocent wild animals, though it seemed he was not nearly as distressed by it as Jojonah.

"Even stubborn Francis agrees that we have made up the time lost by the detour," Master Jojonah went on. "Though he had little argument against us when Father Abbot Markwart agreed with our choice of the eastern road."

"Brother Francis rarely needs support, or even logic, when disagreeing," Braumin remarked, drawing a concurring chuckle from his superior. "He is plotting our new course now, and surprisingly, with the same fervor that he plotted our original course."

"Not so surprising," Master Jojonah replied, lowering his voice to a whisper when he noticed the approach of two younger monks. "Brother Francis will do anything to impress the Father Abbot."

Brother Braumin snickered, but lost his smile when he turned to regard the newcomers, their expressions grave.

"Pray you forgive our intrusion, Master Jojonah," said one of them, Brother Dellman. Both young monks began bowing repeatedly.

"Yes yes," the master prompted impatiently, for it was obvious to Jojonah, too, that something must be terribly wrong. "What is it?"

"A group of monsters," Brother Dellman explained. "Moving from the west, toward that village."

"Brother Francis insists that we can easily avoid them," the other monk interjected. "And so we can, but are we to let those villagers be slaughtered?"

Master Jojonah turned to Braumin, who was shaking his head slowly, as if the very movement pained him profoundly. "Father Abbot Markwart's instructions were clear and uncompromising," the immaculate said uncomfortably. "We are not to engage any, enemy or friend, at least until we have completed our task at the Barbacan."

Jojonah looked down at the village, at the plumes of gray smoke drifting lazily from the chimneys. He imagined how dark that cloud might soon be, black smoke billowing from burning houses; people, children, running about, screaming, in terror and in pain.

And then dying, horribly.

"What is in your heart, Brother Dellman?" the master asked unexpectedly.

"I am loyal to Father Abbot Markwart," the young monk replied without hesitation, straightening his shoulders resolutely.

"I did not ask how you would proceed were the decision yours," Master Jojonah explained to him. "I only asked what was in your heart. What should the monks of St.-Mere-Abelle do when they come upon a situation such as the one before us?"

Dellman started to answer in favor of fighting beside the folk of the village, but stopped, confused. Then he started again, his reasoning moving in a different direction, speaking of the larger goal, the greater good to all the world. But then he stopped again, grunting in frustration.

"The Abellican Order has a long tradition of defending those who cannot defend themselves," the other young monk put in. "In our own region, we have oft welcomed the townsfolk into the safety of our abbey in times of peril, be it powrie invasion or impending storms."

"But what of the greater good?" Master Jojonah asked, stopping the young monk before he could gain too much momentum.

With no answer forthcoming, Jojonah took a different tack. "How many people do you estimate are down there?" he asked.

"Thirty," Brother Braumin replied. "Perhaps as many as fifty."

"And are fifty lives worth the price of defeating our most important mission, a risk that we surely assume if we intervene?"

Again there was only silence, with the two younger monks glancing repeatedly at each other, each wanting the other to seek out the proper answer.

"We know Father Abbot Markwart's position on that," Brother Braumin remarked.

"Father Abbot would insist that they are not worth the potential cost," Master Jojonah said bluntly. "And he would make a strong case for his point."

"And we are loyal to Father Abbot Markwart," Brother Dellman said, as though that simple fact ended the debate.

But Master Jojonah wasn't going to let him off that easily, wasn't going to let Dellman or any of the others hand off the responsibility of this decision; a decision, he believed, that went to the very core of the Abellican Order, and to the very heart of his dispute with Markwart. "We are loyal to the tenets of the Church," he corrected. "Not to people."

"The Father Abbot represents those tenets," Brother Dellman argued.

"So we would hope," replied the master. He glanced at Braumin Herde again, and the man was visibly anxious about the course of Jojonah's questioning.

"What say you, Brother Braumin?" the master asked bluntly. "You have been in the service of the Church for more than ten years; what do your studies of the tenets of the Abellican Order tell you of our course now? By those tenets, are fifty lives, or a hundred lives, worth the risk of the greater good?"

Braumin straightened, honestly surprised that Master Jojonah had put him on the spot, had called him out to reveal publicly what was in his heart. His thoughts whirled back to the powrie battle at St.-Mere-Abelle, to the peasant Father Abbot had possessed, then leaping the body to its death. That act was for the greater good—many powries were destroyed in the action—and yet it still left a lingering foul taste in Braumin's mouth and a cold blackness in his heart.

"Are they?" Jojonah pressed.

"They are," Braumin answered sincerely. "One life is worth the risk. With so important a quest before us, we should not go out of our way to seek those in peril, but when God sees fit to present them before us, we have a sacred obligation to intervene."

The two younger monks gasped in unison, surprised by the words, but also somewhat relieved—an expression, particularly on the face of young Brother Dellman, that Master Jojonah marked well.

"And you two," Jojonah asked of them, "what say you of our course?"

"I would like to save the village," Brother Dellman replied. "Or at least warn them of the impending invasion."

The other monk nodded his agreement.

Jojonah struck a pensive pose, weighing the risks. "Are there any other monsters in the area?" he asked.

The two young monks looked to each other curiously, then shrugged.

"And how strong is this coming force?" Master Jojonah went on.

Again, no answer.

"These are questions we must have answered, and quickly," Master Jojonah explained. "Else we must follow Father Abbot Markwart's decree and be on our way, leaving the villagers to their grim fate. Go then," he bade them both, shooing them away as if they were stray dogs. "Get you to those with the quartz stones. Find me my answers, and be quick about it."

The young monks bowed immediately, turned and sped away.

"You take a great risk," Brother Braumin remarked as soon as the pair were gone. "And more a risk for yourself than for our quest."

"What risk to my soul if I let this pass?" Jojonah asked, a point that temporarily stole Brother Braumin's argument.

"Still," the younger monk said at length, "if the Father Abbot—"

"The Father Abbot is not here," Master Jojonah reminded him.

"But he will be if Brother Francis discovers that you plan to intervene against these monsters."

"I will deal with Brother Francis," Master Jojonah assured him. "And with the Father Abbot, if he does indeed find his way into Francis' body." His tone showed that to be the end of the debate, and, despite his well-

founded fears, Braumin Herde was smiling as Jojonah determinedly walked
ahead of him. The master, his mentor, was taking a stand, Braumin understood. Sometimes, when the heart called loudly enough, one just had to dig
in his heels.

The night was dark; a full moon had risen early, but had been blotted out
by thick and threatening storm clouds. A fitting night, given the monstrous
force approaching Tol Hengor. Nearly two hundred strong, the vicious
band had already overrun two villages, and had no reason to believe that
this next one in line would prove any more difficult. They came into the
western end of the valley in their customary semicircular battle formation,
with goblins forming the frontal shield perimeter, every other one carrying
a torch, and the powries and giants clustered in the middle, ready to support either flank or charge straight ahead. Though they were walking
between two ridges, along lower, less defensible ground, they did not fear
any ambush. The Alpinadoran humans were not bowmen, typically, and
even if the warriors of this village had perfected the art of distance fighting,
their number—reported by scouts at no more than three dozen—would
not be sufficient to cause too much distress. In addition the giants, who
could take many arrow hits, would respond to any flanking attack with a
devastating boulder barrage, turning the ambush back on the ambushers.
No, the powrie leaders knew, Alpinadoran humans were dangerous in close
combat, fighting hand-to-hand with their great strength, and not in hit-and-
run tactics. And so the monsters had chosen this head-on formation rather
than risk breaking the band into smaller, more scattered lines by traveling
over the rougher ground of the ridges.

Thus it was with supreme confidence that the powries moved their combined force through the wide vale, all of them itching for the taste of human
blood, all of the powries wanting to brighten the crimson stain of their
berets.

They couldn't comprehend the power that had come against them in the
form of the monks of St.-Mere-Abelle. A dozen lay in wait on either side of
the vale, Brother Francis leading those on the northern wall, Brother
Braumin in command of those in the south. Master Jojonah sat far in back
of Braumin's group, pressing a hematite, that most useful and versatile of
stones, against his heart. He was the first to fall into the magic, releasing his
soul from its corporeal bonds and drifting out into the night air.

His first task was easy enough. He willed his invisible spirit along at great
speed, moving down to the west end of the valley, meeting the coming
force, scouting out its strength and formation. The spirit whisked back the
way it had come, first to the northern ridge and Brother Francis, then
across the way to Brother Braumin, relaying the information to both
groups. Then, with a thought, Master Jojonah was gone again, back to the
approaching monsters.

Now came the master's more difficult assignment: to infiltrate the monstrous force. Invisible and silent, he glided past the front goblin line and into the central group, going after a powrie body, but wisely reconsidering. Powries, so the ancient tomes declared, were especially resistant to magic, and particularly to any form of possession. They were tough and intelligent and strong of will.

Still, Master Jojonah did not want to get into a goblin body. He could cause a bit of mischief in one, of course, but nothing substantial, likely. Goblins were always an unpredictable and traitorous type, so the powries and giants wouldn't even be caught too much by surprise when one of them suddenly turned against the group, and a frail goblin body wouldn't do much damage against the likes of a tough powrie, let alone a giant.

That left one option for Master Jojonah, who knew he was venturing into wholly unexplored territory. He had never read of any possession of a giant, and knew very little about the behemoths, except for their bad temperaments and tremendous battle prowess.

His spirit moved cautiously beside the handful of fomorians. One in particular, a huge specimen indeed, seemed to be in control of the group, bullying the others and hurrying them along.

Jojonah thought out the different tactics he might use in this attempt, which led him to believe that one of the other behemoths might prove a better target. None of the group, not even the apparent leader, seemed overly intelligent, but one stood out at the other end of the spectrum, a big loping creature, wagging its head and giggling at the sound made by its flapping lips.

Jononah's spirit slipped into the monster's subconscious.

Duh? the giant's will asked.

Give me your form! Jojonah telepathically demanded.

Duh?

Your body! the monk's will commanded. *Give it to me! Get out!*

"No!" the horrified giant roared aloud, and its will locked with Jojonah's, instinctively trying to expel the monk.

Do you know who I am? Jojonah explained, trying to calm the behemoth before its companions could catch on that something was suddenly very wrong. *If you understood, fool, you would not deny me!*

Duh?

I am your god, Jojonah's spirit coaxed. *I am Bestesbulzibar, the demon dactyl, come to aid in the slaughter of the humans. You are not honored that I chose your body as my vessel?*

Duh? the giant's spirit asked again, but this time the tone of the telepathic inquisition was markedly different.

Get out, Jojonah prompted, sensing the weakness, *or I will find another vessel and use it to utterly destroy you!*

"Yes, yes, my master," the giant blubbered aloud.

Silence! Jojonah demanded.

"Yes, yes, my master," the giant repeated in an even louder voice.

Jojonah, partially entrenched now, could hear the world through the behemoth's ears, could hear the sound of the other giants gathering about this one, asking questions. He felt it as if it was his own shoulder when the giant leader pushed the loud and confused behemoth.

The targeted giant, convinced that this was indeed the demon dactyl, was trying desperately to comply, though it had little idea how it might vacate its own body. Jojonah knew he had to work fast, for possession, even upon a willing vessel, was never an easy task. He fell deeper into the hematite, used its magic to infiltrate every aspect, every synapse, of the giant's brain. The giant's id instinctively recoiled and fought back, but without the giant's conscious will backing it, it had little power.

Jojonah felt the blow keenly when the biggest giant laid his new form low.

"Shut yer mouth!" the big brute demanded.

"Duh, yes, master," Jojonah responded. Truly, the heavy jowls and heavy limbs proved an awkward experience for the monk as he tried to talk and pull himself up from the ground.

The big giant hit him again and he lowered his head submissively. "I be quiet," he said softly.

That seemed to mollify the leader for the time being, and the group moved along, back into their place in the formation, oblivious to the fact that they had picked up an extra spirit in the process.

The dozen monks on each side of the valley stood in a line, hands joined, the fourth and tenth of each group holding a graphite, and Brother Francis, in a concession made by Jojonah to quiet the man's outrage, holding a small diamond. Francis was the guidepost to both groups, the one who would select the time. The monks had to strike hard and unerringly; any retaliation from the monsters could cost them dearly.

Francis let the front rim of the goblin semicircle pass below him. The key to victory, they had all agreed, was to destroy the powries quickly and to hurt the giants enough to steal their heart for the fight. With the leaders eliminated, the reasoning went, the cowardly goblins would show little desire for any battle.

Francis was the only one in his line with his eyes open, the rest falling into the magic of the two graphites. He saw the goblins passing, some less than twenty yards away, and he could make out the towering silhouettes of a handful of giants. Francis took a deep breath and called forth the power of the diamond, flashing a brief signal to waiting Brother Braumin across the way.

"Now, brethren," Francis whispered. "It is time." And then Francis, too, fell into the communal magic, transferring his energy through the line to the graphites.

Brother Braumin's words to his group were nearly identical.

A split second later the first thundering bolt erupted from the hand of the fourth monk in Francis' line, followed by a blast from across the way, and then from the tenth in Francis' line, and then again from across the way. Back and forth the lightning barrage went, each monk in sequence loosing his energy into the combined pool of power of his respective line. Many of the younger monks could not even use such stones on their own, but in their mental joining with Francis and Braumin and the older students, their energy was tapped, each in turn.

The whole of the valley trembled with the thunderous report; each successive searing flash revealed fewer monsters scrambling about.

In the center of the enemy formation, powries scrambled and were thrown down repeatedly, staggered and jolted. The giants, larger targets by far, took even more hits, but their great forms withstood the assault much better, and four of the five were still standing after the first complete volley, with only one taken down—and that one by a falling tree, not by a direct hit of magical lightning.

The largest of the giant group, ignoring its trapped and screaming companion, pointed up the northern slope and called for a boulder retaliation. Its intent and its expression changed quickly, though, when the giant beside it lifted a huge rock high into the air and then smashed it down upon its head.

Master Jojonah felt the sudden protests of the possessed giant's true spirit. *I kill him and we be leader!* he telepathically improvised, and that calmed the stupid giant considerably. Still, for all the giant's efforts to remain in the background and let what it believed to be the dactyl control its corporeal form, it simply didn't know how to let go. Thus, the giant was giggling louder than ever as Jojonah instructed the arms to hit the giant leader again and again, finally beating the dazed creature to the ground.

The two remaining giants howled and moved to restrain him.

Jojonah tucked the boulder into his chest, then flung it out into the face of the nearest attacker, staggering the giant. The other hit him with a flying tackle, though, the pair squashing one of the few remaining powries as they tumbled to the ground.

Hey, the possessed giant's spirit protested, and Jojonah sensed that the dim-witted creature was finally catching on. *Hey!*

The giant's will took up the struggle for dominance anew, attacking Jojonah. And then the second lightning volley began.

Jojonah forced the giant form to its feet and ran right in the path of the searing lightning. Then, as he felt the burning energy blast against his chest, he relinquished the battered body to its rightful owner and his spirit flew free, hovering in the empty air to regard the scene.

The largest giant, blood pouring from its head, somehow managed to stagger back to its feet—only to be hit by the next lightning bolt, and then another right after that. The behemoth tumbled to the ground again, all strength and resilience gone, and waited for death to take it.

The lightning continued to roll in, each blast weaker than the previous, as the monks expended their magical energy. But there would be no significant retaliation, Master Jojonah recognized, for all that remained of the monstrous force were less than half of the goblins, a dozen powries, and a single giant, and all of those were too frightened, too battered, and too surprised to even think of continuing the fight. Scattered torches marked their flight back to the west, back out of the valley the way they had come in.

In their retreat, the monsters made their way past one other silent observer, a man who had thought to come in for quiet attacks at the rear of the formation. Any who inadvertently ventured too close to the ranger found death at the end of a huge sword. And when Andacanavar discovered that one of the giants remained alive, he moved in on the limping behemoth, hitting it a series of fierce blows that laid it low before it even realized that the man was there.

When at last the valley fell silent, Brother Francis led his monks quietly across the way to rejoin their peers. Then the whole of the group moved back from the southern ridge, back to the wagons and Master Jojonah, where they quickly formed up their train and started away, not wanting to be discovered by either monster or Alpinadoran.

Andacanavar watched it all with a mixture of hope and confusion.

CHAPTER

❖ 9 ❖

Old Friends Well Met

"So it is true!" the portly man cried, seeing Elbryan and Pony as they walked into the encampment beside the returning archers.

"Belster, my old friend," the ranger replied. "How good it is to see you faring well."

"Well indeed!" Belster declared. "Though we've been a bit short of rations of late." He patted his ample belly as he spoke. "You will see to that, I am sure."

Both Pony and Elbryan chuckled at that remark—ever did Belster O'Comely have his priorities in order!

"And where is my other friend?" Belster asked. "The one whose appetite rivals my own?"

A cloud passed over Elbryan's face. He turned to Pony, who was even more distressed.

"But the reports from the forest spoke of great stone magic," Belster protested. "Magic such as only the Mad Friar used to hurl. Do not tell me that he died this very night! Oh, what tragedy!"

"Avelyn has passed from this life," Elbryan replied somberly. "But not this night. He died in Aida, when he destroyed the demon dactyl."

"But the reports from the forest . . ." Belster stuttered, as though trying to use logic against the ranger's words.

"The reports of the fighting were correct, but spoke of Pony," Elbryan explained, putting his arm across the woman's shoulders. "It was she who put the stones to their powerful use." He turned to his love and lifted his other hand to stroke her thick golden mane. "Avelyn taught her well."

"So it would seem," Belster remarked.

The ranger pulled himself away from the woman and struck a determined pose, staring back at Belster. "And Pony is ready to carry on the work where Avelyn finished," he declared. "In the bowels of smoky Aida, Avelyn destroyed the demon dactyl and turned the tide of this war, stealing the binding force from our enemies. Now it lies before us to finish the task, to rid our lands of these wicked creatures."

To all those around, the ranger seemed to grow a bit taller as he spoke, and Belster O'Comely smiled knowingly. This was the charm of Elbryan, the mystique of Nightbird. Belster knew that the ranger would inspire them all to new heights of battle, would guide them as one pointed and focused force, striking hard at every weakness among their enemy's ranks. Despite the news about Avelyn, despite his mounting fears about the missing Roger Lockless, it seemed to Belster that the world got a bit brighter that night.

The tallies of the victory proved impressive. The forest was littered with the bodies of dead goblins and powries, and several giants. Six men had been wounded, one gravely, and three others were missing and presumed dead. Those who had carried in the worst of the wounded did not expect the man to live through the night—indeed, they had only carried him back that he might say his farewells to his family and be properly buried.

Pony went to him with the hematite, working tirelessly hour after hour, willingly sacrificing every ounce of her own energy.

"She will save him," Belster announced to Elbryan a short time later, when he and Tomas Gingerwart found the ranger as he tended to Symphony, wiping the horse down and cleaning the hooves. "She will," the former innkeeper repeated over and over, obviously trying to convince himself.

"Shamus Tucker is a good man," Tomas added. "He does not deserve such a fate."

All the while he was speaking, Elbryan noted, Tomas looked directly at him, almost accusingly. It seemed to Elbryan that Tomas considered Pony's work with the wounded man to be some kind of a test.

"Pony will do all that is possible," the ranger answered simply. "She is strong with the stones, nearly as strong as was Avelyn, but she used most of her energy in the battle, I fear, and has not much left to give to Shamus Tucker. When I am done with Symphony, I will go to her to see if I can be of any assistance."

"You tend to the horse first?" There was no mistaking the open accusations in Tomas Gingerwart's tone.

"I do as Pony instructed me," the ranger replied calmly. "She wished to start the healing process alone, for in that solitude she might find deeper levels of concentration, and thus a more intimate bond with the wounded man. I trust in her judgment, and so should you."

Tomas cocked his head, regarding the man, and gave a slight and unconvincing nod.

A nervous Belster cleared his throat and nudged his stubborn companion. "Do not think us ungrateful—" he started to apologize to Elbryan.

The ranger's laugh cut him short and he blustered with surprise. He looked to Tomas, who was obviously angry, thinking he was being mocked.

"How long have we lived like this?" Elbryan asked Belster. "How many months have we spent in the forest, fighting and running?"

"Too many," Belster replied.

"Indeed," said the ranger. "And in that time, I have come to understand much. I know why you are mistrusting, Master Gingerwart," he said bluntly, turning from Symphony to stand directly before the man. "Before Pony and I arrived, you were one of the unquestioned leaders of this band."

"Do you imply that I cannot see the greater good?" Tomas asked. "Do you believe that I would place my own desire for power above—"

"I speak the truth," Elbryan interrupted. "That is all."

Tomas nearly choked on that proclamation.

"You are fearful now, and so you should be," the ranger went on, turning back to his horse. "Anytime one in your position of great responsibility senses a change, even a change that appears to be for the good, he must be wary. The stakes are too high."

Belster hid his smile as he studied the change that came over Tomas. The ranger's simple reasoning, honesty, and straightforward manner were truly disarming. Tomas' agitation had passed its peak now, with the man visibly relaxing.

"But understand," Elbryan went on, "that I, and Pony, are not your enemies, nor even your rivals. We will help out where we may. Our goals, as are your own, are to rid the land of the dactyl's evil minions, even as we helped rid the world of the demon itself."

Tomas nodded, seeming somewhat placated, if a bit confused.

"Will the man live?" Belster asked.

"Pony was hopeful," the ranger replied. "Her work with the hematite is nothing short of miraculous."

"Let us hope," Tomas added sincerely.

The ranger finished tending to Symphony soon after, then sought out Pony and the wounded man. He found them under the shelter of a lean-to, the man sleeping comfortably, his breathing steady and strong. Pony was asleep, too, lying right across the man, one hand still holding tight to the soul stone. Elbryan thought to take the hematite and try to do some healing of his own on Shamus Tucker, but changed his mind, reasoning that sleep might be the best cure of all.

The ranger moved Pony slightly, trying to make her more comfortable, and then he left them. He went back to Symphony, thinking to make his bed there, and to his relief found Belli'mar Juraviel waiting for him.

"I led the small group back to Caer Tinella," the elf explained, his voice grim. "And there found a hundred powries, a like number of goblins, and several more giants waiting to join in the chase."

"More giants?" the ranger echoed incredulously, for it was not common for the behemoths to gather in numbers above a handful. The sheer potential for devastation of such a force stole Elbryan's breath. "Do you think they mean to march on Palmaris?" he asked.

Juraviel shook his head. "More likely they are using the towns as staging areas for smaller excursions," he reasoned. "But we should keep careful watch on Caer Tinella. The leader there is a powrie of apparently great renown; even the giants bow before him, and in all the time I spent hiding in the shadows in the town, I did not hear a single word of dissent against him, even when reports began coming in of the disaster in the forest."

"We haven't stung them so hard, then," the ranger remarked.

"We have stung them," Juraviel replied, "and that may serve to only make them more angry. We should watch the south and watch it well. The next force coming to find your friends will be overwhelming, I am sure."

Elbryan instinctively glanced to the south, as though expecting a horde of monsters to be tearing through the trees.

"There is another matter," Juraviel went on, "concerning a particular prisoner the powries have taken."

"It is my understanding that the powries have many prisoners in many towns," Elbryan replied.

"This one may be different," Juraviel explained. "This one knows of your friends in the forest; indeed, he is highly regarded among them, much as you were among the people of Dundalis and the other towns of the Timberlands."

On the edge of the clearing, sheltered by the thick boughs of a pine, Belster O'Comely watched the ranger curiously. Beside him, Tomas was more animated, and only the portly innkeeper's constant prodding prevented the man from getting them both discovered.

Elbryan was talking, to himself, it appeared, though Belster suspected he might know the reason. The ranger was looking up into a tree, to an apparently empty branch, and holding a conversation, though they could not come close to making out the words.

"Your friend's a bit of a loon?" Tomas whispered in Belster's ear.

Belster shook his head resolutely. "All the world should be so crazy," he replied.

Too loudly.

Elbryan turned and cocked his head, and Belster, knowing the game was up, led Tomas from behind the pine. "Ah, Elbryan," the portly man said. "There you are. We have been searching all about for you."

"Not so hard to find," the ranger replied evenly, suspiciously. "I went to Pony—your friend is resting well and appears as though he will survive—and then back here to Symphony."

"To Symphony and . . ." Belster prompted, nodding toward the tree.

The ranger stood calm and did not answer. He wasn't sure how Tomas might react to Juraviel, though Belster had seen the elf and several other Touel'alfar during the time he fought with Elbryan in the north.

"Come now," Belster went on, "I know Elbryan well, and would not expect him to be standing alone and talking to himself."

You should sit with me at Oracle, the ranger thought, and gave a slight chuckle.

"You've brought a friend, unless I miss my guess," said Belster. "A friend whose special talents bode well for me and my companions."

Elbryan motioned for the two men to join him by the tree, and Belli'mar Juraviel, picking up the cue, hopped from the branch, using his nearly translucent wings to flutter down to a soft landing beside his ranger friend.

Tomas Gingerwart nearly jumped out of his boots. "What in all the dark holes in all the strange world is that?" he bellowed.

"That is an elf," Belster calmly explained.

"Touel'alfar," Elbryan added.

"Belli'mar Juraviel, at your service," the elf said, bowing low to Tomas.

The big man only nodded stupidly, wagging his head, wagging his lips.

"Come now," Belster said to him. "I told you of the elves that fought with us at Dundalis. I told you of the catapult caravan, where Brother Avelyn nearly blew himself up, and of the elves who stung our enemies from the trees."

"I . . . I . . . I did not expect . . ." Tomas stuttered.

Elbryan looked to Juraviel, who seemed almost bored by the typical reaction.

With a loud sigh, Tomas managed to steady himself.

"Juraviel has been to Caer Tinella—" Elbryan began to explain.

"I would have asked him to do so if he had not," Belster interrupted anxiously. "We fear for one of our own, Roger Lockless by name. He went into town this very evening, shortly before the monsters came out after us."

"Either their march toward our position began as a search for him, or they have him, it would seem," Tomas added.

"The latter," Elbryan informed them. "Juraviel has seen your Roger Lockless."

"Alive?" both men asked together, their tone showing true concern.

"Very much so," the elf replied. "Wounded, but not too badly. I could not get close; the powries have him under tight and watchful guard."

"Roger has been a thorn to them since they arrived," Tomas explained.

Belster then recounted the many tales of Roger's adventures, the thievery, the mocking jokes left behind, his common practice of having goblins take the blame for his nighttime raids, and the freeing of Mrs. Kelso.

"You will need to fill large shoes, Nightbird," Tomas Gingerwart said gravely, "if you are to replace Roger Lockless."

"Replace him?" the ranger balked. "You speak as if he is already dead."

"In the clutches of Kos-kosio Begulne, he may as well be," Tomas replied.

Elbryan glanced to Juraviel, the two exchanging wry smiles. "We shall see," the ranger said.

Belster nearly hopped for joy, his hopes soaring.

Elbryan was surprised to find Pony up and waiting for him when he arose the next morning, the eastern sky just beginning to brighten with the hint of dawn.

"I would have expected you to sleep the day away after your efforts with the stones," the ranger said.

"I would, were this not so important a day," Pony replied.

Elbryan wore a puzzled expression, but only for a moment as he considered Pony's stance, her sword belted at her hip. "You wish to learn the sword-dance," he reasoned.

"As you agreed," said Pony.

The ranger's lack of enthusiasm showed clearly. "There are so many matters to attend to," he explained. "Roger Lockless, an important figure to these folk, is held prisoner in Caer Tinella, and we have to take a reckoning of the band, to see who can fight and who cannot."

"So you do not intend to do your own sword-dance this morning?" Pony asked, and the ranger knew he was caught by her logic.

"Where is Juraviel?"

"He was gone when I awoke," Pony replied. "But is he not gone every morning, after all?"

"To his own sword-dance, likely," said the ranger. "And to scout the area. Many of the Touel'alfar prefer this time of day, just before the dawn."

"As do I," said Pony. "A fine time for *bi'nelle dasada*."

Elbryan could not hold out against her persistence. "Come along," he said. "Let us find a place where we might begin."

He led her through the dark forest and down into a small shallow where the ground was flat and clear of any large brush.

"I have seen you fight," he explained, "but I have never really found the chance or the cause to examine your style. A few simple attack and defense routines should suffice." He motioned for her to step out into the clearing to give the demonstration.

Pony eyed him curiously. "Should we remove our clothes?" she asked coyly.

Elbryan blew a frustrated sigh. "You intend to keep teasing me?" he asked helplessly.

"Teasing?" Pony replied too innocently. "I have seen you at the sword-dance, and—"

"Are we here to learn or to play?" the ranger said firmly.

"I was not teasing," Pony retorted in a voice just as determined. "I only

mean to keep you interested as the weeks of this war drag on." She stepped
into the clearing then and drew out her sword, setting herself in a low
crouch.

But then she was grabbed by the shoulder and turned about, to find
Elbryan, his expression perfectly serious, staring into her eyes. "It was not
my choice to abstain," he said quietly, seriously. "Nor yours. It was a decision made necessary by circumstance, and one I tolerate, but do not enjoy.
Not at all. You need not worry about keeping me interested, my love. All
my heart is yours, and yours alone." He bent to her and kissed her softly,
but didn't allow that to melt into something deeper and more passionate.

"We will find our time," Pony promised him as they broke the embrace.
"A time and place for me and for you, when we do not need to act for the
betterment of the whole world. A time when you can be Elbryan Wyndon,
and not Nightbird, and when our love can safely bring us children."

They held the pose for a long while, staring at each other, both taking
such great pleasure and comfort in the other's mere presence. Finally the
tip of the sun came above the eastern rim and broke the trance.

"Show me," the ranger bade her, stepping back.

Pony fell back into her crouch, spent a long moment steadying herself,
mentally preparing herself, then went into a routine of attack and defense,
her sword whipping expertly through the air. She had spent years in the
King's army perfecting these maneuvers, and her swordplay now was
nothing short of spectacular.

But it was typical, Elbryan knew, so indicative of the fighting style
common throughout the land, a style mimicked by goblins and powries.
Pony's hips turned repeatedly as she brought her weight behind each
slashing cut, wading forward and then scampering back in defense.

When she finished, she turned, her face red from the effort, her smile
wide with pride.

Elbryan walked up beside her, drawing out Tempest. "Strike that
branch," he bade her, indicating a low limb three feet away.

Pony settled, then stepped ahead, one, two, sword going high and back,
then rushing forward.

She stopped in mid-swing as Tempest stabbed past her, sticking deep
into the branch. She had taken a full step before Elbryan had even started
the movement, and yet he had beaten her to the mark easily.

"The lunge," he explained, holding the pose, his body fully extended,
right arm out straight, left arm turned down behind his trailing shoulder.
He retreated suddenly, settling back into a defensive posture in a mere
second. "Your weaving and slashing maneuvers are excellent, but you must
add the lunge, that sudden, swift stab that no powrie, no opponent, can
expect or deflect."

In response, Pony assumed the ranger's stance, balancing herself perfectly, knees out over her feet, legs angled perpendicular to each other. She stepped out suddenly with her right leg, left arm dropping, right arm extending, mimicking Elbryan's move almost perfectly.

The ranger didn't even try to hide his surprise, or his approval. "You have been studying me," he said.

"Forever," Pony answered, falling back to defensive posture.

"And you almost got it right," Elbryan remarked, deflating her obvious pride.

"Almost?"

"Your body led the way," the ranger explained. "And yet it is your sword which should pull you forward."

Pony looked down at her blade skeptically. "I do not understand."

"You will," Elbryan said with a grin. "Now come along. Let us find a better area where we might properly execute *bi'nelle dasada*."

They found a proper clearing soon after, Elbryan going off to the side to prepare himself, affording Pony some measure of modesty as she undressed. Then they met on the field with their weapons, the ranger leading the dance, Pony attuning herself to his every move.

For a long while Elbryan watched her, gauging her fluidity and grace, marveling at how easily she picked up the dance. Then he let himself fall into his own meditative trance, his own routine, let the song of *bi'nelle dasada* flow through his body.

For a short while Pony tried to keep up, but soon she was only watching, awestruck by the beauty, the interplay of muscle, the continually shifting but always perfect balance.

When he finished, he was covered in sweat, as was Pony, the gentle wind tickling their skin. They stood regarding each other for a long while, and it seemed to each of them as if they had just achieved a level of intimacy no less than lovemaking.

Elbryan reached up and tenderly stroked Pony's cheek. "Every morning," he said. "But take care that Belli'mar Juraviel does not learn of this."

"You fear his reaction?"

"I do not know if he would approve," the ranger admitted. "This is among the highest rituals of the Touel'alfar, and only they have the right to share it."

"Juraviel admitted that you were not *n'Touel'alfar*," Pony reminded him.

"And I feel no guilt," the ranger replied, somewhat convincingly. "I will teach you—I only wish the decision to be kept mine alone."

"To protect Juraviel," Pony reasoned.

"Go and dress," Elbryan said with a smile. "The day will be long and arduous, I fear."

Pony walked back to the brush at the side of the field, satisfied with her morning's work, though truly exhausted. For all these weeks she had desired to begin the sword-dance, and now that she had completed her first experience with it, she was surely not disappointed.

Somehow, the sword-dance felt to her like the training she had received with the magical stones, a gift, a growth, moving her to her potential, moving her closer to God.

PART TWO

THE PECKING ORDER

Once again, Uncle Mather, I am amazed by the resilience of people pushed into a desperate situation. As it was in Dundalis, I have found here a group willing to fight and to die—men and women, young children even, and older folks who should be spending their days telling stories of their long-past adventures. I have seen some terrible suffering, and yet have heard little in the way of complaint—other than the sounds of stomachs rumbling for lack of food.

And with the common suffering comes an altruism that is truly heartwarming and inspiring. As it was with Paulson, Cric, and Chipmunk, who gave their lives for a battle that really wasn't for them to fight, as it was with gallant Bradwarden, who certainly could have chosen a different path, it is now with Belster and Tomas, Roger Lockless and all the others.

I have my fears, though, mostly for an unintentional rivalry that may spring up between myself and the leaders of this band. When I led the fighters in the forest back to the refugee encampment after our great victory, I sensed true tension with Tomas Gingerwart, who, until my arrival, acted as one of the leaders of the forest band, perhaps the strongest voice of all. A calm conversation quickly cured that potential ill, for Tomas has been seasoned by years and experience. As soon as he was assured that he and I both fought for the same goal—the benefit of the people under his care—the rivalry was no more.

But not so, I fear, with another of the band whom I have not yet even met, an impetuous young fellow named Roger. By Belster's words, Roger is young and proud, and has ever been insecure in his position among the refugees, even to the point that he considered Belster and the folk from the northland as potential rivals. What will he think when he meets Pony and me? How will he react when he sees the respect afforded us, particularly from those who knew us in the north, or from those who followed us in the battle in the forest?

In truth, Uncle Mather, I think it ironic that these displaced folk think of me as a hero. For when I see their faces, every one, the expressions of men and women put to the test for perhaps the first time, I see the truest heroism.

Because that is something that cannot be judged by the quality of training and the quality of weapons, Uncle Mather. Simply because I was trained by the Touel'alfar and carry with me weapons of great power, am I any more heroic than the woman who throws herself between danger and her children, or the farmer who trades plowshare for sword to defend his community? Am I more heroic because my chances of winning the battle are greater?

I think not, for heroism is measured in strength of heart, not strength of arm. It is a marker of the conscious decisions, the selflessness, the willingness, to sacrifice everything, in the knowledge that those who follow you will be better off for your efforts. Heroism is the ultimate act of community, I think, the sense of belonging to something bigger than one's own mortal coil. It is rooted in faith: in God, or even in the mere belief that the whole of the goodly folk is stronger when each individual part cares for the others.

It is an incredible thing to me, this resilience, this inner strength, this human spirit. And in admiring it, I realize that we cannot lose this war, that in the end, even if that end be a thousand years hence, we will triumph. Because they cannot kill us, Uncle Mather. They cannot kill the resilience. They cannot kill the inner strength.

They cannot kill the human spirit.

I look into the faces of the men and women, the children, too young for such trials, the aged, too old for such battle, and I know this to be true.

—ELBRYAN WYNDON

❖ 10 ❖

The Holiest of Places

The terrain became more difficult by noon on the day after the fight in the valley. Master Jojonah tried to keep the spirits of his comrades high, reminding them of the good they had done, of the suffering they had prevented by intervening. But all of the monks were tired from their nighttime trials, particularly concerning the further use of magic, and, given the rough terrain, magic this day would have proven a great help.

One thing that neither Jojonah nor Brother Francis would compromise on, though, was the use of the quartz gemstones for scouting. Exhausted as they were, the monks simply could not afford to let down their guard, not in this wild region. Master Jojonah did end the ride early, before the sun had set, and called for his brothers to sleep well and long, to gather their strength that they might attack the road more vigorously the next day.

"We would have had the strength to travel much later," Brother Francis pointedly told the master, as usual, planting himself by Jojonah's side as if keeping a wary eye on the older man, "had we not engaged in an affair that was not our own."

"It seems to me that you enjoyed the rout of the monstrous force as much as any, brother," the Master responded. "How can you doubt the wisdom of our actions?"

"I'll not deny the pleasure I garner in destroying enemies of my God," Brother Francis replied.

That high-browed proclamation raised Jojonah's eyebrows.

"Yet," Brother Francis went on before the portly monk could reply, "I know what Father Abbot Markwart dictated."

"And that is all that matters?"

"Yes."

Master Jojonah silently groaned over the brother's blind faith, a fault so prevalent in the Abellican Order these days, a fault that he, too, had been guilty of for so many years. Master Jojonah, like all the masters and immaculates of St.-Mere-Abelle, had known that the ship hired to carry the brothers to the isle of Pimaninicuit would never be allowed to leave the harbor at All Saints Bay, and that all aboard her would be killed. Like all the others—all except for Avelyn Desbris—Jojonah had accepted that grim outcome as the lesser of two evils, for the monks simply could not have allowed any with such knowledge as the location of Pimaninicuit to sail away. Similarly, Jojonah knew that Brother Pellimar had been allowed to die of an infection from a wound he had suffered on the voyage to that island—though hard work by the older monks with a soul stone certainly could have saved him—because the man could not keep his mouth shut concerning that all-important voyage. But again, at the time, Pellimar's demise had seemed to Jojonah the lesser of two evils.

In reflecting on his own decision, Master Jojonah could not fully blame the zealous Brother Francis now. "We saved many families last night," he reminded. "And for that, I cannot be sorry. Our mission has not been compromised."

"Your pardon, Master Jojonah," came a call from the side of the wagon.

Both men turned to see a trio of younger monks, Brother Dellman among them, cautiously approaching.

"I have detected a presence in the area," Brother Dellman explained. "Not a goblin, not a monster at all," the young monk quickly added, seeing the sudden and frantic reaction. "A man, shadowing our every move."

Master Jojonah sat back, not too concerned, and more interested at that moment in studying the young man who had delivered the news. Brother Dellman was going out of his way to make himself quite useful of late, was working harder than any other in the caravan. Jojonah liked the potential he saw there, in the young man's eyes, in the idealistic attitude.

"A man?" Brother Francis echoed, seeing that Master Jojonah was making no move to reply. "Of the Church? Of Palmaris? Of the village?" he snapped impatiently. Francis, too, had noticed Dellman's work of late, but he wasn't sure of the young monk's motives. "Who is it, and where has he come from?"

"Alpinadoran, obviously," Brother Dellman replied. "A huge man, with long flaxen hair."

"From the village, no doubt," Brother Francis said with a huff aimed directly at the master. "Perhaps you spoke too soon, Master Jojonah," he added curtly.

"He is a man," the older monk argued. "Just a man. Probably trying to find out who we are and why we saved his village. We will send him away and that will be the end of it."

"And is he a precursor?" Brother Francis said. "A spy sent to unveil our weaknesses? Never has Alpinador called itself an ally of the Abellican Church. Need I remind you of the tragedy at Fuldebarrow?"

"You need remind me of nothing," Master Jojonah replied sternly, but

Brother Francis' point was well-taken. Fuldebarrow was an Alpinadoran town, larger than the one from the previous night, wherein the Church, the Abbey of St. Precious of Palmaris, had tried to establish a mission. All had gone well for nearly a year, but then, apparently, the Abellican missionaries had said or done something to offend the Alpinadoran barbarians, probably some insult to the god-figure of the northern people. None of the monks were ever found—physically at least. St. Precious had turned to St.-Mere-Abelle for help in the investigation, and using their magical talents, soul stones to locate the spirits of the dead, the masters of the larger abbey discovered that the missionaries had been brutally executed.

But that incident was nearly a hundred years old, and sending missionaries into any heathen territory was ever a dangerous course.

"Let us be rid of this spy efficiently," Brother Francis said, rising to his feet. "I will—"

"You will do nothing," Master Jojonah interrupted.

Brother Francis straightened as if slapped. "It is curious that I was not able to contact Father Abbot Markwart before the fight at the village," he remarked, the implications obvious, given his sly look Jojonah's way. "Distance is supposed to be irrelevant where hematite is concerned."

"Perhaps you are not as powerful with the stones as you believe," Master Jojonah said dryly. Both men knew better, though. Both knew that Master Jojonah, who possessed a small but effective sunstone, the stone of antimagic, had interfered with Brother Francis' attempt to enlist the Father Abbot against the notion that they would defend the Alpinadoran village from the monsters.

"What are we to do with this troublesome shadow, then?" Francis demanded.

"What indeed?" was all Master Jojonah could answer.

"He knows of us, and thus he looms as a threat," Brother Francis pressed. "If he is a spy, as I believe, then he will likely send a powerful force against us, and letting him live now will not seem so merciful in light of the dozens of men who will pay for our generosity with their lives." He paused, and it seemed to Jojonah that he was almost pleased by that prospect, as if he had just convinced himself that it would be better to let the man live.

It was a passing thought for Brother Francis, though. "Or even if he is not a spy," the fiery monk went on, "he remains a threat. Suppose he is captured by the powries. Do you doubt that he will divulge information about us to the monsters in the false hope of mercy?"

Master Jojonah looked to the three younger monks, all of them wearing startled expressions at the increasingly heated exchange. "Perhaps it would be better if you left us now," the master bade them. "And you, Brother Dellman, well done. Back to the gems with you, the soul stone this time, that you might watch our uninvited guest more closely."

"Uninvited and unwanted," Brother Francis said under his breath as the three younger monks moved away, passing Braumin Herde, who was coming to join Francis and Jojonah.

"Do not underestimate this Alpinadoran," Brother Braumin remarked as he neared. "Were it not for the soul stone, we would never have known he was shadowing our every move, though even as we speak he is less than fifty yards from our encampment."

"Spies are practiced at such tactics," Brother Francis remarked, drawing a sour expression from both Jojonah and Braumin.

"What do you believe?" Master Jojonah asked of Braumin.

"He is from the village, I would guess," the immaculate replied, "though I place less sinister value on that notion than does my brother."

"Our mission is too vital for us to let down our guard," Francis argued.

"Indeed it is," Master Jojonah agreed. He eyed Brother Braumin directly. "Possess the man," he instructed. "Convince him that he should be gone, or, if that should fail, use your power to walk his physical body far, far from here. Let him regain his physical consciousness back in the deep Timberlands, too exhausted to return anytime soon."

Brother Braumin bowed and started away, not thrilled by the prospect of possession, but relieved that Brother Francis did not get his way. He had not journeyed all these miles to play a role in the murder of a human.

Brother Braumin went to Dellman first, and bade the man to pass the word that all activity with quartz should cease, and that Dellman should forgo his searching with the soul stone—possession was tricky enough without the prospect of another disembodied spirit floating about! Then Braumin went to his wagon and prepared himself.

Andacanavar crouched low in the brush, confident that he was too well concealed for any of the nearby monks to locate him. Visually, at least, for the ranger had no experience with magic, other than that of the Touel'alfar, and did not know the potential of the ring stones.

But Andacanavar was sensitive to his environment, extremely so, and he did indeed sense the presence about him, an intangible presence, the feeling that he was being watched.

How strong that sensation became when Brother Braumin's spirit moved right up to the ranger, when Brother Braumin's spirit tried to move right into the man!

Andacanavar looked all about, eyes darting to every shadow, to every conceivable hiding place. He knew he was not alone, and yet all of his physical senses showed him nothing.

Nothing.

The intrusion grew stronger; the ranger almost cried out, despite his better judgment. That near outburst surprised him, and led him to the horrifying and inescapable conclusion that some other will was forcing itself over him.

Andacanavar had participated in the communal gatherings of the Touel'alfar, the joining of the entire elven community into a single harmony. That had been a beautiful thing, a mental sharing, a most intimate experience. But this . . .

Again the ranger almost cried out; but he stopped himself, understanding that the intruding will likely wanted him to yell out and surrender his position.

The ranger searched inside himself, tried to find something tangible, something identifiable. He recalled the communal elven song, a hundred voices joined as one, a hundred spirits blended in harmony. But this . . .

This was rape.

The ranger fell low to the ground, growling softly, fighting back in the only manner he understood. He put up a wall of sheer rage, a red barrier, denying all action. Andacanavar was completely in control of his will, on every level. He used the discipline of *bi'nelle dasada*, the sword-dance, used in his years of training in Caer'alfar. And through that grim determination, that sheer strength of will, the ranger identified his spiritual enemy, located the intruding will. A picture formed in Andacanavar's mind, a map of his own thought process, and he mentally placed an enemy marker whenever a trail on that map was accessed.

The enemy, the will of Brother Braumin, soon showed clear to the man, and then suddenly he and the monk were on equal footing, an open battle of wills, with the advantage of surprise no more. Brother Braumin, disciplined and trained in the stones, fought well, but the ranger was the stronger by far, and the monk was soon expelled, and soon in retreat.

Andacanavar was truly frightened by this strange experience, this unknown magic, but, with his typical courage, he would not let the opportunity pass. He felt a channel, a pathway left by the departing spirit, and he sent his thoughts along it, soaring free of his body.

Soon he was in the monk encampment, and then in one of the wagons. There sat the source of the intrusion, a man, a monk of about thirty winters, sitting cross-legged, deep in meditation.

Without hesitation, Andacanavar continued along the mental pathway, following the spirit right back into the monk's body, resuming the battle. Now the battleground was more difficult, a terrain far more familiar to his enemy, but the ranger pressed on, focused his will. Only one thought slowed him, and that only temporarily: if he dominated this body, would it leave his own open to intrusion?

The ranger had no way of knowing, and the hesitation almost ended his fight.

But then, using the same determination that had sustained him through all these years and all these trials of the unforgiving land of Alpinador, Andacanavar pressed on tenfold, driving hard into the monk's mind, pushing the monk away wherever he found him, pushing, pushing, stealing every pathway, every corner, every hope and every fear.

It was not a good feeling, was too strange and too out of place, and, for the noble ranger, was simply wrong. Despite any rationalization that he had been protecting his very soul, or any that reminded him of his duty to his fellow Alpinadorans, Andacanavar could not rid himself completely of the guilt. Possessing another's body, whatever the reasons, assaulted the ranger's sense of right and wrong profoundly.

But he persevered, and took some comfort in the small and smooth gray stone he held in his unfamiliar hand. This stone was the conduit, Andacanavar recognized, the pathway between the spirits, and with it in his possession, both physical and spiritual, he felt confident that the portal to his own corporeal body was closed to any others. Acclimating himself to the new coil, he dragged himself to the back of the wagon, peering out into the encampment, listening carefully to any passing conversations. He remained there for some time, was greeted by and returned the salutation of many other monks—and truly the ranger was glad that the elves had bothered to teach him the language of Honce-the-Bear! Then, gaining confidence, he dared to exit the wagon, walking openly in the midst of the foreigners.

He didn't have a difficult time in determining rank; in this group, it was apparently based on age, and Andacanavar had always been good at determining a man's years. Between these impressions and the respectful manner in which others greeted him, he confirmed his belief that he was in the body of one of high stature among the monks.

"Master Jojonah wishes to speak to you," one young man offered and another later confirmed, but of course Andacanavar had no way of knowing who this mysterious Master Jojonah might be. So he continued to wander about the encampment, gathering what information he could find. He soon realized that he was being followed—not by any corporeal being, but by the displaced spirit. Again and again the disembodied spirit tried to get back in, and though Andacanavar repelled the assaults, the ranger understood that he was growing weary and would not be able to hold out for long.

He spotted a much older man then, and guessed him to be the leader of the group, perhaps the one the others had spoken of. Beside the man, wearing an angry expression, was another monk of about the same age as the one he had possessed.

"Finished already?" Master Jojonah asked, coming over to him.

"Yes, Master Jojonah," Andacanavar answered respectfully, hoping that his tone, and his guess about the man's identity, were correct.

"And are we rid of the spy?" the other monk asked sharply.

Andacanavar resisted the urge to punch the surly man in the face. He stared at the monk long and hard, purposefully ignoring the question in the hope that the pair would further elaborate.

"Brother Braumin?" Master Jojonah prompted. "The Alpinadoran is gone?"

"What would you have me do?" Andacanavar asked sternly, pointing his ire at the younger of the two, for it seemed obvious to him that this man and the one he had possessed were not on good terms.

"What I would have you do is irrelevant," Brother Francis answered, casting a telltale sidelong glance at Master Jojonah.

"Since you have had no time to walk the Alpinadoran far away from here, I assume you imparted a convincing suggestion that he should depart," Master Jojonah said calmly.

"Perhaps we should have invited him in," Andacanavar dared to respond. "He knows the lay of the land, no doubt, and might have been able to better guide us." The ranger eyed Brother Francis as he spoke, and recognized a budding suspicion there, for the man wore an expression now of total surprise and even of horror.

"I considered that course," Master Jojonah admitted, defusing his hotheaded companion's mounting rage. "But we must adhere to the Father Abbot's decree."

Brother Francis snorted.

"If we brought him in, he would ask questions," Master Jojonah went on, ignoring Francis so completely that Andacanavar recognized that the older monk was quite used to this young monk's impertinence.

"Questions we cannot afford to answer," Jojonah continued. "We will pass through Alpinador quickly, and better not to involve any of the northmen in our quest. Better not to open any old wounds between our Church and the barbarians."

Andacanavar didn't press the issue, though he was indeed relieved to learn that this powerful contingent was not in the northland for any reasons hostile to Alpinador.

"Go back and look over our scouting friend," Master Jojonah instructed, "and see that your suggestion is being followed."

"I will do it," Brother Francis interrupted.

The ranger wisely held back his initial reaction, for that reply would have been too sharp and insistent, even desperate. He had no desire to battle yet another spirit this day. "I am capable of finishing the task assigned to me, Master," he said to the man.

The other monk's expression showed the ranger his slip; that title was reserved, he realized now, for the older man alone. Brother Francis went from angry to suspicious to incredulous, staring hard through narrowed eyes at the ranger in the monk's body. Andacanavar tried to cover his miscue, turning quickly to the older man, the true master, but he found Jojonah wearing a similar doubting expression.

"Pray give me the stone, brother," Master Jojonah said.

Andacanavar hesitated, considering the implications. Could he get back to his own body without that stone? Would the master use it to discover the truth of the ruse?

As though it sensed the ranger's sudden hesitance, the disembodied spirit took that opportunity to attack once more.

The ranger knew it was time to leave.

Master Jojonah and Brother Francis leaped forward to grab the body of faltering Brother Braumin as his eyes flickered and his legs buckled. Brother Francis went right for the hematite, pulling it free of the man's hand.

But Andacanavar's spirit had no trouble locating the ranger's body, or in reentering. He was up and moving almost immediately, though he wondered where he might hide from probing spiritual eyes.

Back in the camp, Brother Braumin steadied himself, then bent over, hands on knees, gasping for his breath.

"What happened?" Master Jojonah asked.

"How did you fail against one who is not even trained—" Brother Francis started to demand, but Jojonah cut him short with a glare.

"Strong," Brother Braumin remarked between gasps. "That one, that Alpinadoran, is strong of will and quick of thought."

"You would have to say that," Brother Francis said dryly.

"Go out yourself with the soul stone," Brother Braumin snapped at him. "It would do you well to find humility."

"Enough of this!" Master Jojonah demanded. He lowered his voice as he noticed that many others were gathering about. "What were you able to learn?" he asked Braumin.

The younger monk shrugged. "He learned from me, I fear, not the other way around."

"Wonderful," remarked a sarcastic Francis.

"What did he learn?" Master Jojonah demanded.

Again Brother Braumin could only shrug.

"Ready the teams," Master Jojonah instructed. "We must be far from this place."

"I will find the spy," Brother Francis offered.

"We will search for him together," Master Jojonah corrected. "If this man defeated Brother Braumin, hold no illusions that you are a match for him."

Brother Francis fumed, trying to find some retort. He turned away, as if to depart.

"Shall you join in the search?" Master Jojonah asked bluntly.

"I am seeing no need for that," came a resonating voice, and all the monks turned as one to see the giant Alpinadoran striding confidently into their camp, crossing through the ring of wagons without so much as a sidelong glance at those monks standing guard. "I am in no mood for any more of this spiritual dueling this day. Let us speak openly and plainly, as men."

Master Jojonah exchanged incredulous looks with Brother Francis, but when they turned to Brother Braumin, the only one who had made any true contact with the ranger, they found that he was not surprised. Nor did he look overly pleased.

"He is a man of honor," Master Jojonah said with some confidence. "Would you agree?"

Brother Braumin was too preoccupied to reply. He had locked stares with the Alpinadoran, the two sharing an almost primal hatred. They had battled intimately, seen each other's soul bared in hatred. For Andacanavar, this man had tried to violate him; for Brother Braumin, this man had proven himself the stronger in a way so personal that it brought him shame.

So they stood and stared at each other, and all the others around them, even Brother Francis, let the moment linger, recognizing the need for it.

Then Brother Braumin moved past his turmoil, reminding himself that the man, after all, had only been defending himself. Gradually, the monk's visage softened and he gave a slight nod. "My attempt to convince you seemed the safer way," he apologized. "For you most of all."

"I'd be finding a horde of giants less threatening than what you tried to do to me," Andacanavar replied, but he, too, gave a nod, a forgiving gesture, and turned his attention to Master Jojonah.

"My name is Andacanavar," he said. "And my land is beneath your boots. Many are my titles, but for your own purposes, you might be thinking of me as the protector of Alpinador."

"A haughty title," Brother Francis remarked.

The ranger let the comment pass. He found it curious that though the other young monk was the one who had tried to steal his body, he liked that man, and certainly respected him, more than this one. "I am no spy," he began, "for there is nothing sinister in my motives. I followed you from the valley for I have seen your strength and cannot be letting you walk the land free. Such power as you have shown could rain disaster on my people."

"We are not enemies of Alpinador," Master Jojonah replied.

"So I have learned," said Andacanavar. "And so I have come to you openly, walking into yer camp as a friend, perhaps an ally, with my weapon on my back."

"We have asked for no help," Brother Francis remarked in a stern tone, drawing a glare from Master Jojonah.

"I am Master Jojonah," the older monk quickly interjected, wanting to shut up the troublesome Francis, "of St.-Mere-Abelle."

"Your home is known to me," the ranger said. "A great fortress, by all the tales."

"The tales do not lie," Brother Francis said grimly. "And each of us here is well-versed in the arts martial."

"As you say," the ranger conceded, again turning his focus to Master Jojonah, who seemed by far the more reasonable man. "You know I came among you, using his body," he explained. "And in so doing, I learned that you mean to pass right through my land. I might be helping you on that matter. None knows the way better than Andacanavar."

"Andacanavar the humble?" Brother Francis remarked. "Do you name that as one of your titles?"

"You know that you are offering insults a bit too freely," the ranger replied. "Perhaps you should be careful, else those lips get ripped off."

Too proud to stand for such a threat, Brother Francis steeled his gaze and took a bold stride forward.

The ranger exploded into motion, too quickly for any of the monks to even cry out. He pulled a small axe from his belt, then lurched to the side so he could throw it in an underhand motion. The axe spun end over end, flying right between the legs of startled Brother Francis, then soared on, embedding itself deep into the sideboard of a wagon some twenty feet behind Francis.

The stunned monk, all the monks, turned about to regard the throw, then turned back to Andacanavar, every one of them wearing an expression of greater respect.

"I might have thrown it a bit higher," the ranger said with a wink. "And then your voice'd be sounding a bit higher."

Brother Francis did well to prevent himself from trembling, both from rage and fear. His face was white, though, revealing his true emotions.

"Move back, Brother Francis," Master Jojonah scolded in no uncertain terms.

Francis looked at the older man, matched Andacanavar's sly grin with an angry stare. Then he did move back in place, feigning a frustrated rage, though in truth—and everyone knew it—he was glad that Master Jojonah had intervened.

"You see, I have also had a bit of training in what you call the arts martial," the ranger explained. "But I am hoping to keep my skills for powries and giants and the like. Your Church and my people have not been friends—and I am seeing no reason to change that now—but if your enemies are the powries, then name Andacanavar among your allies. If you want my help, then know I will get you through my land along the safest and swiftest path. If you do not want my help, then say it now and I leave you." He gave Brother Braumin a sly look, and chuckled as he finished, "And know that I can walk myself far, far away, and am in need of no help from the lot of you."

The young monk blushed deeply.

Master Jojonah looked to his two companions and, predictably, found two different silent messages coming back to him. He turned to the huge stranger, knowing that ultimately this was his own decision to make. "I am not at liberty to tell you our destination," he explained.

"Who's asking?" replied a grinning Andacanavar. "You are going north and west, and intending to leave my land. If you're planning to hold that course, I can show you the swiftest and easiest way."

"And if we do not mean to hold that course?" Brother Francis interjected. He glared at Master Jojonah as he spoke, making clear his position concerning the stranger.

"Oh, but you do," the ranger replied, holding firm his grin. "You are heading for the Barbacan, for Mount Aida, by my guess."

Supremely disciplined, none of the three monks standing before the ranger offered any hint concerning his blunt assumption, but the open-mouthed expressions worn by many of the younger monks surely confirmed Andacanavar's suspicions.

"That is only your guess?" Master Jojonah asked calmly, figuring the man must have heard as much while in Brother Braumin's body. Andacanavar had just become a more dangerous person, the old monk realized, and lamented, for he feared that he might have to let Brother Francis have his way and kill this noble man. "And just a guess?"

"My reasoning," Andacanavar clarified. "If you are meaning to strike at the backs of the monsters that are attacking your homeland, then you are too far to the north and east. You should have gone back to the west before you ever set foot in Alpinador. But you would not have made such a mistake, not with your magics as guide. And so you are heading for the Barbacan, it seems plain to me. You want to know about the explosion there, about the great cloud of gray smoke that covered the land for more than a week and even put some of its ash on my homeland."

Jojonah's fears fast shifted to curiosity. "Then there truly was an explosion?" he asked bluntly, despite his fears of giving away too much information.

Beside him, Brother Francis nearly choked.

"Oh, but the biggest explosion the world has known since I have been in it!" the ranger confirmed. "Shook the ground under my feet, though I was standing hundreds of miles away. And a mountain of clouds rolled up, debris from a whole mountain blown into the sky."

Master Jojonah digested the confirmation, then found himself in a truly terrible dilemma. Father Abbot Markwart's edicts on this matter were clear enough, but Jojonah knew in his heart that this man was no enemy, and might indeed prove to be of great assistance. The master looked around at his entire entourage—for all the monks were gathered about by that time—finally settling his gaze on Brother Francis, who, of course, would likely prove the most troublesome.

"I have seen into his heart," Brother Braumin put in after a long, uncomfortable silence.

"Too much so for my own liking," the ranger remarked dryly.

"And for my own," the monk replied, managing a weak smile. He turned back to Jojonah and, putting aside his inner turmoil with the man, a conflict he knew to be illogical, said, "Let him lead us through Alpinador."

"He knows too much!" Brother Francis argued.

"More than we know!" Brother Braumin shot back.

"The Father Abbot—" Brother Francis began in threatening tones.

"The Father Abbot could not have foreseen this," Brother Braumin was quick to interrupt. "A good man is Andacanavar, a powerful ally, and one who knows the way. A way we could easily lose in this jagged terrain," he added, speaking loudly so all could hear. "One errant turn in a mountain pass could defeat us, or cost us a week of backtracking."

Brother Francis started to respond, but Master Jojonah held up his hand, indicating he had heard enough. The monk, feeling very old indeed, rubbed his hands over his face, then looked at his two companions, then at the ranger. "Dine with us, Andacanavar of Alpinador," he bade the man. "I'll not confirm our destination, but will tell you that we must indeed be out of your land to the north and west, and as soon as is possible."

"A week of hard driving," the ranger said.

Master Jojonah nodded, though he knew that with their magic they could cut that time by more than half.

By noon of the next day, Master Jojonah no longer held any doubts about the wisdom of letting Andacanavar lead the caravan. The road remained rough, for western Alpinador was an unforgiving place, a land of ice-broken stones and jagged mountains, but the ranger knew his way well, knew every trail and every obstacle. The monks, after their long rest, eased the trails with magic, lightening wagons with levitational malachite, clearing debris from the road with strokes of lightning, and of course they continued to bring in the wild animals.

It took Andacanavar a while to catch on to this subtle trick. At first he wondered what trickery the monks were using to hunt the game, but when the caravan left a pair of deer behind them on the trail, both animals nearly dead from exhaustion, the ranger was truly perplexed—and far from happy. He went back to the deer and examined them.

"What do you call this?" he asked of Brother Braumin when the monk, on Jojonah's instructions, joined the curious ranger on the trail.

"We use the energy of the wild animals," the monk explained honestly. "Like food for our horses."

"And then you leave them to die?" the ranger asked.

Brother Braumin shrugged helplessly. "What are we to do?"

The ranger gave a great sigh, trying hard to sublimate his anger. He pulled a large and thick knife from a sheath on the back of his belt and methodically and efficiently killed both deer, then knelt in the dirt and offered a prayer for their spirits.

"Take that one," he instructed Brother Braumin, while he lifted the larger animal by the hooves and slung it over his shoulder.

The two caught up to the wagons soon after, Andacanavar dropping his carcass right in front of Jojonah's team. The master called for a halt and went out to the man.

"You take their life energy and leave them to die?" the ranger accused.

"An unpleasant necessity," Master Jojonah admitted.

"Not so necessary," the ranger came back. "If you have to kill them, then use them, all of them, else you are insulting the animal."

"We are hardly huntsmen," Master Jojonah replied. He gave a sidelong glance as Brother Francis moved up to join them.

"I will show you how to skin and dress them," Andacanavar offered.

"We have no time for that!" Brother Francis protested.

Master Jojonah bit his lip, not knowing how to proceed. He wanted to berate Francis—they could not afford to lose this very valuable guide—but feared that the damage was already done.

"Either you find the time to do it or you kill no more of my animals," the ranger replied.

"These are your animals?" asked a doubtful Brother Francis.

"You are in my land, that much I told you," the ranger replied. "And so I am claiming guardianship on the animals." He turned to face Jojonah squarely. "Now, I'll not stop you from hunting; I have done as much myself. But if you are to take the animal, you cannot let it waste to death on the road. That's an insult, and cruel by any measure of decency."

"Lectured on cruelty by a barbarian," Brother Francis remarked with a snort.

"If you need the lesson, take it where you find it," Andacanavar replied without missing a beat.

"We need no food, or skins," Master Jojonah said calmly. "But the energy is vital to our team. If these horses cannot get us to our destination and back again, then we are stranded."

"And is it necessary for you to take so much from each animal that it hasn't enough left to live?" the ranger asked.

"How are we to know when to stop?"

"Suppose I can show your men that?"

Master Jojonah smiled widely. He had never liked this killing of innocent animals. "My friend, Andacanavar," he said, "if you could instruct us on how we might complete our most vital mission without leaving a single animal on the trail dead behind us, I would be forever grateful."

"So would more than a few deer," the ranger replied. "And as for these you have already killed, know that you will be eating well tonight, and you will find a use for the skins when you get more to the north, for even in high summer the night wind blows a bit chill up there."

Andacanavar then showed the monks how to skin and dress the deer carcasses. A short while later the caravan was on the move again, and several more deer were brought in. The ranger monitored each animal carefully as the monks transferred the energy, and as soon as he saw the creature going into distress, he called a halt to the process, and then the animal, weary but very much alive, was allowed to wander back into the forest.

Only Brother Francis showed any signs of dissent, and it seemed to Master Jojonah and Brother Braumin that even pouting Francis was a bit relieved to be rid of the unpleasant practice.

"A fine trick if you do it right," Andacanavar said to Master Jojonah as they rode along. "But finer it would be if you brought in a moose or two. That would get your horses running!"

"A moose?"

"Big deer," the ranger explained with a wry smile.

"We have brought in some big—" Master Jojonah stared to say, but Andacanavar cut him short.

"Bigger," he said, and hopped down from the wagon and ran off into the brush.

"He is an active old man," Brother Braumin remarked.

The ranger returned to the wagons nearly an hour later. "You tell your spirit-walking friends to go and look down that way," he said, indicating a shallow dell west of the trail. "Tell them to look for something big and dark, with a rack of antlers twice as wide as a man is tall."

Both Jojonah and Braumin gave doubtful looks.

"Just you tell them," Andacanavar insisted. "Then you will see if I am lying."

A short while later, when a huge bull moose wandered onto the trail under the control of the soul stones, both monks offered silent apologies for their doubts.

And how the horses ran when they left the tired moose by the side of the road!

By day they rode, long and hard, and by night all of the monks gathered about their fires, listening to the ranger's tales of the north. Andacanavar's jovial manner and spirited stories won them all over, even Brother Francis, who did not even bother to carry through with his threat to contact the Father Abbot to lodge a complaint.

And so it was on the fourth day of their travels together, when the ranger announced that he would leave as they set their camp, that a pall came over the caravan.

"Bah, you should not be so despairing," Andacanavar told them. "I will show you a road to the Barba—" He stopped and caught himself, giving a wry grin. "If that is where you are going, I mean," he added slyly.

"I cannot confirm," Master Jojonah put in, and he, too, was grinning. He had full confidence in Andacanavar now, had seen the man's heart and knew it to be akin to his beliefs. Of course the man knew where the monks were heading—where else would someone go this far into the Wilderlands?

"A road straight and sure," the ranger went on, "and, if you are not finding any powries or giants blocking the way, you will get there, and soon enough."

"By my maps, our destination is many, many miles from Alpinador's western border," Brother Francis remarked, his tone toward the ranger more respectful now. "We have a long road ahead of us, I fear."

Andacanavar held out his hand, and Brother Francis turned over the parchment, a map of the immediate region. The ranger lifted an eyebrow as he considered it, for it was quite detailed and fairly accurate.

"Your maps are telling you true," Andacanavar agreed. "But we put Alpinador's western border behind us before we set camp the night before the last. So take heart, my friends, for you are almost there—not that I would be taking heart if I was heading into the place where the demon is said to roost!" He bit the tip of one finger then, and with his blood drew another line on the map, the road to the Barbacan, ending it with an X to mark their present location.

He handed the map back to Francis, and with that, and a final bow, Andacanavar left them, running into the underbrush, laughing all the while.

"Were it not for his stature, I'd think him an elf," Brother Braumin remarked. "If there were such a creature as an elf."

Andacanavar's last words concerning their present position came as a relief to offset the monks' sadness at losing their most excellent guide. They ate their evening meal—wonderful venison again—said evening prayers and slept well, then were on the road again, anxiously, before the next dawn.

The land remained rugged—less mountainous, but more heavily forested. Still, using the blood line on the map as a guide, the monks soon came upon a wide and clear road, not just a narrow trail. All wagons stopped there, with the caravan's leaders going out to investigate.

"This swath was cut by the monstrous army on their march to the south," Master Jojonah reasoned.

"Then backtracking it should get us right to the source of the monstrous army," said Brother Braumin.

"A dangerous course," remarked Brother Francis, looking all about. "We are in the open."

"But a swift course, no doubt," Brother Braumin replied.

Master Jojonah thought about it for only a short while, considering most of all that Andacanavar had put them on this trail. "Have the spirit scouts out far and wide," he instructed. "Both our wagons and our horses could use the reprieve of a smooth road."

Brother Francis put every quartz and hematite to use, sending monks out far and wide for fear that they were riding right into an enemy encampment.

Two days later they had still not encountered a single monster, though they had put a hundred miles and more behind them. Now before them they saw the towering mountains that ringed the Barbacan, and all the monks feared they would have a terrible time indeed in getting the wagons through those barriers.

But the road continued on, to the base of the mountains, and right up into the mountains, climbing through a wide pass. Setting a camp in that place was more than a bit disturbing, but again no monsters came forward to challenge them, and those monks with the quartz stones discovered that there weren't many wild creatures about, either. The land seemed strangely dead, and eerily silent. By mid-morning of the next day the end of the mountains was in sight, with only a single ridge blocking their view beyond. Master Jojonah called for a halt, then motioned for Brothers Braumin and Francis to accompany him.

"We should go in spiritually," Brother Francis noted.

It was a good suggestion, a prudent suggestion, but Master Jojonah shook his head anyway. He had a feeling that what lay ahead was incredibly important, and he felt that it should be viewed physically, both body and soul. He motioned the pair to his side, asked the other immaculates to join them, and started the climb.

The younger monks followed the group, not so far behind.

When Master Jojonah crossed the last barrier, coming to a point where he could view the wide valley that was the heart of the Barbacan, his spirits both sagged and soared. The monks filtered away from each other, hardly noticing each other's movements, stunned by the scene, for the devastation looming before them was total. Where once had stood a forest, there was now a field of gray ash littered with charred logs. All the valley was gray and barren, and the air hung thick with the reek of sulfur. It seemed to them all a preview of the end of the world, or a premature glimpse of the place their Church defined as hell. Most shaken of all were the younger monks as they, too, came over the ridge, several crying out in despair.

But when that initial despair passed into a grim acceptance, other, more positive, thoughts found their way into every mind. Could anything have survived this blast? Perhaps their suspicions, their hopes, of a "beheaded" monstrous army were true, for if, as believed, the demon dactyl had called the Barbacan its home, if the demon dactyl had been here at the time of the explosion, then the demon dactyl was surely gone.

Even Brother Francis was too stunned to speak for a long, long time. Gradually he made his way back to Master Jojonah's side.

"Can we take this scene of devastation as proof enough that the demon dactyl is destroyed?" the master asked.

Francis looked down into the ash-filled bowl. It wasn't hard to discern the source of the explosion: a flat-topped mountain standing alone in the middle of the ash field, a thin line of smoke still wisping from its top. "I do not believe this to be a natural occurrence," Francis said.

"There have been volcanoes before," Master Jojonah countered.

"But at this critical time?" Brother Francis asked doubtfully. "Dare we hope that a volcano erupted at the precise moment we most needed its help, and at the precise location of the enemy leader?"

"You doubt divine intervention?" Master Jojonah asked. He sounded serious, though he, too, held great doubts. There were fanatics in the Order who seemed to expect God's thumb to slip down from the heavens and squash the opponents of the Church at every turn; Jojonah had heard one young monk standing at the seawall of St.-Mere-Abelle during the powrie invasion invoking God repeatedly, literally calling out for that punishing thumb. Master Jojonah also believed in the power of God, but he thought of it as an analogy for the power of good. He believed that good would win out in the end of every great struggle, because, by its very nature, good was a stronger force than evil. He suspected that Francis held similar feelings on the subject, for, despite his other shortcomings, the man was a thinker, a bit of an intellectual, who always edged his faith with logic.

Francis eyed him slyly now. "God was on our side," he said. "In our hearts and in the strength that guided our weapons, and surely in the magic that crushed our enemies. But this . . ." he said, opening his arms dramatically as he scanned the devastated valley. "This may have been the work of God, but it was precipitated by the hand of a godly man, or was the result of the demon dactyl's overextending its call to the earth magic."

"Likely the latter," Master Jojonah replied, though he hoped differently, hoped that Brother Avelyn had played a part in this.

Brother Braumin, coming to join the pair, heard the last few comments and now stared long and hard at Brother Francis, surprised by the man's reaction. He turned his perplexed expression to Master Jojonah, and his superior only smiled and nodded, for he was not quite as surprised. At that moment Master Jojonah discovered Brother Francis' redeeming qualities and found that there might indeed be something about the man that he liked. He paused for a bit to silently wonder if Brother Francis might be steered in a new direction.

"Whatever happened here came from that mountain," Brother Francis reasoned. "Mount Aida, by name."

The other two looked at him curiously.

"That is what the Alpinadoran named it," Brother Francis explained. "And indeed, that name corresponds to many old maps that I studied. Aida, the lone mountain within the ring, the lair of the demon."

"It will not be easy to get to it," Brother Braumin remarked.

"Could we have expected differently?" Brother Francis asked with a laugh.

Again the two others only looked to each other and shrugged. It seemed to them as if this explosion might have rid the world of the dactyl demon, and might have rid Brother Francis of a few internal demons, as well.

They let it go at that, though, taking Francis' good mood as a blessing. They could only hope it would endure.

The journey across the ash field was not as difficult as they had feared, for though the gray stuff had settled thick in many places, it had been blown clear in many others. As they neared the mountain, the lead driver made a horrible discovery.

His cry brought the monks running, to find several bodies encased in ash, lying along the side of the twisting trail.

"Powries," Brother Braumin explained, going over to examine them. "And a goblin."

"And that one is . . . was, a giant," said another monk, pointing ahead on the trail to a huge leg protruding from a berm of ash.

"So our enemies were here," Master Jojonah noted.

"Were," Brother Francis emphasized.

They went on to the very base of the mountain and ringed the wagons there. Master Jojonah instructed half of them to set the camp, the other half to begin a thorough search of the area, looking particularly for any way in, or up, the mountain. With torches and a single diamond in hand, a group of monks entered one winding cave that very night, snaking their way into Aida. They returned in less than an hour with news that the tunnel led to a dead end, the way blocked by a solid wall of stone.

"No doubt it traveled farther before the explosion," Brother Dellman told Master Jojonah.

"Let us hope that not all of the tunnels have so collapsed," Jojonah replied, trying to sound hopeful. In looking at blasted Aida, though, the monk had to temper his optimism.

Brother Dellman led his troupe into a second tunnel, and when that one again abruptly ended, the young monk, undaunted, headed into a third.

"He has promise," Brother Braumin remarked to Jojonah as Dellman started off that third time.

"He has heart," Master Jojonah agreed.

"And faith," said the other. "Great faith, else he would not attack his tasks with such determination."

"Is there any more determined than Brother Francis?" Master Jojonah reminded.

Both men looked over to Francis, who was busy marking some parchments, detailing the nuances of the Barbacan.

"Brother Francis, too, has faith," Brother Braumin decided. "He just follows it down errant paths. But perhaps he will find a truer way; it seems as though his time with the honorable Alpinadoran did him well."

Master Jojonah offered no reply, just sat staring at Francis. It did indeed seem as if some of Andacanavar's jovial spirit had rubbed off on the man, but Jojonah wasn't counting Francis as a convert just yet.

"Where do we search next if we find no tunnels open into the mountain's heart?" Brother Braumin asked. "And if the flat top yields no valuable information?"

"Then we search with the hematite," the master replied.

"I had thought we would do that first."

Master Jojonah nodded, expecting as much, for he, too, had thought that the initial search of Aida would be more easily accomplished if the monks used the soul stones. He had changed his mind and their course, considering Brother Braumin's experience with Andacanavar. Jojonah couldn't be certain that the demon dactyl's spirit wasn't lingering about this place, and if the unmagical Alpinadoran could use such a spiritual connection to find his way into their midst, what might the demon dactyl do?

"Let us use our wits and our bodies," the old monk replied to Braumin. "If they do not suffice, then we will utilize the soul stones."

The younger man, trusting fully in Master Jojonah, was satisfied with that. "When will Brother Francis make contact with Father Abbot?" he asked.

"I bade him to wait until the morning," Master Jojonah explained. "I do not think it prudent to open channels to one's spirit in this forsaken place."

That explained much to Brother Braumin, particularly concerning Francis' fine mood, and he let the matter drop. He put a hand on Jojonah's large shoulder, then walked off, for there was much work to be done.

After three hours the monks at camp began to grow nervous about Brother Dellman and the missing party. After four, Master Jojonah considered it might be time to put the hematites to use. He was about to give in and do just that when the monks scouting just west of the camp shouted that they saw torchlight.

Master Jojonah saw it soon after, a single monk exiting the tunnel in the foothills of Aida, moving with all speed back to the camp.

"Brother Dellman," Braumin explained to Jojonah as the man came closer, running full speed down the slope, nearly losing his balance and pitching headlong more than once.

"Gather together, and ready for enemies!" Master Jojonah called.

The monks went into a practiced drill, handing off the appropriate stones to the appropriate wielders. Others strapped on weapons, or went to secure the horses.

Brother Dellman stumbled into camp, gasping, trying to catch his breath.

"Where are the others?" Master Jojonah asked him immediately.

"Still . . . inside," Dellman replied.

"Alive?"

The young monk straightened and tilted his head back, gulping air, calming himself. When he looked back at Jojonah, the master's fears lessened considerably. "Alive, yes," he said calmly. "No danger in there, unless the rubble shifts again."

"Then why are you out here?" Jojonah asked. "And why are you so agitated?"

"We found something . . . someone," Brother Dellman replied. "A man, or half a man, and half horse."

"A centaur?" asked Brother Braumin.

Brother Dellman shrugged, never having heard the term before.

"A centaur wears the body of a man, torso, shoulders, arms and head," Brother Francis explained. "But from the waist down it wears the coil of a horse, four legs and all."

"A centaur," Brother Dellman agreed. "He was in the cave when the mountain fell in on him. Tons and tons of stone."

"You dug him out?" asked Master Jojonah.

"We know not where to begin," Brother Dellman replied.

"Poor creature," Brother Braumin remarked.

"Then leave him to his grave," Brother Francis said callously, seeming quite like the old Francis again. Neither Braumin nor Jojonah missed that fact, and they offered each other a resigned shrug.

"But Brother Francis," Brother Dellman protested, "he is not dead!"

"But you said—" Master Jojonah started to reason.

"Tons," Brother Dellman finished for him. "Oh, he should be dead. He should! Nothing could have survived that crush. And surely, he looks as if he should be dead, all withered and broken. Yet the creature lives. He opened his eyes and begged me to kill him!"

The three older monks stood open-mouthed, while the younger men about them whispered excitedly.

"And did you?" Master Jojonah asked at length.

"I could not," Brother Dellman replied, seeming horrified at the very thought. "His pain must be great, I do not doubt, but I could not end his life."

"God does not give us more than we can bear," Brother Francis recited.

Master Jojonah gave him a sour, sidelong glance. At times that old line sounded like nothing more than an excuse Church leaders used on common folk, the peasants wallowing in poverty while those same leaders lived in luxury.

But that was an argument for another day, Jojonah realized, and so he made no comment on it. "You did well, and right," he said to Dellman. "The others remained with this centaur?"

"Bradwarden," Brother Dellman replied.

"What?"

"Bradwarden," the monk repeated. "That is his—the centaur's—name. I left the others with him, offering what meager comfort they might."

"Let us go and see what we might do," Master Jojonah said. To Brother Braumin, he instructed, "Gather all stones, except duplicates, and take them with us. Brother Francis," he called loudly, so that all about heard clearly, "you will hold the defense of the wagons."

Now it was Francis' turn to wear the sour look, but Master Jojonah wasn't paying him any heed, the old monk already motioning Brother Dellman back the way he had come, back to see this Bradwarden creature, this somehow immortal being.

The path was not long, and Dellman set a swift pace, so that Jojonah was huffing and puffing by the time they came in sight of the other torches. Jojonah walked by the younger monks reverently, to kneel before the twisted, emaciated body.

"You should be dead," Master Jojonah said matter-of-factly, doing well to hide his horror and his revulsion. Only the creature's human torso and the front half of its equine part was exposed, with the rest of it buried, squashed, under a huge slab of rock that climbed right up out of the low corridor and into the collapsed mountain. The creature was bent weirdly, back in on itself, with its eyes facing the very stone that had crushed its lower half. Where once Bradwarden's arms had bulged with strong muscles, they were slack now, withered, as though the centaur's body was consuming itself for lack of food. Master Jojonah moved very close and crouched as low as his portly form would allow, studying and sympathizing.

"Oh, but be sure that I'm feeling like I am dead," Bradwarden replied, his agony reflected clearly in his normally resonant but now shaky voice. "Or at least, heading that way. Ye canno' know me pain." He managed to turn his head about then, to glance upon the newcomer, and he tilted his head curiously at the sight, eyeing Jojonah closely, then gave a pained chuckle.

"What do you see?" the master asked him.

"Do ye have a son, then?" Bradwarden asked.

Master Jojonah looked back over his shoulder to Brother Braumin, who held his hands out helplessly. Why this creature, at this time and in this predicament, would ever ask such a question was beyond his understanding.

"No," Master Jojonah answered simply. "Nor a daughter. My heart was given to God, and to no woman."

The centaur gave a chuckle. "Ah, but what ye've missed," Bradwarden said with a sly wink.

"Why should you ask that?" Master Jojonah inquired, for he wondered suddenly if it might be more than coincidence.

"Ye remind me o' one I knew," Bradwarden replied, his tone revealing fond memories for the old friend.

"A monk?" Jojonah pressed, more urgently now.

"A mad friar, by his own admission," the centaur replied. "A bit too friendly with the drink, but a good man he was—or is, if he found a way out of this cursed place."

"And did you know his name?" asked Master Jojonah.

"Me own brother, he was," the centaur went on, talking more to himself than to the others, and seeming as if he was in some distant place, delirious, perhaps. "By deed, if not by blood."

"His name?" Brother Braumin prompted loudly, moving close and bending near Bradwarden's face.

"Avelyn," the centaur calmly replied. "Avelyn Desbris. A most excellent human."

"He must be saved at all cost," came a voice behind them. All the monks turned about to see Brother Francis, a diamond glowing brightly in his palm, standing at the back of their line.

"You were instructed to command the defense of the encampment," Master Jojonah said to the man.

"I take no orders from Master Jojonah," came the reply, and Jojonah realized then that Father Abbot Markwart had taken Francis' body and come among them. "We must extricate him from this place," he continued, looking to the huge slab.

"Ye're not big enough to lift a mountain," Bradwarden said dryly. "As I wasn't big enough to hold it up while me friends ran off."

"Your friend Avelyn?" Markwart asked impatiently.

"Me other friends," the centaur replied. "I'm not for knowing—" He stopped and grimaced, for his movement in turning about to face the men had caused the rock to shift slightly. "No, ye're not for lifting this," he groaned.

"We shall see," said the Father Abbot. "Why are you still alive?"

"Not for knowing."

"Unless you are no mortal creature," Markwart went on, his tone sly and accusing. He moved past the others to crouch beside Master Jojonah.

"An interesting thought," Bradwarden replied. "Always was told I was a bit headstrong. Might be that I just refused to die."

Markwart was not amused.

"Now me daddy, he died," the centaur recounted. "And me mum, as well, a score and more years ago. She took a hit o' the lightning—now that's an odd way to die! So, no, I'd be guessing that I'm not immortal."

"Unless an immortal spirit has found its way into your body," Markwart pressed.

"Are not all spirits immortal?" Master Jojonah dared to interrupt.

Markwart's glare ended that discussion before it could begin. "Some spirits," he said evenly, looking at Bradwarden, but offering the words as much to Jojonah, "can transcend physicality, can keep a body animated, though it should be dead and still."

"Only spirit in me is me own, and a bit o' the boggle," the centaur assured him with a strained smile and a wink. "And a bit more o' the boggle might be easing me pain, if ye got any."

Markwart's expression didn't change in the least.

"I'm not for knowing why I'm not dead," Bradwarden explained seriously. "Thought I was, when the rock bent me legs and slid down. And suren that me groaning stomach spent a week and more o' tellin' me to die."

Father Abbot Markwart was hardly listening then. He had slipped another stone into his hand, a small but effective garnet, a stone used to detect the subtle emanations of magic, and he was using it now to survey the trapped creature. He found his answer almost immediately.

"You have magic about you," he announced to Bradwarden.

"That, or luck," said Master Jojonah.

"Bad luck," the centaur remarked.

"Magic," the Father Abbot said again, forcefully. "About your right arm."

It took quite an effort for Bradwarden to turn his head enough so he could view his upper right arm. "Oh, by the damned dactyl and all its sisters," he grumbled when he saw the red armband, the piece of cloth that Elbryan had tied about him. "And the ranger thought to be doing me a favor. Two months o' suffering, two months o' hunger, and the damned thing won't let me die!"

"What is it?" Master Jojonah asked.

"Elven healing cloth," Bradwarden replied. "Seems the damned thing is fixing me wounds as fast as the damned mountain's giving them to me! And even the lack o' food and drink won't take me!"

"Elven?" Brother Braumin gasped, reflecting the feelings of all in attendance. Bradwarden deciphered their expressions and was surprised to find that they were surprised.

"Don't ye be telling me that ye're not for believing in elves?" he said. "Nor centaurs, I'm guessing? And how about powries, or maybe a giant or two?"

"Enough," Father Abbot Markwart bade him. "Your point is well taken. But we have never encountered an elf, nor a centaur, until this time."

"Then yer world's become a better place," Bradwarden said, offering another wink, though it ended in a pained grimace.

Markwart rose then and motioned for the others to follow him away from the centaur. "It will be no easy task in getting him out of there," he said once they were out of the range of Bradwarden's hearing.

"Impossible, I'd say," remarked Brother Braumin.

"We can levitate the stone using malachite," Master Jojonah reasoned. "Though I fear that all of our strength combined may not be enough to budge such an obstacle."

"I fear more that when we do lift the stone, the pressure will be relieved so that the centaur's lifeblood will pour from him too fast for his elven arm-band, and our efforts, to compensate," the Father Abbot pointed out.

"But still, we must try," said Brother Braumin.

"Of course," Markwart agreed. "He is too valuable a prisoner, too great a source of information—not only for what happened here, but for the fate of Brother Avelyn—for us to let him die."

"I was thinking more of compassion for his predicament," Braumin dared to add.

"I know you were," Markwart replied without hesitation. "You will learn better."

The Father Abbot stormed away then, motioning for the others to follow. Brother Braumin and Master Jojonah exchanged sour looks, but had little choice in the matter.

On orders from Markwart, who was tiring from the possession and needed a reprieve, they did not make the attempt until late the next day, when they were all rested and mentally prepared. Markwart came back into the body of Brother Francis then, and led the procession, clutching a malachite and a hematite.

In position, all the monks of the caravan, except for Master Jojonah, who also held a hematite, joined in communion within the depths of the soul stone, then channeled their combined energy into the malachite, and when that energy had reached its apex, Father Abbot Markwart released it, aiming it at the slab over Bradwarden.

Master Jojonah only then realized the great risk that Markwart had taken—for the monks of the caravan and not for his own body, which was safely back at St.-Mere-Abelle. As the stone slab groaned under the sudden release of pressure, many smaller stones and clouds of dust fell down into the corridor, and Jojonah feared that all the tunnel might collapse. They should have taken a few days to shore it up, he realized, but that lack of preparedness only emphasized for him the sheer desperation of the Father Abbot to find Avelyn Desbris.

The monks pressed on and the slab shifted again. Bradwarden cried out and went into convulsions, and Jojonah was fast to him, hooking his arms under the broad shoulders of the centaur and pulling with all his might.

He found, to his horror, that he couldn't budge the huge centaur. Even in his emaciated state, Bradwarden weighed well over four hundred pounds. Into the hematite went Jojonah, not to attack the centaur's wounds, as they had planned, but to intercept the thoughts of the other monks, pleading with them to lend some of their energy to the centaur's form that he might drag the huge creature free.

It got tricky then, and Jojonah feared that the slab would tumble back down, but Markwart, so incredibly powerful with the stones now, led the monks in the effort, shifting some of the levitational forces onto the centaur.

Jojonah pulled him free, then fell back into the hematite, going at the centaur's wounds with fervor. He was hardly conscious of the movement as Markwart and the others grabbed both him and Bradwarden and dragged them on their way, rushing out of the unstable tunnel.

And then Master Jojonah was no longer alone in his efforts to save the creature, as Markwart's spirit, and Brother Braumin's and several others, joined him, attacking Bradwarden's every wound.

More than five hours later Master Jojonah lay on the ground just outside Aida, thoroughly exhausted, with Brother Braumin beside him. There they slept, and only woke up late the next morning, to find Brother Francis— and it was indeed Francis—standing over them.

"Where is the centaur?" Master Jojonah asked.

"Resting, and more comfortable than we might have hoped," Brother Francis replied. "We fed him—tentatively at first, but then he ate pounds of meat, half our store of venison, and drank gallons of water. Strong indeed must be the magic of that armband, for already he seems more solid."

Master Jojonah nodded, sincerely relieved.

"And we have found a way up the mountain," Brother Francis added.

"Is there still a need?"

"You will be interested in what we have there discovered among the ashes," Brother Francis said sternly.

Master Jojonah held his next question, instead pausing to take a measure of the man. Whatever progress Francis might have made seemed to have been erased now—probably by the visit of Father Abbot Markwart. The man's expression was cold again; the laughter in his eyes was no more. All business.

"I need to rest, I fear," Master Jojonah said at length. "I will talk to Bradwarden this day; we can climb Aida tomorrow."

"No time," Brother Francis replied. "And none are to speak to the centaur until we return to St.-Mere-Abelle."

Master Jojonah didn't even need to ask where that order had come from. And he came to understand more clearly Brother Francis' shift of mood. When they had first viewed the blasted Barbacan, Francis had proclaimed that the devastation was either the work of a godly man or an overextension of the demon dactyl's magic. Now it seemed clear that Brother Avelyn had indeed been involved, and Master Jojonah did not doubt for a second that the Father Abbot had made it clear to Francis that Brother Avelyn was no godly man.

"We go up the mountain this day," Brother Francis went on. "If you cannot make it, then Brother Braumin will go in your stead. When that duty is finished, we are back on the road."

"It will be dark before you get back down," Brother Braumin said.

"We will ride day and night until we are returned to St.-Mere-Abelle," Brother Francis answered.

The course seemed quite silly to Master Jojonah. The answers were here, of course, or perhaps nearby. To go all the way back to St.-Mere-Abelle made no sense—unless he factored in Father Abbot Markwart's profound distrust of him. The discovery of an eyewitness had changed everything, and Markwart wasn't about to let him take control of this very delicate situation. Jojonah looked to Braumin then, both men wondering if the time had come to make a stand against the Father Abbot, against the Church itself.

Master Jojonah shook his head slightly. They could not win.

He was not surprised, but was surely pained, when he returned to the wagons to find Bradwarden in chains. Still, the centaur's renewed vigor surprised him and gave him hope.

"Ye might at least let them give me me pipes," the centaur begged.

Master Jojonah followed Bradwarden's longing gaze to a set of dusty bagpipes lying on the seat of a nearby wagon. He started to say something, but Brother Francis cut him short.

"He will have food, and he will have healing, and nothing more," the monk explained. "And as soon as he seems fully recovered, the armband will be taken."

"Ah, but Avelyn was a far better man than the lot o' ye put together," Bradwarden remarked, and he closed his eyes and began humming a quiet tune, pausing once to offer a sly look and mutter, "Thieves."

Master Jojonah, eyeing Brother Francis all the while, walked over and took up the bagpipes, then handed them to the centaur.

Bradwarden returned a respectful look and a nod, then took to playing, hauntingly beautiful music that had all the monks, except stubborn Francis, listening intently.

Master Jojonah somehow found the strength to accompany Francis and six others up Aida that afternoon. The top of the mountain was now a wide black bowl, but the ash and molten stone had hardened enough for the monks to walk across it without much difficulty.

Brother Francis led them directly to the spot: a petrified arm sticking from the black ground, fingers clutched as though they had held something.

Master Jojonah bent low and examined the arm and hand. He knew them! Somehow, he knew who this was, somehow he felt the goodness of this place, an aura of peace and godly strength.

"Brother Avelyn," he gasped.

Behind him the others, except for Francis, nearly fell over.

"That is our guess," Brother Francis replied. "It would seem that Avelyn was in league with the dactyl, and was destroyed when the demon was destroyed."

The obvious falsehood overwhelmed Master Jojonah. He rose and spun on Brother Francis powerfully, and nearly struck the man.

But Jojonah held his blow. Father Abbot Markwart would persist with a campaign of lies against Avelyn, he realized, for if it was discovered that Avelyn had given his life in destroying the dactyl, as Jojonah knew to be true, then Markwart's many claims and position in the Church might be in jeopardy. That was why, Jojonah realized, conversations with the centaur were to be limited until the creature was safely back at St.-Mere-Abelle, under Markwart's control.

Master Jojonah forced himself to calm down. This fight was only beginning; now was not the time to wage the battle openly.

"What do you think he was holding?" Brother Francis asked.

Jojonah looked back to the arm and shrugged.

"There is little magic about this man," Brother Francis explained. "A couple of stones, perhaps—we will know that when we exhume the body—but not enough strength to account for the hoard that Avelyn stole."

Exhume the body. The notion screamed out at Jojonah as simply wrong. This place should be marked as a holy shrine, a place of renewing faith and finding character. He wanted to scream out at Francis, to punch the man in the mouth for even uttering such a blasphemous thought. But again he reminded himself that this was not the time to wage the battle, not that way.

"The stone about the arm is solid," he reasoned. "Blasting it will prove no easy task."

"We have graphite," Brother Francis reminded him.

"And if there is a crevice or chasm beneath the body, such violent intrusion will likely drop all the stones away from us forever."

A panicked expression crossed Brother Francis' face. "Then what do you suggest?" he asked sharply.

"Search with the hematite and the garnet," Master Jojonah replied. "It should be no difficult task in determining if there are any stones about this man, and what they might be. Put a brilliant diamond light into the crack about the arm, then let your spirit enter that place."

Brother Francis, not recognizing the larger reasons Father Abbot Markwart might have for destroying this potential shrine, thought about it for a few moments, then agreed.

He also agreed to let Master Jojonah spiritually accompany him into the crevice, since the Father Abbot was too weary to return to his body anytime soon, and Jojonah was the only one who could identify Brother Avelyn; Francis had only seen the man a couple of times, for Avelyn had deserted the abbey shortly after Francis had entered it.

Soon after, the identity was confirmed, along with the knowledge that only one stone, a sunstone, was anywhere near the man, though Master Jojonah sensed the residual magical emanations of another stone, the giant amethyst. The master said nothing of the amethyst to Francis, and had no trouble convincing the younger monk that a simple sunstone, which were already in abundance at St.-Mere-Abelle, was not worth the trouble, risk, and lost time of exhuming the body.

With Francis leading, they left Avelyn then.

Master Jojonah was the last to turn to go, pausing at the sight, reflecting on his own faith and remembering the young monk who had inadvertently taught him so very much.

When they got back to camp, Jojonah pressed a diamond into Brother Braumin's hand, whispered directions to him, and bade him go and see the sacred place. "I will delay Brother Francis long enough for you to return," he promised.

Brother Braumin, not quite understanding, but recognizing from Jojonah's tone the importance of the journey, nodded and turned to go.

"And Brother Braumin," the master said, turning the man about. "Take Brother Dellman with you. He, too, should see this man, and this place."

Brother Francis was in a foul mood indeed when he learned they would be delayed in leaving, for a wagon had somehow broken a wheel.

Still, they were on the move before the dawn. The centaur, seeming fit again—though Francis hadn't yet dared to remove the armband—and playing his pipes, trotted behind Brother Francis' wagon, chained to the frame and with several monks keeping close guard on him.

Neither Brother Braumin, Master Jojonah, nor Brother Dellman spoke a word that night and all the next day, their voices stolen by an image they would carry for the rest of their lives, and by a barrage of profound reflections on their purpose and their faith.

CHAPTER

❖ 11 ❖

Roger Lockless, I Presume

Wincing in agony, Roger bit hard on the piece of wood he had stuck between his teeth. He had torn a sleeve from his shirt, tied it tight about his leg, just below the knee, and knotted it about a second piece of wood. Now he turned that wood, tightening the tourniquet.

He nearly swooned more than once, flitting in and out of consciousness. If he passed out now, he would surely bleed to death, he reminded himself, for the bite of the Craggoth hound was deep, the blood spurting.

Finally, mercifully, the blood flow stemmed, and Roger, cold and clammy, sweating profusely, slumped back against the earthen wall of his cell. He knew this place well, a root cellar close to the town center, and knew there was only one way in or out: a trapdoor at the top of a rickety wooden ladder. Roger stared at it now, lines of meager daylight streaming through. The late afternoon sun, he realized, and he thought that he should try to make his break when the light was gone, under cover of night.

He recognized immediately the foolishness of that notion. He wasn't going anywhere this night, could hardly find the strength to pull himself away from the wall. Chuckling at the futility of it all, he slumped down to the floor, and then he slept all the night through, and would have remained asleep for many, many more hours if the door to his jail had not banged open and the dawn's light poured in.

Roger groaned and tried to straighten himself.

A powrie appeared on the ladder, followed by another, Kos-kosio Begulne himself. The dwarf in front went right to Roger and pulled him up to his feet, slamming him hard against the wall.

Roger teetered, but managed to hold his balance, realizing that if he fell over, the dwarf would just hoist him up again, probably even more roughly.

"Who uses the magic?" Kos-kosio Begulne asked, coming up to Roger, grabbing him by the front of his torn and bloody shirt and pulling him low, so his face was barely an inch from the leathery, wrinkled, imposing

157

visage of the dwarf, close enough that Kos-kosio's foul breath was hot in Roger's face.

"Magic?" Roger replied.

"Get the hounds!" Kos-kosio Begulne cried.

Roger groaned again at the sound of barking.

"Who uses the magic?" the powrie leader demanded. "How many, and how many stones?"

"Stones?" Roger echoed. "I know of no stones, nor of any magic."

Another bark came from above.

"I promise," Roger added, his tone frantic. "I could just lie and give you a name, any name, and you would not know if I spoke truly until, or unless, you found that person. But I do not know of any magic. None!"

Kos-kosio Begulne held Roger close a bit longer, the dwarf growling low—and Roger feared that the fierce powrie would bite his nose off. But then Kos-kosio shoved him back hard against the wall and spun toward the stairs, convinced by the simple logic of Roger's defense. "Ye tie him up!" the leader barked at the other powrie. "Strangle knot. We wants to make our guest comfortable."

Roger wasn't quite sure what Kos-kosio Begulne had in mind, but the other powrie's grin, wide with evil glee, was not promising. The dwarf produced a thin, rough-edged rope and advanced on him.

Roger slumped to the floor. The dwarf kicked him over onto his belly, then yanked his arms roughly behind his back.

"Nah, put the damned hounds away," Kos-kosio Begulne commanded yet another powrie who had come to the top of the root cellar's ladder, leading a Craggoth hound on a short leash. "He's just a weak human, and won't be living through much more pain." Kos-kosio looked back from his perch on the lower rungs, meeting Roger's glare. "I'm wanting to find a bit more fun with this one before I let him die."

"Lucky me," Roger muttered under his breath, and that only got him an even harder tug from the dwarf with the rope.

The "strangle knot," as Kos-kosio Begulne had called it, proved to be a devilish twist of the rope. Roger's arms were bound tightly behind his back, bent at the elbow so his hands nearly touched the back of his neck. The nasty cord then looped over both his shoulders and down the front of his body, wrapping painfully underneath his groin and then up his back once more, finally looping about Roger's throat. So expertly was he tied, and so tightly, that the slightest shift of his arms not only sent waves of pain into his groin, but cut off his air supply, as well.

"Well, human lock-picker, let's be seeing if ye can get yer way outta this." The powrie laughed, set a torch in a wall sconce, lit it, and went to the top of the ladder, calling out to some comrades. "Kos-kosio's not wanting this one to get away!"

"Double lock?" one of the dwarves up above asked.

"Double lock," the powrie on the stairs confirmed. "And then sit the damned hound on it! And ye get one to come and take me seat before the sun's too low. I'm not wanting to miss me supper sitting with this smelly human."

"Quit yer bitching," the other dwarf replied, and closed the heavy trapdoor with a resounding bang. Roger listened carefully as chains and locks were set in place on the door. He studied the powrie coming down the stairs.

One mistake, the young man silently berated Kos-kosio Begulne. *You let this one keep a weapon.*

The powrie made straight for Roger. "You just lie still," the dwarf instructed, and then, to accentuate the point, the nasty creature kicked Roger hard in the ribs.

Roger squirmed—and that only choked him all the more.

Laughing, the dwarf moved across the way and sat down under the burning torch. The wicked creature took off its crimson beret, twirling it about with one finger, letting Roger see it clearly, as if to promise him that his blood, too, would soon enhance the hue. Then the powrie put its gnarly hands behind its head and leaned against the wall, closing its eyes.

Roger spent a long, long while getting his bearings. He fought away the nausea and the pain, then tried to figure a way to get out of the ropes. That would be the easy part, he decided, because even if he got free, even if he then took the dwarf's weapon and killed the creature, where might he go? The cellar bulkhead was locked and chained, and he didn't have to be reminded of what lay in wait atop it.

Truly, the task before him seemed daunting, but Roger forced himself to calm and to concentrate, trying to break things down one step at a time.

Sometime in late afternoon the powries changed guards. The new one gave Roger a bit of food and a drink—nearly drowning him in the process—and then took a seat in much the same place as the previous sentry.

Within an hour this one, too, was snoring contentedly.

Determined not to spend another night as Kos-kosio Begulne's guest, Roger decided that the time to act was upon him. One small step at a time, he reminded himself as he braced his shoulder against the hard wall. He had to angle himself just right, so his weight and not his strength would do most of the work. With a glance at his powrie jailor to make sure the creature was sleeping soundly, Roger closed his eyes and mustered his nerve.

Then he dove against the wall, suddenly, powerfully, hitting with the front of his shoulder, the jolt driving his arm back. Roger's muscles and weight worked in a coordinated manner then, driving him ahead.

He heard a loud pop as his shoulder dislocated, and waves of pain rolled through his body, nearly laying him low. He fought them away, though, and with his arm thus contorted, the rope was loosened enough for him to slip it over the shoulder.

In a matter of seconds he was lying on the floor, free of the rope, gasping for breath. Then, after a moment's respite, he went back to work, jamming his shoulder the other way, popping it back in place—a useful little trick the thief had perfected over the years. Again he spent a moment letting the waves of pain subside, and then gathered up the rope and moved to the sleeping powrie.

"Hey," the dwarf protested a few minutes later, opening its sleepy eyes to see Roger standing before it, the dwarf's short sword in hand. "And what're ye meaning to do with that?" the powrie asked, climbing to its feet and drawing a dagger from its boot. Both the dwarf and Roger understood that even thus armed, the man was no match for the battle-seasoned powrie.

Roger hopped backward on his good leg, falling against the far wall; the powrie growled and charged, raising its dagger before it.

As that arm came up, the dwarf realized that a rope was looped about its wrist, a short leash fastened to a root sticking from the earthen wall near to where the dwarf had been sitting.

"What?" the powrie said, even as the loop tightened and held, pulling the dwarf's arm low, right between its legs, flipping the dwarf over to land heavily on its back.

Roger came off the wall even as the dwarf began its somersault, sliding in beside the prone creature.

"What?" the dwarf bellowed again, just before the pommel of its short sword smashed down on its hard head. The powrie thrashed, trying to pull its arm free, trying to grab at Roger with its other hand.

Roger pounded away with the pommel again and again, until finally the stubborn dwarf lay still. The man nearly fell away from the pain then, and the exertion, flitting in and out of consciousness.

"Not much time," Roger reminded himself stubbornly, dragging himself to his feet.

The powrie stirred; Roger slammed it again, and then once more.

"Not much time," he said again, more insistently, shaking his head at the sheer resilience of the hardy dwarf.

Now things got more complicated; Roger played through the entire scenario, trying to figure every obstacle and every item he would need to overcome them. He took the dagger from the dwarf's hand and the belt from around its waist, and reset the rope to better secure the creature. Then he moved to the ladder, trying to get a measure of the bulkhead's strength. At the center of that trapdoor, on the inside, was a support beam, a strong log. Roger went at this first, or rather, at the wood above it, scraping a hollow area wide enough to loop the rope over the beam. Then he began an expert assault on the boards, whittling at their supports on either end. At one point he heard the growl of the wary Craggoth hound, and had to pause for a long while before the vicious dog would quiet down.

One scratch at a time, one broken splinter, one loosened peg. Again Roger had to stop, this time because his leg was throbbing so badly he could not remain on the ladder. And then again he had to wait, for the powrie was coming back to consciousness and needed to be clunked on the head one more time. Stubbornly Roger went back to work, and finally the boards to either side of the central support were loosened.

The moment was upon him; he hoped he wouldn't faint away from the pain at a critical juncture.

He went back to the dwarf and gathered more tools, then spent a long moment replaying the expected scenario. He checked his gear one final time—the short sword and the dagger, the post from the dwarf's belt buckle, the leather laces from the dwarf's boots, and finally, one of those smelly boots—and then took a deep steadying breath and moved back to the ladder. He pressed slightly on each of the loosened bulkhead boards, trying to get a better feel of where the hound might be. Of course, if there was more than one dog, or if there were any powries in the immediate area up above, the game would end quickly, and likely, painfully, Roger realized, but he decided he had to take the chance. In his mind, he had nothing to lose, for Kos-kosio Begulne would never let him go, and Roger held no illusions about his captivity: as soon as the powrie leader decided he was no longer useful, he would be tortured to death.

He had already looped the rope over the beam from right to left, but then, realizing that the hound was more to the left, he reversed the direction. Down the ladder Roger went, positioning the dazed powrie at the base and to the left-hand side.

Back up on the ladder, in place below the trapdoor, Roger rubbed his hands anxiously, reminding himself over and over that his timing had to be perfect. Using splinters from the worked boards, he set the noose in place just under the right-hand board. Then he took up the boot in one hand and put his other hand firmly against the right board, up through the noose.

A final deep breath and Roger pushed hard, partially dislodging the board, enough so he woke the hound fully and offered it an opening through which it could attack.

And attack it did, jaws snapping right for the boot that Roger pushed up into its face. As soon as the dog latched on, Roger, holding the other end of the boot in both hands, jumped from the ladder, drawing the stubborn hound in through the opening, in through the noose.

The snare worked perfectly, tightening about the hound as it came falling through, hooking about the dog's neck and under one paw about the shoulder. Down they went, Roger in a tumble—a painful tumble!—and the hound dropping to the end of the rope length. The sudden jerk lifted the powrie at the rope's other end to its knees and left the hound dangling, one of its back feet just brushing the floor.

The Craggoth hound bit hard on the boot, shaking its head violently side to side, seemingly oblivious to the fact that it was hanging. Roger was there in a split second, taking the opportunity to loop the leather shoelace about the creature's closed jaws, wrapping it tightly many times and then tying it off.

"Bark now," he taunted, then flicked his finger against the hound's nose. With a last quick check on the powrie, and one more slug to the head for good measure, Roger struggled back up the ladder.

All was quiet outside, but considering the pain in his leg, Roger didn't think he would have much luck trying to slip through the narrow opening he had broken in the trapdoor. He did get his hands out, though, enough to feel along the chains to the two padlocks. Always pleased by his own cleverness, smiling Roger took the narrow post of the powrie's buckle in hand and went to work.

Nightbird waited for the signal whistle, then moved quickly and quietly up to the tree in which his small friend was perched. From this vantage point they could see most of Caer Tinella, and Juraviel's estimate of the number of monsters within that town seemed conservative to the ranger.

"Do you have any idea where they would hold him?" he asked.

"I said that I heard them speak of him, not that I actually saw him," the elf replied. "He could be in any building, or more likely, considering the events of last night, he could be dead."

Nightbird wanted to argue, but held his tongue, for he found that he could not logically disagree with Juraviel. An entire day had passed—he and the elf couldn't risk coming into Caer Tinella in broad daylight—giving Kos-kosio Begulne plenty of time to sort out the details of the disaster in the forest and to lay the blame for it at the feet of his valuable prisoner.

"We should have come right in," Juraviel went on. "As soon as the fight was over, with still two or three hours of darkness before us."

"Pony had to tend the wounded," the ranger replied.

"She is not here anyway," the elf reminded. Nightbird had hoped she would accompany them, but Pony was still exhausted from the overuse of magic. After their sword-dance that morning, she had slept through most of the day, and would likely sleep well again that night.

"But this is," the ranger answered, holding up the hematite. "Roger Lockless might need it."

"More likely, Roger Lockless needs burying," the elf said dryly.

The ranger didn't appreciate the sarcasm, but again he said nothing, except to motion ahead and tell Juraviel to lead on.

The elf was gone in an instant, and a few seconds later another whistle moved the ranger even closer. They held their next position for some time, as a large group of powries and giants filtered out of the town, heading more to the west than the north.

"The fewer left in town, the better our chances," Juraviel remarked, keeping his voice to a tiny whisper now that they were so close.

The ranger nodded and motioned for Juraviel to move along. The next hop put them at the railing of a corral; the next after that put them right beside a barn on the northeastern edge of town. Now they moved together, both holding bows. They froze when they heard voices within the barn, some goblins complaining about work and one grumbling about a broken chain.

"He could be in there," Juraviel said softly.

The ranger didn't think that a reputedly wise powrie leader would be foolish enough to put so valuable a prisoner on the outskirts of the town, but he wanted to leave an open path out of Caer Tinella anyway, and so he gave a little tug on his bowstring and nodded toward the barn.

Juraviel led the way around the side, coming up on the front corner. They passed a pair of doors at the level of the ranger's head, used for throwing hay bales out to the cows, but there were no handles on the outside and so they paid the portal no heed—none, at least, until the two doors swung out, one slamming Nightbird about the shoulders, forcing him to fall back, the other swinging right above Juraviel's head. The poor goblin who had swung the doors didn't realize that a human was blocking one from opening all the way, didn't even realize that anybody was outside, until Juraviel, ducking and turning under the swinging door, lifted his bow and put an arrow right between the creature's eyes. The elf skipped right in, fluttering up with his wings. He grabbed the fast-dying goblin by the front of its ragged tunic and propped it in place.

Nightbird groaned and grumbled, finally getting around the awkward door, only to see Juraviel patting a finger frantically against pursed lips and pointing inside.

The ranger kept his calm and moved to the edge of the opening, peering around. He saw one other goblin, working with a block and tackle and a chain. There may have been others, for the inside of the barn was too cluttered by stalls and bales, a wagon and many other items, for the ranger to be sure. Leaning Hawkwing against the wall, he drew out Tempest and eased beside the goblin, then up to the tier inside the window. Silent as a hunting cat, the ranger made his careful way right behind the goblin working the block and tackle.

"Do you need help?" he asked.

The goblin spun, eyes wide.

Tempest cut it down.

But there was indeed another goblin in the barn, and it came racing out of a nearby stall, trying to run right past the ranger. It jerked and stumbled as an arrow hit it, then staggered again, nearly going to its knees and slowing enough for Nightbird to catch up. The strong ranger grabbed the thing about the head, clamping his hand over its mouth, and pulled it down to the ground.

"Where is the prisoner?" he whispered in its ear.

The goblin squirmed and tried to scream out, but Nightbird grabbed it all the tighter, jerked its head back and forth. Then Juraviel was beside them, the elf holding his bow up beside the goblin's head, his arrow creasing the creature's temple. The goblin calmed considerably.

"If you yell out, you die," the ranger promised, and he eased his hand away.

"It hurts us! It hurts us!" the goblin moaned pitifully, and the two friends could hardly blame it, for it carried one of Juraviel's arrows in its shoulder, another in its thigh. Still, the ranger pressed his hand over the creature's mouth once more.

"The prisoner," he prompted, easing his hand away. "Where is the prisoner?"

"Kos-kosio Begulne have many prisoners," the goblin countered.

"The new prisoner," the ranger clarified. "The one Kos-kosio Begulne hates most of all."

"Nasty arrow from nasty elf!"

"Tell me," the ranger growled, "or my friend will put another arrow into you!"

"In the ground," the goblin squeaked. "In a hole in the ground."

"Buried?" the ranger asked anxiously. "Did Kos-kosio Begulne kill him?"

"Not buried," the goblin replied. "Not dead yet. In a room in a hole."

The ranger looked to Juraviel. "To store food," the ranger explained, figuring out the riddle. "We did as much in Dundalis when I was a boy."

"A root cellar," the elf agreed, and both of them turned back to the prisoner.

"Where is this hole?" Nightbird asked, giving the goblin a shake.

The goblin shook its head; the ranger tightened his grip. "You will tell—" Nightbird started to say, but Juraviel, glancing out a small window beside the barn's front door, the one facing the town proper, interrupted him.

"Time is short," the elf explained. "The powries are astir."

"Last chance," Nightbird said to the goblin. "Where is the hole?"

But the goblin feared Kos-kosio Begulne more than it feared anything these two could do to it. It squirmed and started to cry out, and when the ranger clamped his hand over its mouth, it promptly bit him, struggling wildly to get away. It could not break free of the ranger's strong hold, though, so it tried to bite again, and started to cry out, however muffled the call might be.

A well-aimed thrust of Juraviel's dagger-sized sword ended that; the creature slumped to the floor and died.

"And how are we to find Roger Lockless now?" Nightbird asked.

"The goblin would not have told us more, even if it knew more," the elf replied. "It knew that I would kill it as soon as the information was divulged."

The ranger looked at his companion curiously. "And if we had promised its life in exchange?" he asked.

"Then we would have been lying," Juraviel replied evenly. "Speak not to me of mercy where goblins are concerned, Nightbird. I'll not suffer a goblin to live. Nor should you, who lived through the massacre of Dundalis, and through all the horrors since then."

Nightbird looked down at the dead goblin. Juraviel was right about the wicked race, of course, though as soon as they had taken the goblin prisoner and demanded information, it somehow seemed to change things. Goblins were horrid things, evil and merciless. They lived to destroy, and would attack humans on sight—any humans, including . . . especially, children—as long as they believed they could win the fight. The ranger had never felt guilty about killing them, but if he had given this one his word that if it offered the information it would not be killed . . .

It was a perplexing thought, but one that would have to wait for another time, the ranger realized when he moved over to glance out the window beside the door. Juraviel hadn't been lying; a large group of powries and other monsters was moving through the town, heading generally north. The ranger got the distinct impression they were searching for someone.

"What are you doing?" he asked the elf when he turned about to see Juraviel scampering about the barn, retrieving torches and their sconces.

Juraviel didn't bother to answer. Using rope, he secured the sconces to a board, then put the board across a beam in line with the front window, laying the torches in loosely over a thick blanket of hay.

"A diversion for the way out," the ranger reasoned.

"If indeed we come this way," the elf added.

Nightbird only nodded and did not press the point, trusting in his friend. In a few moments they set out, going through the same hay window that had brought them into the barn, carefully closing the doors behind them. They crept to the front edge of the building and peered around. Many enemies were about, mostly powries, and most of these were carrying blazing torches.

"Not the most promising of situations," the ranger offered, but he did see a way to get closer to the town center. Now, using the cat's-eye, he led the way, moving to the side of another building, then cutting through a narrow alley between it and another. Around the next corner, they came upon a powrie.

Tempest slashed down, angling in from the shoulder, cutting deep into the side of the creature's neck; Juraviel's sword stabbed in under the bottom rib, slanting upward to steal the creature's breath. Still, despite the coordinated and perfect attacks, the dwarf gave a stifled cry as it died.

The two companions exchanged nervous glances at the sound. "Move along, and quickly," the elf bade his friend.

Stepping fast, the ranger was looking down more than up, searching for some bulkhead that would indicate a root cellar, while Juraviel skittered off to the side, trying to keep track of any nearby monsters. That was why the normally alert Nightbird was surprised indeed when he heard a voice above him.

"Looking for something?" it casually asked.

Up went the ranger's eyes, up went his sword, but he halted the swing abruptly when he realized that it was no powrie, no goblin or giant talking, but a human, a skinny and short man reclining on the narrow ledge above a back door. The ranger quickly scanned the form, noting the wound on his leg, the scab and bruises on his face and on the one arm that was exposed. And yet, despite his obvious pain and the precarious, at best, perch, the man held himself easily, comfortably, with an air of confidence and ease. There could be only two answers to this riddle, and it seemed unlikely to the ranger that any human was in league with the powries.

"Roger Lockless, I presume," Nightbird said quietly.

"I see that my reputation has spread wide indeed," the man replied.

"We must be on the move," a nervous Juraviel remarked, coming out of the shadows. One look at the elf, and Roger, eyes going wide and mouth dropping open, overbalanced and tumbled from the ledge. He would have hit the ground hard, but the ranger was there below him, catching him and easing him to his feet.

"What is that?" Roger gasped.

"Answers will wait," the ranger replied sternly.

"We must be quick," Juraviel explained. "The monsters tighten their perimeter about us. They are searching door-to-door."

"They would not have caught me," Roger said with all confidence.

"Many powries," said the elf, "with torches to light the night as if it were day."

"They would not have caught me," Roger said again.

"They have giants to look on rooftops," Juraviel added.

"They would not have caught me," the unshakable thief repeated a third time, snapping his fingers in the air.

A baying split the night air.

"And they have dogs," the ranger remarked.

"Oh, that," said Roger, deflating fast. "Get me away from this cursed place!"

The three started back down the alley, but it became obvious that Roger could not move quickly, could hardly support himself. Nightbird was right beside him, hooking the man's arm across his strong shoulder for support.

"Find me a walking stick," Roger begged.

The ranger shook his head, realizing that a walking stick wouldn't help much. He ducked low suddenly, pulling Roger's arm farther across his shoulders and hoisting him across his back.

"Lead on," the ranger bade Juraviel. "And with all speed."

The elf skittered to a corner, peered around it, then ran off almost at once, sprinting to the next building, and then the next in line. They heard a shout, the resonating voice of a giant, and though they couldn't be certain that the monster was even calling out about them, Juraviel, and then the ranger right behind him, broke into a dead run. The elf fitted an arrow to his bowstring as he went, and when they neared the barn, he slowed, took aim, and let fly, the arrow diving through the window beside the door, nocking hard into the loose board Juraviel had put in place and dropping the burning torches into the bed of hay. Before the three had even gone past the front corner of the barn, the light inside increased dramatically. Before they were out the other side, running along the fence of the corral, the flames burst through the front window and were licking through cracks in the roof.

They passed the corral and were soon into the woods, the ranger in front now and running with all speed, despite the man slung over his shoulder. They could hear the wild commotion back in Caer Tinella, powries, goblins, and giants running all about and calling out orders, most screaming for water, others for a chase of the escaping human. And then they heard, more pointedly, the howling of several hounds closing on their trail.

"Run in, straight to the others," Juraviel instructed. "I will rid us of the troublesome dogs."

"Not so easy a task," Roger gasped as he bounced about.

"Not for one who has no wings," the elf replied with a wink, though Roger's balance was too precarious for him to notice.

Juraviel doubled back then, and the ranger ran on, disappearing into the forest night. The elf waited a moment, gauging the flight of his friend and the sound of the approaching dogs. He picked a tall and wide oak, the ground around it relatively free of brush. He scampered all about its base, making the scent thick, then used his wings to lift him to the lowest branch, carefully rubbing his smell on the bark all the way up. Then he ascended again to a new perch, and then again higher, and was halfway up when the leading hound reached the tree's base. It sniffed and whimpered, then stood up with its forepaws on the trunk and howled excitedly.

Juraviel called down to it, taunting it, and then for good measure put an arrow into the ground right beside the hound.

More hounds arrived, sniffing and circling, taking up the call.

Up higher went the elf, to the very top of the tree, to branches that hardly supported even his lithe form. He paused a moment to revel in the view, all the dark treetops spread far and wide before him. And then, secure that these hounds would remain howling at the scented tree, Juraviel let his wings carry him to a tree farther on, a long flight for an elf. Still, as soon as he found his perch, Juraviel knew he couldn't stop and rest, and so he flew off again to the next tree in line, and so on, until the calls of the hounds were far behind him. He came down then, needing to give his wings a rest, and scampered away on light feet through the forest night.

Later on, from the edges of the human camp, Juraviel saw that Elbryan and Roger had arrived safely. Many others were gathered about the pair, despite the late hour, listening to the tale of the rescue—or of the escape, to hear Roger tell it. Satisfied about a mission well done, Juraviel moved deeper into the forest, to the thick and soft boughs of a pine tree, and settled down for the night.

He was surprised when he awoke, before the dawn, to find that both Elbryan and Pony were already awake and gone from the camp.

The elf gave a smile, thinking that they needed some time alone with each other, a respite for lovers.

He wasn't far from the truth, for Elbryan and Pony were indeed intimate that morning—but not in the way Juraviel imagined. They were out in a secret clearing, performing *bi'nelle dasada*.

That morning, and every morning thereafter, and each time they danced, Pony followed Nightbird's movements a bit longer. It would be years before she could find his level of perfection, if ever, she knew, but she took heart, for each day brought improvement—each day her lunge went a bit faster and a bit farther, her aim a bit more sure.

As the days passed, the ranger noted a change in the dance, subtle but definite. At first he worried that taking Pony under his guidance was perverting this very special gift of the Touel'alfar, but then he realized that the shift, far from undesirable, was a wonderful thing. For each day, he and his companion grew a bit more in tune with each other, each sensing the other's movements, learning to supplement and compliment every routine with the proper support.

Indeed their dance was beautiful, a sharing of heart and soul and, mostly, of trust.

❖ 12 ❖

Unexpected Guests

*T*his *cannot be! It makes no sense whatsoever,* Abbot Dobrinion Calislas of St. Precious Abbey in Palmaris kept telling himself, trying to convince himself through logic, despite the very real reports from reliable monks, that Father Abbot Dalebert Markwart, the leader of the Abellican Church, was waiting for him in the chapel of his abbey.

"Markwart is too old to be traveling to Palmaris," Abbot Dobrinion said aloud, though no one was nearby to hear. He fumbled with his robes as he stumbled down the circular stairs from his private quarters. "And surely he would have given notice of his visit long in advance. Such men do not move helter-skelter about the countryside!

"And such men should not come unannounced!" Dobrinion added. He was no fan of Father Abbot Markwart; the two had been at odds for several years concerning the canonization process of one of St. Precious' former monks. Though it was the second oldest abbey in all the order, behind St.-Mere-Abelle, St. Precious boasted of no saints from its order, a tragic oversight that Abbot Dobrinion was working hard to correct—and one that Father Abbot Markwart had opposed from the very moment Brother Allabarnet's name had been entered.

Dobrinion's voice rose as he finished the frantic thought, the abbot opening the heavy door of the chapel at the same time. His round cheeks flushed, for he feared that the man standing before him, Father Abbot Dalebert Markwart, had heard him.

And it was indeed Markwart, Abbot Dobrinion knew without doubt. He had met the man on more than a dozen occasions, and though he had not seen Markwart in more than a decade, he recognized him now. He glanced around at Markwart's entourage, trying to make some sense of it all. Only three other monks were in the chapel, and one of them was of St. Precious. The other two, both young, one slender and nervous, the other barrel-chested and obviously strong, stood near the Father Abbot in similar poses, their arms crossed in front of them, one hand clasping the other wrist. A defensive position, Dobrinion noted, and it seemed to him that these two were more like bodyguards than escorts. On previous occasions when the Father Abbot had traveled, whether it was Markwart or any of his predecessors, the entourage was huge, no less than fifty monks, and a fair number of them masters, or even abbots. These two were neither, Dobrinion knew, for they were hardly old enough to even have attained half the years of an immaculate.

"Father Abbot," he said solemnly, dipping a respectful bow.

"My greetings, Abbot Dobrinion," Father Abbot Markwart replied in his nasal voice. "Forgive my intrusion into your excellent abbey."

"Indeed," was all that the sputtering, flustered abbot could reply.

"It was necessary," Markwart went on. "In these times ... well, you understand that we must often improvise with an enemy army marching about our lands."

"Indeed," Dobrinion said again, and he wanted to pinch himself, thinking that he sounded incredibly stupid.

"I am to be met here by a caravan," the Father Abbot explained, "which I diverted on its return to St.-Mere-Abelle, for there is little time."

A caravan from St.-Mere-Abelle this far out? Dobrinion thought. And I knew nothing about it!

"Master Jojonah leads it," Father Abbot Markwart said. "You remember Jojonah; you and he went through your training together."

"He was two or three years my junior, I believe," Abbot Dobrinion replied. He had met Jojonah subsequently at Church gatherings, and had once spent a night drinking heavily with the man, and with a hawkish master by the name of Siherton.

"Are any other masters with this caravan?" he asked. "Siherton, perhaps?

"Master Siherton is dead," Father Abbot Markwart said evenly. "He was murdered."

"Powries?" Dobrinion dared to ask, though it seemed from Markwart's tone that the man did not want to elaborate.

"No," Father Abbot said curtly. "But enough of that unpleasant situation; it was a long time ago. Jojonah is the only master on the caravan, though he has a trio of immaculates beside him. They are twenty-five strong, and have with them a most extraordinary prisoner. What I require from you is privacy, for myself, for my fellows of St.-Mere-Abelle, and most of all, for the prisoner."

"I will do all that I can—" Abbot Dobrinion began to respond.

"I am sure that you will," Markwart cut him off. "Have one of your trusted lessers instruct these two—" He indicated the young monks flanking him. "—concerning our accommodations. We will not likely be here for long. No more than a week, I should guess." His face grew very serious and he advanced on Dobrinion, speaking in low, even threatening, tones. "I will have your assurances that there will be no interference," he said.

Abbot Dobrinion rocked back on his heels, studying the old man, surprised by all of this. For St.-Mere-Abelle to even be operating in this region without Dobrinion's knowledge and approval was contrary to Church etiquette. What was this mysterious mission all about, and why hadn't he been informed? And what of this prisoner? With hematite, the Father Abbot surely could have contacted him sooner!

Abbot Dobrinion did well to sublimate his anger. This was the Father Abbot, after all, and Honce-the-Bear was embroiled in a desperate war. "We will do as we are instructed," he assured his superior, bowing his head respectfully. "St. Precious is yours to command."

"I will take your quarters for the duration of my stay," Father Abbot Markwart said. "My lessers will help you to move your necessary items to other accommodations."

Dobrinion felt as though he had been slapped in the face. He had been the abbot of St. Precious for three decades, and that was no small position. St. Precious was the third largest abbey in the Abellican Church, behind St.-Mere-Abelle and St. Honce of Ursal. And because Palmaris was on the edge of the true civilized lands, there was perhaps no abbey more influential to its congregation. For the thirty years of his rule, Abbot Dobrinion had been pretty much left alone—St.-Mere-Abelle was too concerned with the Ring Stones and with general Church doctrine, and St. Honce too embroiled in politics with the King. Thus, Abbot Dobrinion's only rival for power in all the wide northern reaches of Honce-the-Bear was Baron Rochefort Bildeborough of Palmaris, and that man, like his predecessor, in addition to being a close friend to Dobrinion, was quiet and unassuming. Rochefort Bildeborough was a man easily appeased as long as his personal luxuries were secured. Even in the matter of this war that had come to Palmaris, he had turned over defense of the city to the captain of the city guard, instructing that man to report to Abbot Dobrinion, while he kept himself secure in his palace-fortress, Chasewind Manor.

Thus Abbot Dobrinion was not used to being talked to in such superior tones. But again, he remembered his place in the Abellican hierarchy, a pyramid that placed the Father Abbot at its pinnacle. "As you say," he replied humbly, bowing one last time and starting away.

"And perhaps we will have time to discuss the matter of Brother Allabarnet," the Father Abbot said just before Abbot Dobrinion crossed out of the room.

Dobrinion stopped, realizing that he had just been thrown a morsel, a teasing carrot dependent upon his cooperation. His initial thought was to throw that carrot back at the Father Abbot, but he quickly pushed that notion away. Abbot Dobrinion was an old man, and though he was not as old as Markwart, he feared that Markwart would outlive him. By his own estimation, all that he had left to accomplish in his life was to see Brother Allabarnet, a monk of St. Precious, sainted, and that feat would not be easy, perhaps not even possible, without the help of Father Abbot Markwart.

"St. Precious?" Brother Braumin's incredulous tone echoed the emotions of Master Jojonah when Brother Francis announced the new destination.

"The Father Abbot does not wish to lose any time in speaking with the centaur," Brother Francis went on. "He will meet us in Palmaris. In fact, he was on his way to that place when he contacted me, and I suspect that he is already settled in St. Precious."

"Are you certain of this?" Master Jojonah asked calmly. "Was it truly Father Abbot Markwart who told you of this change?"

"You imply that others might somehow get into my mind?" the younger monk retorted.

"I recognize that we have been to the lair of the demon," Master Jojonah explained, again taking pains so that his voice was not accusing. If Father Abbot Markwart had indeed come to Brother Francis with new orders, then Jojonah and all the others had no practical choice but to go along.

"It was the Father Abbot," Brother Francis said firmly. "Would it appease you if I contacted him again? Perhaps I could loan him my body that he tell you personally."

"Enough, brother," Master Jojonah said, waving his hand in surrender. "I do not question your judgment; I only thought it prudent to make certain."

"I am certain."

"So you have said," Master Jojonah replied. "And so our destination shall be St. Precious. Have you determined our course?"

"I have others working with the maps even now," Brother Francis replied. "It is not too far, and once we have crossed the Timberlands, we should find a fairly easy road."

"A road choked with monsters," Brother Braumin put in dryly. "The reports from this area have spoken of abundant fighting."

"We will move too quickly and quietly for them to ever engage us," Brother Francis said.

Master Jojonah only nodded. If the Father Abbot wanted them in Palmaris, then to Palmaris they would go, whatever the obstacles. For Jojonah, though, the greatest obstacle of all would likely find them at the end of the trail, in the person of Dalebert Markwart.

With typical efficiency, Brother Francis completed the plotting and the caravan adjusted its course, wheels humming. They were past the Timberland towns in a couple of days, and though they did indeed find monsters along the way, the creatures never knew of their passage, or realized it too late to possibly catch up to the speeding procession.

*   *   *

"A caravan of monks," Roger Lockless explained. The young man was feeling well again, for Pony had used the hematite extensively on his dog bites and other wounds. He had hardly thanked the woman, though, had just grunted and walked away after their two-hour session. Neither Pony nor Elbryan had seen Roger in the four days since that occasion, until now. "I know monks, and am certain!"

Elbryan and Pony exchanged grim looks, both suspecting that Brother Avelyn might have something to do with this, that these monks might be in search of the stones the companions now held.

"Moving swiftly, so swiftly," Roger went on, sincerely awed. "I doubt that Kos-kosio Begulne even knew they were in the area—or, if the powrie did learn of their passing, they were too far gone by that point for him to do anything about it. They must be halfway to Palmaris by now."

Elbryan started to question that, for Roger had only seen this caravan a couple of hours before. The ranger held the thought quiet, though, for he knew that, whether the estimate of the speed was accurate or not, Roger believed what he was saying.

"A pity that we did not learn of this sooner," Belster O'Comely put in. "What aid might these men of God have given us? What comfort? At the very least, they might have taken our most infirm with them to the safer lands in the south."

"You would not even have learned of them at all had I not been so vigilant," Roger replied angrily, defensively, taking Belster's comment as an insult to his scouting prowess. "How come the great Nightbird knew nothing about them? Or the woman who proclaims to be a great wizardess?"

"Enough, Roger," Elbryan bade him. "Belster was lamenting the reality, not placing blame. It is indeed a pity that we could not enlist the aid of such powerful allies, for if they were moving as swiftly as you say—and I do not doubt that they were," he added quickly, seeing Roger's expression go sour, "then they are likely strong with magic." The ranger was only half serious, though, for while he would have liked to facilitate the passage of their infirm members to Palmaris, he wasn't so sure that these monks would have proven themselves allies—at least not for him and Pony.

"They were moving even faster than you believe," Roger replied. "I cannot describe their true speed. Their horses' legs were but a blur; one rider at the back of the wagon moved so fast that to my eyes he seemed to be a blend of horse and man."

That perked up the ears of all the folk of the Dundalis region, all the folk who knew of the Forest Ghost, who had fought beside Bradwarden and taken comfort in his hauntingly beautiful piping. Elbryan and Pony deflated their brightening expressions, though, shaking their heads at the thought. They had seen the end of Bradwarden, so they both believed.

"You are certain that the caravan kept moving?" the ranger asked Roger.

"Halfway to Palmaris by now," the man replied.

"Then they are no concern of ours," Elbryan reasoned, though silently he vowed to keep an eye out for the monks. If this caravan had come to the north searching for Avelyn and the stones, and if they had garnered some answers through the use of magic, he and Pony might already be considered outlaws.

The caravan arrived at St. Precious with no fanfare, no recognition; Abbot Dobrinion wasn't even there to greet them. That was Father Abbot Markwart's pleasure, along with his pair of bodyguards, quietly meeting the brothers from St.-Mere-Abelle at the abbey's back gate.

Master Jojonah wasn't surprised by Markwart's choice of traveling companions, Brothers Youseff and Dandelion, the two monks in training to replace the late Brother Quintall as Brother Justice. Of all the lesser students in St.-Mere-Abelle, Jojonah had come to like these two the least. Brother Youseff, a third-year student, was from Youmaneff, Avelyn's home town, but there the similarity ended. He was a small and slender man, a vicious fighter who found every advantage in the training arena, no matter how deceptive and unpleasant. His companion, Brother Dandelion, who had only been at the monastery for two years, was physically the opposite of the small man, a huge bear with arms the size of a meaty thigh. Brother Dandelion often had to be restrained in the sparring matches, for once he gained an advantage, he continued to press it to the point of injuring his opponent. In the days of sanity at the monastery, such action might have led to dismissal, but in these dark times, the Father Abbot only chuckled at the man's enthusiasm. Markwart had many times dismissed Jojonah's complaints about Brother Dandelion, assuring Jojonah they would find a fitting place for the savage man.

Brother Jojonah often wondered how Dandelion, or Youseff, for that matter, had even passed the grueling process of elimination to get into the monastery. Every class was whittled down from one or two thousand to twenty-five, and it seemed obvious to Jojonah that there had to be many among those other hundreds more fitting in temperament, intelligence, and piety.

But both these young monks had been sponsored by the Father Abbot himself. "The son of a dear friend," Markwart had said of Dandelion. Master Jojonah knew better. Brother Dandelion had been brought in for his unparalleled physical prowess and for no other reason. He was Markwart's replacement for Quintall, one of the personal bodyguards surrounding the Father Abbot.

As for Youseff, Markwart had explained that Youmaneff, with the loss of Avelyn, was not represented at all in St.-Mere-Abelle, an oversight that had to be corrected if the abbey meant to retain tight control over the small town.

Master Jojonah could only shake his head and sigh; it was all moving beyond his control.

The caravan was put up in the courtyard, with all the monks shown to their quarters, conveniently separated from the brothers of St. Precious. Master Jojonah found himself in a quiet room in a far corner of the great structure, removed from all the others of his troupe, particularly Brother Braumin, who was all the way to the other side of the abbey. The closest to Jojonah was Francis—to keep an eye on him, the master knew.

Still, that very night, Jojonah managed to slip away, meeting quietly with Brother Braumin on the triforium, a decorated ledge twenty feet above the floor of the abbey's great chapel.

"I suspect he is in the lower dungeons," Master Jojonah explained, running his hands over the details of a statue of Brother Allabarnet, whom the monks here called Brother Appleseed. Jojonah could feel the love that had gone into this artwork, and that, he subconsciously understood, was the true work of God.

"In chains, no doubt," agreed Brother Braumin. "A great sin rests on the shoulders of the Father Abbot if his treatment of the heroic centaur is ill."

Master Jojonah quieted the man with a waving hand. They could not afford to be caught speaking against the Father Abbot, no matter how great their ire.

"Have you inquired?" Brother Braumin asked.

"The Father Abbot tells me little now," Jojonah replied. "He knows where lies my heart, though my actions do not overtly oppose him. I am scheduled to meet with him in the morning, at first light."

"To speak of Bradwarden?"

Jojonah shook his head. "I doubt that subject will be breached," he explained. "We are to talk of my departure, I believe, for the Father Abbot has hinted that I will move on ahead of the caravan."

Brother Braumin caught the note of dread in Master Jojonah's voice, and his thoughts went immediately to Markwart's dangerous lackeys. Might the Father Abbot have Jojonah killed on the road? The thought assaulted Braumin's sensibilities, seeming so utterly ridiculous. But try as he might, he could not dismiss it. Nor did he speak it aloud, for it was obvious to him that Jojonah was aware of the situation.

"What do you wish of me?" asked Brother Braumin.

Master Jojonah chuckled and held up his hands in defeat. "Stay the course, my friend," he replied. "Keep true in your heart. There seems little else before us. I do not agree with the direction of our Order, but the Father Abbot does not stand alone. Indeed, those who follow the present course far outnumber those of us who believe the Church has strayed."

"Our numbers will grow," Brother Braumin said determinedly, and in light of the vision he had found at the top of blasted Mount Aida, he truly believed the words. That sight, Avelyn's arm and hand protruding from the blasted rock, had tied together all the words for Braumin, all the stories of Avelyn and the hints that the current Church was off course. In viewing Avelyn's grave, he knew the direction of his life, and that direction would likely bring him into great conflict with the leaders of the Church—a fight Brother Braumin was ready to wage. He squared his shoulders determinedly as he finished with all confidence, "For our course is the most godly."

Master Jojonah would not disagree with the simple logic of that statement. In the end, good and truth would prevail—he had to believe that, for it was the most basic tenet of his faith. How many centuries might it take to turn the Abellican Church back to its proper course, though, and how much suffering would the present course facilitate?

"Keep true in your heart," he said again to Braumin. "Quietly spread the word, not against the Father Abbot or any others, but in favor of Avelyn and those of like heart and generous spirit."

"With the centaur as prisoner, it may go beyond that," Brother Braumin reasoned. "The Father Abbot might force our hand, to stand against him openly or to forever remain silent."

"There are degrees of silence, brother," Master Jojonah replied. "To your room now, and fear not for me. I am at peace."

Brother Braumin spent a long while staring at this dear man, his mentor, then he bowed low, even moved to Jojonah's hand and kissed it, then turned and left.

Master Jojonah spent another hour and more up on that quiet triforium, looking at the statues of saints past, and at the newest construction, the likeness of Brother Allabarnet of St. Precious, who more than a century before had walked the wide land planting apple trees, that settlers might find abundance. The canonization process for Allabarnet was sponsored by Abbot Dobrinion, who dearly wanted to see it through before he died.

Master Jojonah knew well the tales of kindly Allabarnet, and thought the man truly deserving. But given the current conditions of the Church, those stories of generosity and sacrifice would probably work against him.

Master Jojonah's fears about Bradwarden's condition were all too true, for the centaur had been brought to the lower catacombs of St. Precious, and there, in the dark and damp, was shackled to the wall. Still dazed from his brutal experiences in the collapsed mountain, and thoroughly exhausted from the run south, during which the monks had enacted magic spells upon him to make him run faster, Bradwarden was in little condition to resist physically.

And mentally; Bradwarden was caught exhausted and off his guard when Father Abbot Markwart, hematite in hand, came to him that very first night.

Without a word to Bradwarden, the Father Abbot fell into the power of the soul stone, released his mind from its physical bonds and invaded the thoughts of the centaur.

Bradwarden's eyes went wide when he felt this most personal of intrusions. He struggled against the chains, but they would not yield. He fought back mentally—or at least he tried to, for he had no idea where to even begin.

Markwart, this wretched old human, was there in his mind, probing his memories.

"Tell me of Avelyn," the Father Abbot prompted aloud, and though Bradwarden had no intention of offering any answers, the mere mention of Avelyn conjured images of the man, of the trip to Aida, of Pony and Elbryan, of Belli'mar Juraviel and Tuntun, of Symphony, and of all the others who had fought the monsters about Dundalis.

Only gradually did Bradwarden begin to temper and control his thoughts, and by that time the Father Abbot had learned so very much. Avelyn was dead and the stones gone, but these other two, this Elbryan and Pony, had left the devastation of Aida, or at least had left the tunnel wherein the centaur had been trapped, very much alive. Markwart focused on these two as the inquisition continued, and discovered that they were both from a small Timberland town called Dundalis, but had both lived the bulk of their years outside of Dundalis.

Pony, Jilseponie Ault, had lived in Palmaris.

"Ye're a wretch!" Bradwarden fumed when at long last the mental connection was broken.

"You might have offered the information an easier way," the Father Abbot replied.

"To yerself?" the centaur balked. "Ah, but Avelyn was right about ye, about all o' yer stinkin' Church, now wasn't he?"

"Where did this woman, Jilseponie, live when she was in Palmaris?"

"Ye're calling yerselves men o' God, but no good God'd approve of yer works," Bradwarden went on. "Ye took from me, ye thievin' wretch, and for that I'll see that ye pay."

"And what of these diminutive creatures?" Father Abbot Markwart calmly asked. "Touel'alfar?"

Bradwarden spat at him.

Markwart lifted another stone, a graphite, and slammed the bedraggled centaur against the stone wall with a burst of electricity. "There are easy ways, and there are difficult ways," the Father Abbot said calmly. "I will take whatever path you open for me."

He started for the low, open archway that led to the main area of the catacombs. "You will speak with me again," he threatened. Both Markwart and Bradwarden understood the limitations of that threat. The centaur was strong of will and would not be caught by surprise again, and Markwart would find no easy task in getting into his mind.

But Bradwarden feared that he might have already surrendered too much information about his friends.

"You cannot begin to comprehend the importance of this!" the Father Abbot roared at Abbot Dobrinion the next morning, the two men alone in Dobrinion's study—though it was the Father Abbot who was sitting at Dobrinion's large oak desk.

"Palmaris is a large city," Abbot Dobrinion said calmly, trying to appease the man. Markwart hadn't told him much, just that he needed information on a young woman, perhaps twenty years of age, who went by the name of Pony, or Jilseponie. "I know of no one named Pony—except for one stableboy who earned that as a nickname."

"Jilseponie, then?"

Abbot Dobrinion shrugged helplessly.

"She came from the north," Father Abbot Markwart pressed, though he hadn't wanted to reveal even this much to the potentially dangerous Dobrinion. "An orphan."

That hit a chord with the Abbot. "And can you tell me what she looks like?" he asked, trying hard not to let on that he might know something.

Markwart described the woman, for Bradwarden had unintentionally offered him a very clear picture of her, the thick golden hair, the blue eyes, the thick lips.

"What is it?" Markwart demanded, seeing the recognition flash across Dobrinion's chubby face.

"Nothing, perhaps," the abbot admitted. "There was a girl—Jill, she was called—who came from the north, orphaned in a goblin raid. But that was perhaps a decade ago, perhaps more."

"What happened to her?"

"I married her to Master Connor Bildeborough, nephew of the Baron of Palmaris," Abbot Dobrinion explained. "But it did not consummate and the girl was declared an outlaw for her refusal. She was indentured to the Kingsmen," Dobrinion declared, thinking that might be the end of it, and hoping it would be, for he was not pleased at all by the Father Abbot's actions, nor by the man's desperate and secretive attitude.

The Father Abbot turned away and rubbed a hand across his pointy chin, only then noticing that he had not shaved in many, many days. The woman had been in the army—that, too, fit with the centaur's recollections.

The pieces were falling into place.

Markwart, and not Dobrinion, remained in the abbot's study after their discussion had ended. The next in line to see him was Brother Francis, and the Father Abbot's orders to the monk were simple and to the point: keep everyone, even Abbot Dobrinion, away from the centaur, and keep Brad-warden exhausted. They would meet later that day in the dungeon, to continue the interrogation.

When Francis left, Master Jojonah entered. "We must discuss your treatment of the centaur," he said without even formally greeting his superior.

Father Abbot Markwart snorted. "The centaur is none of your concern," he replied casually.

"It would seem that Bradwarden is a hero," Master Jojonah dared to say. "He, along with Avelyn Desbris, saw to the destruction of the dactyl."

"You have it wrong," the Father Abbot retorted, working hard to keep the anger from his voice. "Avelyn went to the dactyl, that much is true, and Bradwarden and these other two, Elbryan and Pony, accompanied him. But they did not go there to do battle, but rather to form an alliance."

"So the destroyed mountain would indicate," Master Jojonah said sarcastically.

Again Markwart snorted. "They overstepped the bounds of magic and of reason," he declared. "They reached into that crystal amethyst which Avelyn stole from St.-Mere-Abelle, and with it, combined with the hellish powers of the demon dactyl, they destroyed themselves."

Master Jojonah saw the lie for what it was. He knew Avelyn, perhaps better than anyone else at St.-Mere-Abelle, and knew that Avelyn would never have gone over to the side of evil. How he might convey that message over the ranting of the Father Abbot, he did not know.

"I have a mission for you," Markwart said.

"You hinted that I would return to St.-Mere-Abelle ahead of the rest," Master Jojonah replied bluntly.

Markwart was shaking his head before the man finished. "You will leave ahead of us," he explained. "But I doubt that you will see St.-Mere-Abelle before us. No, your course is south, to St. Honce in Ursal."

Master Jojonah was too surprised to even respond.

"You are to meet with Abbot Je'howith to discuss the canonization of Allabarnet of St. Precious," the Father Abbot explained.

Master Jojonah's expression was purely incredulous. Father Abbot Markwart had been the primary opponent of the process; were it not for his protests, Allabarnet would already be named a saint! Why the reversal? the master pondered, and it seemed to him that Markwart was trying to strengthen his ties with Dobrinion, and also to conveniently get him out of the way.

"In these trying times, a new saint might be just what the Church needs to reinvigorate the masses," the Father Abbot went on.

Master Jojonah wanted to ask how any such process could be nearly as important as the very real issues before them, including the continuing war. He wanted to ask why a lesser monk couldn't carry this message to Ursal. He wanted to ask why Markwart was reversing himself on this issue.

But all of those questions ran into the same solid wall, Jojonah realized. Father Abbot Markwart was following his own agenda, one bent on retrieving the stones Avelyn had stolen and discrediting the renegade monk at any costs. As he looked at the man now, it seemed to him that Markwart was spiraling down, down, into depths of blackness, that every word the Father Abbot spoke carried him further from the path of God.

"I will go and pack my belongings," Master Jojonah said.

"Already done," Father Abbot Markwart replied as the man turned to leave. "They await you at the abbey's back door."

"Then I will go and speak with—"

"You will go straightaway to the back door," the Father Abbot said calmly. "All the arrangements have been made, all the supplies secured."

"Magic stones?"

"My friend," Markwart said, standing and moving around the side of the desk, "you will be traveling through civilized lands. You will need no magical assistance."

Master Jojonah felt as though he was at a pivotal moment in his life. To go all the way to Ursal without any magical assistance, and on a mission that could become so very complicated, given the sheer paperwork of the canonization process, could keep him out of St.-Mere-Abelle, where he felt that he was desperately needed, for a year and more. Yet his only recourse would be to challenge Markwart here and now, perhaps to make it a public display, calling the man out concerning his beliefs, demanding proof that Brother Avelyn Desbris had gone to Aida to work with the dactyl demon.

His allies would be few indeed, Master Jojonah realized. Brother Braumin would stand behind him, perhaps even young Dellman. But what of Abbot Dobrinion, and thus the hundred and fifty monks of St. Precious?

No, Markwart had beaten him to that, Jojonah understood. He was leaving to discuss a situation near and dear to the heart of St. Precious, the sainthood of one of their own. Dobrinion wouldn't go against Markwart, not now.

Master Jojonah spent a long time staring at this wrinkled old man, his onetime mentor who had become his nemesis. But he had no answers and no recourse—or perhaps, he feared, it was just a lack of courage. How old he felt at that moment, how beyond his days of action!

He went to the back door of the abbey, then walked, for Markwart had not even secured donkey or cart, down the roads of Palmaris, exiting by the southern gate.

❖ 13 ❖

The New Enemy

L ate in the afternoon of his tenth day with the refugee band, Elbryan sought out Oracle for the first time in more than a week. The passing of the monkish caravan had unnerved him, but so had a new detail that was presented that very morning: Roger Lockless walking back into the refugee camp at the head of fifteen former prisoners of Kos-kosio Begulne. The young man, learning in his scouting that the prisoners had been moved from Caer Tinella to Landsdown, took the opportunity to slip into the less defended town and bring the men out.

Still, despite the powrie leader's error in moving the prisoners to the weaker community, disaster had almost found Roger in the woods, for another Craggoth hound remained with the prisoners and was hot on his trail, and only the arrival of Juraviel had allowed Roger and the fleeing prisoners to get away into safety.

That was a detail Roger was quick to omit when he described the events of the previous night to an excited and thrilled gathering of refugees.

The ranger saw a new problem here, a deeper and potentially more devastating problem, and so he went to his uncle Mather to sort things out.

It is as I feared, Uncle Mather, he began when the image appeared to him in the mirror in the near dark gloom. *The rivalry with Roger Lockless heads toward disaster. Just this morning he came into the camp at the head of fifteen people, prisoners of the powries whom he had freed the previous night. Of course we all rejoiced at their appearance, but in speaking with them afterward, I came to understand just how great a chance Roger had taken, with his life and with theirs, in going after them. For though we all desire to relieve the powries of their every prisoner, there seemed to be no pressing need for such a desperate act at this time. The prisoners were safe enough, by all indications, for the moment at least, and we might have formulated a wider-reaching plan that would have facilitated not only their escape, but the downfall of Kos-kosio Begulne and his evil brethren, as well.*

But I understand what drove Roger into the town last night, and so does

Pony. By his erroneous thinking, he has lost his rank among his people. Where they used to look to him, he sees them looking to me.

The ranger paused and contemplated that meeting when Roger had first returned. He considered the man's bluster, the way Roger puffed out his chest when he spoke, the way he looked, particularly at Pony, when he recounted his daring efforts. "Pony," Elbryan said with a great sigh.

He looked back to the mirror, to the perceived ghostly image within its edges. *Pony,* he repeated. *Roger has taken a fancy to her. Or perhaps he merely views her responses as the greatest indicator of his worth. Pony is my partner, as all know well, and if he can win her approval, then perhaps he believes they all will rank him above me.*

With the realization of Roger's "crush" on Pony, the ranger saw just how dangerous the situation might soon become. Roger, with his obvious talents, could be an incredibly valuable addition to their group, but with his immaturity, he might bring disaster upon them all.

"He and I will fight," Elbryan said quietly, aloud. "I fear it will come to that."

The ranger left the room soon after, to see that night had come in, the fires of the encampment burning brightly not far away. He approached at once, and was accosted by loud voices before he drew near.

"We should strike at them," Tomas Gingerwart, full of fire, argued. "And hard! Drive them from our lands and back to their dark mountain holes."

Elbryan came into the ring of firelight to see most heads nodding agreement with Tomas' assessment. He noted Pony, sitting to the side of Tomas, a distressed look on her face.

All the talk paused then, in deference to the ranger, all eyes turning his way, as if awaiting his judgment. As soon as Elbryan and Tomas locked stares, they both understood that they would be on opposite sides of the debate.

"They are without prisoners," Tomas said. "The time to strike is upon us."

Elbryan paused for a long while, truly sympathizing with the man, remembering his own feelings, that desperate need for revenge when his home of Dundalis had been burned to the ground. "I understand—" he started to say.

"Then put the warriors in line," Tomas growled back at him, a response echoed many times over throughout the group.

"Yet I fear that you underestimate the strength of our enemies," the ranger went on calmly. "How many of us, of our friends, will die in such a raid?"

"Worth it," cried one man, "if Caer Tinella is freed!"

"And Landsdown!" cried another, a woman from that more southern settlement.

"And if they are not?" the ranger calmly asked. "If, as I fear, we are repelled, slaughtered on the field?"

"What then for those who cannot fight?" Pony added, and that simple logic, that reminder of the larger responsibility, defeated many retorts.

Still, the argument went on and on, and ended out of exhaustion and not agreement. Elbryan and his side could claim a minor victory, though, for no battle plans were yet being drawn. They were all excited now, the ranger realized, about the arrival of three new powerful allies, the victory in the forest fight, the safe return of Roger Lockless, and Roger's subsequent stealing the rest of Kos-kosio's prisoners. Now, in the security of these new developments, the folk dared to think of reclaiming their homes and punishing the murderous thieves who had come to Caer Tinella and Landsdown. Hopefully, as things settled down once more, logic would replace emotion.

Pony understood and agreed with the rationale, and so she was quite surprised later on, when she and Elbryan met with Juraviel in a pine grove some distance to the south of the encampment, and the ranger announced, "The time to strike hard at our enemy is upon us."

"You just argued against such a course," the woman retorted.

"Our enemies are wounded and disorganized," Elbryan went on, "and a furious attack upon them now might send them running."

"Might," Juraviel echoed grimly. "And it might cost us many of our warriors."

"Our entire existence is a risk," the ranger replied.

"Perhaps we should consider sending those too infirm to fight to the south, to Palmaris, before we plan an attack on Caer Tinella and Landsdown," the elf reasoned. "We might even find allies in the southern cities."

"We have allies in the southern cities," said Elbryan. "But they are concerned for their own borders, and rightly so. No, if we can hit Kos-kosio Begulne hard now and drive him from the towns—"

"That we might hold them?" the elf put in sarcastically, for the mere thought of their ragtag band holding a defensible position was ludicrous.

Elbryan put his head down and sighed deeply. He knew that Juraviel was playing a vital advocate role here, more to help him see through his formulating ideas and work out the finer points than to discourage him, but talking to the Touel'alfar and their pragmatic, if stilted, way of looking at the world was always a bit discouraging to one who saw the world through human eyes. Juraviel didn't understand the level of frustration in Tomas and the others, didn't understand how dangerous that frustration might soon become.

"If we drive Kos-kosio Begulne and his powries from the two towns," the ranger began slowly, deliberately, "it is possible, even likely, that many of their allies will desert the dangerous powries, perhaps even abandon the war altogether. Neither goblins nor giants have any love for powries—they hate the dwarves at least as much as they hate humans—and it is only the strength of the powrie leader, I believe, that is now binding them into a singular force. And even though giants and goblins have been known to ally in the past, there has never been a great fondness between them, by any reports. Giants have been said to eat goblins on occasion. So let us discredit this powrie leader, this binding force, and see what may transpire."

Now it was Juraviel's turn to sigh. "Always are you looking for the greatest possible advantage," he said quietly, his tone edged with resignation. "Always pushing yourself and those around you to the very limits."

A wounded Elbryan looked at the elf curiously, surprised that Juraviel would criticize him so.

"Of course," the elf went on, perking up and a sly smile widening on his angular face, "that is exactly what the Touel'alfar taught you to do!"

"We are agreed, then?" Elbryan asked anxiously.

"I did not say that," Juraviel replied.

Elbryan gave a frustrated growl. "If we do not hit at them, if we do not take advantage of our advantage—and it will prove a fleeting thing, I believe—then we will likely find ourselves in exactly the same desperate situation we just wriggled our way out of. Kos-kosio Begulne will regroup and reinforce and come back at us, forcing another fight in the forest, and sooner or later one of those battles will turn against us. The powrie leader is outraged, no doubt, by the defeat in the forest and the loss of his prisoners."

"He might even suspect that Nightbird has come to the region," Pony added, drawing curious looks from the elf and the ranger.

"I remember the name, and so do you, if you pause long enough to think about it," Pony explained. "Kos-kosio Begulne remembers us from Dundalis."

Juraviel nodded, recalling the ambush the monsters had once set for Nightbird, destroying a pine vale that the ranger dearly loved to draw him out of the forest. That ambush had been turned back against the monsters, though, like every tack they took against the ranger and his cunning and powerful friends.

"It is even possible that the monkish caravan which Roger spoke of was running from something," Elbryan went on.

"We could use our temporary advantage to slip around the towns and flee to the south," Juraviel reasoned. He did not miss the look, almost one of alarm, that passed between Pony and Elbryan at that notion.

"What else?" the elf asked bluntly.

"Anything that would make the monks, with their powerful magic, flee so, must be a considerable force," Pony put in, but she was far from convincing to the perceptive elf.

"Still more rationale that we should simply flee to the south, as did the monks," Juraviel pressed. He noted again the look between his companions. "What else?" he asked again. "There is something more to the passage of the monks. I know you too well, Nightbird."

Elbryan laughed in concession to that point. "Pony and I cannot remain in the area," he admitted. "Nor would we dare to go south."

"Brother Avelyn's stones," Juraviel said.

"It might be that the monks Roger spoke of were looking for us," said Pony. "Or at least looking for the stones that I hold in my possession. When Brother Justice was searching for Avelyn, he used this stone," she explained fishing a red garnet out of her pouch and holding it up for Juraviel to see. "This stone detects the use of magic, thus Avelyn's conjuring powers led Brother Justice right to him."

"And you feel that your use of magic has put the monks on your trail," Juraviel reasoned.

Pony nodded. "It is possible, and too important for us to take any chances."

"The last act of Brother Avelyn's life was to entrust us with the sacred stones," Elbryan put in determinedly. "We will not fail him in this."

"Then perhaps the three of us should be on our way now," Juraviel said. "Are these stones, then, more important than the refugees we now lead?"

Elbryan looked to Pony, but she had no answers for him. "In the measure of history, they may well be," the ranger said.

A noise from the brush, a gurgling, angry sound, brought all three on their guard. Juraviel moved fast, lifting his bow as he disappeared into the flora, then returning a moment later, a furious Roger Lockless beside him.

"You are naming rocks as more important than the people you pretend to lead!" the young man fumed. As he spoke he moved farther from Juraviel, obviously not comfortable near the diminutive creature.

"You need not fear him," Pony remarked dryly, thinking it ridiculous that Roger would act so skittish around one of the two who had rescued him from Kos-kosio Begulne's cruel grasp. She recognized that the young man's hesitance to embrace Juraviel was wrought of more than fear. "Belli'mar Juraviel, indeed all the Touel'alfar, are allies."

"So I've come to understand your meaning of the word," Roger snapped at her.

Pony started to respond, but Elbryan stepped in front of her. "As I was explaining," he said evenly, staring hard at the young man, "these stones are as vital—"

"More vital, you said," Roger interrupted.

"Do not underestimate their importance!" Elbryan yelled right back in his face. The ranger noted Juraviel's disapproving expression then and calmed himself down. "The stones represent much more than even the great power stored within them," Elbryan went on, his voice controlled and even. "They may well be more important than my life, or Pony's, or yours, or the lives of all the people of our band."

"Those are your foolish thoughts—" Roger started to yell back, but Elbryan cut him short with an upraised hand, a movement so quick and so forceful that the end of the young man's sentence came out as a startled gurgle.

"However," the ranger went on calmly, "having said all of that, and truly believing it, I cannot leave this situation as I have found it. I must get these people to the safety of the southland, or at least make certain that the road there is clear ahead of them."

"You name yourself as leader," Roger accused.

"Thus you wish to strike, and strike hard, against Kos-kosio Begulne," Juraviel reasoned, ignoring the petty turn of Roger's argument. "If we hit them hard in the two towns and scatter them to the forest, the whole of this band can flee south in relative safety, without Nightbird guiding them."

"For there, Nightbird would not be wise to go," said Pony. "And yet," she added, looking squarely at her lover, "you just argued against that very course."

"I did," Elbryan agreed. "And I still do argue against a fight that will send all of the warriors, even the majority of them, against the towns."

Pony started to ask what he might be talking about, but then she caught on. Elbryan had just gone into Caer Tinella to rescue Roger, and so now he was thinking of going back, with just his most powerful friends about him, and tilting the balance of power.

Juraviel, also catching on, nodded. "I will go into Caer Tinella this night and gather information," he agreed.

"I can go," said Roger.

"Juraviel is better suited to the task," Elbryan was quick to respond.

"Have you forgotten that I was in Caer Tinella just two nights ago?" Roger protested. "That I returned with the prisoners?"

The other three watched him closely, noting how he emphasized that personal pronoun.

"If the prisoners were still in there, you could not even think of attacking the town!" Roger finished.

Elbryan nodded, conceding the point. Roger's action had indeed set the stage for this possible strike. But still, especially after speaking with the freed prisoners and hearing of their desperate run through the dark forest, Elbryan remained convinced that Belli'mar Juraviel was better suited for the task. Juraviel had told him that one hound, at least, might still be alive, and if that creature had come forth on the trail, none of them, not Roger nor the prisoners, would have likely returned. "Juraviel is the choice," the ranger said calmly.

Pony noted the young man's expression and realized that Elbryan had just further compromised Roger's standing and hurt his inflated pride.

"Can you fly from treetop to treetop when the hounds sniff your trail?" Elbryan asked bluntly before Roger could begin to protest.

Roger chewed his bottom lip; both Elbryan and Pony thought he would strike out at the ranger. He only stamped his foot, though, and turned to leave.

"Stop!" Pony cried, surprising all three. She was coming to understand Roger, and while she did not dislike him, she recognized that he was young and too full of pride and self-importance for his own good.

Roger spun about, eyes wide and blazing with anger.

Pony took out a gemstone, carefully concealing it in her hand so he could not see it clearly, and walked up before him. "What you have overheard is private," she explained.

"Now you deign to order me?" Roger asked incredulously. "Are you my queen, then? Should I kneel?"

"You should be wise enough, even at your age and with your lack of experience, to recognize friend from enemy," Pony scolded. She wanted to go on, laying bare to Roger his shortcomings concerning their relationship, but she realized that such lessons must be truly learned, and not explained, to be fully appreciated. "Yet I see that you cannot, that for some reason you have decided that we are not your friends. So be it."

The woman reached into another pouch, and Roger backed off a step. Not far enough, though, for Pony's hand came out and up fast, and with a yellow-hued weed she marked an X on Roger's forehead. Then she lifted her hand with the gem before him and spoke a series of phrases that sounded very much like some ancient incantation.

"What have you done to me?" Roger demanded, nearly falling over as he continued his retreat.

"I have done nothing to you unless you betray us," Pony replied calmly.

Roger's face screwed up with confusion. "I owe you nothing," he said.

"As I owe you nothing," Pony replied sternly. "Thus I have just evened our relationship once again. In your eavesdropping, you heard things which do not concern you, and as such, it is your responsibility to forget them."

Roger had no answer, other than to shake his head.

"Or to remain silent on the issue, at the very least," Pony went on. "However, if you cannot, you will find a most unpleasant consequence."

"What are you talking about?" Roger asked, and when Pony smiled wickedly, the young man looked past her to speak to Elbryan. "What has she done to me?" he demanded.

Elbryan honestly didn't know, and so his shrug was sincere.

"Tell me!" Roger yelled in Pony's face.

Elbryan closed his eyes as Roger started to reach up for Pony, fully expecting that his love would knock the foolish little man out cold. Roger, though, did not carry through with the movement, and simply stood before Pony, fists clenched in frustration.

"I have put a curse on you," Pony said quietly. "But a curse with a contingency."

"What do you mean?" he asked, his angry tone showing a hint of fear.

"I mean that as long as you do the right thing and remain silent about that which you should not know, nothing ill will befall you," the woman calmly explained. Her expression changed abruptly, grew dark and ominous, and she closed the distance between herself and Roger and rose up tall and terrible on her toes, towering over the small man. "Betray us," she warned in a voice so grave that it raised the hairs on the back of Elbryan's neck, and sent shivers through Roger's body, "and the magic I have put on you will melt the brains in your head so that they will flow out of your ears."

Roger's eyes widened. He knew little of magic, but those displays he had seen were certainly impressive enough for him to believe that the woman was capable of carrying out her threat. He stumbled backward, nearly fell over, turned and ran away.

"Pony!" Elbryan scolded. "How could you do such—"

"I did nothing except mark his forehead with dandelion," the woman replied. "I've done as much to your chin in the buttercup game we played as children."

"Then—" Elbryan stopped and chuckled, somewhat surprised by his companion.

"Was that really necessary?" Belli'mar Juraviel asked dryly.

Pony's expression was dead serious as she nodded in response. "He would have betrayed us to the others," she explained. "And I do not wish it to become public knowledge that we two are outlaws in the eyes of the Abellican Church."

"And is our secret so terrible?" Elbryan put in. "I learned long ago to trust these people."

"Like Tol Yuganick?" Pony retorted, referring to a man who had betrayed her and Elbryan and all the folk of Dundalis before the journey to Aida.

Elbryan had no answer to that, but Pony, recognizing that her cynicism had stung her lover, continued. "I, too, trust Belster and Tomas and all the others," she admitted. "But Roger would have told the story in a way to bolster himself, and that, I fear, might have put us in an unfavorable light. Who knows what tales might then be spun when the folk are safely in Palmaris?"

Elbryan, who was also beginning to understand Roger Lockless, couldn't disagree with that.

"You did well," Juraviel decided. "The time is too critical for us to take such a chance. Young Roger may have had difficulty recognizing the right course, but I think that you painted for him a fairly clear signpost."

Elbryan snorted. "And here I was for all my life believing that morality was somehow tied to conscience."

"And so it is," Pony replied.

"Ideally," Juraviel added. "But do not underestimate the power of fear. Your own Church has used the threat of an afterlife in fiery brimstone to keep its congregation in line for more than a thousand years."

"Not my Church," Elbryan replied. "Not the Church that Avelyn espoused."

"No, the Church that pursued the renegade monk, as much to silence his radical ideals as to retrieve the gemstones, do not doubt," Juraviel replied without hesitation.

Elbryan looked to Pony, to find her nodding her assent with the elf's every word. He gave a chuckle, unable to argue the point. "The Church that pursues Pony and me," he remarked.

"The monks that came through were heading south—and quickly, so Roger said," Pony put in. "I have used the garnet, but can detect no magic in the area, so I assume that Roger's guess about their speed was correct."

"I hope that they continued right past Palmaris," Elbryan added. "But in any case, our time here is limited. I hope to make the most of it."

"Caer Tinella and Landsdown," Belli'mar Juraviel said.

Elbryan's face was dead serious, even grim, as he nodded and gave his reply. "We will meet with you back here at dusk, perhaps to attack before the next dawn."

"As you wish, my friend," the elf said. "I am off to scout out the towns, then. Prepare the attack—and do reconcile, a bit at least, with Roger Lockless. He has done great things for these people, to hear Belster O'Comely speak, and I would guess that he has great things ahead of him, if he does not let his pride hinder him."

"We will take care of Roger," Pony answered.

"Paint the signpost clearly," Juraviel said with a laugh and a snap of his fingers, and then he was gone, disappearing into the underbrush so completely that Pony blinked and rubbed her eyes, wondering if they had deceived her. Elbryan, though, more accustomed to the Touel'alfar, and more knowledgeable in the ways of the forest, was not surprised.

"It is him," Kos-kosio Begulne insisted. "I'm knowin' 'is ways, the bastard!"

Maiyer Dek pondered the words for a long time, as he always did when speaking of anything even remotely important. The huge fomorian was quite impressive for one of his race, both physically and mentally. Though not as sharp-witted as his powrie peer, not even as wise as Gothra, who had ruled the goblins, Maiyer Dek understood his shortcomings and so took his time, examining everything slowly and deliberately.

The giant's silence did little for the anxious Kos-kosio Begulne's already foul mood. The powrie paced the floor of the great barn, picking his nose with one hand, the other slapping repeatedly against his hip.

"There might be other humans like Nightbird," the giant offered.

Kos-kosio Begulne snorted at the notion. "If that's so, then we'd've been kicked all the way back to Aida by this time!"

"One other, then," the giant replied.

"I'm hopin' not," the powrie answered. "And I'm thinkin' not. This one be him. I can smell the bastard. It's Nightbird come a'calling, don't ye doubt. So are ye to give me yer prisoners, or aren't ye?"

Again Maiyer Dek went into a long, drawn-out consideration. He and the other three giants who had accompanied him had just returned from the southland, where they had waged a huge battle against the Kingsmen, just to the west of Palmaris. Many giants had died in the fight, and many more humans, and Maiyer Dek and his surviving cohorts had taken a host of men prisoner. "Traveling foodstuffs," the giant leader called them, and indeed, ten of the two-score men they had taken were eaten by the time the cruel fomorians got to Caer Tinella. Now Kos-kosio Begulne wanted the remaining thirty as bait for the Nightbird, and in truth, Maiyer Dek wasn't overly fond of human flesh. But still, the giant remembered vividly the disastrous battle in the pine vale the last time he and his fellow leaders had baited this man called Nightbird. Did Kos-kosio Begulne really want to bring him in?

"Ye got to give 'em to me," Kos-kosio Begulne said suddenly. "We got to settle with Nightbird now, afore half the force leaves us. Already the goblins're rumbling about going home, and me own folks long for the Weathered Isles."

"So go, all of us," replied the giant, who had never been too keen on coming south to Honce-the-Bear in the first place. Before the dactyl had awakened, Maiyer Dek had enjoyed a comfortable existence in the mountains north of the Barbacan, with a tribe of four-score giants—including twenty females for his whims—and plenty of goblins about for good hunting and better eating.

"Not yet," the powrie retorted sharply. "Not until the damned Nightbird's paid for our troubles."

"You never even liked Ulg Tik'narn," the giant said without even his customary pause.

"Not the point!" Kos-kosio Begulne shot back. "He was a powrie leader, and a good one! Nightbird killed 'im, so I'm meaning to kill Nightbird."

"Then we go?"

"Then we go," the powrie agreed. "And once we're past the human lands, me and me folk'll not protect the goblin scum from yer belly."

That was all Maiyer Dek needed to hear.

By the time Juraviel returned from the towns, Elbryan and Pony had the folk in full agreement with delaying the attack—a difficult proposition given the success of the fight in the woods and the return of Roger and the other prisoners. All of the folk were eager to be done with this adventure, to be sitting in a comfortable common room exaggerating their fireside tales, and if going through Caer Tinella and Landsdown meant they might soon be in the safety of Palmaris, then they were more than ready for the fight.

Pony was still with them, working out details should the attack on Caer Tinella or Landsdown commence, when Elbryan returned to the pine grove.

As soon as the ranger saw Juraviel come down from the tree, he knew something was wrong.

"They have fortified," the ranger reasoned.

"Indeed," Juraviel answered with a nod of his head. "There are three new scout towers about the edge of the town, north, southwest, and southeast, and an impromptu barricade has been erected about the whole of the place, a barrier of barrels, torn walls, anything they could find. It seems solid enough, standing near to the height of a man, but not too thick."

"Enough to slow down a charge," the ranger said.

"Perhaps a bit," Juraviel admitted, though he was not too concerned or impressed with the fortification. "Still, with the new ally that has arrived, I doubt that they feel the need to fortify."

"Another group of powries?" Elbryan asked.

"Giants," Juraviel replied. "Including the biggest and ugliest of those big and ugly brutes I have ever seen. Maiyer Dek, he is called, and even the powries, even Kos-kosio Begulne himself, gives him great respect. His armor is special, I fear, perhaps even magical, for it seems almost to have an inner fire."

Elbryan nodded; he had battled with giants similarly outfitted—and he remembered the name of Maiyer Dek from the Timberlands. The armor was earth magic, forged by the demon dactyl for its elite soldiers.

"We cannot allow these people to go against Caer Tinella," the elf went on. "We might skirt the town in the dark of night, or we might hit at Landsdown, whose garrison does not seem as formidable. But to send these people, untrained warriors all, against giants, particularly this new monstrosity, would be folly. Even your own plans to do battle pose a great risk."

Elbryan had no argument against the simple logic. He had fought enough giants to understand the possibility for complete catastrophe. "If we flee around the towns, they will likely catch our trail," he reasoned. "We would never get all the way to Palmaris ahead of them."

"A wider berth, then?" the elf asked, but he suspected that the ranger wouldn't be easy to convince.

"We can send them," Elbryan replied tentatively.

"But you still wish to go to the town and wage your fight," Juraviel reasoned.

"If this giant, Maiyer Dek, is as powerful and as revered as you indicate, perhaps he and I should speak," the ranger explained.

"Speak?" Juraviel echoed doubtfully.

"With weapons," Elbryan clarified. "How great a blow do you suppose it will prove to our enemies if Maiyer Dek and Kos-kosio Begulne are both slain?"

"Great indeed," the elf admitted. "I do not know what holds the giants and goblins together with each other and even more so with the powries, if not the strong leadership of those two. But still, think wisely, my friend. It will be no easy task to even get to the giant and powrie leaders, and even if you can, even if you somehow find a way to fight them without their minions swarming over you, you may find yourself overmatched. Turn your own question about: What will the refugees do without Nightbird to lead them?"

"They did well enough without Nightbird to lead them until very recently," the ranger reminded. "And they will have Juraviel."

"Whose business this is not!"

"Who chose to come to the aid of the humans," Elbryan replied with a wry grin.

"Who chose to follow his protégé, Nightbird, to make sure the young man did not act foolishly," the elf corrected, smiling widely; and Elbryan knew from that smile that he had Juraviel on his side. "I have too many years invested in your training—and you carry an elven sword and a bow made by my own father—to let you get yourself killed."

"Some call it foolish, others daring," the ranger said.

"Or perhaps they are one and the same," Juraviel put in.

Elbryan clapped the elf on the shoulder, and both were still laughing when Pony moved through the pine grove to join them.

"The news from the towns is good, then?" she reasoned.

"No," both Elbryan and Juraviel said in unison.

Pony rocked back on her heels, caught by surprise, given their jovial attitudes.

"We were just discussing the folly of your Elbryan's intentions," Juraviel explained. "To walk into the middle of an enemy encampment and slay both their leaders, though one is a powrie, as tough and stubborn a creature as ever lived, and the other a huge and mighty giant."

"And you find this amusing?" Pony asked Elbryan.

"Of course."

The woman nodded, and sincerely wondered if the stress of their existence was finally getting to her companion.

"I'll not walk right in," the ranger corrected, staring hard at the elf. "I will sneak, of course, quiet as a shadow, uninvited as death."

"And dead as a piece of wood," Juraviel finished, and both started laughing again.

Pony, who understood that there was a measure of truth beneath their levity, was not amused. "Enough foolishness," she scolded. "You have a hundred warriors pacing anxiously, wondering if they will die this night, awaiting your decree."

"And my decree—which I will insist upon—is that they stand down," Elbryan said, his tone serious.

"I am not certain they will listen," Pony admitted, for in the time the ranger had been away, the talk had again reached a fever pitch, in favor of driving the monsters far away.

"We cannot attack the towns," the ranger explained, "for the powries have found more giant allies, including one attired in the earth magic armor of the dactyl."

Pony sighed deeply and hoped that the folk would listen. She remembered that armor from the fight at the Barbacan, and knew that any of the refugees who came against this new ally would fall quickly. She looked to Elbryan and recognized the dangerous expression on his face.

"We need only explain that they must wait another day or two for the fight, until we can discern the power of our new enemies," Elbryan reasoned.

"But you still plan to go in, and fight, this very night," Pony stated.

"I wish to find a way to destroy this giant, and Kos-kosio Begulne," Elbryan admitted. "It would be a great blow to our enemies, and might cause enough confusion for us to scatter the remaining monsters and get these people to Palmaris."

"Then let us discern how we might accomplish this task," Pony said calmly, moving before Juraviel and bending low. She took up a stick, handed it to the elf, and cleared away the pine needles from the ground before her. "A map, to start," she instructed.

Juraviel looked to Elbryan, both surprised that Pony, usually more conservative than the ranger, had so easily agreed, given the new monsters in town. And Juraviel wondered, too, if this turn of events had changed Elbryan's thinking. Did he still mean to include his love on so dangerous a mission?

The ranger nodded, his expression grim, in answer to that unspoken question. He and Pony had been through too much together for him to even think of excluding her from this important fight. While he had intended to keep Juraviel out of it—an elf's diminutive weapons were not much use against a giant, after all—he had planned all along to execute the attack with Pony beside him.

The daylight was fast fading by that time, so Pony took out her diamond and brought forth a minor globe of light. In a short while Juraviel had the town of Caer Tinella mapped out.

"I cannot be certain where Kos-kosio Begulne will be," the elf explained. "But there are only three buildings high enough to hold a giant." He tapped each in turn on the map. "Barns," he explained. "And this one is the most likely for the giant leader." His pointer settled on the marker for a large structure near the center of town.

"They had no organized defense, as far as I could tell," the elf went on. "Other than the barricades and a few posted sentries."

"Powries are usually prepared," Pony said. "More likely, their defenses are well-concealed."

"But this group has had little trouble of late," Juraviel replied.

"Except for the fight in the forest," said Elbryan.

"And the theft of prisoners," Pony added.

"But no real attacks against the town," the elf explained. "And I doubt they'll expect one, with the fomorian giants so visible to any who think to attack."

"But with Roger, who has shown his ability to get into town at will, gone from their grasp, the ring about the leaders, particularly Kos-kosio Begulne, might be tight," Pony reasoned.

"And that is precisely where I intend to go," Elbryan added.

"No easy task," Juraviel said.

"It never is," the ranger replied.

"But you intend to go anyway," the elf remarked.

Elbryan looked to Pony. "This very night," he explained. "I will seek out Belster and Tomas Gingerwart first and tell them of our plans, and of what they should do, depending on whether Pony and I succeed or not."

"And my role?" the elf asked.

"You will serve as my liaison to Belster," Elbryan explained. "You will learn quickly the outcome of the fight, no doubt, and the sooner Belster is informed, the better he will be able to react."

Juraviel spent a long while staring hard at Elbryan, at the man who had earned the title of Nightbird from the Touel'alfar. The elf felt that doubting Tuntun was with him then, admitting wholeheartedly that she had been wrong in her initial assessment of Elbryan Wyndon, the "blood of Mather," as she had so often sarcastically referred to him. Tuntun had never thought that Elbryan would make the grade as a ranger, had thought him stupid and uncoordinated. She had learned differently, though, so much so that she willingly gave her life to save the young man—and elves were not often altruistic toward humans! And if she were here now, Juraviel knew, to witness the calm determination and sincere sense of duty with which Elbryan was approaching this incredibly dangerous fight, she might well call him "blood of Mather" once again, but this time with sincere affection.

"Your role in this battle will be with the stones alone," Elbryan said to Pony as they made their slow way toward Caer Tinella. Belster and Tomas had agreed that the battle should be delayed while more information was gathered, but did not know that the ranger meant to wage it on his own.

Pony eyed him skeptically. "I have been training hard," she replied. "And well."

"But you do not trust me to fight with sword?"

Elbryan was shaking his head before she finished. "You are between fighting styles," he explained. "Your head tells you the next proper move, but your body is still trained in the other style. Will you lunge or slash? And in the moment it takes you to decide, an enemy weapon will find you."

Pony bit her lip, trying to find some logical response. She could do the sword-dance quite well now, but that was in slower motion than she would find in a real fight. At the end of every session, when Elbryan speeded up the process, she could not keep up, caught, as he had said, between her thoughts and her muscle memory.

"Soon enough," Elbryan promised her. "Until then, you remain most effective with the stones alone."

Pony didn't argue.

The pair came upon Juraviel on a hillock overlooking Caer Tinella from the northeast, the high vantage point affording them a view of all the town. It appeared remarkably as Juraviel had described it, the new barricades wrapping all the central structures, but all three found their gazes locked to a huge bonfire burning in the southeastern corner, all the way to the other side.

"I will investigate it," the elf volunteered.

Elbryan nodded and looked to Pony. "Find them with the soul stone," he said to her, and then to Juraviel added, "If Kos-kosio Begulne and Maiyer Dek are in the barn, then that is where Pony and I will go. You watch our progress into the town, then return here to gather Symphony, for I suspect that I'll leave the horse behind. And then you need only wait and watch."

"You wait," Juraviel corrected, his tone showing that he did not intend to be dissuaded. "There is nothing ordinary about that bonfire; you would do well to let me discern its meaning before you go into the town."

"We may only get one chance at these two," Pony said to Elbryan, nodding her agreement with Juraviel's assessment. "Let us make certain that the time is right."

"Be quick, then," anxious Elbryan said to them both.

Before Juraviel could respond, the quiet of night was stolen by a call from the town.

"Another to the flames!" came the thunderous roar, a giant's voice. "Are you watching, Nightbird? Do you see the men dying because of you?"

All three peered into the distance, focusing on the flames. They saw the silhouettes of three forms, two powries and a man, they seemed, and watched in horror as the man was thrown onto the burning pyre.

His agonized screams rent the air.

Elbryan let out an angry growl, reached around and pulled Pony down from the horse and in the same fluid movement had his bow in hand.

"No, ranger!" Juraviel said to him. "That is exactly what they want!"

"What they think they want," the ranger retorted. "Lead me with your arrows, straight for the wall!" He drove his heels hard into Symphony's sides and the great stallion leaped away, thundering down the hillock, charging for the town. Juraviel sped off in pursuit, half running, half flying, and Pony changed gemstones, putting her hematite away.

Nightbird came out of the cover of the trees in full gallop, crossing the small field before the impromptu wall, Hawkwing up and ready. His first arrow took an unsuspecting goblin in the side of the head, throwing the creature right over. His second got another goblin in the chest just as it lifted its arm to throw a spear.

But his element of surprise was gone, and now the wall teemed with enemies, goblins and powries. Roaring, too angry and too desperate to consider a different course, the ranger bent low over Symphony's neck, spurring the great horse on.

Then both horse and rider stumbled, Symphony nearly going down as a blast of lightning thundered right beside them, smashing into the barricade, splintering wood, throwing goblins and powries all about.

The ranger and his steed recovered quickly, with little momentum lost. Back in full stride, churning the turf, the powerful stallion leaped the six-foot barrier, soaring over the dead and stunned monsters, hitting the ground in a dead run. Arrows buzzed past the ranger as he cut the horse in a tight turn, charging between two buildings. He cut another fast corner, seeing still more enemies rising before him. Down an alley, he broke out into the town square, but turned on his heel again, for the place was swarming with powries, and sped down yet another alleyway.

As he neared one low roof, Nightbird slung Hawkwing over his shoulder, drew out Tempest, and climbed to a standing position, legs far apart and bent for balance. Through the turquoise stone set in the horse's chest, he communicated with Symphony, bidding the horse to keep a steady run and move in close to the building on their right-hand side.

A goblin was just rising as Nightbird came in. Tempest's slash nearly decapitated it, and the ranger was quick to withdraw the sword, yanking it free, then stabbing back out, nailing a second goblin under the chin.

Nightbird dropped back to a sitting position, slid Tempest between thigh and saddle and readied his bow once more, firing as he rode. A powrie leaped out in his path, another on the roof to the left. Nightbird focused on the higher target, driving an arrow into its chest even as it launched a spear his way. Symphony took care of the powrie on the ground, running the dwarf down, nearly stumbling, but holding strong.

Nightbird managed to get his bow across to partially deflect the well-aimed spear, and that defensive movement surely saved his life, though the spear struck home anyway, a grazing hit across the shoulder. It hooked his shirt as the fabric tore away, and with a growl Nightbird reached around and pulled it free, thinking to drop it.

He tucked it under his arm instead, lancelike, as he bore down on an open doorway, a powrie charging out to meet him. Up came the powrie's shield, but not quick enough, and the spear tip glided over the top, catching the screaming dwarf right in the mouth, bashing in its teeth, then sinking deeper, right out the back of the head and into the wood of the doorjamb.

Nightbird let go of the weapon and had not even the time to look back and regard his work.

The powrie, stuck in a standing position, twitched repeatedly as it died.

Nightbird cut a fast corner, then another, angling for the northeastern edge of town. Around yet another bend, he found himself in trouble, for there, blocking the path before him, stood a pair of giants, behemoths no single arrow would fell and that Symphony could not hope to run down.

By the time Juraviel got to the battered barricade, it was clear of monsters, for those few that had survived the ranger's charge and Pony's blast were scattered to the streets of Caer Tinella, chasing Symphony's swift and elusive run. A flutter of his wings sent Juraviel over the wall, to the roof of one of the buildings it connected at this juncture. Across the way stood a goblin, leaping up and down and shouting directions to its comrades on the ground as it spotted the rushing rider.

Juraviel crept up to within five paces, bow in hand. He went down to one knee to better angle the shot, and his arrow caught the goblin right under the base of its skull, driving upward. The creature flipped from the edge of the roof and landed hard on its back, quite dead, in the street.

A movement from behind sent the elf in a spin, another arrow ready to fly. He held the shot, and luckily so, for the form scrambling over the edge of the roof was not that of a goblin or powrie, but of a man, slight of build and climbing nimbly.

"What are you doing here?" the elf whispered as Roger came up to crouch beside him.

"A question I could also be asking you," the young man answered. His gaze focused on the line of prisoners. "There must be thirty of them," he said, and he started at once for the southeastern corner of the roof.

Juraviel let him go and did not follow. The more angles from which they struck out at the monsters, the more confusion they would likely cause, and that confusion might be the only thing that would allow foolish Nightbird to get out of this place alive!

Fluttering wings brought the elf silently to another rooftop, farther into the town and more to the north, and from there he found many opportunities. Off went his arrows, one, two, three, hitting powrie and giant, and yet another powrie on the other side, killing none—though his last arrow had hurt the dwarf badly—but bringing screams of outrage and taking the focus, for these nearby groups at least, off his friend. Monsters closed on the building from every direction.

Juraviel went straight up, into the darkness of night, angling his flight slightly so he landed on yet another building. Then he ran to the far edge of that roof, put an arrow into an unsuspecting goblin for good measure, then fluttered off to yet another building, the large central barn.

In his wake he left monsters screaming and howling, and no longer believing that the ranger had come into the town alone.

Symphony's hooves sent dirt flying wide as the horse angled hard, the ranger trying to pass the giants on the right side. The closest behemoth raised its club, but the ranger was quicker, sliding Tempest back in hand and slashing across, catching the giant's uplifted arm right below the elbow.

The giant roared in pain and could not finish the attack, and so Nightbird and his horse rushed past and seemed to break clear.

But then yet another giant stepped out to block the path, and the trail was narrower up ahead, giving the ranger nowhere to run. He dropped Tempest across his lap and went back to Hawkwing, fitting an arrow and leveling the bow in the blink of an eye.

He would only get one shot.

He had to be perfect.

The arrow, fired from barely fifteen feet away, got the giant right in the eye, and how it howled! It clutched at its face and spun halfway about, shrieking and screaming.

"Run on!" Nightbird commanded the horse. Out flashed Tempest; the ranger tightened his legs about the powerful stallion, and Symphony, understanding Nightbird's commands, understanding the desperation of the situation, willingly obliged and never slowed, hitting the behemoth in full gallop.

The ranger got a strike in at the same moment, his sword slashing hard at the side of the tumbling giant's neck. Down the brute went, and Symphony, stunned, held his balance, Nightbird tugging hard to turn the horse about as the other two came in.

"Keep this one out of the fight," the ranger bade Symphony, and then he tossed his sword to the ground and took up his bow, diving into a roll from the horse's back, fitting an arrow as he went and letting fly as he came rolling around back to his feet. The missile drove deep into a giant shoulder, but the behemoth seemed hardly to notice it.

The ranger conjured images of the poor prisoners on the other side of the town, men being roasted alive on the powrie bonfires, and from those scenes he drew rage, and from his rage he drew strength. He reached out

for Tempest, and the magical blade, hearing his silent call, flew to his hand
and flared with inner power. Nightbird, too focused to even notice the
spectacle of his sword, charged straight ahead.

His attack surprised the giants, enough for the ranger to slide in on one
knee, ducking beneath the sidelong swipe of one brute. Out flashed his
sword, smacking off the behemoth's kneecap, and as the creature instinctively lifted its leg to grab at the wound, the ranger ran forward, right under
the upraised heavy boot, diving past the other leg, out of reach of the
second behemoth as it came around the first for a swing.

Nightbird pivoted and struck once and then again, scoring two stabbing
hits on the giant's buttocks. The brute spun and swung wildly, holding its
club in one hand, its free hand alternately holding its arrow-stuck shoulder,
its slashed knee, its stabbed butt.

The club came nowhere near to hitting the nimble ranger. He dropped
into a squatting position, letting it soar over his head, then came up hard,
chasing the hand, striking out and hitting again, right on the giant's wrist.

The behemoth howled; the club went flying free.

But the move had put Nightbird in a sorry position with the second
giant, and he could not completely avoid the brute's swinging club. It
clipped him on the shoulder and sent him flying, tumbling right over in
the air, coming down head first and tumbling again, and then again after
that as he hit the ground in a desperate attempt to absorb some of the
shock.

He came around in a roll, studying his foe. Truly this was the ugliest
giant he had ever seen, with one lip torn away and a garish tattoo of a goblin
ripped in half covering its forehead. One ear was also missing and the other
sported a large gold earcap. Grinning wickedly, the brute looked to its
stung companion, nodding as the behemoth indicated that it was still ready
for the fight. The ugly brute slowly stalked in.

Even for the elven-trained ranger, two giants were more than a match.

But at least it would remain only two, Nightbird noted, glancing at Symphony. The giant on the ground was trying to rise, but the horse reared
repeatedly over its head, front hooves pounding away.

The giant, blind in one eye, reached out desperately, then tried to rise
again as Symphony spun about.

The horse was only lining the brute up for a kick, though, and the giant
wasn't halfway to standing when Symphony lashed out with both rear legs,
connecting solidly on the giant's face and laying it out straight.

Then the horse came right over the head again, front legs tapping a
steady beat.

Nightbird didn't see the last move, too concerned with scrambling away
from the closest giant's sudden rain of blows, overhand chops that could
not be ducked. The ground shook with each tremendous impact.

The other giant retrieved its club, but seemed in no hurry to join its companion.

Still, Nightbird heard the pursuit closing from all around and knew he was running out of time.

Pony had not been idle. After her lightning blast rocked the barricade, clearing the way for Elbryan and then Juraviel—and then, though she hadn't known it, for Roger Lockless—the woman ran down the slope, angling to the north. She tried to keep track of the ranger's movements within the town, following the sound of shouting monsters and the ringing silverel as Tempest did its work, and she was fairly certain that her love was also making his way around the northern edge.

Pony's run became a series of short bursts, moving from cover to cover, looking back toward the town, trying to gain some information. She saw the heads of two giants, saw one lurch suddenly and cry out in pain, and knew that Nightbird had come upon them. When a third giant's head and shoulders appeared, towering above the low buildings, Pony realized that her love was in serious trouble.

The woman fumbled about her pouch of stones, trying to find one that might help. The ruby was no good, for she hadn't the time to go to Elbryan's side. She might use the graphite to skim a lightning bolt off the rooftops, but that, she feared, might also sting her love, especially if he was in close battle.

"Malachite," the woman decided, pulling forth the green, ringed stone. She would levitate one of the brutes, float him up high into the air, and make the odds a bit more even.

As she pulled out the stone, though, she saw another, the lodestone, and thought it even more clever.

Pony lifted her hand and took aim, focusing her vision through the magic of the gem, seeking out a metallic target at which she could launch her missile.

But there seemed to be nothing; the giants wore no armor and were wielding wooden clubs!

Pony growled and looked deeper, and still found nothing. She was about to change back to the malachite—her heart soared when she saw another giant go down—when at last she found a slight pull coming from the side of the remaining giant's head, from the area near its ear.

Nightbird leaped ahead and to the side, avoiding yet another downward smash. Out flashed Tempest, a sudden lunge, but the giant was already turning its huge body, moving limbs and torso safely out of reach.

This one was skilled, the ranger realized. He gave a nervous glance to the side, to see the other giant watching.

Then he and the ugly brute went through a second round of attack and counter, again with no decisive winner, though this time Nightbird did score a minor hit. Still, the giant only howled—with laughter and not with pain—and its companion seemed even more bolstered and ready to join.

"Argh, get ye in here!" the ugly behemoth bellowed, but the words ended abruptly as the giant's head suddenly snapped to the side. The monster's head came back up straight, but its eyes were no longer seeing the ranger, were suddenly veiled in darkness. Without a movement to brace its fall, the giant dropped face first into the dirt.

The earcap was missing, Nightbird noted. No, not missing, but pushed in, driven right through the giant's skull and into its brain!

Not missing a beat, the ranger spun on the last giant and roared in victory, and the fomorian fell all over itself, burying a powrie that came around the corner as it tried to get away.

The ranger understood this mystery quite clearly. He said a little thank-you to Pony, whom he knew to be the source, then split the giant's skull in half with Tempest and pulled the magnetite from the gore.

"Symphony!" he cried, and ran to retrieve his bow.

The great horse whinnied and spun, pausing only to launch another double kick into the prone giant's face. Symphony came by Nightbird in a canter and the ranger leaped up and pulled himself into his saddle, sliding Tempest under his thigh and putting Hawkwing to the ready in one fluid movement.

He shot the powrie the giant had trampled as it stubbornly tried to regain its footing, then ran over the unfortunate dwarf with Symphony for good measure, breaking into the clear behind it, then turning fast down another alley, and the chase was on once more.

Unlike the ranger, Roger Lockless was doing all he could to avoid drawing attention to himself. The nimble thief worked his way carefully from rooftop to rooftop when the buildings were close enough, or down the side of one structure and up the side of another when they were not. Twice he found himself unintentionally on the same roof as an enemy, but both times he kept calm and as quiet as a shadow and moved along without being noticed, for that enemy, be it goblin or powrie, was inevitably distracted by the tumult of the ranger's passing.

The bonfire guided Roger, leading him unerringly across Caer Tinella until he was perched on a roof no more than twenty feet from the ragged prisoners, a score and a half of them, sitting on the ground, in deep despair, chained together at the ankles. Many monsters were about, and two in particular, a huge giant, the largest Roger had ever seen, and a nervous Koskosio Begulne, caught his attention—and, it seemed, caught the attention of all the other monsters in the area.

"Doomed we are!" the powrie wailed. "Nightbird's come and all the world's a cursed place!"

The giant shook its huge head and calmly bade the powrie to be quiet. "Are you not the one who wanted to bring him in?"

"Ye're not knowing!" the powrie snapped back. "Ye wasn't there, in the middle o' the fight, when he killed us in the valley."

"I wish he had," the giant said dryly. That gave Roger pause. A giant with wit? The mere thought of it sent a shudder down his spine; a giant's only weakness was often between its ears.

With a shrug, the young man slipped down the back side of the building, shadowed from the light of the fire, then tiptoed into the line of human prisoners, slipping to a seat right between a pair of very surprised and very beleaguered men. They did well to keep quiet, and Roger, lockpick in hand, went right to work on the shackles.

"Doomed, says I!" the powrie wailed. "Both of us!"

"You're half right," the giant said quietly. With a sudden move, Maiyer Dek lifted Kos-kosio into the air and tossed the thrashing powrie onto the burning pyre. The dwarf wailed and scrambled out of the flames, but they stubbornly followed, grabbing at clothes, at hair, eating flesh; even the magical bracers the dwarf had taken from fallen Ulg Tik'narn could not save Kos-kosio Begulne from a horrible death.

All the monstrous gathering was in tumult then, some screaming for the death of the prisoners, others—powries all—for a revolt against the giant.

And in the middle of it all Roger Lockless calmly went about his work, shifting down the line, one man at a time, opening shackles and bidding the men to stay calm until all were free.

"Hear me!" Maiyer Dek roared, and it was impossible for any within a hundred yards to not hear the booming, resonant voice. "This is only one human, one puny human. A hundred pieces of King's gold and ten prisoners to the one that brings me the head of Nightbird!"

That put the monsters in line, had them leaping and crying out excitedly, had many of them running off to find the fighting.

For just a split second Roger Lockless entertained the thought of those monsters catching and killing Elbryan. With a low growl the young man quickly berated himself for even thinking such things, and silently thanked the ranger for again allowing him the distraction he needed to finish his work here. And while he opened the next shackle, Roger Lockless prayed for Elbryan's safe escape.

"I am with you, Nightbird," came a most-welcome voice above the ranger as he turned tight about a building, monsters in close pursuit. He heard the twang of an elvish bow, and then the flutter of wings, and a moment later Belli'mar Juraviel was on Symphony behind him, bow in hand.

"You shoot those in front, I will cover flanks and rear," the elf offered, letting fly another arrow even as he made the statement. His bolt hit the mark, scoring solidly on a giant's face, but the behemoth only roared and brushed the insignificant hit away. "Though I fear I'll run out of arrows in an attempt to kill even one giant!" Juraviel added.

It didn't matter too much, anyway, for none of the monsters behind would get near the fast-running Symphony. Head down, nostrils puffing, the stallion tore up the ground, and the ranger, telepathically linked to the horse through the turquoise, did not need his hands to guide him. Those monsters who came out in front, or at an angle where they might intercept, met with the thunder of Nightbird's magnificent bow and the pounding of Symphony's hooves, and the companions ran on, soon turning into the lane that ran the extent of Caer Tinella's western side, just inside the barricade.

Symphony, and the ranger wholeheartedly agreed, skidded to an abrupt stop.

"We cannot get to them," Juraviel said, looking past the ranger to the bonfire, and to the dozens of monsters swarming all about the path ahead of them.

Nightbird growled and moved to kick the horse's flanks.

"No!" Juraviel scolded. "Your run was magnificent and brave, but to go on is purely foolish. And what hope will be left those men if they see Nightbird cut down before them? Over the wall with us, I say! It is the only way!"

Nightbird studied the scene before him, heard the monsters closing from behind and from the east. He could not disagree, and so he grabbed the reins hard and jerked the horse's head to the west, toward the barricade and the open night beyond.

Out in that darkness, only a few feet from the wall, Pony stood perplexed, desperately trying to find some way to improvise. She didn't know exactly where the ranger was, though she was fairly sure he had come to this edge of town, and didn't have the time to use the quartz or the hematite to try and find out. Thus, she could not risk a bolt of lightning or any other substantial magical attack.

But this?

In her hand she held a diamond, the source of light and of warmth. There was a delicate balance in this gemstone's magic, Pony understood, for within its depths light and dark were not absolutes, but were, rather, gradations of each other. Thus a diamond could bring forth a brilliant shine or a quiet glow. But what might happen, Pony wondered, if she tilted the balance in the other direction?

"This is a wonderful time for experiments," she whispered sarcastically, but even as she finished the thought, she was falling into the magic of the stone, finding that balance, picturing it as a circular plate perched atop the tip of a knitting needle. If she turned the closest edge of that plate up, she would bring forth light.

She turned it down instead.

* * *

The great fire dimmed; all the torches seemed to flicker and lessen, until they were no more than tiny pinpricks of light. At first Nightbird thought a gust of wind must have swept through—just over his head, he guessed, since he had felt no breeze. It made no sense, though, for what wind might so easily defeat so large a fire as the burning pyre?

Then it was dark, just dark, and Symphony, heading still for the western wall, hesitated, unable to see the barricade to make the leap.

"Jilseponie with the stones," Juraviel reasoned, though the elf feared differently, feared that this darkness might be the trademark of the demon dactyl. Juraviel had met the beast once before, soon after he had left the ranger's expedition to take some refugees to the safety of Andur'Blough Inninness, and on that occasion the dactyl had been surrounded by a cloud of darkness. Not quite like this one, though; the blackness of the dactyl was more a wave of despair over the heart than a lack of light to the eyes.

"They are blinded," Nightbird replied, noting the frantic movements of the monsters along the lane. They could no longer see him, he realized, could no longer see the ground at their feet or the walls before them.

"As am I," Juraviel was quick to answer, and that gave the ranger pause. He had thought, or hoped, that Pony had indeed enacted some enchantment to blind his enemies, but why, then, was Juraviel affected, and why was he still able to see?

"The cat's-eye," he reasoned, feeling the gem-set circlet about his head. That had to be the answer, but whatever the case, Nightbird was not going to let this turn of fate go to waste. He communicated with his horse, bade Symphony to turn back down the lane, back toward the fire and the prisoners, and then he guided the stallion with the turquoise, as he had so often done before, letting Symphony "see" through his eyes.

"Hold on tightly," Nightbird bade the elf, and Juraviel was willing to comply, since he could not put his bow to use anyway.

Down the path they charged, Nightbird working hard to keep Symphony veering around scrambling goblins and powries, and to keep far away from the two giants that were feeling about one of the buildings. They came out of the enchanted area of darkness suddenly, without warning, right before the bonfire. Most of the monstrous host was behind them, but gigantic Maiyer Dek was not, the behemoth standing near the fire, waving a huge sword easily in one hand.

Nightbird managed to look past the giant, to see Roger among the far end of the prisoner line, working furiously on some shackles.

"I have waited too long for this," the giant said quietly.

"As have I," the ranger answered grimly, needing the bravado to hold this one's attention, and the gazes of all those nearby.

"As have I!" came a cry behind the ranger, and Juraviel leaned out to the side and let fly an arrow for Maiyer Dek's face.

The giant lurched, but in truth he didn't even have to, for though Juraviel's bolt headed straight in, it swerved at the last instant, flying harmlessly to the side.

"Impossible," the elf remarked.

Nightbird groaned softly; he understood, had seen this before. When he had fought Ulg Tik'narn in the woods, for some reason that he could not understand, his arrows and his blows could not strike the powrie.

Apparently Maiyer Dek was similarly armored. And even if the giant was naked, and without a weapon other than its hands, this one would prove a challenge, Nightbird knew without doubt.

"Come along, Nightbird!" the giant roared, and it threw back its head and bellowed with mocking laughter.

That mirth ended abruptly, though, as Maiyer Dek's comrades started shouting with alarm as all the remaining prisoners, and Roger as well, leaped up and scattered, some pausing to tackle nearby enemies and grab their weapons, others just running full out or climbing the closest barrier.

"What trick is this?" the huge giant roared, glancing all about. "Forget them!" he howled, pointing at the ranger. "Forget them all, but this one! This is the Nightbird! I will have his head!"

Nightbird kicked Symphony into a run—not for Maiyer Dek, for the ranger did not think it wise to tangle with that one at this time, but in a circuitous route of the area, trampling monsters, slashing with Tempest, while Juraviel's bow went to work once more. The situation now demanded confusion, and the two riders and their magnificent stallion answered that call perfectly.

Nightbird winced as he saw one man chopped down by a powrie hammer, then another squashed by a giant club. But many more were running free, many more were over the wall and scrambling into the cover of the forest. On the top of the wall directly across the fire, Nightbird spotted Roger. The man smiled and offered a salute, and then he was gone.

Back down the lane the darkness enchantment went away. Nightbird spun Symphony about and charged that way, scattering the confused closest monsters. Then he turned the horse sharply to the east, back into the heart of the town, trying to draw attention to himself and take some of the danger from the fleeing prisoners.

Around and around they went, Symphony always seeming to be one stride ahead of the pursuit—which included an outraged Maiyer Dek. Juraviel began to sing a taunting song, accenting each verse with a well-aimed bowshot.

After several minutes, Symphony puffing hard and the monstrous ring tightening about them, the ranger wisely decided that the game was up. He angled the horse for the nearest barricade, the eastern wall, and over they went, into the night. Nightbird thought to go out to the east and south, then swing back to the refugee encampment after a long while. He would have to trust Roger and Pony to get the prisoners away.

His plans changed, though, when he saw the huge form of Maiyer Dek stepping over the southern wall and then running off into the woods.

Perhaps he would get his fight with the giant after all.

"We must keep them guessing," Juraviel reasoned, lifting off Symphony's back to fly to a nearby branch.

"You keep them confused," Nightbird replied. "I have urgent business to the south."

"The giant?" Juraviel asked incredulously. "He has an enchantment about him!"

"I have seen this magic before," Nightbird answered. "And I know how to defeat it. He wishes a fight with me, and so he shall have it!"

Juraviel offered no argument as the ranger kicked Symphony into a run.

The pursuit was not organized, was just a mob of scrambling monsters, turning about in circles as often as they moved in any one direction. Many soon gave up the chase altogether, not sure of whom they were supposed to be chasing, and not wanting to get caught out alone against the Nightbird.

Stubborn Maiyer Dek did not turn back, though, just pressed on, calling for the ranger to come out and face him squarely.

Following those calls, Nightbird had little trouble in gaining ground on the giant, and he was pleased to discover that the rest of the monstrous pursuit was nowhere to be seen, that the giant leader, in its rage, had struck out alone. The ranger wondered if he should first seek out Pony. "Sunstone," he muttered, remembering how Avelyn had brought down the magical defenses of Kos-kosio Begulne, and recalling, too, that he and Pony had not retrieved any such magic from Avelyn's cache, that the sunstone had been lost in the destruction of Aida.

The ranger looked to his sword, to the gemstone set in the pommel, which was truly a magically constructed mixture of several types of stones, sunstone among them.

Up ahead the huge fomorian came into view, breaking through the last line of brush and pine trees onto a meadow.

"Work for me, Tempest," the ranger whispered, and he brought Symphony around the area, stepping out of the trees on the opposite end of the field when the giant was halfway across.

Maiyer Dek stopped in his tracks, surprised that the man dared to meet him so openly.

"You came out here after me," the ranger explained calmly. "And so you have found me. Let us be done with it."

"Done with yourself!" came the thunderous retort. Maiyer Dek glanced all around suspiciously.

"I am alone," the ranger assured him. "At least, as far as I know. You were trying to follow me, but I followed you." He passed along some telepathic instruction to Symphony then, bidding the horse to be ready to come to his side should the sunstone fail. Then he slipped down from the saddle, Tempest in hand, and started a slow and steady walk toward the fomorian.

Maiyer Dek's grin widened with each passing step. The giant suspected there would be trouble back in the town—he had thrown the powrie leader into the bonfire, after all—but wouldn't they all, giants, goblins, and even the stubborn powries, bow down to him when he walked in with Night-bird's head! And, to Maiyer Dek's thinking, there was no way he could possibly lose. He wore the spiked bracers, the gift of the demon dactyl, and with their magic, no weapon could strike him.

So the giant's surprise was complete, then, when Nightbird rushed across the last fifteen feet, fell into a balanced skip and lunged fast, stabbing him hard in the belly, the glowing Tempest tearing through clothes and leather girdle and slipping nearly half its blade length into Maiyer Dek's abdomen.

Nightbird pulled the blade right out and slashed across, smacking Maiyer Dek across the kneecap. Then, as the giant's leg went predictably wide, the ranger darted right between the treelike limbs, falling into a head-long roll as Maiyer Dek's huge sword swished harmlessly behind him.

He came up in a half turn, legs tucked under him, and leaped back at the giant as it started to turn about, scoring yet another hit, this one deep into the giant's hamstring. Then he ran out the back side of the behemoth, into the clear again, spinning on his heel to face Maiyer Dek squarely.

The giant was clearly confused and in pain, one huge hand holding tight to its spilling guts.

"You believed that your demon armor would defeat my attacks," the ranger said. "And so the gift of Bestesbulzibar worked against you, Maiyer Dek, for my magic, the magic of the goodly God, is stronger by far!"

In response, Maiyer Dek roared and charged.

Nightbird leaped straight ahead, sword up as if he meant to block the attack. He could not hope to stop the sheer power of Maiyer Dek's sword strike, and he knew it, and so at the last moment he leaped out to the side, then charged in behind the swish of the sword, stabbing again at the giant's wounded abdomen.

Maiyer Dek brought the great pommel of his sword in tight fast enough to partially defeat the attack, and then, in a fluid movement, snapped that sword arm out wide, pommel clipping a dodging Nightbird on his already bruised shoulder and sending him into a roll.

The ranger came up in perfect balance, but truly his right shoulder throbbed from the heavy hit, and Maiyer Dek, recognizing a slight advantage here, was quick in pursuit, but this time with his sword at the ready, and not swinging wildly.

The giant put out a lazy swing, testing the ranger's defenses. Tempest banged hard against the huge blade, once and then again, forcing it wide.

"You move your skinny blade well," the giant remarked.

"Except when it is embedded in your belly," the ranger replied.

Predictably, Maiyer Dek came on ferociously, sword slashing across at just the right height to take the ranger's head from his shoulders.

But Nightbird was no longer standing, had dropped to his knees, then came up as the blade flashed over head. Left, right, left went Tempest, then in a straight-ahead thrust, once and again, and then a third time, angled up for the abdomen once more.

Down went the ranger in a desperate dive, the giant reversing its swing for a sudden backhand, and this time with the blade so low that Nightbird had to fall flat on the ground.

Maiyer Dek rushed ahead, lifted his massive booted foot and stamped down, thinking to grind Nightbird into the dirt.

The ranger went over in a roll, then again as the giant continued to stamp at him. Then a third time, and when he came over, he put one leg under him. As Maiyer Dek lifted his foot and turned it yet again, the ranger sprang up, bracing Tempest, pommel in both hands, against his breast, driving it hard into the bottom of Maiyer Dek's foot before it began its downward momentum.

The blade gored through the leather as if it was paper and drove upward, into flesh and bone. Maiyer Dek tried to pull away, but the ranger stayed with him, driving on.

All the ground shook when Maiyer Dek fell over backward, hitting with a tremendous jolt. The giant felt the ranger then, leaping atop his thigh, running up his torso. He tried to reach out with his empty hand, but Tempest slashed away, taking one finger at the knuckle and gashing the others.

Nightbird sprang to the giant's massive chest, then leaped ahead, landing right above the behemoth's shoulder, slashing hard with Tempest at the side of Maiyer Dek's neck. Then he leaped again, into a backward roll, came up to his feet and ran up above the prone giant, narrowly avoiding the great sword as Maiyer Dek rolled about.

Nightbird was twenty feet away when the giant staggered to its feet. The ranger noted the blood pouring freely down the side of Maiyer Dek's neck, and knew that the outcome was decided.

"Ah, but you'll pay for this, little rat!" Maiyer Dek spouted. "I'll cut you in half! I'll—" The giant stopped and put its torn hand up to its neck, then brought the hand out in front of its face, staring incredulously at the complete bloodstain. Stunned, Maiyer Dek looked back to the ranger, to see him mounting Symphony, his sword in its sheath.

"You are dead, Maiyer Dek," Nightbird declared. "The only thing that could save you is the magic of the goodly God, and He, I fear, will show little mercy to one who has committed so many terrible crimes."

Nightbird turned his horse and rode away.

Maiyer Dek moved to follow, but stopped, again lifting his hand, and then, when he discerned that the blood was verily spouting from his neck, he grabbed at the wound tightly, trying to stem the flow, then ran off for Caer Tinella.

He felt the cold creeping into his body before he ever got off the field, felt the touch of death and saw the darkness growing before his eyes.

❖ 14 ❖

Right and Wrong

"Oh, but by yer pardon, master sir," the woman stammered. "I'm just not knowing what ye're wanting from poor old Pettibwa."

Father Abbot Markwart eyed the woman suspiciously, knowing that she was not as dim-witted as she was pretending. It made sense, of course, for she was obviously frightened. She, her husband Graevis, and their son Grady, had been pulled from Fellowship Way, their small inn down in the poorer section of Palmaris.

The Father Abbot made a mental note to speak with Brothers Youseff and Dandelion concerning their rough tactics. Using brute force and threats instead of subtle coercion, they had put the three on their guard, and now garnering any information might prove more difficult indeed. In fact, had he not arrived on the scene to oversee the arrest, Markwart feared that his two overly rough lackeys might have seriously injured the three, might even have killed the son, Grady.

"Be at ease, Madame Chilichunk," Markwart said with a phony grin. "We are searching for one of our own, that is all, and we have reason to believe that he might be in the company of your daughter."

"Cat?" the woman asked suddenly, eagerly, and Markwart knew that he had hit a chord, though he had no idea of who this "Cat" might be.

"Your daughter," he said again. "The one you adopted, who was orphaned in the Timberlands."

"Cat," Pettibwa said earnestly. "Cat-the-Stray, that's what we called her, ye know."

"I do not know the name," the Father Abbot admitted.

"Jilly, then," the woman clarified. "That's her real name, part of it anyway. Oh, but I'd love to be seein' me Jilly again!"

Jilly. Markwart rolled the name over in his thoughts. *Jilly . . . Jilseponie . . . Pony.* Yes, he decided. It fit nicely.

"If you help us," he said pleasantly, "you may indeed see her again. We have every reason to believe that she is alive and well."

"And in the Kingsmen," the woman added.

Markwart hid his frustration well. If Pettibwa and her family knew no more than that old news, they wouldn't be of much help.

"But as I telled yer fellow priest, I'm not knowing where they sent me girl," Pettibwa went on.

"Fellow priest?" Father Abbot echoed. Had Brother Justice interrogated this woman already? he wondered, and hoped, for if that was the case, then Quintall must have also discovered the connection between Avelyn and the Chilichunks. "A monk, you mean? Of St. Precious, perhaps?"

"No, I'm knowin' most of them from St. Precious—me Jilly was married by Abbot Dobrinion himself, ye know," Pettibwa offered proudly. "No, this one was wearing the darker brown robes, like yer own, and his accent was o' the eastlands. St.-Mere-Abelle, ye said ye were from, and I'd be guessin' that he was from the same place."

Father Abbot Markwart was pondering how he might properly identify this man—as Quintall, he suspected—without giving anything away, when boisterous Pettibwa rambled on.

"Oh, and a great big fat man, he was indeed!" she said. "Ye must be feedin' them well at yer St.-Mere-Abelle, though yerself could be using a bit o' fattening, if ye don't mind me telling ye so!"

For a moment Father Abbot Markwart was confused, for there wasn't an ounce of fat on the well-honed muscles of the first Brother Justice. But then, suddenly, he understood, and he could hardly contain his excitement. "Brother Avelyn?" he said breathlessly. "Brother Avelyn Desbris of St.-Mere-Abelle came to speak with you?"

"Avelyn," Pettibwa echoed, letting the name roll off her tongue. "Yessir, that's sounding right. Brother Avelyn come a'askin' about me Jilly."

"And she was with you?"

"Oh no, but she was long into the army by then," Pettibwa explained. "But he wasn't looking to find her; he was asking about where she came from, and how she came to live with me and Graevis. Oh, a nice and cheerful fellow he was, too!"

"And did you tell him?"

"Oh, but for sure," Pettibwa said. "I'm not one to be angering the Church!"

"Keep that thought close to your heart," the Father Abbot said dryly. It was all beginning to fit together, and quite nicely, he realized. Avelyn had met this woman, Pony or Jilly, outside of Pireth Tulme after the powrie invasion, and had traveled with her right through Palmaris and to the north, where they had then met the centaur. The woman had survived the explosion at Aida, Markwart believed, and so had this other mysterious fellow, Nightbird, whom Bradwarden had unintentionally described, and they now had the gemstones.

Finding them would not be easy, obviously, but perhaps Markwart could find a way to bring Pony and Nightbird to him . . .

"I could make ye a fine fattening stew," Pettibwa was saying when the Father Abbot tuned back to the conversation. Of course she was preoccupied with such things, Markwart mused, considering her plump form.

"I may just ask you to do that," he replied. "But not now."

"Oh no, couldn't be," Pettibwa agreed. "But ye come by the Way tonight, or whenever ye're getting the chance, and I'll feed ye well."

"I am afraid that you will not be returning to the Way this day," Markwart explained, rising from his seat behind Abbot Dobrinion's huge desk and motioning to Brother Dandelion, who was standing in the shadows at the side of the large room. "Or anytime soon."

"But—"

"You said that you did not want to anger the Church," Markwart interrupted. "I hold you to that, Madame Pettibwa Chilichunk. Our business is most urgent—more so than the health of your pitiful inn."

"Pitiful?" Pettibwa echoed, growing concerned and angry.

"Brother Dandelion will accompany—"

"I'm not thinking so!" the woman snapped. "I'm no enemy of the Church, Father Abbot, but I've got me life and me family."

Father Abbot Markwart didn't bother to reply, had grown quite bored with the woman, actually, and quite frustrated, since she really had only confirmed what he already knew. He motioned again to Brother Dandelion and the man stepped up to Pettibwa's side and took her thick elbow in his hand.

"Ah, but ye just be lettin' me go!" she yelled at him, tugging away.

Dandelion looked to Markwart, who nodded. Then he grabbed the woman again, more forcefully. Pettibwa tried to pull away, but the big man's grip was like iron.

"Understand, Madame Chilichunk," Father Abbot Markwart explained in a deadly serious voice, and moved his wrinkled old face right near the woman, "you will go with Brother Dandelion, whatever tactics he must use."

"And ye're callin' yerself a godly man?" Pettibwa replied, but her anger was gone, replaced by simple fear. She tried to pull away once more, and Brother Dandelion tightened his fingers and popped her hard on the forehead, stunning her. Then the monk cupped his hand over Pettibwa's, bending her fingers under his grasp, and pressed in, forcing the fingers back on their knuckles.

Waves of pain washed over the woman, stealing the strength from her legs. Brother Dandelion hooked his free arm under her shoulder and easily held her up against his side, keeping the pressure on her fingers every step of the way.

Markwart just went back to the desk, unconcerned with her pain.

As the pair left the room, Abbot Dobrinion entered, looking none too pleased.

"This is how you treat my congregation?" he demanded of Markwart.

"This is how the Church deals with those who will not cooperate," the Father Abbot coolly replied.

"Will not?" Dobrinion echoed doubtfully. "Or cannot? The Chilichunk family are an honest and decent lot, by every report. If they could help in your search—"

"In *my* search?" Father Abbot roared in reply, leaping to his feet and slamming the desk. "You believe that this is my search alone? Can you not understand the implications of all this?"

Abbot Dobrinion patted his hand in the air as Markwart fumed on, trying to calm the old man. That condescending action only fueled the Father Abbot's ire, though.

"We have found Avelyn the heretic," Markwart growled. "Yes, we found him, dead as he deserved in the devastation of Mount Aida. Perhaps his ally, the fiend dactyl, turned against him, or perhaps he merely overestimated his own worth and power; pride was ever one of his many faults!"

Abbot Dobrinion could hardly reply, so stunned was he by the information, and by the sheer outrage in Father Abbot's voice as he relayed it.

"And that woman," Markwart went on, pointing a skinny finger at the door Pettibwa and Dandelion had exited, "and her wretched family, may hold answers for us concerning the whereabouts of our stones. Our stones! God-given to St.-Mere-Abelle, and stolen by the thief and murderer Avelyn Desbris, curse his evil name! And such a cache, Abbot Dobrinion! If those stones fall into the hands of enemies of the Church, then we shall know war on an even greater scale, do not doubt!"

Dobrinion suspected that Father Abbot might be exaggerating there. He had already spoken to Master Jojonah concerning the stones, and Jojonah wasn't nearly as worried about them as was Markwart. But Dobrinion, too, was an old man whose time in this world was fast passing, and he understood the importance of reputation and legacy. That was why he was so desperate to see Brother Allabarnet canonized while he presided over St. Precious, and why he was able to accept Markwart's need to retrieve the stones.

He would have said as much, if he had been given the chance, but the Father Abbot was on a roll then, spouting Church doctrine, telling of Master Siherton, so good a man, murdered by Avelyn, and ranting about how the Chilichunks might be the only clue in getting to this treasonous woman and the cache of gemstones.

"Do not underestimate my desire for this," Markwart finished, lowering his voice to a threatening tone. "If you hinder me in any way, I will repay you a thousand times over."

Dobrinion's face screwed up with incredulity; he was not accustomed to being threatened by one of his own Order.

"As you know, Master Jojonah is already on his way to St. Honce to further Brother Allabarnet's canonization," Father Abbot Markwart said calmly. "I can recall him in an instant, and kill this process altogether."

Dobrinion set his feet firmly in place and squared his shoulders. By his estimation, the old Father Abbot had just crossed a very tangible line! "You are the leader of the Abellican Church," Dobrinion conceded, "and thus hold great power. But the canonization process is greater still, and an issue for all the abbots, not just the Father Abbot of St.-Mere-Abelle."

Markwart was laughing before the man even finished. "But the stories I could tell of Brother Allabarnet," he said with a wicked chuckle. "Long-forgotten tales unearthed from the catacombs of St.-Mere-Abelle. The journal of the man's passage through the eastlands, a journey filled with tales of debauchery and womanizing, of excessive drinking and even one case of petty theft."

"Impossible!" Dobrinion cried.

"Quite possible," Markwart replied grimly without hesitation. "To fabricate and to make them look authentic."

"The lie will not stand the test of time," Dobrinion countered. "Similar lies were told of St. Gwendolyn of the Sea, yet they did not defeat the canonization process!"

"They delayed it for nearly two hundred years," Markwart not so gently reminded. "No, perhaps the lies will not stand the test of time, but neither, my friend, will your old bones."

Dobrinion slumped where he stood, feeling as though he had been physically beaten.

"I intend to gather my information," Markwart said evenly. "By whatever means necessary. As of this moment, Graevis, Pettibwa, and Grady Chilichunk are to be held under suspicion of treason against the Church and God. And perhaps I will speak with this Connor Bildeborough, as well, to see if he is a part of the conspiracy."

Dobrinion started to respond, but decided to hold the thoughts to himself. Connor Bildeborough was the favored nephew, treated practically as son and heir, of the Baron of Palmaris, a man of no small means and influence. But Father Abbot Markwart could find that out for himself, Dobrinion decided. The old wretch might just make a very powerful enemy in the process.

"As you wish, Father Abbot" was all the abbot of St. Precious replied, and he gave a curt bow, turned on his heel and left the room.

Markwart gave a derisive snort when the door closed behind Dobrinion, thinking he had put the man in his place.

Dainsey Aucomb was not the brightest light in the sky, the dashing young man knew, but she was observant enough. And besides, Connor Bildeborough was often able to use her dim wits to his advantage. The Baron's nephew had come to the Way that night, as he often did—though, in truth, the relationship between Connor and Pettibwa Chilichunk had been more than a little strained since the annulment of Connor's marriage to Jill. Still, Grady Chilichunk was more than pleased to call the nobleman a friend, and even Graevis couldn't really blame the man for the failure of the marriage; Jill had refused him his marital rights, after all.

And so Connor continued to frequent Fellowship Way, for though a man of his station was welcomed at the most exclusive taverns in Palmaris, in those places Connor was just another nobleman. Among the common rabble in Fellowship Way, he felt important, superior in every way.

He was surprised, as were many other regular patrons, to find the tavern closed that night. The only light showing through the windows came from two of the guest rooms on the second floor, from the kitchen and from a small room in the back of the building, the room that had been Jill's but now belonged to Dainsey.

Connor called to her softly as he knocked lightly on the door. "Do come and answer, Dainsey," he bade her.

No answer.

"Dainsey Aucomb," Connor said more loudly. "There are many patrons growing restless in the street. We cannot abide that, now can we?"

"Dainsey's not here," came the woman's voice, poorly disguised.

Connor rocked back on his heels, surprised by the note of fear he detected in that voice. What was going on here?

"Dainsey, it is Connor . . . Master Bildeborough, nephew of the Baron," he said more forcefully. "I know that you are behind the door, hearing my every word, and I demand that you speak with me!"

No answer came back, other than a slight whimpering.

Connor grew more agitated, more frightened. Something very strange had happened, perhaps something terrible. "Dainsey!"

"Oh, go away, I beg ye, Mr. Bildeborough," the woman pleaded. "I ain't done nothing wrong, and I'm not for knowing what crimes the mister and missus committed to so anger the Church. No sins on me own door, and me bed's been slept in by none but meself—well, except for yerself, and just those two . . . three times."

Connor tried hard to digest all of that. Crimes against the Church? The Chilichunks? "Impossible," he said aloud, then lifted his hand to bang hard on the door. He stopped himself, though, and reconsidered his course.

Dainsey was frightened, and apparently with good cause. If he frightened her more, he doubted he would be able to get any information out of her.

"Dainsey," he said softly, comfortingly. "You know me, and know that I am a friend of the Chilichunks."

"The missus isn't speaking so highly of ye," Dainsey replied bluntly.

"And you know that story," Connor said, fighting hard to hold his calm tone. "And know, too, that I do not blame Pettibwa for being mad at me. Yet I still come to the Way, still consider the place as a home. I am no enemy of the Chilichunks, Dainsey, nor of you."

"So ye're saying."

"Consider that I could be in there if I so chose," Connor said bluntly. "I could have half the garrison with me, and that door would offer you little protection."

"Dainsey's not here," came the reply. "I'm her sister, and know nothing about what ye're saying."

Connor groaned and banged his forehead against the door. "Very well, then," he said a moment later. "I am leaving, and you should be, as well, before those monks now coming down the road arrive." Staying in place right outside the door, Connor lifted his feet alternately, clunking his boots against the wood, more softly with each step so that it sounded as though he was walking away. Predictably, the door cracked open a few seconds later, and the young man was quick to stick his foot into the opening, bracing his shoulder against the wood and pushing hard.

Dainsey was a spirited lass, and strong from carrying heavy trays, and she gave him a good fight, but finally he forced himself into the room, quickly shutting the door behind him.

"Oh, but I'll scream!" the frightened woman warned, backing away, taking up a frying pan as she passed it sitting on her night table, spilling the drippy eggs down her side in the process. "Ye keep yerself back!" she warned, waving the pan.

"Dainsey, what is wrong with you?" Connor asked, advancing a step and then quickly retreating and holding up his hands unthreateningly as the pan started swinging. "Where are the Chilichunks? You must tell me."

"Ye're already knowing!" the woman accused. "Suren that yer uncle's part of it all!"

"Part of all what?" Connor demanded.

"Part of the arrest!" Dainsey cried, tears streaming down her soft cheeks.

"Arrest?" Connor echoed. "They were arrested? By town guards?"

"No," Dainsey explained. "By them monks."

Connor could hardly speak, so amazed was he by this information. "Arrested?" he asked again. "You are sure of that? They were not just escorted to St. Precious on some minor business?"

"Master Grady, he tried to argue," Dainsey said. "Said he was a friend o' yerself and all, but that only made them laugh, and when Master Grady moved to draw his sword, one o' them monks, a skinny fellow, but so fast, got him good and hard, knocked him right to the floor. And then the old one come rushing in, and he was in a fit—"

"Abbot Dobrinion?"

"No, older than him by a cow's life," Dainsey said. "Old and skinny and wrinkled, but wearing robes like Dobrinion, only more decorated. Oh, pretty things, those robes was, even on the old and wrinkled man, even with that ugly look he kept on his face—"

"Dainsey," Connor said suddenly and firmly, trying to get her back on track.

"He, the old one, he yelled good at that skinny fellow, but then he just looked at Master Grady and telled him that if he did a stupid thing like that again, both his arms'd be torn off," Dainsey went on. "And I believed him, too, and so did Master Grady! Went all white in the face, trembling all over."

Connor shuffled over and sat on the bed, thoroughly stunned and trying to sort it all out. He had been in the Way that night a couple of years before when an enormously fat monk, a man of St.-Mere-Abelle, he had heard, and not of St. Precious, had arrived and spoken with Pettibwa. That meeting had seemed calm enough, though the man had spoken of Jill, which somewhat upset the normally jovial woman. Still, on that occasion, the monk had been gentle enough and gracious enough.

"Did they say why they had come?" Connor asked her. "Did they mention what crimes the Chilichunks were being accused of? You must tell me, I beg."

"They asked about the mister and missus's daughter, that's all," Dainsey replied. "They said I was her at first, and then two young ones moved to grab me. But the old one, he said that it wasn't me, and the mister and missus both said so, too."

Connor put his chin in his hand, trying hard, and futilely, to digest it all. Jill? They were looking for Jill? But why?

"Then they said the mister and missus must be hiding her, and so they went through the whole place, makin' a mess o' everything," Dainsey went on. "And then they took 'em, all three."

Connor Bildeborough was not without resources. His network of friends and confidants included people from the palace to the abbey to House Battlebrow, the most notorious brothel—and thus, one of the most powerful houses—in all the city. It was time for him to put that network into action, he realized, time for him to get some answers.

If the Church had come so forcefully for the Chilichunks on a matter concerning Jill, then Connor, too, might find himself under suspicion. These were, after all, dangerous times, and Connor, who had lived all of his thirty years in the presence of the ruling class, understood well how serious the games of intrigue could become.

"You stay here, Dainsey," he decided. "And keep that door closed, and do not even offer an answer to anyone's call, except for mine."

"But how'm I to be sure that it's yerself come a'calling?"

"We'll have a secret word," Connor said mysteriously, and he saw that get Dainsey's attention. Her face brightened at the thought, the frying pan went back on the night table and she plopped down on the bed right beside him.

"Ooh, but that's so exciting," she said happily. "What word, then?"

Connor thought it over for just a moment. "Bymegod," he said with a wicked smile that brought a fierce blush to Dainsey's cheeks. "You will remember that one, will you not?"

Dainsey giggled and blushed even more. She had heard that phrase before, had been known to say it repeatedly at certain times when she and Connor were alone in her room.

Connor gave her a little tickle under the chin, then rose and went to the door. "Speak to no one else," he instructed as he left. "And if the Chilichunks return—"

"Oh, but I'll let them in!" Dainsey cut in.

"Yes, do," Connor said dryly. "And then tell Grady to find me. Can you remember to do that?"

Dainsey nodded eagerly.

"Bymegod," Connor said with a wink as he departed.

Dainsey sat on the bed giggling for a long while.

"You believe this to be a game?" Markwart screamed, sticking his face right up to poor Grady Chilichunk, the old man's bloodshot eyes boring into Grady's.

Grady was chained to the wall by the wrists, with the shackles up high so that he had to stand on his tiptoes the whole time. And it was hot down there in the cellar of St. Precious, with a fire pit and bellows set up in the low-ceilinged, tight room.

"I never even liked her," the prisoner sputtered in reply, sweat and spittle flying out with every word. "I asked for no sister!"

"Then tell me where she is?" Markwart roared.

"If I knew, I would," Grady protested, his voice more controlled, though hardly calm. "You must believe me!"

Father Abbot Markwart turned to the two monks who had accompanied him to the dungeons, Brothers Francis and Dandelion, the huge and vicious younger monk wearing a hooded cloak, an appropriate garment for this dark occasion.

"Do you believe him?" Markwart asked Francis.

"He seems sincere," Brother Francis answered honestly. His perspective was biased, he knew, because he simply didn't want to see any more of this interrogation, truly the most brutal questioning he had ever witnessed. He did believe Grady, and hoped that Markwart would, as well.

Grady's face brightened just a bit, a hint of a smile turning up the corners of his mouth.

"Seems?" Markwart pressed, sounding incredulous. "My dear Brother Francis, on a matter as important as this, do you believe that the appearance of truth is enough?"

"Of course not, Father Abbot," Brother Francis replied with a resigned sigh.

Father Abbot Markwart turned on Grady. "Where is she?" he asked calmly.

The man whined as he searched for an answer that he could not know.

Markwart nodded to the hooded Dandelion. "We must be certain," he said, and then he walked away, Brother Francis in tow.

Brother Dandelion was right before Grady in an instant, his huge fist slamming hard into the man's exposed ribs. "Please," Grady stammered, and then he was hit again, and again, and again, until his words came out as undecipherable groans.

"And when you are finished," Father Abbot Markwart said to Dandelion, "do go to an upstairs hearth and take a poker, then lay it in the fire of this room for a bit. We must test this one's sincerity, after all, and teach him a lesson of obedience to the Church."

"No!" Grady started to protest, but his breath was blasted away by another heavy punch.

Markwart left the room without looking back. Brother Francis did pause before following, staring back at the spectacle. Grady Chilichunk wasn't the only one in this room being taught a lesson.

Another punch brought a pitiful groan, and Francis rushed away, skittering to catch up to Markwart.

"You would not really use a heated poker on the poor fool?" he asked.

Markwart's look stole the blood from his face. "I will do whatever I deem necessary," he said calmly. "Come along, the old man down the hall is near to breaking, I believe. Perhaps we can invade his thoughts once again with the soul stone." Markwart paused, studying the expression on the younger monk's face, recognizing doubts etched there.

"Whenever the business gets unpleasant, all you need do is think of the greater good," he quietly instructed.

"But if they are telling the truth . . ." Francis dared to argue.

"A pity, then," Markwart admitted. "But not so much a pity as the consequences if they are lying and we do not probe deeper. The greater truth, Brother Francis. The greater good."

Still, Francis was having a hard time reconciling his heart with the spectacle. He said no more about it, though, but produced the soul stone and dutifully followed his superior to the next cell in line.

More than an hour later, a painful hour for Grady and Graevis, Francis and Markwart exited the heavy door leading to the narrow stone stairway to the abbey's chapel. They found Abbot Dobrinion waiting for them on the top step.

"I demand to know what you are doing down there," the abbot fumed. "These are my subjects, and loyal to the Church."

"Loyal?" Markwart spat at him. "They harbor fugitives."

"If they knew—"

"They do know!" Markwart yelled in his face. "And they will tell me, do not doubt!"

The sheer intensity, the sheer wildness, of his tone sent Dobrinion back a couple of steps. He stood staring at Markwart for a long while, trying to get a reading of the man, trying to find out just how far this all had gone. "Father Abbot," he said quietly at length, once he was back in control of his own bubbling anger, "I do not doubt the importance of your quest, but I'll not stand idly by while you—"

"While I begin the canonization process for our dear Allabarnet of St. Precious?" Markwart finished.

Again Dobrinion paused, his thoughts whirling. No, he decided, he could not let Father Abbot use that as leverage against him, not in a matter as important as this. "Brother Allabarnet is deserving—" he started to protest.

"As if that matters," Markwart spat. "How many hundreds are deserving, Abbot Dobrinion? And yet only those chosen few ever even get nominated."

Dobrinion shook his head in defiance to every word. "No more," he said. "No more. Choose your course concerning Brother Allabarnet based on the work and life of Brother Allabarnet, not on whether or not the present abbot of St. Precious agrees with your campaign of terror! These are good people, good in heart and in deed."

"What do you know of it?" Markwart exploded. "When enemies of the Church bring St. Precious down around you, or the rot within the Church brings you down inside the walls you thought sacred, or when goblins freely roam the streets of Palmaris, will Abbot Dobrinion then wish he had let Father Abbot Markwart conduct the matters with a just, but iron, hand? Do you even begin to understand the implications of the cache of stolen stones? Do you even begin to understand the power they might bring to our foes?" The Father Abbot shook his head and waved disgustedly at the man.

"I grow weary of trying to educate you, foolish Abbot Dobrinion," he said. "Let me warn you instead. This matter is too important for your meddling. Your actions will not go unnoticed."

Abbot Dobrinion squared his shoulders and eyed the old man directly. Truly, some of Markwart's claims of the potential calamity had shaken a bit of his confidence, but still, his heart told him that this inquisition of the Chilichunks, and of the centaur, could not be a righteous thing. He had no arguments that would stand against Markwart at that time, though. The hierarchy of the Abellican Church did not allow him, as a mere abbot, to seriously question the authority of the Father Abbot, even within the walls of his own abbey. He gave a curt bow, then turned and walked far, far away.

"Who is Dobrinion's second at St. Precious?" Father Abbot Markwart asked Brother Francis as soon as the other man was gone.

"In line for the position of abbot?" Francis reasoned, and then, when Markwart confirmed that to be what he had in mind, Francis shook his head and shrugged. "No one of any consequence, certainly," he explained. "There is not even a master now in service at St. Precious."

Markwart's face screwed up with curiosity.

"They had two masters," Brother Francis explained. "One was killed on the battlefield to the north; the other died of the red fever just a few months ago."

"An interesting void," Father Abbot Markwart remarked.

"In truth, there is no one in St. Precious ready for such a succession," Brother Francis went on.

Father Abbot smiled wickedly at the thought. He had a master at St.-Mere-Abelle who might be ready for such a position, a man whose hand was no less iron than his own.

"Impeaching him of his title will thus prove all the more difficult," Brother Francis reasoned, thinking he saw where Markwart's thoughts were leading him.

"What?" Markwart asked incredulously, as though the idea never crossed his mind.

"The College will never strip Abbot Dobrinion of his abbey, given that there is no logical successor at St. Precious," Brother Francis reasoned.

"There are plenty of masters at St.-Mere-Abelle ready to assume the role of abbot," Father Abbot Markwart replied. "And at St. Honce."

"But history tells us clearly that the College would not strip an abbey of its abbot without another within the abbey ready to assume the title," Brother Francis argued. "The Twelfth College of St. Argraine was faced with just that prospect, concerning an abbot whose crimes were clearly more egregious than Abbot Dobrinion's."

"Yes yes, I do not doubt your understanding of the matter," Father Abbot Markwart interrupted, somewhat impatiently. He looked in the direction in which Abbot Dobrinion had departed, still showing that smile. "A pity," he muttered.

Then he started away, but, as in the dungeon, Brother Francis paused before following, surprised, when he considered it more closely, that Father Abbot Markwart would even entertain such thoughts. The impeachment of an abbot was no light matter, most decidedly not! It had only been attempted a half-dozen times in the thousand-year history of the Church, and two of those were prompted by the fact that the abbot in question had been proven guilty of serious crimes, one a series of rapes, including the assault on the female abbess of St. Gwendolyn, and the other a murder. Furthermore, the other four impeachment attempts had been in the very early days of the Abellican Order, when the position of abbot was often for sale or an appointment made as a matter of political gain.

Brother Francis gave a deep sigh to steady his nerves and dutifully followed his superior once more, reminding himself that the Church, indeed all the kingdom, was at war, after all, and that these were indeed desperate times.

Brother Braumin Herde was not in good spirits. He knew what was going on in the dungeons of the abbey, though he wasn't allowed anywhere near the lower levels. And even worse, he knew he was now alone in his stance, should he choose to take one against the Father Abbot. Master Jojonah was long gone, taken from him as his old mentor had warned might happen. Father Abbot Markwart knew his enemies and had the upper hand, a position he had no intention of relinquishing.

So Brother Braumin, avoiding monks of his own abbey for fear that they would run to Markwart to report any discussion, spent his hours among the brothers of St. Precious. They were a more jovial bunch than the serious students of St.-Mere-Abelle, he discovered, despite the fact that they had been hearing the sounds of battle not too far to the north for many weeks now. Still, on the whole, St. Precious was a brighter place. Perhaps it was the weather, Brother Braumin thought, for Palmaris was normally much more sunny than All Saints Bay, or perhaps it was the fact that St. Precious was built more aboveground than the larger St.-Mere-Abelle, with more windows and breezy balconies. Or maybe it was the fact that these monks were less secluded, being housed, as they were, in the midst of a huge city.

Or maybe, Brother Braumin mused—and he thought this to be the most likely explanation—the fact that St. Precious was lighter of heart than St.-Mere-Abelle was a reflection of the mood of the respective abbots. Dobrinion Calislas, by all accounts, was a man not unaccustomed to smiling; his great belly laugh was well-reported in Palmaris, as was his love of the wine—elvish boggle, some said—his penchant for games of chance—among friends only—and his love of officiating a grand wedding where no expenses had been spared.

Father Abbot Markwart didn't smile much, Braumin knew, and on those occasions when he did, those not in his favor grew very ill at ease.

Late that afternoon, Braumin stood in the carpeted hallway outside the door of Abbot Dobrinion's private quarters. Many times he lifted his hand to knock on the door, only to let it fall silently by his side. Braumin understood the chance he would be taking if he went in to speak with the man now, if he told Abbot Dobrinion of his fears concerning Markwart and of the quiet alliance that had been forged against the Father Abbot. On the one hand, Braumin felt he had little choice in the matter. With Master Jojonah gone, and on a long road that would keep him out of Braumin's life for years, it appeared, Braumin was powerless to make any moves against Father Abbot Markwart's decisions, particularly the decision that had sent Jojonah away in the first place. Making an ally of Abbot Dobrinion, who by all indications was not having a good time of it on his own against the Father Abbot, might greatly strengthen the cause for both men.

But on the other hand, Braumin Herde had to admit that he really didn't know Abbot Dobrinion very well, particularly the man's politics. Perhaps Abbot Dobrinion and Father Abbot Markwart were bickering over control of the prisoners simply because each wanted the glory of recovering the stones. Or perhaps Abbot Dobrinion's objections were borne on the wings of simple anger that Markwart had come into St. Precious and usurped a good deal of his power.

Brother Braumin spent nearly half an hour standing in that hall, contemplating his course. In the end Master Jojonah's words of wisdom proved the deciding component. "Quietly spread the word," his beloved mentor had bade him, "not against Father Abbot or any others, but in favor of Avelyn and those of like heart."

Patience, Brother Braumin decided. This was the long war of Mankind, he knew, the internal struggle of good and evil, and his side, the side of true goodness and godliness, would win out in the end. He had to believe that.

Now he was miserable and feeling so very alone, but that was the burden the truth in his heart forced upon him, and going to Abbot Dobrinion at this dangerous time was not the proper course.

As it played out in the weeks ahead, Brother Braumin Herde would come to regret this moment when he walked away from Abbot Dobrinion's door.

CHAPTER

❖ 15 ❖

Pride

"Maiyer Dek and the powrie, Kos-kosio," Pony said, feeling very pleased at the outcome in Caer Tinella. She, Elbryan, Tomas Gingerwart, and Belster O'Comely were sitting about a campfire in the refugee encampment, eagerly awaiting the return of Roger Lockless and the other scouts, trying to get a full measure of the impact of this night's raid on the monsters. The news would be good, all of them fully suspected. Several other monsters in addition to the two leaders had been slain, but they, even the three giants, were not overly important, not compared to the giant leader and the powrie leader—and especially given the fact that Maiyer Dek had been the one to kill Kos-kosio, and in full view of many powrie allies! Before the coming of the demon dactyl, giants and powries had rarely allied, indeed had hated each other as much as each hated the humans. Bestesbulzibar had halted that feud, and with the fall of the demon, the alliance had only continued out of necessity, since both armies were deep into the human lands.

But it was a strained thing, an alliance waiting for an excuse that it might turn into a feud.

"If we had convinced Maiyer Dek to join with us, we could not have gotten him to aid us any more than he did," Elbryan remarked with a chuckle. "My hopes soared when I saw him throw the powrie leader into the fire."

"And with Maiyer Dek and three of his giant kin dead," Pony added, "we can expect that the powries, angry at the giants, now have the clear upper hand."

"Except that goblins are more friendly to giants than to the wicked dwarves," Tomas Gingerwart noted. "Even though giants often eat them!"

"True enough," Elbryan admitted. "Perhaps the sides are fairly equal, then, for Caer Tinella was swarming with the wretched goblins. But unless one of great charm can be found among the ranks, and quickly, I suspect the fighting in the town has only just begun."

"Here's hoping they kill each other to the last," Belster O'Comely said, lifting a mug of ale—compliments of Roger Lockless—into the air, then taking a tremendous swallow, draining the mug.

"So they are weaker, and our force has grown by a score ready to fight," Tomas put in.

"A score ready to help the others get past the towns and to the south-land," Elbryan corrected. "We, all of us, have seen enough battle."

"To Palmaris!" Belster roared, finishing with a loud belch.

Tomas Gingerwart was not amused. "A month ago, even a week ago, even two days ago, I would have been satisfied with that," he explained. "But Caer Tinella is our home, and if our enemies are truly weakened, it may be time for us to reclaim the town. That was the plan, was it not? To wait until we took a measure of our enemies and then strike?"

Elbryan and Pony exchanged nervous glances, then looked back to the resolute man, truly empathizing with his desires.

"This is a discussion for later," the ranger said calmly. "We do not know how strongly the monsters remain entrenched in Caer Tinella."

Tomas snorted. "You got in," he said. "How much more devastating might the raid have been if all of our warriors were there to fight beside you?"

"Devastating to both sides, I fear," Pony replied. "We stung the mon-sters and freed the prisoners only because of the element of surprise. If Maiyer Dek had seen a greater force approaching, he would have ordered every one of the captured men slain, and the defense of Caer Tinella would have been more stubborn by far."

Tomas snorted again, not wanting to hear the negative posturing. By his thinking, if Elbryan and Pony, their little unseen friend Juraviel and Roger Lockless, could exact such a toll, then he and his warriors could finish the task.

Elbryan and Pony looked to each other again, and silently agreed to let it go at that. They understood Tomas's feelings, recognized that he had to believe that his home was not lost to him, and they both trusted that the man was sensible enough to listen to their argument if skirting the town and running to the south seemed the more prudent move.

Belster O'Comely, fearing mounting tension, led the discussion in another direction then, pondering the fate of the monstrous army across all the lands. "If we've been hitting at them so hard here, then it seems to me that others are taking them down, as well," he said. "Ho, but I'll be back in the Howling Sheila in Dundalis in the next spring, I'm betting!" he fin-ished, then filled and drained his mug once again.

"It is possible," the ranger said earnestly, his optimism surprising Pony. "If the monstrous army disintegrates, the King will wish the Timberlands quickly reclaimed."

"And Sheila will howl again!" Belster roared, for in his drink-induced state, he had forgotten all pledges to live out his life quietly in the safety of

Palmaris. His excitement brought others over to the campfire, most bearing foodstuffs and beverages.

The conversation took a lighthearted turn then, became the retelling of anecdotes from happier times, before the monstrous invasion, and what had started as a serious wait for important information became a sort of victory celebration. Elbryan and Pony said little, preferring to sit back and listen to the chatter of the others, often looking to each other and nodding. They had already arranged a meeting with Juraviel at the break of dawn in the meadow by the pines, and after they heard what the elf had to say, after they came to understand the truth of their enemy's strength in the two towns, they could make their decisions.

The night deepened, the fires burned low, and most of the folk retired to their bedrolls. Finally, only an hour before the dawn, the scouts returned, led by an exuberant Roger Lockless. "All the giants are gone," the young man proclaimed. "Every one! Driven off by the powries—and they hardly even put up a fight!"

"They did not want to be here in the first place," Pony reasoned. "They prefer their holes in the steep mountains of the Wilderlands."

Tomas Gingerwart gave a shout of victory.

"And what of the goblins?" Elbryan asked calmly, interrupting the celebration before it could begin. He didn't want Roger's excitement to steal the moment and lead Tomas and all the refugees down a course to absolute destruction. Even without giants, the remaining powries might prove too formidable.

"There was a fight and some were killed," Roger replied, not missing a beat. "Others went scattering into the forest."

"And still others remained with the powries," Elbryan reasoned.

"Yes, but—"

"And few, very few, powries were killed?" the ranger pressed.

"The goblins who remained will flee at first sign of battle," Roger said confidently. "They only stay because they're afraid of the bloody caps."

"Armies have won great victories inspired purely by fear," Pony said dryly.

Roger glared at her. "They are ready to be taken," he said evenly.

"We are a long way from making such a claim," the ranger was quick to reply, pointedly cutting off Tomas Gingerwart with an upraised hand as he spoke. Elbryan rose to stand before Roger. "Our responsibilities are too great to make such a quick judgment."

"As you made when you went into Caer Tinella alone?" the young man spat back.

"I did what I thought necessary," Elbryan replied quietly, calmly. He could feel the gazes of many people settling on him and Roger, and any conflict between them would obviously prove a source of great discomfort.

These people had come to trust and love Roger Lockless, and he had truly done much for them in the weeks of their exile. But if he was wrong now, if he was letting his desire to lead the folk to victory overrule good sense, then all of his previous exploits would be for naught, for all of the refugees would likely soon be dead.

"As did I in rescuing the thirty captured soldiers!" Roger said forcefully, and loudly.

"All by yourself?" Pony had to put in.

Elbryan put up his hand, quieting Pony, quieting all about him. "It is too early to make the judgment of whether to attack the towns or circumvent them," he announced. "We will know more, much more, with the light of day." The ranger, thinking and hoping that the discussion was finished then, turned and started away.

"We take back Caer Tinella," Roger Lockless declared, and there were more than a few agreeing calls. "And Landsdown," the young man went on. "And when we have the towns in our possession once more, we send word to Palmaris, that the King's army might reinforce our position."

"The Kingsmen will not come this far north," Pony argued. "Or at least, that is not something upon which we should stake our entire existence. Not yet. Not while Palmaris is under threat of invasion."

"How can you know?" Roger asked sternly.

"I served in the King's army," Pony admitted. "In the Kingsmen and in the Coastpoint Guards. I understand their priorities, and I can assure you that measured against the value of Palmaris, second city of Honce-the-Bear and the gateway of the Masur Delaval, Caer Tinella and Landsdown are not among those priorities. If Palmaris falls, then the way is open all the way to the King's seat in Ursal."

That took a bit of Roger's bluster away. He fidgeted for a few moments, thinking up a retort, but before he could deliver it, Tomas Gingerwart cut in. "We are all weary," the man said loudly, commanding the attention of all nearby. "It is said that good news can be as tiring as bad, and either as tiring as a week of hard work."

"Oh, true enough," Belster O'Comely agreed.

"So our spirits are heightened, our thoughts hopeful," Tomas went on. "But the ranger and Jilseponie are correct. This is not the time to decide."

"Our enemies are disorganized and reeling," Roger argued.

"As they will remain, for another day at least," Tomas answered bluntly. "We'll not attack the towns in the light of day anyway, so let us get our rest now, and hopefully we will see things more clearly in the morning."

Elbryan locked gazes with Tomas and nodded, sincerely grateful that the man had taken such levelheaded control. Then he motioned to Pony and the pair walked off, heading for the pines and the meadow, and a clearer picture of what remained of their adversaries.

Roger Lockless waited in the camp for a short while, then, when no one was paying much attention to him, he stole away, on the trail of the ranger and the woman and, he knew, their private scout.

He caught up to Elbryan and Pony in a meadow lined with pine trees, and blushed deeply, reconsidering his course, when the man and woman embraced each other and kissed passionately. Roger breathed easier when they broke off the clench.

If he had examined his feelings a bit more closely, and more honestly, Roger would have realized that the kiss bothered him more than it should have, that not only did he not wish to spy on such a private moment, but especially not one involving this beautiful woman. But Roger wasn't capable of that level of introspection where these two newcomers were concerned, not yet, and so, seeing the embrace finished, he crept closer into position, and was not surprised in the least when a melodious voice came down to the pair from the branches of a nearby pine.

"Fortune favored us this night," Juraviel explained. "For the giants are gone, all of them, and a fair number of goblins, too. The only better scenario would have been an open brawl between the giants and the powries."

"But that did not happen," Elbryan replied. "Thus, we must assume that the powrie force is still considerable."

"Indeed it is," Juraviel confirmed. "Though their leader has been roasted!"

"The folk wish to attack Caer Tinella, to reclaim it as their home," Pony put in.

"Is that not correct, Roger Lockless?" Elbryan added, recognizing that the young man was about.

Roger went even lower to the ground, put his face right in the grass.

"I do grow weary of this one's spying," Juraviel remarked, fluttering down from the tree.

"Well, come out, then," said Pony. "Since you wished to hear what we would say, you should at least join in the conversation."

Roger told himself repeatedly that there was no way these three could see him, no way that Elbryan and Pony could know, without doubt, that he had followed them.

"Stay with your face buried in the grass, then," Elbryan said with a chuckle. "I am against the attack," he offered to Juraviel.

"And with good reason," the elf replied. "If the war was still a stalemate, then we might consider striking such a blow. But I doubt that Caer Tinella serves as anything more than a temporary home for the powries and few goblins that remain. Certainly, it is not a supply base for any coordinated monstrous force. I see nothing to gain by attacking—the thought of reclaiming and holding the town at this point is purely foolhardy—and everything to lose. Let us not underestimate the strength of the force remaining in Caer Tinella."

"I think it wiser to skirt the town and flee to the southland," Elbryan added.

"It is likely that the road south will prove open all the way to Palmaris," Juraviel replied. "Though how long it will remain that way, I cannot say."

"Convincing the townsfolk to abandon their homes will not be easy," Pony explained.

"But we shall," Elbryan assured her. He looked in the direction of Roger Lockless as he spoke, thinking that the proclamation might at last bring the lad from hiding.

"Perhaps you cared not for your own home!" the young man said, jumping up and storming across to face the ranger. "But we are loyal to Caer Tinella!"

"And so you shall return to Caer Tinella," Elbryan said calmly. "This war will not last much longer, and as soon as the region about Palmaris is declared secure, then I expect the King to send the army north."

"And what will they find?" Roger said, moving right up to the much larger Elbryan. "Burned-out skeletons of our homes?"

"Rebuild," Elbryan calmly replied.

Roger scoffed at the notion.

"Our own home of Dundalis was sacked years ago," Pony said. "Then it was rebuilt, by Belster and his companions. And now it has been sacked again."

"And so it shall be built again," Elbryan said resolutely. "Houses can be put back up; people are forever lost."

"My own family was lost in such a raid," Pony said, taking the young man gently by the elbow.

"And my own," Elbryan added. "And all of our friends."

Roger's visage softened for just a moment as he regarded Pony, but then he pulled away, anger again filling his eyes. "Tell me not of your grief," he snapped. "I know all about losing family and friends. And I am not afraid now. The dwarves are in Caer Tinella, my home, and so I shall go there and get rid of them, every one! You delayed this, but after the success of our attack, you cannot stop it. The folk will follow me, Nightbird," he said, poking himself in the chest. "You think yourself the leader, but it was Roger Lockless, not you, who rescued the prisoners in the last raid, just as it has been Roger Lockless all along, feeding the folk, stealing right from under the big nose of stupid Kos-kosio Begulne. Me!" he yelled, poking his chest again. "And you will not steer them away from Caer Tinella. They will follow me."

"To their doom," the ranger said evenly. "Is this about Caer Tinella, Roger, or is it about who leads?"

Roger waved a hand at him dismissively. "We're not done with this, Nightbird," he said, spitting the elvish title with contempt, and he turned and walked back across the field.

Pony started to follow, her face tight with anger, but Elbryan held up his arm to stop her. "He is young and confused," the ranger explained. "He thought he had his place carved out among the folk, and then we came along."

"He was never formally a leader of the group," said Juraviel. "That lies more to Tomas Gingerwart and Belster O'Comely. Roger was, rather, working outside the limits of the band. Your arrival should not have affected that role."

"In his own mind, he was the hero of the group," Pony reasoned.

"He *is* indeed," Elbryan corrected.

"Agreed," said Juraviel. "But he does not understand that there is room for others."

"Roger Lockless!" Elbryan called loudly.

Roger, at the far edge of the meadow, stopped in his tracks and turned about.

"This must be settled, here and now," the ranger called. "For the good of all the folk." Even as he spoke the words with determination, though, his expression revealed his trepidation. "Give Juraviel your sword," he instructed Pony with a weary sigh.

The woman considered the request, and the look on her lover's face. "Now is not the time," she replied.

"It has to be," the ranger said. "Give Juraviel your sword." He paused and looked from Pony to the approaching Roger, trying to get an even deeper measure of Roger's motivations. "And be gone from here," he added to Pony. "You should not be a witness to this. For his sake."

Pony slid her small sword from its sheath and handed it to the elf, all the while staring Elbryan in the eye. "If you hurt him . . ." she warned, and she turned and walked into the cover of the pines.

Elbryan was wise enough to worry when Pony left a threat unfinished.

"Be careful," Juraviel cautioned. "There may be grim consequences if you take all of the man's dignity."

"I hope it does not come to that," Elbryan said sincerely. "For I do indeed fear the consequences. But this split cannot continue between us. We cannot ask folk in so desperate a situation to make a choice between Roger and me."

"You think Roger will listen to you?"

"I will make Roger listen to me," Elbryan assured him.

"You walk a fine line here, Nightbird," the elf said.

"A line that you and Tuntun showed me well," the ranger replied.

Juraviel nodded, conceding the point. "Make him start it," the elf advised. "If it is to happen."

Elbryan nodded and then straightened as Roger, bold as ever, strode defiantly to stand right before him.

"I grow weary of our bickering, Roger Lockless, who claims leadership of the group," Elbryan called. "In the last raid on Caer Tinella, we showed that we can work well together."

"We showed that my priorities, and not your own, are for the betterment of the folk," the young man replied.

Elbryan took the insult in stride, recognizing the frustration behind it. "We both served valuable functions in the town," he said quietly and calmly. "You freed the prisoners, and for that, all of us, myself included, are indeed grateful. And I defeated Maiyer Dek, a blow from which our enemies will not soon recover."

"But I could have accomplished my task all the more easily if you were not there!" the young man said accusingly. "Yet did you even ask me to go? Where my skills were the ones most needed, did the great Nightbird even inquire if I might be interested in the mission?"

"I did not even know that they held prisoners," the ranger replied honestly. "Else my plan would have been greatly different."

"*Your* plan," Roger spat. "Since you arrived I have heard nothing but your plans!"

"And are we not better off?"

Again Roger spat, this time on Elbryan's feet. "I do not need you, Nightbird," he sneered. "I wish that you and your strange little friend would just disappear into the forest."

"But not Jilseponie," Juraviel noted.

Roger's face turned red. "Her, too!" he said unconvincingly.

Elbryan realized that it would be better to get off of this delicate subject. "But we are not leaving," he said. "Not until the folk are safe in Palmaris, or until the army has marched north to reclaim the towns. I am a fact of your life, Roger Lockless. And if I am put in a position of leadership, one that I have earned through my work in the northland and through my experience, then know that I will not abandon that position for the sake of your foolish pride."

Roger moved as if to strike out, but held his anger, though his face continued to flush.

"My responsibility is to them, not to you," Elbryan calmly explained. "There is a place for you among this band, a very valuable place."

"As your lackey?"

"But know this," the ranger went on, ignoring the foolish comment, "I will argue against any fight for Caer Tinella at this time. Fleeing from the area is the proper course for the folk, and I expect and demand that you will support me in this decision."

Roger eyed the man directly, obviously surprised that the ranger had presumed to give him a direct command.

"I will accept nothing less from you, Roger Lockless."

"You threaten me? As did Pon . . . Jilseponie with her stupid curse?"

"I tell you the truth, and nothing less," Elbryan replied. "This is too important—"

Before the ranger could finish, Roger exploded into motion, launching a punch at his jaw. Not surprised in the least, Elbryan knifed a hand up in front of his face and pushed it out slightly, just enough to deflect Roger's blow harmlessly wide of the mark. The ranger's open hand then shot forward, slapping Roger hard across the face, staggering him backward.

Roger drew out a dagger and started forward, but skidded to a quick stop, facing the angry glow of Tempest.

"A fight between us would be pointless," the ranger said. "You have admitted that you have never killed, yet, regrettably, I have lived by the sword for a long, long time." That said, Elbryan calmly sheathed Tempest.

"I can fight!" Roger yelled at him.

"I do not doubt that," Elbryan replied. "But your real talents lay elsewhere, in scouting, in hindering our enemy with your wits."

"Wits you apparently do not trust with any important decision!"

Elbryan shook his head. "This is battle, not thievery."

"And I am nothing more than a common thief?"

"You act now like a spoiled child," the ranger said. "If you attack me, and kill me, or if I kill you, then what might be the cost to those folk who look to us two to lead them?"

"I do not wish to kill you," Roger informed him. "Only to hurt you!" And on he came, dagger extended.

Elbryan's left hand slapped out right under the blade, catching Roger by the forearm. Before the young man could react, the ranger whipped his free hand across in front of him and brought his left, and Roger's arm, across the other way. Roger felt a sting in his hand, and then suddenly he was free. He caught his balance immediately and tried to come up with a countering strike, but noticed he was no longer holding the dagger, that Elbryan held it in his right hand.

The ranger's left shot out, slapping Roger three times in rapid succession. "You care to try again?" Elbryan asked, flipping the knife back to Roger's nimble grasp.

"Dignity," Juraviel whispered behind the ranger.

Realizing that he might be pushing this too far, that he was insulting the young man, Elbryan reached back and took Pony's sword from Juraviel, then turned and threw it so it stuck in the ground at Roger's feet. "If you wish to continue this, then take up a real weapon," he said.

Roger reached for the sword, then hesitated, looking up to match the ranger's gaze. "I can fight," he said. "But these are your weapons, and not mine. You offer me Pony's ordinary and small sword, while you wield the magical blade—"

Before he could finish his protest, Elbryan, in one fluid movement, drew out Tempest and stuck it in the ground next to Pony's sword, then took the other sword in hand.

"This will be finished, here and now," the ranger said evenly. "It should be so without a fight, but if that is what it takes . . .

"Pick up the weapon, Roger Lockless," Elbryan said. "Or do not. But either way, understand that in the matter of Caer Tinella, my decision shall stand. And that decision is to bypass the town, and Landsdown, as well, and get these folk to the safety of Palmaris."

Roger was hardly listening to anything beyond the ranger's first sentence. This was not about Caer Tinella, it was about pride. It was about a position of leadership that Roger thought he deserved, and it was about a woman—

Roger stopped his train of thought, not willing to go there. He glanced up at Elbryan only briefly, then put his hand about the crafted hilt of Tempest, the silverel pommel wrapped in blue leather. This was about his passage to manhood, he decided, about his courage or fear, about being in control or being controlled—and not by Elbryan, but by his own cowardice.

He pulled the blade from the ground and fell back to a balanced stance, Tempest at the ready.

"First blood?" he asked.

"Until one yields," Juraviel explained, to Roger's surprise. Under the normal guidelines, the sword etiquette, first blood would put an end to such a challenge, but in this instance Juraviel wanted to make certain that Roger Lockless learned a valuable lesson.

Elbryan held his ground calmly; he could tell from Roger's expression that the impatient young man would strike first and strike hard. Predictably, Roger charged, skidding up short and launching Tempest in a wide-swinging arc.

Elbryan reached across his body with the blade of his sword inverted, angled down. As Tempest connected, the ranger skillfully "caught" the sword with his own blade and retracted his arm to somewhat absorb the shock of the strike—else, he feared, Tempest might have shorn his blade in two! Then the ranger smoothly turned his blade up, lifting his hand as he went so that Roger's attack sailed harmlessly high.

Elbryan could have stepped ahead then, and with a short stroke ended the fight. He started to make that exact move, but remembered Juraviel's warning and stepped back instead.

On came Roger, not even realizing that he had already lost the contest. The young man's sword work this time was more deceptive, Tempest stabbing for Elbryan up high, then down low, then low again, and, after a feint up high, low a third time in succession.

Elbryan simply moved his head to avoid the first attack, slapped at the blade once and again to defeat the next two, then hopped the last. Now the ranger did counter, coming forward suddenly as soon as he landed from his slight jump and swinging at Roger in a wide arc, allowing the young man the time to get Tempest in the way to parry.

Elbryan worked furiously, in widely exaggerated and clearly revealed moves, and nimble Roger easily picked off each attack, even managed to counter on two occasions, the first surprising Elbryan and almost slipping through his defenses. The ranger recovered quickly, though, slapping his free hand against the flat of Tempest's blade, though he did get a slight nick on the side of his hand in the process.

"In a contest of first blood, I already won," Roger bragged.

The ranger sublimated his pride and let the insult pass. He had no time nor desire for such taunting games, for he had to focus on the challenge of this particular fight—not concerning whether he would win or lose, but to make sure that neither he nor Roger was injured in the process. Elbryan had to choreograph this one perfectly.

Another flurry ensued, the two men slapping their swords repeatedly in the air between them, picking off each other's blows, with Roger gradually gaining an advantage, the ranger backing steadily. Spurred by the gain, Roger pressed onward even more forcefully, launching Tempest in mighty swings, inadvertently opening his defenses.

Elbryan did not take any of those openings, just continued to back, and to bend a bit, allowing the smaller man to rise above him.

Roger yelped with satisfaction and came on hard, slashing Tempest in a downward, diagonal manner.

Up came the ranger, flipping his sword to his left hand and parrying strong, then, in the blink of an eye, turning the blade right over Roger's halted sword, then diving the tip back under, and whipping the blades out wide so forcefully that Tempest flew from Roger's grasp. Elbryan let his own blade fall free, as well.

The young man dove for the sword; Elbryan dove right in front of him, rolling a somersault, pivoting as he landed and coming right back in. As Roger reached for the sword, his right arm was jerked back, bent at the elbow, Elbryan's right arm sliding under it. Before the young man could react with his free left arm, Elbryan's left slipped under his armpit, then up and around the back of Roger's neck. At the same time, the ranger stepped one leg past Roger and jerked him to the side, over his knee. They went down hard, Elbryan on top of Roger, the young man's arms helplessly pinned behind his back.

"Yield," the ranger instructed.

"Not fair," Roger complained.

Elbryan stood up, hauling Roger to his feet with him, then released him, shoving him forward. Roger immediately went for Tempest.

Elbryan started a silent call to the sword, which would have floated it back to his hand, but decided against the move, letting Roger retrieve the blade, then spin, facing him squarely.

"Not fair," Roger gasped again. "This is a sword fight, not a contest of wrestling strength."

"The hold was merely a continuation of the swordplay," Elbryan replied. "Would you have preferred getting stuck with a sword?"

"You could not!" Roger argued. "Your parry cost us both our weapons!"

Elbryan turned to Juraviel, and saw that the elf recognized the truth of the situation, that he had fairly won. But the elf said, "The lad is correct," and Elbryan, seeing that Roger had learned no lesson here, understood and approved. "Thus the fight is not ended."

"Go and retrieve your sword," Roger said to Elbryan.

"No need," Juraviel interjected, and his tone was a bit too jovial for Elbryan's liking. "The swords were dropped and you were the first to retrieve. Take the advantage, young Roger!"

Elbryan glared at Juraviel, thinking the elf might be pushing things a bit.

Roger came ahead three steps, sword raised in line with Elbryan's face. "Yield," the young man said, smiling widely.

"Because you have the advantage?" Elbryan replied. "As you had with the dagger?"

The poignant reminder sent Roger leaping ahead, but the ranger sprang out, too, soaring in a dive right past Roger, spinning up to his feet and scrambling to his sword before the young man could reverse direction and catch up.

Roger charged right in, though, furious at his own mistake, swinging wildly. Metal rang against metal many, many times, Elbryan neatly picking off every blow.

Fast tiring, Roger tried one of the ranger's tricks, flipping Tempest to his left hand and slashing in.

Elbryan's backhand parry nearly knocked him in a complete circle, and when Roger recovered, raising Tempest defensively before him, he found that the ranger was not there.

And then he felt the tip of a sword against the back of his neck.

"Yield," Elbryan instructed.

Roger tensed, calculating a move, but Elbryan only dug the tip in a bit deeper, ending any such thoughts.

Roger threw Tempest to the ground and stepped away, turning an angry glare on the ranger—a look that grew even darker when Elbryan unexpectedly starting laughing.

"Well fought!" the ranger congratulated. "I did not think you would be so strong with the blade. It seems that you are a man of many talents, Roger Lockless."

"You easily defeated me," the young man spat back.

Elbryan's smile was unrelenting. "Not as easily as you might believe," he said, and he looked to Juraviel. "The shadow dive," he explained.

"Indeed," replied the elf, cuing in to the ranger's reference, remembering when he had seen Elbryan beaten on the sparring field by Tallareyish Issinshine, the elf using just such a move. "It is a move that will work two out of three times," Juraviel went on, speaking to Roger. "Or at least, in two out of three attempts, it will not bring absolute disaster."

Juraviel turned back to Elbryan. "It does not do my old heart well to see you, Nightbird, whom we elves trained to the highest levels, forced to resort to such a desperate maneuver to save defeat at the hands of a mere child!" he scolded.

Elbryan and the elf looked to Roger, both thinking they had done well here, that the issue about the towns, and the pecking order between the two of them, had been settled.

Roger glowered at the ranger and the elf for a few moments, then spat on the ground at Elbryan's feet, turned and stormed away.

Elbryan gave a great sigh. "He is not an easy one to convince," he said.

"Perhaps he recognized your deception as easily as did I," Juraviel reasoned.

"What deception?"

"You could have beaten him at any time, in any manner," the elf stated bluntly.

"Two out of three," the ranger corrected.

"When you fought Tallareyish, perhaps," Juraviel was quick to answer. "In that instance, however, Tallareyish's maneuver had been wrought purely of desperation, for you had clearly gained the upper hand."

"And this time?"

"This time the shadow dive was used for no better reason than to save some of Roger's dignity, a tactic I am not certain will prove effective."

"But—" Elbryan started to protest, for Juraviel had bade him do just that before the fight began.

"Just take care that your 'lesson' doesn't impart a false sense of ability in Roger," the elf warned. "If he goes into battle against a powrie, he'll not likely come out of it alive."

Elbryan conceded that point, looking to the place where Roger had exited the field. That seemed the least of their troubles, however, for, given Roger's attitude, it seemed it would not be easy to convince the folk to go around the two occupied towns.

"Go and give Pony back her blade," Juraviel instructed.

Too caught up in the moment, trying to figure out how he might better correct this situation with Roger, Elbryan didn't even reply, just retrieved and sheathed Tempest and walked off into the night.

"While I go and have a talk with Roger Lockless," Juraviel finished under his breath when the ranger had walked away.

The elf caught up with Roger soon after, in a root-strewn clearing beneath the heavy boughs of a wide-spreading elm tree.

"Etiquette and simple good manners would have demanded that you congratulate the winner," Juraviel explained, lighting on a branch right above the young man.

"Be gone, elf," Roger replied.

Juraviel hopped down to the ground right in front of the young man. "Be gone?" he echoed incredulously.

"Now!"

"Save your threats, Roger Lockless," the elf answered calmly. "I have seen you fight and am not impressed."

"I brought your wonderful Nightbird to a near standstill."

"He could have beaten you at any time," the elf interrupted. "You know that."

Roger stood up, and though he was not tall by human standards, he still towered over the elf.

"Nightbird is as strong as any man alive," the elf went on. "And, trained by the Touel'alfar, he is as nimble with the blade as any. He is the complete warrior, and could have turned your own blade back in your face, had he so chosen. Or he might have simply caught your arm and crushed it in his iron grasp."

"So says his lackey elf!" Roger cried.

Juraviel scoffed at the absurdity of the statement. "Have you already forgotten your first fight?"

Roger's expression screwed up with curiosity.

"What happened when you went at Nightbird with the dagger?" the elf asked. "Is that not proof enough?"

A thoroughly frustrated Roger punched out at Juraviel. The elf stepped inside the blow, caught Roger by the wrist, then went right behind the young man, turning Roger's arm behind his back and grabbing him by the hair with his free hand. A tug on both arm and hair had Roger turning about, and Juraviel promptly slammed his face into the trunk of the elm.

"I am not Nightbird," Juraviel warned. "I am not human, and hold little compassion for fools!" With that, Juraviel slammed Roger into the tree once more, then spun the man about and hit him with a backhand that sat him on the ground.

"You know the truth, Roger Lockless," he scolded. "You know that Nightbird is your better in these matters, and that his judgment concerning our course should be heeded. Yet you are so blinded by your own foolish pride that you will doom your own people before admitting it!"

"Pride?" Roger yelled back. "Was it not Roger Lockless who went into Caer Tinella to rescue—"

"And why did Roger Lockless go into Caer Tinella?" Juraviel interrupted.

"On both occasions. For the sake of the poor prisoners, or out of fear that he would be upstaged by this new hero?"

Roger stuttered over a response, but Juraviel wasn't listening anyway. "He could have beaten you at any moment, in any manner," the elf said again, and then he turned and walked away, leaving battered Roger sitting under the elm tree.

❖ 16 ❖

To the Father Abbot's Amusement

"A bbot Dobrinion grows increasingly uneasy," Brother Francis offered to Father Abbot Markwart. The younger monk was obviously agitated; every word that came from him was strained, for in speaking them, Brother Francis was caught somewhere between fear and horror. Of course Abbot Dobrinion was uneasy, he realized, for they were torturing the abbot's subjects in the very dungeons of this holy place!

"It is not my place to say, perhaps," Francis went on, pausing often, trying to gauge impassive Markwart's reaction, "but I fear—"

"That St. Precious is not friendly to our cause," the Father Abbot finished for him.

"Forgive me," Brother Francis humbly said.

"Forgive?" Markwart echoed incredulously. "Forgive your perceptiveness? Your wariness? We are at war, my young fool. Have you not yet realized that?"

"Of course, Father Abbot," Francis said, bowing his head. "The powries and goblins—"

"Forget them!" Markwart interrupted. "And forget the giants, and the dactyl demon, as well. This war has become much more dangerous than any matter concerning mere monsters."

Brother Francis lifted his head and stared long and hard at Markwart.

"This is a war for the heart of the Abellican Church," Markwart went on. "I have explained this over and over to you, and yet you still do not understand. This is a war between traditions which have stood for millennia, and usurpous ideas, petty contemporary beliefs concerning the nature of good and the nature of evil."

"Are those not timeless concepts?" a very confused Brother Francis dared to ask.

"Of course," Markwart replied with a disarming chuckle. "But some, Master Jojonah among them, seem to believe they can redefine the terms to fit their own perceptions."

"And what of Abbot Dobrinion?"

"You tell me of Abbot Dobrinion," Markwart instructed.

Brother Francis paused, contemplating the implications. He wasn't quite sure how the Father Abbot viewed Dobrinion, or anyone else, for that matter. Back at St.-Mere-Abelle, Markwart had argued often with Master De'Unnero, and often violently, and yet, despite their differences, it was no secret that De'Unnero was the Father Abbot's closest adviser, next to Francis himself.

"Brother Avelyn the heretic used to analyze every question," Father Abbot Markwart remarked. "He could not simply speak what was in his heart, and that, I fear, was his undoing."

"Abbot Dobrinion will fight us," Brother Francis blurted. "I do not trust him, and think him more akin to Master Jojonah's definitions of good and evil than to yours . . . ours."

"Strong words," Markwart said slyly.

Brother Francis paled.

"But not wholly untrue," Markwart went on, and Francis breathed easier. "Abbot Dobrinion has ever been an idealist, even when those ideals fly in the face of pragmatism. I thought that his craving for the sainthood of Brother Allabarnet would allow me to keep him in line, but apparently he is possessed of greater weakness than I believed."

"He will fight us," Brother Francis said more firmly.

"Even as we speak, Abbot Dobrinion petitions for the release of the Chilichunks," Markwart explained. "He will go to the Baron of Palmaris, likely to the King himself, and of course, to the other abbots."

"Have we a right to hold them?" Brother Francis dared to ask.

"Is the Abellican Order more important than the fate of three people?" came the curt response.

"Yes, Father Abbot," Brother Francis replied, bowing his head once more. When Markwart put it that simple way, it was easy for Francis to put aside his private feelings about the treatment of the prisoners. Indeed the stakes were high here, too high for him to let foolish compassion get in the way.

"And what, then, shall we do?" the Father Abbot asked, though it was obvious to Brother Francis that the old man had already made up his mind.

Again Brother Francis hesitated, thinking through the problem. "An Abbot College," he began, referring to the gathering of all the Church hierarchy, a process necessary if the Father Abbot meant to remove Abbot Dobrinion.

"There will indeed be such a gathering," Markwart replied. "But it will not convene until mid-Calember."

Brother Francis considered the words. Calember was the eleventh month, still more than four months away. "Then we must leave St. Precious at once," he reasoned at length, guessing, correctly, that the Father Abbot was fast running out of patience with him. "We must take our prisoners to St.-Mere-Abelle, where Abbot Dobrinion shall have no say in their treatment."

"Well spoken," Markwart congratulated. "Indeed, we must be gone from St. Precious tomorrow, the centaur and the Chilichunks in tow. See to the arrangements, and plot our paths."

"A straight run," Brother Francis assured him.

"And make it public, very much so, that we are leaving," the Father Abbot went on. "And see to it that Connor Bildeborough is taken, as well, for that is news which will spread wide."

Brother Francis wore a doubting expression. "That may invite trouble from the crown," he warned.

"And if so, we will release him," Markwart replied. "Until that happens, the gossip may reach the ears of the woman we seek."

"But she may not care about Bildeborough," Brother Francis reasoned. "Their union was short, and unpleasant, so it is said."

"But she will come for the Chilichunks," Markwart explained. "And for that ugly half-horse creature. The arrest of Master Bildeborough will only serve to publicize our other prisoners."

Brother Francis considered the reasoning for a moment, then nodded. "And what of Abbot Dobrinion?" he asked.

"A smaller thorn than you would believe," Markwart replied quickly, and it seemed to Francis that the man already had a plan in mind for the venerable abbot of St. Precious.

Connor Bildeborough paced the small room—a rented flat in the lower section of Palmaris. Though the man was of noble blood, he preferred the excitement of the docks and the rougher taverns. The only adventure he found at his uncle's palace was the occasional fox hunt, and those he considered foolish, an ego-propping exercise that did not even qualify, in his mind, as sport. No, Connor, quick with his wits and quick with his sword, preferred a good fight in a tavern, or a brush with would-be muggers in a dark alleyway.

To that end, he had been spending a considerable amount of time in the fields north of Palmaris, trying to earn a warrior's reputation in skirmishes with the many monsters to be found up there. His uncle had presented him with a magnificent gift at the outset of the war, a slender sword of unmatched craftsmanship. Its blade gleamed of some silvery metal that could not be identified, and inset along its golden basket pommel were several tiny magical magnetites so the weapon could be used beautifully for parrying, practically attracting an opponent's blade. Its name was Defender, and where his uncle had ever found such a blade, Connor could not know. The rumors about the sword were many, and impossible to confirm. Most agreed it had been forged in the smithies of the first King of Honce-the-Bear—some said by a cunning powrie who had deserted its kindred on the Weathered Isles. Other tales claimed that the mysterious Touel'alfar had helped in its creation, and still others claimed that both races had played a role, along with the best human weaponsmiths of the day.

Whatever the truth of the blade's origins, Connor understood that he now possessed a most extraordinary weapon. With Defender in hand, just a week before he had led a contingent of Kingsmen against a horde of powerful giants, and though the results had been somewhat disastrous—as can be expected in a fight with giants—Connor had done quite well, could even claim two kills by his sword. What glories he had found in the north!

Now, though, in this room with his good friend Abbot Dobrinion, Connor understood that he should be keeping his attention a bit closer to home.

"It is about Jill," the abbot insisted. "Father Abbot Markwart believes she is in possession of the gemstone cache which was stolen from St.-Mere-Abelle."

Jill. The name hit Connor hard, tugged at his memories and at his heart. He had courted her for months, wonderful months, only to have their marriage disintegrate in a matter of hours. When Jill had refused him his marital rights of consummation, Connor could have demanded her death.

But of course he could not have done that, for he had indeed loved the spirited, though troubled, woman. He had settled for the judgment that she should be indentured to the King's army, and how his heart had broken when his Jilly left Palmaris.

"I had heard that she was far, far away," the young nobleman said somberly. "In Pireth Tulme, or Pireth Danard, serving in the Coastpoint Guards."

"So she may be," Abbot Dobrinion conceded. "Who can tell? The Father Abbot is searching for her, and believes she was in the north, back in Dundalis, and even farther, accompanied by Avelyn of St.-Mere-Abelle, who stole the sacred gemstones."

"Do you know this man?" Connor asked suddenly, again wondering about this first monk who had visited Pettibwa Chilichunk.

"Never met him," Abbot Dobrinion replied.

"A description, then?" Connor pressed.

"A large man, big of bone and, they believe, big of belly, as well," the abbot replied. "So said Master Jojonah."

Connor nodded, digesting the information. The monk who had visited with Pettibwa was indeed large, of bone and of belly. Could it be that Jill had come back through Palmaris in this man's company? Could Jilly, his Jilly, have been so close, without him ever knowing it?

"The woman is in trouble, Connor, very great trouble," Abbot Dobrinion remarked gravely. "And if you know anything concerning her, where she might be, or if she is indeed in possession of the stones, the Father Abbot will seek you out. And his techniques of interrogation are not pleasant."

"How could I know anything about Jill?" Connor replied incredulously. "The last time I saw her was at her trial, when she was sent away to join the King's army." His statement was true enough—the last time he had seen Jill was on the occasion of their annulment, and her indenture—but of late Connor had traveled out of Palmaris often, to the north to do battle, to make a name for himself in what many agreed were the waning days of the war. He had heard tales of a rogue band operating farther to the north, near the towns of Caer Tinella and Landsdown, using tactics and magic to wreak havoc with the monsters. Might Jill and the monk Avelyn, with their stolen gemstones, be the source of that magic?

Of course, Connor meant to keep his suspicions private, even from Abbot Dobrinion.

"The Father Abbot means to find her," Dobrinion said.

"If Jill has made more trouble for herself, then there is little I can do to rectify the situation," Connor replied.

"But by the simple fact that you were once wed to the woman, you are involved," Dobrinion warned.

"Ridiculous," said Connor, but even as he spoke the word, the door to the room burst open and four monks, Youseff and Dandelion, Brother Francis, and the Father Abbot himself, entered.

Dandelion went right for Connor; the man moved to draw his slender sword, only to find it lifting of its own accord from its scabbard. Connor grabbed at the handle, but when he caught it by the pommel, he found his arm pulled up high, and in a moment he was standing on his tiptoes, and for all his strength and all his weight, he could not bring the sword back down to a defensive posture.

Dandelion hit him a short, sharp blow, then yanked his hand from the sword hilt and wrapped him in a tight hug. The sword drifted away, weightless, and Connor couldn't comprehend it until he noticed that the fourth monk, Brother Francis, was using a green-ringed gemstone.

"Do not resist, Master Connor Bildeborough," the Father Abbot instructed. "We wish to speak with you, that is all, on a matter of tremendous importance, a matter concerning the security of your uncle's holdings."

Connor instinctively tried to break free of the hold, but found his efforts futile, for Dandelion was too strong and too skilled to allow him any openings. Besides, the other young monk, Youseff, was standing at the ready, a small and heavy club in hand.

"My uncle will hear of this," Connor warned Markwart.

"Your uncle will agree with my decision," the Father Abbot replied confidently. He gave a nod to his two lackeys and they dragged Connor away.

"You tread on dangerous ground," Abbot Dobrinion warned. "Baron Rochefort Bildeborough's influence is not to be taken lightly."

"I assure you that one of us is indeed treading on dangerous ground," the Father Abbot calmly replied.

"You knew that we were looking for Connor Bildeborough," Brother Francis accused, walking over to take the sword from midair. "Yet you came out to warn him?"

"I came out to find him," the abbot corrected. "To tell him that he must come in and speak with you, that any information he might have—and he has none, I can assure you—might prove important to winning the war."

Father Abbot Markwart chuckled snidely throughout Dobrinion's halfhearted protest. "Words are often such pretty things," he remarked when Dobrinion was finished. "We use them to speak the truth of facts, yet to hide the truth of intent."

"You doubt me?" Dobrinion asked.

"You have made your position concerning this matter quite clear to me," Markwart replied. "I know why you came looking for Connor Bildeborough. I know what you wished to accomplish, and know, too, that your goals and my own are not in accord."

Abbot Dobrinion huffed in reply and strode defiantly past the pair. "The Baron must be informed," he explained, moving to the door.

Brother Francis grabbed him roughly by the arm, and he spun, glaring in disbelief at the young man's brazen action.

Francis returned that look with a murderous stare, and for a moment Dobrinion thought the brother would lash out at him. A motion from Father Abbot Markwart ended the tension of the moment, though, and Francis let go of the abbot with his hand, if not with his glare.

"The manner of the telling is all important," Markwart said to Dobrinion. "Do explain to the Baron that his nephew is not charged with any crime or sin, and had merely volunteered to answer our questions on this important matter."

Abbot Dobrinion stormed away.

"His report to the Baron will not be flattering," Brother Francis remarked as Youseff and Dandelion dragged Connor away.

"As he will," the Father Abbot conceded.

"Baron Bildeborough could prove a difficult adversary," Brother Francis pressed.

Again Markwart did not seem overly concerned. "We will see what happens," he replied. "By the time Rochefort Bildeborough is even informed, we will have discerned what Connor knows, and the mere fact of his arrest will publicize our presence and the identity of our other prisoners. After that, this man means little to me."

He started away then, and Brother Francis, after a short pause to consider the ramifications of this meeting, to consider the strain between Markwart and Dobrinion and the dire consequences that rivalry might hold for the abbot of St. Precious, turned to follow.

"Are we to do battle in the streets of Palmaris?" a frustrated Brother Francis fumed at Abbot Dobrinion. They had barely begun questioning Connor Bildeborough—using polite and friendly tactics—when a host of soldiers arrived at the gates of St. Precious, demanding the man's release.

"I told you that arresting the nephew of Baron Bildeborough was no small matter," the abbot shot back. "Did you not believe that his uncle would react with force?"

"Enough, enough, from both of you," Father Abbot Markwart scolded. "Bring to me the emissary of Baron Bildeborough that we might settle this."

Both Dobrinion and Brother Francis started for the door, then stopped, glaring at each other.

"And you, Abbot Dobrinion," the Father Abbot went on, drawing the man's attention, then motioning for Francis to go and complete the task. "You are needed with the centaur. He wishes to speak with you."

"My place is here, Father Abbot," Dobrinion replied.

"Your place is where I deem it to be," the old man said. "Go to the pitiful creature."

Abbot Dobrinion stared hard at Markwart, not pleased at all. He held no reservations about speaking with Bradwarden, but the centaur's cell was far below, perhaps the farthest point in all the abbey from their present position, and by the time he got down there and back, even if his conversation with Bradwarden lasted but a few words, the meeting with Bildeborough's men could be long over.

He did as he was instructed, though, bowing to his superior and storming out of the room.

Brother Francis entered a moment later. "Brother Youseff will bring the emissary presently," he explained.

"And you will go right off to Connor Bildeborough," Father Abbot Markwart said, tossing a gray soul stone to Francis. "Or near to Connor, though not where you can be seen. Go to him in spirit only, at first, and be not gentle. See what secrets his mind might hold. Then bring him to me. I will delay the Baron's soldiers for as long as possible, but they will not leave here without Connor."

Brother Francis bowed and ran off, and had just exited when another man burst in.

"Where is Abbot Dobrinion?" the gruff soldier asked, pushing past Brother Youseff to stand before Father Abbot Markwart. He was a burly man, dressed in the overlapping leather armor bearing the house insignia, the eagle, of House Bildeborough. That emblem was emblazoned on his metal shield, as well, and on the crest of his shining helm, a tight-fitting affair that pulled low over his ears, with a single strip running down between his eyes to fit over his nose.

"And you are?" Markwart prompted.

"An emissary from Baron Bildeborough," the man said imperiously. "Come to secure the release of his nephew."

"You speak as if young Connor had been arrested," Markwart remarked casually.

The burly soldier rocked back on his heels, taken a bit off guard by Markwart's cooperative tone.

"The Baron's nephew was only asked in to St. Precious that he might answer some questions concerning a previous marriage," Markwart went on. "Of course he is free to leave at his leisure; the man has committed no crime against the state or the Church."

"But we were informed—"

"Erroneously, it would seem," Father Abbot Markwart said with a chuckle. "Please, sit and take some wine—fine boggle from Abbot Dobrinion's private stock. My man has already been sent to retrieve Master Connor. They should join us within a few minutes."

The soldier looked around curiously, not really knowing how to react to it all. He had come out with a contingent of more than fifty armed and armored warriors, ready to do battle, if necessary, to pull Connor Bildeborough from his imprisonment.

"Sit," Father Abbot Markwart bade him again.

The soldier pulled a chair from a side table, while Markwart retrieved a bottle of boggle from a cabinet at the side of the room. "We are not enemies, after all," the Father Abbot said, again in an innocent tone. "The Church and King are allied, and have been for generations. It amazes me that you would be so impetuous as to come to the gates of St. Precious thusly armed." He popped the top from the bottle and poured a generous amount in the soldier's glass, then just a bit for himself.

"Baron Bildeborough wastes no effort where young Connor is concerned," the soldier replied, taking a sip, then blinking repeatedly as the potent wine washed down.

"Still, you came here looking for battle," the Father Abbot went on. "Do you know who I am?"

The man took another sip—a larger one this time—then eyed the wrinkled old man. "Another abbot," he answered. "From some other abbey, St.-Mere-Able, or something like that."

"St.-Mere-Abelle," Markwart confirmed. "The mother abbey of all the Abellican Church."

The soldier drained his glass and reached for the bottle, but Markwart, his expression changing dramatically to one of outrage, pulled the boggle away. "You are a member of the Church, are you not?" he asked sharply.

The soldier blinked a couple of times, then nodded.

"Then you should be aware that you are now addressing the Father Abbot of the Abellican Order!" Markwart screamed at him. "With a snap of my fingers I could have you banished and branded! With a word to your King, I could have you declared an outlaw."

"For what crime?" the man protested.

"For any crime I choose!" Markwart yelled back at him.

Brother Francis entered the room then, Connor Bildeborough right behind him, the nobleman looking somewhat unsettled, though not physically harmed.

"Master Connor!" the soldier said, rising so quickly that his chair toppled behind him.

The Father Abbot rose as well, and moved about the desk, coming to stand right before the obviously intimidated soldier. "Do not forget what I told you," the old priest said to the man. "With just a word."

"Now you threaten the soldiers of my uncle's house?" Connor Bildeborough said. His presence and the forcefulness of his tone bolstered the soldier's resolve, the man straightening and looking Father Abbot Markwart in the eye.

"Threatening?" Markwart echoed, and that laugh came again, but this time it held a sinister edge. "I do not threaten, foolish young Connor. But I think that it would do you well, would do your uncle well, and would do the soldiers of your uncle's house well, to understand that these are matters quite beyond their understanding. And interference.

"I am not surprised that a willful young man, so full of pride, such as yourself, would not look past his own importance to comprehend the gravity of our present situation," Markwart went on. "But it does surprise me that the Baron of Palmaris would act so foolishly as to send an armed contingent against the leaders of the Abellican Order."

"He thought that those leaders had acted improperly, and dangerously," Connor stated, working hard to keep from seeming defensive. He had done nothing wrong, after all, and neither had his uncle. If there had been criminal conduct in all of this, it was perpetrated by the old man standing before him.

"He thought . . . you thought," Markwart said dismissively. "It seems that all of you make your own judgments, and act upon them as though God Himself blessed you with special vision."

"You deny that you came and took me?" Connor asked incredulously.

"You were needed," Markwart replied. "And were you mistreated, Master Bildeborough? Were you tortured?"

The soldier puffed out his chest and clenched his jaw.

"No," Connor admitted, and the burly man relaxed. "But what of the Chilichunks?" he asked. "Do you deny that you hold them, and that their treatment has not been so kindly?"

"I do not," Markwart replied. "They have, by their own actions, become enemies of the Church."

"Rubbish!"

"We shall see," the Father Abbot replied.

"You mean to take them from Palmaris," Connor accused.

No answer.

"That I will not allow!"

"You hold jurisdiction in such matters?" the Father Abbot asked sarcastically.

"I speak for my uncle."

"How pretentious," Markwart said with a snicker. "And tell me, Master Connor, are we to do battle in the streets of Palmaris, that all the city might learn of the rift between the Church and their Baron?"

Connor hesitated before responding, realizing the potentially disastrous implications. His uncle was held in high regard, but most of the common folk in Palmaris, and in any other city in Honce-the-Bear, truly feared the wrath of the Church. But still, the fate of the Chilichunks was at stake here, and for Connor that was no small matter. "If that is what is necessary," he said sternly.

Markwart continued to laugh, his agitated trembling hiding the movement as he slipped his hands into a pouch on the sash of his voluminous robes, drawing forth a lodestone. Up came the hand, and a split second later the magnetite shot out to smash the soldier's helmet on the nose guard. The burly man yelped and grabbed at his face, blood pouring freely from both nostrils, waves of pain rolling over him, driving him down to one knee.

At the same moment, Brother Youseff leaped forward, tightening his hand as though it was a blade and driving it into the kidney of unsuspecting Connor Bildeborough, dropping him to his knees, as well.

"Possess him," Father Abbot Markwart instructed Brother Francis. "Use his mouth to instruct the soldiers to let us pass." He turned to Youseff. "The prisoners are ready for transport?"

"Brother Dandelion has all the caravan loaded and readied in the back courtyard," Youseff replied. "But Abbot Dobrinion, before he went down into the dungeons, set many guards about that yard."

"They will not battle us," Markwart assured him.

The soldier groaned and tried to stand as the Father Abbot retrieved the lodestone, but Youseff, the alert watchdog, was right there, launching a series of vicious, snapping blows to the man's face that laid him low on the floor.

Markwart looked to Brother Francis, who stood staring at Connor but apparently taking no action. "Brother Francis," the Father Abbot prompted sternly.

"I did get into his thoughts," Brother Francis explained. "And learned some things which might prove valuable."

"But . . ." Markwart prompted, recognizing the hesitant tone.

"But only when he was caught unawares," Brother Francis admitted.

"And only for a second. He is strong of will and readily expelled me, though he knew not the nature of the attack."

Father Abbot Markwart nodded, then stepped closer to the still-dazed Connor. Out shot the old man's fist, brutally snapping Connor's head to the side, and he crumbled to the floor. "Now possess him," the Father Abbot said impatiently. "It should not prove too difficult!"

"But I will learn nothing when he is in this state," Brother Francis argued. It was true enough; an unconscious or dazed man might be relatively easily possessed, but of body only, with no invasion of memory or desire. When consciousness returned, the fight for control would begin anew.

"We need nothing more of this one's mind," Markwart explained. "We need only his body and his voice."

"Evil doings," Brother Braumin whispered to Brother Dellman as the two stood solemnly in the courtyard of St. Precious, surrounded by their brothers of St.-Mere-Abelle, and with the four prisoners close by. Brother Braumin was not surprised by the sudden order to ready the wagons, for he had been watching the Father Abbot and his lackey Francis closely in their interactions with Abbot Dobrinion, and knew their welcome at St. Precious was wearing quite thin.

What did surprise the monk, though, was the presence of armed soldiers at all of the abbey's gates, a force sent to contain them, he realized, and particularly to contain their prisoners. Whispers among the ranks had spoken of a new captive, a nobleman, though none save Markwart, Brother Francis, and the Father Abbot's two personal bodyguards had been allowed anywhere near the man. Still, given the appearance and the demeanor of the soldiers, it wasn't hard to understand that the Father Abbot might have overstepped his bounds here.

"Why have they come?" Brother Dellman whispered back.

"I do not know," Braumin replied, not wanting to involve this promising young monk too deeply in the intrigue. Brother Braumin feared that he and his brothers would be leaving, and if the soldiers tried to stop them, Palmaris would see a display of magical devastation heretofore unknown in the city.

What should I do? the gentle Brother Braumin wondered. If the order came from Father Abbot Markwart to battle the soldiers, what course should he follow?

"You seem distressed, brother," Dellman remarked. "Do you fear that these soldiers will attack us?"

"Exactly the opposite," Brother Braumin replied in exasperation. He growled and smacked his hand against the wagon. How he wished that Master Jojonah were here to guide him!

"Brother," Dellman said, putting a hand on Braumin's shoulder to calm him.

Braumin turned to face the younger monk squarely, took him by the shoulders and locked his gaze. "Watch closely the coming events, Brother Dellman," he bade the man.

Dellman stared at him quizzically.

Braumin Herde sighed and turned away. He wouldn't openly accuse the Father Abbot to this young man. Not yet. Not until the evidence was overwhelming. Such an accusation, such a declaration that so much of what Dellman thought holy was a lie, might break the man, or send him running to Father Abbot Markwart for comfort.

Then Braumin Herde's heart would be known, and he, like Master Jojonah, would quickly be neutralized.

The monk knew then what he would do if the order came. He would fight with his brothers, or at least would give the appearance of fighting. He could not reveal his heart, not yet.

"Forgive me, Master Jojonah," he mumbled under his breath, and then, on impulse, he added, "Forgive me, Brother Avelyn."

Soon after, the grim-faced guards of Baron Bildeborough stood aside, on orders from the man they had come to rescue, as the caravan from St.-Mere-Abelle rolled out of the abbey's back gate. The three Chilichunks were bound and gagged in the back of one wagon, with Brother Youseff standing dangerous guard over them, while Brother Dandelion sat atop the back of battered Bradwarden, the centaur's upper, human torso covered in blankets. The monks had tied Bradwarden close to the wagon in front of him, and brutal Dandelion forced the centaur to bow low and forward, so that nearly all of that telltale human torso was inside the leading wagon.

Father Abbot Markwart and Brother Francis were likewise hidden from sight, the Church leader not wishing to be bothered with common soldiers, and Brother Francis deep in the throes of maintaining his possession of Connor. When the caravan was safely away, moving steadily to the eastern dock area of the city, then turning north, Francis walked Connor's body back into the abbey and relinquished control, and the man, still dazed from the pounding Markwart had given him, slumped to the floor.

The caravan encountered no resistance as it exited the city altogether, moving through the north, and not the east gate. Markwart turned them east almost immediately, and soon they were running clear of Baron Bildeborough's domain. Again the monks used their levitating malachite to cross the strong flowing waters of the Masur Delaval, avoiding any possible trouble at the well-guarded ferry.

From the moment he reached the lower dungeons, to find that Bradwarden had been removed by Markwart's men more than an hour before, Abbot Dobrinion knew that trouble was brewing up above. His first instincts started him running back for the stone stair, crying for guards.

Pragmatic Dobrinion calmed and slowed, though. What could he do? he asked himself honestly. If he even managed to get to the courtyard before the caravan's departure, would he lead the fight against Markwart's men?

"Yes, my Abbot!" a young monk, a man barely more than a boy, whom Dobrinion recognized as a newcomer to St. Precious, cried enthusiastically, skidding to a stop right before the tired old abbot. "At your bidding."

Dobrinion pictured this young man as a smoking husk, a charred corpse left in the wake of a magical fireball. Markwart carried such stones, he knew, and so did Brother Francis. And those two younger men, Youseff and Dandelion, were trained killers, or, as the Church called such assassins, Brothers Justice.

How many dozens of Dobrinion's flock would be slaughtered this day if he went above and refused to allow Markwart to leave? And even if they proved successful in defeating the monks from St.-Mere-Abelle, then what?

Dalebert Markwart was the Father Abbot of the Abellican Order.

"There is no reason to guard these empty cells," Dobrinion said quietly to the young monk. "Go and find some rest."

"I am not weary," the monk replied, wearing a wide and innocent smile.

"Then rest for me," Dobrinion said in all seriousness, and he started a long and slow walk up the stone stairs.

❖ 17 ❖

Edicts from on High

Elbryan blew a long sigh and looked helplessly to Pony. He knew that Juraviel, too, was watching him, though the elf remained far from the firelight where the leaders of the band had gathered.

"Once Caer Tinella and Landsdown are secured," Tomas Gingerwart said, obviously trying to placate the adamant ranger, "we will follow your lead to the south, those of us who are not fit to remain and defend our homes, at least."

Elbryan wanted to grab the man by the shoulders and shake him hard, wanted to yell into his face that even if the two towns were taken, there would likely be few remaining to stand in defense. He wanted to remind Tomas and all the others that if they went after the towns and failed, and the powries then pursued them, it was likely that all would be lost: all the fighters, all the elderly, and all the children. But the ranger kept silent; he had made the argument over and over, had spoken it in every manner he could think of, and every time, it had fallen on deaf ears. How bitter this impotence was for Elbryan, to think that all of his efforts to ensure that the fate that befell his own home and his own family would not be repeated here, might prove to be in vain because of foolish pride. They wanted to save their homes, they claimed, but if there could be no security in a place, how could it be called home?

His frustration now was not lost on one of the men sitting nearby. "Are ye not to argue with him, then?" Belster O'Comely asked.

The ranger looked at his old friend and merely threw up his hands.

"Then you will join us in our fight," Tomas reasoned, and that notion brought a cheer from the gathering.

"No," Pony said sternly, and unexpectedly. All eyes, even Elbryan's turned to regard her.

"I'll not go," the woman said firmly.

Surprised gasps turned to angry whispers.

"I've never shied from a fight, you know that," Pony went on, crossing her arms resolutely. "But to agree to go and do battle for the two towns would only bolster your belief that you are following the correct course. And you are not. I know this, and Nightbird knows it. I am not going to now make the same arguments that you have ignored for the last days, but neither will I fall in line for the slaughter. I wish you well in your folly, but I will remain with the infirm, trying somehow to usher them to safety when the powries roll out of Caer Tinella into the forest, hunting, and with no one to stand against their hordes."

It seemed to Elbryan that Pony might be exaggerating just a bit, but her strong words prompted many whispered conversations, some angry but others doubting the course of attack. The ranger had thought to go along for the attack, and thought Pony would surely stand outside the town proper, launching devastating magical attacks. Her resolve not to participate—and he knew this to be no bluff—had caught him by surprise. As he considered it over the next few seconds, though, he came to understand her point.

"Nor will I join you," the ranger said, drawing more comments, angry and astonished. "I cannot condone this course, Master Gingerwart. I will remain with Jilseponie and the infirm, and if the powries come out, I, we, will do what we may to hold them at bay and get the infirm to safety."

Tomas Gingerwart verily trembled as he looked to Belster O'Comely, his expression openly accusatory.

"Reconsider, I beg," Belster said to Elbryan. "I, too, have seen too much of this war, my friend, and would prefer a course around the powries to Palmaris. But the decision is made, fairly and by vote. The warriors will go after their homes, and we, as allies, have a responsibility to aid in that fight."

"Even if it is folly?" Pony asked.

"Who is to say?" Belster replied. "Many thought your own attack on the towns to be folly, yet it turned out for the better, by far."

Elbryan and Pony locked stares, the ranger drawing strength from the resolute woman. Pony had made up her mind and it would not be changed, and so Elbryan, too, decided to stay the course.

"I cannot participate in this," he said calmly. "When I went into Caer Tinella, my actions brought no threat to those who could not fight."

Belster looked to Tomas and shrugged, having no practical argument against that simple logic.

Roger Lockless, looking bedraggled, walked into the camp then. He stared at Elbryan for a long while, and all in attendance, the ranger included, thought he would seize the moment to paint Elbryan as the coward, or as the traitor.

"Nightbird is right," the young man said suddenly. He stepped past a stunned Elbryan and Pony to address the whole gathering. "I have just returned from Caer Tinella," he said loudly. "We cannot attack."

"Roger—" Tomas started to protest.

"The powries have reinforced," Roger went on. "They outnumber us, perhaps two or three to one, and they are entrenched in strong defensible positions. Also, they have great spear-throwing contraptions hidden among the walls. If we attack, even if Nightbird and Pony join with us, we will be slaughtered."

The grim news quieted the gathering for a while, then inspired many more whispered conversations, though these were neither agitated nor angry, but rather subdued. Gradually, the looks from every man and woman fell onto the shoulders of Tomas Gingerwart.

"Our scouts said nothing of this," the man explained to Roger.

"Were your scouts, before me, within the town?" Roger replied.

Tomas looked to Belster and to the other leaders of the band for some help, but all of them just shook their heads helplessly.

"If you decide to go to battle, then I, too, will remain with Nightbird and Pony," Roger finished, stepping back to stand at the ranger's side.

That was enough, for Tomas and for all the proud and stubborn folk.

"Get us to Palmaris," Tomas said grudgingly to Elbryan.

"We break camp at first light," the ranger replied, then looked to Roger, nodding his approval as the gathering dispersed. Roger didn't return the look with a smile or a nod; he had done what he had to do, and nothing more. Without meeting the ranger's stare, without a word to either Elbryan or Pony, the young man walked away.

Soon Elbryan and Pony were alone at the fire, and Juraviel came down from the trees behind to join them.

"What did you say to him?" the ranger asked, guessing that the elf had spent some private time with the surprising Roger Lockless.

"The same thing I said to you at the milking trough when you were blinded by pride," Juraviel replied with a sly look.

Elbryan blushed deeply and looked away from Pony and the elf, remembering all too clearly that embarrassing moment. He had just fought with Tuntun—a real fight and not a planned sparring match—accusing the female elf of cheating at a contest that left him with a cold meal. Tuntun had summarily battered him, but the young Elbryan, blinded by anger and pride, had not accepted the defeat well, had spouted foolish words and idle threats.

Belli'mar Juraviel, his mentor, and the closest thing he could then call a friend in all of Andur'Blough Inninness, had promptly thrashed him, putting him into the cold water of the trough several times.

"A painful lesson," Juraviel said at length. "But one that stayed with you all these years."

Elbryan couldn't deny the truth of that.

"This young Roger has promise," the elf went on. "It was no small matter for him to come in here and side with you, even though he knew that you were right."

"He is maturing," Pony agreed.

Juraviel nodded. "I will begin scouting our path this night," he explained.

"A wide berth of the powries," Pony said.

The elf nodded again.

"One last question," Elbryan begged as ever-elusive Juraviel started back to the trees. The elf turned to regard him. "Have the powries really reinforced?"

"Would it make a difference in your choice?" the elf asked.

"None."

Juraviel smiled. "To my knowledge—and that knowledge is great concerning this matter, do not doubt—Roger Lockless has been nowhere near Caer Tinella this night."

The ranger had suspected as much, and the confirmation made him admire Roger's choice all the more.

There was no sign of pursuit; as Father Abbot Markwart had figured, Baron Bildeborough, Abbot Dobrinion, and indeed all of Palmaris, were simply glad to be rid of the monks from St.-Mere-Abelle. They set camp that night across the Masur Delaval, the lights of Palmaris clear in the distance.

After conferring with Brother Francis and learning of the man's discoveries from his brief time inside the thoughts of Connor Bildeborough, the Father Abbot spent a lot of time alone, pacing, fighting hard to control his mounting anxiety. Just a score of feet away, inside the ring of wagons, the firelight blazed and the monks talked happily of returning to their home. The Father Abbot blocked it all out, had no time for such petty matters. Connor Bildeborough knew of the search for the woman, and furthermore, he believed the woman to be operating, with the magical stones, not too far away in the battleground north of Palmaris. Francis had caught the name Caer Tinella in that brief invasion of Connor's thoughts, and a quick look at his maps confirmed that to be a town along the road to the Timberlands, a town Francis and the caravan had passed on their wild run to Palmaris.

The goal was close, so close, the end of the troubles of Avelyn Desbris, the restoration of Father Abbot Dalebert Markwart's good name in the annals of the Abellican Church. Youseff and Dandelion would complete the task and retrieve the stones, and then all that would be left for Markwart would be the complete denunciation of the heretic Avelyn. He would destroy the legend as the explosion at Aida had destroyed the body.

Then all would be well, would be as it had been before.

"Or will it?" the Father Abbot asked himself aloud. He sighed deeply and considered the potential trail of problems his expedition had set for him. Jojonah was no ally and would likely oppose him, perhaps even going so far as to speak positively and publicly concerning dead Avelyn! And Abbot Dobrinion was no longer even neutral on the matter. The abbot of St. Precious was surely outraged at the abduction of the Chilichunks, and at his own treatment by the contingent from St.-Mere-Abelle. Particularly the latter, the Father Abbot mused, thinking that the abbot was more concerned with his wounded pride than his tortured subjects.

And what of Baron Bildeborough, who was already prepared to do battle with the Church for the sake of his nephew?

As he rolled the problems over and over in his thoughts, they each appeared to Markwart as a huddled black creature, and each seemed to grow with every rethinking, mounting powerfully, until they were black walls surrounding him, choking him, burying him!

The old man stamped the ground and issued a stifled cry. Would all the world and all the Church turn against him? Was he alone in his understanding of the truth? What conspiracies had that wicked Jojonah and that fool Dobrinion launched? To say nothing of the rot started by the evil Avelyn Desbris!

Markwart's mind whirled, looking for holes in those black walls, seeking some way to fight down the darkness. He must call Jojonah back from the trail to Ursal, bring him back into St.-Mere-Abelle, where he could watch over the man's every move. Yes, that was necessary.

And he must set Youseff and Dandelion on the trail at once, settling the issue of Avelyn's cache, returning the gemstones to their rightful place in St.-Mere-Abelle. Yes, that would be prudent.

And Connor and Dobrinion would prove to be trouble. They had to be persuaded, or . . .

The Father Abbot stood very still in the small clearing outside the wagon ring, steadying his breathing. The strength was back in his heart now, the will to fight on, to do whatever necessary to gain the desired end. Gradually he was able to open his eyes, and then to unclench his taut fists.

"Father Abbot?"

The call came from behind, a familiar voice and not an enemy. He turned to see a very concerned Brother Francis staring at him.

"Father Abbot?" the man said again.

"Go and tell Brothers Youseff and Dandelion to come to me," the old man instructed. "And then you join in the discussion within the wagon ring. I must know the mood of my brothers."

"Yes, Father Abbot," Francis replied. "But should you be out here alone, with monsters—"

"Now!" Markwart growled.

Brother Francis disappeared behind another wagon, into the more common area within the ring. A moment later two forms, one hulking, the other lithe, appeared, moving silently to bow before their master.

"It is time for you to put your training to use," Markwart said to them. "Brother Justice is your title now, for each of you, the only name that you will know, the only name by which you will refer to each other. You cannot comprehend the urgency of this matter; the fate of all the Church rests on your actions these next few days.

"Brother Francis has come to believe that the stolen gemstones are in the hands of the woman, Jilseponie Ault, who is referred to as Jill or Pony by her friends," the old man went on. "And she, we believe, is in the region about Caer Tinella, north of Palmaris, along the road to the Timberlands."

"We go straightaway," Youseff replied.

"You go in the morning," Father Abbot Markwart corrected. "In disguise, and appearing as no monk. You go by ferry across the river, then into Palmaris. The journey north will wait one day."

"Yes, Father Abbot," the pair said in unison, cuing on the old man's hesitation.

"Or five days," Markwart went on, "if that is what it takes. You see, we have a problem in Palmaris, one which you must eliminate."

Again Markwart hesitated, considering the course. Perhaps he should split the pair, that if one of them failed in this matter, the other might still get to the stones. Perhaps he should bypass Palmaris and concentrate on the gemstones, and then, when that issue was settled, he could send the pair back out.

No, he realized. By that time the conspiracy against him would be fully entrenched, perhaps even expecting trouble from him, and even worse, Connor knew of the woman and might find her before the monks.

"Connor Bildeborough," he said suddenly. "He has become a problem to me, to all the Church. He seeks the gemstones for his personal gain," he lied.

"The problem is to be eliminated," Brother Youseff reasoned.

"Leave no trail."

After a long silence the two men bowed and turned about, starting away.

Markwart hardly noticed the movement, as he considered his last words. *Leave no trail.*

Would that be possible with a suspicious Abbot Dobrinion in Palmaris? Dobrinion was no fool, nor was he weak with the few stones he possessed, one of which was a soul stone. The man might even find Connor's spirit before it flew far from the world, and from it learn the truth.

But Dobrinion was alone, isolated. There wasn't another monk at St. Precious of any consequence, not another who could use hematite for so difficult a task.

"Brothers Justice," Markwart said.

The two men spun about, running back to stand before their superior.

"The trouble is deeper than Connor Bildeborough, for he is in league with another who might put the stones to devastating use," Markwart explained. "If this man gets the gemstones, he will claim leadership of the Church, and will assume his place in St.-Mere-Abelle."

It was all preposterous, of course, but the two men, their minds bent by the expert work of Master De'Unerro, hung intent on every word.

"It pains me greatly," the Father Abbot lied. "Yet, I have no choice in the matter. You must kill two men in Palmaris, the other being Dobrinion Calislas, abbot of St. Precious."

Just a hint of surprise showed on the alert face of Brother Youseff, while Brother Dandelion accepted the order as easily as if Markwart had just told him to throw away the dinner scraps.

"It must appear to be an accident," Markwart went on. "Or an act of our monster enemies, perhaps. There can be no mistakes. Do you understand?"

"Yes, Father Abbot," Brother Dandelion replied at once.

Markwart studied Youseff, who wore a wicked smile. The man nodded, and it seemed to Markwart that he was enjoying the prospect of this immensely.

"Your reward awaits you at St.-Mere-Abelle," Markwart finished.

"Our reward, Father Abbot, is in the service, in the act itself," Brother Youseff declared.

Now Father Abbot Markwart, too, was smiling wickedly. And feeling much better. Suddenly, as with his earlier reflections, everything seemed to come clear to him, as though he had found a deeper level of concentration where all the worries could be put aside, all distractions ignored, and problems could be resolved logically and with foresight. He reconsidered his course about recalling Master Jojonah. Let the man be gone to Ursal until he died, for all he cared, for without Dobrinion's backing, Master Jojonah seemed no real threat.

Yes, if all went well with the Brothers Justice, the elimination of two potential problems and the retrieval of the stones, the issue would be settled, as would his own place in the history of the Abellican Order. Now the Father Abbot was agitated again, excited. He knew that he could not sleep this night and had to find some distraction, something to allow him to believe he was working toward that most coveted goal. He went to Brother Francis then, bidding the man to collect Grady Chilichunk and meet him outside the wagon ring. When Francis arrived, verily dragging the protesting Grady, Markwart motioned for him to follow and then led the pair far away from the ring.

"Is this safe?" Brother Francis dared to ask.

"Brothers Youseff and Dandelion are shadowing our every move," Markwart lied, for he was little concerned about any monsters, sensing somehow that few were about. Like the revelations that had come to him, he just somehow knew there was no danger out here.

Not for him, anyway. Poor Grady Chilichunk could not claim the same.

"You were her brother, for years," Markwart said to him.

"Not by choice, nor by blood," Grady replied, spitting every word with contempt.

"But by circumstance, and that is equally damning," Markwart came back.

Grady chuckled and turned away, but Francis was there in an instant, forcing the man's head back so he looked Markwart in the eye.

"You are not repentant," Markwart remarked.

Grady tried to look away again, and this time Francis not only forced his head back, but kicked him hard in the back of the knees, dropping him to a kneeling position before the Father Abbot. The young monk stayed right beside Grady, keeping him in that position, grabbing him by the hair and turning up his head so he could not look away from his superior.

"I have committed no crime!" Grady protested. "Nor, certainly, have my parents. You are the unholy one!" Grady Chilichunk had never been a brave man. He always followed the course of luxury, willingly serving as lackey to men of higher position, particularly Connor Bildeborough, that his own life be easier. Nor had he ever been a dutiful son, turning his back on his parents and their business—except for the monies it provided him— for many years. But now, helpless and hopeless on the road with the brutal and powerful monks, something changed within Grady, some sense of responsibility. He cared little for his own comfort at that time, focusing rather on the fact that his parents, his mother, were being so ill-treated. All the world had gone crazy, it seemed, and Grady somehow understood that all the whining and pleading and cooperating he could muster would not get him, and certainly not his parents, out of this trouble. With hopelessness came anger, and that anger in Grady sparked action—a rare thing for the cowardly man. He spat up at Markwart, hitting the Father Abbot in the face.

Markwart only laughed, unconcerned, but Francis, horrified that this common peasant would do such a thing to the Father Abbot, drove his elbow into the side of Grady's head. The man groaned and tumbled, and Francis was on him, kicking him hard, again in the head, then falling atop him, rolling him over onto his belly and yanking his arms painfully behind his back.

Grady said nothing, was too dazed to even offer a protest.

"Enough, Brother Francis," Markwart said calmly, patting his hand in the air. "His actions only verify that this one has turned his back on the Abellican Church and all the goodliness in the world."

Still Grady only lay limply beneath Brother Francis, groaning softly.

"Well, it seems as though we'll get nothing important from this one this night," Markwart remarked.

"I am sorry, Father Abbot," Francis said with alarm, but again Markwart was making no complaints. Given the events he had set into motion, the Father Abbot was simply in too fine a mood to let anything upset him.

"Take him back and put him in his bed," Markwart said.

Brother Francis hauled Grady to his feet and started away, but then stopped, realizing that Markwart wasn't following.

"I will enjoy the peace of the night," the Father Abbot explained.

"Alone?" Francis asked. "Out here?"

"Be gone," Markwart bade him. "There is no danger out here."

Francis found that he had little choice but to follow the command. He left slowly, looking back often, and every time seeing his Father Abbot standing calmly, unafraid.

For indeed Father Abbot Markwart was absolutely certain of his safety, for though he didn't know it, he was not alone.

The spirit of Bestesbulzibar was with him, relishing in his choices this dark night, guiding those decisions.

Much later on, Markwart slept contentedly, so much so that when Francis came to rouse him at the dawn, he instructed the brother to go away, and to let the others sleep in, as well. Several hours later Markwart did rise, to find most of the camp astir and a very nervous Brother Francis pacing back and forth near the three wagons that each held one of the Chilichunks.

"He'll not awaken," the brother explained to Markwart when he came over to see what was the matter.

"Who?"

"The son, Grady," Francis explained, shaking his head, then nodding toward the wagon that held the man. Markwart went in, and came back out grim-faced.

"Bury him by the side of the road," the Father Abbey said. "A shallow grave, unconsecrated ground." And he walked by Francis as though nothing out of sorts was going on, as though this had just been another routine order. He stopped just a few steps away and turned back on Francis. "And make certain that the other prisoners, particularly the dangerous centaur, know nothing of this," he explained. "And Brother Francis, you bury him yourself, after the caravan has departed."

A panicked look came over Francis, to which Markwart only chuckled and walked away, leaving the brother alone with his guilt.

Francis' thoughts whirled. He had killed a man! The night before, he must have hit Grady too hard, or kicked him too hard. He replayed the events over and over, wondering how he had done such a thing, or what he might have done differently, all the while fighting hard not to scream out aloud.

He was trembling, eyes darting all about. He felt the sweat on his forehead as he saw the Father Abbot coming back toward him.

"Be at peace, brother," Markwart said. "It was an unfortunate accident."

"I killed him," Francis gasped in reply.

"You defended your Father Abbot," Markwart answered. "I will perform a ceremony of absolution back at St.-Mere-Abelle, but I assure you that your penitential prayers will be light."

Trying to hide his grin, Markwart left the man.

Brother Francis was not so easily calmed. He could understand the logic of Markwart's argument—the man had, after all, spat in the face of the Father Abbot of the Abellican Church. But while Francis could logically argue that this had indeed been an unfortunate accident, his own actions justified, the rationalization could not take root in his heart. The pedestal had been knocked out from under him, that pervasive self-belief that he was above all other men. Francis had made mistakes before, of course, and he knew it, but not to this extreme. He remembered all the times of his life when he had imagined that he was the only real person, and that everyone else, and everything else, was merely a part of his dream of consciousness.

Now, suddenly, he felt as if he was just another man, a very small player in a very large script.

Later that morning, as the caravan moved far away, Brother Francis pushed the dirt on the pale face of Grady Chilichunk. In one blackened corner of his heart, Francis knew then that he was a damned thing.

Subconsciously that heart and soul ran to the Father Abbot then, for in that man's eyes, there had been no crime, no sin. In that man's view of the world, Brother Francis could hold his illusions.

PART THREE

THE DEMON
WITHIN

I cried for the death of Brother Justice.

That was not his real name, of course. His real name was Quintall; I know not if that was his surname or his birth-given name, or if he even had another name. Just Quintall.

I do not think that I killed him, Uncle Mather—not when he was human, at least. I think that his human body died as a consequence of the strange broach he carried, a magical link, so Avelyn discovered, to that most evil demon.

Still, I cried for the man, for his death, in which I played a great part. My actions were taken in defense of Avelyn and Pony, and of myself, and given the same situation, I have no doubt that I would react similarly, would battle Brother Justice without hearing any cries of protest from my conscience.

Still, I cried for the man, for his death, for all the potential lost, wasted, perverted to an evil way. When I consider it now, that is the true sadness, the real loss, for in each of us there burns a candle of hope, a light of sacrifice and community, the potential to do great things for the betterment of all the world. In each of us, in every man and every woman, there lies the possibility of greatness.

What a terrible thing the leaders of Avelyn's abbey did to the man Quintall, to pervert him so into this monster that they called Brother Justice.

After Quintall's death, I felt, for the first time, as though I had blood on my hands. My only other fight with humans was with the three trappers, and to them I showed mercy—and mercy well repaid! But for Quintall there was no mercy; there could not have been even if he had survived my arrow and his fall, even if the demon dactyl and the magical broach had not stolen his spirit from his corporeal form. In no way short of his death could we have deterred Brother Justice from his mission to slay Avelyn. His purpose was all-consuming, burned into his every thought by a long and arduous process that had bent the man's free will until it had broken altogether, that had eliminated Quintall's own conscience and turned his heart to blackness.

Perhaps that is why the demon dactyl found him and embraced him.

What a pity, Uncle Mather. What a waste of potential.

In my years as a ranger, and even before that in the battle for Dundalis, I have killed many creatures—goblins, powries, giants—yet I shed no tears for them. I considered this fact long and hard in light of my feelings toward the death of Quintall. Were my tears for him nothing more than an elevation of my own race above all others, and if so, is that not the worst kind of pride?

No, and I say that with some confidence, for surely I would cry if cruel fate ever drove my sword against one of the Touel'alfar. Surely I would consider the death of a fallen elf as piteous and tragic as the death of a fallen man.

What then is the difference?

It comes down to a matter of conscience, I believe, for as in humans, perhaps even more so, the Touel'alfar possess the ability, indeed the inclination, to choose a goodly path. Not so with goblins, and certainly not with the vile powries. I am not so sure about the giants—it may be that they are simply too stupid to even understand the suffering their warlike actions bring. In either case, I'll shed no tears and feel no remorse for any of these monsters that falls prey to Tempest's cut or to Hawkwing's bite. By their own evilness do they bring their deaths. They are the creatures of the dactyl, evil incarnate, slaughtering humans—and often each other—for no better reason than the pleasure of the act.

I have had this discussion with Pony, and she posed an interesting scenario. She wondered whether a goblin babe, raised among humans, or among the Touel'alfar in the beauty of Andur'Blough Inninness, would be as vile as its wild kin. Is the evil of such beings a blackness within, ingrained and everlasting, or is it a matter of nurturing?

My friend, your friend, Belli'mar Juraviel, had the answer for her, for indeed his people had long ago taken a goblin child into their enchanted land and raised the creature as if it were kin. As it matured, the goblin was no less vicious and hateful, and no less dangerous than its kin raised in the dark holes of distant mountains. The elves, ever curious, tried the same thing with a powrie child, and the results were even more disastrous.

So I'll cry not for goblins and powries and giants, Uncle Mather. I shed no tears for creatures of the dactyl. But I do cry for Quintall, who fell into evil ways. I cry for the potential that was lost, for the one terrible choice that pushed him to blackness.

And I think, Uncle Mather, that in crying for Quintall, or for any other human or elf that cruel fate may force me to slay, I am preserving my own humanity.

This is the scar of battle, I fear, that will prove to be the most everlasting.

—ELBRYAN THE NIGHTBIRD

❖ 18 ❖

Enemies of the Church

The only magic they carried was a garnet, for detecting the use of the enchanted gemstones, and a sunstone, the antimagic stone. In truth, neither of the pair was very proficient with gemstones, having spent the bulk of their short years in St.-Mere-Abelle in rigorous physical training and in the mental incapacitation necessary for one to truly claim the title of Brother Justice.

The caravan had gone back to the east that morning, while the two monks, changing out of their robes to appear as common peasants, had gone south, to the Palmaris ferry, catching the first of its three daily journeys across the Masur Delaval at the break of dawn. They were in the city by mid-afternoon, and wasted no time in going out to the north, over the wall and not through the gate. By the time the sun was low on the western horizon, Youseff and Dandelion had spotted their first prey, a band of four monsters—three powries and a goblin—setting camp amidst a tumble of boulders less than ten miles from Palmaris. It quickly became obvious to the monks that the goblin was the slave here, for it was doing most of the work, and whenever it slowed in its movements, one of the powries would give it a sharp slap on the back of the head, spurring it to motion. Even more important, the monks noted that the goblin had a rope, a leash, tied about its ankle.

Youseff turned to Dandelion and nodded; they would be able to take advantage of this arrangement.

As the sun was slipping below the horizon, the goblin exited the camp, followed closely by a powrie holding the other end of the rope. In the forest, the goblin began foraging for firewood, while the powrie stood quietly nearby. Youseff and Dandelion, silent as the lengthening shadows, moved into position, the slender monk going up a tree, the heavier Dandelion slipping from trunk to trunk, to close ground on the powrie.

"Yach, hurry it up, ye fool thing!" the powrie scolded, kicking at the leaves and dirt. "Me friends'll eat all the coney, and there'll be nothing but bones for me to gnaw!"

The goblin, a truly beleaguered creature, glanced back briefly, then scooped another piece of kindling. "Please, master," it whined. "Me arms is full and me back is hurtin' so."

"Yach, shut yer mouth!" the powrie growled. "Ye're thinkin' ye got all ye can carry, but it's not enough for the night fire. Ye're wanting me to come all the way back out here? I'll flog yer skin red, ye smelly wretch!"

Youseff hit the ground right beside the startled powrie, plopping a heavy bag over its head in the blink of a surprised eye. A moment later Dandelion, in full run, slammed the dwarf from behind, hoisting it in a bear hug and taking it on a fast run, face first into the trunk of the nearest tree.

Still the tough powrie struggled, throwing back an elbow into Dandelion's throat. The big monk hardly noticed, just pressed all the harder, and then, when he saw his companion's approach, he hooked his arm under the powrie's and lifted the dwarf's arm up high, exposing ribs.

Youseff's dagger thrust was perfectly aimed, sliding between two ribs to pierce the stubborn dwarf's heart. Dandelion, holding fast the thrashing powrie, managed to free one hand so he could wrap the wound, not wanting too much blood to spill.

Not here.

Youseff, meanwhile, turned to the goblin. "Freedom," he whispered excitedly, waving his hand for the creature to run away.

The goblin, on the verge of a scream, looked curiously at the human, then at its armload of wood. Shaking from excitement, it tossed the wood to the ground, slipped the rope from its ankle and sped off into the darkening forest.

"Dead?" Youseff asked as Dandelion let the limp powrie slump to the ground.

The big man nodded, then went to tighten the bindings on the wound. It was imperative that no blood would be spilling when the pair returned to Palmaris, and particularly not when they entered St. Precious. Youseff removed the powrie's weapon, a cruel-looking serrated and hooked blade as long and thick as his forearm, and Dandelion put the dwarf in a heavy, lined sack. With a glance about to make sure the other powries had not caught on to the ambush, they went on their way, running south, the load proving hardly a burden to the powerful Dandelion.

"Should we not have taken the goblin for Connor Bildeborough?" Dandelion asked as they slowed their pace, nearing the city's north wall.

Youseff considered the question a moment, trying hard not to laugh at the fact that his dim-witted friend had only mentioned it now, more than an hour after they told the goblin to run away. "We need only one," Youseff assured him. The Father Abbot had made his needs quite clear to Brother Youseff. Any action against Abbot Dobrinion had to either appear as simply an accident or lead suspicion in a direction far removed from Markwart; the implications within the Church should St.-Mere-Abelle seem connected in any way, after all, could prove grave. Connor Bildeborough, though, was not such a problem. If his uncle, the Baron of Palmaris, even suspected the Church in Connor's demise, he, in his ignorance of the rivalries between the abbeys, would be as likely to blame St. Precious as St.-Mere-Abelle, and even if he did turn his attention to the abbey on All Saints Bay, there would be little, very little, he could do.

It was hardly an effort for the skilled assassins to get over the city wall and past the eyes of weary guardsmen. The battlefield had been pushed back, and though rogue bands like the one the monks had encountered were still about, they were not thought to be much of a threat by the garrison entrenched in the city—a garrison strengthened in recent days by a full brigade of Kingsmen from Ursal.

Now Dandelion and Youseff changed back into their brown robes and, with heads humbly bowed, made their solemn way through the streets. They were bothered only once, by a beggar man, and when he would not leave them alone, even going so far as to threaten them if they would not give him a silver coin, Brother Dandelion calmly tossed him against an alley wall.

It was long after vespers and St. Precious was quiet and dark, but the monks took little comfort in that fact, understanding that the men of their Order would prove more vigilant than the slothful city guards. Again, though, the Father Abbot had prepared them properly. On the southern wall of the abbey, where the wall was in fact a part of the main building itself, there were no windows and no visible doors.

In truth, there was a single door, carefully concealed, from which the abbey's kitchen workers brought out the scraps from the day's meals. Brother Youseff brought forth the garnet, using it to find the invisible doorway, for the portal, in addition to being magically concealed, was magically sealed against opening from the outside.

The door was also conventionally locked—or should have been—but before the monks of St.-Mere-Abelle had departed St. Precious, Brother Youseff had gone to the kitchen, ostensibly for supplies, but in truth to destroy the integrity of the portal's binding. Apparently the Father Abbot had recognized that they might need a quiet way into St. Precious, he pondered now, and was indeed impressed by his master's foresight.

Using the sunstone, Youseff defeated the meager magical lock and carefully pushed open the door. Only one person was inside, a young woman singing and scrubbing a pot over a sink of steaming water.

Youseff was behind her almost immediately. He paused, listening to her carefree song, taking pleasure in the evil irony of that lively tune.

The woman stopped singing, sensing the presence.

Youseff basked in her fear for just a moment, then grabbed her by the hair and drove her face into the water. She struggled and thrashed, but to no avail against the efficient assassin. Youseff smiled as she slumped to the floor. He was supposed to be a passionless killer, a mechanical tool for the Father Abbot's will, but in truth the monk found that he enjoyed the killing, enjoyed the victim's fear, enjoyed the absolute power. Looking down at the dead young woman, he only wished he had been granted more time, that he could have savored the preliminary game, the terror leading up to the death.

Death, by comparison, was such a bland and easy thing.

St. Precious was quiet that night, as if the whole of the place, the abbey itself, was relaxing after the trials of the Father Abbot's visit. Through the hallways stalked Youseff and Dandelion, the Brothers Justice, with powerful Dandelion carrying the sacked powrie over one shoulder. They saw only one monk, and he didn't see them, all the way to the door of Abbot Dobrinion's private quarters.

Youseff went down to one knee before the door, a small knife in hand. Though he could easily pick the meager lock, he scraped and scratched at the wood about it, whittling it down, making it appear as if the door had been forced.

Then they were in, and through another door, this one less sturdy and not locked, to Dobrinion's bedside.

The abbot awoke with a start. He began to scream out, but fell strangely silent when he considered the pair, when he saw the heavy serrated blade waving tantalizingly inches from his face, its metal gleaming in the soft light of the moon spilling in through the room's lone window.

"You knew we would come for you," Youseff teased.

Dobrinion shook his head. "I can speak with the Father Abbot," he pleaded. "A misunderstanding, that is all."

Youseff held a finger to pursed lips, smiling wickedly behind it, but Dobrinion pressed on.

"The Chilichunks are criminals—that is obvious," the abbot spouted, and he hated the words as he spoke them, hated himself for his cowardice. Abbot Dobrinion fought a great battle then, his conscience vying against his most basic survival instinct.

Youseff and Dandelion watched his torment, not understanding the source of it, but with Youseff surely enjoying it.

Then Dobrinion calmed and stared at Youseff squarely, seeming suddenly unafraid. "Your Markwart is an evil man," he said. "Never was he truly Father Abbot of the Abellican Church. I call on you now, in the name of the solemn vow of our Order—piety, dignity, poverty—to turn against this evil course, to find again the light—"

His sentence ended as a gurgle, as Youseff, too far lost to even hear such conscience-tugging pleas, ripped the serrated edge across the abbot's throat, opening it wide.

The pair went to the powrie then, dropping it to the floor. Dandelion unwrapped and then picked at its wound, removing all sign of scabbing, while Youseff searched about the abbot's quarters. He found at last a small knife, used for cutting seals from letters. Its blade was not as broad as the one of his dagger, but the knife fit fairly snugly into the powrie's mortal wound.

"Take him from the bed," Youseff instructed Dandelion. As the big man dragged Dobrinion toward the desk, Youseff walked alongside, cutting a series of smaller wounds on Dobrinion's corpse, making it seem as if the abbot had put up a great struggle.

Then the two killers were gone, silent death, two shadows flowing out from St. Precious into the black night.

Word of the abbot's murder spread throughout the city the very next morning, frantic cries sweeping along the fortified walls, teary-eyed soldiers blaming themselves for allowing a powrie to slip past them. Whispers of doom crossed from tavern to tavern, street corner to street corner, each retelling the rumors, embellishing the tale. By the time Connor Bildeborough, waking in a bed in the infamous brothel, House Battlebrow, heard the story, an army of powries was reputedly on the outskirts of Palmaris, ready to rush in and slaughter all of the people in their time of grief.

Half naked, dressing as he went, Connor exited the house and flagged down a carriage, demanding that the driver take him at once to Chasewind Manor, the home of his uncle.

The gates were closed; a dozen armed soldiers, their weapons drawn, surrounded the carriage as the horse skidded to an abrupt stop, and both Connor and the poor frightened driver felt the eyes of many archers upon them.

Recognizing Connor, the guards relaxed and helped the nobleman down, then ordered the driver away in no uncertain terms.

"My uncle is well?" Connor asked desperately as the guards escorted him through the gate.

"Unnerved, Master Connor," one man answered. "To think that a powrie could so easily get through our defenses and slay Abbot Dobrinion! And all of this coming right behind the troubles in the abbey! Oh, what dark days are upon us!"

Connor made no move to reply, but he listened carefully to the man's words, and the unspoken, probably even unrealized, implications behind them. He rushed through the manor house then, down the heavily guarded halls and into his uncle's audience room.

Fittingly, the soldier standing guard beside Baron Rochefort Bildeborough's desk was the burly man, face heavily bandaged, whose nose had been smashed under a magical assault by none other than Father Abbot Dalebert Markwart himself.

"My uncle knows of my arrival?" Connor asked the man.

"He will join us presently," the guard replied, his voice slurred, for his mouth, too, had been battered by the magnetite missile.

Even as he finished speaking, Connor's uncle entered the room through a side door, his face brightening as he gazed upon his nephew.

"Thank God himself that you are alive and well," the man said generously. Connor had always been Rochefort Bildeborough's favorite relative, and since the man had no children, it was a common belief in Palmaris that Connor would inherit the title.

"Should I not be?" Connor asked in his typically casual manner.

"They got in to kill Abbot Dobrinion," Rochefort replied, taking his seat opposite the desk from Connor.

Connor did not miss the effort his uncle required for the simple action. Rochefort was overweight and suffered from severe pains in the joints. Until the previous summer, the man had ridden his fields every day, rain or shine, but this year he had been out only a couple of times, and never two days in succession. Rochefort's eyes, too, showed the sudden aging. They had always been gray in hue, but they were dull now, filmed over.

Connor had wanted the title of Baron of Palmaris since he was old enough to understand the prestige and entitlement that came with it, but now, as that moment seemed to be drawing near, he had discovered that he could wait—and many years. He would rather that he kept his present position, and that his dear uncle, the man who had been as a father to him, remained alive and well.

"How would the monsters even know to look for me?" Connor replied calmly. "The abbot is a clear target for our enemies, but myself?"

"The abbot and the Baron," Rochefort reminded.

"And indeed I am glad to see that you have taken all the proper precautions," Connor said quickly. "You may be a target, but not I. To the knowledge of our enemies, I am nothing more than a common tavern-hunter."

Rochefort nodded, and seemed relieved by the logic of Connor's reasoning. Like a protective father, he didn't fear for himself half as much as he feared for Connor.

Connor, though, was not really convinced by his own words. The powrie slipping into St. Precious at this tension-filled time, so soon after the horrible Father Abbot's departure, seemed a bit too convenient to him, and he only grew more uneasy as he looked upon the broken face of his uncle's principal guard.

"I want you to stay at Chasewind Manor," Rochefort said.

Connor shook his head. "I have business in the city, Uncle," he replied. "And I have been battling powries for months now. Fear not for me." As he finished, he patted Defender, comfortably sheathed at his hip.

Rochefort stared long and hard at the confident young man. That was what he liked about Connor, the confidence, the swagger. He had been so much like Connor in his own youth, bouncing from tavern to tavern, from brothel to brothel, living life so fully, taking each moment to the very limits, of life, of danger. How ironic, he thought, that now, growing older, and with less pleasure, less excitement, less life, ahead of him, he should be more protective of his life. Connor, indeed so much like a younger Rochefort, with so much more to lose, thought little of potential danger, felt immortal and invulnerable.

The Baron laughed, and dismissed the thought of ordering Connor to stay at Chasewind Manor, for that, he realized, would steal all that he loved from the spirited young man. "Keep one of my soldiers beside you," he offered in compromise.

Again Connor resolutely shook his head. "That would only outline me as a potential target," he reasoned. "I know the city, Uncle. Know where to garner information and where to hide."

"Go out! Go out!" the Baron cried in defeat, laughing all the while. "But know that you carry more than the responsibility of your own life with you." He rose with considerably less trouble than he had found in sitting, and rushed about the desk, clapping Connor on the shoulder roughly a couple of times, then letting his big hand rest intimately about his nephew's neck. "You carry my heart with you, boy," he said solemnly. "If they find you as they found Dobrinion, then know that I will surely die of a broken heart."

Connor believed him, every word. He gave the man a hug and a pat, then strode confidently from the room.

"He will soon be your baron," Rochefort said to the soldier.

The man snapped to attention and nodded, obviously approving of the choice.

"Open it."

"But Master Bildeborough, I see no reason to disturb the sleep of the dead," the monk replied. "The coffin has been blessed by Brother Talumus, our highest ranking—"

"Open it," Connor repeated, locking the young man in his unrelenting glare.

Still the young monk hesitated.

"Should I bring my uncle?"

The monk bit at his lip, but surrendered to the threat, bending low to grasp the wooden lid. With a look back to the resolute Connor, he slid the cover aside. There lay the woman, her complexion chalky blue in death.

To the monk's horror, Connor reached in and grabbed her by the shoulder, lifting and turning the corpse, his face low, impervious to the stench as he studied her intently. "Wounds?" he asked.

"Just the drowning," the monk replied. "In the sink. Hot water, too. Her face was all red at first, but now the blood, and all the life, is gone from it."

Connor gently shifted the body back into place and stood back, motioning to the monk that he could close the coffin. He put his hand to his mouth, running his thumbnail between his teeth, trying to make sense of it all. The monks of St. Precious had been very accommodating when he showed up at their gate. They were frightened and confused, he knew, and the presence of so important a representative of Baron Bildeborough had helped to settle them.

In Abbot Dobrinion's room Connor had found little in the way of clues. Both bodies were still there, the abbot's cleaned and carefully placed in state on his bed, and the powrie's right where the monks had found it. The blood of both corpses was liberal about the room, despite all efforts to clean the place. When Connor protested the changes in the room, the monks took great pains to describe the struggle, as they had interpreted it, in great detail: the abbot had been wounded first, and several times, probably taken by surprise while he lay asleep on his bed. One of the wounds was mortal, a slash across the throat, but still the brave Dobrinion had managed to struggle across the room to retrieve the small knife.

How proud were the monks of St. Precious that their abbot had been able to take revenge on his killer!

To Connor, who had battled the tough powries, it seemed unlikely at best that a single thrown dagger could have so perfectly taken one down, and that Dobrinion, given the viciousness of the slashed throat, could even have gotten to the desk. The scenario was not beyond belief, though, and so he kept his thoughts to himself, accepting the description with a noncommittal nod and a simple word of praise for gallant Dobrinion.

When he subsequently inquired about how the powrie might have gained access, Connor learned of a second victim, a poor girl who had been ambushed and drowned in the kitchen. It remained a mystery to the monks as to how the powrie had gained entrance, for the door was magically sealed against being opened from the outside, and indeed it was little known, being invisible against the abbey's bricked wall. The only explanation they could find was that the foolish girl had been in league with, or more likely, been duped by, the powrie and had let the dwarf in.

That, too, seemed acceptable to Connor, though a bit of a stretch, but now, in looking at the girl, her skin unbroken, the young nobleman's fears and suspicions rose high about him. Still he said nothing to the monks, understanding that without the guidance of the only man of any authority in all the abbey, they could do little.

"Poor girl," was all he muttered as the monk escorted him from the abbey's cellar—just a pair of stairways up from where the Chilichunks had been held as prisoners, Connor continually reminded himself.

"Your uncle will help us to secure the abbey from further intrusion?" one of the monks waiting in the chapel for the pair inquired.

Connor asked for parchment and quill, then scribbled out a request for such aid. "Take this to Chasewind Manor," he instructed. "Of course the family Bildeborough will do all that we can for the security of St. Precious."

He bade the monks farewell then, and swept out into the streets of Palmaris, the place of whispers and rumors, the place where he might truly find his answers.

Questions and images haunted him throughout the afternoon. Why would the powries go after Abbot Dobrinion, who had not been very much engaged in the fighting? Only a handful of monks had gone out from St. Precious to the fighting in the north, and they had been far from decisive in any battles. Given that, and the fact that St. Precious had played more of a healing role in the war, it seemed unlikely that any of Dobrinion's actions would have spurred the powries to such a dramatic action.

The only explanation Connor could think of was that the monks of St.-Mere-Abelle, who had reportedly come in from the north, had skirmished with the monsters, probably destroying many, and thus inadvertently set up the abbot as a target for assassination.

But after his experiences with Markwart, Connor didn't believe that possible scenario. The words "too convenient" echoed in his mind whenever he considered every piece of evidence or any seemingly logical conclusions.

That night, Connor found his way to Fellowship Way, which he had convinced Dainsey Aucomb to reopen the previous night, explaining to her that the Chilichunks would be in desperate straights indeed when they returned to Palmaris—even though Connor did not believe they would ever return to Palmaris—if their business had not been maintained. The place was bustling, all the locals eager for gossip about what had happened to Abbot Dobrinion and to Keleigh Leigh, the poor drowned kitchen girl. Connor kept quiet through most of the discussion, more interested in listening than in speaking, trying to find someone who might have some important and valid information—no small matter in this sea of rumor. Though he worked hard to keep a low profile, he was approached often, the commoners suspecting that the nobleman would know more than they.

Through all their inquiries, Connor only smiled and shook his head. "I know only what I have heard since entering the Way," he'd reply.

The night rolled on without progress; frustrated Connor put his back against the wall and closed his eyes. Only one fellow's call of "newfolks," the term commonly applied to visitors who had not been previously seen in the Way, stirred him from his respite.

It took him a few moments to focus his vision, to shift his gaze through the crowd toward the door and the two men, one large, the other small and slender, but walking with the perfect balance and absolute alertness of a trained warrior. Connor's eyes went wide. He knew these men, and knew that their present dress, that of common peasants, was not fitting.

Where were their robes?

The mere sight of Youseff brought back pain in Connor's kidney, and given his last meeting with the two, the nobleman thought it wise to slip even further into the crowd. He motioned to Dainsey first, bringing her to the bar opposite him.

"See what they want," he instructed, indicating the two newfolks. "And tell them that I have not been in the Way all the week."

Dainsey nodded and slid back the other way, while Connor faded toward the back wall. He tried to stay close enough to catch any snatches of conversation between Dainsey and the two as they predictably approached the hostess, but the noise of the packed tavern allowed for very little eavesdropping.

Until Dainsey—wonderful Dainsey!—raised her voice pointedly and called out, "Why, he's not been in here all the week!"

Connor's suspicions were confirmed, the monks were looking for him—and he could guess why easily enough. And now he knew why Keleigh Leigh had not been cut, why no powrie had dipped its beret in her spilling blood, a tradition that, according to everything Connor had ever heard about the cruel bloody caps, no powrie would ever forsake. He dared to turn about and steal a glance back toward Dainsey, and she looked at him out of the corner of her eye, then "inadvertently" brushed her other hand down the front of her blouse, opening it wide, catching the attention of every man nearby, the two monks included.

Good girl, Connor thought, and he used the distraction to make some ground, slipping, weaving, toward the door. It took him more than a minute to cover the twenty feet, so crowded was the Way, but then he was out in the salty air of the Palmaris night, the wide sky clear and crisp overhead.

He glanced back into the tavern, to see the crowd jostling, as though someone was trying to get to the door.

Connor didn't wait to discern who that might be; if the monks recognized Dainsey's move as a diversion, they would understand where to turn next. The nobleman rushed to the corner of the Way, then went around the corner, turning and peering back to the door.

Sure enough, Youseff and Dandelion burst out onto the street.

Down the alley went Connor, his thoughts spinning. He wasted no time, climbing the gutter work to the roof, then falling flat on his belly, shaking his head as the two monks came around the corner on his trail. He turned away, crawling quietly.

Up here, with the sky seeming so close, the lights of the city night below him, Connor couldn't help but fall back in time. This place had been Jill's special spot, her hideaway from the world. She had come up here often, to be alone with her thoughts, to seek out past events too painful for her fragile mind to find.

A metal scraping sound blew away those thoughts of Jill; one of the monks, Youseff likely, had started to climb.

Connor was away in an instant, leaping the far alley to the roof of the next building, rushing over the peak and sliding down, turning, catching the lip of the roof as he went over, then dropping to the street. He went on in full flight, running scared, thinking of Jill, thinking of all the craziness that had come to his little world.

Abbot Dobrinion was dead. Dead! And no powrie had done it.

No, it was these two, the lackeys of Father Abbot Dalebert Markwart, the leader of all the Abellican Church. Markwart had killed Dobrinion because of the abbot's resistance, and now had set his assassins on him.

The enormity of that line of reasoning at last hit Connor, and nearly laid him low. He considered his course—should he seek protection at Chasewind Manor?

Connor dismissed that, fearing to implicate his uncle. If Markwart had gotten to Dobrinion, could anyone, even the Baron of Palmaris, be safe? These were powerful enemies, Connor understood; if all the legions of the King of Honce-the-Bear were turned against him, they would be no more dangerous enemies than the monks of the Abellican Church. Indeed, by many standards, not the least of which concerned those mysterious and little understood magical powers, the Father Abbot was a more powerful man than the King.

The scope of this all, the incredible idea that the Father Abbot would order—had ordered!—Dobrinion murdered, assaulted the nobleman's sensibilities, kept his mind whirling as he vanished into the Palmaris night.

But still, Connor knew that he would run out of places to hide. These two, and others, if there were more in the city, were professional assassins. They would find him and kill him.

He needed answers, and he thought he knew where he might find them. Besides, someone else was in danger here, the real target of Markwart's wrath. He did turn to Chasewind Manor then, crossing the gate into the courtyard, but veering from the main house to the stables. There he quickly saddled Greystone, his favorite hunting horse, a beautiful and thick-muscled palomino with a long blond mane. With eager Greystone under him, Connor rode out of Palmaris' northern gate before the night had crossed its midpoint.

❖ 19 ❖

Change in Direction

The traveling was easy—or should have been, for the road stretching along the western bank of the Masur Delaval south of Palmaris was the finest causeway in all the world. And early on Jojonah found a ride with a caravan that traveled for two days, through both day and night. Master Jojonah, though, was not having a good time of it. His old bones ached badly, and some two hundred miles south of Palmaris he had taken ill, beset by terrible cramps and nausea, and by a low fever that kept him sweating continually.

Bad food, he supposed, and hoped in all seriousness that this journey and illness would not be the end of him. He still had much he meant to do before he died, and in any case, dying alone on the road halfway between Ursal and Palmaris, two cities of which he had never been overly fond, was not appealing in the least. So with typical stoicism the old master staggered along from town to town, walking slowly, leaning heavily on a sturdy stick, and chastising himself for letting his belly grow so thick. "Piety, dignity, poverty," he said sarcastically, for truly he felt less than dignified, and it seemed he was carrying this vow of poverty way too far. As for piety . . . Jojonah wasn't sure what that word meant anymore. Did it mean following blindly the lead of Father Abbot Markwart? Or following his heart, using those insights that Avelyn, by example, had given to him?

The latter, he decided, but in truth, that solved little, for Jojonah wasn't sure exactly what course he might take to make any real difference in the world. Likely he'd just get himself demoted in Church rank, perhaps even banished, perhaps even burned as a heretic—the Church had a long history of turning like a ravenous animal on a proclaimed heretic, torturing such men to death. A shudder coursed Jojonah's spine as he considered that thought, like some grim premonition. Yes, Father Abbot Markwart was in a foul mood of late, and the more foul it became by far if ever someone mentioned the name of Avelyn Desbris! Thus the master found a new enemy, despair, on that long road to Ursal. But he plodded on, putting one foot in front of the other.

He awoke on the sixth day out to find the sky thick with dark clouds, and by mid-morning a cool rain had begun. Jojonah was at first glad of the cloud cover, for the previous day had been brutally hot. But as the first raindrops began to fall, as the chilly water touched his feverish skin, he grew miserable indeed, and even considered returning to the town in which he had slept the previous night.

He didn't reverse direction, though, but simply slogged along a puddle-filled road, turning his attention inward, to Avelyn and Markwart, to the direction of the Church and any course he might follow to alter that dark path. As the minutes turned to an hour, then two, the master was so deep in thought that he never heard the wagon approaching fast from behind.

"Be clear the road!" the driver cried, pulling hard on the reins, then yanking them to the side. The wagon swerved, narrowly missing Jojonah, spraying him with a great wash as he tumbled to the muddy ground in surprise and terror.

Off to the side went the wagon, sinking deep into the mud—and only that mud, grabbing at the wheels like some living creature, kept the cart from overturning as the frantic driver fought to gain control. Finally the team slowed and the wheels slipped to a messy halt. The driver leaped down at once, taking only a quick glance at his stuck rig, then rushing back across the road to where Jojonah sat.

"My pardon," the monk stammered as the man, a handsome fellow of about twenty years, splashed over to him. "I did not hear you in the rain."

"No pardon's needed," the man said pleasantly, helping Jojonah to stand and brushing some of the mud from his soaked robes. "Sure that I been fearing that since I taked the road outta Palmaris."

"Palmaris," echoed Jojonah. "I, too, just came from the most excellent town." The monk noted that the man's expression soured at the mention of the word "excellent," and so Jojonah quieted, thinking it prudent to listen and not to speak.

"Well, the quicker I'm coming from the same place," the man replied, glancing back helplessly at his wagon. "Or was," he added despondently.

"We will not easily extract it from the mud, I fear," Jojonah agreed.

The man nodded. "But I'll find villagers to help," he said. "There be a town a three-mile back."

"The folk are helpful," Jojonah said hopefully. "Perhaps I shall accompany you; they would be quick to help a priest of the Church, after all, and were quite kind to me last night, for that is where I slept. And then, after we have extracted your wagon, perhaps you'll take me along. My destination is Ursal, and I've a long road ahead, I fear, and a body not taking well to the travel."

"Ursal's me own ending," the man said. "And ye might help in me message, since it concerns yer own Church."

Jojonah perked his ears up at that remark and cocked an eyebrow. "Oh," he prompted.

"Truly 'tis a sad day," the man went on. "So sad a day that sees the death of Abbot Dobrinion."

Jojonah's eyes went wide and he staggered, catching hold of the man's sleeve for support. "Dobrinion? How?"

"Powrie," the man answered. "Little rat devil. Sneaked into the church and killed him to death."

Jojonah could hardly digest the information. His mind started whirling, but he was too sickly and too confused. He sat down again, plop, onto the muddy road, and dropped his face into his hands, sobbing, and didn't know if he was crying for Abbot Dobrinion or for himself and his beloved Order.

The driver put a comforting hand on his shoulder. They left together for the town, the man promising he would spend the night there even if the folk managed to clear his wagon of the mud. "And ye'll be riding with me the rest o' the way to Ursal," he said with a hopeful smile. "We'll get ye blankets to keep ye warm, Father, and good food, lots of good food, for the road."

One of the families in the small town put Jojonah and the driver up for the night, giving him a warm bed. The monk retired early, but couldn't immediately fall asleep, for a crowd was gathering in the house, with all the folk of the area coming to hear the driver's sad tale of the death of Abbot Dobrinion. Jojonah lay quiet and listened to them for a long while, then finally, shivering and sweating, he drifted off to sleep.

Youseff and Dandelion did not make the return trip.

Master Jojonah awoke with a start. The house was quiet and, since the clouds hung low outside, dark. Jojonah looked all around, narrowing his eyes. "Who is there?" he asked.

Youseff and Dandelion did not make the return trip! he heard again, more emphatically.

No, not heard, Jojonah realized, for there was not a sound, save the pat of heavy raindrops on the roof. He felt the words, in his mind, and he recognized the man who was putting them there.

"Brother Braumin?" he asked.

I fear that the Father Abbot put them on your trail, the thoughts imparted. *Run, my friend, my mentor. Flee back to Palmaris if you are not far away, to the court of Abbot Dobrinion, and do not allow Brothers Youseff and Dandelion entrance into St. Precious.*

The communication was weak—which Jojonah understood, for Braumin wasn't very practiced with the hematite, and likely the man was using it now under less than ideal circumstances. *Where are you?* he telepathically asked. *St.-Mere-Abelle?*

Please, Master Jojonah! You must hear my call. Youseff and Dandelion did not make the return trip!

The contact was lessening—Braumin was getting tired, Jojonah realized. Then, abruptly, it was gone altogether, and Jojonah feared that perhaps Markwart or Francis had happened upon Braumin.

If it really was Braumin, he had to remind himself. If it was anything at all beyond the delirium of his fever.

"They did not know," the master whispered, for he realized only then that Braumin's message had mentioned nothing about Dobrinion. Jojonah scrambled out of bed, groaning for the effort, and made his way quietly through the house. He startled the lady first, nearly tripping over her as she slept on a mattress of piled blankets on the common room floor. She had given up her own bed for him, he realized, and truly he did not wish to disturb her now. But some things simply couldn't wait.

"The driver?" he asked. "Is he in the house, or did he take shelter with another family?"

"Oh, no," the woman said as pleasantly as she could. "Sure that he's sleeping in the room with me little boys. Snug as bugs in a rug, so the sayin' goes."

"Get him," Master Jojonah instructed. "At once."

"Yes, Father, whatever ye're needing," the woman replied, untangling herself from her bedroll and half walking, half crawling across the room. She returned in a few moments, the bleary-eyed driver at her side.

"Ye should be sleeping," the man said. "Not good for yer fever, being up so late."

"One question," Jojonah prompted, waving his hands to quiet the man, to make sure he was paying close attention. "When Abbot Dobrinion was murdered, where was the caravan of St.-Mere-Abelle?"

The man cocked his head as if he didn't understand.

"You know that monks of my abbey were visiting St. Precious," Jojonah pressed.

"A bit more than visiting, by the trouble they bringed," the man said with a snort.

"Indeed," Jojonah conceded. "But where were they when the powrie killed Abbot Dobrinion?"

"Gone."

"From the city?"

"Out to the north, some say, though I heared they crossed the river, and not on the ferry," the driver replied. "They were out a day and more afore the abbot fell to the powrie."

Master Jojonah rocked back on his heels, stroking his large chin. The driver started to elaborate, but the monk had heard enough and stopped him with an upraised palm. "Go back to bed," he bade both the man and the lady of the house. "As will I."

Back in the solitude of his dark room, Master Jojonah did not fall off to sleep. Far from it. Convinced now that the contact with Braumin was not a dreamy, imagined thing, Jojonah had too much to think about. He was not fearful, as Braumin had been, that Youseff and Dandelion had been set on his trail. Markwart was too close to his goal, or at least the obsessed man thought he was, to delay the killers. No, they would go north of Palmaris, not south, onto the battlefield in search of the stones.

But apparently they had made one brief stop on the way, long enough to fix a bit of Markwart's trouble in Palmaris.

Master Jojonah rushed to the one window in the room, pushed open the shutters and vomited onto the grass outside, sickened by the mere thought that his Father Abbot had ordered the execution of another abbot!

It rang as preposterous! Yet, every detail that was filtering to Jojonah led him inescapably in that direction. Was he, perhaps, clouding those details with his own judgments? he had to wonder. *Youseff and Dandelion did not make the return trip!*

And Brother Braumin had no idea that Abbot Dobrinion had met such an untimely end.

Truly Master Jojonah hoped he was wrong, hoped that his fears and his feverish delirium were running wild, hoped that the leader of his Order could never have done such a thing. In any case, there seemed only one road ahead of him now, back to the north, and not south, back to St.-Mere-Abelle.

Finally all two hundred were on the move, swinging west and then south of the two towns still in powrie hands. Elbryan directed the march, keeping scouts well ahead of the caravan and holding his forty best warriors in a tight group. Of all the ragged caravan, only about half could fight even if pressed, the other half being simply too old or two young, or too ill. The general health of the group was good, though, thanks mostly to the tireless efforts of Pony and her precious soul stone.

No resistance came out at them from the two towns, and as the afternoon of the fifth day began to wane, they were almost halfway to Palmaris.

"Farm and a barn," Roger Lockless explained, coming back to meet with Elbryan. "Just a mile ahead. The well's intact, and I heard chickens."

Several of the people nearby groaned and cooed and smacked their lips at the thought of fresh eggs.

"But no one was about?" the ranger asked skeptically.

"None outside," Roger replied, and he seemed a bit embarrassed that he couldn't have discerned more. "But I was not far ahead of you," he hastily explained. "I feared that if I tarried too long, you would get in sight of the structures, and any monsters inside, if there are any, would see you."

Elbryan nodded and smiled. "You did well," he said. "Hold the group in check here while Pony and I go in and see what we might learn."

Roger nodded and helped Pony climb on Symphony's back behind the ranger.

"Strengthen the perimeter, particularly in the north," Elbryan instructed the young man. "And find Juraviel. Tell him where to find us."

Roger accepted the orders with a nod. He slapped Symphony on the rump and the horse bounded away. Roger hardly watched the departure, was already moving to instruct the folk of the caravan to settle into a defensive posture.

The ranger found the structures easily enough, and then Pony went to work, using the soul stone to spirit-walk into first the barn and then the farmhouse.

"Powries in the house," she explained when she came back into her own body. "Three, though one is sleeping in the back bedroom. Goblins hold the barn, but they are not alert."

Elbryan closed his eyes, seeking a deep, meditative calm, transforming, almost visibly, into his elven-trained alter ego. He indicated a small copse of trees to the left of the barn, then slipped down from Symphony, helping Pony do the same. Leaving the horse, the pair moved cautiously to the shadows of the copse, and then the ranger went on alone, continuing his advance, moving to stumps, to a water trough, to anything that would conceal him. Soon enough he was at the farmhouse, his back to the wall beside a window, Hawkwing in hand. He peered around, then looked back in Pony's direction and nodded, fitting an arrow.

He turned abruptly and let fly, scoring a hit on the back of the head of a powrie as the unsuspecting dwarf cooked over a stove. The momentum drove the creature's head forward, forcing its face right into the sizzling grease in the frying pan.

"What're ye doing!" the dwarf's companion howled, rushing to the stove.

That dwarf skidded to a stop, though, noting the quivering arrow shaft, then spun about to find Nightbird and Tempest waiting.

Down swept the mighty sword as the powrie reached for its weapon. As its arm fell free of its body, the howling dwarf tried instead to charge ahead, barreling into the ranger.

A sure thrust of Tempest skewered the creature right through the heart, the lunging ranger putting the blade in all the way to its hilt. After a couple of wild spasms, the powrie slid dead to the floor.

"Yach, ye're waking me up!" came a roar from the bedroom.

Nightbird smiled, then waited a minute, slipping quietly to the door. He paused a few moments longer, making sure that the dwarf had settled down once more, then slowly pushed open the door.

There lay the powrie, on a bed, its back to him.

The ranger came out of the house soon after, giving a quick wave to Pony. He retrieved Hawkwing and began a cautious circuit of the barn. Of note was the hayloft, with one door cracked open and a rope hanging to the ground.

The ranger glanced all around, to see Pony moving to a new position, one that allowed her to view both the main door and the hayloft. He was truly blessed to have such a competent companion, he knew, for if he got into trouble, Pony would always be there.

And now, both of them understood the plan. Pony could have charged straight into the barn, of course, using serpentine and the explosive ruby to blow the place away, but the smoke of such a fire would not be a good thing. Instead she held her position, magnetite and graphite in hand, as Nightbird's backup.

And the ranger did not underestimate the amount of discipline it took for her to accept that position. Every morning, she performed the sword-dance beside him, and her blade work was truly becoming magnificent. She wanted to fight, to stand beside Elbryan, to dance now for real. But Pony was truly disciplined and patient. The ranger had assured her that she would get her chance to use the new techniques—both knew that she was almost ready.

But not yet.

Nightbird tested the rope to the hayloft, then began a cautious and quiet climb. He paused just below the door, listening, peeking in at the loft level, then waved one finger up in the air for Pony to see.

Up he went, level with the door, putting one foot gingerly in the small crack, though he had to continue to hold on to the rope. He had to move fast, he realized, and wouldn't likely have time to draw any weapon.

Again the ranger took a deep, steadying breath, found his center and his necessary calm. Then he hooked his foot about the bottom of the door and yanked it out, hurling himself into the loft, into the surprised goblin standing a nonchalant guard within.

The goblin gave a cry, muffled almost immediately as the ranger clamped a strong hand over its mouth, his other arm wrapping tight the goblin's weapon hand. Nightbird clamped his hand over the creature's face, squeezing hard, then turned his wrist and drove the goblin to its knees.

A cry from below told him he was out of time.

With a sudden jerk, Nightbird brought the goblin back up to its feet, then twisted and threw, launching the creature out the open door to dive the ten feet to the ground. It landed hard and groaned, then tried to get back up, tried to call out. At the last instant it spotted Pony, the woman standing calm, hand extended.

A lodestone traveling many times the speed of a sling bullet blasted right through the metal amulet the creature had around its neck, a piece of jewelry it had stolen from a woman who futilely begged for her life.

Inside the barn, Nightbird set Hawkwing to deadly work, blasting goblins from the ladder as they tried to gain the loft. A moment later the startled ranger found out he was not alone, as a second archer joined him.

"Roger told me of your plans," Belli'mar Juraviel explained. "A good start!" he added, plunking an arrow into a goblin that had foolishly scurried into view.

Recognizing that there was no way they could possibly get up that ladder, the remaining goblins went for the main door instead, pushing it wide and scrambling out into the daylight.

A bolt of streaking lightning laid most of them low.

Then the elf was above them, at the doors to the loft, firing down at those who continued to scramble.

The ranger did not join his friend, but took a different route, slipping down the ladder. He hit the ground in a roll, avoiding a spear throw by one creature, and was firing Hawkwing as he came around, taking the goblin right in the face, then again, taking out a second as it ran for the door.

Then all was quiet, inside at least, but Nightbird sensed he was not alone. He put his bow to the ground and drew out his sword, moving slowly, silently.

Outside, the cries diminished. Nightbird came to a bale of hay, put his back against it and listened hard.

Breathing.

Around he went suddenly, holding his swing just long enough to make sure that it was indeed another goblin and not some unfortunate prisoner, then lopping the creature's ugly head from its shoulders with a single stroke. He came out into the daylight afterward, finding Pony and Juraviel walking Symphony toward the barn, their business finished.

The elf stayed with Elbryan, securing a new perimeter, while Pony galloped the stallion back to gather the group.

"I canno' be turning back now," the driver replied when Jojonah told him of the plans the next morning. "Though suren I'd love to be helping ye. But me business—"

"Is important. Indeed," Jojonah finished for him, excusing him.

"Yer best way back is with the ships," the driver went on. "Most o' them are heading up north and to the open sea for the summer season. I'd've come down on one meself, but few be coming south just now."

Master Jojonah stroked his stubbly chin. He had no money, but perhaps he could find a way. "The nearest port, then," he said to the driver.

"South and east," the man replied. "Bristole by name. A town built for fixing and supplying the boats and not much else. She's not too far outta me way."

"I would be obliged," the monk answered.

So they were off again, after a hearty breakfast, supplied for free by the goodly townsfolk. Only when the wagon began rambling down the road did Master Jojonah comprehend how much better he was feeling physically. Despite the bumpy nature of the ride, his breakfast had settled well. It was as if the news of the previous night, the implication that things were darker by far than he had ever imagined, had pumped strength back into his frail body. He simply could not afford to be weak now.

Bristole was as small a town as Jojonah had ever seen, and seemed strangely unbalanced to the monk. The dock areas were extensive, with long wharves that could accommodate ten large ships. Other than that, though, there were but a few buildings, including only a pair of small warehouses. It wasn't until the wagon pulled into the center of the cluster of houses that Jojonah began to understand.

Ships going up- or downriver would need no supplies at this point, since the trip from Palmaris to Ursal was not a long one. However, the sailors might desire a bit of relief, and so the ships would put in here for restocking of a different nature.

Of the seven buildings clustered together, two were taverns and two were brothels.

Master Jojonah said a short prayer, but was not overly concerned. He was an accepting man, ever willing to forgive the weakness of the flesh. It was, after all, the strength of the soul that counted.

He bade farewell to the generous driver, wishing he could give the goodly man more than words for his efforts, and then turned to the business at hand. Three ships were in; another was approaching from the south. The monk walked down to the riverbank, his sandals clapping against the extensive boardwalk.

"Hail, good fellows," he called as he neared the closest ship, seeing a pair of men bending low behind the taffrail, working hammers on some problem he could not see. Jojonah noted that this ship was in stern first, an oddity, and, he hoped, an omen that it would soon depart.

"Hail, good fellows!" Jojonah yelled more loudly, waving his arms to get their attention.

The hammering stopped and one old sea dog with wrinkled brown skin and no teeth looked up to regard the monk. "And to yourself, Father," he said.

"Are you heading north?" Master Jojonah asked. "To Palmaris, perhaps?"

"Palmaris and the Gulf," the man answered. "But we're not heading anywhere at all anytime soon. Got an anchor line that won't hold; chain's all busted."

Jojonah understood why the ship was in dock backward. He looked around, back at the town, searching for some solution that would get this ship sailing. Any worthy port would have held the proper equipment— even the meager docks of St.-Mere-Abelle were supplied with such items as chains and anchors. But Bristole was no town for ship repairs, was more a place for "crew repairs."

"Got a new one sailing up from Ursal," the old seaman went on. "Should arrive in two days. Are you looking for passage, then?"

"Yes, but I cannot delay."

"Well, we'll take you, for five pieces of the King's gold," the old man said. "A fair price, Father."

"Indeed it is, but I've not the gold to pay, I fear," Jojonah replied. "Nor the time to delay."

"Two days?" the sea dog balked.

"Two days more than I have to spare," Jojonah answered.

"I do beg your pardon, Father," came another voice, from the ship next in line, a wide and sturdy caravel. "We shall be sailing north this very day."

Master Jojonah waved to the two on the damaged vessel and walked around to get a better view of the newest speaker. The man was tall and lean and dark-skinned—not from the sun, but from his heritage. He was Behrenese, and, given his complexion, likely from a region of southern Behren, far south of the Belt-and-Buckle.

"I am afraid that I have no gold to pay," Jojonah replied.

The dark man flashed a pearly smile. "But Father," he said, "why would you be needing the gold?"

"I'll work for my passage, then," Jojonah offered.

"All on my ship could use a good prayer, Father," the Behrenese man replied. "More, I fear, after our little stop here. Come aboard, I beg you. We were not to leave until late in the day, but I've only one man out and he can be retrieved easily. If you are in a hurry, then we are in a hurry!"

"Very generous, good sir—"

"Al'u'met," the man answered. "Captain Al'u'met of the good ship *Saudi Jacintha*."

Jojonah cocked his head at that curious name.

"It means Jewel of the Desert," Al'u'met explained. "A bit of a joke on my father, who wished me to ride the dunes, not the waves."

"As my own father wanted me to serve ale, not prayer," Jojonah replied with a laugh. He was more than a bit surprised to find a dark-skinned Behrenese in command of an Ursal sailing ship, and even more surprised to see the man pay so much respect to one of the Abellican Order. Jojonah's Church was not prominent in the southern kingdom; indeed, missionaries had many times been slaughtered for trying to impose their vision of divinity on the often intolerant priests—*yatols* in the Behren tongue—of the deserts.

Captain Al'u'met helped Jojonah over the last step of gangplank, then dispatched two of his crewmen to go and find the one missing sailor. "Have you bags to bring aboard?" he asked Jojonah.

"Only what I carry," the monk replied.

"And how far north will you be sailing?"

"Palmaris," Jojonah replied. "Or across the river, actually; I can ride the ferry. I am needed at St.-Mere-Abelle on most urgent matters."

"We may be sailing past All Saints Bay," Captain Al'u'met said. "Though you will lose a week at least traveling by sea."

"Then Palmaris it is," the monk said.

"Exactly where we were going," Captain Al'u'met replied, and, smiling still, he pointed to the cabin door leading under the poop deck. "I have two rooms," he explained. "Surely I can share one with you for a day or two."

"You are Abellican?"

Al'u'met's grin widened. "For three years," he explained. "I found your God at St. Gwendolyn of the Sea, and as fine a catch as Al'u'met has ever known."

"But another disappointment for your father," Jojonah reasoned.

Al'u'met put a finger to pursed lips. "He does not need to know such things, Father," he said slyly. "Out on the Mirianic, when the storms blow high and the waves break twice the height of a tall man above the forward rail, I choose my own God. Besides," he added with a wink, "they are not so different, you know, the God of your land and the one of mine. A change in robes would make a priest a *yatol*."

"So your conversion was one of convenience," Jojonah teased.

Al'u'met shrugged. "I choose my own God."

Jojonah nodded and returned the wide smile, then made his slow way toward the captain's cabins.

"My boy will show you your quarters," Al'u'met called after him.

The cabin boy was just within the shelter of the room, throwing bones, when Master Jojonah opened the door. The lad, no more than ten years of age, scrambled frantically, collecting his dice and looking very guilty—he had been caught derelict from his chores, the monk knew.

"Set our friend up, Matthew," Captain Al'u'met called. "See to his needs."

Jojonah and Matthew stood staring at each other, sizing each other up for a long time. Matthew's clothes were threadbare, as was the lot for anybody working aboard a ship. But they were a fine cut, better than the attire of most crewmen the monk had met. And the boy was cleaner than most cabin boys, his sun-bleached hair neatly trimmed, his skin golden tanned. There was one notable blemish, though, a black patch on the boy's forearm.

Jojonah recognized the scar, and he imagined the pain the boy must have felt. The patch had been caused by the second of the three "medicinal" liquids—rum, tar, and urine—kept on the sailing ships. The rum was used to kill the worms that inevitably found their way into foodstuffs, to kill the aftereffects of bad food, and simply to forget the long, long, empty hours. The urine was used for washing, clothes and hair, and as disgusting as that thought was, it paled in comparison to the liquid tar. This was used to patch torn skin. The boy, Matthew, had obviously gashed his arm, and so the sailors had applied tar to the wound to seal it.

"May I?" Jojonah quietly asked, reaching for the arm.

Matthew hesitated, but dared not disobey, cautiously holding the arm up for inspection.

A fine job, the monk noted. The tar had been sanded flat with the skin, a perfect patch of black. "Does it hurt?" Jojonah asked.

Matthew shook his head emphatically.

"He does not speak," came Captain Al'u'met's voice, the man having moved up right behind the distracted monk.

"Your work?" Jojonah asked, indicating the arm.

"Not mine, but Cody Bellaway's," Al'u'met answered. "He serves as healer when we are far from port."

Master Jojonah nodded and let the issue drop—openly, at least, for in his mind the image of Matthew's blackened arm would not so quickly fade. How many hematites were locked away in St.-Mere-Abelle? Five hundred? A thousand? The number was considerable, Jojonah knew, for when he was a younger monk, he had done an inventory of just that stone, easily the most common stone returned from Pimaninicuit over the years. Most of these soul stones were of far less power than the one the caravan to the Barbacan had taken along, but still, Jojonah had to wonder how much good might come of these if they were given to the sailing ships with one or two men on each vessel taught how to bring forth their healing powers. Matthew's wound had been considerable, no doubt, but Jojonah could have easily sealed it with magic, not tar. With hardly an effort, much suffering could have been avoided.

That line of thinking made the master wonder on a grander scale. Why weren't all the communities, or at least one community in each general region of the kingdom, given a hematite, with their chosen healers trained in its use?

He had never discussed such a thing with Avelyn, of course, but somehow Master Jojonah understood that Avelyn Desbris, if the choice had been his, would without hesitation have distributed the small hematites to the general populace, would have opened up St.-Mere-Abelle's horde of magic for the betterment of all, or at least distributed the most minor hematites, stones too weak to be used for diabolical purposes such as possession, stones too weak to be used in any real malevolent way.

Yes, Jojonah knew, Avelyn would have done it if given the chance, but of course Father Abbot Markwart would never have given him the chance!

Jojonah patted the mop of Matthew's blond hair and motioned for the lad to show him to his room. Al'u'met left them then, calling for his hands to ready the ship for departure.

Saudi Jacintha slipped out of Bristole soon after, her sails fast filling with wind, pushing her against the considerable current. They would make good time, Al'u'met came and assured the monk, for the south winds were brisk, with no sign of storm, and as the Masur Delaval widened, the pull of the water was not so strong.

The monk spent the bulk of the day in his cabin, sleeping, gathering the strength he knew he would need. He did get up for a short while, and with a friendly nod convinced Matthew to play dice with him, assuring him the captain wouldn't mind if he took a short break from his chores.

Jojonah wished that the boy could talk, or even laugh, in the hour they spent throwing dice. He wanted to know where the lad had come from and how he had wound up on a ship at so tender an age.

Likely his parents, poverty-stricken, had sold him, the monk knew, and he winced at the thought. That was how most ships acquired cabin boys, though Jojonah hoped that Al'u'met had not been the one to purchase him. The captain claimed to be a religious man, and men of God did not do such things.

A light rain came up that night, but nothing that impeded *Saudi Jacintha*'s progress. This crew was well-trained and knew every turn in the great river, and on the ship plowed, her prow spray foaming white in the moonlight. It was at that forward rail, in that same night after the rain had stopped, that Master Jojonah fully accepted the truths that were forming in his heart. Alone in the darkness with the splash of the prow, the croaking of the animals on the bank, the flutter of the wind in the sails, Master Jojonah found his course come clearer.

He felt as if Avelyn was with him, hovering about him, reminding him of the three vows—not just the empty spoken words, but the meaning behind them—that supposedly guided the Abellican Order.

He stayed up all through the night and went to bed again right before the dawn, after coaxing a sleepy-eyed Matthew to go and fetch him a good meal.

He was up again at dinnertime, dining beside Captain Al'u'met, who informed him they would reach their goal early the next morning.

"You might not wish to stay up all the night again," the captain said with a smile. "You will be back to land in the morning, and will not travel far, I will guess, if you are asleep."

Still, later on that evening, Captain Al'u'met found Jojonah again at the forward rail, staring into the darkness, looking into his own heart.

"You are a thinking man," the captain said, approaching the monk. "I like that."

"You can tell such things simply because I am standing out here alone?" Jojonah replied. "I might be thinking of nothing at all."

"Not at the forward rail," Captain Al'u'met said, taking a spot right beside the leaning monk. "I, too, know the inspiration of this place."

"Where did you get Matthew?" Jojonah asked abruptly, blurting out the words before he could even consider them.

Al'u'met gave him a sidelong glance, surprised by the question. He looked back to the prow spray and smiled. "You do not wish to think that I, a man of your Church, purchased him from his parents," the perceptive man reasoned. "But I did," Al'u'met added, standing straighter and looking directly at the monk.

Master Jojonah did not return the stare.

"They were paupers, living near St. Gwendolyn, surviving on the scraps your Abellican brothers bothered to toss out for them," the captain went on, his tone deepening, growing somber.

Now Jojonah did turn, eyeing the man severely. "Yet this is the Church you chose to join," he stated.

"That does not mean that I agree with all of those who now administer the doctrine of the Church," Al'u'met calmly replied. "As to Matthew, I purchased him, and at a handsome price, because I came to think of him as my own son. He was always at the docks, you see—or at least, he was there at those times when he could escape his wrathful father. The man beat him for no reason, though little Matthew had not seen his seventh birthday at the time. So I purchased him, took him aboard to teach him an honest trade."

"A difficult life," Jojonah remarked, but all animosity and hints of accusation were gone from his voice.

"Indeed," the large Behrenese agreed. "A life some love and others loathe. Matthew will make up his own mind when he is old enough to better understand. If he comes to love the sea, as I do, then he will have no choice but to stay aboard ship—and hopefully he will choose to stay with me. *Saudi Jacintha* will outlive me, I fear, and it would be good to have Matthew to carry on my work."

Al'u'met turned to face the monk and went quiet, waiting until Jojonah looked at him directly. "And if he does not love the smell and the roll of the waves, he will be free to go," the man said sincerely. "And I will make sure that he has a good start wherever he chooses to live. I give you my word on this, Master Jojonah of St.-Mere-Abelle."

Jojonah believed him, and his return smile was genuine. Among the tough sailors of the day, Captain Al'u'met surely stood tall.

They both looked back to the water and stood in silence for some time, save for the splashing prow and the wind.

"I knew Abbot Dobrinion," Captain Al'u'met said at length. "A good man."

Jojonah looked at him curiously.

"Your companion, the wagon driver, spread word of the tragedy in Bristole while you were seeking passage," the captain explained.

"Dobrinion was indeed a good man," Jojonah replied. "And a great loss it is for my Church that he was killed."

"A great loss for all the world," Al'u'met agreed.

"How did you know him?"

"I know many of the Church leaders, for, given my mobile profession, I spend many hours in many different chapels, St. Precious among them."

"Have you ever been to St.-Mere-Abelle?" Jojonah asked, though he didn't think Al'u'met had, for he believed that he would remember this man.

"We put in once," the Captain replied. "But the weather was turning, and we had far to go, so I did not get off the docks. St. Gwendolyn was not so far away, after all."

Jojonah smiled.

"I have met your Father Abbot, though," the Captain went on. "Only once. It was 819, or perhaps 820; the years do seem to blend as they pass. Father Abbot Markwart had put out a call for open-seas sailing ships. I am not really a river-runner, you see, but we took some damage last year—powrie barrelboat, for the wretched dwarves seemed to be everywhere!—and were late getting out of port this spring."

"You answered the Father Abbot's call," Jojonah prompted.

"Yes, but my ship was not chosen," Al'u'met replied casually. "Truthfully, I think it had something to do with the color of my skin. I do not believe that your Father Abbot trusted a Behrenese sailor, especially one who was not, at that time, an anointed member of your Church."

Jojonah nodded his agreement; there was no way that Markwart would have accepted a man of the southern religion for the journey to Pimaninicuit. The monk found that notion ironic, laughable even, given the carefully planned murderous end of the voyage.

"Captain Adjonas and his *Windrunner* were the better choice," Al'u'met admitted. "He was riding the open Mirianic before I ever learned to work an oar."

"You know of Adjonas, then?" Jojonah asked. "And of the end of the *Windrunner*?"

"Every seaman on the Broken Coast knows of the loss," Captain Al'u'met replied. "Happened just outside of All Saints Bay, so they say. A rough bit of water, to be sure, though I am amazed that a man as sea-seasoned as Adjonas got caught too near the shoal."

Jojonah only nodded; he could not bring himself to reveal the awful truth, to tell this man that Adjonas and his crew had been slaughtered in the sheltered waters of All Saints Bay by the holy men of the religion Al'u'met had freely joined. Looking back at that now, Master Jojonah could hardly believe that he had gone along with the plan, the terrible tradition. Had it always been that way, as the Church insisted?

"A fine ship and crew," Al'u'met finished reverently.

Jojonah nodded his agreement, though in truth, he hardly knew any of the sailors, had met only Captain Adjonas and the first hand, Bunkus Smealy, a man he did not like at all.

"Go and get your sleep, Father," Captain Al'u'met said. "You've a hard day of walking ahead of you."

Jojonah, too, thought that to be a good time to break the conversation. Al'u'met had inadvertently given him much to think about, had rekindled memories and put them in a new light. *That does not mean that I agree with all of those who now administer the doctrine of the Church*, Al'u'met had said, words that rang as truly prophetic to the disillusioned master.

Jojonah slept well that night, better than he had since he had first arrived in Palmaris, since all the world had spun completely over. A cry concerning dock lights woke him with the sun and he gathered his few possessions and raced onto the deck, thinking to see the long wharves of Palmaris.

All that he saw was fog, a heavy gray blanket. All the crew was abovedecks, most at the rail, holding lanterns and peering intently into the gloom. Looking for rocks, or even other ships, Jojonah realized, and a shudder coursed his spine. The sight of Captain Al'u'met calmed him, though, the tall man standing serenely, as though this situation was nothing out of the ordinary. Jojonah made his way to join him.

"I heard a cry for dock lights," the monk explained, "though I doubt that any might have been spotted in this fog."

"We saw," Al'u'met assured him, smiling. "We are close, and getting closer by the second."

Jojonah followed the captain's gaze out over the forward rail, to the gloom. Something—he couldn't quite identify it—seemed out of place to him, as though his internal direction sense was askew. He stood quiet for a long while, trying to sort it out, noting the position of the sun, a lighter splotch of grayness ahead of the ship.

"We are traveling east," he said suddenly, turning to Al'u'met. "But Palmaris is on the western bank."

"I thought that I would save you the hours on the crowded ferry," Al'u'met explained. "Though they might not even run the ferry in this gloom."

"Captain, you did not have to—"

"No trouble, my friend," Al'u'met replied. "We would not be allowed into Palmaris port until the fog rolled back anyway, so rather than set anchor, we turned to Amvoy, a smaller port and one with less rules."

"Land to forward!" came a call from above.

"Amvoy's long dock!" another sailor agreed.

Jojonah looked to Al'u'met, who only winked and smiled.

Soon after, *Saudi Jacintha* glided easily into position beside the one long dock at Amvoy, the skilled sailors expertly tying her in place.

"I wish you well, Master Jojonah of St.-Mere-Abelle," Al'u'met said sincerely as he led the monk to the gangplank. "May the loss of good Abbot Dobrinion strengthen us all." He shook Jojonah's hand firmly, and the monk turned to go.

At the edge of the plank he stopped, torn, prudence battling conscience.

"Captain Al'u'met," he said suddenly, turning about. He noted several other sailors in the vicinity, all listening to his every word, but didn't let that deter him. "In the coming months you will hear stories of a man named Avelyn Desbris. Brother Avelyn, formerly at St.-Mere-Abelle."

"The name is not known to me," Captain Al'u'met replied.

"But it will be," Master Jojonah assured him. "You will hear terrible stories of the man, naming him as a thief, a murderer, a heretic. You will hear his name dragged through the very fires of hell."

Captain Al'u'met made no reply at all as Jojonah paused and swallowed hard on his words.

"I tell you this in all sincerity," the monk went on, realizing that he was crossing a very delicate line here. Again he paused, swallowing hard. "The stories are not true, or at least, the manner in which they will be told will be slanted against the actions of Brother Avelyn, who was, I assure you, a man following his God-inspired conscience at all times."

Several of the crewmen merely shrugged, thinking that the words meant little for them, but Captain Al'u'met recognized the gravity in the monk's voice and understood that this was a pivotal moment for the man. From Jojonah's tone, Al'u'met was wise enough to understand that these tales of this monk he did not know might indeed affect him, and everyone else associated with the Abellican Church. He nodded, not smiling.

"Never has the Abellican Church fostered a better man than Avelyn Desbris," Jojonah said firmly, and he turned and left the *Saudi Jacintha*. He understood the chance he had just taken, realizing that the *Saudi Jacintha* would likely find its way to St.-Mere-Abelle again one day, and that Captain Al'u'met, or more likely, one of the eavesdropping crewmen would speak with men at the abbey, would perhaps speak with Father Abbot Markwart himself. But for some reason, Jojonah didn't try to qualify the story, or retract it. There, he had said it, openly. As it should be.

Still, the monk's words followed him as he entered Amvoy, filling him with doubts. He secured a ride to the east on a wagon, and though the driver was a member of the Church, and a man as friendly and generous as Captain Al'u'met, at their parting three days later, only a few miles from the gates of St.-Mere-Abelle, Master Jojonah did not recount his tale of Avelyn.

It wasn't until he came in sight of the abbey that the master's doubts vanished. From any perspective, St.-Mere-Abelle was an impressive place, its walls ancient and strong, a lasting part of the mountainous coastline. Whenever he looked upon the abbey from out here, Jojonah was reminded of the long, long history of the Church, of traditions that preceded Markwart, and even the last dozen Father Abbots before him. Again Jojonah felt as if Avelyn's tangible spirit was about him and in him, and he was overcome with a desire to dig deeper into the Order's past, to look for the way things had once been so many centuries before. For Master Jojonah could hardly believe that the Church as it now existed could have become such a dominant religion. These days, people were drawn to the Church out of heritage;

they were "believers" because their parents had been, their grandparents had been, their grandparents' parents had been. Few were like Al'u'met, he understood, recent converts, members out of their heart and not their heritage.

It could not have been like that in the beginning, Jojonah reasoned. St.-Mere-Abelle, so vast and impressive, could not have been built with the few who would have agreed, in heart, with the teachings of the present-day Church.

Bolstered by his insight, Master Jojonah approached the strong gates of St.-Mere-Abelle, the place he had called home for more than two-thirds of his life, the place that now seemed to him a facade. He did not yet understand the truth of the abbey, but, with Avelyn's spirit guiding him, he meant to find it out.

❖ 20 ❖

Following the Bait

onnor Bildeborough didn't feel nervous in the least as he left the familiar and safe, until now, confines of Palmaris behind. He had been in the open northland many times in the last months, and was confident he could avoid any trouble from the large numbers of monsters still to be found up there. The giants, with their dangerous rock-throwing abilities, had become quite scarce, and goblins and powries did not ride horses and would never catch Greystone.

Even when he set camp that first night, some thirty miles north of the city, the nobleman wasn't concerned. He knew how to conceal himself, and since it was summer, he didn't even need a fire. He reclined under the boughs of a bushy spruce, his horse nickering softly nearby.

The next day and night were much the same. Connor avoided the one real road that ran up this way, but he knew where he was going, and found enough level and clear ground to keep the pace swift.

On the third day, well over a hundred miles north of Palmaris, he came upon the ruins of a farmhouse and barn, and the tracks in the area told the experienced hunter exactly what had happened: a goblin troupe, a score at least, had come this way within the last couple of days. Fearing rain and an obscurement of the tracks, for the sky was heavy, Connor was back on his horse at once, following the easy trail. He caught up to the raiding band late that afternoon, a light rain just beginning to fall. While Connor was glad to see that it was indeed only goblins, their numbers were twice his estimate and they were outfitted for war and marching with some measure of discipline. The nobleman considered their course, north-by-northwest, and thought it prudent to follow them. If what he suspected, if what the rumors had told him, were true, then these foolish goblins might lead him to the warrior band, and to the person using the magical gemstones operating in the area.

He rested within half a mile of the noisy goblin encampment. At one point, late in the night, he dared to sneak close to the perimeter—and was again impressed by the professionalism shown by the normally slovenly creatures. Still, Connor managed to get close enough to hear pieces of various conversations, complaints mostly, and a confirmation that most of the giants had gone home and the powries were too concerned with their own welfare to worry about any goblins.

Then Connor listened with great interest as a pair of goblins argued about their destination. One wanted to go north, to the encampment at the two towns—Caer Tinella and Landsdown, Connor realized.

"*Argh!*" the other scolded. "Yer knowin' that Kos-kosio's dead and gone, and so's Maiyer Dek! Ain't nothing up there but that Nightbird and his killers! The towns're all but lost, ye fool, and gettin' hit with balls o' fire every day!"

A smile widened on Connor's face. He went back to his impromptu camp and his horse and managed to steal a few hours sleep, but was up and ready to go well before the dawn. He followed the goblin troupe again, thinking to swing wide to the west with them, just in case, then turn back to explore the area near Caer Tinella and Landsdown.

The rain was back, heavier this day, but Connor hardly cared.

They took their rest under the shelter of the buildings, using the well, and they did indeed find fresh eggs and fresh milk for their enjoyment. They also found a wagon in the barn, and oxen to pull it, some whetstones to hone their blades and a pitchfork, which Tomas thought would look fine tucked into the belly of a giant. Roger, snooping about every corner of the barn, found a thin but strong rope and a small block and tackle, small enough that he could carry it without trouble. He had no idea what he might use it for, except maybe to rescue the wagon from some mud, but he took it anyway.

And so when the refugees left the farmhouse later that same night, they were refreshed and ready for the last leg of their flight to safety.

As usual, Roger and Juraviel moved into the point position, the elf scrambling nimbly along the lower branches of the trees, the tireless young Roger running a sweeping arc, always alert, always looking for signs of danger.

"You did well today," Juraviel said unexpectedly, catching Roger off his guard.

The young man looked up at the elf curiously. The two hadn't spoken much since Juraviel's thrashing of Roger, other than to agree to plans for their common scouting routes.

"After you spotted the farmhouse and barn, you accepted the position Nightbird gave to you without question," the elf explained.

"What was I to do?"

"You could have argued," the elf replied. "Indeed, the Roger Lockless I first met would have seen the duty of staying with the caravan as a slight to his abilities, would have grumbled and complained and probably run off to

the farmhouse anyway. In fact, the Roger Lockless I first met would not
even have come to Nightbird and the others with the news, not until he had
first had his way with the powries and the goblins."

Roger considered the words for a moment, and found that he could not
disagree with the assessment. When he had first spotted the farmhouse, his
instincts goaded him to go in for a better look, and a bit of light-fingered
fun, perhaps. But that course had screamed as dangerous to Roger, not so
much for him, but for the others, who were moving along not so far behind.
Even if he hadn't been caught—which seemed to him likely, whatever monsters might have been inside—he might have had to lay low and stay put,
and thus the caravan would not have been warned in time, and a fight—not
on favorable terms—might have ensued.

"You understand, of course," the elf went on.

"I know what I did," Roger replied curtly.

"And you know that you did well," Juraviel said, and then, with a sly
smile, he added, "You learn quickly."

Roger's eyes narrowed as he snapped his angry gaze over the elf; he certainly didn't need to be reminded of the "lesson."

Juraviel's continuing smile defeated him, though, put his pride in its
proper place. Roger knew then that they had come to an understanding, he
and this elf. The lesson had taken, he had to admit. The cost of failure in
this situation was bigger than his own life, and thus he had to accept directions from those more experienced than he. He relented his angry glare,
and even managed a nod and a grin.

Juraviel perked up his ears suddenly, his eyes darting to the side. "An
approach," he said, and then he was gone, slipping into the tree cover so
quickly that Roger blinked many times.

Then the young man moved fast, finding cover. He spotted the
"approach" soon after, and relaxed when he recognized the source, a
woman of his group, also out scouting. He startled her so much when he
stepped out from behind a tree that she nearly drove her dagger into his
chest.

"Something has put you on edge," Roger understated.

"A group of enemies," the woman replied. "Moving west, south of our
position."

"How strong?"

"There are quite a few, two score, perhaps," she answered.

"And what manner of enemies?" came a question from the trees above.

The woman looked up, though she knew she would not catch a glimpse
of this ever-elusive friend of Nightbird. Few of the advance scouts had seen
Juraviel, though all had heard his melodic voice from time to time. "Goblins," she replied. "Just goblins."

"Back to your place, then," the elf bade her. "Find the next in line, and he, the next in line, that all the scouts are linked, that word can be passed quickly."

The woman nodded and sped away.

"We could let them pass," Roger offered as Juraviel came back in sight on a lower branch.

The elf was not looking at him, was staring far away. "Go back and tell Nightbird to prepare a surprise," he instructed Roger.

"By Nightbird's own words, we are not to engage," Roger argued.

"Just goblins," Juraviel replied. "And if they are part of a larger band, they might be flanking us, and thus should be defeated quickly. Tell Nightbird that I insist we attack."

Roger looked long and hard at the elf, and for a moment Juraviel thought he would refuse the order. And that was exactly what Roger was thinking. The young man bit back that response, though, nodded and ran off.

"And Roger," Juraviel called, stopping him before he had gone five strides. He turned back to regard the elf.

"Tell Nightbird that this was your plan," Juraviel said. "And that I approve completely. Tell him that you believe we must hit the goblins fast and hard. The plan is yours to claim."

"That would be a lie," Roger protested.

"Would it?" asked the elf. "When you heard of the goblins, did you not first think that we should attack? Was it not only your obedience to the words of the ranger that stopped you from saying so?"

The young man pursed his lips as he considered the words, the simple truth of them.

"There is nothing wrong with disagreeing," Juraviel explained. "You have proven repeatedly that your opinion in these matters is truly valuable, and Nightbird understands this, as does Pony, as do I."

Again Roger turned and sped off, and this time with a noticeable spring in his step.

"My baby!" the woman screamed. "Oh, do not hurt him, I beg of you!"

"Duh?" one goblin asked its leader, scratching its head at the unexpected voice. This band had come from the Moorlands, and were not well-versed in the common language of the land. From their dealings with powries, they knew enough words to understand the general meaning of it all, though.

The goblin leader saw its band shuffling anxiously. They were thirsty for blood, though in no mood for any real battle, and now, delivered into their hands, it seemed, was an easy kill. The overcast had finally broken, and a bright full moon illuminated the night.

"Please," the unseen woman went on. "They are all just children."

That was all the goblins could stand. Before the leader of the band even gave the word, they were off and running into the forest, each wanting to be the first to claim a kill.

Another cry came out of the shadows, but seemed no closer. The goblins continued their blind charge, crashing through the brush, tripping over roots, but scrambling right back to their feet and running on. Eventually they all came into a small clearing, bordered on the back by a tumble of boulders, on the left by a stand of pines, and on the right by an equally thick mix of oak and maple.

From somewhere behind those pines came the woman's voice, but now it did not seem so frantic as she sang:

> *Goblins, goblins, running hard,*
> *Delivering songs unto the bards.*
> *For in your folly you've come to play*
> *And every goblin dies this day!*

"Duh?" the goblin asked its leader again.

Another voice, melodious and clear, the voice of an elf, picked up the impromptu tune from somewhere within the shadows of the oak.

> *Dies from arrow, dies from blade,*
> *From magic woven, the toll is paid.*
> *For every person who at your hands*
> *Was murdered most foul while you walked these lands,*
> *We take revenge, we cleanse the night,*
> *That dawn might bring a shining light.*

More verses came at the confused monsters as many others took up the song, and laughter followed some of the lines, particularly the ones insulting to the goblins. Finally a resonating, powerful voice joined in, in a tone calm and deathly serious, and all the forest went quiet, as if to hear the words:

> *By your own evil have you brought this hour,*
> *And by my hands and by my power,*
> *Beg not for mercy, for judgment is passed,*
> *We cut you down unto the last.*

As he finished, the man walked his shining black stallion out from the shadows behind the boulders, in plain view of the stunned goblins.

"Nightbird," more than one creature whispered, and they knew then, every one, that they were truly doomed.

*   *   *

From a hillock not so far away, Connor Bildeborough watched the unfolding spectacle with more than a passing interest. For that first voice, the woman's, haunted the man, a voice he had listened to for so many wonderful months.

"I would give you a chance to surrender," the ranger said to the goblins. "But I am afraid that I have no place to put you, nor do I trust the likes of smelly goblins."

The goblin leader strode forward boldly, clenching tight its weapon.

"Are you the leader of this ragged band?" the ranger asked.

No answer.

"Impertinence!" the Nightbird shouted, and he pointed his finger at the goblin's helmeted head. "Die!" he commanded.

The sharp retort had every goblin jumping, and then staring incredulously as their leader's head snapped violently to the side, as this powerful goblin who had bullied its way to a position of prominence simply fell over dead!

"And who is now the leader?" the ranger asked ominously.

The goblins went into a frenzy, scrambling every which way, most turning about, trying to run out the way they had come in. But Nightbird's band had not been idle during the minutes of the taunting song, and a strong contingent of archers was now in place in the forest behind the monsters. As they turned to the trees, they were met by a hail of stinging arrows, and then, when they scrambled yet another way, a sizzling bolt of lightning thundered out of the pines, blinding them all and killing several.

On came Nightbird, on came his warriors, charging down on the confused and disorganized band.

And on came Connor Bildeborough, as well, Defender in hand. The nobleman had seen and heard enough, and galloped headlong into the battle, the name of Jilly ringing from his lips.

Nightbird seemed to be everywhere he was most needed, bolstering his soldiers wherever the goblins appeared to have gained any advantage.

From the oak stand, Belli'mar Juraviel, so sure of hand and eye, peppered the monsters with his small arrows, even stinging several who were engaged in close combat.

Across the way from the elf, Pony held her magic in check, conserving her strength, thinking, fearing, that she would have to use the healing soul stone soon enough.

By the time he got near the clearing, Connor was truly impressed. No ragtag band this! The lightning, the arrows, the perfect timing of the ambush—he lamented that if the King's soldiers were as well-trained, this war might have ended long ago!

He hoped to find Jilly when he came onto the clearing, but she was not about and he couldn't rightly go looking for her. His sword was needed now, and so he kicked Greystone into a short burst, slashing one goblin as he passed and then trampling a second who had put a man to the ground.

The horse stumbled and Connor lost his seat, tumbling hard to the ground. No matter, though, for he was not badly hurt and he was up and ready with his sword in an instant.

Luck was not with the nobleman, though, for several goblins had chosen this particular place as their exit point, and now only Connor stood between them and the forest. He raised his sword and bravely assumed defensive posture, slipping his thoughts to the magnetites, activating their attracting magic.

A goblin sword slashed in, but Defender easily got in its path, blade against blade. When the goblin tried to retract its weapon, it found the blade somehow stuck to the nobleman's sword.

A deft twist and swing of Defender, a release of the magnetite magic, and the goblin's sword was flying free.

But Connor was far from free, for other goblins pressed in, and many carried not metal weapons, but thick wooden clubs.

A small arrow zipped out from behind Connor, taking one goblin in the eye. Before he could even glance back to discern the source, the warrior astride the stallion was there beside him, his magnificent sword glowing of its own magical light.

The goblins turned about, shouting "Nightbird!" and "Doom!" repeatedly, and seemed not to care that they were running from two men into the whirling swords of two score.

It was over in a matter of minutes, and the wounded—and there weren't many, and only one or two appeared seriously injured—were quickly ushered back to the forest in the north, into the pines.

Connor went to his horse, carefully inspecting the beast's legs and breathing a deep sigh indeed when he discerned that beautiful Greystone had not been seriously injured.

"Who are you?" the man on the stallion asked him, walking near. His tone was not threatening, was not even suspicious.

Connor looked up to see that many of the warriors were about him, eyeing him curiously.

"Forgive us, but we have not found many allies so far from the more populated lands," the ranger added calmly.

"I am a friend from Palmaris, it would seem," Connor answered. "Out hunting goblins."

"Alone?"

"There are advantages to riding alone," Connor answered.

"Then hail and good greetings," Elbryan said, sliding down from Symphony and walking to stand directly before the man. He took Connor's hand in a firm shake. "We have food and drink, but we will not be stopping for long. Our road leads to Palmaris, and we plan to use the hours of the night to our advantage."

"So it would seem," Connor said dryly, looking at the many goblin dead.

"You are welcome to join us," Elbryan said. "In fact, we would consider it an honor and a great favor."

"I did not prove myself so worthy a fighter in that battle," Connor remarked. "Not measured next to the one called Nightbird," he added, offering the ranger a smile.

Elbryan only smiled in reply, and started away, Connor falling in beside him. He went to the first kill, the goblin who had led the band, and bent low, pulling aside the creature's bent and torn helmet.

"How far to the city?" another man, young and slight, asked.

"Three days," Connor replied. "Four, if you have any who will slow you down."

"Four, then," Roger replied.

Connor looked from him to the ranger just in time to see the large man dig a gemstone out of the goblin's smashed head.

"Then you are the worker of magic," the nobleman reasoned.

"Not I," replied Elbryan. "I can use the stones to some small degree, but pale indeed beside the true wielder."

"A woman?" Connor asked breathlessly.

Elbryan turned and rose, facing Connor directly, and Connor realized that his question had touched some nerve, had unsettled this man as surely as a threat. As eager as he was, Connor was wise enough to let the matter drop for now; these folks, the magic-user at least, were outlaws in the eyes of the Church, and they might know it, and might be more than a little suspicious of anyone asking too many probing questions.

"I heard the woman's song," Connor went on, deflecting his true intent. "I am a nobleman, and have seen magic before, but never have I witnessed such a magnificent display."

Elbryan didn't reply, but his visage softened somewhat. He looked around, to see that the refugees were efficiently ending the suffering of those goblins who had not yet succumbed to their wounds, then going about the task of taking whatever supplies they could find among the dead monsters. "Come," he bade the stranger. "I must ready the folk for the continuing march."

He led Connor, Roger in tow, into the forest then, moving to an area where the undergrowth was not so dense. Several fires were burning, guiding the people as they went about their work, and beside one such blaze Connor saw her.

Jilly, working over the wounded. His Jilly, as beautiful—more beautiful!—than she had been back in Palmaris, before the war, before all the pain. Her blond hair was shoulder-length now, and so thick that he felt as if he could lose himself in it, and even in the dim light of the fires her eyes shone blue, sparkling and rich.

All color left Connor's handsome face and he broke away from Elbryan, walking as if in a daze toward her.

The ranger caught up to him in an instant, taking him by the arm. "Are you wounded?" Elbryan asked.

"I know her," was Connor's breathless reply. "I know her."

"Pony?"

"Jilly."

Still the ranger held him firmly, more firmly, in place, turning him and eyeing him directly. Elbryan knew that Pony had married a nobleman in Palmaris, with disastrous consequences. "Your name, sir," the ranger inquired.

The man straightened. "Connor Bildeborough of Chasewind Manor," he answered boldly.

Elbryan didn't know how to react. One part of him wanted to punch the man in the face, to lay him low . . . because he had hurt Pony? No, that wasn't the reason, the ranger had to admit, to himself if not openly. He wanted to punch Connor out of sheer jealousy, out of the fact that, for a time at least, this man had found Pony's heart. She may not have been in love with Connor as she now loved him, may not even have consummated their relationship, but she had cared deeply about Connor Bildeborough, had even married him!

The ranger closed his eyes for a brief moment, finding his center and his calm. He had to consider how Pony would feel if he clobbered the man now, had to consider how she would feel at the mere sight of Connor Bilde-borough. "Better to wait until she is finished with the wounded," he explained calmly.

"I must see her and speak with her," Connor stuttered.

"To the detriment of those who just battled the goblins beside her," the ranger said firmly. "You will prove a distraction, Master Bildeborough, and the work with the stones requires absolute concentration."

Connor glanced back to the woman, even took a step that way, but the ranger tugged him back insistently back, with strength that frightened the man. He turned again to face Elbryan, and understood he would not get near Jilly now, that this man would drag him away forcibly, if need be.

"She will be finished within the hour," Elbryan said to him. "And then you may see her."

Connor studied the ranger's face as he spoke, and realized only then that there was something more than friendship between this man and the woman who had been his wife. He sized up Elbryan in light of his new observation, taking a measure of the ranger should they come to blows.

He didn't like the prospect.

So he followed the ranger as the man went about the business of preparing for the move. Connor glanced over at Jill often, as did Nightbird, and neither of them doubted that they were thinking much the same things. Finally Connor broke away from the ranger and moved to the far end of the encampment, putting as much distance, and as many people, between himself and Jill as possible. The sight of her, the realization that she was once again so near, was finally settling in on the nobleman; he had gone past the pleasant recollections to that one horrible night, their wedding night, when he had almost raped his unwilling bride. And then he had paid for an annulment, and forced charges against Jill for refusing him, an accusation that had taken her from her family and indentured her to the King's army. How would she feel about seeing him again? he wondered, and worried, for Connor could not believe that she would return his wistful smile.

They were on the road for nearly half an hour before Connor finally mustered the courage to ride up beside the woman, who was riding Symphony, the ranger walking along beside her.

Elbryan saw him coming first. He looked up at Pony, locking her gaze. "I am here in support of you," he said. "For whatever you need of me, even if that means that I must leave you alone."

Pony eyed him curiously, not understanding, then heard the hoofbeats. She knew that a stranger had joined in the battle, a nobleman from Palmaris, but Palmaris was a big city, and she had never imagined that it might be . . .

Connor.

Pony nearly toppled from Symphony at the sight of the man; her arms and legs went weak, her stomach churned. The black wings of remembered pain fluttered up about her, threatening to bury her. It was a part of her life that she did not want to recall, a memory better lost. She had survived the pain, had even grown from the pain, but she did not wish to relive it, especially not now, with the future so uncertain and so full of challenges.

Still, she could not avoid those images. She had been held down, like an animal, her clothes torn from her and her limbs held steady. And then, when he, this man who had professed to love her, could not follow through, she had been summarily dismissed, dragged from her bedchamber. Even that was not enough for him, for then Connor—this man, this gallant-looking figure so splendid on his well-groomed riding horse, with jewels in his sword belt and clothes cut of the finest cloth—had ordered both the handmaidens to return to him for his pleasure, had cruelly shot the barb right into her heart.

And here he was, astride his horse right beside her, a smile finding its way onto his undeniably handsome face. "Jilly," he blurted, so full of excitement.

CHAPTER

❖ 21 ❖

In the Bowels of St.-Mere-Abelle

"Y ou would allow your beloved husband to be tortured for the sake of your outlaw, adopted daughter?" Father Abbot Markwart asked the poor woman.

Pettibwa Chilichunk was a wretched sight. Dark bluish bags circled her eyes and all of her skin seemed to sag, for she had not slept more than a few hours in many days, ever since Grady had died on the road. Pettibwa had been heavy for many years, but had always carried her round form with grace and a light bounce in her step. No more. Even during those times when sheer exhaustion laid the woman low, she was ultimately awakened by horrible nightmares, or by her captors, who seemed as wicked as any dream could ever be.

"We will take his nose first," Father Abbot Markwart went on. "Right to here," he added, running his finger along the crease of a flared nostril. "It makes for a gruesome sight indeed, and assures that poor Graevis will be forever an outcast."

"Why would ye be doin' such a thing, and yerself claimin' to be a man o' God!" Pettibwa cried. She knew that the old man was not lying, that he would do exactly what he had threatened. She had heard him just minutes before, in the adjoining room in the southernmost cellar of St.-Mere-Abelle, formerly a storage area but now converted to hold the two Chilichunks and Bradwarden. Markwart had gone to Graevis first, and Pettibwa heard the agonized screams quite clearly through the earthen wall. Now the woman wailed and repeatedly made the holy sign of the evergreen, the symbol of the Abellican Order.

Markwart was unrepentant and unimpressed. He came forward suddenly, powerfully, moving his leering visage to within a hair's breadth of

Pettibwa's face. "Why, you ask!" he roared. "Because of your daughter, foolish woman! Because your dear Jilly's evil alliance with the heretic Avelyn could bring about the end of the world!"

"Jilly's a good girl!" Pettibwa yelled back at him. "Never would she do—"

"But she has!" Markwart interrupted, growling out every word. "She has the stolen gemstones, and I will do whatever is necessary—pity Graevis!—to see that they are returned. Then Pettibwa can look upon her disfigured outcast husband and know that her own foolishness condemned him, as it condemned her son!"

"Ye killed him!" Pettibwa cried, tears streaming down her face. "Ye killed me son!"

Markwart's expression went perfectly cold, stone-faced, and that, in turn, seemed to freeze the woman, locked her in his gaze. "I assure you," the Father Abbot said in even tones, "that your husband, and then you, will soon envy Grady."

The woman wailed and fell back—and would have fallen right to the ground had not Brother Francis been behind to support her. "Oh, what're ye wantin' o' poor Pettibwa, Father," she cried. "I'll tell ye. I'll tell ye!"

A wicked smile crossed the Father Abbot's face, though he had been looking forward to cutting off the stupid Graevis' nose.

St.-Mere-Abelle was buttoned up tight, with guards, young monks armed with crossbows, and the occasional older student armed with a potent gemstone, graphite or ruby, patrolling every section of wall. Master Jojonah, recognized by all and liked by most, had no trouble getting back into the abbey, though.

Word of his arrival preceded him, and he was met in the main hall almost as soon as he entered by a very sour-looking Brother Francis. Many other monks were in that hall, as well, curious as to why Jojonah had returned.

"The Father Abbot will speak with you," the young monk said curtly, looking around as he spoke, as though playing to the audience, showing them which of them, he or Jojonah, was truly in the favor of Markwart.

"You seem to have forgotten respect for your superiors," Master Jojonah replied, not backing off an inch.

Francis snorted and started to reply, but Jojonah cut him short.

"I warn you, Brother Francis," he said gravely. "I am sick and have been too long on the road and too long in this life. I know that you fancy yourself Father Abbot Markwart's adopted son, but if you continue this attitude toward those who have attained a higher rank than you, toward those who, by their years of study and the wisdom of simple age, are deserving of your respect, I will bring you before the College of Abbots. Father Abbot Markwart may protect you there, in the end, but his embarrassment will be considerable, as will his vengeance upon you."

All the hall went deathly silent, and Master Jojonah pushed past the stunned Brother Francis and exited. He needed no escort to Markwart's room.

Brother Francis paused for a long while, regarding the other monks in the room, their suddenly condescending stares. He responded with a threatening glare, but for now, at least, Master Jojonah had stolen the bite from this dog's bark. Francis stormed out of the main hall, feeling the eyes of his lessers upon him.

Master Jojonah entered the Father Abbot's room with hardly a knock, pushing through the unlocked door and moving right up to the desk of the old man.

Markwart shifted aside some papers he had been studying and sat back in his chair, sizing up the man.

"I sent you on an important matter," the Father Abbot stated. "Surely you could not have completed your mission in Ursal and returned to us already."

"I never got near to Ursal," Master Jojonah admitted. "For I was taken by illness on the road."

"You do not seem so sick," Markwart remarked, and not kindly.

"I was met on the road by a man with news of the tragedy in Palmaris," Master Jojonah explained, eyeing Markwart closely as he spoke the words, trying to see if the Father Abbot would inadvertently offer any clue that the death of Abbot Dobrinion had not been unexpected.

The old man was too sly for that. "Not so much a tragedy," he replied. "The issue was settled with the Baron amicably, his nephew returned to him."

A knowing grin made its way onto Master Jojonah's face. "I was speaking of the murder of Abbot Dobrinion," he said.

Markwart's eyes widened and he came forward in his chair. "Dobrinion?" he echoed.

"Then news has not reached St.-Mere-Abelle," Jojonah reasoned, going with the obvious bluff. "It is good that I have returned."

Brother Francis bumbled into the room.

"Yes, Father Abbot," Jojonah went on, ignoring the younger man. "Powries, or a single powrie, at least, entered St. Precious and murdered Abbot Dobrinion." Behind him, Brother Francis gasped, and it seemed to Master Jojonah that the news was a true surprise to the younger man. "As soon as I heard, of course, I turned back for St.-Mere-Abelle," he went on. "It would not do for us to be caught so unawares; it would seem that our enemies have singled out their prey, and if Abbot Dobrinion is a target, it only stands to reason that the Father Abbot of the Abellican Order—"

"Enough," Markwart interrupted, putting his head down in his arms. Markwart realized what had just happened here, understood that Jojonah, ever the clever one, had just turned his feigned surprise back against him, had just justified his return to St.-Mere-Abelle beyond any question.

"It is good that you returned to us," Markwart said a moment later, looking back to the man. "And a tragedy indeed that Abbot Dobrinion met with such an untimely end. But your business here is finished, and so prepare again for the road."

"I am not physically able to make the journey to Ursal," Jojonah replied. Markwart eyed him suspiciously.

"Nor do I think such a move prudent, given the demise of the chief sponsor for Brother Allabarnet's sainthood. Without Dobrinion's backing, the process will be set back years, at least."

"If I order you to go to St. Honce, then you shall go to St. Honce," Markwart answered, the rough edge of his ire beginning to show through.

Still, Master Jojonah didn't back away. "Of course, Father Abbot," he replied. "And by the code of the Abellican Order, when you find justification to send a sickly master halfway across the kingdom, I will willingly go. But there is no reason for that now, no justification. Just be pleased that I was able to return in time to warn you of the potential danger from the powries." Jojonah turned on his heel suddenly, putting his smirking face right in front of Brother Francis.

"Step aside, brother," he said ominously.

Francis looked past him, to Father Abbot Markwart.

"This young monk moves dangerously close to a trial before the College of Abbots," Jojonah said calmly.

Behind him, Father Abbot Markwart motioned for Brother Francis to get out of the master's way. Then, when Jojonah was gone, Markwart motioned for the flustered young monk to close the door.

"You should have sent him back out on the road," Brother Francis argued immediately.

"For your convenience?" Markwart replied sarcastically. "I am not the supreme dictator of the Abellican Order, but only the appointed leader, forced to work within prescribed guidelines. I cannot simply order a master, particularly a sickly one, on the road."

"You did so before," the young monk dared to put in.

"With justification," Markwart explained, rising from his seat and walking around the desk. "The canonization process was very real, but Master Jojonah is correct in saying that Dobrinion was its chief sponsor."

"And it is true that Abbot Dobrinion is dead?"

Markwart gave the young man a sour look. "So it would seem," he replied. "And thus, Master Jojonah was correct in returning to St.-Mere-Abelle, and is correct in refusing to go back out at this time."

"He did not look so sickly," Brother Francis remarked.

Markwart was hardly listening. Things had not played out as he had hoped; he wanted Jojonah settled at St. Honce in Ursal long before news of the abbot's death reached him. Then he would have sent news to Abbot Je'howith to use the master as his own, giving a temporary appointment of Jojonah to St. Honce—a temporary appointment that Markwart meant to make last until the portly master had died. Still, this scenario did not seem so terrible to him. Jojonah was a thorn in his side—one growing sharper and longer daily, it seemed—but at least with Jojonah here, he could keep an eye on him.

Besides, it was hard for Markwart to be upset. Youseff and Dandelion had completed part of their mission, at least, and certainly the most dangerous part in Palmaris. By Jojonah's own words, a powrie was being blamed. One very formidable enemy had been eliminated, and the other had no proof that Markwart had been involved. All the Father Abbot needed now was the return of the stolen stones and his position would be secured. He could deal with Jojonah, could crush the man if need be.

"I will attempt contact with the Brothers Justice," Brother Francis offered. "We should keep abreast of their progress."

"No!" Markwart said suddenly, sharply. "If the thief with the stolen stones is wary, such contact might be detected," he lied, noting Brother Francis' questioning stare. In truth, Markwart meant to use a soul stone himself to speak with Youseff and Dandelion; he didn't want anyone else, including Brother Francis, to contact them, to perhaps learn of their doings in Palmaris.

"Keep an eye and an ear bent always toward Master Jojonah," he instructed Francis. "And be wary, too, of your peer, Brother Braumin Herde. I want to know with whom they converse during their free time, a complete list."

Brother Francis hesitated a long while before nodding his understanding. So many things were going on about him, he realized, things of which he knew so very little. But again, as was typical for the man, he saw the opportunity to impress his Father Abbot, saw the course toward personal growth, and he was determined that he would not fail.

The news was not so disconcerting to Father Abbot Markwart as Brother Youseff had feared. Connor Bildeborough had escaped and could not be found. He had gone underground, into the bowels of the city, or perhaps out to the north.

Go for the gemstones, Markwart telepathically instructed the young monk, and with that, Markwart imparted a clear picture of the woman who went by the various titles of Jill, Jilly, Pony, and Cat-the-Stray. Pettibwa had been quite helpful that morning. *Forget the Baron's nephew.*

As soon as Youseff's reply of understanding came back to him, the weary Father Abbot broke the connection, let his spirit fall back into his own body.

But there was something else . . .

Another presence, Markwart feared, thinking that his lie to Brother Francis about Avelyn's protégé sensing the magic of the soul stone might hold more truth than he believed.

He relaxed, and quickly, though, for he came to recognize the intrusion as just another part of his own subconscious. Monks had traditionally used the soul stones for the deepest forms of meditation and introspection, though rarely in these times, and it seemed to Markwart that he had inadvertently stumbled down that path.

So he followed the course to the destination, thinking he was laying bare his own innermost feelings, thinking that perhaps in this state he might find needed moments of pure clarity.

In his thoughts he saw Master Jojonah and the younger monk, Brother Braumin Herde, plotting against him. Of course this didn't surprise Markwart; hadn't he just sent Brother Francis to keep a close watch over them?

But then something else came into the scene: Master Jojonah with a handful of stones, walking toward a door, a door that Markwart knew, Markwart's own door. And in the master's hand . . . graphite.

Jojonah kicked open the door and released a tremendous bolt of energy at the Father Abbot as he sat quiet on his chair. Markwart felt the sudden flash, the burn, the jolt, his heart fluttering, his life rushing away . . .

It took Markwart several agonizing seconds to separate imagination from reality, to realize it was only insight and not actually happening. Before this moment of enlightenment, he had never imagined just how dangerous Jojonah and his wicked cohorts could be!

Yes, he would watch them closely, and would act against them in a brutal and definitive manner if need be.

But they would grow strong, his inner voice told him. As the war ended, the great victory achieved, the still little known fight at Mount Aida would be whispered and then spoken openly, and, with Jojonah's prodding, Avelyn Desbris might be held up as a hero. Markwart could not tolerate that possibility, and he understood then that he must move quickly against the memory of the thief and murderer, must paint such a dark portrait of Avelyn—one that put him in league with the demon dactyl—that the whispers would speak of fortunate infighting between enemies at Aida, not the actions of a heroic man.

Yes, he must thoroughly discredit Avelyn and put the heretic in his proper place in the thoughts of the people and in the annals of Church history.

Markwart came out of his trance suddenly, realizing only then how tightly he was clutching the soul stone, his withered old knuckles gone white from the strain.

He smiled, thinking himself clever for attaining such a high level of concentration, then put the stone back in the secret drawer of his desk. He was feeling much better, caring not at all that the bothersome Connor had apparently gotten away—the man could do him no harm in any case.

Dobrinion, the true threat in Palmaris, had been taken care of, and now Markwart understood the true nature of Jojonah and his cohorts. As soon as the Brothers Justice delivered the stones, his own position would be secured. And from such a position of strength, Markwart knew he could easily deal with any trouble Jojonah put his way. Yes, he decided, he would begin the preemptory strike against Jojonah soon, would speak with Je'howith, who was a longtime friend and a man as dedicated to the preservation of the Order as he was, and through the influence of the abbot of St. Honce, Markwart thought, he could enlist the aid of the King.

At the other end of the broken connection, the spirit of Bestesbulzibar, the demon dactyl, was satisfied. The supposed spiritual leader of the human race was in his palm now, was accepting the precepts that Bestesbulzibar fed to him as though they were his own thoughts and beliefs.

The demon remained bitter about the defeat at Aida, about the loss of its corporeal form—which it had not yet figured out how to replace or recover—but found this puppet game with the Father Abbot of the Abellican Church, the institution that had ever been the demon's greatest foe, quite pleasant, a distraction that allowed Bestesbulzibar to forget the defeat.

Almost.

"Why are we down here?" Brother Braumin asked, glancing nervously at the flickering shadows cast by his torch. Rows of bookcases filled with dusty ancient texts were crowded all about the two men, and the ceiling, too, closed in on them, for it was low and thick.

"Because here is where I will find my answers," Master Jojonah replied calmly, seeming oblivious to the tons and tons of rock hanging thick over his head. He and Brother Braumin were in the sublibrary of St.-Mere-Abelle, the oldest section of the abbey, buried deep beneath the newer levels, almost down at the level of the waters of All Saints Bay. In fact, in the abbey's earliest days, there had been a direct exit from this section of rooms to the rocky beach, a tunnel connecting to the corridor and portcullis Master De'Unnero had defended against the powrie attack, but that ancient passageway had been closed off as the abbey moved upward on the mountainside.

"With Abbot Dobrinion dead and the canonization process at least delayed, the Father Abbot has no excuse to send me out of St.-Mere-Abelle," Jojonah explained. "But he will keep me quite busy, if he has his way, and no doubt Brother Francis or some other will hover about my every move."

"Brother Francis would not be quick to come down here," Brother Braumin reasoned.

"Oh, but he will," Master Jojonah replied. "In fact, he has, and recently. In these ancient rooms, Brother Francis found the maps and texts to guide our journey to Aida. Some of those maps, my friend, were drawn by Brother Allabarnet of St. Precious himself."

Brother Braumin cocked his head, not quite catching on.

"I will assume the role as chief sponsor of Brother Allabarnet for sainthood," Master Jojonah explained. "That will allow me room from the Father Abbot's intrusions, for no doubt he intends to keep me so busy that I have little time for any mischief. When I announce publicly that I will sponsor Allabarnet, the Father Abbot must concede time to me or risk the enmity of St. Precious, thus freeing me even from my normal duties."

"That you might spend your days down here?" Brother Braumin asked doubtfully, for he saw no gain in being in this place; indeed, he wanted to run out of there at once, back into the daylight, or at least into the lighter and more hospitable rooms of the upper abbey. This place was too much like a crypt for his liking—and in fact there was a crypt nearby, in several of the adjoining rooms! Even worse, in the far corner of this very library stood a shelf of very old books, ancient tomes of sorcery and demon magic that the Church had banned. Every copy that had been discovered save these— preserved that the Church might better investigate the workings of its enemies—had been burned. Braumin wished that none had been spared, for the mere presence of these ancient tomes sent a shudder through him, a palpable aura of cold evil.

"This is where I must be," Master Jojonah explained.

Brother Braumin held out his arms, his expression purely incredulous. "What will you find down here?" he asked, and subconsciously glanced at the shelf of horrible tomes.

"I do not honestly know," Jojonah replied. He noted the direction of Braumin's glance but thought little of it, for he had no intention of going anywhere near the demonic volumes. Drawing Braumin's attention, he moved to the nearest shelf and reverently lifted one huge volume, its cover holding on by barely a strand. "But here, in the history of the Church, I will find my answers."

"Answers?"

"I will see as Avelyn saw," Jojonah tried to elaborate. "The attitudes I witness now among supposedly holy men cannot be the same as those who founded our order. Who would follow Markwart now, were it not for traditions that root back a millennium and more? Who would adhere to the doctrines of the leaders of the Abellican Church if they could see past their blindness and recognize the men as merely men, full of the failings adherence to the higher order of God is supposed to erase?"

"Strong words, Master," Brother Braumin said quietly.

"Perhaps it is time that someone spoke those strong words," Jojonah replied. "Words as strong as Avelyn's deeds."

"Brother Avelyn's deeds have branded him as a thief and a murderer," the young monk reminded.

"But we know better," Jojonah was quick to reply. He looked back to the ancient tome again, brushing the dust from the battered cover. "And so would they, I believe. So would the founders of the Order, the men and women who first saw the light of God. They would know."

Jojonah fell silent, and Brother Braumin spent a long time digesting the words. He knew his place here, though, that of portraying the worst-case scenario, and so he had to ask, "And if your studies show that they do not, that the Church is as it has always been?"

The words hit Master Jojonah hard, and Brother Braumin winced as the older man's round shoulders visibly slumped.

"Then my life is a waste," Jojonah admitted. "Then I have followed errantly that which is not holy, but humanly."

"Heretics have spoken such words," Brother Braumin warned.

Master Jojonah turned and eyed him directly, locked his gaze with the most intense stare the immaculate had ever seen from the normally jovial man. "Then let us hope the heretics are not correct," Jojonah said gravely.

The master turned back to the texts, and Braumin again paused, letting the words sink in. He decided that to be enough of that line of questioning—Master Jojonah had embarked upon a course for which there could be no retreat, one of enlightenment that would lead to justification or to despair.

"Brother Dellman has been asking many questions since we departed St. Precious," Brother Braumin said, trying to lighten the conversation.

That notion brought a welcome smile to Master Jojonah's face.

"The Father Abbot's actions concerning our prisoners seem out of place, of course," Brother Braumin went on.

"Prisoners?" Jojonah interrupted. "He brought them?"

"The Chilichunks and the centaur," Brother Braumin explained. "We know not where they are being held."

Master Jojonah paused. He should have expected as much, he realized, but in the commotion over Abbot Dobrinion's death, he had almost forgotten about the unfortunate prisoners. "St. Precious did not protest the taking of Palmaris citizens?" he asked.

"Rumors say that Abbot Dobrinion was not pleased at all," Brother Braumin replied. "There was a confrontation with Baron Bildeborough's men, over his nephew, who was reportedly once married to the woman who accompanied Brother Avelyn. And many say that Abbot Dobrinion was in league with the Baron against the Father Abbot."

Jojonah chuckled helplessly. It all made sense, of course, and now he was even more certain that no powrie had murdered Abbot Dobrinion. He almost said as much to Brother Braumin, but wisely held his tongue, understanding that such terrible information might break the man, or launch him on a course so bold as to get him killed.

"Brother Dellman has paid attention to the events, then?" he asked. "He is not closing his eyes and ears to the truth about him?"

"He has asked many questions," Brother Braumin reiterated. "Some bordering on being openly critical of the Father Abbot. And of course, we are all concerned about the two brothers who did not make the return trip to St.-Mere-Abelle. It is no secret that they were in the Father Abbot's highest favor, and their demeanor has ever been a conversation point among the younger brothers."

"We would all do well to watch closely the hunting dogs of Father Abbot Markwart," Master Jojonah said gravely. "Do not trust Brother Youseff or Brother Dandelion. Go now to your duties, and do not visit me unless your news is most urgent. I will contact you when I see the opportunity; I will wish to hear of Brother Dellman's progress. Pray ask Brother Viscenti to befriend the man. Viscenti is enough removed from me that his conversations with Brother Dellman will not be noticed by the Father Abbot. And Brother Braumin, do find out about the prisoners, where they are and how they are being treated."

Brother Braumin bowed and turned to go, but stopped as Master Jojonah called to him once more.

"And keep in mind, my friend," Jojonah warned, "that Brother Francis and some of those other, less obvious hunting dogs of Father Abbot Markwart will never be far away."

Then Master Jojonah was alone with the ancient texts of the Abellican Order, parchments and books, many of which had not been viewed in centuries. And Jojonah felt the ghosts of his Church in the adjoining crypts. He was alone with that history now, alone with what he had spent his life accepting as divine guidance.

He prayed he would not be disappointed.

❖ 22 ❖

Jilly

"Jilly," Connor repeated, as softly and gently as he could.

The look on the woman's face was caught somewhere between sheer incredulity and horror, the expression of a child faced with impossible and terrible circumstances.

Elbryan, gazing up at his love, had seen that expression on her face only once before, up on the north slope overlooking Dundalis, when their first kiss had been interrupted by the sounds of their town dying. He put a hand firmly on Pony's thigh, supporting her, holding her in place, for she was surely swaying unsteadily on Symphony's broad back.

The moment passed; Pony pushed aside the troubling emotions and found the same inner resolve that had carried her through the trials of so many years. "Jilseponie," she corrected. "My name is Jilseponie, Jilseponie Ault." She glanced down at Elbryan, gathering strength from his unending love. "Jilseponie Wyndon, actually," she corrected.

"And once, Jilly Bildeborough," Connor said quietly.

"Never," the woman spat, more sharply than she had intended. "You erased that title, proclaiming before the law and before God that it had never been. Is it now convenient for the noble Connor to reclaim that which he disposed of?"

Again the ranger patted her firmly, trying to calm her down.

Her words stung Connor profoundly, but he accepted them as earned. "I was young and foolish," he replied. "Our wedding night . . . your actions hurt me, Jilly . . . Jilseponie," he corrected quickly, seeing her grimace. "I—"

Pony held up her hand to stop him, then glanced down at Elbryan. How painful this must be to him, she realized. Certainly he did not need to suffer through a recounting of the night she was wed to another man!

But the ranger stood calm, his bright eyes showing nothing but sympathy for the woman he so loved. He didn't even let those green orbs reflect his anger, jealous anger, toward Connor, for he knew that to do so would be unfair to Pony. "You two have much to discuss," he said. "And I have a caravan to watch over." He patted Pony's thigh one more time, this time gently, almost playfully, showing her that he was secure in their love, and then, with a playful wink, the perfect gesture to lessen the tension, he walked away.

Pony watched him go, loving him all the more. Then she glanced about, and, seeing that others were too near and might overhear, she kicked Symphony into a walk. Connor and his mount followed closely.

"It was not meant against you," Connor tried to explain when they were alone. "I did not mean to hurt you."

"I refuse to discuss that night," Pony said with finality. She knew better, knew that Connor had indeed tried to hurt her, but only because her refusal to make love with him had wounded his pride.

"You can so easily dismiss it?" he asked.

"If the alternative is to dwell on that which needs no explanation and can only bring pain, then yes," she answered. "What is past is not as important as what is to come."

"Then with your dismissal, allow forgiveness," Connor begged.

Pony eyed him directly, looked deeply into his gray eyes and remembered those times before the disastrous wedding night, when they had been friends, confidants.

"Do you remember when we first met?" Connor asked, reading her expression. "When I came out into the alley to protect you, only to find rogues raining down about me?"

Pony managed a smile; there were some good memories, many good ones, mixed in with the ultimately painful ending. "It was never love, Connor," she said honestly.

The man looked as though she had slapped him with a wet towel.

"I did not know what love was until I came back and found Elbryan," Pony went on.

"We were close," the man protested.

"We were friends," Pony replied. "And I will value the memory of that friendship before we tried to make it more than that. I promise you."

"Then we can still be friends," Connor reasoned.

"No." The answer came straight from Pony's heart before she could even spend a moment to consider it. "You were friends with a different person, with a little lost girl who did not know from where she had come, and did not know to where she was going. I am not that person anymore. Not Jilly, not even Jilseponie, in truth, but Pony, the companion, the lover, the wife, of Elbryan Wyndon. My heart is his, and his alone."

"And is there no room in that heart for Connor, your friend?" the man asked gently.

Pony smiled again, growing more comfortable. "You do not even know me," she replied.

"But I do," the nobleman argued. "Even when you were, as you proclaim, that little lost girl, the fire was there. Even when you were most vulnerable, most lost, there was, behind your beautiful eyes, a strength that most people will never know."

Truly Pony appreciated the sentiment. Her relationship with Connor had never been properly resolved, had been left on a note too sour to do justice to the enjoyable months they had spent together. Now, with his simple words, she felt a sense of closure, a true sense of calm.

"Why did you come out here?" she asked.

"I have been out north of the city for months," Connor replied, a bit of the swagger finding its way back into his voice. "Hunting goblins and powries—and even a few giants, I dare say!"

"Why did you come out here now?" the perceptive woman pressed. She had seen it on his face: Connor had not been nearly as surprised to see her as she to see him, and yet, given the last each knew of the other's whereabouts, the surprise to him should have been greater. "You knew, did you not?"

"I suspected," Connor admitted. "I have heard tales of magic being used against the monsters up here, and you have been linked to the enchanted gemstones."

That gave Pony pause.

"Call back your . . . husband," Connor said. "If you are, as you say, ready to let go of the past and pay attention to the future. I did indeed come out here for a reason, Jill . . . Pony. And more of a reason than to see you again, though I would have traveled the length and breadth of Honce-the-Bear for that alone."

Pony bit back her response, questioning why, then, Connor had not done just that in all the years she had been indentured to the army. There was no need for such bickering, no need to tear the scabs from old wounds.

They met shortly thereafter, Connor, Pony, and Elbryan, and with Juraviel comfortably tucked within the sheltering boughs of a nearby tree.

"You remember Abbot Dobrinion Calislas," Connor started, after pacing nervously for what seemed like an hour, trying to figure out where to begin.

The woman nodded. "The abbot of St. Precious," she said.

"No more," Connor explained. "He was murdered a few nights ago, in his own room at the abbey." The nobleman paused, studying their reactions, and was at first surprised that none of them seemed overly concerned. Of course, Connor realized, they did not really know Dobrinion and his good heart; their experience with the Church was less than enamoring.

"They said a powrie did it," Connor went on.

"Dark times indeed if a powrie can so easily get into what should be the most secure building in a city braced for war," Elbryan remarked.

"I think that he was killed by the Church he served," Connor said outright, watching the ranger closely. Now Elbryan did lean forward a bit, growing more than a little intrigued. "The monks from St.-Mere-Abelle were in Palmaris," Connor explained. "A great contingent, including the Father Abbot himself. Many had just returned from the far north, from the Barbacan, so it is said."

He had their attention now.

"Roger Lockless saw such a caravan flying swiftly to the south past Caer Tinella and Landsdown," Pony reminded.

"They are looking for you," Connor said bluntly, pointing to Pony. "For those gemstones, which they claim were stolen from St.-Mere-Abelle."

Pony's eyes went wide. She stuttered a few undiscernible words as she turned to her lover for support.

"We feared as much," Elbryan admitted. "That is why we were insistent on bringing the folk to the safety of Palmaris," he explained to Connor. "Pony and I cannot remain with them—the risk for the folk is too great. We would see them to safety, then go our own way."

"The risk is greater than you believe," Connor put in. "The Father Abbot and most of his companions have left, heading back to their own abbey, but he left a pair—at least a pair—behind, men trained to kill, do not doubt. I believe it was those two who killed Abbot Dobrinion. They came after me, as well, for my connection to Pony is known to them, but I managed to elude them, and now they will hunt for you."

"Brother Justice," the ranger reasoned, shuddering at the thought of dealing with another like Quintall—apparently a pair of them this time.

"But why would they murder Abbot Dobrinion?" Pony asked. "And why would they come after you in such a manner?"

"Because we opposed the Father Abbot's methods," Connor replied. "Because . . ." He paused and cast a truly sympathetic look Pony's way. She would not like this news, not at all, but she had to be told. "Because we did not approve of his treatment of the Chilichunks—treatment he had planned for me, as well, before my uncle the Baron intervened."

"Treatment?" Pony replied, leaping to her feet. "What treatment? What does that mean?"

"He took them, Pony," Connor explained. "In chains, back to St.-Mere-Abelle, along with the one called Bradwarden, the centaur."

Now the stunned Elbryan was on his feet, as well, moving before Connor, too overwhelmed to even voice the question.

"Bradwarden is dead," came Juraviel's voice from the trees.

Connor spun about but saw nothing.

"He was killed in Aida," the elf went on. "Upon the defeat of the demon dactyl."

"He was not killed," Connor insisted. "Or if he was, then the monks found a way to resurrect him. I have seen him with my own eyes, a belea-guered and pitiful creature, but one very much alive."

"As I saw him," put in Roger Lockless, coming out of the trees to join the group. He moved to Elbryan's side and dropped a hand on the man's strong shoulder. "The caravan, at the back of the caravan. I told you as much."

Elbryan nodded, remembering well Roger's description, remembering his own emotions when Roger had told of the monks' passage by the two towns. He turned to Pony then, who was eyeing him directly, those telling fires burning brightly behind her blue orbs.

"We must go to them," she said, and the ranger nodded, their path sud-denly clear.

"The monks?" Roger asked, not understanding.

"In time," Connor interrupted. "And I will go with you."

"This is not your affair," the ranger said suddenly, wanting to retract the words, words prompted by his desire to get this man far from Pony as soon as possible, even as he spoke them.

"Abbot Dobrinion was my friend," the nobleman argued. "As are the Chilichunks, all three. You know this," he said, looking to Pony for sup-port, and the woman nodded. "But first, we, you, must deal with the killers. They are not to be taken lightly. They got to Dobrinion and made it look enough like a powrie assassination to deflect all attention. They are cunning and they are deadly."

"And they will be dead, soon enough," the ranger said with such deter-mination that none would dare offer a doubt.

"We will meet again," Elbryan assured Belster O'Comely early the next morning, taking the man's hand firmly. Belster was holding back tears, Elbryan knew, for he suspected, and Elbryan could not disagree, that this was the last time they would see each other. "When the war is settled and you open your tavern again in the Timberlands, then know that Nightbird will be there, drinking your water and scaring away your other patrons."

Belster smiled warmly, but he didn't expect that he would be making the journey back to Dundalis even if the monsters were driven away very soon. He was not a young man, and the pain of the memories would be great indeed. Belster had fled Palmaris because of debt, and only because of debt, but that time seemed many centuries ago, given all that had hap-pened, and he was quite sure he could open an establishment right in the city without fear of his past coming back to haunt him. There was no reason to tell all of that to the ranger, though. Not now, and so he only held fast his assuring smile.

"Lead them well, Tomas," the ranger said to the man standing beside Belster. "The road should be clear, but if you find trouble before you find Palmaris, then I trust you will see them through."

Tomas Gingerwart nodded gravely, and stamped his new weapon, the pitchfork, on the ground. "We owe you much, Nightbird," he said. "As we owe Pony, and your little unseen friend, as well."

"Do not forget Roger," the ranger was quick to reply. "To him the folk of Caer Tinella and Landsdown owe perhaps the most of all."

"Roger would never let us forget Roger!" Belster said suddenly, jovially, in a voice that reminded Elbryan so much of Avelyn.

That gave them all a laugh, a proper note to end the discussion. They shook hands and parted as friends, Tomas running to the front of the caravan and calling for them to move along.

Pony, Connor, and Juraviel joined Elbryan soon after, watching the train depart, but not so far down the road Tomas stopped the group momentarily and a lone figure moved away, running back toward the ranger and his friends.

"Roger Lockless," Pony said, not surprised. Behind him the caravan started away once more, drifting to the south.

"You were to serve as Tomas' principle guide," Elbryan said when Roger moved to join him.

"He has others who can serve in that role," the young man replied.

The ranger's look was stern and uncompromising.

"Why is he to stay?" Roger protested, pointing to Connor. "Why are you, with Palmaris only three days march? Would not Elbryan and Pony prove of great value to the city's garrison in these dark times?"

"There are other matters which you do not understand," Elbryan said calmly.

"Matters that concern him?" Roger asked, pointing again at Connor, who resisted the urge to walk over and punch the young man.

Elbryan nodded gravely. "You should go with them, Roger," he said, speaking in the tone of a friend. "We cannot, for there is a matter that must be settled before any of us show our faces in the city. But trust me when I say that the danger here is greater for you by far than any danger you might find in Palmaris. Be quick now, and catch Tomas and Belster."

Roger shook his head resolutely. "No," he answered. "If you are to stay up here, fighting on, then so am I."

"There is nothing left for you to prove," Pony put in. "Your name and reputation are secured and well-earned."

"Name?" Roger balked. "In Palmaris, soon enough, I will be Roger Billingsbury again. Just Roger Billingsbury. An orphan, a waif, a cast-aside."

"My uncle the Baron would value one of your talents," Connor offered.

"Then when you are able to return to your uncle to tell him about me, I will join you," the young man quickly replied with a smirk. That flippant look disappeared at once, though, and he cast a very serious stare at Elbryan. "Do not make me return," he begged. "I cannot go back to being Roger Billingsbury again. Not yet. Out here, fighting monsters, I was able to find a side of myself that I never knew existed. I like that side of me, and fear to lose it in the mundane life of a secure city."

"Not so secure," Connor quipped under his breath.

"You'll not lose your new mantle," the ranger said in all seriousness. "You will never go back to being that person you were before the invasion of your home. I know this, better than you can imagine, and I tell you honestly that, here or in Palmaris, you are, and will remain, Roger Lockless, hero of the north." He looked over to Pony and considered the weight of such a responsibility, thought of the vow of celibacy that he and his lover had been forced by circumstance to accept, and added, "That may not be as grand a thing as you believe, Roger."

The young man straightened a bit and managed a nod, but his overall expression, begging for acceptance, did not change, leaving the issue squarely on the shoulders of the ranger.

Elbryan looked to Pony, who nodded.

"There are two men hunting for Pony and for me," the ranger began. "And for Connor; they tried to kill him in Palmaris, which sent him on the road in search of us."

"He knows you two?" Roger asked. "And knew you were up here?"

"He knows me," Pony put in.

"He came in search of the one wielding magic, though he knew not who that might be," the ranger explained. "We are outlaws, Roger, both Pony and me. You heard us express as much that time we spoke with Juraviel soon after the caravan passed the northern towns. The Church wants the magic stones back, yet on the grave of our friend Avelyn, we'll not return them. Thus have they sent assassins in search of us, and they are not far away, I fear." Despite the grim words, the ranger flashed a comforting smile to Roger. "But easier will our task be if Roger Lockless desires to join in our cause."

Roger's grin nearly took in his big ears.

"Understand that you, too, will then be considered an outlaw in the eyes of the Church," Pony remarked.

"Though my uncle will remedy that situation when this is finished," Connor was quick to add.

"Do you plan to run from them, or fight them on your own terms?" Roger asked determinedly.

"I'll not spend my days glancing over my shoulder for assassins," the ranger replied in a tone so grim that it sent a shudder coursing along Connor's spine. "Let them look back for me."

*   *   *

Her spirit walked through the shadowed forest. She saw Belli'mar Juraviel working his way along the mid-level boughs of a grove and brushed right past him. The perceptive elf perked up his ears, for though Pony's spirit was invisible and silent, Juraviel's keen senses felt something.

Then down to the ground the woman went, flying as if on the wind. She found Connor, pacing his golden horse in a defensive perimeter about the small encampment. She even saw her own body, sitting cross-legged, far behind the man. And even farther back, behind her corporeal form, she saw the large elm, and the dark hole at its base. Elbryan was in that hole, at Oracle, and Pony did not dare enter and disturb that deepest of concentrations.

Instead her thoughts lingered on Connor, trying to gain some perspective on all that had happened between them. She found his protectiveness of her as he paced his horse somewhat comforting, and indeed the nobleman had touched her simply by coming out here to find her and warn her. He had known all along that it was she with the gemstones, or at least had suspected as much, and knowing, too, that those stones were the Church's main focus, he could have gone south, to more populated regions, in his flight from the assassins. Or had he betrayed her openly, he might have remained in the comforts of Palmaris, for the Church would not even consider him an enemy. But he had not; he had come north, to warn her. And had stood behind his friends, the Chilichunks.

Pony had never hated Connor, not even on the morning after their tragic wedding night. He had been wrong, she believed with all her heart, but his actions were based on very real frustrations that she had inspired. And in the final analysis of that night, Connor had not been able to follow through with forcing himself upon her, had cared for her too much to take her in that way.

So Pony had forgiven him, long ago, within the first days of her service in the King's army.

But what did she feel now, in looking on this man who had been her husband?

It wasn't love, was never that, she understood, for she knew how she felt when she looked upon Elbryan and that was something very different, very much more special indeed. But she did care for Connor. He had been a friend when she had needed one; because of his gentleness in those months of courting, she had begun the road to recovery of her memory and her emotional health. If things had been better on her wedding night, she would have stayed married to him, would have borne him children, would have—

Pony's line of thought ended abruptly as she realized she no longer regretted the events of that wedding night. For the first time, she came to understand the benefits of what she had deemed a horrible experience.

That night had set her on a course to become who she now was, had put her in the army, where she received superb training and discipline for her natural fighting talents. That experience had subsequently brought her to Avelyn's side, where she learned of deeper truths, where she gained her spirituality, and that turn of events in Palmaris had, ultimately, brought her back to Elbryan. Only now, measuring her feelings for the ranger against the feelings she had held for another man in another time, did Pony realize just how special was their love.

They had battled for months against the invading monsters, had lost dear friends, and now her adoptive family and another friend were apparently in danger, and still Pony would not trade who she was, this very moment, this very place, for any feasible alternative. The lessons in life were often bitter, but they were necessary building blocks.

So Pony was warmed by the sight of Connor Bildeborough pacing a stoic guard about her—and about Elbryan. At that moment she put her past to rest.

But she knew she could not linger and savor the scene, and so her spirit went out again, into the forest. She found Roger, and then Juraviel above him, and she went out ahead, searching the shadows, looking for some sign.

I do fear the weight of the Church, Uncle Mather, Elbryan admitted, sitting back against a stone in the cramped cave, staring into the depths of the barely visible mirror. *How many of these assassins will come after us?*

The ranger leaned back and sighed. The Church would not give up, that much was obvious to him, and eventually, some day in some remote place, he and Pony would lose. Or they would lose in St.-Mere-Abelle, where Elbryan knew they must go for the sake of Bradwarden and the Chilichunks, who had been Pony's family.

But I have to fight on, he said to the ghost of his uncle. *We have to fight on, for the sake of Avelyn's memory, for the truth that he found within the twisted ways of his Order. And soon we will take that fight right to the spider's web.*

But first . . . ah, Uncle Mather, one Brother Justice nearly defeated me and Pony and Avelyn before. How might we handle the likes of two such expert killers?

Elbryan rubbed his eyes and stared into the mirror. Images came back to him of the first fight with the Church, when Avelyn's old classmate Quintall, carrying the title of Brother Justice, had battled him in a cave. First the assassin had sealed that cave from magic using a sunstone, the same gem that was on the pommel of Elbryan's sword.

And he had used a garnet to locate Avelyn, for that stone detected magic. A garnet . . .

A smile found its way onto Elbryan's face, the answer coming clear before him. He leaped out of his chair and squirmed out the narrow cave opening, rushing to Pony and shaking her vigorously, trying to break her trance.

Her spirit, sensing the disturbance at her corporeal body, soared back, and in but a few moments she blinked open her physical eyes.

Elbryan stood over her; behind him, Connor was slipping down from his horse, coming to see what the commotion was about.

"No more use of the soul stone," the ranger explained.

"With my spirit freed, I can scout out far more than the others," the woman argued.

"But if our enemies are using garnet, they will feel the vibrations of your magic," Elbryan reasoned.

Pony nodded; they had already talked about that potential problem.

"We have garnet," Elbryan explained. "The one taken from Quintall. How much more effective will your search be with the broader sight of that stone?"

"If they are using magic," Pony reasoned.

"How could they hope to find us in this vast land without such aid?" the ranger countered.

Pony paused and studied him for a long moment, and Elbryan noted the look of curiosity that came over her face.

"You seem very sure of yourself suddenly," she noted.

Elbryan's smile widened.

"Quintall was a deadly enemy," Pony reminded. "Alone he nearly defeated me, you, and Avelyn."

"Only because he shaped the battlefield to his liking," the ranger replied. "He held the element of surprise, and in a place of his choosing and his preparation. These two killers will prove formidable in battle, but if we hold the element of surprise, in a place of our choosing, then the battle will be decided quickly, I do not doubt."

Pony did not seem convinced.

"One fault in Quintall's plan was arrogance," the ranger explained. "He played his hand early, in the Howling Sheila, because he felt that he was supreme, that his training had elevated him above all others in matters of battle."

"There was some truth in that belief," said Pony.

"But his training, and that of our present foes, does not equal that which I received at the hands of the Touel'alfar, that which you have received by me and by Avelyn, and that which we have both learned through months of fighting. And we have three powerful allies. No, my fear for this situation has lessened considerably. If you can use the garnet to track our adversaries, we will bring them in to a place we have prepared and to a battle for which they cannot be prepared."

It made perfect sense to Pony, and she believed she could indeed track the assassins in the manner Elbryan had described. The monks would be using magic to detect magic, and thus she could use magic to detect their magic.

"And once we have located them, we will know that they have likewise seen us," the ranger went on. "We will know their destination, but they will have little understanding of ours."

"The time and the place will be ours to choose," Pony said. She went to work immediately, and soon sensed the use of magic, the monks probably employing garnet. It was short-lived, though, and Pony figured that the pair had sensed her magic use and altered their general direction accordingly.

"They put up a sunstone shield, I would guess," the woman explained to Belli'mar Juraviel, opening her eyes to see that the elf had come to join her.

"But is this not also magic use?" the elf inquired. "Can you not detect it as well?"

Pony's face crinkled at the simple but somehow errant logic. "Not the same," she tried to explain. "Sunstone is antimagic. I could enact such a shield using the stone in the pommel of Tempest, and our enemy's use of garnet would be for naught."

Juraviel shook his delicate head, not believing a word of it. "All the world is magic, so say the elves," he explained. "Every plant, every animal, is possessed of magical energy."

Pony shrugged, seeing no sense in arguing the point.

"If sunstone defeats all magic, there will be a hole in the continuum," Juraviel explained. "An empty spot, a hole in the blanket of magic that fills all the world."

"I cannot—" Pony began.

"Because you have not learned to see the world through the eyes of the Touel'alfar," the elf interrupted. "Join with me in spirit, as you and Avelyn used to join, that we might search together, that we might find the hole, and thus our enemies."

Pony thought it over for just a minute. Her joining through hematite with Avelyn had been personal, intimate, and left her incredibly vulnerable, but when she considered her elven friend, she felt no threat whatsoever. She didn't believe that Juraviel was right about this matter, thought that his perspective was just that—a different way of looking at the same things—but she did produce the soul stone, and then together the pair went out through the garnet.

Pony was quickly amazed at how vibrant all the world seemed, a glow of magic about every plant and every animal. Soon, very soon, they found the hole Juraviel had described, tracking the monks as easily as if the pair was using garnet instead of sunstone.

Guide me, Juraviel imparted to her, and then she sensed that he was physically gone from the spot, following the trail out to meet their foes.

When he returned to the encampment, barely three hours later, his report of the monks exceeded anything Elbryan could have hoped for. The elf had found them and studied them from the hidden boughs of the trees.

Of particular note were their weapons, with nothing of range, except one or two small daggers and any magical stones they might possess. Juraviel had even overheard some of their conversation, a discussion about capturing Pony, that she might be brought to Father Abbot Markwart alive.

The ranger smiled. With their bows and Pony's gemstones, they could more than counter any such distance attacks, and their discussion of taking a captive proved to him that these two did not comprehend the power that would come against them. "Lead them in to us," he bade Pony. "Let us prepare the battleground."

The small plateau seemed an obvious choice for an encampment, set on a ledge on a rocky hillside with but one approach, and that being steep and dangerously exposed. There was one open area, a small campfire burning, surrounded on three sides by more rocks and on the fourth by a small copse of trees.

Brother Youseff smiled wickedly; the garnet indicated that magic was in use up there. He put the stone away in a pouch on the rope belt of his brown robes, which he and Dandelion had donned again when they left the city, and took out the sunstone, bidding Dandelion to take his hand, that they might combine their powers to make the antimagic shield that much stronger.

"They will try to use magic against us," Youseff explained. "That is their primary weapon, no doubt, but if we are strong enough to defeat that use, then their conventional weapons will prove worthless against our training."

Dandelion, so physically strong and skilled, grinned at the prospect of some solid hand-to-hand fighting.

"We kill the woman's companions, first," Youseff explained. "Then we go after her. If we must kill her, then so be it. Otherwise we will take her and the gemstones and be on our way."

"To Palmaris first?" Dandelion asked, for he wanted another chance at Connor Bildeborough.

Youseff, understanding the supreme importance of this part of their mission, shook his head. "Straight through the city and back to St.-Mere-Abelle," he explained. He closed his other hand over Dandelion's. "Concentrate," he instructed.

A few moments later, the antimagic shield strong and in place, the pair began easily scaling the rocky cliff, moving silently and confidently.

Near the top they peeked over the ridge, and both smiled even wider, for there, sitting beside the woman, was Connor Bildeborough—all the eggs in one basket, it seemed.

With a look to each other to coordinate the movement, the two monks hauled themselves over the lip, landing gracefully and in a defensive posture.

"Welcome!" Connor cried, his tone light—and to the monks, confusing. "Remember me?"

Youseff glanced at Dandelion, then took a sudden stride forward, covering a third of the distance to the still-sitting man. Then he lurched, a small arrow boring into the back of his calf, cutting right into the tendon.

"Oh, but my friends will not allow you to approach," Connor said happily.

"You do not understand how hopeless your situation is," added Roger Lockless, stepping out from behind some rocks directly behind Pony and Connor. "Have you, by chance, met the one called Nightbird?"

On cue, the ranger, looking splendid atop Symphony and with Hawkwing in hand, stepped out of the copse of trees.

"What are we to do?" Brother Dandelion whispered.

Youseff snapped his angry glare over Connor. "You have discredited and disgraced your uncle and all your family," he growled. "You are an outlaw now, as surely as are these ragged fools you call friends."

"Brave words for one in your position," Connor replied casually.

"Think you that?" Youseff remarked, suddenly calm. With the hand that was clenching his wounded leg, he gave a subtle signal to Dandelion.

Suddenly, brutally, Dandelion charged past his companion, springing upon Connor as the man rose and drew out his sword, moving too quickly for anyone to react. He slapped aside Connor's sword, then laid the man low with a wicked forearm smash to the throat. Then he ran right over the falling Connor, forcing Roger back against the stones.

Youseff sprang forward from his good leg right behind Dandelion, thinking to get to the woman, to put her in a deadly hold that he might bargain his way out. But as in the initial assault, the confident monk underestimated his opponent, did not appreciate just how powerful Pony was with the gemstones. The antimagic shield was still strong, though not as much so with both its creators otherwise engaged, but even if Youseff and Dandelion were doing nothing but concentrating on the sunstone, they would not have defeated Pony's power.

Youseff felt his feet slip out from under him, not to fall, but rather to rise, harmlessly, into the air. His momentum continued to carry him forward, toward Pony, but when he reached for her in this unfamiliar weightless state, he tumbled headlong, turning a half somersault. Then he felt the sudden sting in his back as Pony rolled over and kicked out, both feet landing squarely, propelling Youseff back the way he had come, back out over the cliff to dangle helplessly in midair.

Overwhelmed by the charge, Roger was in no position to counter as Dandelion swung back the other way, again smashing Connor as the man tried to rise, then falling down atop him, pinning him to the ground. Up came the big man's arm, fingers stiff and straight, poised for the killing slash into defenseless Connor's exposed neck.

Connor growled and tried to cry out, tried to wriggle free. He closed his eyes for just an instant.

The blow did not fall. Connor opened his eyes to see Dandelion still poised above him, struggling to drop the punch, a look of absolute incredulity on his face that anything could so hold back his powerful arm.

Nightbird held him fast by the wrist.

Dandelion spun with amazing agility for one so large, turning and putting his feet under him, at the same time dipping his shoulder to bowl the ranger over. But Elbryan, too, was moving, spinning right under Dandelion's arm, turning about with a vicious jerk that popped the man's elbow out of joint.

Howling with pain, Dandelion spun about and launched a heavy punch—which never came near to hitting Nightbird, the ranger sidestepping, then wading right back in with a powerful combination of blows on Dandelion's face and chest.

On came the big monk, growling past the pain in his arm, accepting more punches, that he could get close enough to wrap Elbryan in a tight hug.

The ranger cupped Dandelion's chin with one hand, grabbed the back of the man's hair with the other, meaning to turn him aside. He stopped, though, feeling a curious prodding in his chest. At first he thought Dandelion had somehow deceived him and brought a dagger to bear, but when he looked past the man, to Connor Bildeborough standing behind him, the ranger understood.

Dandelion, Connor's sword right through his back and chest, slumped in the ranger's arms.

"Bastard," Connor muttered grimly, shifting to keep his hold on the sword as dead Dandelion rolled to the ground.

Nightbird let the man fall free, then went to Symphony and took up Hawkwing, fitting an arrow and turning his attention to Youseff. He leveled and drew back.

But the threat was ended, the monks obviously defeated, and Elbryan could not simply kill this man.

"Do not," Pony said, in full agreement as the ranger eased his bowstring back to rest.

"I will kill him," Connor said grimly, finally extracting his sword from the heavy corpse.

"As he hangs there helpless?" Pony asked skeptically.

Connor kicked at the ground. "Drop him to the rocks, then," he said, but he wasn't serious; he could no more kill this helpless man than could Elbryan.

Pony was glad for that.

"We are going to find our friends," the ranger said to Youseff, "whom your Father Abbot has unjustly imprisoned."

Youseff scoffed at the sheer folly of such a claim.

"And you will lead us, every step," the ranger finished.

"To St.-Mere-Abelle?" the monk replied incredulously. "Fool. You cannot begin to comprehend the power of such a fortress."

"As you could not comprehend the force prepared against you in this place," Elbryan calmly replied.

That hit Youseff hard. He narrowed his eyes dangerously and glared at Elbryan. "How long can you hold me here?" he asked, his voice even and deathly calm. "Kill me now, fools, else I promise to avenge—"

His bluster was lost suddenly as a small form rushed past him, spinning him over in the air. He flailed and tried to respond, and realized that he had lost his grip on the sunstone. When he finally straightened out again, Youseff saw the winged elf land easily on the ledge beside the others.

"Sunstone, as you guessed, Nightbird," Juraviel said, displaying the pilfered stone. "I suspect the garnet is in his belt pouch, if not on the dead man."

Elbryan watched Youseff closely as Juraviel spoke, and saw that the elf's words, too, were unnerving the man.

"He may have a soul stone, as well," Pony interjected. "Some way to keep in contact with his leaders."

"Of course, we'll not let him use that," Connor said with a chuckle. "But I must disagree with your decision," he said to the ranger. "He'll not lead us to St.-Mere-Abelle, but will be returned to St. Precious, where he can answer for the murder of Abbot Dobrinion. I will take him myself, with Roger Lockless beside me, and let the Church learn the truth of its Father Abbot!"

Elbryan looked long and hard at Connor, considering for just a moment the implications of his actions, which had saved the man's life. If he had hesitated for just an instant, then Connor Bildeborough, this man who had so wronged Pony, would also be dead.

The ranger would tolerate no such weakness within himself, and so he dismissed those dark thoughts out of hand, and knew in his heart that he would have thrown himself in the way of the deadly monk's strike if that was the only way to save Connor, or any of his companions.

He looked back to Youseff then, and considered the truth of Connor's words. He remembered the fervor of the first Brother Justice, and understood that Youseff would be no willing guide, no matter the threats. But if they did as Connor suggested, then perhaps they would not be alone in their quest to free their friends. Would not the Church have to admit its complicity, thus discrediting the Father Abbot?

It seemed plausible. "Bring him in," the ranger instructed.

Belli'mar Juraviel flew out from the ledge, moving behind the dangling Youseff. Using his bow as a pole, the elf prodded the man toward the ledge. At first Youseff offered no resistance, but then, as he neared the lip, as the drop beneath him became not so far, he spun suddenly, grabbed at the elf and caught hold of the bow as Juraviel wisely let it go. The monk had no way to stop his momentum, though, and so he continued to rotate right around.

To see Elbryan at the edge of the lip, fist cocked.

The blow sent Brother Youseff spinning head over heels away from the ledge, and sent the man's mind flying into unconsciousness.

Juraviel, laughing at the outrageous sight, retrieved his bow and prodded the now limp monk to the ledge.

❖ 23 ❖

The Other Brother Francis

Of all the duties for the young monks at St.-Mere-Abelle, Brother Dellman found this one the most painful. He and two other monks were braced against spokes on a giant wheel crank, bending their backs to turn the thing, grunting and groaning, digging in their heels, but slipping often against the tremendous weight.

Down below, far, far below, supported by heavy chains—which themselves weighed more than a thousand pounds—was a great block of stone. Good stone, solid, taken from an underground quarry just inside the southernmost courtyard of St.-Mere-Abelle. The wide expanse of that quarry was reached through the lower tunnels of the original abbey—in fact, Master Jojonah, huddled in the lower libraries, could sometimes hear the chipping of the stones—but the best way to bring stones needed for the upper walls of the abbey was by use of this crank.

The pain and the struggle was good for the young monks, in the eyes of the masters and the Father Abbot.

Another day, Brother Dellman might have agreed with that. Physical exhaustion was good for the soul. But not today, not so soon after his return from a long and difficult journey. He wanted nothing more than to go to his eight-foot-square chamber and curl up on his cot.

"Push on, Brother Dellman," scolded Master De'Unnero in his sharp voice. "Would you force brothers Callan and Seumo to do all the work?"

"No, Master De'Unnero," Brother Dellman grunted, bending his shoulder to press harder against the spoke and driving on, the muscles in his legs and back straining and aching. He closed his eyes and issued a long and low groan.

But then the weight seemed to grow suddenly, the wheel pushing back. Dellman's eyes popped open wide.

"Hold it fast, brother!" Dellman heard Callan cry. He saw the man, lying on the ground, then noted Seumo skittering, off-balance, to the side.

"Peg it!" Master De'Unnero shouted, meaning that someone, anyone, should drive the locking peg back into the crank.

Poor Dellman fought with all his strength, pressed as hard as he could against the wheel. But his feet were inevitably beginning to slide. Why wasn't Callan back at the wheel? he wondered. And why wouldn't Seumo get up? Why were they moving so slowly?

He thought to let go and spring out of harm's way, but knew that to be impossible. With no one bracing the wheel, the spin would be too fast, too sudden, and he would be smashed and thrown.

"Peg it!" he heard De'Unnero cry again, but everyone seemed to be moving in so slowly!

And the wheel was winning now, Dellman's muscles strained past their breaking point.

Then he was moving backward, bending over, all his joints seeming to go the wrong way. He heard the sudden snap, like a whip, as one of his legs exploded in pain, and then he was rolled over backward. One of his arms was hooked, though, and the spinning wheel took him on a wild ride, finally throwing him far and wide, to smash hard against a water trough, shattering its side, and his shoulder.

He lay there, barely conscious, drenched and covered with mud and blood.

"Carry him to my private chambers," he heard a voice, De'Unnero's, he thought.

Then the master was right before him, leaning over, seeming truly concerned. "Fear not, young Brother Dellman," De'Unnero said, and though it appeared he was trying to be comforting, his voice still held that wicked edge. "God is with me, and by His power I will help to mend that broken body."

The pain grew more intense suddenly as Callan and Seumo took the battered young monk by the arms and lifted him. Waves of agony rolled over poor Brother Dellman, fires ignited within every muscle of his body. And then he was sinking, sinking, into a profound blackness.

The days blended into one, for he did not notice their passing. Time held no meaning for Master Jojonah now. He left the lower library only when the physical needs of his body forced him out, and returned as soon as possible. He had found nothing useful among the stacks and stacks of tomes and parchments, but knew he was close. He felt it, in his heart and soul.

He glanced often at the shelf of forbidden books, wondering if, perhaps, they had been placed off-limits not because of any evil penning, but because they held a truth that would prove damning to the present leaders of the Abellican Order. After many such musings, even one point where he rose and took a few steps for the shelf, Master Jojonah laughed aloud at his own paranoia. He knew those books, for he had helped to inventory them as one of his requirements before he attained the rank of immaculate. There were no hidden truths there; those were the books of evil, of dactyl earth-magic and of perverting the powers of the sacred stones for evil purposes, for summoning demons or animating corpses, for causing plague or withering crops—unacceptable practices even in times of war. From a private Masters' Gathering, Jojonah knew that one of the books, in fact, described a massive crop destruction the Church leveled on the southern kingdom of Behren in God's Year 67, when Behren and Honce-the-Bear had been embroiled in a bitter war for control of the passes through the Belt-and-Buckle mountain range. The famine had turned the tide of battle, but the cost in terms of innocent lives and lasting enmities had not, in retrospect, been worth the gain.

No, those books shelved in the dark corner of the lower library held no measure of justice and truth, unless that was in the lessons to be learned from terrible past mistakes.

But Jojonah had to remind himself of that quite often as the days wound on without any dramatic success. And one other thing began to nag at the sensibilities of the gentle master, growing in him until it proved a tremendous distraction: the plight of Markwart's prisoners. They were paying dearly, perhaps had already paid the supreme price, for the sake of his delay here. A large part of Jojonah's conscience screamed at him to go and see to those poor people and to the centaur, who, if he had been with Avelyn when the dactyl demon was defeated, was indeed heroic.

But Jojonah could not pull himself away, not yet, and so he had to sublimate his worries about the prisoners. Perhaps his work here would save them, he told himself, or perhaps it would prevent any such atrocities from being committed by the Church in the future.

He was beginning to make some progress, at least. The library was not as haphazardly laid out as he had first believed. It was divided into sections, and those, roughly, were set out chronologically, dating from the very earliest days of the Church to the time less than two centuries before, when the newer libraries were constructed and this place became a vault and not a working area. Fortunately for Jojonah, most of the writings of the time in which Brother Allabarnet lived, at least those collected from outside St.-Mere-Abelle, were stored down here.

As soon as he discovered the general layout, Master Jojonah began his search among the very earliest tomes, those dating back before God's Year 1, the Great Epiphany, the Renewal, which separated the Church, Old Canon and New Canon. Jojonah figured that his answers might lie in the time before the Renewal, at the very inception of the organized Church, the time of Saint Abelle.

He found no answers there; what few pieces remained—and fewer still that remained legible—were decorous works, songs mostly, exalting the glory of God. Many were written on parchments so brittle that Jojonah did not dare to even handle them, and others were carved on tablets of stone. The writings of Saint Abelle were not down here, of course, but were on display in the higher library. Jojonah knew them by heart, and remembered nothing about them that would help in his quest. The teachings were general mostly, wise words about common decency, and open to many interpretations. Still, the master vowed to go and view them again, when the time presented, to see if he might read them in a new light with his new insights, to see if they might afford him some hint of the true precepts of his Church.

What Jojonah most wanted down here was to find the Abbot's Doctrine of that momentous year of the Great Epiphany, but he knew that to be impossible. It was one of the great travesties of the Abellican Order that the original Abbot's Doctrine had been lost, centuries before.

So the master went on with what was available, moving to the writings immediately following the creation of the New Canon. Jojonah found nothing. Nothing.

A man of lesser heart would have surrendered to the daunting task, but the thought of quitting never entered Jojonah's mind. He continued his chronological scan, found some promising hints among the writings of the early Father Abbots, a turn of a phrase, for instance, that he could never imagine Markwart saying.

And then he found a most interesting tome indeed, a small book, bound in red cloth, and penned by a young monk, Brother Francis Gouliard in God's Year 130, the year after the first journey to Pimaninicuit following the Great Epiphany.

Jojonah's hands trembled as he gingerly turned the pages. Brother Francis—and how ironic that name seemed!—had been one of the Preparers on that journey, and he had returned and penned his story!

That alone hit Jojonah profoundly; monks returning from Pimaninicuit now were discouraged, indeed even prohibited, from ever speaking of the place. Brother Pellimar had come back wagging his tongue, and not coincidentally, he had not survived for long. Yet back in Francis Gouliard's time, the Preparers were encouraged, according to the text, to detail their accounts of the journey!

Though it was cool in the dark room, Jojonah felt sweat beading on his forehead, and he took care so that it did not drop on the delicate pages. Fingers trembling, he gingerly turned the page and read on:

> to finde thee thy smallst stones of greye and redde, that thee may prepare ample to bringe Godly healing to all the knowne worlde.

Master Jojonah sat back and took a deep and steadying breath. Now he understood why the abbey held such a huge cache of small hematites, the small stones of gray and red! The next passage, in which Brother Francis Gouliard wrote of his fellow voyagers, struck the master even more profoundly:

> *Thirty-and-three brothers did crewe the* Sea Abelle, *men younge and stronge, trained well and trusted well to bringe we two Preparers to Pimaninicuit and back.*
> *And then did all thirty-and-one (for two had died on the voyage) join in the final cataloguing and preparing.*

"Brothers," Jojonah mouthed softly. "On the *Sea Abelle*. They used monks." The master found it hard to speak through breath that would not come. A flood of tears streamed down his face as he recalled the fate of the *Windrunner* and her unfortunate crew, hired men, and one woman, and not brothers. It took him a long time to compose himself and read on. Brother Francis Gouliard's style was difficult, many of the words too arcane for Jojonah to decipher, and the man tended to pen in a stream-of-consciousness manner, instead of purely chronologically. A few pages on and Francis was describing the departure from St.-Mere-Abelle, the beginning of the voyage.

And there it was before Jojonah, an edict from Father Abbot Benuto Concarron in his farewell speech to the good ship and crew, demanding that the Abellican Order spread the wealth of God, the gemstones, along with the word of God.

Piety, dignity, poverty.

The tears came freely; this was the Church that Jojonah could believe in, the Church that had coaxed in a man as pure of heart as Avelyn Desbris. But what had happened to so alter this apparent course? Why were the *stones of greye and redde* still within St.-Mere-Abelle? Where went the charity?

"And where is it now?" he asked aloud, thinking again of the poor prisoners. Where had the Church of Brother Francis Gouliard and Father Abbot Benuto Concarron gone?

"Damn you, Markwart," Master Jojonah whispered, and he meant every word. He tucked the book under his voluminous robes and left the cellars, going straight to the privacy of his room. He thought that he should look in on Brother Braumin, but decided that course could wait, for there was another matter that had been weighing heavily on Jojonah for several days.

So he was soon descending once more into the lower levels of St.-Mere-Abelle, on the other side of the great abbey, down to the rooms Father Abbot Markwart had converted into dungeons. He was not really surprised when he was met by a monk standing guard, the young man moving to block his path.

"I'll not stand and argue with you, young brother," Jojonah blustered, trying to sound imposing. "How many years have passed since you traveled the Gauntlet of Willing Suffering?"

Indeed the formidable master was imposing to the poor young brother! "One year, Master," he said softly. "And four months."

"One year?" Jojonah boomed. "And yet you dare to block my way? I attained the rank of master before you were born, and yet you stand before me now, telling me that I cannot go on."

"The Father Abbot—"

Jojonah had heard enough. He reached across, bringing his arm along the young monk's side, and bulled his way past, staring hard at the young man, daring him to try and stop the move.

The young monk stuttered over a few protests, but only stamped his foot in impotent frustration as Jojonah continued on down the stairs. At the bottom two more young monks stood to block Jojonah's way, but he didn't even bother to speak with them, just continued on, pushing through, and again they didn't dare try to physically stop him. One did follow, though, complaining every step, while the second ran back the other way—to inform Father Abbot Markwart, Jojonah knew.

He was treading on dangerous ground here, Jojonah knew, perhaps pushing the Father Abbot too far. But the book he had found had only bolstered his resolve to stand strong against Markwart's injustices, and he vowed silently that he would not be turned away, whatever the punishment, that he would check on the poor prisoners, just to make sure they were alive and not being treated too badly. Jojonah was risking a great deal, and could rationally argue that the long-term greater good called for him to continue to remain quiet and obscure. But that course would not do much to help the poor Chilichunks and the heroic centaur; that argument, Jojonah knew, was one that men such as Markwart often used to justify ungodly or cowardly actions.

So he didn't even care that he might be pushing Markwart to the very edge of rage. He pressed on, through one door, by another startled young monk, and down another stair. Then he paused, Brother Francis standing before him.

"You should not be down here," Francis remarked.

"By whose command?"

"Father Abbot Markwart," Francis answered without hesitation. "Only he, myself, and Master De'Unnero are to be allowed past the lower stairs."

"A worthy crew," Master Jojonah said sarcastically. "And why is that, Brother Francis? That you might torture the poor innocent prisoners in privacy?" He said it loudly, and took some satisfaction in the uncomfortable shuffling of feet he heard from the young guard standing behind him.

"Innocent?" Francis echoed skeptically.

"Are you so ashamed of your actions that they must take place down here, away from all prying eyes?" Master Jojonah pressed, moving forward another step as he spoke. "Yes, I have heard the tale of Grady Chilichunk."

"An accident on the road," Francis protested.

"Hide thy sins, Brother Francis!" Jojonah replied. "Yet they remain sins all the same!"

Francis snorted derisively. "You cannot comprehend the meaning of this war we wage," he protested. "You show pity for criminals, while innocents pay dearly for their crimes against the Church, against all of Mankind!"

Master Jojonah's answer came in the form of a heavy left hook. Brother Francis was not caught completely unawares, though, and managed to turn so the blow only grazed his face, and as Master Jojonah overbalanced from the miss, the younger monk leaped behind him, locking him in a tight choke hold and twisting hard, stealing the man's balance.

Master Jojonah squirmed and twisted, but only for a moment, for the blood supply was cut short and his brain, starved, fast drifted into unconsciousness.

"Brother Francis!" the younger monk yelled, panicking, and he rushed forward, trying to separate the two. Francis willingly let go, allowing the heavy Jojonah to slump to the floor.

He heard the footsteps sharp against the wood. Pacing, pacing, and he fell into the rhythm of that stride, went along with it, let it carry him back to the world of the living. The light seemed harsh to his eyes, which had known so much darkness in the previous days, but as soon as he found his focus, he knew exactly where he was: propped in a chair in the private room of Father Abbot Markwart.

Markwart and Brother Francis stood before him, neither appearing very pleased.

"You attacked another monk," Father Abbot Markwart began curtly.

"An impertinent subordinate needing a scolding," Master Jojonah replied, rubbing the bleariness from his eyes. "A brother desperately in need of a good thrashing."

Markwart looked over at the smug Brother Francis. "Perhaps," he agreed, merely to deflate the puffy young man. "And yet," Markwart continued, turning his attention squarely back to Jojonah, "he was only acting as I instructed."

Master Jojonah fought hard to maintain control, for he wanted, desperately wanted, to burst loose of his pragmatic bonds and tell Markwart, wicked Markwart, exactly what he thought of him and his so off-course Church. He just chewed his lip and let the old man continue.

"You abandon your duties to support the cause of Brother Allabarnet," the Father Abbot fumed. "A worthy cause, so I thought, given the fate of poor Abbot Dobrinion, for the monks of St. Precious are in need of some morale at this dark time. And yet you abuse the free time I allowed you and find yourself across the whole of the abbey, meddling in affairs which do not concern you."

"Am I not to care that we have innocent prisoners hanging from dungeon walls?" Master Jojonah replied, his voice firm and strong. "Am I not to care that people who have committed no crimes and no sins, and a centaur who may indeed be a hero, stand in this supposedly holy sanctuary's dungeons in chains, and are subjected to torture?"

"Torture?" scoffed the Father Abbot. "You know nothing of it!"

"Thus I tried to find out," Jojonah countered. "Yet you would deny me that, would deny all eyes."

Again Markwart scoffed. "I would not subject the frightened Chilichunks and the potentially dangerous Bradwarden to the private inquisitions of others. They are my responsibility."

"Your prisoners," Jojonah corrected.

Father Abbot Markwart paused and took a deep breath. "Prisoners," he echoed. "Yes, they are. No sins, say you, yet they are in league with the thieves who hold the stolen stones. No crimes, say you, yet we have every reason to believe that the centaur was in league with the demon dactyl, and only the accidental destruction of Aida prevented him from joining in the rampage against all the godly people of the world!"

"Accidental destruction," Jojonah echoed incredulously, sarcastically.

"That is the decision of my investigation!" Markwart yelled suddenly, moving very near the sitting master, and Jojonah thought for a moment that the man meant to strike him. "You chose at this time to pursue another course."

If only you understood the truth of that, Jojonah silently replied, and was quite glad then that he had hidden the ancient book in his room before he tried to get to the prisoners.

"And yet you could not even hold true to that course!" Markwart went on. "And while you were at your work, buried in ancient writings that bear no importance to the present dangerous situation, one of our younger brothers nearly met his doom!"

That perked up Jojonah's ears.

"In the courtyard," Markwart went on. "Doing work that Master Jojonah would normally oversee, but that Master De'Unnero had to watch over, in addition to the other laborers he was directing. Perhaps that was why he could not react in time when two of the three brothers slipped off the wheel, when the third, poor Dellman, was nearly broken in half by the sudden weight."

"Dellman!" Jojonah cried, nearly coming out of his seat, forcing Markwart to take a step back. Panic crept through Jojonah's mind; he worried suddenly for Brother Braumin, whom he had not seen in days. How many "accidents" had there been?

He realized, though, that his excitement only implicated Dellman as a fellow conspirator, and so he worked hard to control himself, to settle back into his chair. "The same Brother Dellman who accompanied us to Aida?" he asked.

"The only Brother Dellman," Markwart sternly replied, seeing right through the ruse.

"Such a pity," Jojonah remarked. "He is alive, though?"

"Barely, and perhaps not for long," the Father Abbot answered, going into his pacing once more.

"I will see to him."

"You will not!" the Father Abbot snapped. "He is under the care of Master De'Unnero. I forbid you from trying to so much as speak to him. He does not need to hear your apologies, Master Jojonah. Let the guilt of your absence weigh on your mind. Perhaps that will lead you back to your true duties and purpose."

The thought that he was somehow responsible was preposterous, of course, but Jojonah understood the subtle meaning behind it. Markwart was only using that excuse to keep him away from Brother Dellman, to keep his influence from the man while De'Unnero, the master so proficient at bending the minds of the brothers sent on Avelyn's trail, worked his wicked way.

"You are my witness to this, Brother Francis," Markwart said. "And I warn you, Master Jojonah, if I hear that you go anywhere near Brother Dellman, the consequences will be dire—for you and for him."

It surprised Jojonah that Markwart had drawn so clear a line in the sand, had all but openly threatened him. Things were going Markwart's way, it seemed to Jojonah, so why had he taken such a bold step as that?

He didn't press the issue, simply nodded and left, and had no intention of crossing Markwart's line anytime soon. It would be better for Brother Dellman, he reasoned, if he broke all connection with the man for the time being. Besides, Jojonah was only beginning his work. He took a quick meal, went to his room and sighed profoundly in relief to find the tome still in place. Then he went right back to the lower stairs, heading again for the ancient libraries, for more pieces to this ever-more-interesting puzzle.

The doors were sealed, barred by heavy planks. One young monk, a man Jojonah did not know, was standing guard.

"What is the meaning of this?" the master asked.

"No entrance to the lower libraries at this time," the man mechanically replied. "By order of—"

Before he had even finished, Master Jojonah stormed away, taking the stairs two at a time. He was not surprised to find Father Abbot Markwart waiting for him in his private quarters, this time alone.

"You said nothing about ending my work," Master Jojonah began, feeling his way cautiously into this fight, for he believed this one might prove conclusive.

"Now is not the time to worry about Brother Allabarnet's sainthood," the Father Abbot replied calmly. "I cannot afford to have one of my masters wasting precious time in the dungeons."

"A curious choice of words," Jojonah came back, "considering that you have many of your most trusted brothers wasting time in dungeons of another sort."

He saw the flicker of anger in the old man's eyes, but Markwart got it quickly under control. "The canonization process will wait until the war is ended," he said.

"By all reports, it may already be over," Jojonah was quick to reply.

"And until the threat to our Order is ended," Markwart added. "It is reasonable to assume that if a powrie could get to Abbot Dobrinion, then none of us are safe. Our enemies are desperate now, for their war is going badly, and it is prudent to believe that they might begin a larger campaign of assassinating important leaders."

Jojonah had to fight very hard to hold his tongue, to stop from accusing Markwart then and there of facilitating Dobrinion's murder. He didn't care anymore for his personal well-being, would have laid into Markwart openly, publicly, beginning an internal struggle that would likely cost him his life. But he could not, he reminded himself many times in the next few seconds. There were others to consider—Dellman, Braumin Herde, Marlboro Viscenti, and the poor prisoners. For their sake, if not his own, he could not begin the open battle against Markwart.

"The process will also wait until the stolen gemstones are returned," Markwart went on.

"Thus I will sit idle, wasting my time in the upper levels," Jojonah did dare to remark.

"No, I have other plans for you," Markwart replied. "More important matters. You are obviously well again—fit enough to attack another monk—and so you should prepare yourself for the road."

"You just said that the sainthood would wait," Jojonah responded.

"So I did," Markwart replied. "But your destination is no longer St. Honce. You will go to Palmaris, to St. Precious, to witness the appointment of a new abbot."

Master Jojonah could not completely hide his surprise. There was no monk at that abbey prepared for the job, and thus, as far as he knew, nothing of succession had even been discussed, and would be a matter for the College of Abbots later that year.

"Master De'Unnero," Father Abbot Markwart answered his unspoken question.

"De'Unnero?" Jojonah echoed incredulously. "The junior master in all of St.-Mere-Abelle, a man prematurely promoted due to the death of Master Siherton?"

"The murder of Master Siherton, by Avelyn Desbris," Markwart was quick to remind.

"He will assume the leadership of St. Precious?" Jojonah continued, too engrossed to even feel the sting of that last verbal barb. "Surely that position is of utmost importance, given the fact that Palmaris remains closest to the lines of battle."

"That is exactly why I chose De'Unnero," Markwart replied calmly.

"You chose?" Jojonah echoed. There was little precedence for such a move; the appointment of an abbot, even one coming from within the ranks of the affected abbey, was no small matter, one open to the collective reasoning of the College of Abbots.

"There is no time to convene the College prematurely," Markwart explained. "Nor can we wait until the scheduled meeting in Calember. Until then, acting on what I deem to be emergency circumstances, I have appointed Master De'Unnero as Dobrinion's replacement."

"Temporarily," Jojonah said.

"Permanently," came the stern reply. "And you, Master Jojonah, will accompany him."

"I just returned from many weeks on the road," Jojonah protested, but he knew he was defeated, and understood that he had erred in trying to get to the prisoners, in pushing hard against Markwart. And now he would pay. Markwart had been well within his rights to halt the canonization process for the time being, and whether or not the Father Abbot's choice of De'Unnero for abbot would stand would be decided at the fall College of Abbots, and not before. Jojonah was out of excuses and out of dodges.

"You will remain at St. Precious to aid Master . . . Abbot De'Unnero, as his second," Markwart went on. "If it pleases him, you may return to St.-Mere-Abelle with him for the College."

"I outrank him."

"No more," Markwart replied.

"I . . . the College will not stand for this!" Jojonah protested.

"That will be determined in mid-Calember," Markwart replied. "If the other abbots and their voting seconds see fit to overrule me, then perhaps Jojonah will be appointed abbot of St. Precious."

But by that time, Jojonah knew, Markwart would likely have his gemstones back, and all of those monks (who had been in league with, or even friendly to, Jojonah's cause,) would have been weeded out of St.-Mere-Abelle, the victims of "accidents" like the one that befell Brother Dellman, or converted to Markwart's way of thinking by a barrage of lies and threats. Or, for those brothers of conviction like himself, Markwart would find missions in faraway, dangerous lands. Until this moment, Master Jojonah had not truly appreciated how formidable a foe the old Father Abbot would prove to be.

"Perhaps we will meet again," Markwart said, waving his hand dismissively. "For the sake of peace of mind for both of us, I hope not."

And so it ends, Master Jojonah thought.

❖ 24 ❖

Resolution

They came in sight of the clusters of houses, farms mostly, just to the north of Palmaris, and were heartened indeed to see that many of the folk had come out of the walled city and returned to their homes.

"The region is returning to normal," Connor remarked. He was sitting astride his horse, riding next to Pony, who along with Belli'mar Juraviel was up on Symphony, while Elbryan and Roger walked in front, flanking Brother Youseff, whose hands were bound tightly behind his back. "We will know peace again, and soon," Connor promised, and that seemed a likely notion to all the others, for they had seen no monsters all the way to this point.

"Caer Tinella and Landsdown may have been the last monstrous strongholds in the region," the ranger reasoned. "What few remain there should prove of little trouble to Palmaris' garrison." The ranger stopped then, taking Symphony's bridle and bringing the horse to a halt. He looked up at his two friends, and both Pony and Juraviel understood.

"We do not dare enter the city," Elbryan said to Connor. "Nor even get close enough that those folk in the farms might see us." He looked at Brother Youseff as he finished the thought. "Even knowing of us seems to endanger people."

"Because you recognize that you are rightly branded as outlaws," Brother Youseff retorted sharply. "Do you believe that the Church will cease its hunt for you?" He laughed wickedly, seeming not at all the prisoner here.

"It may be that the Church will have other, more pressing problems when the truth of your actions at St. Precious becomes known," Connor put in, stepping Greystone up between the monk and the ranger.

"And you have proof of these absurd accusations?" Brother Youseff was quick to reply.

"We shall see," Connor answered, and turned back to Elbryan and the two on Symphony. "Roger and I will deliver him to my uncle," he explained. "We will use the secular channels of power before trying to decide how much of the Church will side with this dog and his masters."

"You might be starting a small war," Pony reasoned, for it was well-known that the Church was nearly as powerful as the state—and some who had witnessed the magical powers of St.-Mere-Abelle considered the Church even more powerful.

"If such a war is to begin, then it was started by those who murdered Abbot Dobrinion, not by me or my uncle," Connor replied with conviction. "I am only following the proper course in response to that heinous act, and in defense of my own life."

"We will wait for word," Elbryan put in, not wanting to belabor this point any longer.

"Roger and I will return to you as soon as possible," Connor agreed. "I know that you are anxious to be on your way." He was careful to end the thought there, for he did not want the dangerous monk prisoner to know that Elbryan intended to go straightaway to St.-Mere-Abelle. Given the wonders he had seen of stone magic, Connor had thought it foolish that the ranger openly declared to Youseff that they would be going after their captured friends. The less precise information this dangerous man held, the better for all of them.

Connor motioned to Elbryan and turned his horse aside, the ranger walking beside him, away from the others. "If I cannot get back out to you, then farewell, Nightbird," the nobleman said in all sincerity.

Elbryan followed the nobleman's gaze back to Pony.

"I would be a liar if I did not admit that I was envious of you," Connor went on. "I, too, loved her; who could not, after witnessing her beauty?"

Elbryan had no practical response, and so he said nothing.

"But it is obvious where lies Jill's . . . Pony's heart," Connor added after a long and uncomfortable pause. "That heart is for you," he said, looking the ranger in the eye.

"You do not intend to return to us," Elbryan suddenly understood. "You will deliver the monk, then stay in Palmaris."

The man shrugged noncommittally. "It is painful to see her," he admitted. "Painful and wonderful all at once. I have not yet decided which is the more prominent emotion."

"Farewell," Elbryan replied.

"And to you," said Connor. He looked again to Pony. "May I say my good-byes to her privately?" he asked.

Elbryan offered a consenting smile—not that he considered this in any way his decision. If Pony wanted to speak privately with Connor, then she would do so, whatever, he, Elbryan, might think of it. He made things easier for Connor, feeling some honest sympathy for the man, by walking back to Pony and delivering the message. After waiting for Juraviel to slip down from Symphony, the woman urged the horse out to join the man.

"I may not return," Connor explained.

Pony nodded, still unsure why Connor had come out in the first place.

"I had to see you again," he went on, understanding her unspoken question. "I had to know that you were well. I had to . . ." He paused and sighed deeply.

"What do you need from me?" Pony asked bluntly. "What can we say that has not been said?"

"You can forgive me," Connor blurted, and then tried desperately to explain. "I was hurt . . . my pride. I did not want to send you away, but could not stand to see you, to know that you did not love me . . ."

Pony's smile silenced him. "I never blamed you, so there is nothing for me to forgive," she replied quietly. "I find what happened between us to be tragic, for both of us. We had a special friendship, and I shall always treasure that."

"But what I did, on our wedding night . . ." Connor protested.

"It is what you did not do that allowed me to place no blame," said Pony. "You could have taken me, and if you had, I would never have forgiven you—indeed, I might have used my magic to cut you down on the field when first I saw you again!" She knew that to be a lie as soon as she heard the words come out of her mouth. Whatever her feelings toward Connor, she could not use the gemstones, the sacred gifts of God, in such a vengeful way.

"I am sorry," Connor said sincerely.

"As am I," Pony replied. She leaned over and kissed the man on the cheek. "Farewell, Connor Bildeborough," she said. "You see the enemy plainly now. Fight well." And she turned her horse about and walked back to Elbryan.

Soon after, Pony, Elbryan, and Juraviel were heading back to the north, full of hope, but making plans for a journey that they knew might be as dark as their trip to Aida to face the demon dactyl. They hoped Connor's mission would be fruitful, and quickly, and that the King, and the sensible and godly members of the Abellican Order, if there were any left, would turn against this wicked Father Abbot who had so wrongly imprisoned Bradwarden and the Chilichunks. They hoped, too, to find their friends healthy and free before they ever entered St.-Mere-Abelle.

But practicality told them otherwise, for such political actions might take months, even years. Bradwarden and the Chilichunks could not wait, did not deserve to wait, and so the three planned to set off for the abbey on All Saints Bay as soon as Roger, and perhaps Connor, returned to them.

It was with equal determination that Roger and Connor strode toward Palmaris. Connor held great faith in his uncle Rochefort. Ever since he was a child, Connor had looked up to the man as someone who could get things done, a great man who shaped life in the city. All the many times Connor had gotten himself into trouble, his uncle Rochefort had taken care of things quietly and effectively.

Brother Youseff recognized that confidence in the man, both from his boasts of what his uncle would now accomplish and the swaggering manner in which he sat in his saddle.

"You should understand, Master Bildeborough, the ramifications of being in league with those two," the monk taunted.

"If you do not shut your mouth, I will gag you," Connor promised.

"But the embarrassment to your uncle!" Youseff pressed. "What fun it shall be when the King learns that Baron Bildeborough's nephew is traveling with outlaws."

"I am indeed," Connor said, looking down at the man. "Now."

Brother Youseff was not amused. "Your accusation is ridiculous, of course," he said. "And your uncle will recognize that fact and apologize profusely to the Church—and perchance the Church could be persuaded to accept the apology and not excommunicate him."

Connor scoffed openly, not really impressed, and certainly not believing this dangerous monk's words. Fear did lick at Connor's thoughts, though, for himself and for his uncle. He tried to hold fast to his confidence in the great man, the Baron of Palmaris, but reminded himself repeatedly not to underestimate the power of the Church.

"Perhaps even you two could be forgiven," Youseff went on slyly.

"Forgiven for defending ourselves?" Roger quipped.

"Neither of you was involved," Youseff replied. "Only the girl and the other one. And perhaps the elf—no such creature was known to us, and thus his fate is yet to be determined."

Again Connor scoffed. For this man who had stalked him at the Way, who had tried to catch him to kill him, to insist that he wasn't involved was purely ridiculous.

"Ah yes, the girl," Brother Youseff went on, changing his tone, looking up out of the corner of his eye to measure Connor's response. "How sweet that capture will prove," he said lewdly. "Perhaps I might find time to take pleasure with her before I present her to my superiors."

The monk saw the strike coming—indeed he had invited it!—and he didn't waver now, but let Connor smack him across the back of his head. It wasn't a hard blow, but one that Youseff could convincingly use as he dove down to the ground, slamming his left shoulder squarely and pushing through the blow. He heard the popping sound as the bone dislocated, felt the waves of pain washing over him, and he cried out, seemingly from the pain, but really to cover the movements as he brought his arms closer together behind his back, changing the angle of the bindings.

"We are almost to the city!" Roger scolded. "Why did you hit him?"

"Did you not want to do exactly the same thing?" Connor replied, and Roger had no answer. Roger went for the fallen monk then, as did Connor, sliding down from Greystone.

The security of Youseff's ties depended on not being able to bring his arms farther back behind him, but now, with the shoulder popped out of place, that was no longer true. He got his left hand free in moments, but held his position, keeping his hands close together, ignoring the numbing pain in his left shoulder.

Roger was beside him first, stooping to put his arms around the man.

Youseff bided his time—this one was not the most dangerous of the pair.

Then Connor was there, helping Roger hoist the monk back to his feet.

Faster than either of them could realize, Brother Youseff tucked his feet under him and came up straight. The binding ropes flew wide as his right arm swung about, fingers and thumb locked in a rigid C position. That deadly hook drove right into Connor's throat, stunning the man, smashing against his exposed flesh, then driving right through so that Youseff held Connor's windpipe in his hand.

He looked the nobleman right in the eye, unblinking, uncaring, then tore out Connor's throat.

Connor Bildeborough fell away, clutching at his mortal wound, gasping for breath that would not come, trying futilely to stem the explosion of blood that rose about him in a crimson mist, that backed down his open windpipe into heaving lungs.

Youseff spun and struck, knocking stunned Roger to the ground.

The young man wisely discerned that he could do nothing for Connor and little against the powerful monk. He was moving as soon as he hit the ground, and while Youseff turned back to taunt the dying Connor, Roger managed to get to the horse.

"I think I will go and kill your uncle next," Youseff said with an evil grin.

Connor heard him, but only from far, far away. He was falling, he felt, slipping deeper and deeper into a blackness, deeper within himself. He felt cold and alone, all noises diminishing to nothingness. His vision narrowed, became points of light.

Bright and warm.

He found one place of great comfort, one place of hope: he had made his peace with Jill.

Everything was gone now, except the light, the warmth. Connor's spirit walked toward it.

Roger held on dearly to one stirrup as Connor's frightened horse bolted, dragging him along. Behind him he heard the monk coming hard; Youseff had taken up the chase.

Growling against the pain, Roger pulled himself closer to the horse as he ran alongside it. He strengthened his grasp on the saddle, then reached back and slapped Greystone hard, spurring the horse on. He managed to glance back as he did, and saw Youseff, running fast, closing ground.

Using all of his agility, every ounce of his strength, Roger pulled himself up, up. He somehow got his feet off the ground, and with the drag gone, the horse put some ground between itself and the running monk.

Roger didn't even try to gain a proper seat, but just pulled himself over the saddle sidelong, hanging head down, grimacing with each painful jolt.

The fine horse left the monk behind.

A frustrated Brother Youseff kicked hard at the ground. He glanced up and down the road, both ways, wondering which course he should take. He could go back to Palmaris—with Connor dead, there would likely be no accusations raised against him concerning the murdered abbot. Certainly the word of the rogues in the north would not be sufficient to bring such charges against the Abellican Church.

But while he didn't fear the Baron of Palmaris or the monks of St. Precious, the thought of reporting back to Father Abbot Markwart with news of the disaster made the hairs on the back of Youseff's neck stand up. Dandelion was dead, but so was the troublesome Master Bildeborough.

Youseff looked the way Roger had gone, to the north. He had to get to him before Roger could rendezvous with the others, had to ensure complete surprise when he sprang back upon the woman. And Youseff knew he would indeed go back after her, and her two companions. They had only beaten him the first time because they knew he was coming, but now . . .

Then he could report back to the Father Abbot.

Brother Youseff started to run, legs pumping tirelessly, carrying him over the miles.

Roger was riding easily, but quickly. The monk hadn't given up, he suspected, for they both knew that Roger meant to get back to Elbryan and Pony, which Youseff could not allow. Still, Roger was not too worried, for with the horse he could keep ahead.

But barely, he saw when he climbed the side of one hillock, looking back down the road to see the monk, far in the distance, but still running!

"Impossible," Roger muttered, for they must have covered more than five miles by then. Yet the monk's speed seemed as great as if he had just taken up the chase!

Roger climbed back on the horse and started away at a faster pace. He could tell that the mount was tired—sweat glistened on the golden coat—but he couldn't afford to let Greystone slow down. He glanced back many times, hoping, praying, that the monk could not outlast his mount. On and on he went, staying to the road, more concerned with speed than stealth, knowing that the monk, incredible as the man was, could not match his horse's pace.

He was riding easily again soon after, confident that he had left his pursuer far behind, and plotting the best course to find his friends; they had arranged to meet at an abandoned farmhouse no more than ten miles farther.

The horse stumbled, and Roger's eyes went wide when he saw the gleam of metal to the side of the road. Greystone was limping now, having thrown a shoe.

Roger was down to the ground in an instant, running to retrieve the shoe, then back to the horse to see what leg it had come from. The answer was obvious before he even approached, for the horse was limping badly now, favoring its rear left leg. Gingerly, Roger hooked his arm about that limb and bent it up at the knee.

The hoof was in bad shape. Roger didn't know much about horses, but realized that this one couldn't go on unless that shoe was replaced. And there was no way he could do that.

"Bloody powrie luck," the young man cursed, glancing back nervously down the road. It took all of Roger's willpower to control his mounting fears, to force himself to think clearly, to reason through the problem. First he considered running, but he dismissed that thought, sensing that the monk would find and catch him long before he got to Elbryan and the others. He then wondered if any houses this far north were inhabited once more, thinking he might find someone to replace the shoe, but again he understood that he had not the time.

"The fight is mine," Roger said aloud, needing to hear the words as he continued to gaze back down the road. He went to the saddlebags then, for he and Connor had collected many items on the journey south, looking for something—anything!—that might help him now.

Most of the items were simply general supplies for the road: ropes and a grapnel, a small shovel, pots and pans, extra clothing and the like. One item caught his attention, though. At the last stop, at the very farm where Elbryan and the others would wait, Roger had taken a come-along, a small block-and-tackle unit favored by farmers for hoisting bales, or even for pulling in stubborn bulls.

Roger held the item in his hand, studying it, trying to find some way to put it to use. Several images flashed in his mind, and he focused at last on one in particular, one that utilized his abilities. He couldn't outfight the monk, he knew, but he might be able to outwit the man.

By the time Brother Youseff got to that spot, Roger and the horse were gone, but the horseshoe remained, right in the middle of the road. The monk stopped and examined the shoe, then stood and glanced all about curiously. He couldn't imagine that the young man had been so foolish as to leave the telltale item behind.

Youseff searched ahead on the road and saw no fresh tracks beyond a dozen or so feet. To the side of the trail, he easily found signs of the limping horse's passage, and on the other side, a spot of blood and a lighter set of tracks, the footprints of a light man. Now it made sense to the monk. The horse had thrown the shoe and had then thrown the young man. Smiling widely, the monk started down the sloping ground, toward a copse of trees, in which, he suspected, he would find his second victim.

From high in one of those trees, Roger Lockless, rope, grapnel, and come-along in hand, watched the monk's confident approach. Youseff slowed as he neared the trees, moving with more caution, darting from cover to cover.

Roger lost sight of the monk when he entered the copse. Again he was amazed when Youseff emerged at another point, quite far into the trees, for the man had traveled many yards without even stirring the thick underbrush. Roger looked to his items, to the finger he had purposely pricked to leave a blood trail, and wondered if his wits would be enough.

It was too late to change his mind about his plans, though, for Youseff was right at the base of the tree now and had spotted the last drop of blood.

The monk's head slowly turned up, staring through the leafy shadows, his gaze at last settling on the dark shape high among the branches, hugging tight to the trunk.

"If you come down, I will spare your life," the monk called.

Roger doubted that, but still, he almost began a negotiation.

"If you make me climb all the way up there to drag you out, then know that your death will be most unpleasant," Youseff went on.

"I never did anything against your Church!" Roger replied, playing the part of a frightened child, which at that moment did not seem to him to be too much of a stretch.

"And thus I will spare your life," Youseff repeated. "Now come down."

"Go away," Roger cried.

"Come down!" Youseff yelled. "I give you one last chance."

Roger didn't reply, other than to whimper loudly enough for the monk to hear him.

As Youseff started to climb, following a predictable course among the branches, Roger watched the monk closely. He tugged on one rope for the hundredth time, testing it. One end was tied fast to the tree, the other secured to one end of the come-along. A second rope, fastened to the grapnel, was tied to the come-along's other end.

The knots were secure and the ropes were the right length, Roger reminded himself, but still, when he considered the enormity of his plan, the need for perfect timing and more than a bit of luck, he nearly swooned.

Youseff was more than halfway up now, fully twenty feet from the ground.

"One more branch," Roger muttered.

Up came the monk, planting his feet on the last solid limb of the lower trunk. He would have to pause there, Roger knew, and map out the rest of the climb, for he was in an open area that afforded no ready branches.

As soon as Youseff was in place, Roger Lockless took his rope firmly in hand and leaped out. He plummeted between a pair of branches, getting a few nasty scratches in the process. Then, some feet out from the trunk, he hit another branch, as he had planned, and kicked out, launching himself on a circuitous route about the tree. He crashed and bounced repeatedly but held fast to his circular, descending course, passing the startled Youseff barely an arm's length away.

How Roger breathed easier as he continued around, for Brother Youseff had been too surprised to leap out at him.

"Damn you!" the monk cried. Youseff had at first thought that Roger was using the rope to get ahead of him to the ground, but suddenly, as the loop tightened about him, pinning him to the trunk, as Roger swung around and below, he understood.

On the last turn, Roger, holding the rope in only one hand now, took up the other rope and launched the grapnel at a cluster of white birch. Then, hoping it would catch, Roger braced his feet as he came around the base of the trunk, the first length of rope playing out to the end. He dug in then, pulling with all his strength to keep the rope taut about Youseff.

He knew he didn't have long, for with the many branches interfering with the pull, the rope was not tight enough to hold the agile and strong monk for long.

Not yet.

Roger pulled on the rope in the birch trees with one hand, using the other to crank the come-along and take up some slack. He groaned aloud as he felt the grapnel slipping through tangle. Finally, though, it caught fast.

Up above, Youseff was laughing and trying to extricate himself. He had the rope up above his elbows now and would soon slip under it.

Roger gave one final tug, and then, seeing that the slack was nearly gone, he dove for the come-along, cranking hard and fast with both hands.

Youseff had just started to lift the rope over his head when it snapped taut, slamming him back against the tree trunk. "What?" he asked, for he knew that the skinny little man couldn't pull so powerfully. He could see well enough below to know that no horse had come into the area, and so he stubbornly pushed back against the rope.

He heard the crack of a branch below, breaking under the strain, and was loose for just an instant before the rope pulled hard again, squeezing him against the trunk. Youseff's left arm was free and under the rope now, but the binding crossed diagonally down his shoulder, right under his other arm, pinning him tightly. He continued his stubborn fight as the rope tightened even more.

Roger wasn't looking up, was just pulling on the come-along's crank with all his strength. The rope was no longer even vibrating, was out straight and tight, and so Roger finally stopped, fearing he would pull one of the birch trees right out of the ground.

He stepped out from under the tree and looked up to see the squirming, helplessly pinned monk. Now he did smile, with absolute relief. "I will return," he promised. "With friends. It seems that you now have two murders to answer for!" And he turned and ran off.

Youseff paid the words little heed, just continued struggling against the impossibly tight binding. He squirmed and shifted, thought to try and slip out under the rope.

He realized that to be a foolish move almost immediately—but too late—as the rope slipped up an inch, creasing the side of his neck.

Belli'mar Juraviel was first into the copse, moving ahead of Elbryan, Pony, and Roger. The sun was low in the sky now, its bottom edge dipping below the horizon. The group had hurried back to the spot as soon as Roger had come to them, wanting to capture and secure the dangerous monk before nightfall.

Elbryan and the others waited outside the cluster of trees, the ranger watching Pony closely. She had been silent all the way back to this place; the news of Connor's death had hit her hard.

Strangely, her mourning did not incite any jealous feelings within Elbryan, only an empathy for her. He understood, truly understood, the relationship between Pony and the nobleman, and he knew now that with Connor's death, the woman had lost a part of herself, had lost that time of healing in her life. So Elbryan vowed silently to keep his own negative feelings private, to focus on Pony's needs.

She sat straight and tall on Symphony now, cutting a stoic and strong figure in the fading light. She would get through this, as she had come through the first massacre at Dundalis, as she had come through the bitter war and all the losses, particularly the death of Avelyn. Once again the ranger found himself marveling at the woman's strength and courage.

He loved her all the more for it.

"He is dead," came a call from the tall grass, Juraviel returning to the group. The elf cast a glance at Roger, one that perceptive Elbryan didn't miss, and explained, "He was just about free when I came upon him, stuck in the tree just as you described. I had to cut him down—it took several arrows."

"You are sure he is dead?" Roger asked nervously, not wanting anything more to do with that one.

"He is dead," Juraviel assured him. "And I believe that your horse, Connor's horse, is just over there," the elf added, pointing across the road.

"He threw a shoe," Roger reminded.

"Which can be easily repaired," Juraviel replied. "Go and get him."

Roger nodded and started away, and Pony, on Elbryan's signal, kicked Symphony into a trot after him.

"Your quiver is full," the ranger noted when he and the elf were alone.

"I retrieved my arrows," Juraviel replied.

"Elves do not retrieve arrows that have hit the mark," the ranger replied. "Not unless the situation is desperate, which ours, now that the monks are both dead, is not."

"Your point?" Juraviel asked dryly.

"The man was dead when you went into the copse," Elbryan reasoned.

Juraviel agreed with a nod. "He apparently tried to get out of the bindings, choking himself," he explained. "Our young Roger did well in tightening the bonds, and was quite clever in capturing the man in the first place. Too clever, perhaps."

"I have battled with one called Brother Justice before," Elbryan said. "And you saw the fanaticism at our ambush. Did you doubt that it must end like this, with the death of the monk?"

"I wish he had not died at young Roger's hands," Juraviel replied. "I do not believe that he is ready for that."

Elbryan glanced to the road, to see Pony and Roger walking together, leading Symphony and Connor's limping horse.

"He must be told the truth," the ranger decided, and he looked to Juraviel, expecting an argument.

"He'll not take it well" was all the elf warned, but Juraviel did not disagree with the ranger. The road ahead for all of them would be dark, no doubt, and perhaps it was better to get this unpleasantness over with here and now.

When the pair arrived with the horses, Juraviel took Greystone and, after examining the injured hoof, led the creature away, motioning for Pony to take Symphony and follow.

"Juraviel did not kill the monk," Elbryan said to Roger as soon as the others were gone.

Roger's eyes widened in panic and he glanced all around, as if expecting Brother Justice to leap out at him at any moment. The man had unnerved Roger more than any other foe, even Kos-kosio, ever had.

"You did," Elbryan explained.

"You mean that I was the one who defeated him," Roger corrected. "And that the kill by Juraviel was no large matter."

"I mean that you killed him," the ranger said firmly. "I mean that you tightened the rope and it somehow slipped about his neck, choking the life from him."

Roger's eyes widened again. "But Juraviel said—" he started to protest.

"Juraviel feared for your sensibilities," Elbryan bluntly replied. "He was not certain how you would accept such grim reality, and thus feared to speak plainly."

Roger's mouth moved but no words came forth. The weight of the truth was hitting him hard, Elbryan realized, and he could see that he was swaying.

"I had to tell you," Elbryan said, softly now. "You deserve to know the truth, and must get beyond it if you are to handle the responsibilities that have now been put on your young shoulders."

Roger was hardly listening, was swaying more pronouncedly now and seemed as if he might simply topple over.

"We will speak later," Elbryan said to him, walking up to him and dropping a comforting hand on his shoulder. Then the ranger continued past, going to join Juraviel and Pony, leaving Roger alone with his thoughts.

And with his pain, for truly Roger Billingsbury—and suddenly he craved for that title again and not the foolishly pretentious Roger Lockless—had never been hit by anything like this. He had known grief many times, too many times, in his young life, but that pain was different. That pain allowed him to keep himself up on a pedestal, to continue to view himself as the center of the universe, as somehow better than everyone else. In all the pain and all the many trials young Roger had ever known, he had been able to hold on to his somewhat childish Roger-centric view of the world.

Now, suddenly, that pedestal had been kicked out from under him. He had killed a man.

He had killed a man!

Without conscious choice, Roger was sitting in the grass. Desperately, his rational side battled against his conscience. True, he had killed a man, but what choice had the man given him? The monk was a killer, pure and simple. The monk had killed Connor right before his own eyes, brutally, evilly. The monk had murdered Abbot Dobrinion!

But even those truths did little to assuage Roger's sudden sense of guilt. Whatever the justifications, and in spite of the fact that he had not intentionally killed Brother Justice, the man was dead, and the blood was on his hands.

He put his head down, laboring hard for breath. He craved all those things that had been torn from him at too young an age: family warmth and the reasonable, comforting words of adults he could look up to. With that thought, he looked over his shoulder to his three friends, to the ranger who had so bluntly told him of his crime and then left him alone.

For a moment Roger hated Elbryan for that. But it could not hold; soon enough he understood that the ranger had told him out of respect for him, out of confidence in him, and had then left him alone because an adult—and he was an adult now—had to work through such pain, at least in part, alone.

Pony came for him soon after, saying nothing of the monk's death, but only informing him they were going to gather up the fallen monk and then go south to retrieve Connor's body.

Silently, Roger fell into line, purposefully averting his eyes from the spectacle of Brother Justice, slung over Greystone's back. The horse was walking better now, for Juraviel had shaved its hoof to level, but still the pace was slow. Night fell in full, and still they walked, determined to get to Connor's body before he was torn apart by some scavenging creature.

With some difficulty, for the night was quite dark, they at last found the man.

Pony went to him first, and gently closed his eyes. Then she walked away, far away.

"Go to her," Juraviel said to Elbryan.

"You know what to do with him," the ranger replied, and the elf nodded. Then, to Roger, Elbryan added, "Be strong and be sure. Your role is perhaps the most important of all now."

And then he walked away, leaving Roger staring at Juraviel for an explanation.

"You are to take Connor, the monk, and the horse and head straight out to Palmaris," the elf explained.

Roger inadvertently glanced at the dead monk, at the image that so shook his self-perception.

"Go to the Baron, not the abbey," the elf explained. "Tell him what has happened. Tell him of Connor's belief that these monks, and not any powrie, murdered Abbot Dobrinion, and that they chased Connor out of Palmaris, for he, too, had unwittingly become an enemy of the wicked Church leaders."

"And then what for me?" the young man asked, wondering if this was the last time he would see these three.

Juraviel glanced around. "We could use another horse—another two," he added, "if you plan to ride with us."

"Does he want me to?" Roger asked, nodding toward the distant Elbryan.

"Would he have told you the truth if he did not?" Juraviel replied.

"And what of you, then?" Roger quickly asked. "Why did you lie to me? Do you think me a foolish young boy, unable to take responsibility?"

"I think you a man who has grown much in the last weeks," the elf replied honestly. "I did not tell you because I was not sure of what Nightbird—and do not doubt that he is the leader of this group—had planned for you. If we meant to leave you in Palmaris, in safety with Tomas and Belster, if we had determined that your role in this fight was at its end, then what good would it have done you to let you know that you had the blood of a dead man on your hands?"

"Is the truth not absolute?" Roger asked. "Do you play God, elf?"

"If the truth is not in any way constructive, then it can wait for a better time," Juraviel replied. "But since your course is yours to determine, then you needed to know now. Our road will be dark, my young friend, and I do not doubt that we will find other Brother Justices in our path, perhaps for years to come."

"And each successive kill gets easier?" Roger asked sarcastically.

"Pray that is not the case," Juraviel replied in a severe tone, eyeing Roger unblinkingly.

That demeanor set the young man back on his heels.

"Nightbird thought that you were emotionally strong enough to know the truth," the elf added. "Take it as a compliment."

Juraviel started to walk away.

"I do not know if he was right," Roger admitted suddenly.

The elf turned about to see Roger, head down, shoulders bobbing in sobs. He went to stand beside him, put his hand on the small of Roger's back. "The other monk was only the second man Nightbird ever killed," he said. "He did not cry this time because he shed all those tears after killing the first, the first Brother Justice."

The notion that this stoic and powerful ranger had been equally shaken hit Roger profoundly. He wiped his eyes and stood straight, looked to Juraviel and nodded grimly.

Then Roger was on the road south, too agitated to sit and wait out the remainder of the night. He had to move quite slowly, for the injured Greystone carried both bodies, but he was determined to speak with Baron Bildeborough before the midday meal.

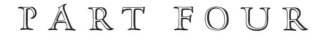

PART FOUR

DOWN THE ROAD OF SHADOWS

As I learned more about the Church that Avelyn served—the Church of my parents and of every fellow human I have ever known—and as I met more of the Abellican monks, I began to recognize just how subtle the nature of evil might be. I had never spent time considering this before, but is the evil man inherently evil? Is he even aware that his actions are evil? Does he believe them to be, or has he tainted his perspective so that he believes himself to be in the right?

In these times, when the dactyl awoke and the world knew chaos, many, it seems, have come to question the very essence of evil. Who am I, or who is anyone, they might say, to judge which man might be considered evil and which good? When I ask, is the evil man inherently evil, I am supposing an absolute distinction that many people refuse to acknowledge. Their concept of morality is relative, and while I'll admit that the moral implications of many actions might be dependent upon a certain situation, the overall moral distinction is not.

For within that truth, I know a larger one. I know that there is indeed an absolute difference between good and evil, with individual perspective and justification notwithstanding. To the Touel'alfar, the common good is the measuring stick—putting the good of the elven folk first, but considering the good of all others, as well. Though the elves desire little contact with humans, they have for centuries taken humans under their tutelage and trained them as rangers, not for any gains to Andur'Blough Inninness, for that place is beyond the influence of the rangers, but for the betterment of the world at large. The elven folk are not aggressors, never that. They fight when they must, in defense and against imperialism. Had the goblins not come to Dundalis, the elves would never have sought them out, for though they have no love of goblins or powries or giants, and indeed consider the three races to be a scourge upon the very world, the elves would suffer them to live. To go to the mountains and attack these monsters, by elven standards, would reduce the Touel'alfar to the level of that which they despise above all else.

Conversely, the powries and the goblins have shown themselves to be warring and wicked creatures. They attack whenever they find advantage, and it is little wonder that the demon dactyl sought out these races for its minions. I tend to view the giants a bit differently, and wonder if they are, by nature, evil, or if they simply look at the world in a different way. A giant may look at a human and, like a hungry hunting cat, see its next meal. Still, as with powries and goblins, I feel no remorse in killing giants.

None at all.

Among the five races of Corona, then, I consider the humans most *shrouded in mystery. Some of the very best people in all the world—Brother Avelyn, as a prime example—were human, as were, and possibly are, some of the very worst tyrants. In general, my own race is a goodly one, but not as predictable and disciplined as the Touel'alfar, certainly! Still, in temperament and general beliefs, we are much closer to the elves than to the other three races.*

But those shades of gray . . .

Perhaps nowhere is the confusing concept of evil more evident than in the ranks of the Abellican Church, the accepted moral leader of the majority of humankind. Likely it is because this body has been entrusted with so high a standard, no less than to serve as the vanguard of human souls. An error in perspective among the Church leaders is a disastrous thing indeed, as Avelyn proved. To them he was a heretic, though in truth, I doubt there has ever been a man more godly, more charitable, more generous, more willing to sacrifice everything for the common good.

Perhaps the Father Abbot, who sent Brother Justice after Avelyn, can justify his actions—to himself, at least—by claiming them to be for the betterment of all. A master was killed in Avelyn's escape, after all, and Avelyn had no legal claim to the stones he took.

But the Father Abbot is wrong, I say, for though Avelyn might be technically labeled a thief, the stones were his on purely moral grounds. Having watched his work, even before he sacrificed himself to rid the world of the demon dactyl, I have no doubt of this.

The capacity of any individual to justify his or her actions will forever amaze me, I fear.

—ELBRYAN WYNDON

❖ 25 ❖

A Choice for Roger

By the time he neared the northern gate of Palmaris city proper, Roger Lockless and his grim luggage had attracted more than a little attention. Several farmers and their families, alert to anything moving in the area in these dangerous times, had noted the man's passage, and many even came out to follow him, pestering him with questions.

He offered few explanations all the way to the gate, grunting his answers to general questions, such as, "Did you come from the north?" or "Any goblins up there?" The farmers accepted the vague answers without complaint, but the guards at the gate proved much more insistent. As soon as Roger drew near and it became apparent he had two human bodies strapped across his hobbled horse, one of the two great city gates cracked open and a pair of armored soldiers rushed out to intercept him.

Roger was very much aware of the fact that other guards watching from the walls had their bows drawn and ready, and aimed at his head.

"Your doing?" one of the soldiers snapped, moving to inspect the bodies.

"Not that one," Roger quickly replied as the man lifted Connor's head, his eyes widening in recognition and horror.

The other soldier was at Roger's side in an instant, sword drawn and brought level with the man's neck.

"Do you think I would walk openly into Palmaris bearing the body of the Baron's nephew if I had killed the man?" Roger calmly asked, wanting these soldiers to understand that he knew the identity of the nobleman. "I have been called many things, but I do not number 'fool' among them. And besides, I considered Connor Bildeborough a friend. That is why, though I have other pressing business, I could not leave him on the road for the goblins and buzzards to pick over his corpse."

"What about this one?" snapped the soldier standing beside the horse. "He is from the abbey, is he not?"

"Not from St. Precious, no," Roger replied. "He is from St.-Mere-Abelle."

The two soldiers looked to each other with trepidation; neither of them had been among those sent to St. Precious when the trouble with the Father Abbot had begun, but both had heard well the stories, and that put a sinister spin indeed on their suspicions when viewing the two bodies draped across Roger's horse.

"You killed this one?" the soldier asked.

"I did," Roger replied without pause.

"An admission of guilt?" the other soldier was quick to interrupt.

"For if I did not, then he surely would have killed me," Roger finished calmly, looking the accusing soldier right in the eye. "I should think that, given the identity of these two, this conversation would be better served in the home of the Baron."

The soldiers looked to each other, unsure of how to proceed.

"Unless you think it better to have the common folk pawing over Connor Bildeborough," Roger added, a sharp edge to his tone. "Perhaps one will find proper use for Defender, or it might be that their rumors will reach the Baron, or the abbot of St. Precious, and who can tell what intrigue that might bring?"

"Open the gates," the soldier standing beside the horse called to the guards on the wall. He motioned to his companion, and the man put his sword away. "Be gone to your homes," he scolded the excited and whispering onlookers, and then he and his companion flanked Roger and started toward the city, grim baggage in tow. They stopped when they got inside the gate, other guards shutting it behind them. Out of sight of the farmers—for they weren't sure whether or not this stranger had any allies among those folk—they grabbed Roger roughly and slammed him up against the wall, frisking every inch of his body and removing anything that even resembled a weapon.

A third guard brought out blankets to cover the bodies, then took hold of the horse's reins and led the beast, while the first two grabbed Roger roughly by the elbows and half carried, half dragged him through the city streets.

Roger spent a lot of time alone in Chasewind Manor, the palatial home of Baron Rochefort Bildeborough. He wasn't physically alone, but the two grim-faced soldiers assigned to guard him seemed in no mood for conversation. So he sat and waited, sang songs to himself, even counted the boards of the hardwood floor three times, as the hours passed.

When the Baron finally entered, Roger understood the delay. The man's face was puffy, his eyes sunken, the hollow look of grief all about him. The news of Connor's death had hit him hard, very hard; apparently Connor had not been exaggerating when boasting of his standing with his uncle.

"Who killed my nephew?" Baron Bildeborough asked before he had even taken his seat in the chair opposite Roger.

"His killer has been delivered to you," Roger replied.

"The monk," Baron Bildeborough stated more than asked, as though that fact held little surprise.

"That man and one other of St.-Mere-Abelle attacked us," Roger began.

"Us?"

"Connor, myself, and . . ." Roger hesitated.

"Go on with your tale about Connor," Baron Bildeborough said impatiently. "The details will wait."

"In the fight, the monk's companion was killed," Roger explained. "And this monk was captured. Connor and I were taking him to you—we were on the very outskirts of the city—when he broke free and killed your nephew, a single thrust of his fingers to the throat."

"My healer tells me that Connor has been dead longer than your story would suggest," Baron Bildeborough put in, "if you then killed the monk, on the outskirts of my city."

"It did not happen quite that way," Roger stuttered. "Connor was dead immediately; I could see that, and so, being no match for the monk, I fled, taking Connor's horse."

"Greystone," said Rochefort. "The name of the horse is Greystone."

Roger nodded. "The monk would not give up his pursuit, and when Greystone threw a shoe, I knew that I would be caught. But I beat him with wits where my strength would not, and though I had only meant to capture him, that he might come back and stand open trial for his crimes, he was killed in the process."

"I have been told that you are long on wits, Roger Billingsbury," the Baron said. "Or do you prefer the name Lockless?"

The stunned young man had no reply.

"Fear not," Baron Bildeborough reassured him. "I have spoken with a former companion of yours, a man who holds you in the highest regard and made no secret to me of your exploits against the powries in Caer Tinella."

Still dumbstruck, Roger could only shake his head.

"By simple coincidence, I employ the daughter of a Mrs. Kelso on my staff," Rochefort explained.

Roger relaxed and even managed a smile. If Baron Bildeborough trusted Mrs. Kelso, then he had nothing to fear from the man.

"I warned Connor—what an impetuous and cocky young man he was!" Rochefort said quietly, lowering his head. "If the powries could get to Dobrinion, then none of us was safe, I told him. But this rogue monk," he added, shaking his head. "How could he have expected such an assassin? It makes no sense to me."

"No powries got to Abbot Dobrinion," Roger replied firmly, drawing the man's attention. "And this monk was no rogue."

The Baron's expression was caught somewhere between outrage and confusion as he looked directly at the surprising Roger.

"That is why Connor and I were coming fast to see you," Roger explained. "Connor knew that the monks, and no powrie, murdered Abbot Dobrinion. With the captured monk in tow, he thought he had his proof."

"A monk of the Abellican Order killed Dobrinion?" Rochefort asked skeptically.

"This is much bigger than Abbot Dobrinion," Roger tried to explain. He knew he had to be careful not to give away too much information about his three companions. "It is about stolen gemstones and a struggle within the Church powers. It is all beyond me," he admitted. "All too complicated concerning areas with which I have little knowledge. But the same two monks who attacked my friends and me in the northland killed Abbot Dobrinion. Connor was certain of that."

"What was he doing in the northland?" Rochefort wanted to know. "Did you know him before this incident?"

"Not I, but one of my companions," Roger admitted, and then he took a deep breath and took a chance. "She was married to Connor once, for a short time."

"Jilly," Rochefort breathed.

"I can say no more, and please, for her sake, for my sake, for all our sakes, do not ask," said Roger. "Connor came to warn us, that is all you need to know. And in saving us, he forfeited his own life."

Baron Bildeborough sat back in his chair, digesting all that he had heard, weighing it beside the recent disturbances at St. Precious concerning the Father Abbot and his fellows of St.-Mere-Abelle. After a long while he looked back to Roger, then patted an empty chair beside him. "Come and sit with me as a friend," he said sincerely. "I want to know everything about Connor's last days. And I want to know all about Roger Billingsbury, that we two might discern our best course of action."

Roger tentatively shifted to the chair closer to the Baron, taking more than a little hope in the fact that Bildeborough had referred to them as a team.

"That is him," Juraviel insisted, peering down from the hillock with his keen eyes. "I can tell by the awkward way he sits in the saddle." The elf gave a snicker. "It amazes me that a human as agile as Roger can appear so clumsy on a horse."

"He does not understand the animal," Elbryan explained.

"Because he chooses not to," the elf replied.

"Not everyone was trained by the Touel'alfar," the ranger said with a grin.

"Nor is everyone blessed with a turquoise stone that they might learn the heart of their mount," Pony added, giving Symphony a gentle stroke on the neck.

The horse nickered softly.

The three friends and Symphony went down from the hillock, moving at an angle to intercept Roger.

"It went well!" he called excitedly, delighted to have found them. He kicked his horse into a faster trot and pulled harder on the reins of the horse trailing behind him, a horse the companions had seen before.

"You saw Baron Bildeborough," Elbryan reasoned.

"He gave me the horses," Roger explained. "Including Fielder here," he added, patting the horse that had been Rochefort's favorite. It struck Roger then how generous the Baron had been, almost mentorlike.

"Greystone is for you," Roger said to Pony, pulling Connor's beautiful palomino ahead. "Baron Bildeborough insisted that Connor would want you to have him. And this," he added, taking a sword, Connor's magnificent blade, Defender, from the side of his saddle.

Pony turned her wide-eyed expression to Elbryan, who only shrugged and said quietly, "It seems fitting."

"But then the Baron knows of us," Juraviel reasoned in less content tones. "Or of Pony, at least."

"I did not tell him much," Roger replied. "I promise. But he needed answers—Connor was as a son to him, and the sight of Connor dead nearly broke him." He turned to Elbryan, whom he figured would judge his actions most critically of all. "I came to like the Baron," he said. "And trust him. I do not think he is an enemy of ours, especially considering the identity of Connor's killer."

"It seems that the Baron came to like Roger Lockless, as well," the ranger remarked. "And to trust him. These are no small gifts."

"He understood the message," Roger replied. "And the intent of the messenger. Baron Bildeborough knows that he is in dire straits when measuring his own strength against that of the Abellican Church. He needs allies as badly as we do."

"How much did you tell him of us?" Juraviel interrupted, his voice still stern.

"He did not ask very much at all," Roger calmly replied. "He did come to trust that I was a friend, and an enemy of his enemies. He asked nothing of your identities, other than what I offered about you," he finished, motioning to Pony.

"You did well," Elbryan decided after a few moments. "Where does it all stand now?"

Roger shrugged, fearing to face that question. "The Baron will not let the matter drop, of that I am sure," he said. "He promised me that we would take it to the King, if need be, though I believe he fears to incite a war between crown and Church."

" 'We'?" Pony asked, picking up the cue.

"He wants me to bear witness," Roger explained. "He bade me to come back to him presently, that we might plan a journey to Ursal, should his private conferences with some trusted monks of St. Precious fail to give him satisfaction.

"Of course I told him that I could not," Roger added, seeing the curious expressions.

Now Roger was confused, as those expressions turned from curious to disapproving.

"We are on to St.-Mere-Abelle, so I believed," Roger said. "Baron Bildeborough wants to be in Ursal before the turn of the season, for he has learned that a College of Abbots is to be assembled in mid-Calember and he is determined to speak with the King before Abbot Je'howith of St. Honce journeys north. Yet there is no possible way that I can go all the way to St.-Mere-Abelle beside you, finish our business there, and then return to Palmaris in time for the Baron's departure."

Still their expressions remained doubting.

"You don't want me to go!" a horrified Roger reasoned.

"Of course we do," Pony replied.

"But if the greater good will be served by having you at Baron Bildeborough's side, then there you should be," Elbryan added, both Pony and Juraviel nodding their assent.

"I have earned my place beside you," Roger protested, lapsing back into his childish nature once again, a prideful mindset which screamed at him that being left out was an affront. "We have learned to fight well together. It was I who killed Brother Justice!"

"Everything you say is true," Pony answered, moving next to the young man and draping her arm about him. "Everything. You have earned your place, and we are glad and grateful to have you beside us, and surely we would be the better off for your particular abilities as we try to make our way into St.-Mere-Abelle."

"But . . ." Roger prompted.

"But we do not think we can win," Pony answered bluntly, her candor catching Roger by surprise.

"Yet still you go."

"They are our friends," said Elbryan. "We must go. We must try every means possible to get Bradwarden and the Chilichunks out of the Father Abbot's clutches."

"Every means," Juraviel emphasized.

Roger started to argue, but stopped abruptly, closing both his eyes and his lips tightly as the point finally came through. "And if you cannot rescue them by force, then their only chance will come from an intervention by the King, or by those forces in the Church not under the Father Abbot's wicked influence," he reasoned.

"You may come with us if you desire," Elbryan said sincerely. "And we will be glad to have you along. But only you have spoken with Baron Bildeborough, and thus only you can decide which course is the most important for Roger Lockless."

"Only I can decide which course is the most important for Bradwarden and the Chilichunks," Roger corrected. He went quiet then, and the others did, too, allowing him his private thoughts. He wanted to go to St.-Mere-Abelle, to take part in this grand adventure. Desperately.

But his reason overruled that desperation. Baron Bildeborough needed him more than did Elbryan, Pony, and Juraviel. Juraviel could more than fill his niche as scout, and between Elbryan's sword and Pony's magic, any contributions he might make should battle find them would be nominal at best.

"Promise me that you will find your way back to me when you again pass through Palmaris," the young man said, choking up with every word.

Elbryan gave a laugh. "Could you doubt that?" he said lightheartedly. "Juraviel must come through or near to Palmaris on his road home."

"As will Elbryan and I," Pony added. "For when this is settled, when we again find peace, we will go back to Dundalis, our home, and Bradwarden's. And on our way, I must take my family back to Fellowship Way in Palmaris." Pony offered a quiet smile and hugged the man close, nearly pulling him from his saddle. "And even if our destination lay the opposite way, we would not leave Roger Lockless behind." She kissed the man on the cheek, drawing a deep blush.

"We each have our duties spread clear before us," Pony went on. "Two paths to defeat the one enemy. We will win out, and then we will celebrate—together."

Roger nodded numbly, too overcome to verbally reply. Elbryan came over and patted him on the shoulder, and he looked past the ranger, to see Juraviel offering a confirming nod. He didn't want to leave them! How could he go away from the first real friends—the first friends who had bothered to point out his faults as well as praise his talents—he had ever known?

And yet, precisely because of that, because these real friends were in dire trouble with the powerful Abellican Church, he knew he had to go back to Baron Bildeborough. Roger had known many trials in his life, but never before had he been asked by his own conscience to willingly sacrifice so very much. This time, unlike his jaunt into Caer Tinella behind the raiding Elbryan, his decision was motivated by altruism, and not jealousy, not fear of being outdone by the ranger. This time Roger acted out of love for Pony and Elbryan, and for Juraviel, the most blunt friend of all.

He said not a word, but took Elbryan's hand in a shake that became a hug, then took up Fielder's reins and rode away.

"He has grown," Belli'mar Juraviel observed.

Pony and Elbryan silently agreed; both were as upset by this farewell as was Roger. Pony slipped down from Symphony and went to Greystone; the ranger taking Symphony by the bridle, they walked the horses back to their small camp.

They packed what few supplies they needed and set out on the road south. Juraviel wrapped himself in a blanket to hide his wings and weapons, appearing as a young boy, and took a seat on Greystone behind Pony. They decided to go straight into Palmaris, through the northern gate, for, with the monsters retreating, the city had become more open of late, and they didn't believe they would be denied passage.

There was little conversation among them as they crossed through the northern outskirts, past the houses, most empty, but some with family returned. They actually caught sight of Roger on the road ahead of them several times, but thought it best to let him go in alone. Given what had just transpired between Roger and Baron Bildeborough, approaching the gate beside him would cause unwanted attention.

So much so that, on Juraviel's advice, they decided to set camp outside the city that night, to wait a day and let all thoughts of Roger Lockless pass from the minds of the city guards.

Still, things were quiet between them, and Elbryan in particular seemed in a somber mood.

"Is it Bradwarden?" Pony asked him as they ate supper, a fine stew of coneys Juraviel had shot.

The ranger nodded. "I was remembering his days in Dundalis, before you returned," he admitted. "Or even back before that, when you and I were on the northern slope awaiting our fathers' return from the hunt, when we heard the music of the Forest Ghost."

Pony smiled, recalling that long-past, innocent time. She understood the source of Elbryan's melancholy to be more than simple nostalgia, though, understood, and surely empathized with, the pangs of guilt that resonated through her lover's every word.

Juraviel, sitting off to the side, recognized it, too, and was quick to jump into the conversation. "You thought he was dead," the elf remarked.

Both Pony and Elbryan turned to regard him.

"To blame yourselves is foolish," Juraviel went on. "The mountain fell on him, so you believed. What were you to do, begin digging your way back in with your bare hands? And you, Nightbird, with your arm torn and broken?"

"Of course we do not blame ourselves," Pony argued, but her words sounded hollow, even to her.

"Of course you do!" Juraviel replied with a burst of mocking laughter. "That is the way with humans—and too often for my taste, their self-blame is justified. But not this time, and not with you two. You did all that you could, loyally, valiantly. Even with all you have heard, you doubt that it could be Bradwarden."

"The evidence seems solid," Elbryan remarked.

"But so does the evidence that the centaur was killed," Juraviel replied. "There is something to this which you do not understand, and rightly so, for if it is indeed Bradwarden, then some force beyond your comprehension has kept him alive—or has brought him back from the dead. True?"

Elbryan looked to Pony, then both turned back to Juraviel and nodded.

"That alone should alleviate your guilt," the elf reasoned, catching them in his logic trap. "If you were so certain that Bradwarden was killed, then how can you be blamed, by others or by yourselves, for leaving that foul place?"

"True again," Elbryan admitted, managing a smile, glad indeed that the wisdom of the Touel'alfar remained by his side.

"Then look not to the road behind," Juraviel said. "But to the road ahead. If it is indeed Bradwarden, if he is indeed alive, then he needs you now. And when we are done, when the centaur is freed, how much better all the world shall be."

"And we can return to Dundalis with him," Pony put in. "And all the children of those who return to that town to rebuild will know the magic of the song of the Forest Ghost."

Now they were at ease. They finished their dinner, speaking of the days they would know when this dark road was traveled and put well behind them, speaking of their plans when peace again reigned in Honce-the-Bear, when the Timberlands were reclaimed, when the Church was put aright.

They went to sleep early, vowing to make the gates before the break of dawn, and both Pony and Elbryan slept soundly, their elven friend keeping a watchful guard.

❖ 26 ❖

The Newest Abbot

A frustrated and angry Master Jojonah shuffled down the main hallway in the upper level of St.-Mere-Abelle, the long and grand corridor running along the top of the cliff wall overlooking All Saints Bay. Windows were spaced every few feet to the monk's right, the eastern view, while the left-hand wall was dotted sporadically by wooden doors layered with carvings of intricate detail. Each door told a separate story, one of the fables that formed the basis of the Abellican Church, and usually Jojonah, who had only fully examined a score of the fifty doors in all his decades at St.-Mere-Abelle, would pause and look at a portion of yet another. After an hour of perusal, he might have fully scrutinized a six-inch-square block, reflecting on all of the hidden meanings. This day, though, feeling particularly foul, and in no mood for reflections on his strayed Order, the master just put his head down and rambled on, chewing his lips to keep from mumbling aloud.

He was taken by complete surprise, then, when a man blocked his path. He jumped back, startled, then looked up into the smiling face of Brother Braumin Herde.

"Brother Dellman is doing well," the younger monk informed him. "They believe he will live, and will walk again, though not smoothly."

Master Jojonah didn't blink, his expression holding that angry stare and focusing it, not quite intentionally, on Brother Braumin.

"Is something wrong?" Braumin asked.

"Why would I care?" Jojonah blurted before he could consciously formulate a reply. He silently chastised himself immediately, using the unintentionally sharp retort as a personal lesson concerning just how angry and out-of-control he had become. He had erred badly because of that anger and frustration, had pushed Markwart too far. Of course he cared about Brother Dellman! Of course he was glad that the sincere young man was healing well. And of course, Master Jojonah did not want to take his outrage out on Brother Braumin Herde, in effect, his closest friend. He looked at the hurt and surprised expression on Braumin's face, and formulated an apology.

Jojonah quickly bit back that reply, though, conjuring another image of Brother Braumin, one of the man lying lifeless in a wooden box. That image surely shook the old man, as painful a thought as a father might have for one of his children.

"Brother Braumin, you assume much," Jojonah went on instead, keeping his voice sharp, and loud.

Braumin glanced around nervously, fearing they might be overheard, for there were indeed other monks in the long corridor, though none in the immediate area.

"Brother Dellman was injured badly," Jojonah elaborated. "Through his own foolishness, I have been told. Well, men die, Brother Braumin. It is the greatest truth, the one inescapable fact of our existence. And if Brother Dellman had died . . . well, so be it. Better men than he have gone before."

"What nonsense is this?" Brother Braumin dared to ask, quietly, calmly.

"The nonsense of your self-importance," Jojonah snapped right back at him. "The nonsense to believe that any one man can make a difference, a real difference, in the course of human events." The master snorted and waved his hand dismissively and started by. Brother Braumin reached out to grab him, but Jojonah roughly shoved the arm away.

"Get on with your life, Brother Braumin," Jojonah scolded. "Find meaning where you will and secure your own little corner of the too-big world!"

Jojonah pounded off down the corridor, leaving poor Braumin Herde standing perplexed and wounded to his heart.

And Jojonah, too, was hurting. In the midst of his little speech he had almost succumbed to the despair he was spouting. But it was all for a noble purpose, he reminded himself now, finding again his inner center of harmony, throwing out all the bluster and a good deal of his anger in a great mental belch. He had berated Braumin, loudly, publicly, because he loved the man, because he wanted the man to keep away from him long enough for him to be far along the road with Master De'Unnero before Braumin even figured out that he was gone.

That was the safest course, Jojonah knew, given Markwart's foul mood and increasing paranoia. Braumin had to lay low for the time being, perhaps for a very long time. Given the "accident" that befell Brother Dellman, the course Jojonah had set Braumin on, with his talk of Avelyn and the faults of the Church and his visit to Avelyn's sacred grave, suddenly appeared to Jojonah as incredibly selfish. Battered by his own conscience, he had needed Braumin's support, and thus, in his desperation, had pulled the man into his secret little war.

What consequences that might hold for Brother Braumin Herde stung Jojonah profoundly now. Markwart had won, it seemed, and he had been a fool all along to believe he could beat the powerful man.

The blackness of despair crept up around him again. He felt weak and sick, the same sickness he had known on the road to Ursal, as the strength and righteous determination ebbed away.

He doubted he would live to see the great doors of St. Precious.

Master Jojonah's brutal treatment left Brother Braumin standing stunned in the long corridor. What could possibly have happened to so turn the master around?

Brother Braumin's eyes widened; he wondered if that had indeed been Master Jojonah he had been speaking with, or if, perhaps, Markwart, or even Francis, had taken control of the man's body.

Braumin calmed quickly, dismissing the notion. Possession was difficult enough on the unsuspecting who had never been trained in the use of the stones. Since Jojonah could use the soul stone, and use it well, he had definitely learned how to manipulate his spirit in such ways that would prevent such intrusion.

But what, then, had happened? Why had the master, after all these days, spoken so angrily and rudely to him? Why had the master practically disavowed all that the two of them had tried to accomplish, all that they considered Avelyn to stand for?

Braumin thought of poor Dellman and the unfortunate "accident." Whispers among the younger monks hinted that it was no accident at all, but rather a coordinated maneuver by De'Unnero and the other two monks who had been working on the wheel with Dellman. And that line of thought led Braumin to only one answer: perhaps Jojonah was protecting him.

Braumin Herde was wise enough, and understanding enough of gentle Master Jojonah, to put aside his hurt and believe that to be the case. But still, it made little sense to him. Why would Master Jojonah change his mind now? They had already discussed in length the course this quiet rebellion must take, and that course was not one of great risk for Brother Braumin.

The monk was still standing in the long corridor, staring out the window at the dark waters of the cold bay below, musing over the possibilities, when a sharp voice from behind startled him. He turned to face Brother Francis, and in glancing around, had the distinct feeling that the monk had not been far away all along. Perhaps Jojonah had known of Francis' spying, Braumin hoped.

"Saying your farewells?" Francis asked, smirking with every word.

Braumin looked back to the window. "To whom?" he asked. "Or to what? The world? Did you think I meant to jump out? Or perhaps you were only hoping as much."

Brother Francis laughed. "Come now, Brother Braumin," he said. "We really should not be arguing amongst ourselves. Not when such possibilities loom before us."

"I admit that never have I seen you in so fine a mood, Brother Francis," Braumin replied. "Has someone died?"

Francis let the sarcasm slide off his shoulders. "It is likely that you and I will be working together for many years to come," he said. "We really must learn more of each other if we are to properly coordinate the training of first-year students."

"First-year students?" Braumin echoed. "That is a job for masters, not immaculates . . ." As soon as he heard his own words, Brother Braumin could see where this all was leading, and he didn't care for the path at all. "What do you know?" he asked.

"I know that there will soon be openings for two masters at St.-Mere-Abelle," Francis said smugly. "Since few of the present group seems worthy, the Father Abbot will be left with difficult decisions, perhaps even waiting until those worthy in my class are promoted to immaculate in the spring. I had thought that your ascension to master would be assured, given that you are the highest-ranked immaculate and were chosen as second on the most important mission to Aida, but truthfully, it seems a bit doubtful." He finished with another laugh and turned to leave, but Braumin wouldn't let him get away that easily. He grabbed Francis roughly by the shoulder and spun him about.

"Another mark against you?" Francis asked, eyeing Braumin's hand on his shoulder.

"What two masters?" Braumin demanded. He could guess easily enough that one of the departing masters would be Jojonah.

"Did not your mentor tell you?" Brother Francis replied. "I did see you speaking with him, did I not?"

"What two masters?" Braumin demanded more urgently, tugging hard on Francis' robe as he spoke.

"Jojonah," Francis answered, straightening and pulling away.

"How?"

"He is to depart on the morrow for St. Precious, to accompany Master De'Unnero, who will become the new abbot," Francis was all too happy to explain, and he did indeed enjoy the crestfallen expression on Brother Braumin's face.

"You lie!" Braumin yelled. He fought hard to hold control, reminding himself that he should not openly appear distressed by Jojonah's departure. But this was more than he could bear. "You lie!" he said again, shoving Francis so hard that the man nearly fell to the floor.

"Ah, my temperamental Immaculate Brother Braumin," Francis scolded. "Another mark against your possible promotion, I fear."

Braumin wasn't even listening. He shoved past Francis and started down the corridor, first in the direction Jojonah had gone, but then, too hurt and confused to even think of confronting the man at that time, he spun about and walked briskly, then broke into an open run, to his private room.

Brother Francis watched it all with great amusement.

Despite his protests, Brother Braumin knew that Francis was not lying. The Father Abbot had struck against Master Jojonah, it seemed, in a way that was at least as effective as Brother Dellman's accident. With Master Jojonah far away in St. Precious, an abbey whose stature had been greatly diminished by the death of revered Abbot Dobrinion, and under the watchful eye of wicked De'Unnero, Father Abbot Markwart had all but neutralized the man.

Now Braumin better understood the treatment Master Jojonah had given him in the corridor, the abrupt dismissal and disclaimer of all they had hoped to achieve. Braumin realized that the man was defeated and despairing, and so he put aside his own hurt and anger and sought out Jojonah, going to the master's private room.

"I find it difficult to believe that you would be stupid enough to come here," Jojonah greeted him coldly.

"I should desert my friends when they need me most?" Brother Braumin asked skeptically.

"Need you?" echoed an incredulous Jojonah.

"Blackness has come to your heart and spirit," Braumin pressed. "I see your pain clearly on your face, for I, above all others, know that face."

"You know nothing, and babble like a fool," Jojonah scolded, and truly it hurt him to speak so to Braumin. He reminded himself that it was in the young monk's own interest, and so he pressed on. "Now be gone, back to your duties, before I report you to the Father Abbot and he pushes you even further down the list of promotions."

Brother Braumin paused and considered the words carefully, and then he came to a new understanding. Jojonah talked of the list of promotions and his place on it, and relating that to their last discussion before they had met in the corridor, Brother Braumin could then see another course that the older man was following.

"I had thought that despair had defeated you," he said quietly. "I came to you only because of that."

His change in tone profoundly affected Jojonah. "Not despair, my friend," he said comfortingly. "Only pragmatism. It would seem that my time here is ended, and that my road to Brother Avelyn has taken an unforeseen twist. That bend may make my journey longer, but I'll not stop walking. However, it would seem that our time of walking together has reached its end."

"Then what am I to do?" Braumin asked.

"Nothing," Master Jojonah replied somberly, but without hesitation, for he had thought through this situation quite carefully.

Brother Braumin gave an incredulous, even derisive, snort.

"The situation has changed," Master Jojonah explained. "Ah, Braumin, my friend, I blame myself. When I learned of the plight of the Father Abbot's unfortunate prisoners, I could not keep away."

"You went to them?"

"I tried to go to them, but was stopped, and roughly so," Jojonah explained. "I underestimated the Father Abbot's reaction. In my foolhardiness, I overstepped the bounds of good sense, and have pushed Markwart too, too far."

"Never could compassion be called foolhardy," Brother Braumin was quick to put in.

"But still, my actions have forced Markwart to act," Jojonah replied. "The Father Abbot is too strong and too entrenched. I have not lost my heart or my way, I assure you, and I will go against Markwart openly when I deem the time is right, but you must promise me here and now that you will take no part in that battle."

"How could I ever make such a promise?" Brother Braumin firmly replied.

"If you ever loved me, you will find the way," Master Jojonah replied. "If you believe in what Avelyn says to us from his grave, you will find a way. Because if you cannot make that promise, then know that my road has reached its end, know that I will not follow the course of opposing Markwart. I must be alone in this; I must know that no one else will suffer for my actions."

There came a long pause, and finally Brother Braumin nodded. "I will not interfere, though I feel that your request is ridiculous."

"Not ridiculous, my friend, but practical," Master Jojonah replied. "I will go against Markwart, but I cannot win. I know that, and so do you, if you can put your bravado aside and be honest with yourself."

"If you cannot win, then why raise the fight?"

Jojonah gave a chuckle. "Because it will weaken Markwart," he explained, "and publicly raise issues which may find a root of truth in the hearts of many in the Order. Think of me as Brother Allabarnet, planting seeds in the hope that, in days when I am no more, they will live on and bear fruit for those who follow my footsteps. Think of me as one of the original craftsmen at St.-Mere-Abelle, who knew that they could not live long enough to see their vision of the abbey fulfilled, but who went to their dedicated labors anyway, some spending their entire lives working on the intricate carvings of a single door, or cutting the stone for the original foundation of this magnificent structure."

The poetic words struck Braumin deeply but could not push him past his desire not only to wage battle, but to win. "If we truly believe in Brother Avelyn's message, then we cannot stand alone," he said. "We must take the fight—"

"We do believe and we will, in the end, win out," Master Jojonah interrupted, seeing where this was going and knowing it to be a fool's ending. "I must hold faith in that. But for both of us to go against Markwart now would set our cause far, far back, perhaps beyond retrieval. I am an old man, and feeling older by the day, I assure you. I will begin the war against Markwart, and against the current way of the Church itself, and that will perhaps entice some of the Order to begin looking at our routines, our supposed traditions, in a new light."

"And what is my place in this hopeless war?" Brother Braumin asked, trying to keep the sarcasm out of his tone.

"You are a young man, and will almost certainly outlive Dalebert Markwart," Master Jojonah calmly explained. "That is, forgoing any unfortunate accidents!" He didn't have to speak the name of Dellman to conjure the unpleasant images into Brother Braumin's mind.

"And then?" Braumin asked, his tone growing more composed.

"You will quietly spread the word," Master Jojonah replied. "To Viscenti Marlboro, to Brother Dellman, to all who will listen. Building on the little I will accomplish, you will find allies where you will, but take great care to make no enemies. And above all," Jojonah said, moving to a corner of the rug beside his desk, then pulling it back to reveal a secret compartment in the floor, "you will protect this." He took the ancient text out of the compartment and handed it to a wide-eyed Braumin.

"What is it?" the young monk asked breathlessly, understanding that he was holding something of great importance, that this old book was part of the reason for Master Jojonah's surprising decisions.

"It is the answer," Jojonah replied cryptically. "Read it quietly, secretly, and then hide it safely away and put it out of your thoughts. But not out of your heart," he added, patting Braumin's strong shoulder. "Play along with Father Abbot Markwart's games if you must, even to the extent of ambitious Brother Francis."

Braumin's face screwed up with incredulity.

"I am counting on you to become a master of St.-Mere-Abelle," Jojonah firmly answered that look. "And soon—perhaps even as my replacement. It is not out of the question, because Markwart wants to give open signs that he is waging no private battle against me, and our friendship is widely known. You must find your way to that spot and spend your years in ways that will place you in line for a position as abbot of one of the other abbeys, or perhaps even in line for the position of Father Abbot itself. Aim high, my young friend, because the stakes are so tragically high. Your reputation remains impeccable and impressive beyond Markwart's inner circle. When you have attained the pinnacle of your power, however high that might be, then secure your friends and decide how to continue the holy war that Brother Avelyn began. That might mean passing the book and the dreams along to a younger, trusted ally, and following a course similar to mine. Or the situation might call for you and your allies to openly wage the battle within the Church. Only you will know."

"You ask much."

"No more than I have asked of myself," Jojonah said with a self-deprecating chuckle. "And I believe that you are a finer man than ever was Jojonah!"

Brother Braumin scoffed at that remark, but Jojonah shook his head and would not back down. "It took me six decades to learn what you already have placed firmly in your heart," the old master explained.

"But I had a better teacher," Brother Braumin replied with a grin.

That brought a smile to beleaguered Jojonah's sagging face.

Braumin turned his attention to the book, holding it higher between himself and the master. "Tell me more," he insisted. "What is in here?"

"Brother Avelyn's heart," Jojonah replied. "And the truth of what once was."

Braumin eased the book back down in front of him and tucked it under his voluminous robes, close to his heart.

"Remember all that I told you of the fate of the *Windrunner*, and hold that in comparison to the former ways of our Order," Jojonah explained.

Braumin hugged the book even tighter, giving a solemn nod. "Fare well, my friend, my teacher," he said to Jojonah, fearing he would never see the man again.

"Fear not for me," Master Jojonah replied. "For if I were to die today, I would die contented. I have found my heart and the truth, and have passed that truth on to able hands. We will win out, in the end."

Brother Braumin came forward suddenly and wrapped the large man in a great hug, holding it for a long, long time. Then he turned abruptly, not wanting Master Jojonah to see the moisture that had gathered in his eyes, and rushed out of the room.

Jojonah wiped his own eyes and quietly closed the door behind the man. Later that day, he, De'Unnero, and a score and five young escorts set out from the great gate of St.-Mere-Abelle. It was a formidable force accompanying the would-be abbot, Jojonah noted, twenty-five monks—fourth- and fifth-year students, he recognized—wearing heavy leather protection and well-armed with sword and heavy crossbow. The old master sighed at the sight; he knew that this group was more to ensure De'Unnero's immediate and absolute dominance at St. Precious than to protect the would-be abbot on the road.

But what did it matter? Jojonah did not feel as though he had much fight in him; the road to St. Precious seemed imposing enough.

He hesitated as the gates of the abbey swung closed behind him, wondering if he should go back in and confront Markwart openly, should make his last stand here and now and be done with it, because he felt very mortal this day, as though he was running out of time.

But he felt weak and sick, as well, and did not turn about to go and find Markwart.

He lowered his head, in shame and out of sheer weariness, and gradually tuned in to the speech that sharp-tongued De'Unnero was giving to all the group, himself included. The man barked commands about how they would proceed, a marching order, protocol for the road, and he insisted from one and all, particularly from Jojonah, for he moved right up to stand before the man, that from this moment forward he be addressed as Abbot De'Unnero.

The title assaulted Master Jojonah's every sensibility. "You are not an abbot yet," he reminded the man.

"But perhaps some of you need practice with assigning me the title," De'Unnero retorted.

Jojonah held his ground as the man crowded forward.

"This comes from the Father Abbot himself," De'Unnero stated, unrolling a parchment with a snap of his arm. On it was written Markwart's latest edict, proclaiming that henceforth, Brother Marcalo De'Unnero would be known as Abbot De'Unnero. "Have you anything else to argue, Master Jojonah?" the man asked smugly.

"No."

"Just no?"

Master Jojonah didn't back down, and didn't blink, his gaze boring holes into the accursed document.

"Master Jojonah?" De'Unnero prompted, and his tone explained what he was waiting for.

Jojonah looked up to see that wicked smile, to see that De'Unnero was, in fact, putting him on trial in front of the younger monks. "No, Abbot De'Unnero," he said, hating every word, but realizing that this was not the fight he wanted.

With Jojonah put in his place, De'Unnero motioned for the procession to begin, and so they marched, in precise order, to the west.

It seemed to Master Jojonah that the road had just become much longer.

❖ 27 ❖

The Escape

"Τ hey are gone?" Father Abbot Markwart asked Brother Francis later that same afternoon, the old man remaining in his private room for most of the day, not wanting any confrontations with Master Jojonah, whom he suspected was on the very edge of explosiveness. He had pushed Jojonah right to that edge purposely, and then pushed him out of the way, for Markwart feared that the old master had some fight left in him, a public brawl Markwart did not want. Let Jojonah go to Palmaris and do battle with De'Unnero!

"Master . . . Abbot De'Unnero led them away," Brother Francis explained.

"Now the interrogation of the prisoners might commence in full," Markwart said, with such coldness that Brother Francis felt a shiver run along his spine. "Have you the enchanted armband that was taken from the centaur?"

Brother Francis reached into a pocket and produced the elvish item.

"Good," Markwart said with a nod. "He will need it to survive this day." He started for the door, Francis scurrying to keep up.

"I fear that the other prisoners will need it more," the young monk explained. "The woman, in particular, is looking gravely ill."

"They need it, but we do not need them," Markwart said ferociously, turning on the younger man.

"Perhaps someone could tend them with the soul stone, then," Francis stuttered.

Markwart's laugh pierced him to the heart. "Did you not hear me?" he asked. "We do not need them."

"Yet we'll not let them go," Brother Francis reasoned.

"Indeed we will," Markwart corrected, and before the smile could widen on the younger man's face, he added, "We'll let them go to face the wrath of God. Leave them alone in their dark holes."

"But Father Abbot—"

Markwart's stare silenced him. "You worry about individuals when all the Church is at stake," the old man scolded.

"If we do not need them, then why keep them imprisoned?"

"Because if the woman we seek thinks we have them, she may walk right into our grasp," Markwart replied. "It matters little whether they are alive or dead, as long as she thinks they are alive."

"Then why not keep them that way?"

"Because they can bear witness!" the Father Abbot growled, moving his wrinkled old visage right up to Brother Francis, nose-to-nose. "How might their tale be received? Will those listening understand the greater good served by their suffering? And what of the fate of the woman's son? Would you desire to answer to those charges?"

Brother Francis took a deep breath and steadied himself, reminded once again of the depth of the old Father Abbot's obsession, and of his own deep involvement. Again the young monk found himself at a crossroads, for in his heart, despite what his obedience to the Father Abbot and the Church might be telling him, he knew that this torture of the Chilichunks and the centaur was a wicked thing. Yet he, too, was inescapably a part of that wicked thing, and unless Markwart prevailed, his complicity would be revealed for all the world to see. The woman was sickly because her heart had broken on the road when her son had died.

"The woman's perception is everything," Markwart went on. "It matters not whether her parents are truly alive or dead."

"Whether they are alive or have been killed," Francis corrected aloud, though muttering it under his breath too low for the Father Abbot, who was stalking toward the stairs once more, to hear. The young monk took another deep breath, but when he blew it out, the flickering flame of compassion in his heart went dark yet again. This was a tasteless, nasty business, he decided, but it was all for the good, and he was following the edicts of the Father Abbot of the Abellican Church, the man closest to God in all the world.

Brother Francis picked up his pace, rushing past Markwart to open the doors to the stairwell.

"Pettibwa? Oh, Pettibwa, why don't ye answer?" Graevis Chilichunk called repeatedly. The night before, he had been talking to his wife through the walls of their adjoining cells, and though he couldn't see her, for the darkness was absolute, the sound of her voice had been comforting indeed.

Not that Pettibwa had offered much comfort with the content of her words. Grady's death had grown like a canker in the woman's heart and soul, Graevis knew, and though he had taken the brunt of the punishment, was battered and half starved, his old bones protesting his every movement—and with more than a few of them broken, he was sure—his wife was in worse shape by far.

He called out again and again, pleading with her.

Pettibwa couldn't hear him, for her thoughts and all her sensibilities were turned inward, were locked in the image of a long tunnel and a bright light at its end, in the image of Grady standing at the exit of that tunnel, holding his hand out to her.

"I see him!" she cried. " 'Tis Grady, me boy."

"Pettibwa?" came Graevis' call.

"He's showing me the way!" Pettibwa exclaimed, with more strength than she had shown in many, many days.

Graevis understood what was happening here, and his eyes widened in panic. Pettibwa was dying, was willingly leaving him and all this horrid world! His first instinct was to scream out to her, to bring her back to him, to plead with her not to leave him.

He remained silent; he caught himself in time to realize how selfish such a course would be. Pettibwa was ready to go, and so she should, for surely the next life would be a better place than this.

"Go to him, Pettibwa," the old man called with a trembling voice, tears streaming from his dull eyes. "Go to Grady and hug him, and tell him that I love him, too."

He went quiet then, all the world seemed to hush, so much so that Graevis could hear the rhythmic breathing of the woman in the adjoining cell. "Grady," she muttered once or twice, and then there came a great sigh, and then . . .

Silence.

Sobs shook the old man's broken body. He pulled against his chains with all his strength until one of his wrists popped out of joint and waves of pain made him lean back against the wall. He brought one hand in close to wipe the tears and snot from his face, and then, with strength that he didn't believe he still possessed, Graevis stood straight and tall. This would be his last act of defiance, he understood.

Concentrating, conjuring images of his dead wife to bolster his courage, Graevis tugged with all his might against the shackle holding that injured hand. He ignored the pain, pulling the hand tight into the shackle, and then on some more. He didn't even hear the crack of bone, but just pulled on, like a wild animal, tearing his skin, crushing his hand into the shackle.

Finally, after minutes of agony, the hand pulled free and Graevis' legs went weak beneath him.

"No ye don't," he scolded, lifting himself straight and turning for the remaining length of chain. In one movement Graevis leaped up over his extended hand, twisted and turned and threw that shackled arm up over his head so that when he came back down, the chain was looped about his neck. He was up on his tiptoes and could relieve the choking pressure.

But not for long, he knew as his legs began to weaken and his body slumped, the chain pulling tight about his throat.

He wanted to find that tunnel, wanted to see Pettibwa and Grady beck-
oning to him.

"I told you he was evil!" Father Abbot Markwart roared at Brother
Francis when they came upon the hanging man. "But even I did not understand the depth of it, apparently. To take his own life! What cowardice!"

Brother Francis wanted to agree wholeheartedly, but a nagging part of
his conscience would not let him dismiss it that easily. They had found the
woman, Pettibwa, in the adjoining cell, dead, and not by her own hand.
Francis could only assume that Graevis knew she had died, and that had
been the final burden, the one that pushed the battered old man past all
sanity.

"It does not matter," Markwart said dismissively, calming somewhat now
that the shock of it all had worn off a bit. Hadn't he and Francis just discussed this very probability? "As I explained to you upstairs, neither of
them had anything valuable left to tell us."

"How can you be certain?" Francis dared to ask.

"Because they were weak," Markwart snapped at him. "As this—" He
waved his hand at the limp form hanging against the wall. "—only proves.
Weak, and if they had anything else to tell us, they would have broken
under the strain of our questioning long ago."

"And now they are dead, all three, the family the woman Pony once
knew," Brother Francis said somberly.

"But as long as she does not know they are dead, they remain useful to
us," the Father Abbot said callously. "You will tell no one of their demise."

"No one?" Francis echoed skeptically. "Am I to bury them alone? As I
did with Grady on the road?"

"Grady Chilichunk was your responsibility by your own actions," Markwart snapped at him.

Brother Francis stuttered, searching for a reply but finding none.

"Leave them where they are," Markwart added, after he believed that the
younger monk had squirmed long enough. "The worms can eat them in
here as well as if they are buried in the ground."

Francis started to argue, tentatively this time, to point out the problem of
the stench, but he stopped short as he considered his surroundings. In
these untended dungeons the smell of a couple of rotting corpses would
hardly be noticeable, and would certainly not change the nasty aura of the
place. Still, to leave these two unburied without proper ceremony, particularly the woman, who had done nothing to facilitate her death, struck
Francis hard.

But he, too, was no longer on that holy pedestal, Francis reminded himself. His hands were not clean, and so, like all the other inconsistencies that
assaulted the man who would be Markwart's protégé, Brother Francis

shrugged it away, put it completely out of mind, blew out the candle of compassion yet again.

Markwart motioned to the door, and Francis noted the nervous edge of the movement. They had come to the Chilichunks first, and had yet to establish whether or not Bradwarden, who, by Markwart's estimation was the more important prisoner, was still alive. Francis hustled out of the cell and down the smoky, dirt and stone corridor, fumbling with his keys as he led the way to Bradwarden's cell.

"Be gone, ye dog! I got nothing to tell ye!" came the defiant call from inside as Francis, a very relieved Francis, put the key in the lock.

"We shall see, centaur," Markwart muttered quietly, wickedly. Then of Francis he asked, "Did you bring the armband?"

Francis started to pull the item from his pocket, then hesitated.

But too late, for Markwart saw the movement and reached over and took the armband. "Let us go to our duty," the Father Abbot said, seeming quite amused.

His lighthearted tone sent a shudder along the spine of Brother Francis, for he knew that with the enchanted band secured about his arm, the centaur was in for a long and terrible episode.

CHAPTER

❖ 28 ❖

When Duty Calls

The wind was brisk across the wide waters of the Masur Delaval as Elbryan, Pony, and the disguised Juraviel boarded the ferry in Palmaris, with Juraviel getting more than a few curious looks. Pony held him close, though, pretending he was her son—her ailing son, and since disease was a too common and much feared event in Honce-the-Bear, no one dared move too close.

In truth, Juraviel's moans held more than a little touch of realism, for the heavy blanket wrapped about him was sorely bending his wings.

The huge sails unfurled and the square-decked ship eased out of Palmaris harbor, wood creaking and waves snapping sharply against her low sides. There were more than fifty passengers standing about the wide and flat deck, with the crew of seven working methodically, lazily, having made this passage twice every day, when the weather permitted, for years.

"They say the ferry is a good place to gather information," Juraviel whispered to Elbryan and Pony. "People crossing the river are often afraid, and frightened people often echo aloud their own fears in the hope that another will speak comfort."

"I will move among them," Elbryan offered, and he slipped away from his "family."

"Yer boy sick?" came a question almost immediately when the ranger moved near a group of five adults, three men and two women, fishermen, by the looks of them.

"We have been in the north," the ranger explained. "Our home was sacked, as was our entire village. For a month and more we have been dodging powries and goblins, scraping for food where we might, going hungry more often than not. My boy, Belli . . . Belli ate something foul, a mushroom, I would guess, and has not yet recovered, nor may he ever."

That brought some sympathetic nods, particularly from the women.

"And where are ye going?" the same man asked.

"East," Elbryan answered cryptically. "And you?" he asked quickly, before the man could press the point.

"Just to Amvoy," the man replied, referring to the city across the water, the destination of the ferry.

"We all live in Amvoy," one of the women put in.

"Just visiting friends in Palmaris, now that it's all calmed down," the man added.

Elbryan nodded and looked away, out to the wide waters, the docks of Palmaris fast receding as the lumbering ship found some favorable and strong winds.

"Take care if ye're going beyond Amvoy," the woman offered.

"We are."

"To St.-Mere-Abelle," the fisherman reasoned.

Elbryan snapped an incredulous stare over the man, but was wise enough to hide it quickly, not wanting to give anything definite away.

"That's where I'd go if I had a sick boy," the man went on, and neither he nor his companions caught the expression on the ranger's face. "They say them monks got cures for anything, though they're not quick in giving them out!"

That brought a laugh from his companions, except from the woman who had been talking, who looked at the ranger earnestly. "Ye take care if ye're to go east of Amvoy," she said again, more deliberately. "There've been reports o' powrie bands roving the land. And them monsters're not to care for yer sick boy, don't ye doubt."

"And one nasty band o' goblins," the man added. "Rumor says they were left on their own by the powries, and now they're running scared."

"Nothing more dangerous than scared goblins," another man put in.

The ranger gave her a grateful smile. "I assure you," he said, "I am no novice in dealing with powries, or goblins." With that, he bowed and moved about the deck. He heard again people expressing concerns about roving bands in the east, but garnered nothing truly valuable.

He made his way around, coming back to Pony and Juraviel. The elf reclined with his blanket tightly wrapping him, while Pony was at work tending the horses, for Greystone, in particular, had grown quite uncomfortable with the ferry rolling in the rough water. The horse stamped his foot repeatedly, snorting and whinnying, and sweat was beginning to glisten about his muscled neck.

Elbryan went to him and took a firm hold on his bridle. He gave a powerful tug, straight down, and that steadied the horse momentarily. Soon enough, though, Greystone was right back to stamping and tossing his head.

Symphony, meanwhile, had calmed considerably, and when Elbryan found the moment to consider the stallion, and Pony bent low against Symphony's neck, her cheek to the magical turquoise, he understood. Pony had found communication with Symphony, an understanding, and managed to impress upon the spirited stallion the need for calm.

Greystone gave a tug that nearly launched Elbryan away. The horse tried to rear up, but the ranger dug in and pulled all the harder.

Several other people, a pair of crewmen among them, came over then, trying to help steady the beast, for a nervous horse on an open ship deck could be a dangerous companion indeed.

But then Symphony took control of the situation, pushing past Elbryan and laying his head across the top of Greystone's neck. Both horses snorted and neighed, Greystone stamped the deck again and tried to rear, but Symphony would have none of that, pressing down harder, even lifting one front leg over the smaller stallion's back, holding Greystone in place.

Then, to the amazement of all the onlookers, Elbryan and Pony included, Symphony came down from Greystone's back and nuzzled up to the horse, snorting and shaking his head. Greystone issued a few more protests, but they sounded halfhearted.

And then both horses were calm.

"Good horse," one man muttered to Elbryan as he started away.

Another asked if Elbryan wanted to sell Symphony.

"Avelyn's stone proves itself useful now and then," Pony remarked when the three friends were alone with the horses again.

"I understand the communication between yourself and Symphony, for we have each done that before," the ranger said. "But am I wrong in believing that Symphony actually conveyed your message to Greystone?"

"Something of that nature, so it would seem," Pony replied, shaking her head, for she had no practical answers.

"How full of arrogance you humans are," Juraviel remarked, drawing looks from both of them. "Does it so surprise you that horses can communicate with each other, at least in a rudimentary way? How would they have survived all these centuries if they could not?"

Elbryan and Pony, defeated by the simple logic, just laughed and let it go at that. The ranger's expression, though, changed quickly, back to serious.

"There is talk of powrie bands roving the eastern reaches of the kingdom," he explained. "And of one band of particularly troublesome goblins."

"Could we have expected any less?" Juraviel replied.

"From what I could gather, it would seem that our enemies east of the river are in similar disarray," the ranger went on. "The powries deserted the goblins, so say the rumors, and the goblins are on a rampage as much out of fear as out of their generally wicked nature."

Juraviel nodded, but Pony quickly added, "You mean that it would seem as though *some* of our enemies are in disarray. And by my estimation, neither goblins nor powries rank as our worst enemy at this time."

That painful reminder of their destination and the potential disaster they faced at the place quieted them all and cast a somber pall over the group. They spent the next, and last, hour of the voyage in relative silence, tending to the horses, and all were glad when the ferry at last docked in the small city of Amvoy.

The ship's captain, standing beside the entrance to the gangplank, reiterated warnings about goblins and powries to all the passengers as they disembarked, bidding them all take great care if they traveled out of the city.

Needing no supplies, the friends cut right through the walled city to the eastern gate, where again they were warned about potential dangers in the open lands beyond. Their passage was not hindered, though, and so they rode out from Amvoy that very afternoon, the two horses quickly putting miles behind them.

The terrain here was far less wooded than that north of Palmaris. The land was more cultivated, crisscrossed by wide roads, some covered in cobblestones—not that any were really needed, for the grassy fields were easily crossed. Paralleling the road from a safe distance, the group passed another town that same day, and though it wasn't walled, they could see that its defenses—archers on rooftops, even a catapult in the town square— were securely in place.

Farmers stoically working the fields paused to note their passing, a few even giving a friendly wave or calling to them an offer of a free meal. But the friends pushed on, and as the sun moved low in the sky, they came in sight of yet another town, this one much smaller than the previous, as the land was more sparsely populated the farther they moved from the great river.

They swung around to the east of the settlement and camped with the black silhouettes of the buildings visible in the distance, deciding to keep a watch for the townsfolk that night.

"How far do we have to go?" Juraviel asked as they sat around a low fire, eating their supper.

Elbryan looked to Pony, who had spent years in this area.

"A couple of days," she replied. "No more." She took a stick from the fire and scratched a crude map in the dirt, marking the Masur Delaval and All Saints Bay. "St.-Mere-Abelle is no more than a hundred miles from the river, if I remember correctly," she explained, and then she drew out the land farther to the east, marking Macomber Village and, finally, Pireth Tulme. "I was here, in Pireth Tulme, but after I met up with Avelyn, we went back to the river—not near to St.-Mere-Abelle, but along a course to the south of the abbey."

"Two days," Elbryan mumbled. "Perhaps three. We should begin to formulate our plans."

"There is little to decide," Juraviel said with cavalier flair. "We will walk up to the doors of the abbey and demand our friends be returned. And if they are not, and promptly, we will knock the place down!"

The attempt at humor brought grins, but nothing more, for all of them, Juraviel included, began to recognize how daunting this quest really was. St.-Mere-Abelle was home to hundreds of monks, they knew, many of them proficient in the use of the magical gemstones. If Elbryan, or particularly Pony, was discovered and recognized, the quest would be over, and quickly.

"You should not bring the gemstones into the abbey," Elbryan remarked.

Pony looked at him wide-eyed; her use of the stones was among their most potent weapons, and a valuable scouting and infiltrating tool, as well.

"They might detect any use," the ranger explained. "They might be able to sense the presence of the stones even if you are not using them."

"A surprise strike is our only chance," Juraviel agreed.

Pony nodded her agreement, not wanting to get into that debate just yet.

"And if we are discovered," the ranger went on in grim tones, aiming his remark directly at Pony, "you and I must surrender ourselves, loudly and publicly, calling for an exchange."

"The two of us for the release of the Chilichunks and Bradwarden," Pony reasoned.

"And then Juraviel will retrieve Avelyn's stones and go with them to the west, and then with Bradwarden back to Dundalis," Elbryan continued. "Then you take the stones back to Andur'Blough Inninness," he explained to the elf, "and bid your Lady Dasslerond to hold them forever safe."

Juraviel was shaking his head before Elbryan finished. "The Touel'alfar will not be involved in the matter of the stones," he said.

"You already are involved!" Pony insisted.

"Not so," said Juraviel. "I am helping friends, repaying debts, and nothing more."

"Then help us in this matter," Pony continued, but Elbryan, with his better understanding of the aloof elves, had already given up the fight.

"You ask for political involvement," Juraviel explained. "That we cannot do."

"I ask for you to uphold the memory of Avelyn," Pony argued.

"This is a matter for the Church to settle," Juraviel was quick to answer. "They, and not the Touel'alfar, must decide their own course."

"This is a matter for the humans to settle," Elbryan agreed, putting his hand on Pony's arm to quiet her. She looked him square in the eye, and he shook his head slowly, deliberately, conveying the hopelessness of such an argument.

"I would ask that you retrieve the stones and give them to Bradwarden," the ranger said to the elf. "Let him take them far away and bury them deep."

Juraviel nodded his agreement.

"And return Greystone to Roger," Pony went on. "And Symphony to the forest beyond Dundalis, his home."

Again the elf nodded and a long moment of silence ensued, broken only when Juraviel began to laugh suddenly.

"Ah, but a hopeful group we have become!" the elf said. "We are planning our defeat, not our victory. Is that as you were trained, Nightbird?"

Elbryan's smile widened across his face, shadowed with the stubble of a three-day-old beard. "I was trained to win," he said. "And we will find a way into St.-Mere-Abelle, and be out of the place with Bradwarden and the Chilichunks before the monks can ever know we were there."

They toasted that thought with raised food and drink. Then they finished their meal and went about organizing the camp and its defense, Juraviel going out to scout the night, leaving Elbryan and Pony alone.

"I fear this," Pony admitted. "I feel as though it is the end of the long road I began when first I met Avelyn Desbris."

Despite his earlier bravado, Elbryan could not disagree.

Pony moved close to him then, and he put his arms around her. She looked up into his eyes, slid up to her tiptoes and gently kissed him. Then she moved back, locking his stare with her own, the tension building. She came back and kissed him again, more urgently, and he returned the kiss, brushing his lips against her, feeling her strong back under the press of his arms, his hands massaging the muscles.

"What of our pact?" he started to ask, but Pony put her finger across his lips, silencing him, then kissed him again, and again, pulling him down to the ground beside her.

It seemed to Elbryan that they two were alone in the wide world, under the sparkling stars and with the gentle summer breeze blowing across their bodies, licking their exposed skin, tickling them, cooling them.

They were on the road early the next day, running their horses hard, as dawn pinkened the eastern sky before them. Any discussions of how they might get into St.-Mere-Abelle secretly fell apart before they really began, for they would have no practical understanding of the place until they had glimpsed it and seen its fortifications and its state of readiness. Were the doors opened wide for refugees from any nearby towns, or were they sealed shut, with dozens of armed guards patrolling the monastery's walls?

They could not know, and so, putting their discussion off until it could produce something tangible, they heightened their pace, determined to make the abbey by the next morning.

But then they saw the smoke, rising like demon fingers above a ridge lined with trees. All three had seen such plumes before, and knew it was from no campfire or hearth.

Despite the urgency of their mission, despite the high stakes, no one questioned their course. Elbryan and Pony together turned their mounts to the south, riding hard for the ridge, then up the grassy slope to the tree line. Juraviel, bow in hand, fluttered away from Greystone as soon as they made those trees, the elf climbing high to better scout out the area.

Elbryan and Pony slowed and dismounted, then walked over the lip of the ridge cautiously. Spread below them, along the main road in a bowl-shaped valley, was a caravan of wagons, laden with goods and turned into a defensive, roughly circular formation. Several wagons were burning, and Elbryan and Pony could hear the shouts from the men below, calling for water, or for preparation of the defenses. The pair could see, too, that many people were down, and the agonized screams of the wounded rolled up out of the bowl.

"Merchants," the ranger remarked.

"We should go down to them," Pony said. "Or at the least, I should, bringing the soul stone."

Elbryan looked at her skeptically, not wanting to use that stone, or any other, so near to St.-Mere-Abelle. "Wait for Juraviel's return," he bade her. "I see no dead monsters about the ring, and so it seems likely that this battle has just begun."

Pony nodded her agreement, though the wails of the wounded pained her greatly.

Juraviel was back soon enough, fluttering to a tree limb just above their heads. "The scene is both good and bad," the elf explained. "First and most importantly, the attackers were goblins, and not powries, a lesser foe by far. But they are four score in number, and preparing a second strike." He pointed across the dell, to the southern ridge. "Beyond the trees."

Elbryan, ever the tactician, and understanding goblins' ways, surveyed the area. "They are confident?" he asked Juraviel.

The elf nodded. "I saw few wounded, and none in argument of further attack."

"Then they will come in right over that ridge," the ranger reasoned, "using the down slope to speed their run at the merchants. Goblins never concern themselves about their own dead. They'll not expend the time or the effort to coordinate a more comprehensive attack."

"Nor will they have to," Juraviel added, looking down at the wagons and the pitiful attempt at defense. "The merchants and their guards cannot hope to hold them off."

"Unless we help them," Pony was quick to put in, and her hand subconsciously slipped to the pouch of gemstones, a motion Elbryan did not miss.

He looked Pony in the eye and shook his head. "Do not use the gems unless we absolutely need them," he instructed.

"Four score," Juraviel remarked.

"But they are only goblins," said the ranger. "If we can kill one of four, the rest will likely flee. Let us prepare the battlefield."

"I will go and watch the goblins," the elf said, and he disappeared from sight so quickly that both Elbryan and Pony blinked in disbelief.

The two led the horses around the dell, moving down across the road, out of sight of the merchant wagons, then up the southern slope to the tree line. "They are hungry and frightened," Elbryan noted.

"The merchants or the goblins?"

"Likely both," the ranger replied. "But I speak of the goblins. They are hungry and frightened and desperate, and that makes them doubly dangerous."

"So if we kill one in four, they will not run?" Pony asked.

The ranger shrugged. "They are too far from home, with no prospects of getting back. I suspect the rumors are true, that the powries deserted them out here, in a land filled with enemies."

Pony gave him a sidelong glance. "Do you intend to offer mercy?" she asked.

The ranger chuckled at the thought. "Not for goblins," he said firmly. "Not after Dundalis. I pray they do not flee, for then they will live to cause more sadness. Let four score come over the hill, and let four score die at our hands."

They were up to the top of the ridge by then, and the goblins were in sight, huddled on the side of a ridge half a mile to the south. There weren't many trees between the two positions and the goblins, but both Pony and Elbryan quickly discounted any ideas of spotting Juraviel as he made his way down to them. They turned instead to the tree line, to see what surprises they could put together for the oncoming horde. Pony moved to the underbrush, looking for young trees suitable for snares, while the ranger focused on one large and dead elm, precariously perched on the very edge of the ridge.

"If we could drop this in their midst, it would cause more than a little confusion," the ranger remarked when Pony moved to join him.

"If we had a team of plow horses, we might indeed," Pony replied sarcastically, for the dead tree was indeed huge.

But Elbryan had an answer to that. He reached into a pouch and took out a packet of red gel. "A gift of the elves," he explained. "And I think this trunk might be rotted enough for it to work."

Pony nodded. She had seen Elbryan use that same gel in Aida, to weaken a metal bar so completely that a single swipe of his sword had cut right through it. "I've already set one snare, and I can see possibilities for several more," she said. "Also, a few sharpened sticks in the underbrush might cause some havoc."

The ranger nodded absently, too immersed in his own work to even notice as Pony went back to hers.

Elbryan found the weakest point along the trunk and tested its width and give. He was convinced that with several mighty swings of Tempest, he could fell the tree, but that would not be good enough, for he would never find the time in the midst of a horde of goblins. But if he could properly prepare it now . . .

He took up his sword and gave a light chop, then fell back cautiously as he heard the responding crackles of buckling wood. Again he found the proper place and cut into the tree, and then again. He went to the packet next and tore it open, then smeared a line of the reddish substance—a mixture the elves used to weaken items—across the critical point, putting it in line with a pair of trees farther down the slope.

As he finished, Pony came back to him, riding Greystone. "We should tell them," she said, motioning toward the merchant caravan.

"They know that someone is up here already," the ranger replied.

"But they should know of our plans to help," Pony reasoned, "that they might properly prepare a complementary defense. We cannot hope to stop all the goblins, no matter how effective our traps and swords." She pointed down the slope to a stump barely visible above the tip of the tall grass. "The descent is steep there, and the lead goblins will be at full speed and in range of any bows the merchants might have," she explained. "That could be a critical point. If I can string a trip rope, we could slow the goblins' progress and allow the merchants many more shots."

"Three hundred feet," Elbryan replied, surveying the distance from the stump to the nearest cover.

"The merchants likely have that length of rope and more to spare," said Pony. She waited for his nod, then turned Greystone about and moved cautiously down the slope. Two-thirds of the way, less than fifty yards from the caravan and wide open in the grass, she noted the many bows leveled at her, though more and more were dipping low as the archers recognized that she was no goblin.

"My greetings," she said, moving right up to the wagons and addressing a heavy man wearing clothing of the finest fabrics, who seemed, by his posture, to be one of the leaders of the embattled band. "I am no enemy, but an ally."

The man nodded cautiously, offering no response.

"The goblins have not gone far, and are preparing to come back," Pony said, and she turned and pointed back up the slope. "From there," she explained. "My friend and I are preparing a few tricks for them, but we'll not stop them fully, I fear."

"When did this become your fight?" the merchant asked suspiciously.

"We always make battles against goblins our own," she replied without hesitation. "Unless you would prefer that we do not help, and let the four-score goblins swarm over you."

That took away a good measure of the man's bluster. "How can you know they will come from the south?" he asked.

"We know goblins," was Pony's reply. "We know their tactics, or lack thereof. They are gathered in the south, and have not the patience to swing about and coordinate an attack from several different directions. Not when they think they have their prey cornered and defeated."

"We'll give 'em a fight!" one archer declared, shaking his bow in the air, a movement followed only halfheartedly by the other ten or so holding bows. All told, the caravan could offer less than forty able-bodied fighters, Pony surmised, and a single score of bows, likely wielded by inexperienced and untrained archers, would hardly dent the goblin onslaught before hand-to-hand combat was joined about the wagons. Elbryan could fight goblins three against one, even four to one, with a reasonable expectation of victory, but to the average man or woman, a single goblin could prove too difficult a foe.

Pony knew that, and so, apparently, did the merchant, for his shoulders sagged. "What do you offer?" he asked.

"Have you any rope?"

The merchant nodded to a man nearby, and he ran to a wagon and pulled aside the tarp, revealing loops and loops of fine cord, thin and strong. Pony motioned for him to bring it. "We will try to even the odds," she explained. "And I will slow their charge there, along the line of that stump, well within range of your bows. Shoot well."

She took the rope from the man, then placed it on the saddle behind her and turned Greystone away.

"What is your name, woman?" the merchant asked.

"There will be time for such discussions later," she replied, kicking the horse into a fast canter to the stump.

Up on top of the hill Elbryan was putting the last touches on his array of traps. He made a lasso and tossed it high into the branches of the dead tree, looping it expertly out to the side, then tying it off on the horn of Symphony's saddle. Then he guided the horse to a thick copse far to the side and went about disguising the rope, not wanting to tip off the goblins.

"More company," he heard from above, Juraviel's voice, as he was just finishing.

The ranger looked up, peering intently, finally discerning the lithe form of the elf.

"To the east," Juraviel explained. "A band of monks, a dozen perhaps, approaching cautiously."

"Will they be here in time for the battle?"

Juraviel glanced to the south. "The goblins are already moving," he explained. "Perhaps the monks could get here in time if they hurried, but I saw no sign of that. They cannot have missed the smoke, but I do not know how anxious they are to join in the fray."

Elbryan chuckled, somehow not surprised. "Go and tell Pony," he instructed. "Tell her to keep the stones secure and unused."

"If the situation demands, she will not hold back the magic," Juraviel reasoned. "Nor should she."

"But if she does use them, I suspect we will be fighting a dozen monks soon after the goblins are dispatched," the ranger replied grimly.

The elf worked his way quickly along the edge of the ridge, taking care to stay out of sight of the men at the circled wagons below. He relayed the message to Pony, then rushed back into position, half flying, half climbing—for his small and fragile wings were getting sorely tired—into a tree even as the front-running goblins approached. With some relief, but not much surprise, Juraviel noted their helter-skelter formation, no more than a mob rushing into battle. As the three friends had hoped, the goblins did not pause as they crested the ridge, just rambled over the top and began their charge down the other side, not even taking the time to scout out the defenses of their intended prey.

And hardly noticing the misfortunes of some of their fellows, the elf realized, as a goblin tripped into one of Pony's snares, loosing the bent sapling. The creature shrieked, but it was hardly heard above the battle cries of its companions, and was flipped head over heels and sent spinning into the air, to hang helplessly a few feet from the ground.

Several goblins ran right past their caught companion, paying it no heed, other than to laugh at its misfortune.

To the other side another goblin shrieked in startlement and sudden pain as it plunged into one of the small, nasty trenches Pony had quickly dug and disguised. The creature's leg straightened violently, then bent too far forward, snapping the bone right below the kneecap. The goblin fell back, clutching its throbbing leg and howling, but again its comrades had no time for it.

And then a third went down, roaring in agony, its foot punctured by a carefully concealed spike.

Taking confidence in the goblins' inattentiveness, Juraviel took up his small bow and started picking out his shots. One unfortunate goblin stopped right at the base of the elf's tree, leaning on the trunk as it caught its breath. Juraviel's arrow plowed right into the top of its skull, stunning it, then dropping it to its knees, one hand still braced against the tree trunk. It died in that position.

For all the effort, though, only one in twenty of the goblins had been thus slowed, and the leading runners continued to charge down the grassy slope. Juraviel got another shot, hamstringing a goblin as it broke clear of the tree line, and then he looked out to the west, a bit farther down the hill, to the pair of trees where Nightbird prepared the largest surprise of all.

The ranger was down on one knee, behind the shield of trees, bow leveled horizontally between the trunks. He let the lead goblins get past the trap, trying to hit the main group. In addition to causing the most damage, this would bring the goblins in at the merchants in an even more scattered manner, a few at a time, he hoped.

A dozen goblins came through the trees at the same time, a dozen more right behind them.

Nightbird let fly, but his shot, true to the mark, was intercepted at the last moment by an unsuspecting goblin, the creature taking it in the side. Undaunted, even anticipating that something like that might happen, Nightbird had the second arrow away immediately, this one slipping through the press to drive hard into the prepared trunk.

At that same moment, the ranger gave a whistle to his trusted horse and Symphony lurched forward, pulling the rope taut.

The dead tree gave a series of tremendous cracking noises in protest, and many goblins froze in place, suddenly afraid.

And then it came sweeping down amongst them, tons of wood, dozens of long and wide sharp-ended branches.

Goblins dove left and right, screamed and scrambled, but the ranger's timing had been perfect. Three were killed outright, and many more, a dozen and four, were seriously gashed by splintering pieces, or slammed hard to the ground, or trapped under grabbing branches. About a quarter of the goblins had already gone beyond the area of the trap, and they kept up their run for the wagons. Of those caught in or behind the fallen tree, most simply scrambled on over the newest obstacle, too hungry for human blood to even consider the possibility that this might be an ambush, while others, confused and wary, milled about or searched for cover. That confusion, that breaking of any cohesive ranks, was exactly the outcome Nightbird had hoped for.

Not about to miss the opportunity, the ranger took up Hawkwing again, driving an arrow into a goblin that had wandered a bit too close, and then firing again, taking out a goblin as it tried to extract itself from the prickly branches.

Up the hill, Symphony tugged and pulled, breaking free the piece of the tree that was bound by the rope. One goblin moved near the heavy brush that concealed the great stallion, inspecting the commotion, but Nightbird promptly shot it down.

Symphony broke free of the copse, several goblins spotting him and giving a howl. Down the hill Symphony pounded, rushing to the ranger.

Nightbird, Tempest in hand, ran out to meet the horse, reaching around and cutting the rope with a single swipe of the magical blade. He pulled himself into the saddle, laying Tempest across his lap and readying Hawkwing yet again, fitting an arrow as he settled into his seat.

And how those closest goblins scrambled when they saw that bow come up their way!

Nightbird blew one down, and with a roar of defiance, he kicked

Symphony into a short burst that brought them right into the open, the ranger letting fly another arrow—and scoring another hit—as they went.

The closest goblins skidded to an abrupt halt, some of them hurling spears, but Nightbird was too quick for that, spinning Hawkwing in his hands, then swiping it about like a club, parrying the missiles harmlessly aside.

Up came the bow in a quick circuit, left hand gripping it solidly in the middle as the right fitted yet another arrow. A split second later another goblin went squirming into the dirt.

On the ranger charged. He got one more shot, then set Hawkwing across the saddle horn and took up Tempest, bearing down on a group of three. He turned Symphony hard to the side at the very last second and leaped from the saddle, landing in a roll, coming up in a short run and using the sheer momentum of his charge to drive his slashing sword right through a goblin's blocking club, and halfway through the creature's head, as well.

A snap of his wrist sent the goblin flying away, sent Tempest in a sudden spin back over Nightbird's hand. As the blade came around, he stabbed straight ahead, scoring his second kill, and he tore Tempest free and brought it about in time to block the downward-slicing sword of the third.

One against one, the goblin was no match for Nightbird. The ranger parried another blow, then a third, and this time he hit the goblin's sword so hard that it went up high. Nightbird stepped forward, inside the opening, and, still using Tempest to brace the goblin's sword above its head, he clamped his free hand about the creature's skinny neck.

The ranger drove on, bending the goblin over backward, the tremendous muscles in his arm bulging and cording. With a grunt and a sudden, vicious burst, Nightbird snapped the creature's neck, and dropped it dead to the ground.

More goblins were coming in about him; the ranger welcomed them.

The lead group of goblins heard the fighting but never bothered to look back, too intent on the apparently easy prey of the merchant caravan. Down the slope they ran, full speed, hooting wildly, hungrily. Arrows came out at them—one even went down—but that hardly slowed the fierce charge.

But then, suddenly, those in the lead were sprawling, flying headlong to the ground. More and more tumbled, the whole group becoming entangled and bogged down.

Off to the side, in the brush, Pony urged Greystone ahead, keeping the rope taut as goblin after goblin tripped across it. She had tied one end securely to the stump, then had strewn it across the grass to these trees, carefully noting the angle so that when the horse pulled, the rope would come up at the right height, just under a goblin's knee. Before she tied off the other end to her mount, she had looped it under an exposed root to prevent the jerking of the tripping goblins from affecting Greystone directly. Now the powerful stallion, straining forward, kept the rope taut.

From below, the two-score archers at the caravan had more time to pick their shots, at relatively stationary targets, and their next barrage was far more effective. Even worse for the goblins, those that got back up had lost their momentum, had to begin their rush anew from a standstill barely forty yards from the bowmen.

The merchants and their guards, though not true warriors, were not fools, and several were not firing arrows, but were holding their shots for whatever goblin ventured too near. The monsters came at the wagons in random order, one or two at a time, and without the panic-inspiring confusion of a rushing mob. Thus the archers were able to focus clearly and most of their shots rang true.

Pony knew that her job here was done. She reached back with her sword and cut Greystone free, then turned the horse about, thinking at first to charge out into the midst of those goblins still pulling themselves up from the grass. But then she looked back up the hill and saw her love in the midst of yet another group. Resisting the urge to take out her magical gems, she drove her heels hard into Greystone's flanks and the horse leaped away, thundering up the hill.

With the bulk of the goblin horde moving beyond the ridge, leaving the few dead and wounded behind, Juraviel could more freely pick his shots. At first he concentrated on those creatures battling the ranger, but as the extent of the disaster began to sink in to the goblins, several turned about and tried to flee, running back up over the hill, passing right below the elf's position with no intention of stopping, or even slowing.

Juraviel's bow hummed continuously, arrow after arrow stinging the frightened and fleeing monsters. He shot every goblin he could see, and had nearly emptied his quiver when one creature skidded to a stop at the base of his tree, hopping excitedly and pointing up at him.

Juraviel promptly drove an arrow into its ugly face, dropping it right beside its dead and kneeling companion. Then the elf shot two more of the creatures, who had come to see what the goblin was yelling about.

Juraviel reached back methodically for his quiver, to find that he had only one arrow remaining. With a shrug, he shot yet another, then hooked the bow over a jut in the limb, drew out his slender sword and moved lower in the tree, looking for the proper moment to strike hard.

He realized, though, that this fight was already nearing its end, for more than a score of goblins lay dead on the hill, another score were fast dying down by the merchant caravan, several had gone back over the ridge, and another substantial group were running full out down the slope, but angling to the east. The sight brought great hope to Juraviel, for these were the goblins of old, the cowardly, easily confused enemy that could not hold formation in the face of unexpected resistance. These were the goblins that, though much more numerous than the humans and elves of Corona, had never posed any organized threat of domination.

The goblins' eagerness to get at the exposed warrior waned fast as one after another fell dead at the end of Nightbird's glowing sword.

Fully surrounded by five, the ranger came ahead powerfully, then, seeing those before him falling back and knowing that those behind would be pressing forward, he quickly reversed his direction, spinning about with a powerful slash of his sword, knocking aside a swinging club and a stabbing spear. With the perfect balance of years of *bi'nelle dasada*, the ranger's feet shuffled fast, before those goblins now behind him could come in at his back, and with these two taken by surprise with his sudden shift, he scored a solid stab in the club-wielder's chest.

As that creature fell away, clutching its wound in a futile attempt to hold in its spouting lifeblood, its companion retracted its spear and let fly.

The throw was true, right for the ranger's head, but a subtle twist and duck, and Tempest flashing up diagonally, deflected it harmlessly over his shoulder—harmless for Nightbird, that is, for the missile's continuing flight caused those goblins behind the ranger to dodge aside frantically, slowing their progress, giving the ranger more time to press his newest attack.

The now unarmed goblin threw up its arms in a feeble defense. Tempest flashed three times repeatedly, the first slashing one arm aside, the second stabbing the other shoulder, dropping that defense, and the third going straight for the throat.

Nightbird spun about in time to defeat the charge of the remaining three, and was back in a low and balanced defensive crouch as two more replaced their fallen comrades, again surrounding the ranger, but this time seeming less eager to make the first attack.

Nightbird continued to turn about, ready to defend from every angle. Every so often he let Tempest out in a measured thrust, not to score a hit, but to entice those goblins behind the strike to come in. He thought to play on their mistakes, to let them lead and, inevitably, err, but then he came to a different understanding, a confident smile, so unsettling to the goblins, widening on his face.

They understood his contentment a moment later when Greystone thundered into their midst, plowing them aside, Pony's slashing sword chopping one and then another to the ground. At first the woman moved to rush right beside her love, even freeing up her hand so she could reach down and help him onto the horse behind her.

But the ranger was motioning for her to come down and join in the fun.

Pony threw her leg over the saddle, quickly reversing her feet so her closest foot was in the lone stirrup. She waited for two more goblins to dive aside in the face of Greystone's mighty charge, then she leaped free, slapping the horse to continue its run, and hitting the ground in a fierce charge.

One goblin stood between her and Nightbird, its sword out straight.

Pony's rush was too fast. She went down low and came up hard, her sword lifting the goblin's blade up high, sending it, along with a couple of goblin fingers, flying away. She continued her run, right beside the creature, turning the angle of her blade so it drove right through the goblin's chest as she passed.

The goblin squealed and got yanked about, Pony tearing the sword free, leading her charge with her bloody blade slashing wildly.

Nightbird had not been idle, moving with a ferocity that stunned his enemies, opening the way and positioning himself so Pony could get in to join him. In the span of a few seconds the lovers were standing back-to-back.

"I thought you would stay low on the hill to check on the merchants," Nightbird said, seeming not too pleased that Pony was with him in this dangerous situation.

"And I thought it was past time that I tried out this sword-dance you have been teaching me," she casually replied.

"Do you have the stones ready?"

"We will not need them."

The determination in her voice bolstered the ranger, even brought a smile to his face.

The goblins circled, trying to get a measure of these two. Their many dead companions lying about them vividly reminded them of the consequences of any foolhardy attacks. Still, they outnumbered Pony and Nightbird by more than five to one.

One creature hooted and rushed ahead, launching a spear at Pony. Up flashed her sword, at the last moment, deflecting the weapon high, over her shoulder, and taking most of its momentum. Pony hadn't cried out at all, but she didn't have to, for Nightbird, feeling her muscles against his back, recognized the movement as clearly as if he had made it. He half turned as the spear rebounded over Pony's shoulder, and a quick snap of his hand snared it. In the same fluid movement, the ranger brought the goblin spear past him and heaved it hard right into the chest of another goblin that had ventured too close.

"How did you do that?" Pony asked, though she had never even glanced back to see the movement.

Nightbird only shook his head, and Pony sensed it and went quiet, as well, the two of them settling more comfortably into their defensive stance. They felt an amazing symbiosis growing between them, as though they were communicating through their very muscles as clearly as if using open speech. Pony anticipated every twitch, every bend, of Nightbird's stance.

The ranger felt it, too, and was surely amazed by the intimacy. Despite his logical fears, Elbryan knew enough to trust in this strange extension of *bi'nelle dasada*. He did pause and wonder if the elves even knew that the sword-dance could be taken to this extreme. But his musing lasted only an instant, for the goblins were getting edgy, some skittering closer, another readying a spear as if to throw it—though the goblins across the way, having witnessed the first disastrous attempt, weren't pleased by that prospect.

Pony understood that Nightbird wanted her to go out to the left. A quick glance that way told her the reason: a particularly bold goblin needed to learn a swift and painful lesson. She look a deep breath, eliminating all doubts from her thoughts, for she knew that doubt would bring hesitation, and hesitation would bring disaster. This was the real meaning of their morning ritual, she realized, a dance as intimate as lovemaking, and now was the real test of their trust. Her love wanted her to go out to the left.

Nightbird felt the tension in her back, then the sudden lunge, and as she moved, he moved, rolling around, off her back foot, a complete pivot that took the two goblins rushing in at the apparent opening completely by surprise. The closest goblin was prodding out at Pony with its spear when Tempest slashed down, taking both its arms at the elbows.

The second goblin at least managed to get its club in the way, though the ranger merely slapped the blocking weapon aside and stabbed the creature hard in the belly.

Now Pony was moving, rolling over Nightbird's trailing foot, as he had gone over hers. And again, those goblins coming in at the apparent opening Nightbird's movement had caused were caught by surprise, and by Pony's slashing sword. One fell to the ground, grasping at its torn throat, while two others leaped into a short and hasty retreat.

And Pony and Nightbird were back-to-back again, crouched, in perfect defense and perfect harmony.

From the tree line, Belli'mar Juraviel watched in satisfaction as Symphony ushered the riderless Greystone to safety. Many times the elf had witnessed the intelligence of Symphony, but every time, as now, he was thrilled and awed by the display.

Even more awesome was the spectacle that Juraviel witnessed when he glanced back down to his human companions and saw the harmony of their movements, Pony and Nightbird complementing each other with absolute perfection. To the Touel'alfar, *bi'nelle dasada* was a personal dance, a private meditation of a warrior, but now, watching this, Juraviel soon understood why Nightbird had taught it to Pony, and why they danced together.

Indeed, at that moment on the grassy slope—a slope fast turning red with spilled goblin blood—Pony and Nightbird were as one, a singular warrior.

Juraviel realized that his bow should not be idle, that he should be helping out his friends. They hardly seemed to need it, though, playing off each other's movements so fluidly that the goblin circle was widening, not closing, and was thinning, the creatures giving more and more ground.

Juraviel did finally blink away his awe long enough to retrieve a single arrow, and his shot took a goblin in the back of the neck, just under the skull.

The line around Nightbird and Pony thinned considerably, with more goblins turning and running away than falling to the pair's harmonious dance. Pony scored a kill, and the ranger cut down a goblin stupidly going for her back again as she turned, but then it all seemed to come to a standstill, with no monsters venturing near enough for any attacks.

Nightbird sensed the mounting fear and tension, saw the goblins looking as much behind them now as ahead. They wanted to break and run off, every one, and the battle was about to enter its most critical stage. He started to explain as much to Pony, but she cut him short before he had hardly begun, saying simply, "I know."

And she did know, Nightbird recognized, from the subtle movements of her muscles as she dug herself in, finding balance and positioning her legs for a fast shift.

The spears came in at them in no coordinated fashion; the first goblin let fly, turned and fled, and a shower of missiles followed, the creatures using the barrage to cover their flight.

Nightbird and Pony spun and dove, came up with sword slashing, deflecting and dodging. There was no pause on the part of the ranger or his companion as they came through the volley unscathed, each rushing out at the closest goblins, cutting them down and running on to the next in line. No longer did the two work in concert, but neither did any of the goblins, so every fight became an individual contest. Pony worked her sword marvelously, weaving circles about her opponent until she found an opening, and then striking true, a measured thrust, her second or third hit usually finishing the task.

Nightbird, stronger and more skilled, was less finesse and more sheer power. As goblins raised their weapons to block, he merely smashed through the defense, and usually through the goblin in the same deadly strike. He darted back and forth, rushed ahead and turned completely about, whatever was needed to bring him to his next kill. The goblins should have calmed and organized a coordinated resistance, but they were stupid creatures, and frightened.

They died quickly.

Those few who managed to get up the hill to the tree line ahead of the ranger found yet another foe, a lithe little creature, hardly as tall as a goblin, wielding a sword so slender that it seemed more fitted to a dinner table than a battleground.

The leading goblin swerved to meet this newest foe, thinking it to be a human child, thinking to score a quick kill.

Juraviel's sword smacked against the tip of the goblin's blade, once, and then three more times, so rapidly that the creature had no time to react. And each time, the elf inched ahead, so that when the fourth parry rang out, Juraviel was only a foot from the surprised goblin.

The elf's sword flashed again in rapid succession, once, twice, thrice, driving three holes into the goblin's chest.

Out charged Juraviel, meeting the next, this one unarmed, having thrown its spear at the ranger. The goblin held up its hands.

Belli'mar Juraviel of the Touel'alfar had no mercy for goblins.

The rout on the slope ended at about the same time as the rout at the wagons. The lead group of goblins, the ones Pony had tripped up, fell dead to the last without ever getting into the ring.

There remained one more substantial group, though, running down the road to the east, out of the dale.

Pony spotted Juraviel first, sitting calmly on a low branch up the hill, wiping the blood off his sword with a rag of goblin clothing.

"I counted four who passed beyond me," he called down to his friends. "Taking full flight down the back side of the ridge."

Nightbird whistled, but Symphony was moving to him before he made a sound.

"Are none to get away to carry on the legend of the Nightbird?" Pony teased him as he reached for the saddle. In the northland war, Nightbird had often let one or two monsters run away, to whisper his name in fear.

"These goblins will only cause more mischief," the ranger explained, swinging himself up. "There are too many innocents around whom they might harm."

Pony looked at him quizzically, then to Greystone, wondering if she should join him.

"Keep watch on the merchants," the ranger explained. "They will likely need your talents at healing."

"If I see one close to death, I will use the soul stone," Pony explained.

The ranger conceded the point.

"And what of them?" Pony asked, pointing to the band fleeing to the east. There had to be at least a score of the creatures, maybe thirty or more.

The ranger considered their course and gave a chuckle. "It would seem that the monks may yet be involved," he said. "If not, we will hunt that band down when we are finished here. Our road is east anyway."

He was off before Pony even nodded her assent, thundering Symphony up the ridge and down the back side, preparing Hawkwing as he went. He spotted the first of the goblins running through the grass and closed the distance quickly, meaning to go right past the creature and use his sword. Then he caught sight of the second, running in a completely different direction; the group had scattered.

No time for Tempest, the ranger decided, and up came his bow.

Only three remained.

❖ 29 ❖

Hungry for Battle

"If we join in prayer, a single stroke of God's lightning hand will destroy them all," offered one young monk, who had also been on the expedition to Aida, including the battle outside the Alpinadoran village.

Master De'Unnero's sharp eyes narrowed as he considered the monk and the assenting nods of those nearby, men who had heard the tale of the great victory in the northland, the tale of sparking fingers reaching down from the line of monks to utterly vanquish their enemies.

There was something else inspiring them, too, De'Unnero recognized. Fear. They wanted a clean and quick blow against the approaching goblin force because they were afraid of engaging these relatively unknown creatures in melee. The would-be abbot strode powerfully up to the speaker, his gaze setting the man back on his heels, draining the blood from his face. "Master Jojonah alone will use the magic," he snapped, his head jerking side to side so that all could see his expression, so that none would dare question him. "He is too old and infirm to fight."

Looking at the wretched man, Jojonah had an almost irresistible urge to rush over and prove him wrong.

"As for the rest of us," De'Unnero went on, barking the words, "let us consider this an exercise of valuable training. We may yet see battle in our new home in Palmaris."

"This 'training' could be deadly," Master Jojonah piped in, and the measure of calm in his quiet voice only added to the sarcasm.

"All the more valuable, then," De'Unnero said without hesitation, and when he saw Jojonah shaking his head, he stormed over to stand before him, crossing his strong arms defiantly over his chiseled chest.

Not now, Master Jojonah reminded himself quietly, not wanting to embarrass the man, for that would only make De'Unnero dig in all the more. "I beg of you to be done with this approaching band efficiently and cleanly," he said. "Let us blast them away, a single, combined stroke of lightning, and go see to whoever is beyond that rise." He pointed behind De'Unnero as he finished, to the plume of black smoke still drifting lazily into the air.

In response, De'Unnero handed him a piece of graphite, a single stone. "Use it well, brother," he said. "But not too well, for I wish to have my new attendants properly trained in the pleasures of battle."

"Pleasures of battle?" Jojonah echoed, but under his breath, as De'Unnero spun away, calling to the brothers to ready their crossbows. The old master could only shake his head in disbelief. He rubbed the graphite about his palm, thinking to hit the goblin troupe hard and fast, to kill them or scatter them, that few, if any, of the younger monks would see any real battle. His rubbing became more urgent when the forward scout signaled back that the goblins were approaching, for Jojonah could not feel the power of the stone.

The master fell within himself, seeking that special place of magic—in his mind, that special place of God. He dismissed thoughts of De'Unnero, believing that such negativity might be having an adverse effect. And he rubbed the graphite about his fingers, felt its every groove.

But not its magic. Jojonah opened his eyes to find he was alone in the road. Near panic, he glanced around, and then relaxed somewhat, seeing that De'Unnero had positioned the others in the brush to the side. The lead goblins were in sight now, running hard around a bend in the road. Jojonah looked down at the graphite, incredulous, feeling betrayed.

The goblins came on, their rush changing from one of retreat to a hungry charge.

Jojonah lifted his arm and closed his eye, calling to the stone.

Nothing, no lightning, came forth, not even a sparkle, and the goblins were closer now. Jojonah tried again, but found no source of magic within that graphite. Then he understood the truth of it, that this stone was not enchanted, was just an ordinary rock. Fear gripped Jojonah; he thought that De'Unnero had set him up to die, here on the road. He was an old man and had no weapon, and could not possibly do battle! He gave a cry and turned about, hobbling as fast as his thick legs would take him.

He heard the goblins howling, closing. He expected a spear to take him in the back at any moment.

But then De'Unnero and the brothers struck hard at the goblin mob, monks leaping up from the brush at the sides of the road, firing heavy crossbows designed to take down powries, or even giants, point-blank. Thick bolts tore through goblin flesh, blasting holes in the diminutive creatures, and sometimes even in goblins behind the first victim. The goblin mob was leaping, spinning, falling, and the goblin cries of attack turned fast to screams of surprise and agony.

Jojonah dared to slow and glance back, to see that half the goblins were already down, some squirming, others dead, and that Master De'Unnero had leaped out onto the road in the midst of the rest. De'Unnero was a

perfect killing machine now, leaping and twisting. Out snapped his extended fingers, hand rigid, driving through a goblin throat. He turned as
another tried to club him on the head. Up came De'Unnero's arms in a stiff
cross above his head, catching the downswing between his forearms.
Thrusting the arms out wide, he tore the club from the startled goblin's
grasp, caught it while it spun about, then snapped it hard across the creature's face, and then again, even more forcefully, with a powerful backhand.

De'Unnero kept running, using the club to knock aside a spear thrust,
then around again to smash the first goblin a third time—though it was
already nearly unconscious on its feet—laying it out in the dirt.

Around he came, launching the club at the spear-wielder, then following
the weapon's flight with a quick rush, moving inside the tip of the spear and
pushing it aside, while his free hand rained heavy blows about the creature's face and throat.

Other monks were on the road now, overwhelming the goblins, breaking
them apart. A few monsters scampered out to the side, whining, but
De'Unnero had left several of his warriors in place, and they had their powerful crossbows ready by that time.

And then, with the goblin horde already falling apart, came perhaps the
worst blow of all, as brutal De'Unnero fell into his signature gemstone, the
tiger's paw, as his arms, already deadly, transformed into the mighty limbs
of a tiger and began raking apart those nearest goblins.

It was over before Master Jojonah could even get back to his companions.

When he did return, huffing and puffing, he found De'Unnero in an
excited, almost frantic state, the man rushing all about the line of young
monks, clapping them hard on the back, verily snarling at their great victory.

Only a few monks were down, and the worst injured of the group had
been hit by a crossbow quarrel from across the road, the firing monk not
taking care with the angle of his shot. Several goblins on the road were still
alive, but in no condition to continue any fight, and several more had
escaped, running fast across the fields to the sides of the road.

De'Unnero seemed not to care. The man even found a wide smile for
Jojonah.

"It could not have been quicker even with the use of magic," the would-
be abbot said.

"Something you obviously never intended, other than your personal
stone," Jojonah replied sharply, tossing back the useless stone. "I do not
like being a pawn, Master De'Unnero," Jojonah went on.

De'Unnero glanced around at the young monks, and Jojonah did not miss
the sly grin on his face. "You played a necessary role," De'Unnero argued,
not bothering to scold the man for referring to him as merely a master.

"With a true gemstone, I could have been more useful."

"Not so," said De'Unnero. "Your lightning stroke may have killed a few,
but the rest would have scattered, making our task all the more difficult."

"Several did get away," Jojonah reminded him.

De'Unnero waved the thought away. "Not enough to cause any real mischief."

"So you needed me frightened and running."

"To lure them in," De'Unnero replied.

"Me? A master of St.-Mere-Abelle?" Jojonah pressed, for he understood the more subtle reasoning of Marcalo De'Unnero. The man had humiliated him in front of the younger monks, thus securing his own standing among them; while Jojonah had run like a frightened child, De'Unnero had leaped into the midst of the enemy and personally killed at least a handful.

"Forgive me, my brother," De'Unnero said insincerely. "You are the only one appearing infirm enough to so lure the goblins. The whole troupe of them might have fled from a younger, sturdier man, like myself."

Jojonah went quiet, staring hard at this man, his nemesis. Such an action, such a deception upon an Abellican master, could be brought before higher authorities, with the likely result that De'Unnero would be severely punished for his presumption and for so embarrassing him. But to what higher authorities might he appeal? Master Jojonah wondered. To Father Abbot Markwart? Hardly.

De'Unnero had won this day, Jojonah accepted, but he also determined then and there that this personal fight would be a long, long battle.

"The hematite, if you please," he said to De'Unnero. "We have wounded in need of assistance."

De'Unnero glanced around, seemed less than impressed by the severity of any wounds, then tossed the stone to Jojonah. "Again you prove that you have some value," he said.

Jojonah just turned away.

"You taught her," Juraviel, sitting in a tree, stated accusingly when Elbryan came back to the ridge, his hunting successfully completed.

The ranger didn't have to ask what the elf was talking about, for he knew that Juraviel had watched his dance with Pony, and that no two humans could ever find that level of grace and harmony without *bi'nelle dasada*. Without retort, Elbryan ignored the accusation. He looked down to the circled wagons, to see Pony moving among the merchants, helping out.

Juraviel gave a great sigh and rested back against the trunk. "You cannot even admit it?" he asked.

Now the ranger did snap a glare over the elf. "Admit it?" he echoed incredulously. "You speak as though it was a crime."

"And is it not?"

"Is she not worthy?" Elbryan shot right back, waving his arm out toward the wagons and Pony.

That somewhat deflated the elf's anger, but still he pressed on. "And is Elbryan to be the judge of who is worthy and who is not?" he argued. "Is

Elbryan, then, to become the instructor in place of the Touel'alfar, who perfected *bi'nelle dasada* when the world itself was young?"

"No," the ranger said grimly. "Not Elbryan, but Nightbird."

"You presume much," said Juraviel.

"You gave me the title."

"We gave you your life and more," the elf retorted. "Take care that you do not abuse the gifts, Nightbird. Lady Dasslerond would never suffer such an insult."

"Insult?" the ranger echoed, as though the whole notion was ridiculous. "Consider the situation that I, that we, were put in. Pony and I had just destroyed the dactyl, and now had to fight our way through hordes of monsters, and that just to reach Dundalis. And so, yes, I shared my gift with her, for both our sakes, as she shared the gift that Avelyn had given to her, for both our sakes."

"She taught you to use the stones," Juraviel reasoned.

"I am nowhere near her level of power with them," the ranger admitted.

"Nor is she near to your fighting prowess," said the elf.

Elbryan was about to offer a stinging retort, for he wouldn't suffer such an insult to Pony, especially one so obviously ridiculous, but Juraviel kept on talking.

"And yet, a human who can move with such grace, who can complement one trained by the Touel'alfar so very beautifully, is a rare find indeed," the elf went on. "Jilseponie dances as though she had spent years in Caer'alfar."

That brought a smile to Elbryan's face. "She was trained by the master," he said with a grin.

Juraviel didn't even challenge the joking boast. "You did well," the elf decided. "And yes, Jilseponie is worthy of the dance, as worthy as any human has ever been."

Satisfied with that, the ranger looked down the dale and out to the east. "A large group went out that way," he remarked.

"Likely they ran right into the approaching monks."

"Unless the monks chose to hide and let the goblins pass," Elbryan said.

Juraviel understood his cue. "Go to your companion and see to the merchants," he offered. "I will scout to the east and find out what has become of our goblin friends."

The ranger walked Symphony down the slope to the wagons. One frightened man raised a weapon as if to fend the newcomer away, but another nearby boxed him on the ear.

"Ye fool!" the second man said. "He's just saved yer stinking life. Killed half the goblins by himself!"

The other man dropped his weapon to the ground and began dipping a series of ridiculous bows. Elbryan only smiled and walked Symphony past, right into the ring. He spotted Pony at once and slipped down from the horse, handing the reins to a young woman, barely more than a girl, who rushed over to help him.

"They have many sorely wounded," Pony explained, and indeed at the time she was tending to one man who it seemed would not survive. "From the earlier fight, not the last one."

Elbryan looked up, turning his nervous gaze to the east. "The monks are not far, I fear," he said quietly. When he looked back down, he found Pony staring up at him, chewing her thick upper lip, her blue eyes wide, questioning. He knew what she meant to do, whether he argued against it or not, and realized she was only waiting for him to explain where he stood on the issue.

"Be quiet with the soul stone," he bade her. "Wrap the wound as though you were tending it more conventionally. And use the gem only—" He stopped, seeing the transformation in Pony's expression. She had wanted his opinion, out of respect, but she did not need his commandments. The ranger went silent then, nodding to show that he trusted her judgment.

He watched as she drew out the gray stone from her pouch, clutching it close and bending over the man. Elbryan, too, went down low, taking a bandage and beginning to wrap it about the man's wound, a slash in the right side of his chest, through the ribs and quite deep, perhaps even through a lung. The ranger wrapped the wound, and tightly—he didn't want to bring the man any more pain, but he needed him to cry out a bit to cover Pony's secret work.

The man gasped, Elbryan offered words of comfort, and then, in mere seconds, the man relaxed, looking up at the ranger quizzically. "How?" he asked breathlessly.

"Your wound was not nearly as bad as it looked," Elbryan lied. "The blade did not get past your rib bone."

The man's look was doubtful, but he let it go at that, just relieved that the pain was gone now, or nearly so, and that his breath was coming to him easily once more.

Elbryan and Pony made their way about the camp then, searching out any too injured for conventional methods. They found only one more, an older woman who had been hit in the head, whose eyes stared vacantly across the way, drool running freely from her mouth.

"Senseless," a man attending her said. "I seen it before. The goblin club breaked her head. She'll die tonight, in her sleep."

Pony bent low, examining the wound. "Not so," she replied. "Not if she's properly wrapped."

"What?" the man asked skeptically, but fell silent as Elbryan and Pony went to work, the ranger putting bandages about the old woman's head, while Pony, the soul stone tucked under one palm, put her hands near the wound as if to hold the head together while it was being wrapped.

Pony closed her eyes and fell into the stone, sent the healing magic through her fingers. She felt stings of pain, the tenderness and swelling, but she had tended far worse in the battles of the northland.

She came out of her trance a moment later, the wound reduced so as to not be life-threatening, to the cries of "Approach! From the east!"

"Goblins!" one frightened merchant yelled.

"No!" another cried. "Brothers! St.-Mere-Abelle has come to our aid!"

Elbryan cast a nervous glance at Pony, who quickly pocketed the gemstone.

"I don't know how ye did it, but ye suren saved Timmy's life," said a woman, rushing up behind Elbryan. Both Elbryan and Pony followed her gaze across the way, to the man with the chest wound, who was standing now and talking easily, even managing a laugh.

"It was not so bad," Pony offered.

"It was to the lung," the woman insisted. "Checked it meself, and thought he'd be dead afore the dinner bell."

"You were nervous and shaken," Pony offered. "And rushed, for you knew that the goblins were coming back."

The woman's face brightened with a disarming grin. She was older than the two, perhaps in her mid-thirties, with the worn but pleasant demeanor of an honest worker who had known a hard but satisfying life. She glanced by the pair, to the wounded old woman sitting on the ground, her eyes already showing signs of life once more.

"Not so shaken," she said softly. "I seen much in the battles these last weeks, and lost a son, though me other five children are safe, God be praised. They only asked me along on the caravan to Amvoy because of me reputation for putting broken people back together."

The ranger and Pony exchanged a serious look, something the woman didn't miss.

"I'm not knowing what ye're hiding," she said quietly. "But I'm not for talking. I seen ye up on the hill, fighting for us, though ye know not a one in the group, from what I'm hearing. I'll not betray ye." She finished with a wink and turned away to join the commotion as the procession of monks approached along the eastern road.

"Where is our son?" Pony asked Elbryan with a smirk.

The ranger looked around, though of course Juraviel was nowhere in sight. "Probably behind the monks," he answered dryly. "Or under one of their robes."

Pony, nervous that her use of the stones might have drawn these brothers in and that the quest might soon be over, appreciated the levity. She hooked her arm inside her lover's and led him toward the gathering.

"I am Abbot De'Unnero, departing St.-Mere-Abelle for St. Precious," they heard the lead monk, a man full of so much energy that his eyes verily glowed. "Who is the leader here?" Before anyone could answer, De'Unnero's discerning eye settled on the pair, Elbryan and Pony. Their stride and the weapons they carried distinguished them.

The would-be abbot walked up to them, looking hard.

"We are as new to the group as are you, good friar," the ranger said humbly.

"And you happened upon them by mere chance?" De'Unnero asked suspiciously.

"We saw the smoke rising, as you must have in the east," Pony answered, her tone sharp and showing clearly that she was not intimidated. "And being folk of goodly heart, we rushed to see if we might help. When we arrived, the second fight was brewing, so we made it our own."

De'Unnero's dark eyes flashed, and it seemed to both Elbryan and Pony that he wanted to strike out at her for the implied accusation. She had, for all intents and purposes, just asked the monk why he and his fellows had not hustled to join in.

"Nesk Reaches," came a call from a heavy man in bright clothing, the same man Pony had spoken with when she had first approached the caravan before the fight. The merchant hustled forward, extending his left hand, for his right was bandaged. "Nesk Reaches of Dillaman Township," he said, " 'Tis my caravan, and glad we are to see you."

De'Unnero ignored the man's offered hand, his sharp gaze still scrutinizing Elbryan and Pony.

"Master De'Unnero," a portly old friar interrupted, moving forward to stand beside the forceful man. "They have wounded. Pray give me the soul stone that I might tend them."

Elbryan and Pony didn't miss the flash of outrage crossing De'Unnero's angular face, the man obviously not pleased that this other monk had so openly offered help, and magical help at that. Still, he had been put on the spot, in front of all the merchants and all his own procession, and so De'Unnero reached into his pouch and produced a hematite, handing it over.

"Abbot De'Unnero," he corrected.

The portly monk bowed and walked past him, offering a glance and a smile at Elbryan and Pony as he moved into the group.

Predictably to Pony, for she had already made an accurate assessment of the man, Nesk Reaches started for the portly friar, holding up his slightly injured hand, playing the wound for all it was worth.

De'Unnero wouldn't let the merchant leader go that easily, though. The monk grabbed Reaches roughly by the shoulder and turned him about. "You admit that this is your caravan?" he asked.

The merchant humbly nodded.

"What fool are you to be bringing people out in this danger?" De'Unnero scolded. "Monsters are thick in the region, and are hungry and hunting. The warning has been given across the land, yet here you are, out alone and hardly guarded."

"Please, good friar," Nesk Reaches stammered. "We were in need of provisions. We had little choice."

"In need of good profits, more likely," De'Unnero snapped. "Thinking to turn a few pieces of gold at a time when few caravans are running and goods are more valuable."

Grumbles from the crowd told Elbryan and Pony, and De'Unnero, that the reasoning was sound.

De'Unnero let Nesk Reaches go then, and called out to the portly monk. "Be quick about it! We have been delayed too long already." To Reaches, he added, "Where are you headed?"

"Amvoy," the thoroughly intimidated merchant stammered.

"I will soon be sanctified as abbot of St. Precious," De'Unnero explained loudly.

"St. Precious?" Nesk Reaches echoed. "But Abbot Dobrinion—"

"Abbot Dobrinion is dead," De'Unnero callously stated. "And I will replace him. And, merchant Reaches, I expect that you and your caravan, owing a debt to me, will attend the ceremony. In fact, I insist upon it. And I remind you that you would be wise to be generous in your offerings."

He turned away then to his procession, motioning the monks out of the wagon circle. "Be quick," he called to Master Jojonah, spinning about. "I'll not waste our entire day at this business."

Elbryan used the distraction to slip away to the horses, remembering that Symphony carried a gemstone in his breast which might be quite significant and telling to monks of St.-Mere-Abelle.

Pony, meanwhile, kept her eyes on the portly monk tenderly attending the many wounded. When De'Unnero's group was safely away, she went up to the man, offering to help with conventional healing, tearing bandages and the like.

The monk looked at her sword, at the blood spattered on her pants and boots. "Perhaps you should rest," he said. "You and your companion have done quite enough this day, from what I have heard."

"I am not tired," Pony said with a smile, taking as much of an initial liking to this man as she had a disliking to the other, De'Unnero. She couldn't help but measure that man against Abbot Dobrinion, whom he would apparently replace, and the contrast sent a shudder along her spine. This monk, though, so sincerely at work to relieve the suffering, seemed more like the former abbot of St. Precious, whom Pony had met on a couple of occasions. She bent low and held the hand of the man the friar was attending, applying pressure in just the right spot to slow the bleeding of his torn hand.

She noticed then that the monk was not looking at her, or at the wounded man, but had settled his gaze on Elbryan and the horses.

"What is your name?" he asked Pony, his eyes drifting to study her.

"Carralee," Pony lied, using the name of her infant cousin who had been killed in the first goblin raid on Dundalis.

"I am Master Jojonah," the monk replied. "Well met, I would say, and fortunate for these poor folk that we—particularly you and your companion—came along when we did!"

Pony hardly heard the last few words. She stared hard at the portly man. Jojonah. She knew that name, the name of the one master of whom Avelyn had spoken fondly, the one man at St.-Mere-Abelle, Avelyn had believed, who had understood him. Avelyn hadn't talked much with Pony about his colleagues during his days at the abbey, but he made it a point one night after too many "potions of courage," as Avelyn called his liquor, to tell her about Jojonah. That fact alone relayed to the woman just how dear this old man had been to Avelyn.

"Your work is truly amazing, Father," she remarked as Master Jojonah put a soul stone to use on the injured man. In truth, Pony soon realized that she was more powerful with the gemstones than this master of the abbey, a fact that pointedly reminded her of just how powerful Avelyn Desbris had been.

"It is a minor thing," Master Jojonah replied when the man's gash was mended.

"Not minor to me," the man said, and gave a laugh that sounded more like a cough.

"But what a good man you are to do such work," Pony said enthusiastically. She was acting purely on instinct now, following her heart, though her thoughts were screaming at her to be cautious and shut up. She gave one nervous glance around, to make sure that no other monks had wandered back into the wagon circle, then continued quietly, "I once met another of your Church—St.-Mere-Abelle, is it not?"

"Indeed it is," Master Jojonah replied absently, looking around for any others who might need his healing talents.

"A good man was he," Pony continued. "Oh, such a good man."

Master Jojonah smiled politely, but started to walk off.

"His name was Aberly, I believe," Pony said.

The monk stopped abruptly and turned on her, his expression shifting from polite tolerance to sincere intrigue.

"No, Avenbrook," Pony bluffed. "Oh, I cannot remember his name quite right, I fear. It was years ago, you see. And though I cannot remember the name, I'll never forget the monk. I came upon him when he was helping a poor street beggar in Palmaris, much as you just helped that man. And when the poor man offered to pay him, fishing a few coins out of his raggedy pocket, Aberly, or Avenbrook, or whatever his name might have been, accepted graciously, but then arranged for the coins, along with more than a few of his own, to be returned to the poor man inconspicuously."

"Indeed," Jojonah muttered, nodding his head with her every word.

"I asked him why he did that—with the coins, I mean," Pony went on. "He could have just refused them, after all. He told me that it was just as important to protect the poor man's sense of pride as his health." She finished with a broad smile. The story was true, though it had happened in a tiny village far to the south and not in Palmaris

"Are you sure you cannot remember the brother's name?" Jojonah prompted.

"Aberly, Aberlyn, something like that," Pony replied, shaking her head.

"Avelyn?" Jojonah asked.

"That might be it, Father," Pony replied, still trying not to give too much away. She was encouraged, though, by the warm expression on Master Jojonah's face.

"I said be quick!" came a shout from outside the wagon circle, the harsh bark of St. Precious' new abbot.

"Avelyn," Master Jojonah said again to Pony. "It was Avelyn. Never forget that name." He patted her shoulder as he walked past.

Pony watched him go, and for some reason that she had not yet discerned, she felt a bit better about the world. She moved to Elbryan then, the ranger still standing right against Symphony, hiding the telltale turquoise.

"May we leave now?" he asked her impatiently.

Pony nodded and climbed up on Greystone, and with a wave to the merchant entourage, the pair trotted their mounts out of the wagon circle, going back to the south, up the slope and away from the monks, who were back on the road, heading to the west. Just over the ridge, Elbryan and Pony met up with Juraviel again, and they were quickly heading east, putting as much ground between themselves and the monks as possible.

De'Unnero began scolding Master Jojonah as soon as the older man rejoined the monk procession. His tirade went on and on, long after the group exited the valley.

Jojonah tuned it out almost immediately, his thoughts still with the woman who had helped tend the wounded. He felt warm inside, calm and hopeful that Avelyn's message had indeed been heard. The woman's tale had touched him deeply, had reinforced his positive feelings toward Avelyn, had reminded him once again of all that was—or all that could be—right with his Church.

His smile as he pondered the tale only infuriated De'Unnero even more, of course, but Jojonah could hardly have cared less. At least in this tirade—on the edge of insanity, it seemed—De'Unnero was showing his temperament honestly to the younger, impressionable monks. They might be in awe of the man's fighting prowess—even Jojonah was amazed by that—but his verbal lashing of an old, impassive man would likely sour more than a few stomachs.

Finally realizing that Jojonah's serenity was too entrenched to be shaken, the volatile master backed off and the procession went on its way, with Master Jojonah falling into position at the end of the line absently, trying to conjure images of Brother Avelyn's work with the poor and sick. He thought of the woman again, and was glad, but as he pondered her tale, as he considered her and her companion's obviously mighty role in the battle, his contentment fast shifted to curiosity. It made little sense to him that a man and a woman, obviously powerful warriors, would be making their way to the east from Palmaris—and not in position as guard of one of the few, precious caravans that were trying to get through. Most heroes, after all, were making their name and reputation in the north, where the battle lines were more obvious. It occurred to Master Jojonah that this situation needed more investigating.

"The stone!" Abbot De'Unnero snapped at him from the front of the procession.

The man was hardly paying him any heed, so Jojonah bent low and quietly gathered another stone of similar size, then dropped it into the pouch in place of the hematite. Then he rushed over to De'Unnero, seeming obedient, and handed the pouch over. He breathed easier when the vicious master, no lover of magic other than his signature tiger's paw, tucked the pouch away without a look.

They marched until the sun went down, putting several miles behind them before setting camp. A single tent was propped for De'Unnero, who went inside right after his meal with parchment and ink to further plan the grand ceremony of his appointment as abbot.

Master Jojonah said little to his companions, just moved off by himself quietly and settled amidst several thick blankets. He waited until all the camp had quieted, until several of the brothers were snoring contentedly, and then he took the hematite from his pocket. With one last glance around to make sure no one was taking any notice, he fell into the stone, connecting his spirit to its magic and then using that magic to let his spirit walk free of his body.

Without the corporeal bonds of his aged and too-heavy frame, the master set out at great pace, covering the miles in mere minutes. He passed by the merchant caravan, which was still circled in the valley.

The woman and her companion were not there, and so Jojonah's spirit did not stay, but rather drifted up high, into the air, above the hilltops. He spotted a pair of campfires, one to the north and another in the east, and by sheer luck chose to investigate the eastern glow first.

Perfectly silent and invisible, the spirit glided in. He soon saw the two horses, the great black stallion and the muscled golden palomino, and then, beyond them, huddled about the fire, the two warriors talking to a third figure he did not know. He drifted closer cautiously, giving them all due respect, moving in a circuit about the perimeter of the camp to get a better look at this third member of the band.

If he had been in his corporeal form, Jojonah's gasp would have been audible indeed when he saw the lithe figure, the angular features, the translucent wings!

An elf! Touel'alfar! Jojonah had seen statues and drawings of the diminutive beings at St.-Mere-Abelle, but even at the abbey the writing on the Touel'alfar was indecisive as to whether there really were such beings, or whether they were merely legend. After encountering powries and goblins and hearing the tales of fomorian giants, Jojonah was not logically surprised to learn that there really were Touel'alfar, but the sight of one still startled him profoundly. He spent a long time hovering about that camp, his gaze never leaving Juraviel while he listened to the conversation.

They were speaking of St.-Mere-Abelle, of the prisoners Markwart had taken, particularly the centaur.

"The man was proficient with the hematite," the woman was saying.

"Could you defeat him in a battle of magics?" the strong man asked.

Jojonah had to swallow his pride when the woman nodded confidently, but any anger he might have felt washed away as soon as she explained.

"Avelyn taught me well, better than I had understood before," she said. "The man was a master, indeed the one that Avelyn had called his mentor, the one man that Avelyn had loved at St.-Mere-Abelle. Avelyn always spoke highly of Master Jojonah, but in truth, the man's work with the stones was not so strong, not compared to Avelyn, and not compared to my own."

She had not said it in any boastful way, but merely matter-of-factly, and so Jojonah took no further offense. Instead he considered the deeper, richer implications of it all. She had been trained by Avelyn! And under his tutelage, this woman, who did not look as though she was near her thirtieth birthday, was stronger than a master of St.-Mere-Abelle. That notion, and he found from her tone that he believed her words, served to reinforce Jojonah's continually mounting respect for Avelyn.

He wanted to stay near and continue his eavesdropping, but realized then that time was short and that he would have to cover quite a bit of ground before the dawn. His spirit soared back to his waiting body, and when he was again corporeal, he breathed easier to learn that his out-of-body flight had not been noticed. All the camp was quiet.

Jojonah looked at the soul stone, wondering how to proceed. He might need this, he realized, but if he took it, then De'Unnero would likely make hunting him down a priority even above the journey to St. Precious. On the other hand, if he left the soul stone, then it might be used, much as he had used it this night, to search for him.

Jojonah found a third option. From inside the folds of his voluminous robes he produced parchment and ink, then set about writing a short note explaining that he was going to return to the merchant caravan and escort them to Palmaris. He would take the soul stone, he explained, because the merchants were far more likely to need it than were the monks, especially— and Jojonah took great care to play this part up—since the monks had Master De'Unnero, perhaps the greatest fighter ever to come out of St.-Mere-Abelle, at their head. Also, Jojonah assured De'Unnero that he would make sure that the merchants, and any compatriots they could muster, would attend the ceremony at St. Precious, bearing expensive gifts.

"My conscience will not allow me to leave these people out here all alone," the note finished. "It is the duty of the Church to help those in need, and by so helping, we bring willing contributors into the flock."

He hoped that the emphasis on wealth and power would calm De'Unnero's expectedly vicious response. But he couldn't really worry about that now, not with these three people, so potentially important to everything that he held dear, so very near. Carrying only the soul stone and a small knife, he crept out of the camp, taking care not to be noticed, and set out as fast as his old frame would carry him, back to the east.

His first destination was the valley where the merchants had settled, so he could get his bearings, and also from an honest desire to check in on the battered caravan. When he drew near the place, he found another potential gain. Improvising, Master Jojonah cut a piece of his robe, not a difficult thing to do since the material had grown threadbare from his many days of traveling. He broke a few low branches and scuffled his feet about to make it seem as if a fight had occurred, then cut his own finger, carefully soaking the ripped material in blood and dripping some more about the area.

He quickly sealed the wound with the hematite, then moved over the ridge to the slope above the valley. The camp seemed peaceful enough, a couple of fires burning, several figures moving about calmly, so the monk took a moment to gauge his position, then set out.

He came in sight of the low-burning campfire before the dawn, and crept up. He didn't want to startle these people, certainly not to alarm them, but he figured that his best chance was to get close enough for the woman to recognize him.

He was soon in the bushes about the small campsite, the fire clearly in sight. He thought that he had been silent, and was glad to see the two bedrolls bulging with forms. How to wake them, he wondered, without frightening them into action?

He decided to wait until the dawn, to let them wake up on their own, but even as he started to settle down for perhaps an hour's wait, he sensed that he was being watched.

Master Jojonah spun about as the large form crashed in. Though

Jojonah, like all the monks of St.-Mere-Abelle, was a trained fighter, in the blink of an eye he was on his back, the edge of a very fine sword pressed against his throat, the strong man on top of him, pinning him helplessly.

Jojonah made no move to resist, and the man, upon recognizing him, backed off slightly.

"No others in the area," came a melodic voice—the elf, Jojonah presumed.

"Master Jojonah!" the woman said, coming into view. She rushed over and put a hand on the strong ranger's shoulder, and with a look and a nod, Elbryan got up from the monk and offered his hand.

Jojonah took it and was pulled to his feet with such ease that the man's strength, like his incredible agility, stunned him.

"Why are you here?" the woman asked.

Jojonah looked right into her eyes, their beauty and depth not diminished in the least by the dim light. "Why are you?" he asked, and his tone, one that showed such understanding, gave both Pony and Elbryan pause.

In Search of Answers

"Brother Talumus," Baron Bildeborough went on slowly, calmly, his tone a futile attempt to hide the agitation that bubbled just beneath the surface, "tell me again of Connor's visit here, of every stop he made, of everything he inspected."

The young monk, thoroughly flustered, for it was obvious he wasn't giving the Baron what he wanted, started talking so fast and in so many different directions that his words came out as a jumble. Prompted by the Baron's patting hand, the man stopped and took a deep and steadying breath.

"The abbot's room first," Talumus said slowly. "He was not pleased that we had cleaned it up, but what were we to do?" As he finished the sentence, his voice rose up again with excitement. "The abbot must be in public state—tradition demands it! And if we were to have guests at the abbey—oh, and streams of them!—then we could not leave the room all gory and torn up."

"Of course not. Of course not," Baron Bildeborough said repeatedly, trying to keep the monk calm.

Roger watched his new mentor closely, impressed by the man's patience, by how he was keeping this blubbering monk somewhat on track. Still, Roger could see the underlying tension on Rochefort's face, for the man now understood, as did Roger, that they would get few answers and little satisfaction here. St. Precious, with no ranking masters behind Abbot Dobrinion, was in absolute disarray, with monks running every which way, and discussion of this or that rumor taking the place of even the prayer times. One confirmed bit of news had proven especially unnerving to Roger and Rochefort: St. Precious would soon get a new abbot, a master from St.-Mere-Abelle.

To Roger and to Rochefort, that fact seemed to lend even more credence to Connor's suspicions that the Father Abbot himself had been behind the murder.

"We left the powrie, though," Brother Talumus went on, "at least until after Master Connor had departed."

"And then Connor went to the kitchen?" Rochefort inquired gently.

"To Keleigh Leigh, yes," replied Talumus. "Poor girl."

"And she was not injured other than the drowning?" Roger dared to put in, looking directly at Rochefort as he spoke, though the question was obviously for Talumus. Roger had previously explained to Rochefort that Keleigh Leigh's lack of cuts—for dipping berets—had been a primary clue to Connor that the powrie had not committed these crimes.

"No," replied Talumus.

"None of her blood was spilled?"

"No."

"Go and find me the person who first discovered her body," Baron Bildeborough instructed. "And be quick."

Brother Talumus scrambled to his feet, saluted and bowed, then ran from the room.

"The monk who found her will likely have little to tell us," Roger remarked, surprised by the Baron's request.

"Forget the monk," Rochefort explained. "I only sent Brother Talumus that we might find a few minutes alone. We must decide upon our course, my friend, and quickly."

"We should not tell them of Connor's suspicions, or of his demise," Roger said after a few seconds pause. Baron Bildeborough was nodding as he went on. "They are helpless in the face of this. Not a single monk here, if Talumus is the highest ranking remaining, could possibly stand against the coming master of St.-Mere-Abelle."

"It does seem that Abbot Dobrinion was lax in developing any talents in his lessers," Rochefort agreed. He gave a snort. "Though I might enjoy the sheer tumult of telling Talumus and all the others that St.-Mere-Abelle murdered their beloved abbot."

"Not much of a fight," Roger put in dryly. "From all that Connor told me of the Church, St.-Mere-Abelle would quickly dismantle the order at St. Precious, and then the Father Abbot would be even more entrenched in Palmaris than he will be when the new abbot arrives."

"True enough," Baron Bildeborough admitted with a sigh. He brightened his expression immediately for the sake of the two jittery monks entering the room, Talumus and the first witness. On with the questioning, he decided, but only for appearances—both he and Roger knew they would learn nothing more from this man or any other at St. Precious.

The two were back at Chasewind Manor soon after, Rochefort pacing the floor while Roger sat upon the man's favorite stuffed chair.

"Ursal is a long ride," Rochefort was saying. "Of course, I will want you with me."

"Will we actually meet the King?" Roger asked, a bit overwhelmed by that possibility.

"Oh, but King Danube Brock Ursal is a good friend, Roger," replied the Baron. "A good friend. He will grant me audience and will believe me, do not doubt. Whether or not he will be able to take any overt action given the lack of evidence—"

"I was a witness!" Roger protested. "I saw the monk kill Connor."

"Perhaps you bear false witness."

"You do not believe me?"

"Of course I do!" the Baron replied, again giving that customary pat in the air with his plump hand. "Indeed, boy, else why would I have gone to so much trouble? Why would I have given you Greystone and Defender? If I didn't trust you, boy, you would be in chains, and tortured until I was convinced that you were speaking truly."

The Baron paused and looked at Roger more closely. "Where is that sword?" he asked.

Roger shifted uncomfortably. Had he just compromised that trust? he wondered. "Both sword and horse have been put to good use," he explained.

"By whom?" the Baron demanded.

"By Jilly," Roger was quick to reply. "Her road is darker still, and fraught with battle, I fear. I gave them over to her, for I am no rider, nor much of a swordsman."

"Both can be taught," the Baron grumbled.

"But we've not the time," Roger replied. "And Jilly can put them to good use at once. Do not doubt her prowess . . ." Roger paused, trying to gauge the great man's reaction.

"Again I trust in your judgment," the Baron said at length. "So we'll not speak of this again. Now back to our primary business. I believe you—of course I do. But Danube Brock Ursal will be more cautious in his acceptance, do not doubt. Do you realize the implications of our claims? If King Danube accepted them as truth and spoke of them publicly, he might well begin a war between Church and state, a bloodbath that neither side desires."

"But one that the Father Abbot of St.-Mere-Abelle began," Roger reminded.

A cloud passed over Baron Rochefort Bildeborough's face then, and he seemed to Roger so very old and tired indeed. "And so we must go south, it would seem," he said.

A knock on the door cut short Roger's response.

"My Baron," said an attendant, entering, "word has just come to us that the new abbot of St. Precious has arrived. Master De'Unnero, by name."

"Do you know of him?" the Baron asked Roger, who only shook his head.

"He has already requested your audience," the attendant went on. "At St. Precious this very afternoon at high tea."

Bildeborough nodded and the attendant left the room.

"I must hurry, it would seem," the Baron remarked, glancing out the window at the westering sun.

"I will accompany you," Roger said, rising from the stuffed chair.

"No," Bildeborough replied. "Though I would indeed welcome your impressions of this man. But if the depth of this heinous conspiracy is as far-reaching as we fear, then better that I go alone. Let the name and face of Roger Billingsbury remain unknown to Abbot De'Unnero."

Roger wanted to argue, but he knew that the man was right, and knew, too, that Bildeborough's answer for not taking him was only half of the reason. Roger understood that he was still young and very inexperienced in matters politic, and Bildeborough feared—and Roger could not honestly dismiss those fears as folly—that this new abbot might glean a bit too much information from their high tea.

So Roger sat and waited at Chasewind Manor for the rest of that afternoon.

Mid-Calember was not so far away. Not when Father Abbot Markwart considered the preparations he must make for the momentous proclamations he intended. The old and wrinkled man paced his office at St.-Mere-Abelle, pausing every time he passed the window to view the summer foliage. The events of the last few weeks, particularly the discovery at the Barbacan and the trouble in Palmaris, had forced Markwart to change his thinking on many matters, or at least to accelerate his maneuvers toward his long-terms goals.

With Dobrinion gone, the makeup of the College of Abbots had changed dramatically. Though he would be a new abbot, De'Unnero, by the mere fact that he presided over St. Precious, would be granted a strong voice at the College, possibly even third behind only Markwart and Je'howith of St. Honce. That would give Markwart great power to strike hard.

The old cleric smiled wickedly as he fantasized about that meeting. At the College of Abbots he would forever discredit Avelyn Desbris, would brand the man indelibly as a heretic. Yes, that was important, Markwart realized, for if he did not pass such sanctions against Avelyn, then the man's actions would remain open for interpretation. As long as the brand of heretic had not been formalized, all of the monks, even first-year brothers, remained free to discuss the events of Avelyn's departure, and that was a dangerous thing. Would some be sympathetic to the man? Might the word "escape" wriggle into such discussions in place of the commonly described murder and theft?

Yes, the sooner he made the declaration of heresy and it was approved by the Church leaders, the better. Once the brand was formalized, no discussion of Avelyn Desbris in any positive light would be tolerated at any abbey or chapel. Once Avelyn was declared a heretic, his entry into the annals of Church history would be complete, and ultimately damning.

Markwart blew a long sigh as he considered the road to that coveted goal. He would be opposed, he suspected, by stubborn Master Jojonah—if the man lived that long.

Markwart dismissed the possibility of yet another assassination; if all of his known enemies began dying, then probing eyes would likely turn his way. And besides, he knew that Jojonah was not alone in his beliefs. He could not strike out that hard. Not yet.

But he had to be prepared should the fight come to pass. He had to be able to prove his point about Avelyn's heresy, for the devastation at the Barbacan was certainly open to interpretation. It was true, and indisputable, that Siherton had been killed on the night of Avelyn's flight from St.-Mere-Abelle, but in that, too, Jojonah might be able to find some argument. Intent, and not mere action, determined sin, and only true sin could brand a man a heretic.

Thus Markwart knew he would have to prove more than his interpretation of the events on the night when Avelyn absconded with the stones. To get the complete confirmation of that brand—a brand the Church had never been quick to hand out—he would have to prove that Avelyn subsequently used those stones for ill, that the man's degeneration to the dark side of human nature was complete. But he would never quiet Jojonah, Markwart realized. The man would fight him concerning Avelyn Desbris, would deny his plans to the last. Yes, he saw that now; Jojonah would return with the College of Abbots and would fight him. They were long overdue for that confrontation. Thus Markwart decided that he would have to destroy the master, and not just the man's argument.

Markwart knew exactly where he could find allies to that cause, a preemptive strike against Jojonah. Abbot Je'howith of St. Honce held a position as a close adviser to the King, and could access that power, in the form of the fanatical Allheart Brigade. All that he had to do, Markwart thought, was prep Je'howith properly, have him bring along a few of those merciless warriors . . .

Satisfied, the Father Abbot turned his thoughts to the issue of Avelyn. He did have one remaining witness to Avelyn's actions, Bradwarden, but from his interrogations of the centaur, both verbal and with the soul stone, he had a fair measure of the beast's considerable willpower and feared that Bradwarden would not break, no matter how brutally they tortured him.

With that in mind, the Father Abbot moved to his desk and made a note to Brother Francis that he should work ceaselessly with the centaur until the College convened. If they couldn't trust that Bradwarden had indeed broken and would say whatever they told him to say, then the centaur would be killed before the distinguished guests arrived.

Markwart realized yet another problem as he penned that note. Francis was a ninth-year brother, yet only immaculates and abbots would be allowed to attend the College. Markwart wanted Francis there; the man had his limitations, but he was loyal enough.

The Father Abbot ripped a corner of the parchment and noted a reminder, "IBF," to himself, then tucked it away. As he had broken protocol, due to the emergency of the war, in appointing De'Unnero as abbot of St. Precious and in sending Jojonah to the Palmaris abbey to serve as De'Unnero's second, so he would promote Brother Francis to the rank of immaculate.

Immaculate Brother Francis.

Markwart liked the sound of that, liked the notion of increasing the power of those who obeyed him without question. His explanation for the premature appointment would be simple, and surely accepted: with two masters sent to bolster St. Precious, St.-Mere-Abelle had been left weak at the top echelons. Though the abbey boasted scores of immaculates, few had attained the credentials necessary for promotion to the rank of master, few even continued to strive for such a rank, and Francis, given his vital work with the caravan to the Barbacan, would strengthen that stable considerably.

Yes, the Father Abbot mused. He would promote Francis before the College, and then again, soon after, to the rank of master, to replace . . .

. . . Jojonah, he decided, instead of De'Unnero. For De'Unnero's replacement he would look among the scores of immaculates, perhaps even to Braumin Herde, who was deserving even if his choice of mentors had left a great deal to be desired. Still, with Jojonah so far away and unlikely to ever return—except for the three weeks of the College—Markwart figured that he might be able to bring Braumin Herde tighter into the fold by tempting him with the coveted rank.

The Father Abbot's step lightened as he waded through these problems, as solutions became all too apparent. This new insight he had found, this new level of inner guidance, seemed nothing short of miraculous. Every layer of intrigue seemed to fall away, leaving him with answers crystal clear.

Except for the problem of branding Avelyn quickly, he reminded himself, and he slapped his hand against his desk in frustration. No, Bradwarden would not break, would remain defiant until the bitter end. Markwart, for the first time, lamented the loss of the Chilichunks, for they, he knew, would have been so much easier to control.

An image came to him then, of the small library wherein Jojonah had been digging for information about Brother Allabarnet. Markwart saw the room clearly in his mind, and couldn't understand why—until one area of the back corner, a distant, unused shelf, came clear in the image.

Markwart followed his instincts, followed the inner guidance, first to his desk to retrieve some gemstones, then down from his office, down the damp and dark stairs that led to the ancient library. No guards were posted now, for Jojonah was supposedly far away, and Markwart, glowing diamond in hand, entered cautiously. He went past the shelves of books to the back corner, to the books which the Church had long ago banned. He knew logically that even he, the Father Abbot, should not be perusing these, but that inner voice promised him answers to his dilemma.

He studied the shelf for a few minutes, glancing at every tome, at the labels of every rolled parchment, then closed his eyes and replayed those images.

His eyes stayed closed, but he lifted his hand, trusting that it was being guided to the book he needed. Grasping gently but firmly, Markwart tucked the prize under his arm and shuffled away, and was back in the privacy of his office before he even inspected the work, *The Incantations Sorcerous.*

Roger expected that the Baron would be gone late into the evening, and was rather surprised when the man returned long before the sun had even touched the horizon. He went to meet Bildeborough full of hope that all had gone well, but those hopes were deflated as soon as he saw the huge man, huffing and puffing, his face red from explosive rage.

"In all my years, I have never met a more unpleasant man, let alone a supposed holy man!" Rochefort Bildeborough fumed, storming out of the foyer and into his audience room.

Roger, following quickly, thought he might have to take a second choice of seat this time, for the Baron plopped into his stuffed chair. But then the huge man was right back to his feet, pacing anxiously, and so Roger slipped in behind him to take what was fast becoming his customary seat.

"He warned me!" Baron Bildeborough fumed. "Me! The Baron of Palmaris, friend of Danube Brock Ursal himself!"

"What did he say?"

"Oh, it started well enough," Bildeborough explained, slapping his hands together. "All polite, with this De'Unnero creature hopeful that the transition would be smooth as he took his place in St. Precious. He said that we might work together—" Bildeborough paused and Roger sucked in his breath, recognizing that some important declaration was forthcoming. "—despite the apparent shortcomings and criminal behavior of my nephew!" the Baron exploded, stomping his feet and punching at the air. The exertion overwhelmed him almost immediately, and Roger was quick to his side, helping him into the comfortable chair.

"The dog!" Bildeborough went on. "He does not know of Connor's death, I am sure, though he will certainly learn of it soon. He offered to pardon Connor, on my word that Connor would be more careful of his behavior in the future. Pardon him!"

Roger worked hard to keep the man calm then, fearing that he would simply die of his rage. His face was puffy and bloodred, his eyes wide.

"The best thing that we can do is to go to the King," Roger calmly said. "We have allies that the new abbot cannot overcome. We can clear

Connor's name—indeed, we can put all the blame for these troubles where it rightly belongs."

The reminder did calm the Baron considerably. "Off we go," he said. "To the south, with all speed. Tell my attendants to prepare my coach."

De'Unnero had not underestimated Baron Bildeborough in the least. His forceful demeanor at their meeting had been purposefully designed to garner both information from the man and understanding of the Baron's political leaning, and in De'Unnero's sharp eyes, their conversation had been extremely successful on both counts. Bildeborough's outrage showed that he, too, might prove an open enemy of the Church, more troublesome than either his nephew or Abbot Dobrinion.

And De'Unnero was smart enough to understand the true culprit behind the removal of those troubles.

For, despite his words at the meeting, De'Unnero did indeed know of the death of Connor Bildeborough, and he knew, too, that a young man had brought the body back to Palmaris, along with the body of a man dressed in the robes of an Abellican monk. Again the angry abbot lamented that Father Abbot Markwart had erred in not sending him on the most important mission to retrieve the stones. Had he gone in search of Avelyn, this issue would have been settled long ago, with the gemstones returned and Avelyn and all of his friends dead. How much less a problem Bildeborough would be to him, and to the Church!

For now Markwart and the Church had a problem, a big one, De'Unnero believed. According to those monks of St. Precious whom De'Unnero had already interviewed, and those of St.-Mere-Abelle who had witnessed the near battle in St. Precious' courtyard, Baron Bildeborough had thought of Connor as a son. The accusation of murder had no doubt been laid at the Church's door, and Bildeborough, whose influence went out far from Palmaris, would not be silent on this matter.

The new abbot was not surprised, then, when one of his flock, a fellow monk who had made the journey with De'Unnero from St.-Mere-Abelle, returned from his assigned scouting post to report that a carriage had left Chasewind Manor, riding south, right out of Palmaris, along the river road.

The new abbot's other spies soon returned, confirming the story, one of them insisting that Baron Bildeborough himself was in that coach.

De'Unnero did not betray his emotions, remained calm and went through the few remaining evening rituals as though nothing was amiss. He went to his room early, explaining that he was weary from the ride, a perfectly plausible excuse.

"This is where I hold advantage even over you, Father Abbot," the abbot of St. Precious remarked as he looked out his window to the Palmaris night. "I need no lackeys for my dark business."

He pulled off his telltale robes and dressed in a loose-fitting suit of black material, then pushed open the grate on the window and climbed out, disappearing into the shadows. Moments later he crouched in an alleyway, his favorite gemstone in hand.

De'Unnero fell into the stone, felt the exquisite pain as the bones in his hands and arms began to reshape and twist. And then, spurred by the sheer excitement of the coming hunt, the sheer ecstasy that he could finally act, he fell deeper, and quickly kicked off his shoes as his legs and feet, too, transformed into the hind legs and paws of a tiger. He felt as if he was losing himself in the magic, becoming one with the stone. All his body jerked and spasmed. He raked a paw across his chest, tearing wide his clothing.

Then he was on all fours, and when he tried to protest, a great growl came out of his feline maw.

Never had he gone this far!

But it was wonderful!

The power, oh, the power! He was the hunting tiger now, in body, and all of that sheer power was under his absolute control. Soon he was running swiftly and silently on padded feet, bounding over the high Palmaris wall with ease and charging off down the southern road.

On the very first pages, the general description of the tome, the Father Abbot understood. Only a few months before, Father Abbot Dalebert Markwart would have been horrified at the thought.

But that was before he had found the "inner guidance" of Bestesbulzibar.

He reverently placed the book away in the lowest drawer of his desk, locking it tight.

"First business at hand," he said aloud, drawing clean parchment and a vial of black ink from another drawer. He unrolled the parchment and secured its ends with weights, then stared at it for a long time, trying to determine the best manner of wording. With a nod, he titled the paper:

Promotion of Brother Francis Dellacourt to Immaculate Brother
The Order of St.-Mere-Abelle

Markwart spent a long time preparing that important document, though the final draft was no more than three hundred words. By the time he finished, the day was nearing its end, the other monks gathering for dinner. Markwart swept out of his office, to the wing of St.-Mere-Abelle serving as residence for the newest students. He found the three he wanted and called them off to a private room.

"You will each provide me with five copies of this document," he explained. One of the young brothers shifted nervously.

"Speak your mind," Markwart demanded of him.

"I am not well-versed, nor very skilled, in illumination, Father Abbot," the man stuttered, head bowed. In truth, all three were overwhelmed by the demand. St.-Mere-Abelle boasted of many of the finest scribes in all the world. Most of the immaculates who would never attain the rank of master had chosen the vocation of scribener.

"I did not ask if you were skilled," Markwart replied to the man, to them all. "You can read and write?"

"Of course, Father Abbot," all three confirmed.

"Then do as I asked," the old man said. "Without question."

"Yes, Father Abbot."

Markwart let his dangerous stare linger on each of them individually, then, after what seemed like minutes of silence, threatened, "If any of you speak a word of this, if any of you give anyone else even a hint of the contents of this paper, you will, all three, be burned at the stake."

Again came the silence, Markwart studying the young monks intently. He had decided to use first-year students, and these three in particular, because he was certain that such a threat would carry great influence. He left them, then, confident that they would not dare fail the commandment of their Father Abbot.

Markwart's next stop was the room of Brother Francis. The man had already gone to dinner, but the old monk wasn't deterred, sliding his instructions concerning Bradwarden under the door.

Soon after, back in his private quarters, in a little used room to the side of his bedroom, the Father Abbot set about his next preparation. First he removed all items, even furniture, from the room. Then, with the ancient book, a knife, and colored candles in hand, he went back in and began tracing a very specific pattern, described in great detail in the tome, in the wooden floor.

The forest seemed a quiet place to Roger, full of peace and calm. Something about the very air was different here than in the northland, some serenity, as though all the woodland animals, all the trees and flowers, knew that no monsters were about.

Roger had come out from the small camp beside the wagon to relieve himself, but had stayed out as the minutes passed, alone with his thoughts and with the starry canopy. He tried not to think of his coming meeting with King Danube; he had rehearsed his speech many times already. He tried not to worry for his friends, though he suspected they would likely be approaching St.-Mere-Abelle by now, perhaps had already battled with the Church over the prisoners. For now, Roger wanted only rest, the calm peace of a summer's night.

How many times had he reclined on a branch in the forest near Caer Tinella, alone in the quiet night? Most, if the weather was agreeable. Mrs. Kelso would see him for dinner, and then again for breakfast, and though the mothering woman believed him to be comfortably curled up in her barn, he was more often in the forest.

Try as he may, Roger couldn't find that level of calm now, couldn't find that deep, introspective serenity. Too many worries crept into the corners of his consciousness; he had seen and experienced too much.

He leaned heavily against a tree, staring up at the stars, lamenting his loss of innocence. All during his time with Elbryan, Pony, and Juraviel, they had applauded him for maturing, had nodded approvingly as his decisions became more based in responsibility. But accepting those responsibilities had taken a toll, Roger understood now, for the stars did not twinkle so brightly, for his heart was surely heavier.

He sighed again and told himself that things would get better, that King Danube would put the world aright, that the monsters would be driven far away and he could return to his home and his previous life in Caer Tinella.

But he didn't believe it. With a shrug, he started back for the wagon, back for discussions of important matters, back for responsibility.

He paused, though, before he got near the campsite, the hairs on the back of his neck tingling.

The forest had gone strangely, eerily, quiet.

Then came a low, resonating growl, the likes of which Roger had never before heard. The young man froze in place, listening intently, trying to discern the direction, though the low roar seemed to fill all the air, as though it was coming from everywhere at once. Roger didn't move, didn't breathe.

He heard the draw of sword, another roar, this one more emphatic, and then the screams, sudden and horrible. Now he was moving, running blindly, stumbling on roots, taking more than one branch in the face. He saw the fire-light from the camp, silhouettes darting back and forth before it.

And the screams continued, cries of fear, and now of agony.

Roger came in sight of the camp to see the guards, all three, lying about the fire, torn and broken. He hardly took note of them, though, for the Baron was halfway inside the carriage, struggling mightily to get all the way in that he might close the door.

But even if he could have done so, Roger knew that the door would prove a meager barrier against the creature, a gigantic orange and black striped cat that had a claw hooked about his boot.

The Baron spun over and kicked out, and the tiger let go long enough for the man to get inside. But the man never got close to shutting the carriage door, for the cat had only let go that it might settle back on its haunches, and before Bildeborough had even cleared the line of the door, the tiger sprang into the carriage, atop him, claws raking.

The carriage rocked violently, the Baron screamed, and Roger stared helplessly. He did have a weapon, a small sword, barely more than a dagger, but he knew that he couldn't possibly get to Bildeborough in time to save the man, and in any case couldn't possibly defeat, or even seriously injure, the great cat.

He turned and ran, tears streaming down his face, his breath coming in labored, forced gasps. It had happened again! Just like the incident with Connor! Again he was no more than a helpless bystander, a witness to the death of a friend. He ran on blindly, stumbling, brush and limbs battering him as the minutes became an hour. He ran until he dropped from exhaustion, and even then he dragged himself on, too frightened to even look back to see if there was any pursuit.

❖ 3 1 ❖

Alternate Routes

Backlit by the rising sun, swathed in a veil of morning fog, the great
fortress of St.-Mere-Abelle loomed in the distance, stretching far
along the clifftop overlooking All Saints Bay. Only then, viewing the
sheer size and ancient strength of the place, did Elbryan, Pony, and Juraviel
truly come to appreciate the power of their enemies and the scope of their
task. They had informed Jojonah of their course soon after he arrived at
their campsite.

And then he had told Pony of her brother's demise.

The news hit her hard, for though she and Grady were never close
friends, she had spent years beside him. She didn't sleep well the rest of
that night, but was more than ready for the road before the dawn, a road
that had led them here, to this seemingly indestructible fortress that now
served as prison to her parents and her centaur friend.

The great gates were closed tight, the walls high and thick.

"How many live here?" Pony asked Jojonah breathlessly.

"The brothers alone number more than seven hundred," he replied.
"And even the newest class, brought in last spring, have been trained to
fight. You would not get into St.-Mere-Abelle through use of force, if the
King's army stood behind you. In calmer times, you might find your way in
posing as peasants, or as workers, perhaps, but now, that is not possible."

"What do you plan?" the ranger asked, for it seemed obvious to all that
if Master Jojonah could not get them in, their quest was hopeless. After
their meeting in the wood, Jojonah had promised to do just that, assuring
them that he was no enemy, but a very valuable ally. The four of them had
started off together the very next morning, Jojonah leading the way to the
east, to this place he had known as his home for many decades.

"Any structure this size has less noticeable ways to enter," Jojonah
replied. "I know of one."

The monk led them to the north then, a circuitous route that took them
far around the northern tip of the great structure, then down a winding,

rocky trail to the narrow beach. The water was right up to the rocks, waves licking against the base of the stone, a dance that had continued for centuries untold. Still, the beach was certainly passable, so the ranger plunked one foot in, testing the water.

"Not now," the monk explained. "The tide is coming in, and though we'll get through before the water is too high, I doubt that we'll find the time to return. When the tide recedes later this day, we will be able to make our way along the shore to the dock area of the abbey, a place little used and little guarded."

"Until then?" the elf asked.

Jojonah motioned back up the trail, toward a hollow they had passed, and all agreed they could use the rest after their long day and night of hard travel. They set a small camp, sheltered from the chill sea breeze, and Juraviel prepared a meal, their first in many hours.

The conversation was light at this time, with Pony doing most of the talking, telling the eager master of her travels with Avelyn, retelling parts over and over again at Jojonah's bidding. It seemed he couldn't get enough of her stories, that he hung on every little detail, probing the woman repeatedly to go into more depth, to add her feelings to her observations, to tell him everything about Avelyn Desbris. When Pony at last got to the point where she and Avelyn had met up with Elbryan, the ranger joined in with his own observations, and then Juraviel, too, found much to add as they detailed their efforts against the monsters in Dundalis, and the beginning of the trip to the Barbacan.

Jojonah shuddered when the elf described his encounter with Bestesbulzibar, and then again when Pony and Elbryan told him of the battle outside Mount Aida, of the fall of Tuntun and the final, brutal confrontation with the dactyl demon.

Then it was Jojonah's turn to speak—between bites, for the elf had prepared a wonderful meal. He told of the discovery of Bradwarden, of the centaur's pitiful condition, but one that healed remarkably under the influence of the elven armband.

"Even I, even Lady Dasslerond, I suspect, did not know the true depth of the item's powers," Juraviel admitted. "It is a rare bit of magic, else we would all wear one."

"Like this?" Elbryan said, smiling, and turning his body so his left arm was showcased, the green elven band tight about his muscles.

Juraviel only smiled in reply.

"There is one thing which I have not yet seen," Jojonah interrupted, dropping his gaze over Pony. "Avelyn befriended you?"

"As I have told you," she replied.

"And at his demise, you took the gemstones?"

Pony shifted uncomfortably and looked at Elbryan.

"I know that the stones were taken from Avelyn," the monk went on. "When I searched his body—"

"You exhumed him?" Elbryan asked in horror.

"Never that!" Jojonah answered. "I searched with the soul stone, and with garnet."

"To detect his magic," Pony reasoned.

"And there was little about him," Jojonah said, "though I am certain—even more so from your descriptions of the journey—that he went to the place with a considerable cache. I know why his hand was extended upward, and I know who was first to find him."

Again Pony looked over at Elbryan, and his expression was no less unsure than her own.

"I would like to see them," Jojonah stated flatly. "Perhaps to wield them in the coming fight, if there is to be one. I have considerable talents with the gemstones and will put them to good use, I assure you."

"Not so good as Pony," Elbryan remarked, drawing a surprised look from the monk.

Despite that, Pony reached to her pouch and took the small satchel from it, opening it wide.

Jojonah's eyes sparkled at the sight of the stones, the ruby, the graphite, garnet—taken from Brother Youseff—and serpentine, and all the others. He extended his arm toward them, but Pony shifted her hand away, out of his reach.

"Avelyn gave these to me, and so they are my burden," the woman explained.

"And if I might better use them in the coming fight?"

"You cannot," Pony said calmly. "I have been trained by Avelyn himself."

"I spent years—" Jojonah started to protest.

"I saw your work with the merchant caravan," Pony reminded him. "The wounds were minor, yet they took you tremendous effort to bind. I have measured your strength, Master Jojonah, and I speak now with no intent to insult, or to brag. But I am the stronger with the stones, do not doubt, for Avelyn and I found a connection, a joining of our spirits, and in that bond I came to understand."

"Pony's use of magic has saved me and so many others time and time again," Elbryan added. "She does not boast, but merely speaks the truth."

Jojonah looked from one to the other, then to Juraviel, who was also nodding.

"I did not use them in the fight for the merchant caravan because we knew that monks were in the area, and I feared we would be detected," Pony explained.

Jojonah put his hand up in front of him, a signal that no further explanation was needed; he had heard this same story before when he was spiritually scouting out the three. "Very well," he agreed. "But I do not believe that you should bring them into St.-Mere-Abelle—not all of them, at least."

Pony looked to Elbryan again, and he shrugged and then nodded, thinking that the monk's reasoning, offering the same argument that he and Juraviel had made to Pony earlier, might be sound.

"We do not know if we will get back out," Juraviel reasoned. "But is it better," he asked Jojonah, "that the stones be hidden out here instead of back in the hands of the monks of your abbey?"

Jojonah didn't even have to think about that one. "Yes," he said firmly. "Better that the stones are cast into the sea than to be given into the hands of Father Abbot Markwart. So I beg that you leave them out here, as we will leave these fine horses."

"We shall see" was all that Pony would promise.

The discussion then turned to more practical matters at hand, with the ranger asking what they might expect in the way of guards at this seaside door.

"I doubt that any will be down there," Jojonah replied with confidence. He went on to describe the massive door, backed by the huge portcullis, backed by yet another massive door, though that inner one was likely left open.

"That sounds little like any entrance for us," Juraviel remarked.

"There may be smaller entrances nearby," Jojonah replied. "For that is a very ancient section of the abbey, and at one time the docks were used extensively. The great doors are fairly new, no more than two centuries old, but there once were many other ways into the structure from the docks."

"And you hope to find one of these in the dark night," the elf said doubtfully.

"It is possible that I could open the great doors with the gemstones," Jojonah said, glancing at Pony as he spoke. "St.-Mere-Abelle takes few precautions against magical attacks. If they are expecting a ship, the portcullis, the only obstacle against successful stone use, might be open."

Pony didn't reply.

"Our bellies are full, our fire warm," the ranger remarked. "Let us find some rest now, until the time is right."

Jojonah looked up at Sheila, the bright moon, and tried to recall the latest he had heard concerning the tides. He rose and bade the ranger to accompany him back to the waterfront, and when they got down there, they saw that the water was much calmer and almost back down to the base of the rocks.

"Two hours," Jojonah reasoned. "And then we will have the time we need to get into St.-Mere-Abelle and complete our task."

He made it all sound so easy, Elbryan noted.

"You should not come here," Markwart told Brother Francis when the man arrived at the Father Abbot's private quarters, a place he had frequented often in the last few weeks. "Not yet."

Brother Francis held his arms out wide, truly perplexed by the hostile attitude.

"We must turn our attention wholly to the College of Abbots," Markwart explained. "You will be there, and so will the centaur, if we are successful."

Brother Francis' face screwed up even more with confusion. "I?" he asked. "But I am not worthy, Father Abbot. I am not even an immaculate, and will not attain that title until next spring, when all of the abbots are back in their respective abbeys."

The grin that splayed across the Father Abbot's wrinkled and withered face nearly took in his ears.

"What is it?" Brother Francis asked, his tone edging on frantic.

"You will be there," Markwart said again. "Immaculate Brother Francis will stand beside me."

"But—But—" Francis stuttered, too overwhelmed. "But I have not reached my ten years. My preparations for promotion to immaculate brother are in order, I assure you, but the rank cannot be attained by one who has not yet spent a full decade—"

"As Master De'Unnero became the youngest abbot in the modern Church, so you will become the youngest immaculate brother," Markwart said matter-of-factly. "These are dangerous times, and sometimes the rules must be bent to accommodate the immediate needs of the Church."

"What of the others of my class?" Francis asked. "What of Brother Viscenti?"

Markwart laughed at the notion. "Many will attain their new rank in the spring, as scheduled. As for Brother Viscenti . . ." He paused and grinned even wider. "Well, let us just say that the company he keeps could well determine his future.

"But for you," the Father Abbot went on, "there can be no delays. I must promote you to immaculate before I can then move you into the position of master. Church doctrine is unbending on that point, regardless of situation."

Francis teetered and felt faint. Of course, he had predicted as much to Braumin Herde that day in the seawall corridor, but had no idea that his mentor would move so quickly. And now that he had heard the proclamation out loud, had heard firsthand that Father Abbot Markwart did indeed mean to promote him to one of the two vacant master positions, he was surely overwhelmed.

Brother Francis felt as if he was rebuilding the pedestal of self-righteousness he had broken by killing Grady Chilichunk, as if, by mere fact of his ascension in the Order, he was redeeming himself, or even that he needed no redemption, that it had been, after all, merely an unfortunate accident.

"But you must stay far from me until that the promotion is finalized," Markwart explained. "Better for protocol. I do have a most important job for you, in any case—that of breaking Bradwarden. The centaur will speak for us, against Avelyn and against this woman who now holds the gemstones."

Brother Francis shook his head. "He thinks of them as kin," he dared to disagree.

Markwart brushed the notion away. "Every man, every beast, has a breaking point," he insisted. "With the magical armband, you can inflict upon Bradwarden such horrors that he will beg for death, and that he will give up his friends as enemies of the Church merely on your promise to kill him quickly. Be inventive, immaculate brother!"

The title was indeed inviting, but Francis' face soured anyway at the thought of the distasteful job.

"Do not fail me in this," Markwart said sternly. "That wretched beast may be the keystone of our declaration against Avelyn, and do not doubt that that declaration is vital to the survival of the Abellican Church."

Francis bit his lip, his emotions obviously torn.

"Without the centaur's confirmation against Avelyn, Master Jojonah and others will stand against us, and the very best we might hope for is that the labeling of Avelyn Desbris as a heretic will be taken under consideration," Markwart explained. "Such a 'consideration' process will take years to complete."

"But if he truly was a heretic—and he was," Francis quickly added, seeing the Father Abbot's eyes going wide with rage, "then time is our ally. Avelyn's own actions will damn him, in the eyes of God and in the eyes of the Church."

"Fool!" Markwart snapped at him, and the Father Abbot spun away, as if he couldn't stand the sight of Francis, a gesture that profoundly stung the younger monk. "Each passing day will count against us, against me, if the gemstones are not recovered. And if Avelyn is not openly declared a heretic, then the general populace and the King's army will not aid in our quest to find the woman and bring her to justice."

Francis followed that reasoning; anyone officially deemed a heretic became an outlaw not only of the Church, but of the kingdom as well.

"And I will have those gemstones!" Markwart went on. "I am not a young man. Would you have me go to my grave with this issue unresolved? Would you have my presidency over St.-Mere-Abelle be marred by this black mark?"

"Of course not, Father Abbot," Francis replied.

"Then go to the centaur," Markwart said so coldly that the hairs on the back of Francis' neck stood up. "*Enlist* him."

Brother Francis staggered out of the room, as shaken as if Markwart had physically struck him. He ran his hand through his hair and started for the lower dungeons, determined that he would not fail his Father Abbot.

Markwart moved to the door and shut it, and locked it, scolding himself silently for allowing his office to be so open, given the secret and telling floor design in the adjoining room. He went to that room then, admiring his work. The pentagram was perfect, exactly as it had appeared in the book, scratched into the floor and with the grooves filled by multicolored wax.

The Father Abbot had not slept in more than a day, too engrossed in his work and in the mysteries the strange tome was showing him. Perhaps the Chilichunks would also attend the College of Abbots. Markwart could bring spirits up to reinhabit their bodies, and with hematite he could all but eliminate the natural decay.

It was a risky move, he knew, but it was not without precedence. *The Incantations Sorcerous* clearly spelled out a similar ruse, used against the second abbess of St. Gwendolyn. Two of St. Gwendolyn's masters had turned against the abbess, arguing that no woman should hold such a position of power—indeed, other than the abbey of St. Gwendolyn, women played only a minor role in all the Church. When one of those masters found that the other had died, merely of old age, he understood his predicament, for he knew that he could not battle the abbess alone. But through prudent use of *The Incantations Sorcerous*, the master had not been alone. He had summoned a minor malevolent spirit to inhabit his friend's corpse, and together they waged war on the abbess for nearly a year to come.

Markwart moved back to his desk, needing to sit and consider his course. The Chilichunk imposters would only have to be in front of the College for a short while. It was possible that the deception would succeed, for only he and Francis knew with certainty that the couple had died, and then he would have two strong witnesses against the woman.

But what might be the cost of failure? Markwart had to wonder, and the possibilities seemed grim indeed.

"But I'll not know until I see the animations," he said aloud, nodding. He decided to follow the course. He would bring the Chilichunks—their bodies, at least—under his control, and see how fine the deception appeared. Then he could decide, while watching the progress of Bradwarden's bending, whether or not to present them before the College.

Smiling, rubbing his hands with anticipation, Markwart took up the black book and a pair of candles and went into the prepared room. He placed the candles in the appropriate positions and lit them, then used diamond magic to pervert their glow, having them give off a black light instead of yellow. Then he sat between them, within the pentagram, legs crossed.

Soul stone in one hand, *The Incantations Sorcerous* in the other, Markwart walked free of his body.

The room took on strange dimensions, seemed to warp and twist before his spiritual eyes. He saw the physical exit, and then another, a portal in the floor with a long, sloping passageway behind it.

He took this darker route, his soul going down, down.

Sheila was directly above the abbey, and the water was far, far out when Jojonah led the ranger and his companions to the wharves and the lower door. Symphony and Greystone had been left far behind, as had many of the gemstones, Pony taking only those she thought might prove necessary.

She now held a malachite, the stone of levitation and telekinesis, and a lodestone.

Jojonah led the way to the great doors in front of the wharves, then inspected them closely, even taking the ranger's sword and sliding it under one worn area. As he moved the blade back and forth he felt the barriers— the portcullis was down.

"We should search south along the cliff face," Jojonah reasoned, speaking in a whisper and motioning that there might be guards atop the wall—though that wall was several hundred feet above the companions. "That is the most likely place for us to find a more accessible door."

"Do you suspect that any guards will be posted within this portal?" Pony asked.

"At this time of night, I doubt there are any below the second level of the abbey," Jojonah replied with confidence. "Except perhaps for guards Markwart has posted near the prisoners."

"Then let us try these," Pony replied.

"The portcullis is down," Jojonah explained, trying hard, but futilely, to keep the edge of hope in his voice.

Pony held up the malachite, but the monk wore a doubtful expression.

"Too large," he explained. "Perhaps three thousand pounds. That is why this gate is hardly guarded. The front doors swing in, but they cannot open while the portcullis is down. And of course that portcullis is inaccessible to any lever we might construct while the solid doors are closed."

"Not inaccessible to magic," Pony argued. Before the master could protest, she fished out the soul stone and was soon out of body, slipping through the crack between the front doors to view the portcullis. She went back to her physical coil quickly, not wanting to expend too much energy. "This is the way," she announced. "The inner doors are not closed, nor did I see any sign of guards in the hallway beyond."

Jojonah didn't doubt her; he had done enough spirit-walking to know its potential, and to understand that even in the darkened tunnels, the woman would have been able to "see" clearly enough.

"The front doors are barred, as well as blocked by the portcullis," Pony explained. "Prepare a torch and go and listen carefully, for the lifting portcullis and then the bar. When you hear it rise, go quickly, for I know not how long I can offer you."

"You cannot lift—" Jojonah started to protest, but Pony had already raised her hand with the malachite, had already fallen into the depths of the greenish stone.

Elbryan moved near the master and dropped a hand on his shoulder, bidding him to be quiet and watch.

"I hear the portcullis rising," Juraviel whispered after a few moments, the elf standing with his ear pressed against the large doors. Elbryan and a stunned Jojonah rushed to join him, and despite the monk's protests that it was impossible, he did indeed hear the grating sound of the great gate lifting into the ceiling.

Pony felt the tremendous strain. She had lifted giants before, but nothing of this magnitude. She focused on her image of that portcullis and fell deep, deep within the power of the stone, channeling its energy. The portcullis was up high enough, she believed, above the top of the doors, but then she had to reach even deeper, to grab the locking bar as well and somehow try to lift it.

She trembled violently; sweat beaded on her forehead and her eyes blinked rapidly. She pictured the bar, found it in her mental image, and grabbed at it with all her remaining strength.

Juraviel pressed his ear closer, could hear the bar shifting, one end going up. "Now, Nightbird!" he said, and the ranger put his shoulder to the great doors and heaved with all his strength. The bar fell free, the doors swung open, and Elbryan slipped down to one knee in the passageway, quickly moving to light his torch.

"The locking mechanism is in a cubby down to the right," the monk said to the elf as Juraviel ran past Elbryan.

A moment later the torch came up and the elf announced that the portcullis was secured. Jojonah, back at Pony's side, shook the woman roughly, drawing her from her trance. She came out of it and stumbled, nearly falling over for lack of strength.

"I have seen but one other with such power," Jojonah remarked to her as he led her into the passage.

"He is with me," Pony replied calmly.

The master smiled, not doubting her claim and taking great comfort in the possibility. He quietly closed the inner doors then, explaining that the draft would be felt deep into the abbey if the corridor was left open to the sea.

"Where do we go?" the ranger asked.

Jojonah thought on it for a moment. "I can get us to the dungeons," he said, "but only by going up several levels, then coming back down at another point."

"Lead on," said Elbryan.

But the monk was shaking his head. "I do not like the possibilities," he explained. "If we encounter any brothers, the alarm will be sounded." The notion that they might indeed meet up with some of St.-Mere-Abelle's flock brought a wave of panic over Jojonah, not for this powerful trio and their mission, but for the unfortunate brothers they might encounter.

"I beg you not to kill any," he blurted suddenly.

Elbryan and Pony exchanged curious glances.

"Brothers, I mean," Jojonah explained. "Most are unwitting pawns for Markwart, at worst, and not deserving of—"

"We did not come in here to kill anyone," Elbryan interrupted. "And so we shall not, on my word."

Pony nodded her agreement, and so did Juraviel, though the elf wasn't so sure that the ranger had spoken wisely.

"There may be a better way to the dungeons," Jojonah said. "There are old tunnels off to the side, just a hundred feet in. Most are blocked, but we can pass those barriers."

"And you will know your way along them?" the ranger asked.

"No," Jojonah admitted. "But they all tie together—the oldest parts of the abbey—and I am certain that any course will lead us soon enough to a place I can recognize."

Elbryan looked to his friends for confirmation, and they both nodded, preferring a trek down unused passageways to a course that would likely put them in contact with other monks. First, on Juraviel's reasoning, they also closed the portcullis, preferring to leave no sign that the abbey's security had been breached.

They found the old passageway soon after, and, as Jojonah predicted, had no trouble in getting through the barrier the monks had constructed. Soon they were walking along the most ancient corridors and rooms of St.-Mere-Abelle, sections that had not been used in centuries. The floors and walls were all broken, the uneven angles of stone casting ominous lengthened shadows in the torchlight. Water stood calf-deep in many places, and small lizards ran on padded feet along the walls and ceiling. At one point Elbryan had to draw out Tempest just to cut his way through a myriad of thick webs.

They were intruders here, as any person would be, for these regions had been left for the lizards and the spiders, for the damp and the greatest adversary, time. But the companions plodded on through the often narrow always twisting corridors, spurred by thoughts of Bradwarden and the Chilichunks.

The tunnel was dark and without detail, just a swirling mass of gray and black. Fog drifted up about the spirit of wandering Markwart, and though his form was noncorporeal, in this place he felt the cold touch of that mist.

For the first time in a long, long while, Markwart considered his course and wondered if he was wandering too far from the light. He recalled that time when he was a young man, first entering St.-Mere-Abelle half a century before. He had been so full of idealism and faith, and those qualities had pushed him up through the ranks, attaining immaculate on the tenth anniversary of his entrance to the Order, and master only three short years later. Unlike so many of the previous Father Abbots, Markwart had never left St.-Mere-Abelle to serve as abbot of another abbey, had spent all of his years in the presence of the gemstones, in the most sacred of Abellican houses.

And now, he reasoned, the gemstones had shown him a new and greater path. He was beyond the limits of his predecessors, wandering into regions unexplored and unexploited. And so, after only a moment of doubt, it was with great pride, bolstered by his unwavering confidence in himself, that Markwart continued the descent along the dark and cold tunnel. He understood the perils here, but was certain he would be able to take whatever evils he found and twist them for the sake of good, the end justifying the means.

The tunnel widened to a black plane of swirling gray fog, and among its rolling mounds and stinking mists Markwart saw the huddled forms, blacker shadows among the darkness, hunched and twisted.

Several nearby sensed his spirit and approached hungrily, clawed hands extended.

Markwart held up his hand and ordered them back, and to his satisfaction, they did indeed retreat, forming a semicircle about him, red-glowing eyes staring at him hungrily.

"Would you like to see again the world of the living?" the spirit asked of the two closest.

They leaped forward, cold hands grasping Markwart's ghostly wrists.

A sense of elation filled the Father Abbot's spirit. So very easy! He turned and started back up the tunnel, the demon spirits in tow. He opened his eyes then, his physical eyes, blinking in the sudden candlelight, the twin flames flickering wildly. They were still burning black, but not for long, for they flared red and huge suddenly, great fires spouting up from the meager candles, swaying, dancing, filling all the room with their red-hued light, stinging Markwart's eyes.

But he did not, could not, look away, mesmerized by the black shapes forming within those fires, humanoid shapes, hunched and twisted.

Out they stepped, side by side, the two hideous forms, their hungry, red-glowing eyes boring into the seated Father Abbot. Beside them the candles flared one last time and returned to normal, and all the room was hushed.

Markwart sensed that these demon creatures could spring upon him and rend him to pieces, but he was not afraid.

"Come," he bade them, "I will show you to your new hosts." He fell into the hematite and his spirit walked free of his body once more.

❖ 32 ❖

Pony's Nightmare

T he ranger carefully marked the walls at every intersection, and there were many in this maze of ancient and unused corridors. The four wandered for more than an hour, at one point chopping their way through a door and dismantling a bricked barrier before finally happening upon an area that seemed familiar to Jojonah.

"We are near the center of the abbey," the monk explained. "To the south is the quarry, and the ancient crypts and libraries; to the north, the corridors that used to serve as living quarters for the brothers, but now serve Markwart as dungeon cells." Without any prompting, the master led the way, moving carefully and quietly.

Soon after, Elbryan doused the torch, for the flickering of firelight could be seen up ahead.

"Some of the cells are there," Jojonah explained.

"Guarded?" asked the ranger.

"Possibly," the monk replied. "And it could be that the Father Abbot himself, or one of his powerful lackeys, is nearby, interrogating the prisoners."

Elbryan motioned for Juraviel to take up the point. The elf moved far ahead, returning a few moments later to report that two young men were indeed standing a calm guard in the area of torchlight.

"They are not wary," Juraviel explained.

"They would expect no trouble down here," Master Jojonah said with confidence.

"You stay here," Elbryan said to the monk. "It would not be wise for you to be seen. Pony and I will clear the way."

Jojonah dropped an anxious hand on the ranger's forearm.

"We'll not kill them," Elbryan promised.

"They are trained fighters," Jojonah warned, but the ranger hardly seemed to be listening, already moving ahead, Pony and Juraviel by his side.

As they neared the area, Elbryan moved in front, then went down low to one knee, peering around an earthen bend.

There stood the two young monks, one stretching and yawning, the other leaning heavily against the wall, half asleep.

Suddenly the ranger was between them, elbow lashing out at the leaning monk, slamming him hard into the wall. Up snapped Elbryan's backhand the other way, dropping the yawning monk even as he opened wide his eyes and started to protest. The ranger turned back to the one now slumping even lower against the wall, wrapping the man, spinning him over and putting him facedown to the floor, while Pony and Juraviel came in on the other, who was too dazed from the heavy hit to offer any resistance. Using fine elven twine, they bound the men, and gagged them and blindfolded them using their own monk robes, and the ranger dragged them down a dark side passage.

By the time he returned, Jojonah was back with the group, and Pony was standing outside a wooden door, staring hard at it. As soon as Jojonah had identified it as Pettibwa's cell, Pony started toward it as if she meant to burst right in. But now she could not.

The stench told her the truth, the same smell she had known in sacked Dundalis those many years before.

Elbryan was beside her in an instant, steadying her as she finally lifted the latch and pushed open the door.

The torchlight splayed into the filthy room, and there, amidst her own waste, lay Pettibwa, the skin on her thick arms slack and hanging, her face so very pale and hugely bloated. Pony stumbled to her, fell to her knees beside the woman and moved to cradle Pettibwa's head, but the body would not bend, and so the woman lowered her head to Pettibwa instead, her shoulders bobbing with sobs.

She had known nothing but love for this foster mother, the woman who had seen her into adulthood, who had taught her so much about life and love, and about generosity, for in those years long past, Pettibwa had no practical reason to take in the orphaned Pony. Yet she had accepted Pony into her family fully, shown the girl as much love and support as she gave to her own son, and that was considerable indeed.

And now she was dead, and in no small part because of that loving generosity. Pettibwa was dead because she had been kind to an orphaned child, because she had served as mother to the woman who became an outlaw of the Church.

Elbryan held Pony close and tried to hold together her emotions—so many whirling emotions: guilt and grief, sheer sadness and a great emptiness.

"I need to talk to her," Pony said repeatedly, her words coming out over sobbing gasps. "I need—"

Elbryan tried to comfort her, tried to hold her steady, and grabbed her arm when she reached for the soul stone.

"She has been gone too long," the ranger said.

"I can find her spirit and say good-bye," Pony reasoned.

"Not here, not now," Elbryan softly replied.

Pony started to protest, but finally, with trembling hand, replaced the gem in her pouch—though she kept her hand close to it.

"I need to talk to her," she said more firmly, and turned from her lover to the corpse once more, bending low and whispering farewells to her second mother.

Jojonah and Juraviel watched from the doorway, the monk horrified, though surely not surprised that the woman had not survived the wrath of Markwart. He was embarrassed as well that one of his Order, indeed the very leader of his Order, had done this to the innocent woman.

"Where is the other human?" Juraviel asked.

Jojonah nodded to the next cell in line, and they both went quickly— only to find Graevis hanging dead, the chain still wrapped about his neck.

"He escaped the only way he could," Jojonah said somberly.

Juraviel went right to the corpse, carefully turning it out of the chain choker. Graevis' stiff form contorted weirdly as it fell to the length of the single shackle, but better for Pony to see him like that, the elf reasoned, than in his death pose.

"She needs to be alone," Elbryan said to them, joining Jojonah in the doorway.

"A bitter blow," Juraviel agreed.

"Where is Bradwarden?" the ranger asked Jojonah, his tone stern, forcing the guilt-ridden monk to retreat a step. Elbryan recognized Jojonah's horror at once, though, and so he put a comforting hand on the monk's broad shoulder. "It is a difficult time for us all," he offered.

"The centaur is farther along the corridor," Jojonah explained.

"If he lives," Juraviel put in.

"We will go to him," the ranger said to the elf, motioning for Jojonah to lead on. "You stay close to Pony. Protect her from enemies and from her own turmoil."

Juraviel nodded and came out of the cell as Elbryan and Jojonah made their quiet way along the corridor. Juraviel went back to Pony then, telling her gently that Graevis, too, was dead, then embracing her as sobs of grief washed over her.

Jojonah followed the ranger farther down the low corridor, guiding Elbryan past intersections with soft whispers. They moved around a final bend into another shadowy, torchlit area, where they saw two doors, one on the left-hand wall and another at the very end the corridor.

"You think this is ended, but it has only begun!" they heard a man cry, followed closely by the crack of a whip and a low, feral growl.

"Brother Francis," Jojonah explained. "A lackey of the Father Abbot."

The ranger started ahead, but stopped fast, and Jojonah faded into the shadows, as the door began to open.

The monk, a man of about the same years as Elbryan, stepped out, whip in hand and a very sour expression on his face. He froze in place, eyes going wide as he took note of Elbryan, this stranger standing impassively, sword still in its scabbard.

"Where are the guards?" the monk asked. "And who are you?"

"A friend of Avelyn Desbris," Elbryan replied grimly, and loudly. "And a friend of Bradwarden."

"Oh, by the gods, good show!" came a cry from within the cell, and it surely did Elbryan's heart good to hear the booming voice of his centaur friend again. "Oh, but ye're to get yer due, Francis the fool!"

"Silence!" Francis commanded the centaur. He rubbed his hands together and eased the whip out to its length as Elbryan advanced a step—though the ranger still did not bother to draw his sword.

Francis lifted the whip threateningly. "Your friendships alone show you to be an outlaw," he said, a nervous edge to his voice despite his best efforts to appear calm.

The ranger recognized those efforts, but hardly cared whether this man was confident or not. Bradwarden's voice and the realization that this man had just used that whip on his centaur friend assaulted the ranger's sensibilities, sent him spiraling into that warrior mentality. He continued his advance.

Francis pumped his arm but didn't snap the whip. He shifted uncomfortably and glanced over his shoulder as often as forward.

On came Nightbird, Tempest still sheathed at his hip.

Now the panicking Francis did try to snap the whip, but Nightbird quick-stepped forward, inside its rolling length, and pushed it aside. The monk threw the weapon at him, turned and sprinted for the door at the end of the corridor. He grabbed at the handle and yanked hard, and the door opened about a foot before Nightbird's hand was against it, stopping its momentum.

With frightening strength the ranger slammed the door closed.

Sensing an opening in the ranger's defenses, Francis spun about and launched a straight right punch for the man's exposed ribs.

But even as his right hand pushed the door, Nightbird stiffened his left hand, holding it fingers up and perpendicular to his body, a foot in front of him. A simple, slight shift, perfectly timed, brushed Francis' hand out wide, and then Francis' successive left was turned harmlessly under the ranger's upraised right arm.

Francis tried yet another fast right, and again the ranger picked it off, brushing it out wide with the same blocking hand, only this time he followed it out, keeping the back of his fingers in contact with Francis' arm. It all seemed too slow to Francis, and too easy, but suddenly the tempo changed, Nightbird rolling his hand fast over Francis' forearm, grabbing hard and yanking back across his body. He caught Francis' fist, covering it with his right hand and pulling hard, again with the frightful, undeniable strength.

Francis lurched to the side, his arm drawn right across his body and down, and his breath was blasted away by a short, straight left jab to his side, a punch incredibly jarring, given the mere five inches the ranger's fist traveled. Francis bounced hard against the door and tried to recover, but Nightbird, holding fast the monk's fist, drove his arm up and under Francis', and the sudden movement at so strange an angle brought a loud, bone-jarring pop from Francis' elbow. Waves of pain washed over him. His broken arm was thrown up high as he fell back squarely against the door, and the large ranger waded in, hitting him with a right to the stomach that doubled him over, followed by a left uppercut to the chest that lifted his feet right off the ground.

A devastating flurry followed, left and right in rapid succession, hammering away, jolting Francis against the door or up into the air.

It ended as abruptly as it had started, with Nightbird moving back a step, leaving Francis bent forward from the door, one hand holding his belly, the other hanging limply. He looked up at the ranger just in time to see the roundhouse left hook. It caught him on the side of the jaw, snapped his head violently to the side, and flipped him right over to land on his back on the hard floor.

All the world was spinning into blackness for Francis as the large form moved over him. "Do not kill him!" he heard from far, far away.

Nightbird hushed Jojonah immediately, not wanting his voice to be recognized. He relaxed when he looked closer at his victim, to see that Francis was unconscious. Moving quickly, the ranger dropped a sack over the monk's head and bade Jojonah to bind him, then went charging into Bradwarden's cell.

"Taked ye long enough to find me," the centaur said cheerily.

Elbryan was overcome by the sight, and thrilled, for Bradwarden was indeed very much alive, and looking healthier than the ranger could ever have hoped.

"The armband," the centaur explained. "What a good bit o' magic!"

Elbryan ran over and embraced his friend, then, remembering that time was not their ally, went right for the large shackles and chains.

"I'm hopin' ye found a key," the centaur remarked. "Ye're not for breaking them!"

Elbryan reached into his pouch and produced the packet of red gel, the same substance he had used on the tree against the raiding goblins. He unfolded the packet, then smeared the reddish gel onto the four chains holding the centaur.

"Ah, but ye got more o' the same stuff ye used in Aida," the centaur said delightedly.

"We must be quick," Jojonah remarked, coming into the room. The sight of him put Bradwarden into a fit, but Elbryan was quick to explain that this was no enemy.

"He was with them that took me from Aida," Bradwarden explained. "With them that put me in chains."

"And with them that mean to get you out of these chains," the ranger was quick to add.

Bradwarden's visage softened. "Ah, true enough," he surrendered. "And he did give me me pipes on the long road."

"I am no enemy of yours, noble Bradwarden," Jojonah said with a bow.

The centaur nodded, then turned his head and blinked curiously as his right arm came down from the wall. There stood Elbryan, Tempest in hand, readying to strike at the chain that held the centaur's right hind leg.

"Good sword," Bradwarden remarked, and then, with a single swing, his leg, too, was free.

"Go see to Elbryan," Pony said. She was still kneeling beside the body of Pettibwa, but she resolutely straightened her back.

"I doubt that he needs any assistance," the elf replied.

Pony took a deep breath. "Nor do I," she said, and Juraviel understood that she wanted to be alone. He noted that her hand was again clutched about a stone in the pouch, and that was surely alarming, but in the end he knew that he had to trust in Pony. He kissed her gently on the top of the head, then moved back from her, out the door of the cell but no farther, keeping quiet guard in the torchlit corridor.

Pony tried hard to hold control. She put her hand to Pettibwa's bloated cheek and stroked it gently, lovingly, and it seemed to her as if the dead woman settled easier, as if the pallid color of death was not so obvious.

Pony felt something then, a sensation, a rush, a tickle. Confused, wondering if, in her longing to reach out to Pettibwa, she had unintentionally slipped under the power of the soul stone she once more held tight in her hand. Following that course, Pony closed her eyes and tried to concentrate. Then she saw them, or thought she did, a trio of spirits, one an old man, rushing through the room.

Three spirits: Pettibwa, Graevis, and Grady?

The notion startled Pony as much as it intrigued her, but still not understanding, she became afraid and wisely broke all connection to the soul stone. She opened her eyes and looked down at Pettibwa—to see the woman looking back at her!

"What magic might this be?" Pony muttered aloud. Had she subconsciously reached out so powerfully with the soul stone that she had grabbed Pettibwa's disembodied spirit? Was such resurrection even possible?

She got her terrifying answer as Pettibwa's eyes flared red with demonic flames and the woman's face contorted, a guttural snarl coming from her opened mouth.

Pony rocked back, too confused, too overwhelmed, to immediately react, and her horror only grew as the corpse's teeth elongated into pointed fangs.

Up came the corpse to a sitting position, too suddenly, plump arms shooting out and clamping hard, with superhuman strength, about Pony's throat. The horrified young woman thrashed violently, turning her hands into every possible angle to gain leverage but making no headway in dislodging the demon's powerful grip.

But then Juraviel was there, his slender sword slashing hard against Pettibwa's bloated forearm, opening it wide that the pus and gore could spill out.

Elbryan was just about to sever the last of Bradwarden's chains when Pony's cry reached his ears. He slashed hard with Tempest, spinning on his heel and taking several steps before the chain even fell to the floor, Jojonah close behind. He came around the bend in full speed, heard a tumult within the cell that held the body of Graevis, and kicked open the door.

And then he stopped, stunned, for the animated corpse had bitten right through its one chained wrist and now came toward him, its eyes flaring with red fires, its stump arm leading the way with a spray of blood.

Elbryan wanted to go to Pony—above all else, he wanted to get by her side—but he could not rush off, and took some comfort when Jojonah thundered past behind him on his way to Pettibwa's cell. Out came Tempest and in charged the ranger, meeting the demon creature head on, ignoring the spray of the bloody stump and slashing away viciously at the reaching arms.

"My mum," Pony said repeatedly, falling back against the wall as Juraviel battled the creature. The woman knew rationally that she should go to Juraviel's side, or that she should use the gemstones now, perhaps the soul stone to force this evil spirit from Pettibwa's body. But she could not act, could not get past the horror at seeing Pettibwa, her adopted mother, in this state!

She forced herself to find a level of calm, told herself repeatedly that if she could get into the soul stone, she might learn the truth of this creature. Before she could begin the move, though, Juraviel thrust ahead powerfully, right between the reaching arms, stabbing his sword deep into the corpse's heart, a sight that froze Pony in place.

The demon laughed wildly and batted the elf's hand from the sword hilt, then swatted Juraviel with a backhand that launched him head over heels.

The elf accepted the blow, and was moving with it before it ever connected, diminishing much of the shock. A flutter of his wings, a perfect twist in midair, landed him squarely on his feet, facing the demon creature—which still had the sword sticking from its chest.

Then another form came charging into the small cell, rushing past the elf. Without slowing, Jojonah slammed hard into the demon, burying it under his tremendous weight, taking it heavily into the back wall.

And then Bradwarden entered, and the cell was packed full of bodies!

"What is it about?" the centaur gasped.

With an unearthly roar, the demon launched Jojonah away, but Bradwarden found his answers quickly, and as the creature rushed forward, the centaur spun about and hit it with a double-kick that sent it careening back into the wall. Bradwarden moved right in on the creature, front hooves smashing away, fists pounding hard, a sudden and brutal beating that would not allow the demon to find any time to go on the offensive.

"Get her out of here," Juraviel instructed Jojonah. As the monk scooped Pony into his arms, the elf leveled his bow and waited for an opening.

All the months of Bradwarden's frustration came pouring out in the next seconds as the centaur rained blow after blow on the demon creature, battering it, tearing bloated flesh, smashing bone into pulp. Still, if he was truly harming the creature, it didn't show it, just kept trying to find some way to grab at him.

But then an arrow popped into one of those red-glowing eyes, and how the demon howled!

"Oh, but ye didn't like that one!" the centaur said, using the opportunity to spin about and drive his rear legs right into the demon face. With the head already pressed against the stone wall, the skull exploded in a shower of gore, but still the body fought on, arms flailing wildly.

Jojonah ushered Pony into the hall and set her down against the wall.

"Damned thing, lay down and die!" came Elbryan's voice from the next cell.

The monk charged away to the door and then looked back, a disgusted expression on his face, waving for Pony to stay back.

Inside the cell, Elbryan slashed hard with Tempest, abandoning his normal thrusting style, for he had stabbed the creature several times, driving his sword tip deep into flesh and organs, with little effect. So he had gone to a more conventional style, taking up the mighty sword in both hands and swinging it in devastating, slashing motions. One of the demon's arms was severed at the elbow, and a downstroke of Tempest took the other, right at the shoulder.

Still the creature came on, but a straight-across cut of Tempest stopped its momentum and gave the ranger time to level and line up his backswing.

Jojonah looked away, understanding, as the great sword flashed across, lopping the head off. When the monk looked back, his revulsion was even greater, for that head, lying to the side against the wall, was still biting at the air, fires still burning in the eyes! And the body continued to press the attack.

Elbryan punched out with his fist and knocked the body back, then took up Tempest in both hands, did a complete pivot, coming around with the sword low, taking off one leg. The corpse tumbled to the side, one stump thrashing, one leg kicking, and with the head, just a few inches away, snapping futilely at the air.

The fires in the eyes were diminishing, though, and Elbryan soon realized that the fight was over. He rushed back into the hall, past Jojonah, past Bradwarden and Juraviel as they exited the first cell, to grab up the hysterical Pony in his arms.

"Still kicking," Bradwarden explained to Jojonah when the monk saw that Pettibwa's body, the gory remains of its head flapping about its shoulders, was still flailing against the wall, tearing at the stone.

"But not for knowing which way to turn," the centaur added, closing the door.

Jojonah went to the ranger and the woman. Amazingly, Pony was fast composing herself.

"Demon spirits," the monk explained, looking Pony right in the eye. "Those were not the souls of Graevis and Pettibwa."

"I saw them," Pony stuttered, gasping for breath, her teeth trembling. "I saw them come in, but there were three."

"Three?"

"Two shadows and an old man," she explained. "I thought it was Graevis, though I could not see clearly."

"Markwart," Jojonah breathed. "He brought them here. And if you saw them—"

"Then he saw you," Elbryan reasoned.

"We must be gone from this place, and quickly," Jojonah cried. "Markwart is on his way, do not doubt, and with an army of brothers behind him!"

"Run on," said Elbryan, pushing Jojonah toward the same ancient corridors that had brought them to this cursed place. He glanced back once at the side passage where they had put the guards, then took up the rear of the line, with Pony beside him. They moved as swiftly as the often tight and twisting corridors would allow, and soon came upon the dock doors of the abbey, closed and with the portcullis down, as they had left them.

Master Jojonah started for the crank, but Pony, steadier now and with a grim determination set upon her face, held him back. She took out the malachite once more and fell into its magic, and though she was weary and emotionally battered, she brought up a wall of rage and channeled it into the stone. With hardly an effort, it seemed, the portcullis slid up into the ceiling holes.

Elbryan was right to the great doors, lifting the locking bar and pulling one open. He moved to put the bar aside, but again Pony, still in the throes of the levitational magic, intervened.

"Hold the bar above the locking latch," she instructed. "Quickly."

They could hear the terrific strain in her voice, so Bradwarden ushered Jojonah out the open door, while Juraviel went behind Pony and gently eased her along, as well. As she passed the open door and Elbryan, Pony put her other hand, holding the magnetite, against the outside of the metallic door and fell into that magic as well.

The portcullis shifted dangerously over Elbryan's head, but Jojonah, understanding what the clever woman meant to do, was at Pony's side, easing the magnetite from her hand and strengthening the magnetic pull, through the door and onto the metal locking bar. Pony fell fully into the malachite once more, steadying the portcullis as Elbryan, too, came outside.

The ranger pulled the door closed, and Jojonah released his magnetic magic, then gave a satisfied sigh as the locking bar fell into place across the latches of the two doors. Then Pony gradually let go of her magic, easing the portcullis down, making it look as if these doors had not been breached.

She turned about and blinked in the glare, as did the others, the morning sun low in the sky before her, cutting shafts of light through the thick fog lifting from All Saints Bay. The tide was not in, but it was on the way, and so they set off immediately and at a swift pace, back down the beach and along the trail to their horses.

Snarling with rage, and despite the protests of the two dozen brothers rushing about him, the Father Abbot was the first to crash through the doors to the dungeon area on the lower level.

There was the battered Francis, the hood still tight about his head, struggling to stand, being helped by one of the other guards Elbryan had overpowered. Farther along the corridor, just inside the doors of their cells, lay the destroyed bodies of the Chilichunks, Pettibwa's still thrashing at the floor as the demon spirit struggled to the end.

Markwart was not surprised, of course, since he had seen the intruder, the woman kneeling over Pettibwa, on his escort of the demons, but the other monks could not have expected this grisly scene. Some cried and fell away, others fell to their knees in prayer.

"Our enemies brought demons against us," Markwart cried, waving a hand at the plump woman's body. "Well fought, Brother Francis!"

With some help from another young brother, Francis finally escaped the hood and his bonds. He started to explain that he had done little fighting, but stopped in the face of Markwart's glare. Francis wasn't certain what was going on here, hadn't seen the Chilichunks' animated corpses, and wasn't sure exactly who had destroyed the demons. He had a fair idea, though, and that notion sent many things careening through his thoughts.

* * *

Elbryan grew ill at ease, even frightened, as he watched Pony make her way along the trails. Her grunts were not of weariness, though she surely must have been exhausted after her magical feats, but of anger, a primal rage. The ranger stayed close to her, put his hand on her whenever the trail allowed, but she hardly looked at him, just continually blinked away any hint of tears, her jaw set firmly, her gaze locked ahead.

At the horses, Pony methodically retrieved the rest of her gemstones.

Jojonah offered to use healing hematite on Bradwarden, if the woman would loan him one, but the centaur brushed away that idea before Pony could begin to answer. "I'm just needing a bit o' food," he insisted, and truly, he did look healthy enough, though quite a bit skinnier than the last time the others had seen him. He patted his arm, the red elven armband securely in place. "Good gift ye gave to me," he said to Elbryan with a wink.

"Our road will be long and fast," the ranger warned, but Bradwarden only patted his less than ample belly and laughed. "I'm running all the faster for me lack o' belly," he said cheerily.

"Then let us go," said the ranger. "At once. Before the monks come out of their abbey to search for us. And let us deliver Master Jojonah to St. Precious on time."

"Ride Greystone," Pony bade the monk, handing him the reins.

Jojonah accepted them without protest, for it made sense that the lighter woman, and not he, should climb on the back of the centaur.

But Pony caught them all by surprise, turning not for Bradwarden, but back toward St.-Mere-Abelle, running full out, gemstones in hand.

Elbryan caught up to her twenty yards away and had to tackle her to stop her progress. Now she was indeed crying, shoulders bobbing with sobs, but she fought against him furiously, trying to get free, trying to get back to the abbey to exact some revenge.

"You cannot defeat them," the ranger said to her, holding her tightly. "They are too many and too strong. Not now."

Pony continued to fight, even unintentionally clawed Elbryan's face.

"You cannot dishonor Avelyn like this," Elbryan said to her, and that gave her pause. Gasping, tears streaming down her face, she looked at him skeptically.

"He gave you the stones to keep them safe," Elbryan explained. "Yet if you go back to the abbey now, you will be defeated and the gemstones will fall into the hands of our—of Avelyn's—enemies. They will be taken by the same one who brought such turmoil and pain to the Chilichunks. Would you give him that?"

All strength seemed to fall away from the woman then, and she slumped into her lover's arms, burying her face in his chest. He led her gently back to the others and put her in place atop Bradwarden, with Juraviel behind her to keep her steady.

"Give me the sunstone," he bade her, and when she did, he took it to Jojonah, explaining that they should put up some blocking magic to defeat any magical attempts to find them. Jojonah assured him that such a feat would be easy enough, so the ranger went to Symphony and took the lead as the group thundered away at full gallop, putting St.-Mere-Abelle far, far behind them before the sun climbed high in the eastern sky.

"Find them!" the Father Abbot fumed. "Search every passage and every room. All doors barred and guarded! Now! Now!"

The other monks scrambled, some heading back the way they had come to alert the rest of the library.

When the reports filtered back to Markwart that the back dock doors had apparently not been opened, the search within the library intensified, and by mid-morning nearly every corner of the great structure had been scoured. The outraged Markwart set up a central reporting area in the abbey's huge chapel, surrounded by the masters, each in command of a number of searching monks.

"They had to come in, and depart, through the dock doors," one of the masters reasoned, a sentiment backed by many. His scouting leader had just returned to him to report that no other door in the abbey showed any sign of entry.

"But the doors were closed and barred, an impossible feat from outside the abbey," another master reasoned.

"Unless they used magic," someone offered.

"Or unless someone within the abbey was there to meet them, to open the doors for them, to close the doors behind them," Markwart reasoned, and that thought drew an uncomfortable shift from every man in the room.

Soon after, when it was obvious that the enemies were indeed long gone from the abbey, Markwart ordered half the monks out in searching parties and another two dozen out magically, using quartz and hematite.

He knew the futility, though, for the Father Abbot was finally getting a true appreciation of the cunning and power of his real enemies. With that hopelessness came a pit of rage deeper than Markwart had ever known, one that he honestly believed would overwhelm him forever.

He found relief later that afternoon, though, when he interviewed Francis and the two monks who had been on guard near the cells, when he learned more about these intruders who had come to St.-Mere-Abelle, including one who was no stranger to the place.

Perhaps he wouldn't need the centaur and the Chilichunks after all. Perhaps he could shift the blame, even of the original theft of the gemstones by Avelyn, by theorizing about a larger conspiracy within the Order. Now, he understood. Now, he had a scapegoat.

And Je'howith would be bringing a contingent of Allheart soldiers.

Markwart stood in his private quarters that night, staring out the window. "We shall see," he said, a hint of a grin spreading on his face. "We shall see."

"You're not even to ask for the stones?" Pony said, standing on the streets of Palmaris with Elbryan and Master Jojonah. The group had landed earlier that morning north of the city, traveling across the great river on Captain Al'u'met's *Saudi Jacintha*, which, fortunately, had still been docked in Amvoy. Al'u'met had agreed to Jojonah's request for help without question and without payment, and with a promise that not a word of the impromptu ferry would be spoken to anyone.

Juraviel and Bradwarden were still in the north, while Elbryan, Pony, and Jojonah entered Palmaris, the monk to return to St. Precious, the other two to check on old friends.

"The sacred gems were given into fine care," Jojonah replied with a sincere smile. "My Church owes you much, but I fear that you will get no just rewards from the likes of Father Abbot Markwart."

"And you?" Elbryan asked.

"I go to deal with one less cunning, but equally wicked," Jojonah explained. "Pity all the monks of St. Precious, to have lost Abbot Dobrinion to Abbot De'Unnero."

They parted then as friends, with Jojonah retiring to the abbey and the other two moving along the streets of the city, trying to find some information. Pure luck brought them in the path of Belster O'Comely soon after, the man howling with glee to see them both alive.

"What information about Roger?" the ranger asked.

"He went south with the Baron," Belster explained. "To the King, so I've heard."

That bit of news pleased them immensely and filled them with hope, for word of the Baron's demise had not yet reached the common folk of Palmaris.

With Belster in tow, and Pony leading, they went next to Fellowship Way, the tavern that had been Pony's home for those difficult years after the first sacking of Dundalis. Profound pain assaulted Pony as she looked upon the place, and she could not stay, pleading with Elbryan to get her out of the city, back to the northland where they both belonged.

The ranger agreed, but first turned to Belster. "Go into the Way," he bade the innkeeper. "You have been looking to remain in Palmaris, so you told me. They will need help in there to keep the business open and running smoothly. I can think of none better suited for the job than you."

Before the innkeeper denied the request, he paused long enough to study the ranger and to follow Elbryan's gaze to Pony.

Then he understood.

"The finest tavern in all of Palmaris, so I've been told," he said.

"It was," Pony added grimly.

"And so it shall be again!" Belster said enthusiastically. He patted Elbryan on the shoulder, gave Pony a great hug, then started for the tavern, a noticeable spring in his step.

Pony watched him, even managed a smile, then looked up to Elbryan. "I love you," she said quietly.

The ranger returned her smile and kissed her gently on the forehead. "Come," he said, "we have friends waiting for us on the road to Caer Tinella."

Epilogue

The morning was brisk, despite the brilliant sunlight streaming in from the east. The breeze was not stiff, but Pony felt it keenly across every inch of her bare skin as she danced *bi'nelle dasada* among the falling many-colored leaves. She was not with Elbryan this morning, nor had she been for many days, preferring to dance alone now, for a time, as she used these moments of deep meditation as an escape from her grief and her guilt.

She saw Pettibwa and Graevis, even Grady, as she twirled about the piles of leaves. She remembered those days of her youth, faced them squarely and used them to put the events that had come after into a proper context. For, despite the very heavy burden of guilt, Pony rationally understood that she had done nothing wrong, that she had taken no road which, given the option once more, she would not now take.

And so she danced, every morning, and she cried, and when the grief finally began to lift and her common sense began to take the edge from her guilt, she was left with only . . .

Rage.

The leader of the Abellican Church was her enemy, had started a war from which Pony had no intention of running. Avelyn had given her the gemstones, and through that act of faith she felt well-armed.

She pivoted and turned in perfect balance, throwing a pile of leaves high with her fast-stepping feet. The meditation was deep and strong, a similar sensation as when she fell deep within the embrace of the gemstones. She was getting stronger.

She did not mean to maneuver around that wall of rage; she meant to smash right through it.

Winter came early that year, and by mid-Calember the ponds north of Caer Tinella already showed the shine of ice, and mornings were often greeted by a thin white coating of snow.

Farther to the south, the clouds hung heavy over All Saints Bay, the winter gales beginning to threaten. The water loomed darker, with the whitecaps rolling in against the cliffs contrasting starkly. Only two of the thirty abbots convening for the College at St.-Mere-Abelle—Olin of St. Bondabruce of Entel, and Abbess Delenia of St. Gwendolyn—had come by sea, and they both planned to stay as Markwart's guests throughout the winter, for few ships would brave such perilous waters at that time of year.

Despite the gathering of so many Church dignitaries, and reports that the war was all but over, the mood at the abbey was somber, as gloomy as the season. Many of the abbots had been personal friends of Abbot Dobrinion. Also, there was the general feeling, spurred by many whispers, that this College would prove eventful, even pivotal, to the future of the Church. Father Abbot Markwart's appointment of Marcalo De'Unnero to head St. Precious, and the recent news that a ninth-year brother had been promoted to Immaculate, were not matters without debate or opposition.

And everyone knew that other "guests" would be hovering about the College, a contingent of soldiers from Ursal, men of the fierce Allheart Brigade, by all accounts, on loan from the King to Abbot Je'howith of St. Honce. Such an accompanying force was certainly not without precedent in the Church, but it almost always signaled that some serious trouble was afoot.

Tradition dictated that the College would convene after vespers on the fifteenth day of the month, with all the participants, abbots and masters, spending the whole of the day quietly in reflection, preparing themselves mentally for the coming trials. Master Jojonah took this duty particularly to heart, closing himself in the small room afforded him, kneeling by his bed in prayer in the hopes that he would find some divine guidance. He had been quiet and impassive in his months under De'Unnero at St. Precious, taking no action to anger the new abbot or to even hint of the subversion that was in his heart. Of course, he had been scolded for leaving De'Unnero on the road, but after one brutal confrontation, nothing more had been said of the matter—to Jojonah, at least.

Now was his chance, he knew, perhaps his last chance, but could he find the courage to speak out openly against Markwart? He had heard little concerning the agenda of the College, but he strongly suspected—especially considering the companions the abbot of St. Honce had brought—that Markwart would use this opportunity to get a formal brand against Avelyn.

Markwart apparently had allies in this matter, powerful allies, but still, Jojonah knew what course his conscience dictated should Markwart's declaration against Avelyn come to pass.

But what if it did not?

Jojonah's midday meal was delivered outside his door, with only a single signaling knock, as he had instructed. He went to retrieve the food, and was surprised indeed when he opened the door to see Francis standing in the hall, holding his tray.

"So the rumors are true," Jojonah said distastefully. "Congratulations, immaculate brother. How unexpected." Jojonah took the tray, but held the door with his free hand, as if he meant to close it in Francis' face.

"I heard you," Francis said quietly.

Jojonah cocked his head, not understanding.

"In the dungeons," Francis remarked.

"Truly brother, I know not of what you speak," Jojonah said politely, falling back a step. He started to close the door, but Francis slipped into the room quickly.

"Shut the door," Francis said quietly.

Jojonah's first instinct was to lash out verbally at the upstart young man, but he could not ignore Francis' claim, and so he gently closed the door and moved to his bed, placing the tray on the small table.

"I know that it was you who betrayed us to the raiders," Francis said bluntly. "I have not yet determined who opened the wharf doors for you— and then closed them behind you—for I have witnesses as to the where-abouts of Brother Braumin Herde."

"Perhaps it was God who let them in," Jojonah said dryly.

Francis turned on him and didn't seem to much appreciate the wit.

"Who let you in, you mean," he stated firmly. "I heard you before I lost consciousness, and I assure you that I recognize your voice."

The smile left Jojonah's face, replaced by a determined stare.

"Perhaps you should have let the man kill me," Francis stated.

"Then I would be just like you," Jojonah quietly replied. "And that I fear worse than any punishment, worse than death itself."

"How could you know?" Francis demanded, trembling with rage and advancing a step, as if he meant to strike out at Jojonah.

"Know?" the master echoed.

"That I killed him!" Francis blurted, falling back and breathing hard. "Grady Chilichunk. How could you know that it was I who killed him on the road?"

"I did not know," a disgusted, and surprised, Jojonah replied.

"But you just said—" Francis started to argue.

"I was speaking of your demeanor, and no specific actions," Jojonah interrupted. He paused to study Francis, and saw that the man was torn apart.

"It does not matter," Francis remarked, waving his hand. "It was an accident. I could not know."

The immaculate didn't believe those words for a moment, Jojonah understood, and so he did not press the point as Francis staggered out of the room.

Jojonah didn't even bother to eat his meal then, too consumed by Francis' words. He knew what was to come now, and so he went back to his bedside and prayed, as much the confession of a doomed man as any request for guidance.

That night, the College began with long and uneventful introductions of the different abbots and their escorting masters, all pomp and ceremony that was expected to last through the dawn. This was the only event to which all the monks of the host abbey were invited, and so more than seven hundred had gathered in the great hall, along with the soldiers of the All-heart Brigade who had accompanied Abbot Je'howith.

Jojonah watched it from the back rows of seating, near the exit. He tried to keep an eye on Markwart, who, after the initial prayer and greeting, had retired to the shadows at the edge of the room. On and on it went, and Jojonah even considered running away on more than one occasion. How long might he be gone before Markwart and the others even realized that he had left? he wondered.

Truly that would have been the easier course.

He expected that the night would prove uneventful, and anticipated another long day in his private room, praying, but then held his breath when, just before the dawn, Father Abbot Markwart again took center stage.

"There is one matter which should be breached before the break," the Father Abbot began. "One which all the younger brothers should hear openly addressed before they are dismissed from the College."

Jojonah was on the move, swinging around the back of the seats and down the outside row, moving toward the central area. He took the course because it would bring him right past Braumin Herde.

"Listen carefully," he instructed the immaculate, bending low as he passed. "Record every word in your memory."

"It is no secret to you all that a most important matter, a most important crime, has plagued St.-Mere-Abelle and all of our Order for several years now, a crime that showed the true depth of its wickedness in the rising of the demon dactyl and the terrible war that has brought so much misery and suffering to our lands," Markwart went on, his tone loud and dramatic.

Jojonah continued his slow walk toward the front of the hall. Many heads turned to regard him, many whispered conversations began in his wake, and he was not surprised, for he understood that his sympathies toward Avelyn were not secret, even beyond the walls of St.-Mere-Abelle.

And he saw Je'howith's soldiers, Markwart's stooges, gathered at the side and seeming eager.

"It is the most important declaration possible of this College of Abbots," the Father Abbot finished powerfully, "that the man, Avelyn Desbris by name, be branded openly and formally as a criminal against the Church and state."

"A call for heresy, Father Abbot?" asked Abbot Je'howith of St. Honce, sitting in the front row.

"Nothing less," Markwart confirmed.

Murmurs erupted from every corner of the hall; heads shook and heads nodded, abbots and masters bending low in private conversations.

Jojonah swallowed hard, recognizing that his next step would lead him to a cliff face. "Is this not the same Avelyn Desbris who was once given the highest honor in all the Abellican Church?" he asked loudly, drawing the attention of all, particularly of Brother Braumin Herde. "Was it not Father Abbot Dalebert Markwart himself who named Avelyn Desbris as a Preparer of the sacred stones?"

"Another time," Markwart replied, keeping his cool and calm tone. "More the pity, then, and farther the fall."

"Farther the fall indeed," Jojonah retorted, moving powerfully to the center stage to face his nemesis. "But it was not Avelyn who fell from grace."

In the back of the room Braumin Herde dared to smile and nod his head; from the whispers and reactions of those nearby, it seemed to him as if Jojonah was doing quite well.

"Not only Avelyn, you mean!" Markwart said suddenly, ferociously.

Simple startlement made Jojonah pause, and that gave Markwart the opening he needed to sweep his proclamations back out to the entire audience. "Be it known here and now that the security of St.-Mere-Abelle was again breached this very summer," the Father Abbot cried. "The prisoners I had secured to speak to you against Avelyn were stolen from my very grasp."

More gasps than whispers came from the audience now.

"I introduce now Immaculate Brother Francis," Markwart explained, a name that was not unfamiliar to the gathering—indeed, one of the points of contention that was expected to be raised later in the College concerned the man's premature promotion.

Braumin Herde chewed hard on his lip as he recognized the pain on Jojonah's face. He remembered his promise to his beloved Jojonah, though, pointedly telling himself again and again that this was exactly the scenario Jojonah had predicted. Out of love and respect for Jojonah, he had to remain silent, though if he had gotten one hint that this College might be swayed Jojonah's way, he would have run down to stand beside the man.

That hint never materialized. Markwart's questions were quick and to the point as he prodded Francis for information concerning the escape of the prisoners. Francis described Elbryan in great detail, and went on to confirm that demons had apparently inhabited the bodies of the Chilichunk couple.

And then he looked Jojonah right in the eye.

And then he fell silent.

Jojonah could hardly believe that the man had not betrayed him!

But Markwart still clung to his superior edge as he thanked and dismissed the brother, for he had only used Francis to set up his next witness, one of the guards Elbryan had overpowered, one who had crept up a bit along the side passage to get a glimpse of the intruders, and who could, and did indeed, identify Master Jojonah as a conspirator.

Jojonah fell silent; he knew that he would not be heard at that time no matter how loud his protests.

Abbot De'Unnero came next, detailing the events on the road that had allowed Jojonah to sneak away, opening a timetable during which the master could indeed have gone to St.-Mere-Abelle. "And I spoke with the merchant, Nesk Reaches," De'Unnero insisted, "and confirmed that Master Jojonah had not returned to their encampment."

A strange sense of calm began to wash over Jojonah, an acceptance that this indeed was a fight he could not win. Markwart had come here well-prepared.

He looked over at the fanatical Allheart soldiers and smiled.

Next Markwart called for one of Jojonah's companions on the road to Aida, a monk who would no doubt explain to the gathering how Jojonah had manipulated the group away from Avelyn's body.

Every piece seemed to be falling in place against him.

"Enough!" Jojonah cried, breaking the momentum. "Enough. I was indeed in your dungeons, evil Markwart."

The gasps came louder, accompanied by more than a few shouts of anger.

"Freeing those imprisoned unlawfully and immorally," Jojonah asserted. "I have seen too much of your wickedness. I watched it exact a toll upon gentle—yes, gentle and godly!—Avelyn. I saw it most keenly in the fate of the *Windrunner*."

Master Jojonah paused with that last statement and even laughed aloud. Every abbot, master, and immaculate in this room understood, and approved of, the fate of the *Windrunner*; every leader in this room was complicit in the murders.

Jojonah knew he was doomed. He wanted to rail out against Markwart, to show the ancient texts that described the previous method of collecting stones, to scream out that Brother Pellimar, who had been on that journey to collect the stones, had also been murdered by this supposedly holy Church.

But there was no practical point to it, and he did not want to give everything away. He looked to Brother Braumin Herde then, the man who would take up his torch, and he smiled.

Markwart screamed again for a declaration of Avelyn as a heretic, then added that Jojonah, by his own admission, was a traitor to the Church.

And then Abbot Je'howith, the second most powerful man in the Order, rose tall and seconded the motion, and with a confirming nod from Markwart, motioned to his soldiers.

"By your own words you have committed treason against the Church and the King," Je'howith proclaimed as the soldiers surrounded Jojonah. "Have you any offering of defense?" He turned about to face the congregation. "Will any others speak for this man?"

Jojonah stared up at the gathering, at Braumin Herde, and the man dutifully remained silent.

The Allheart soldiers swarmed over the master, and with Markwart and Je'howith's blessings, so did many monks, beating him, dragging him away. As he was ushered out the door, he saw Brother Francis standing quietly, taking no part, seeming distressed and helpless.

"I forgive you," Jojonah said to the man. "As does Avelyn, as does God." He almost added the forgiveness of Brother Braumin, but could not go that far in trusting Francis.

And then he was gone, dragged from the room as the mob gained momentum.

Many were still in their seats, sitting quiet and stunned, including Brother Braumin. He caught sight of Francis staring up at him, but had only a glare to offer in return.

Later that same cold Calember day, Master Jojonah, stripped naked and placed in an open cage on the back of a wagon, was taken through the streets of St.-Mere-Abelle village, his porters crying out his sins and crimes to the nervous townsfolk.

Insults became spit, became stones hurled Jojonah's way. One man ran up to the cart with a sharpened stick, stabbing the monk hard in the belly, opening a vicious wound.

Brothers Herde, Viscenti, and Dellman, and all the other monks of St.-Mere-Abelle, and all the visiting abbots and masters, watched it solemnly, some with horror, some with satisfaction.

For more than an hour Jojonah was carted about the streets, and he was a battered and broken man, hardly conscious, when the Allheart soldiers at last dragged him from the cart and lashed him to a stake.

"You are damned by your actions," Markwart proclaimed above the frenzy of the excited crowd. "May God show you mercy."

And the pyre was lit beneath Jojonah's feet.

He felt the flames biting at his skin, felt his blood boiling, his lungs charring with every breath. But only for a moment, for then he closed his eyes and he saw . . .

Brother Avelyn, reaching for him with outstretched arms . . .

Jojonah never screamed, never cried out at all.

It was to Markwart, the biggest disappointment of the day.

Braumin Herde watched the whole of the execution as the flames climbed higher, engulfing his dearest friend. Beside him, both Viscenti and Dellman turned to leave, but Herde grabbed them and would not let them go.

"Bear witness," he said, and they were the last three monks to leave the awful scene.

"Come," Braumin Herde bade them when at last it was over, when the flames had died away. "I have a book you must see."

In the crowd of villagers, Roger Lockless also watched. He had learned much since his flight from the road south of Palmaris, from the monster that had destroyed Baron Bildeborough. In the last few hours alone, he had learned of Jojonah and the freeing of the half-man, half-horse prisoner, and while the news had given him hope, this sight had brought only despair and disgust.

But he watched, and understood then that the Father Abbot of the Abellican Order was indeed his enemy.

Far from that place, in the lands north of Palmaris, Elbryan held Pony close on an empty hillock, watching the rise of Sheila. The war with the monsters was over, but the war with the greater enemy, they both knew, was only beginning.

About the Author

R. A. SALVATORE was born in Massachusetts in 1959. His first published novel was *The Crystal Shard*. He has since published more than a dozen novels, including the *New York Times* bestsellers *The Halfling's Gem*, *Sojourn*, *The Legacy*, and *Starless Night*. He makes his home in Massachusetts with his wife, Diane, and their three children.

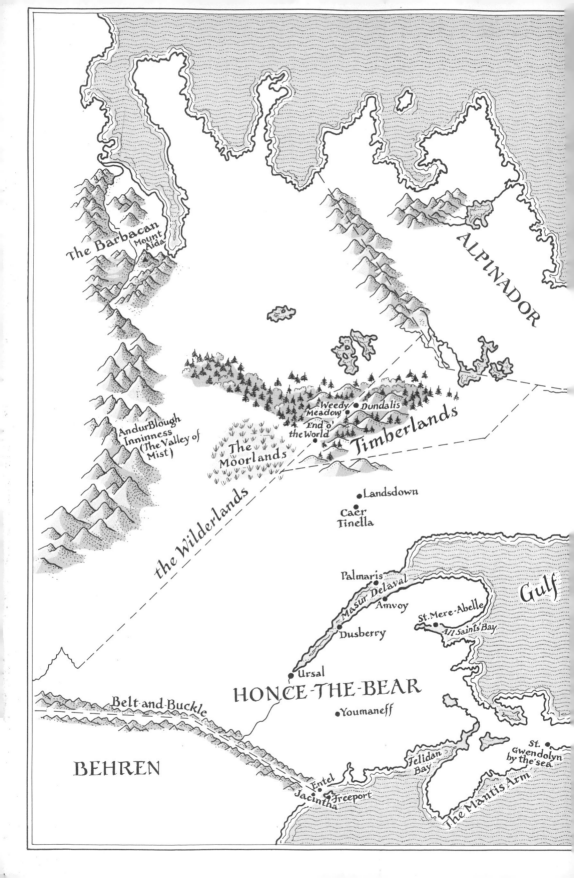